OOK OF LEGENDS

ADAPTED FROM THE WORKS
OF **JAN HAROLD BRUNVAND**
BY **ROBERT LOREN FLEMING**
AND **ROBERT F. BOYD, JR.**

PARADOX PRESS
NEW YORK

THE BIG BOOK OF URBAN LEGENDS
published by Paradox Press. Introduction
Copyright ©1994 Jan Harold Brunvand.
All other material Copyright ©1994 Paradox
Press. All Rights Reserved. Factoid Books
and all story titles, character names and
likenesses and related indicia are trademarks
of Paradox Press. The stories, characters,
and incidents featured in this publication
are entirely fictional. Any use of real
people, places or events is entirely
imaginary. Paradox Press is an imprint of
DC Comics, 1325 Avenue of the Americas,
New York, NY 10019. A division of Warner
Bros. — A Time Warner Entertainment
Company. Printed in USA. First Printing.

Cover collage by Gregory Homs
Cover spot illustration by Roger Langridge
Interior publication design by Brian Pearce
Lettering by Steve Smith
Additional lettering by Gail Beckett

TABLE OF CONTENTS

1 MOVING VIOLATIONS

AUTOMOBILE LEGENDS

2 WILD KINGDOM

ANIMAL LEGENDS

3 CAMPFIRE CLASSICS

HORROR LEGENDS

4 COMIC CALAMITIES

ACCIDENT LEGENDS

5 CAUGHT IN THE ACT

SEX AND SCANDAL LEGENDS

6 CRIMES AND MISDEMEANORS

CRIME LEGENDS

7 OCCUPATIONAL HAZARDS

BUSINESS, PROFESSIONAL AND GOVERNMENT LEGENDS

8 FOAF-A-RAMA

CELEBRITY RUMORS, ACADEMIA LEGENDS AND MISCELLANEOUS

INTRODUC-TION

BY JAN HAROLD BRUNVAND

Is this the climax of my career as a folklorist — to see my collections of urban legends turned into comics?

My mother will be puzzled; after all, she tried to improve my mind by throwing out the big stacks of comics that my brothers and I accumulated when we were kids. But my mentor in folkloristics, the late Professor Richard M. Dorson, probably would have approved; after all, he wrote a lavishly illustrated book, *America in Legend,* for the U.S. Bicentennial, breaking his own rule about not popularizing the science of folklore.

But a comic book! Well, why not? After all, comics are just another manifestation of the same popular culture that gives rise to many urban legends in the first place.

Urban legends (UL's, as I sometimes call them) are true stories that are too good to be true, and they are always said to have happened to a Friend of a Friend (or FOAF). The first UL I remember hearing was "The Death Car," the tale of a $50 Buick cursed with a corpse's stench that the kids in Lansing, Michigan, yearned to locate when I was in high school there in the late 1940s. The first UL that I heard debunked was also "The Death Car" when I took Professor Dorson's "American Folklore" class at Michigan State University in the early 1950s.

I gave up on the $50 Buick (which later became a $500 Corvette) and continued my studies, ending up at Indiana University where I earned a Ph.D. in folklore. Professor Dorson had become the director of the program there, and while helping him to index his book *American Folklore* (1959), I read several versions of a weird little story about a dead cat wrapped in a package. (See "The Dead Cat in a Package" and "Another Dead Cat in a Package" on pages 42 and 43 of this book.) Several months later, the same story appeared as a true incident in the Bloomington, Indiana, *Daily Herald Telephone.*

I clipped the news item, the very first clipping in a file of what were then called "Urban Belief Tales." The more such stories I collected — from oral tradition, the media, students, and from fellow folklorists — the more I wondered *why,* although everyone knew some of these legends, few understood their importance as modern folklore. Gradually, I included more urban legends in my university courses, and eventually I wrote an article on them for *Psychology Today* (June 1980) and proposed a book on the subject to the publisher of my textbook, W.W. Norton & Company.

That book, *The Vanishing Hitchhiker,* appeared in 1981 as a textbook supplement, complete with bibliographic notes, glossary, and guide to self-study of urban legends, but it quickly caught on with the general public and even got me on the David Letterman show. This kicked off an unending series of talk shows, interviews, and queries from journalists trying to verify odd rumors and stories. I hadn't realized that urban legends were so widely told, nor that they would appeal so strongly to media-saturated Americans.

But urban legends are, indeed, so prevailing as a modern narrative form — second only to dirty jokes, in my opinion — that hundreds of readers immediately began to send me favorite stories that I had left out. Following an editor's suggestion, I had included my full address in *The Vanishing Hitchhiker*. Furthermore, I was reminded by folklorists of stories I had missed in the scholarly literature, and then I started to hear a suspicious story about a guard dog choking on two fingers bitten off an intruder. Aha! There were both *old* urban legends I had overlooked and *new* urban legends developing. Enough material for a second book.

The Choking Doberman came out in 1984, and again I included my address, not really expecting that many more ULs would appear. When my research showed that the title story was updated from an ancient traditional legend, I started putting "new" in quotation marks when applied to ULs.

I soon had enough stuff from readers to compile *The Mexican Pet* in 1986, titling the book from yet another "new" legend that surfaced in 1983 and soon achieved worldwide popularity. From 1987 to 1992 I wrote a newspaper column syndicated by United Feature; this yielded the latest two of my UL books, *Curses! Broiled Again!* (1989) and *The Baby Train* (1993). In the latter I included my "Type Index of Urban Legends," an outline of the filing system used in my eight story-stuffed drawers.

There is a seemingly inexhaustible supply of these stories, and old legends are constantly being told, changed, retold, and then told again as new. "The Graveyard Wager," for example (see page 67 in this book), is an ancient folktale, but it's still narrated today at campouts and slumber parties as if it really happened recently to some local kids.

And now, a comic book — a natural-enough transition from folklore to popular culture. After all, urban legends, like comics, present stark, clear plots with morals, and they are tremendously popular, despite their low place on the cultural totem pole. Both genres have given us memorable characters, situations, and even catch phrases ("It's a bird, it's a plane, it's Superman!" versus "I don't know what game you're playing, lady, but I hope your team wins!" — see page 139). But will the 200 urban legends in this book, so vividly illustrated by top comic artists, kill the genre as folklore? Will people now merely *read* the stories and no longer *tell* them?

I doubt it, since I just filed the umpteenth version of the latest descendant of "Red Velvet Cake" (see page 180) taken off a computer net, and a few months ago I heard about a supposed initiation ritual in which gang members drive around with their headlights off, hoping to provoke other drivers to blink at them and invite a "Lights Out" revenge — death! (Rest assured, this has only happened to elusive FOAFs, friends of friends, and never to real people.) Although such stories are now being transmitted via new technologies, they'll probably never become outmoded and disappear.

Folklore, whether age-old or modern, doesn't die out after it's publicized, and I predict a quick response to *The Big Book of Urban Legends* will be letters from readers telling us about stories not included here. Now, *that* would have impressed Professor Dorson.

JAN HAROLD BRUNVAND *is the author of* The Baby Train, Curses! Broiled Again!, The Mexican Pet, The Choking Doberman, *and* The Vanishing Hitchhiker, *which provided the source material for the stories in this volume. He is a professor of English and folklore at the University of Utah.*

CHAPTER ONE

AUTOMOBILE LEGENDS

Richard Dorson, discussing the legend — defined as "the story which never happened told for true" — in 1959, mentioned that contemporary legends "fasten particularly onto the automobile, chief symbol of modern America." Evoking freedom, power, coming-of-age, and more than a hint of sex, the automobile continues to dominate American urban legends, as indeed to affect much of American social life and popular culture as well. So it's no surprise that a goodly portion of the ULs both in this chapter and scattered through others are about Americans' love affairs with their cars, as well as about some love affairs conducted partly *in* their cars.

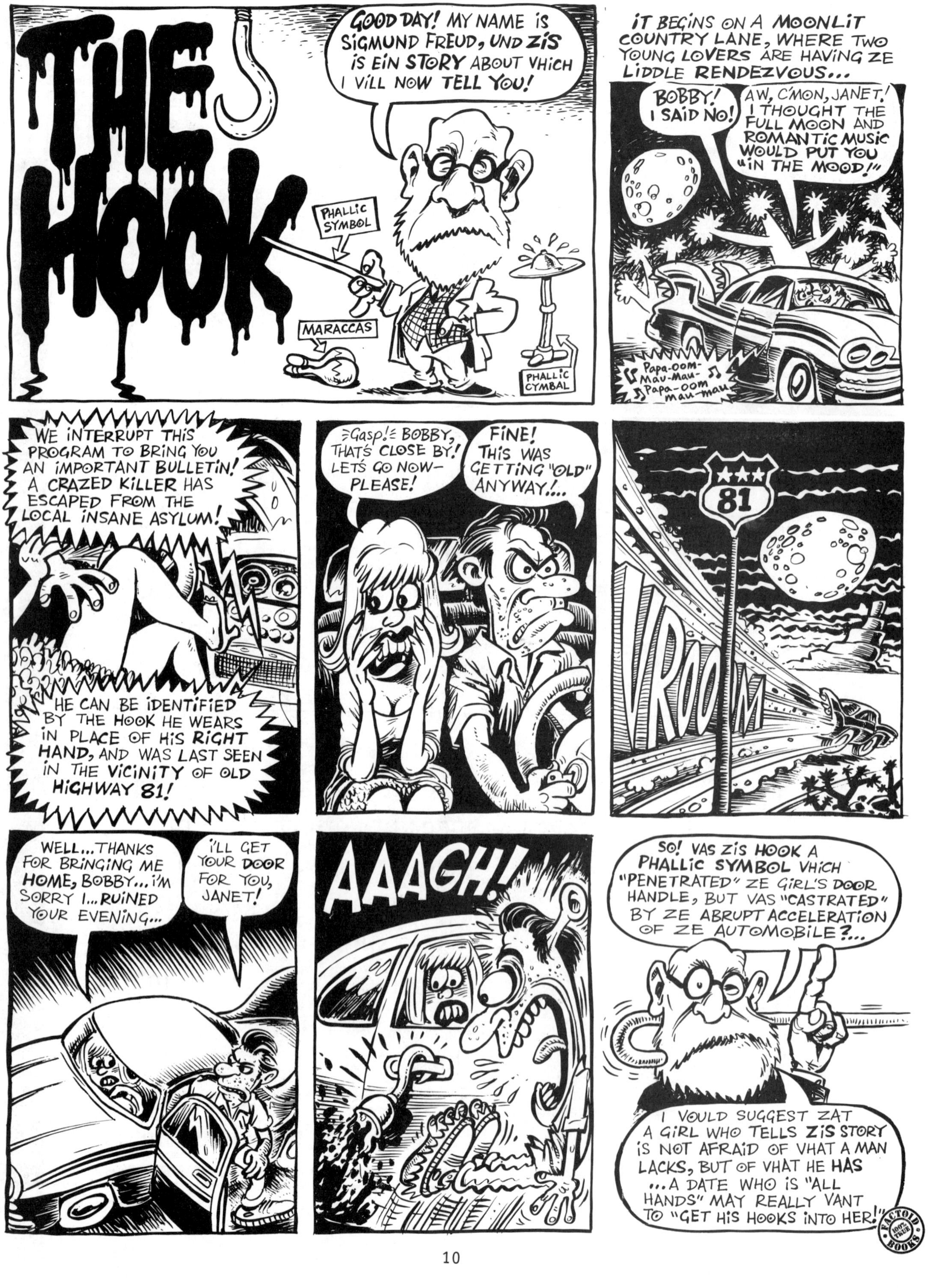
THE HOOK
GOOD DAY! MY NAME IS SIGMUND FREUD, UND ZIS IS EIN STORY ABOUT VHICH I VILL NOW TELL YOU!
PHALLIC SYMBOL
MARACCAS
PHALLIC CYMBAL
IT BEGINS ON A MOONLIT COUNTRY LANE, WHERE TWO YOUNG LOVERS ARE HAVING ZE LIDDLE RENDEZVOUS...
BOBBY! I SAID NO!
AW, C'MON, JANET! I THOUGHT THE FULL MOON AND ROMANTIC MUSIC WOULD PUT YOU "IN THE MOOD!"
Papa-oom-Mau-Mau-Papa-oom mau-mau
WE INTERRUPT THIS PROGRAM TO BRING YOU AN IMPORTANT BULLETIN! A CRAZED KILLER HAS ESCAPED FROM THE LOCAL INSANE ASYLUM!
HE CAN BE IDENTIFIED BY THE HOOK HE WEARS IN PLACE OF HIS RIGHT HAND, AND WAS LAST SEEN IN THE VICINITY OF OLD HIGHWAY 81!
Gasp! BOBBY, THAT'S CLOSE BY! LET'S GO NOW—PLEASE!
FINE! THIS WAS GETTING "OLD" ANYWAY!...
81
VROOM
WELL...THANKS FOR BRINGING ME HOME, BOBBY...I'M SORRY I...RUINED YOUR EVENING...
I'LL GET YOUR DOOR FOR YOU, JANET!
AAAGH!
SO! VAS ZIS HOOK A PHALLIC SYMBOL VHICH "PENETRATED" ZE GIRL'S DOOR HANDLE, BUT VAS "CASTRATED" BY ZE ABRUPT ACCELERATION OF ZE AUTOMOBILE?...
I VOULD SUGGEST ZAT A GIRL WHO TELLS ZIS STORY IS NOT AFRAID OF VHAT A MAN LACKS, BUT OF VHAT HE HAS ...A DATE WHO IS "ALL HANDS" MAY REALLY VANT TO "GET HIS HOOKS INTO HER!"
FACTOID BOOKS 100% TRUE

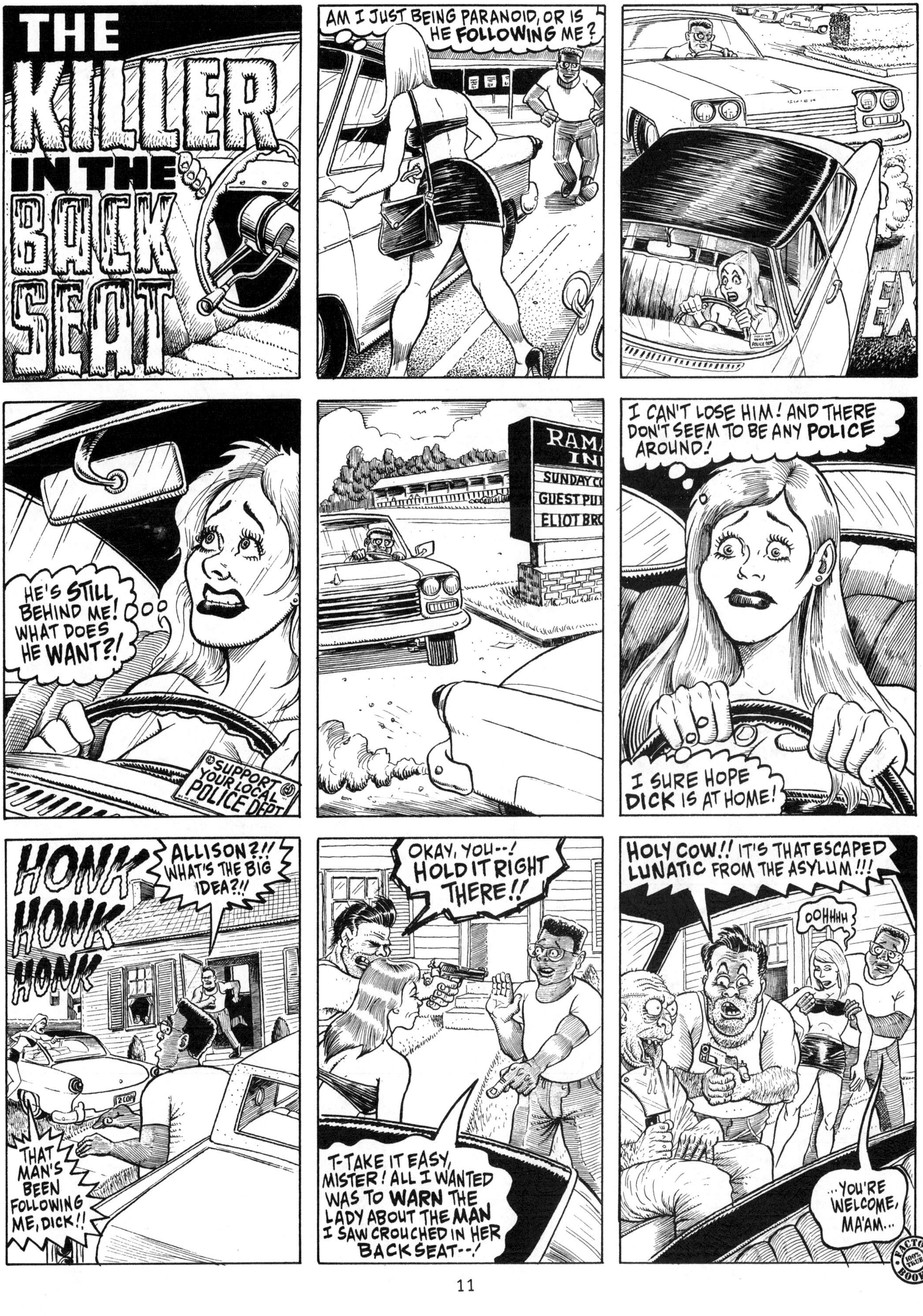

THE KILLER IN THE BACK SEAT
AM I JUST BEING PARANOID, OR IS HE FOLLOWING ME?
EX
HE'S STILL BEHIND ME! WHAT DOES HE WANT?!
SUPPORT YOUR LOCAL POLICE DEPT
RAMA INN
SUNDAY CO
GUEST PU
ELIOT BRO
I CAN'T LOSE HIM! AND THERE DON'T SEEM TO BE ANY POLICE AROUND!
I SURE HOPE DICK IS AT HOME!
HONK HONK HONK
ALLISON?!! WHAT'S THE BIG IDEA?!!
THAT MAN'S BEEN FOLLOWING ME, DICK!!
OKAY, YOU--! HOLD IT RIGHT THERE!!
T-TAKE IT EASY, MISTER! ALL I WANTED WAS TO WARN THE LADY ABOUT THE MAN I SAW CROUCHED IN HER BACK SEAT--!
HOLY COW!! IT'S THAT ESCAPED LUNATIC FROM THE ASYLUM!!!
OOHHHH
...YOU'RE WELCOME, MA'AM...

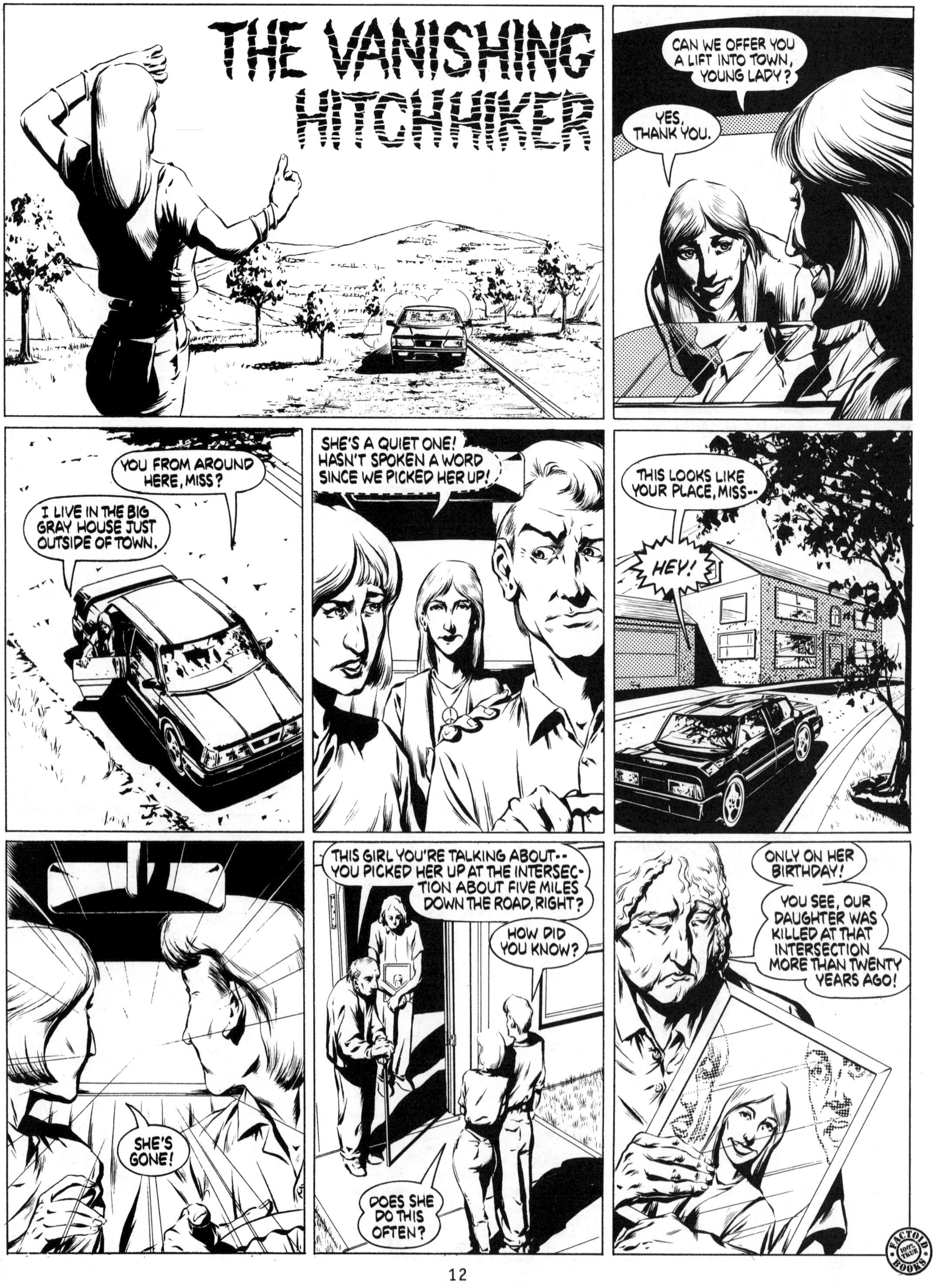
THE VANISHING HITCHHIKER
CAN WE OFFER YOU A LIFT INTO TOWN, YOUNG LADY?
YES, THANK YOU.
YOU FROM AROUND HERE, MISS?
I LIVE IN THE BIG GRAY HOUSE JUST OUTSIDE OF TOWN.
SHE'S A QUIET ONE! HASN'T SPOKEN A WORD SINCE WE PICKED HER UP!
THIS LOOKS LIKE YOUR PLACE, MISS--
HEY!
SHE'S GONE!
THIS GIRL YOU'RE TALKING ABOUT-- YOU PICKED HER UP AT THE INTERSECTION ABOUT FIVE MILES DOWN THE ROAD, RIGHT?
HOW DID YOU KNOW?
DOES SHE DO THIS OFTEN?
ONLY ON HER BIRTHDAY!
YOU SEE, OUR DAUGHTER WAS KILLED AT THAT INTERSECTION MORE THAN TWENTY YEARS AGO!
FACTOID BOOKS 100% TRUE

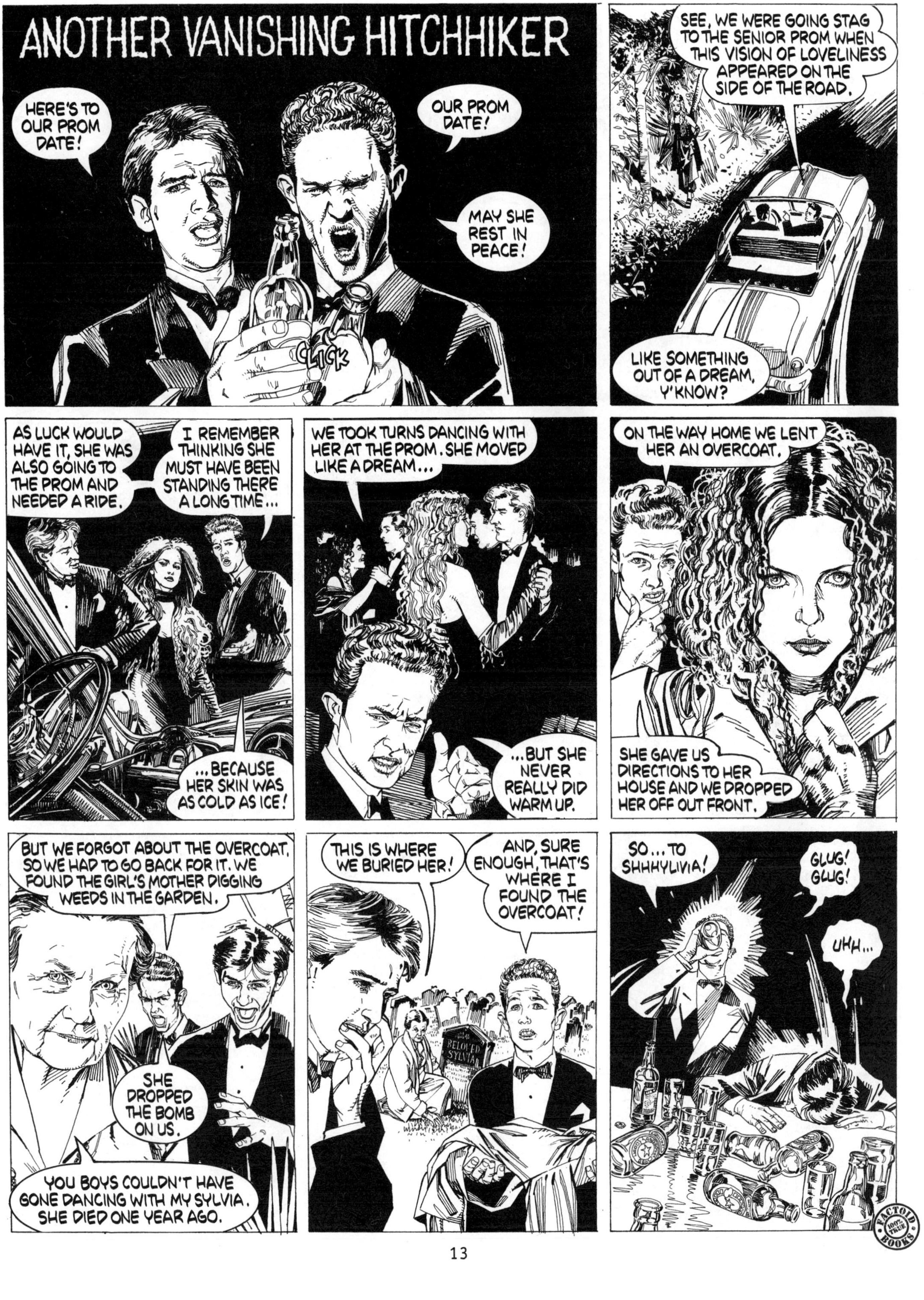
ANOTHER VANISHING HITCHHIKER
HERE'S TO OUR PROM DATE!
OUR PROM DATE!
MAY SHE REST IN PEACE!
CLICK
SEE, WE WERE GOING STAG TO THE SENIOR PROM WHEN THIS VISION OF LOVELINESS APPEARED ON THE SIDE OF THE ROAD.
LIKE SOMETHING OUT OF A DREAM, Y'KNOW?
AS LUCK WOULD HAVE IT, SHE WAS ALSO GOING TO THE PROM AND NEEDED A RIDE.
I REMEMBER THINKING SHE MUST HAVE BEEN STANDING THERE A LONG TIME...
...BECAUSE HER SKIN WAS AS COLD AS ICE!
WE TOOK TURNS DANCING WITH HER AT THE PROM. SHE MOVED LIKE A DREAM...
...BUT SHE NEVER REALLY DID WARM UP.
ON THE WAY HOME WE LENT HER AN OVERCOAT.
SHE GAVE US DIRECTIONS TO HER HOUSE AND WE DROPPED HER OFF OUT FRONT.
BUT WE FORGOT ABOUT THE OVERCOAT, SO WE HAD TO GO BACK FOR IT. WE FOUND THE GIRL'S MOTHER DIGGING WEEDS IN THE GARDEN.
SHE DROPPED THE BOMB ON US.
YOU BOYS COULDN'T HAVE GONE DANCING WITH MY SYLVIA. SHE DIED ONE YEAR AGO.
THIS IS WHERE WE BURIED HER!
AND, SURE ENOUGH, THAT'S WHERE I FOUND THE OVERCOAT!
BELOVED SYLVIA
SO... TO SHHHYLIVIA!
GLUG! GLUG!
UHH...
FACTOID BOOKS 100% TRUE

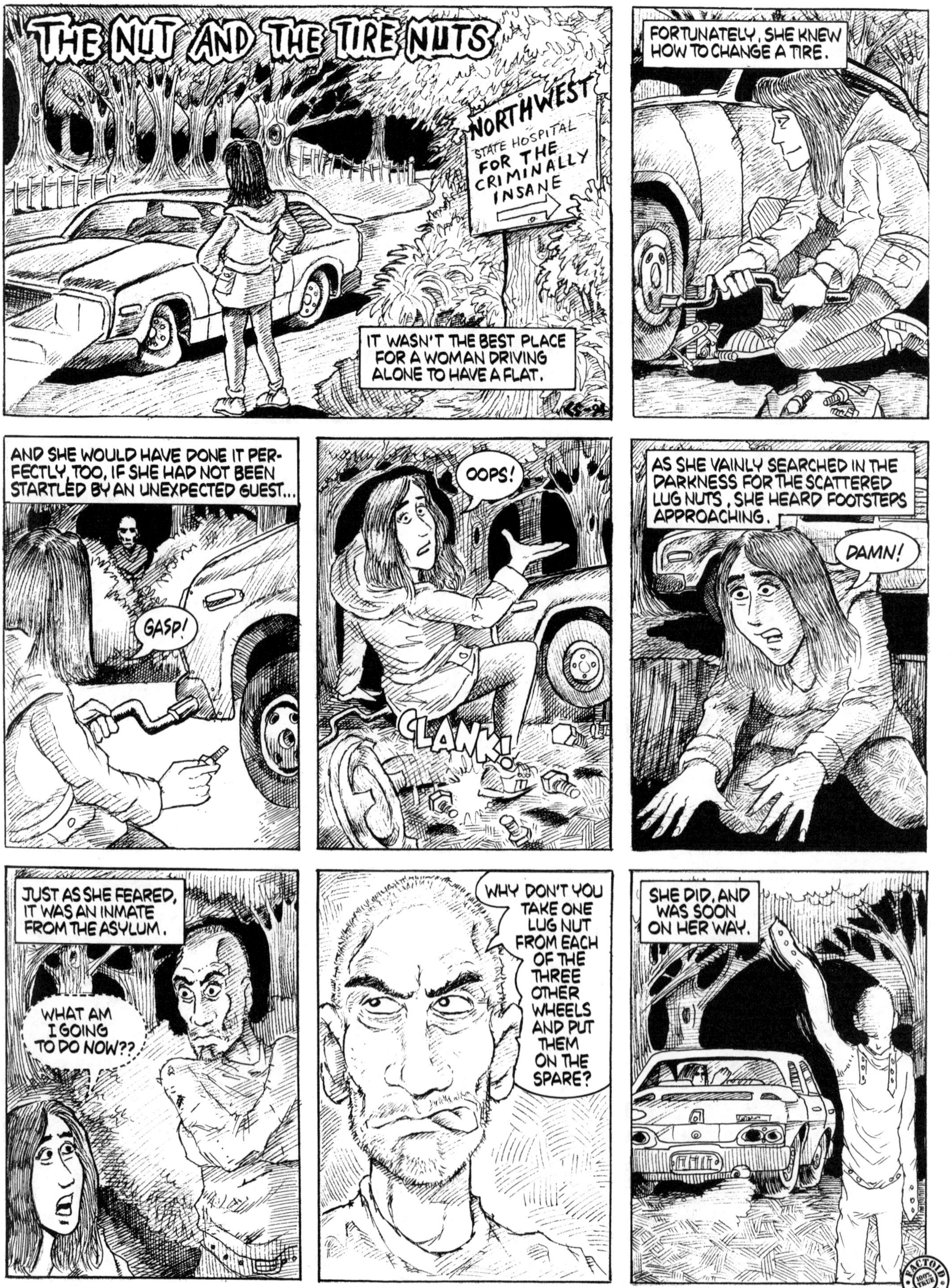
THE NUT AND THE TIRE NUTS
NORTHWEST STATE HOSPITAL FOR THE CRIMINALLY INSANE
IT WASN'T THE BEST PLACE FOR A WOMAN DRIVING ALONE TO HAVE A FLAT.
FORTUNATELY, SHE KNEW HOW TO CHANGE A TIRE.
AND SHE WOULD HAVE DONE IT PERFECTLY, TOO, IF SHE HAD NOT BEEN STARTLED BY AN UNEXPECTED GUEST...
GASP!
OOPS!
CLANK!
AS SHE VAINLY SEARCHED IN THE DARKNESS FOR THE SCATTERED LUG NUTS, SHE HEARD FOOTSTEPS APPROACHING.
DAMN!
JUST AS SHE FEARED, IT WAS AN INMATE FROM THE ASYLUM.
WHAT AM I GOING TO DO NOW??
WHY DON'T YOU TAKE ONE LUG NUT FROM EACH OF THE THREE OTHER WHEELS AND PUT THEM ON THE SPARE?
SHE DID, AND WAS SOON ON HER WAY.
FACTOID BOOKS 100% TRUE

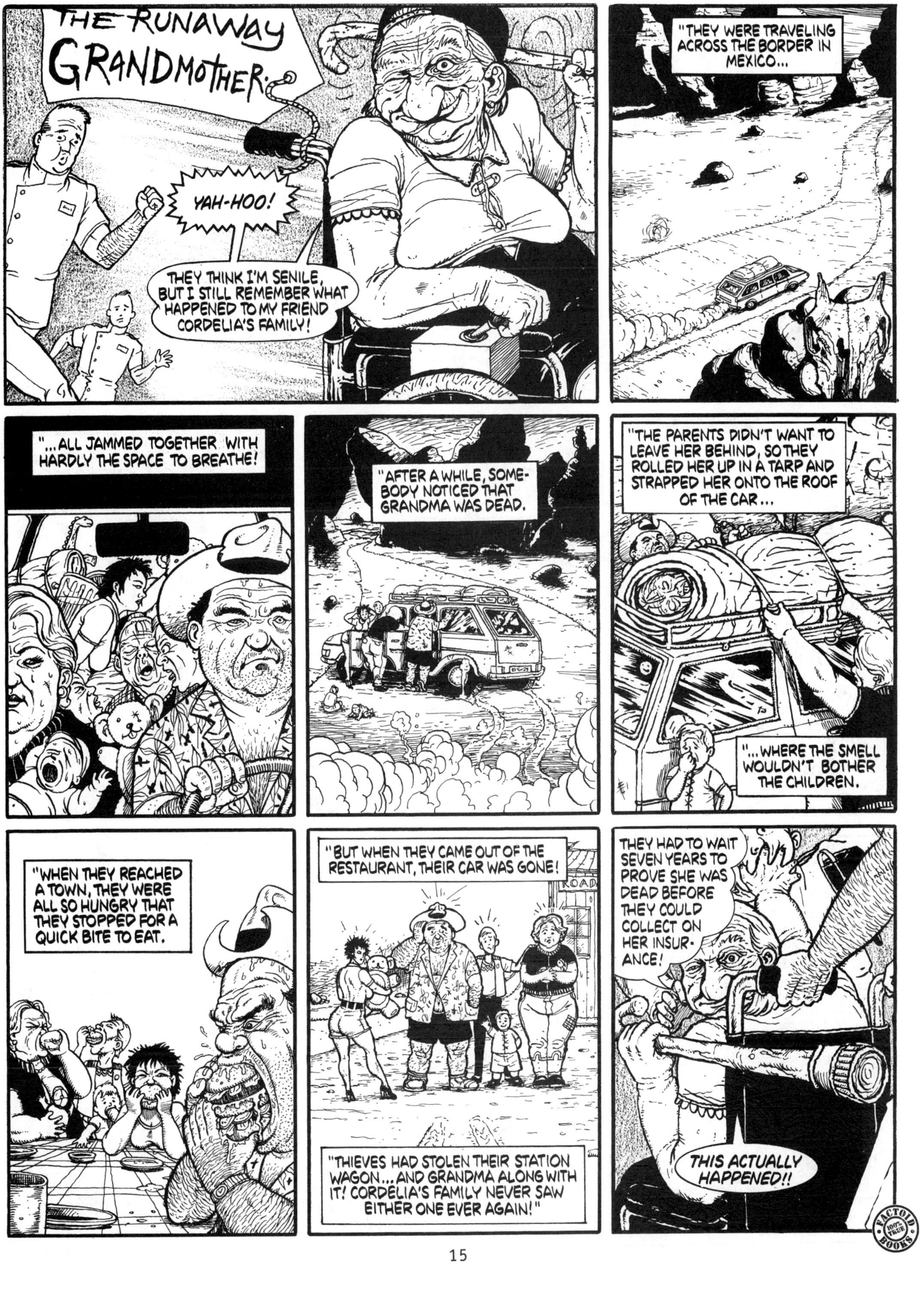
THE RUNAWAY GRANDMOTHER
YAH-HOO!
THEY THINK I'M SENILE, BUT I STILL REMEMBER WHAT HAPPENED TO MY FRIEND CORDELIA'S FAMILY!
"THEY WERE TRAVELING ACROSS THE BORDER IN MEXICO...
"...ALL JAMMED TOGETHER WITH HARDLY THE SPACE TO BREATHE!
"AFTER A WHILE, SOMEBODY NOTICED THAT GRANDMA WAS DEAD.
"THE PARENTS DIDN'T WANT TO LEAVE HER BEHIND, SO THEY ROLLED HER UP IN A TARP AND STRAPPED HER ONTO THE ROOF OF THE CAR...
"...WHERE THE SMELL WOULDN'T BOTHER THE CHILDREN.
"WHEN THEY REACHED A TOWN, THEY WERE ALL SO HUNGRY THAT THEY STOPPED FOR A QUICK BITE TO EAT.
"BUT WHEN THEY CAME OUT OF THE RESTAURANT, THEIR CAR WAS GONE!
"THIEVES HAD STOLEN THEIR STATION WAGON... AND GRANDMA ALONG WITH IT! CORDELIA'S FAMILY NEVER SAW EITHER ONE EVER AGAIN!"
THEY HAD TO WAIT SEVEN YEARS TO PROVE SHE WAS DEAD BEFORE THEY COULD COLLECT ON HER INSURANCE!
THIS ACTUALLY HAPPENED!!
FACTOID BOOKS 100% TRUE

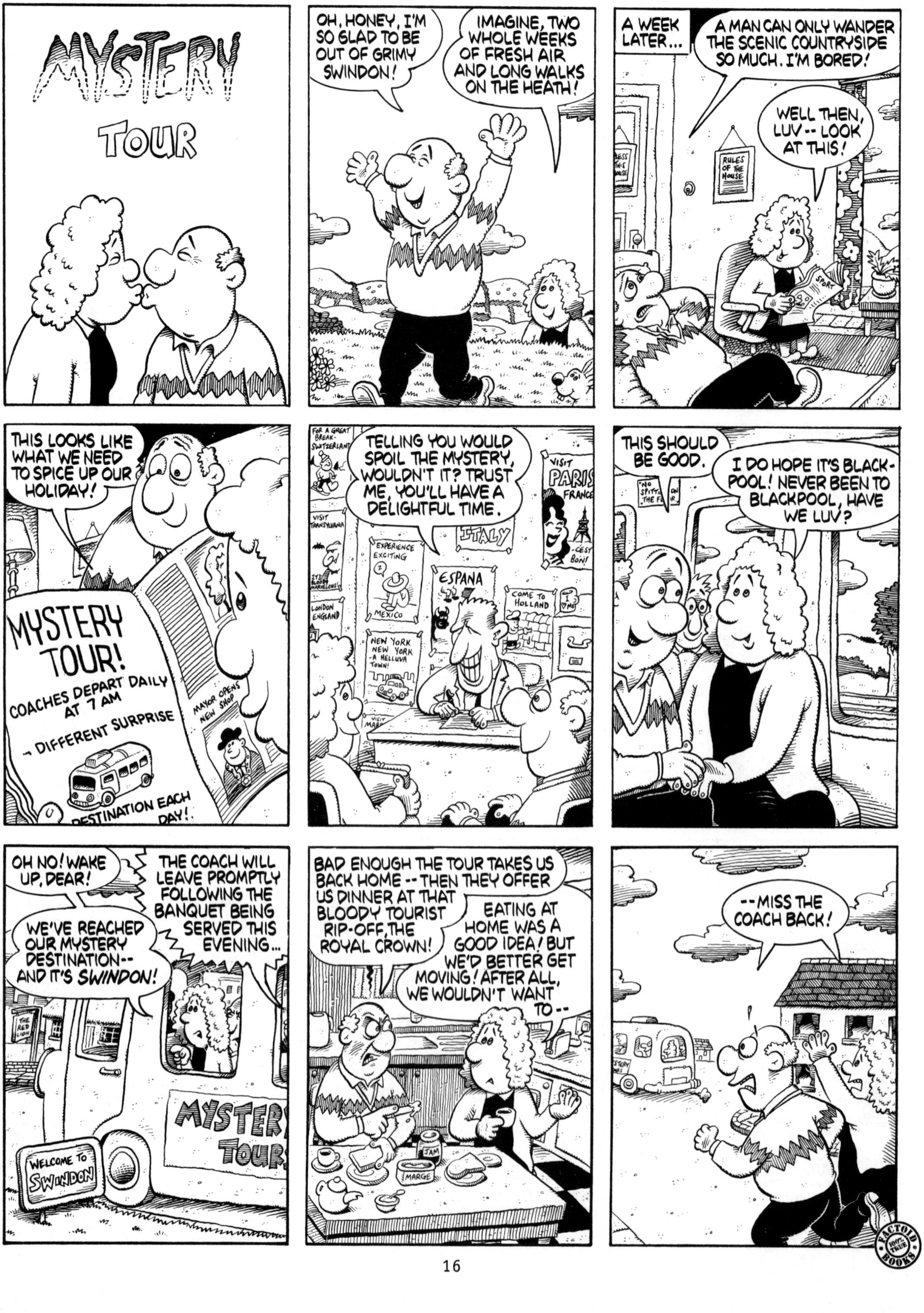
MYSTERY
TOUR
OH, HONEY, I'M SO GLAD TO BE OUT OF GRIMY SWINDON!
IMAGINE, TWO WHOLE WEEKS OF FRESH AIR AND LONG WALKS ON THE HEATH!
A WEEK LATER...
A MAN CAN ONLY WANDER THE SCENIC COUNTRYSIDE SO MUCH. I'M BORED!
WELL THEN, LUV -- LOOK AT THIS!
RULES OF THE HOUSE
SPORT
THIS LOOKS LIKE WHAT WE NEED TO SPICE UP OUR HOLIDAY!
MYSTERY TOUR!
COACHES DEPART DAILY AT 7 AM
- DIFFERENT SURPRISE
DESTINATION EACH DAY!
MAYOR OPENS NEW SHOP
TELLING YOU WOULD SPOIL THE MYSTERY, WOULDN'T IT? TRUST ME, YOU'LL HAVE A DELIGHTFUL TIME.
FOR A GREAT BREAK - SWITZERLAND
VISIT TRANSYLVANIA
EXPERIENCE EXCITING MEXICO
ITALY
VISIT PARIS FRANCE -C'EST BON!
ESPANA
COME TO HOLLAND
I ♥ ME
LONDON ENGLAND
NEW YORK NEW YORK - A HELLUVA TOWN!
THIS SHOULD BE GOOD.
I DO HOPE IT'S BLACKPOOL! NEVER BEEN TO BLACKPOOL, HAVE WE LUV?
OH NO! WAKE UP, DEAR!
THE COACH WILL LEAVE PROMPTLY FOLLOWING THE BANQUET BEING SERVED THIS EVENING...
WE'VE REACHED OUR MYSTERY DESTINATION-- AND IT'S SWINDON!
THE RED LION
MYSTERY TOURS
WELCOME TO SWINDON
BAD ENOUGH THE TOUR TAKES US BACK HOME -- THEN THEY OFFER US DINNER AT THAT BLOODY TOURIST RIP-OFF, THE ROYAL CROWN!
EATING AT HOME WAS A GOOD IDEA! BUT WE'D BETTER GET MOVING! AFTER ALL, WE WOULDN'T WANT TO --
JAM
MARGE
-- MISS THE COACH BACK!
FACTOID BOOKS 100% TRUE

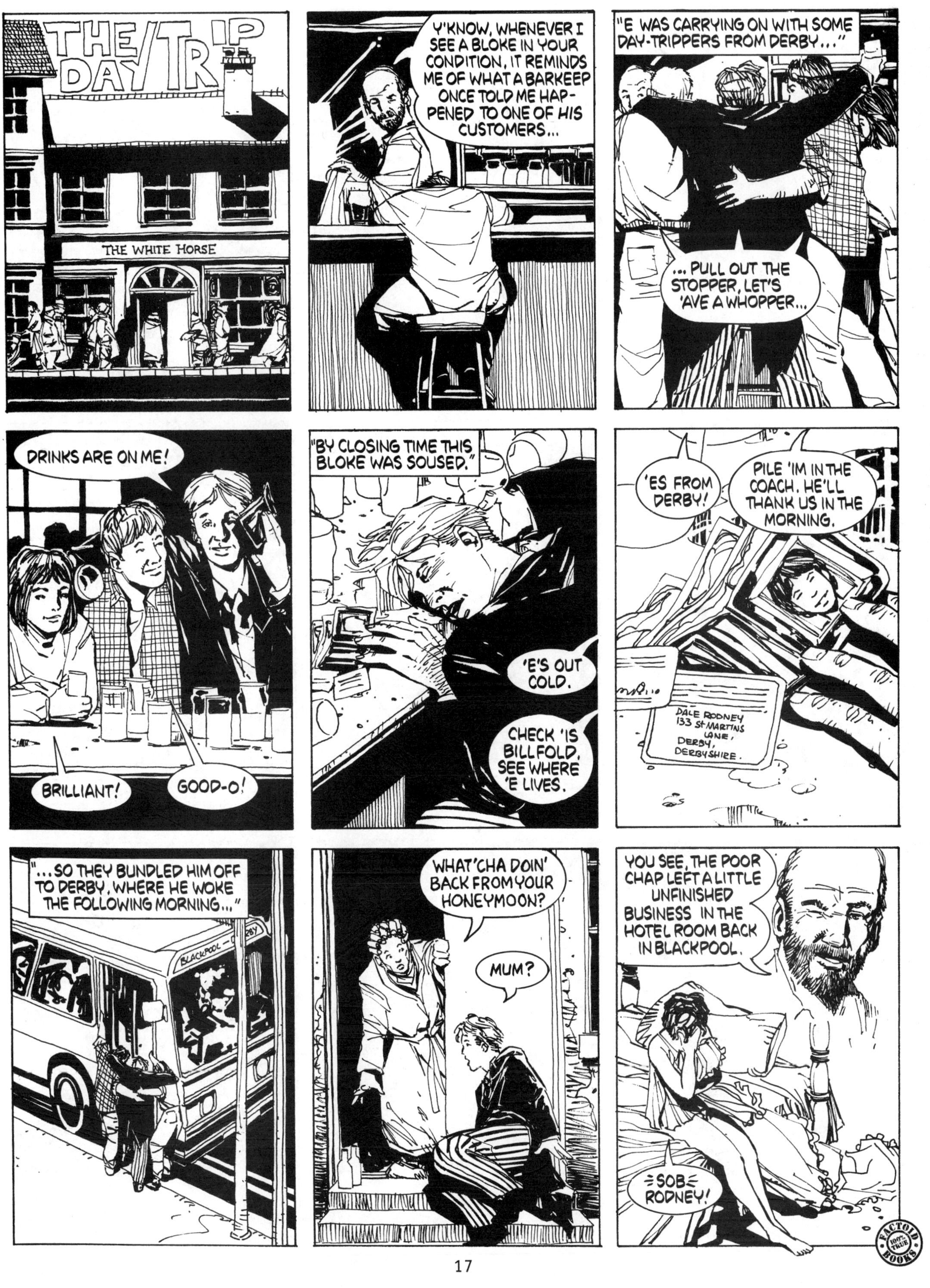
THE DAY TRIP
THE WHITE HORSE
Y'KNOW, WHENEVER I SEE A BLOKE IN YOUR CONDITION, IT REMINDS ME OF WHAT A BARKEEP ONCE TOLD ME HAPPENED TO ONE OF HIS CUSTOMERS...
"'E WAS CARRYING ON WITH SOME DAY-TRIPPERS FROM DERBY..."
... PULL OUT THE STOPPER, LET'S 'AVE A WHOPPER...
DRINKS ARE ON ME!
BRILLIANT!
GOOD-O!
"BY CLOSING TIME THIS BLOKE WAS SOUSED."
'E'S OUT COLD.
CHECK 'IS BILLFOLD. SEE WHERE 'E LIVES.
'ES FROM DERBY!
PILE 'IM IN THE COACH. HE'LL THANK US IN THE MORNING.
DALE RODNEY
133 St MARTINS LANE,
DERBY,
DERBYSHIRE.
"...SO THEY BUNDLED HIM OFF TO DERBY, WHERE HE WOKE THE FOLLOWING MORNING..."
WHAT'CHA DOIN' BACK FROM YOUR HONEYMOON?
MUM?
YOU SEE, THE POOR CHAP LEFT A LITTLE UNFINISHED BUSINESS IN THE HOTEL ROOM BACK IN BLACKPOOL.
SOB RODNEY!
FACTOID 100% TRUE BOOKS

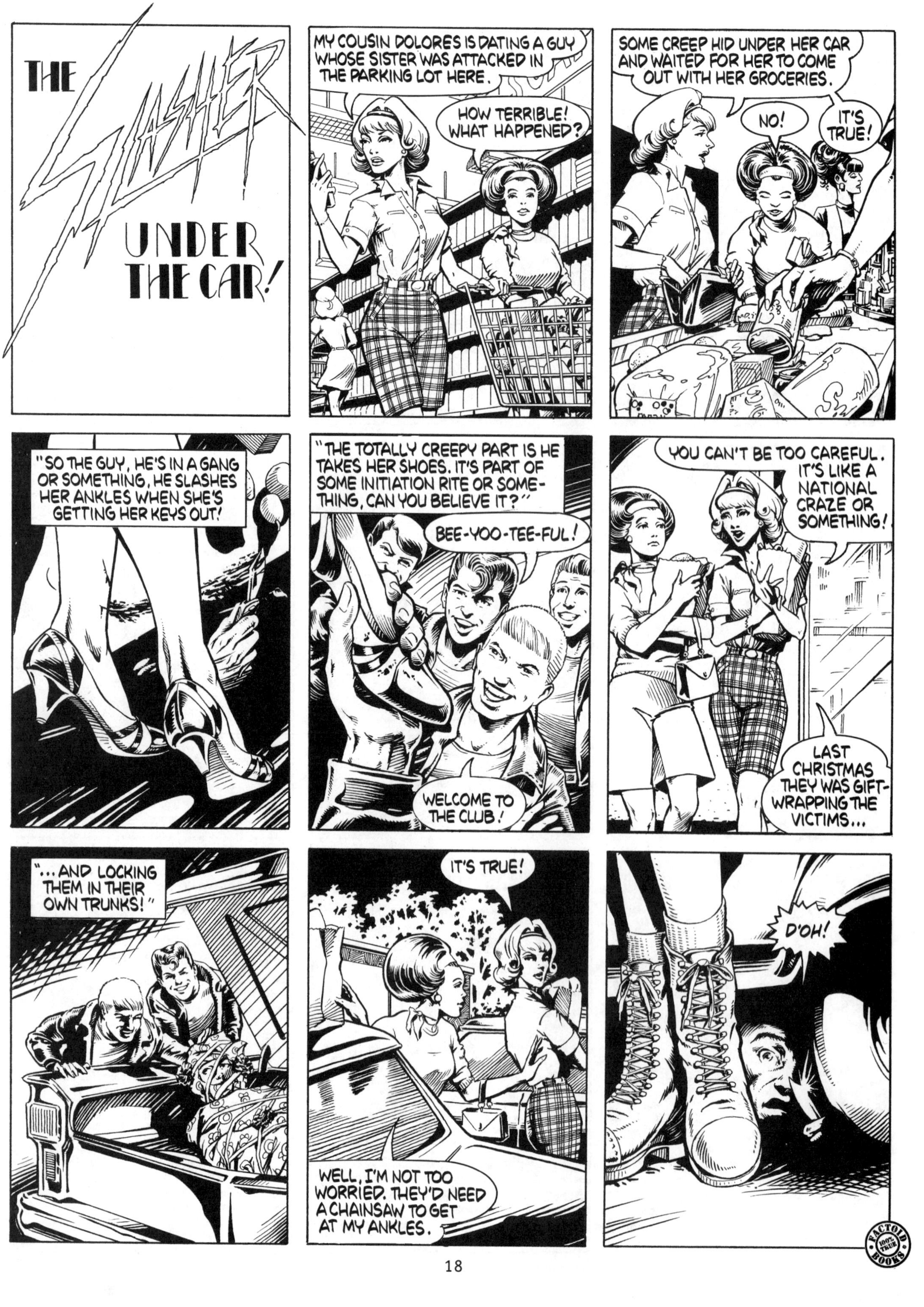

THE SLASHER
UNDER THE CAR!
MY COUSIN DOLORES IS DATING A GUY WHOSE SISTER WAS ATTACKED IN THE PARKING LOT HERE.
HOW TERRIBLE! WHAT HAPPENED?
SOME CREEP HID UNDER HER CAR AND WAITED FOR HER TO COME OUT WITH HER GROCERIES.
NO!
IT'S TRUE!
"SO THE GUY, HE'S IN A GANG OR SOMETHING, HE SLASHES HER ANKLES WHEN SHE'S GETTING HER KEYS OUT!
"THE TOTALLY CREEPY PART IS HE TAKES HER SHOES. IT'S PART OF SOME INITIATION RITE OR SOMETHING, CAN YOU BELIEVE IT?"
BEE-YOO-TEE-FUL!
WELCOME TO THE CLUB!
YOU CAN'T BE TOO CAREFUL. IT'S LIKE A NATIONAL CRAZE OR SOMETHING!
LAST CHRISTMAS THEY WAS GIFT-WRAPPING THE VICTIMS...
"...AND LOCKING THEM IN THEIR OWN TRUNKS!"
IT'S TRUE!
WELL, I'M NOT TOO WORRIED. THEY'D NEED A CHAINSAW TO GET AT MY ANKLES.
D'OH!
FACTOID BOOKS 100% TRUE

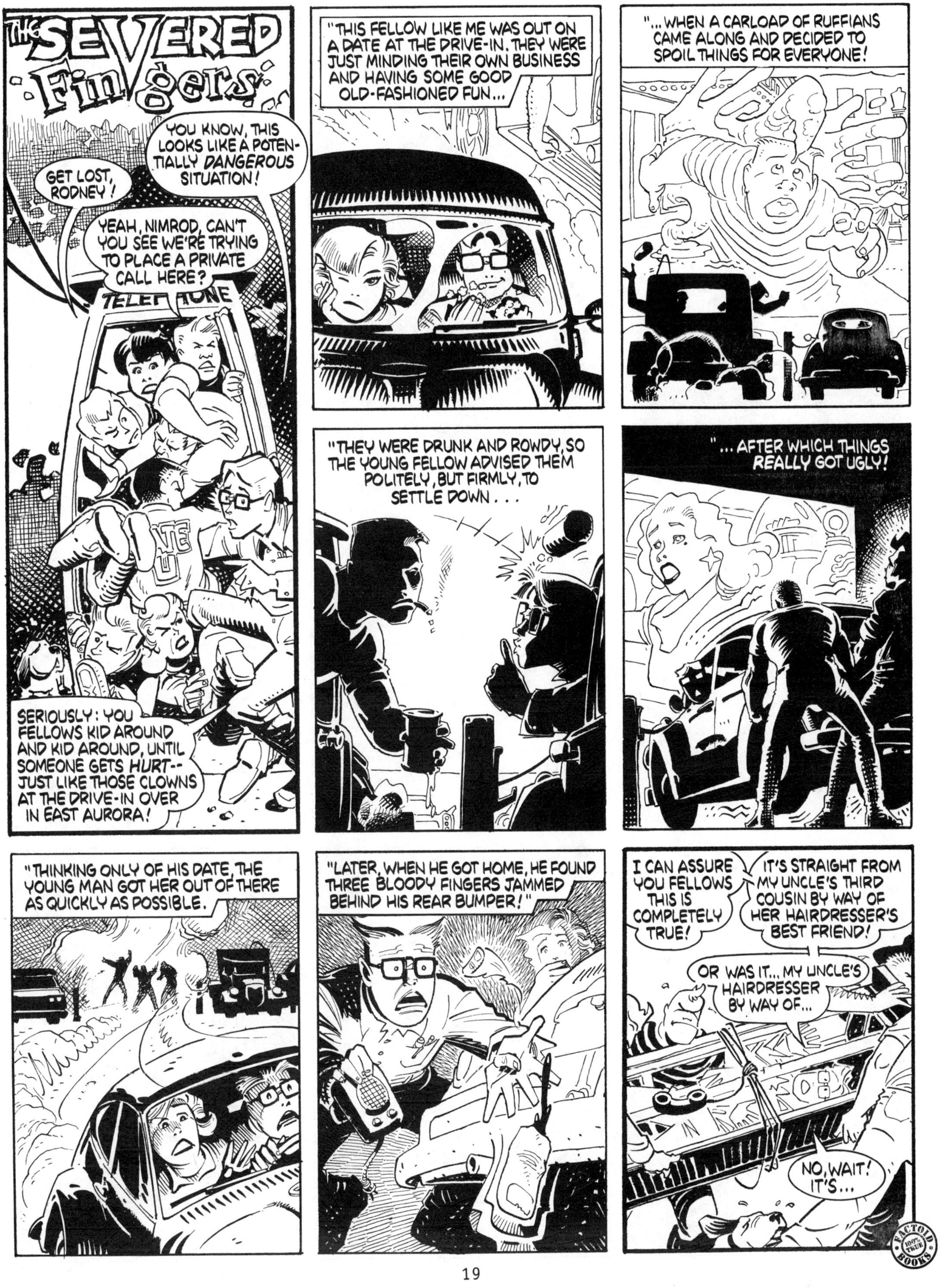
THE SEVERED FINGERS
YOU KNOW, THIS LOOKS LIKE A POTENTIALLY DANGEROUS SITUATION!
GET LOST, RODNEY!
YEAH, NIMROD, CAN'T YOU SEE WE'RE TRYING TO PLACE A PRIVATE CALL HERE?
TELEPHONE
SERIOUSLY: YOU FELLOWS KID AROUND AND KID AROUND, UNTIL SOMEONE GETS HURT-- JUST LIKE THOSE CLOWNS AT THE DRIVE-IN OVER IN EAST AURORA!
"THIS FELLOW LIKE ME WAS OUT ON A DATE AT THE DRIVE-IN. THEY WERE JUST MINDING THEIR OWN BUSINESS AND HAVING SOME GOOD OLD-FASHIONED FUN...
"...WHEN A CARLOAD OF RUFFIANS CAME ALONG AND DECIDED TO SPOIL THINGS FOR EVERYONE!
"THEY WERE DRUNK AND ROWDY, SO THE YOUNG FELLOW ADVISED THEM POLITELY, BUT FIRMLY, TO SETTLE DOWN . . .
"... AFTER WHICH THINGS REALLY GOT UGLY!
"THINKING ONLY OF HIS DATE, THE YOUNG MAN GOT HER OUT OF THERE AS QUICKLY AS POSSIBLE.
"LATER, WHEN HE GOT HOME, HE FOUND THREE BLOODY FINGERS JAMMED BEHIND HIS REAR BUMPER!"
I CAN ASSURE YOU FELLOWS THIS IS COMPLETELY TRUE!
IT'S STRAIGHT FROM MY UNCLE'S THIRD COUSIN BY WAY OF HER HAIRDRESSER'S BEST FRIEND!
OR WAS IT... MY UNCLE'S HAIRDRESSER BY WAY OF...
NO, WAIT! IT'S...
FACTOID BOOKS 100% TRUE

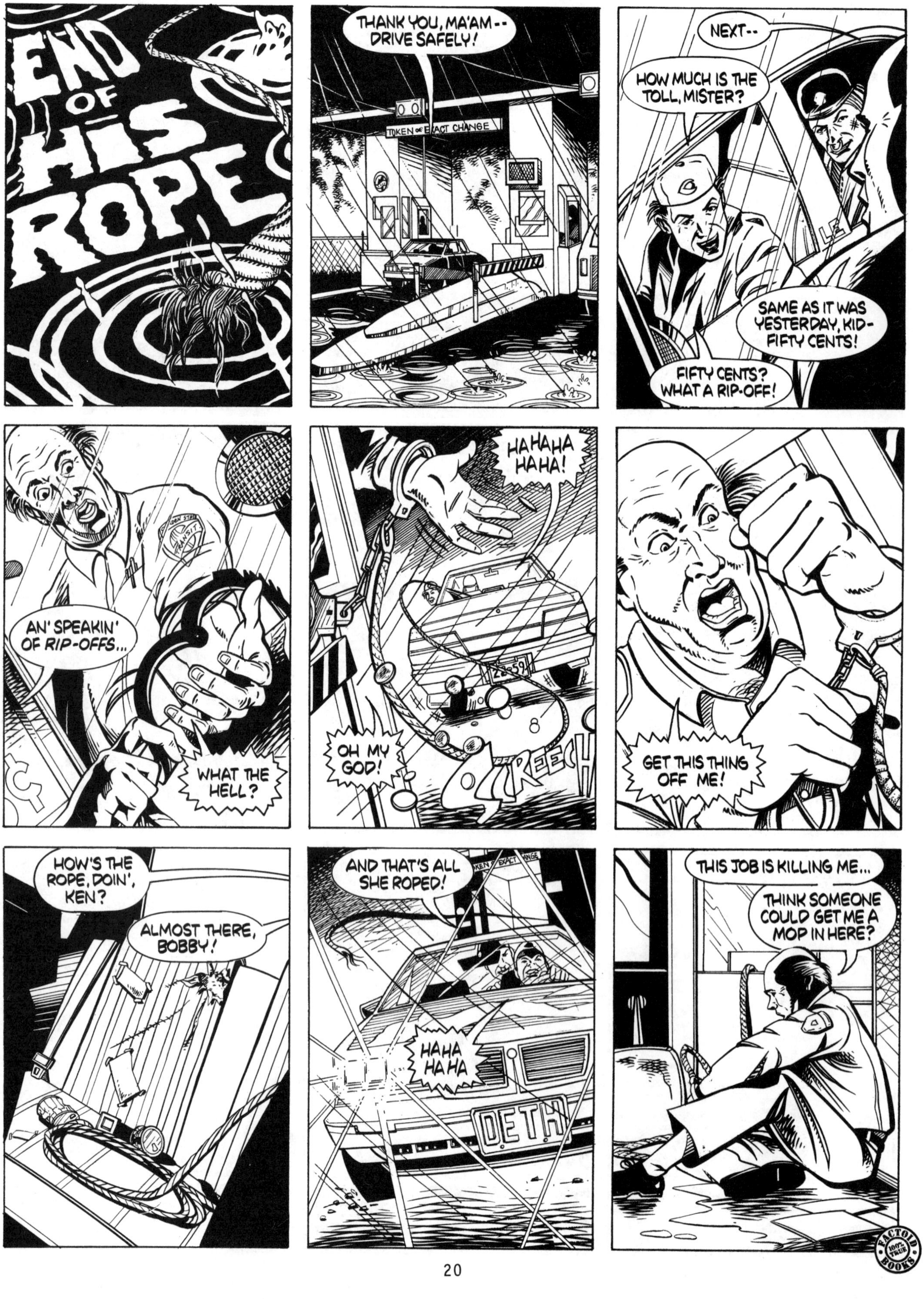
END OF HIS ROPE
THANK YOU, MA'AM -- DRIVE SAFELY!
TOKEN OR EXACT CHANGE
NEXT--
HOW MUCH IS THE TOLL, MISTER?
SAME AS IT WAS YESTERDAY, KID-FIFTY CENTS!
FIFTY CENTS? WHAT A RIP-OFF!
AN' SPEAKIN' OF RIP-OFFS...
WHAT THE HELL?
HAHAHA HAHA!
OH MY GOD!
SKREECH
GET THIS THING OFF ME!
HOW'S THE ROPE, DOIN', KEN?
ALMOST THERE, BOBBY!
AND THAT'S ALL SHE ROPED!
HAHA HAHA
DETH
THIS JOB IS KILLING ME...
THINK SOMEONE COULD GET ME A MOP IN HERE?
FACTOID BOOKS 100% TRUE

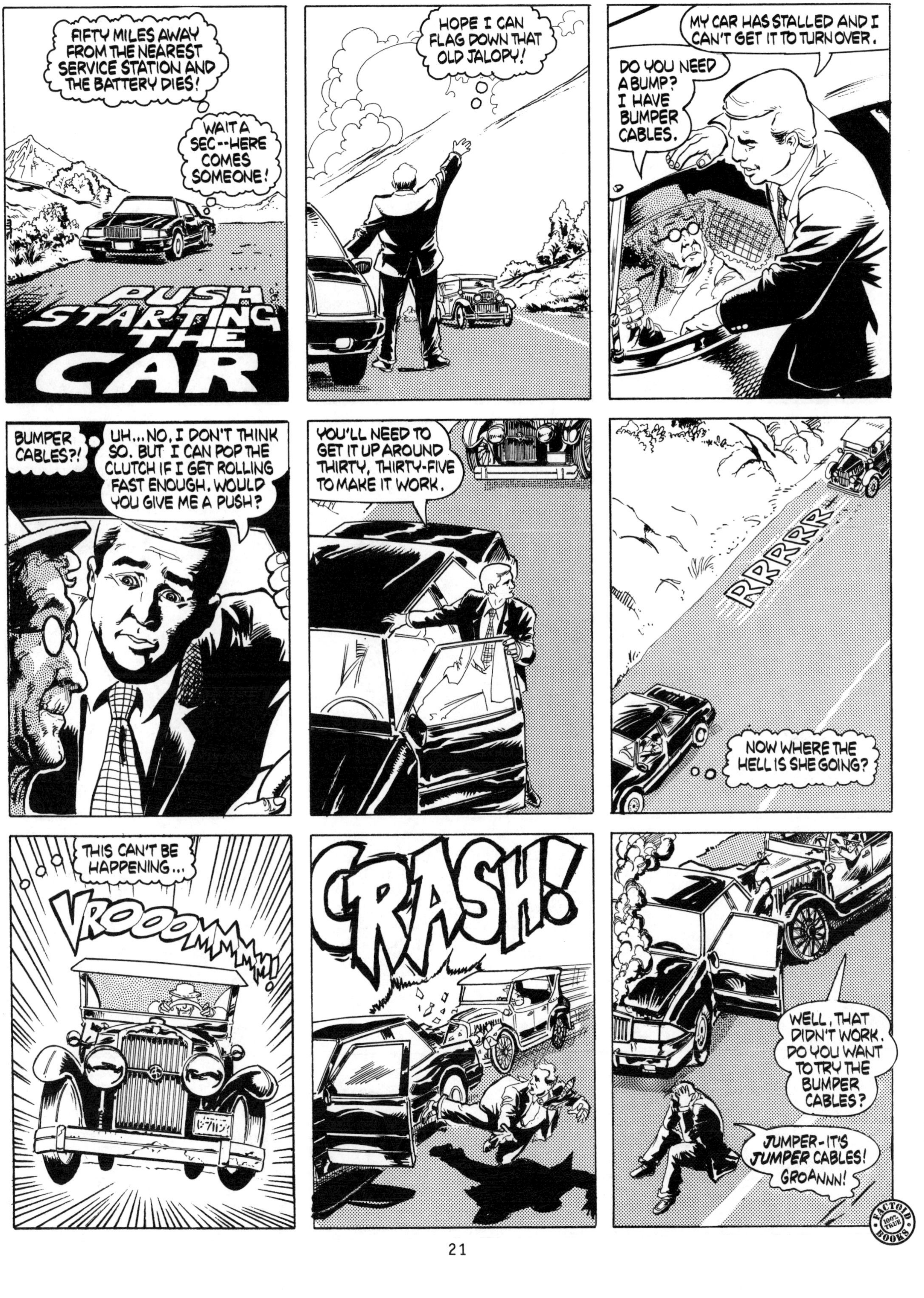
FIFTY MILES AWAY FROM THE NEAREST SERVICE STATION AND THE BATTERY DIES!
WAIT A SEC--HERE COMES SOMEONE!
PUSH STARTING THE CAR
HOPE I CAN FLAG DOWN THAT OLD JALOPY!
MY CAR HAS STALLED AND I CAN'T GET IT TO TURN OVER.
DO YOU NEED A BUMP? I HAVE BUMPER CABLES.
BUMPER CABLES?!
UH...NO, I DON'T THINK SO. BUT I CAN POP THE CLUTCH IF I GET ROLLING FAST ENOUGH. WOULD YOU GIVE ME A PUSH?
YOU'LL NEED TO GET IT UP AROUND THIRTY, THIRTY-FIVE TO MAKE IT WORK.
RRRRRR
NOW WHERE THE HELL IS SHE GOING?
THIS CAN'T BE HAPPENING...
VROOOMMMMM!
CRASH!
WELL, THAT DIDN'T WORK. DO YOU WANT TO TRY THE BUMPER CABLES?
JUMPER-IT'S JUMPER CABLES! GROANNN!

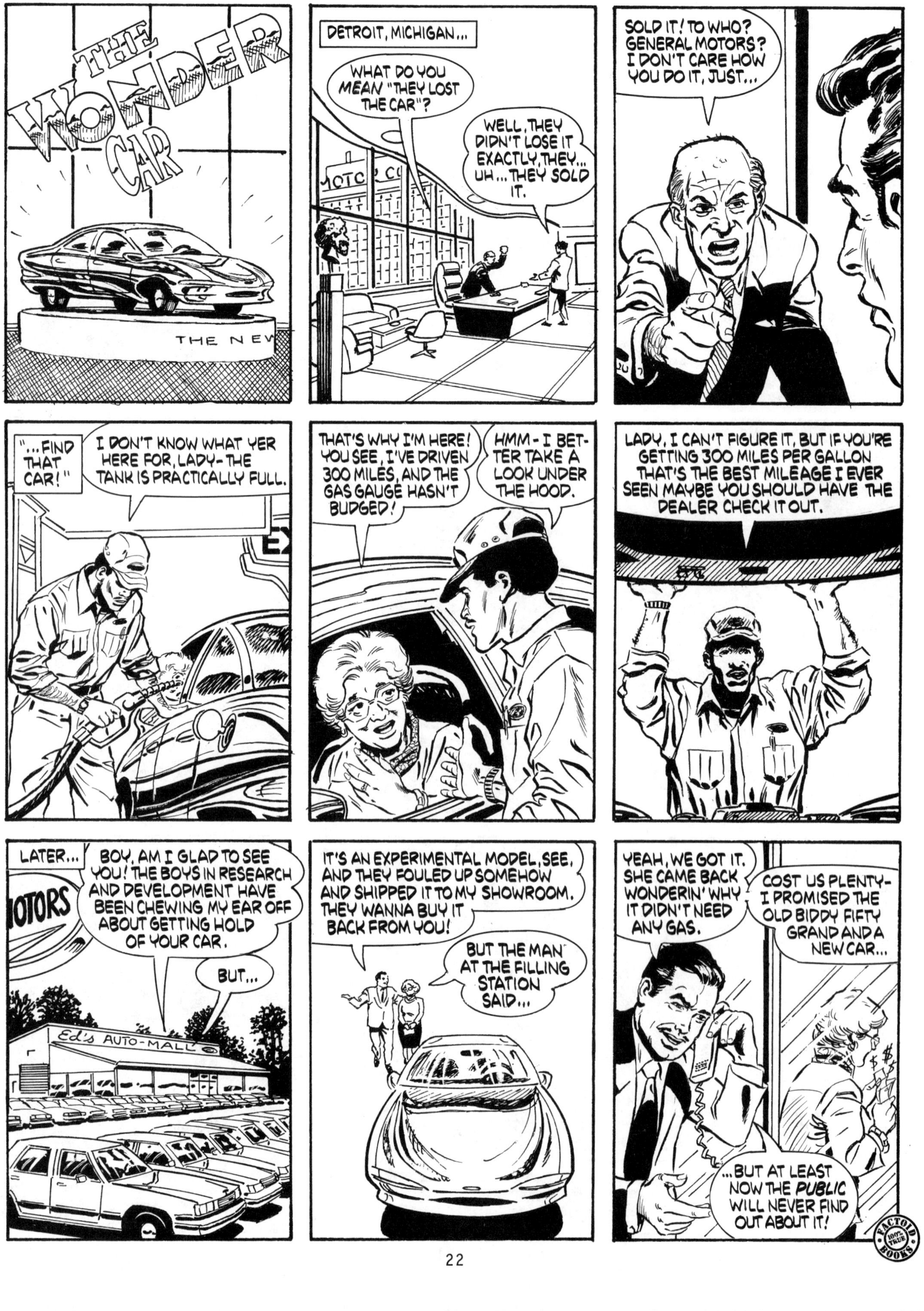
THE WONDER CAR
THE NEW
DETROIT, MICHIGAN...
WHAT DO YOU *MEAN* "THEY LOST THE CAR"?
WELL, THEY DIDN'T LOSE IT EXACTLY, THEY... UH... THEY SOLD IT.
SOLD IT! TO WHO? GENERAL MOTORS? I DON'T CARE HOW YOU DO IT, JUST...
"...FIND THAT CAR!"
I DON'T KNOW WHAT YER HERE FOR, LADY- THE TANK IS PRACTICALLY FULL.
THAT'S WHY I'M HERE! YOU SEE, I'VE DRIVEN 300 MILES, AND THE GAS GAUGE HASN'T BUDGED!
HMM - I BETTER TAKE A LOOK UNDER THE HOOD.
LADY, I CAN'T FIGURE IT, BUT IF YOU'RE GETTING 300 MILES PER GALLON THAT'S THE BEST MILEAGE I EVER SEEN MAYBE YOU SHOULD HAVE THE DEALER CHECK IT OUT.
LATER...
BOY, AM I GLAD TO SEE YOU! THE BOYS IN RESEARCH AND DEVELOPMENT HAVE BEEN CHEWING MY EAR OFF ABOUT GETTING HOLD OF YOUR CAR.
BUT...
Ed's AUTO-MALL
IT'S AN EXPERIMENTAL MODEL, SEE, AND THEY FOULED UP SOMEHOW AND SHIPPED IT TO MY SHOWROOM. THEY WANNA BUY IT BACK FROM YOU!
BUT THE MAN AT THE FILLING STATION SAID...
YEAH, WE GOT IT. SHE CAME BACK WONDERIN' WHY IT DIDN'T NEED ANY GAS.
COST US PLENTY- I PROMISED THE OLD BIDDY FIFTY GRAND AND A NEW CAR...
...BUT AT LEAST NOW THE *PUBLIC* WILL NEVER FIND OUT ABOUT IT!
FACTOID BOOKS 100% TRUE

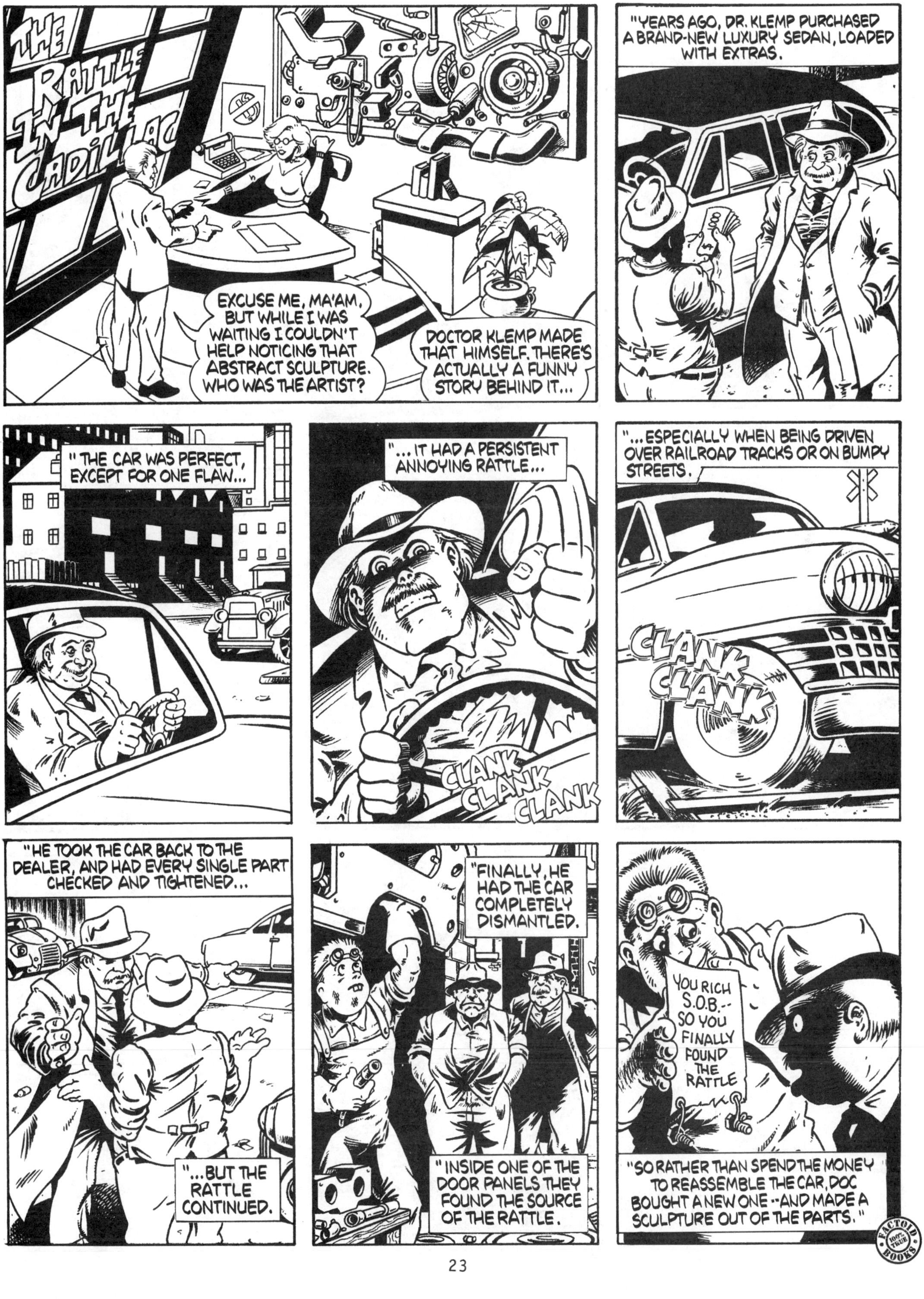
THE RATTLE IN THE CADILLAC
EXCUSE ME, MA'AM, BUT WHILE I WAS WAITING I COULDN'T HELP NOTICING THAT ABSTRACT SCULPTURE. WHO WAS THE ARTIST?
DOCTOR KLEMP MADE THAT HIMSELF. THERE'S ACTUALLY A FUNNY STORY BEHIND IT...
"YEARS AGO, DR. KLEMP PURCHASED A BRAND-NEW LUXURY SEDAN, LOADED WITH EXTRAS.
"THE CAR WAS PERFECT, EXCEPT FOR ONE FLAW...
"...IT HAD A PERSISTENT ANNOYING RATTLE...
CLANK CLANK CLANK
"...ESPECIALLY WHEN BEING DRIVEN OVER RAILROAD TRACKS OR ON BUMPY STREETS.
CLANK CLANK
"HE TOOK THE CAR BACK TO THE DEALER, AND HAD EVERY SINGLE PART CHECKED AND TIGHTENED...
"...BUT THE RATTLE CONTINUED.
"FINALLY, HE HAD THE CAR COMPLETELY DISMANTLED.
"INSIDE ONE OF THE DOOR PANELS THEY FOUND THE SOURCE OF THE RATTLE.
YOU RICH S.O.B.-- SO YOU FINALLY FOUND THE RATTLE
"SO RATHER THAN SPEND THE MONEY TO REASSEMBLE THE CAR, DOC BOUGHT A NEW ONE--AND MADE A SCULPTURE OUT OF THE PARTS."
FACTOID BOOKS 100% TRUE

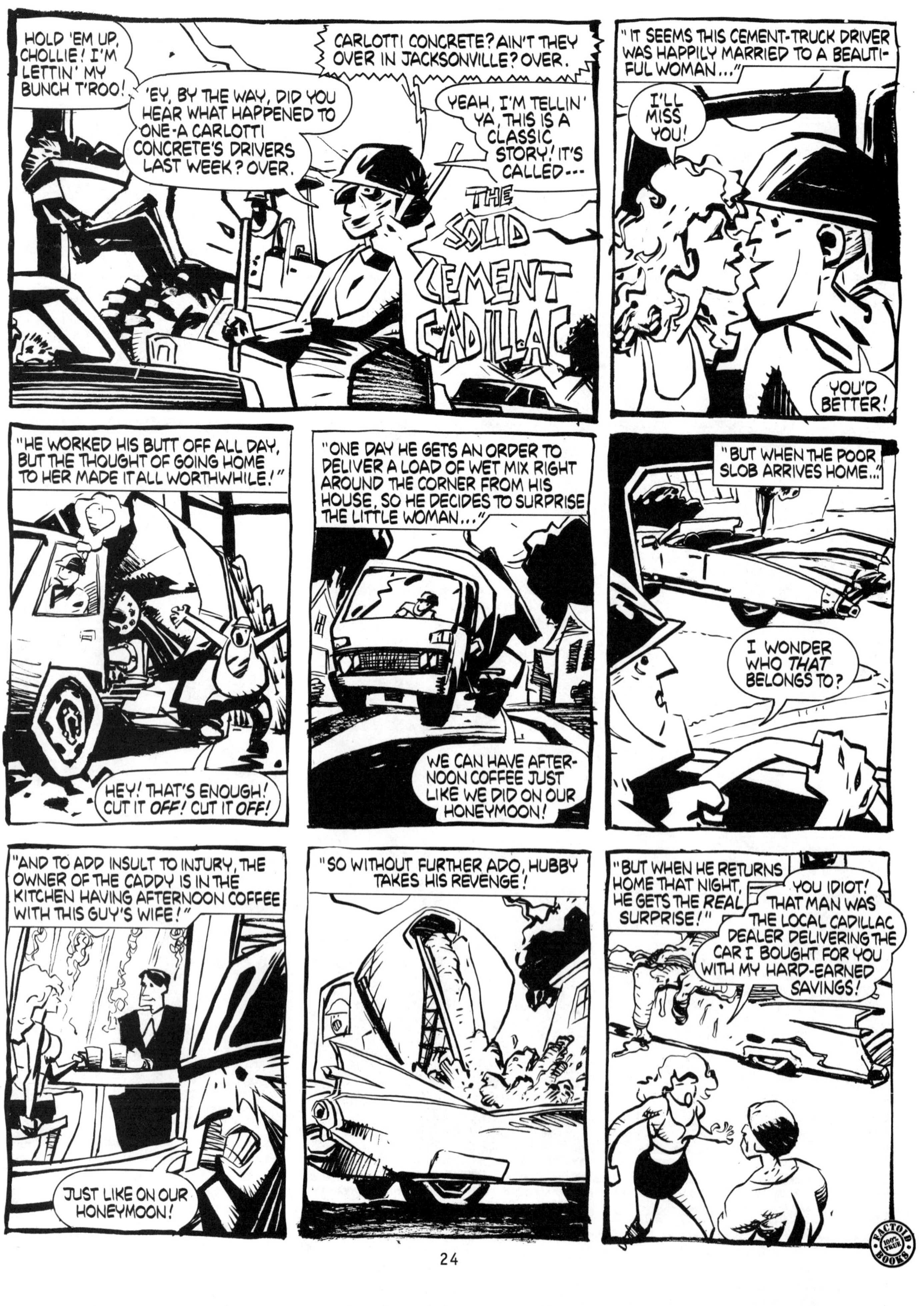
HOLD 'EM UP, CHOLLIE! I'M LETTIN' MY BUNCH T'ROO!
'EY, BY THE WAY, DID YOU HEAR WHAT HAPPENED TO ONE-A CARLOTTI CONCRETE'S DRIVERS LAST WEEK? OVER.
CARLOTTI CONCRETE? AIN'T THEY OVER IN JACKSONVILLE? OVER.
YEAH, I'M TELLIN' YA, THIS IS A CLASSIC STORY! IT'S CALLED---
THE SOLID CEMENT CADILLAC
"IT SEEMS THIS CEMENT-TRUCK DRIVER WAS HAPPILY MARRIED TO A BEAUTIFUL WOMAN..."
I'LL MISS YOU!
YOU'D BETTER!
"HE WORKED HIS BUTT OFF ALL DAY, BUT THE THOUGHT OF GOING HOME TO HER MADE IT ALL WORTHWHILE!"
HEY! THAT'S ENOUGH! CUT IT OFF! CUT IT OFF!
"ONE DAY HE GETS AN ORDER TO DELIVER A LOAD OF WET MIX RIGHT AROUND THE CORNER FROM HIS HOUSE, SO HE DECIDES TO SURPRISE THE LITTLE WOMAN..."
WE CAN HAVE AFTERNOON COFFEE JUST LIKE WE DID ON OUR HONEYMOON!
"BUT WHEN THE POOR SLOB ARRIVES HOME..."
I WONDER WHO THAT BELONGS TO?
"AND TO ADD INSULT TO INJURY, THE OWNER OF THE CADDY IS IN THE KITCHEN HAVING AFTERNOON COFFEE WITH THIS GUY'S WIFE!"
JUST LIKE ON OUR HONEYMOON!
"SO WITHOUT FURTHER ADO, HUBBY TAKES HIS REVENGE!
"BUT WHEN HE RETURNS HOME THAT NIGHT, HE GETS THE REAL SURPRISE!"
YOU IDIOT! THAT MAN WAS THE LOCAL CADILLAC DEALER DELIVERING THE CAR I BOUGHT FOR YOU WITH MY HARD-EARNED SAVINGS!
FACTOID BOOKS 100% TRUE

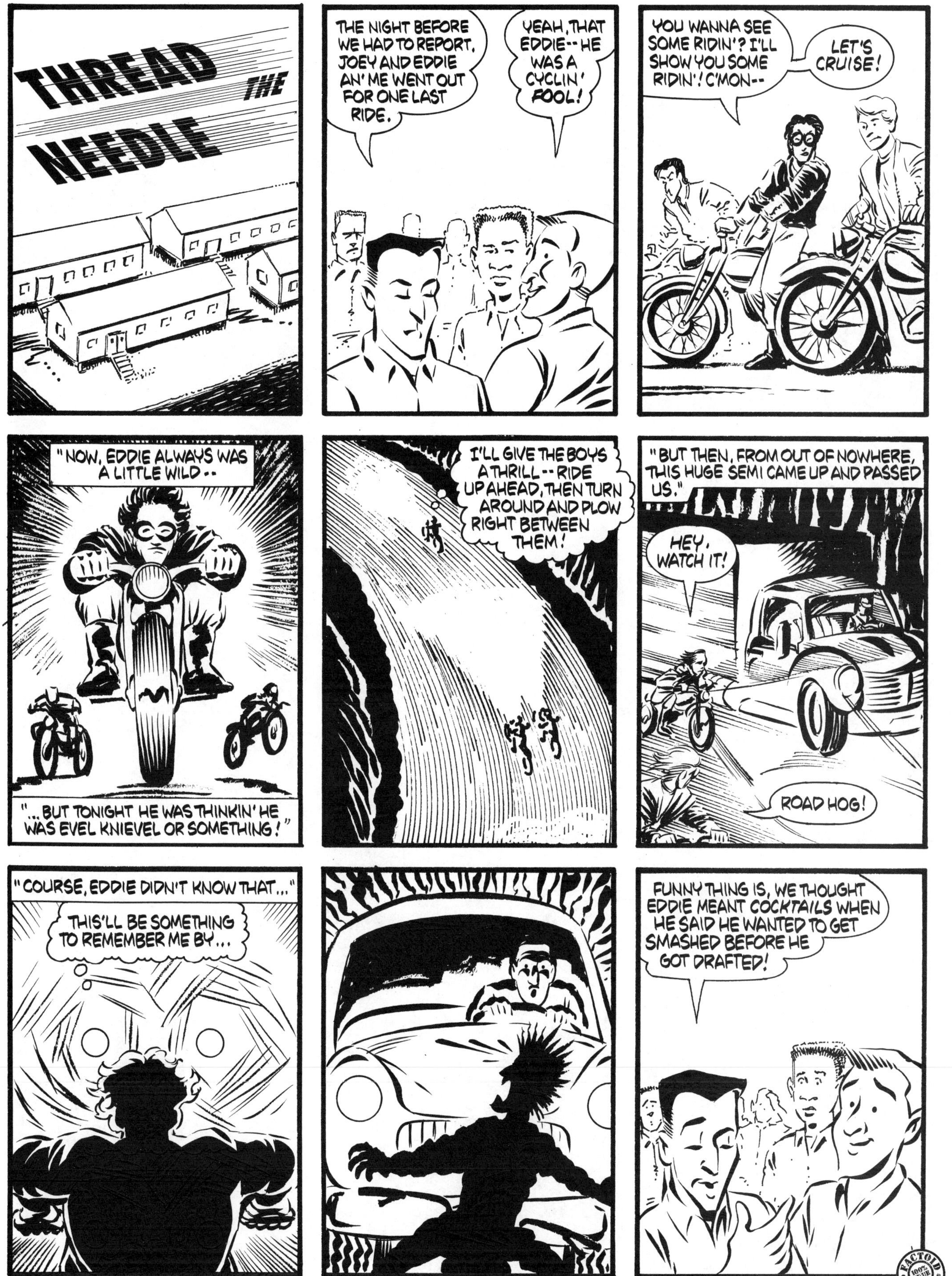
THREAD THE NEEDLE
THE NIGHT BEFORE WE HAD TO REPORT, JOEY AND EDDIE AN' ME WENT OUT FOR ONE LAST RIDE.
YEAH, THAT EDDIE-- HE WAS A CYCLIN' FOOL!
YOU WANNA SEE SOME RIDIN'? I'LL SHOW YOU SOME RIDIN'! C'MON--
LET'S CRUISE!
"NOW, EDDIE ALWAYS WAS A LITTLE WILD--
"...BUT TONIGHT HE WAS THINKIN' HE WAS EVEL KNIEVEL OR SOMETHING!"
I'LL GIVE THE BOYS A THRILL-- RIDE UP AHEAD, THEN TURN AROUND AND PLOW RIGHT BETWEEN THEM!
"BUT THEN, FROM OUT OF NOWHERE, THIS HUGE SEMI CAME UP AND PASSED US."
HEY, WATCH IT!
ROAD HOG!
"COURSE, EDDIE DIDN'T KNOW THAT..."
THIS'LL BE SOMETHING TO REMEMBER ME BY...
FUNNY THING IS, WE THOUGHT EDDIE MEANT COCKTAILS WHEN HE SAID HE WANTED TO GET SMASHED BEFORE HE GOT DRAFTED!
FACTOID 100% TRUE BOOKS

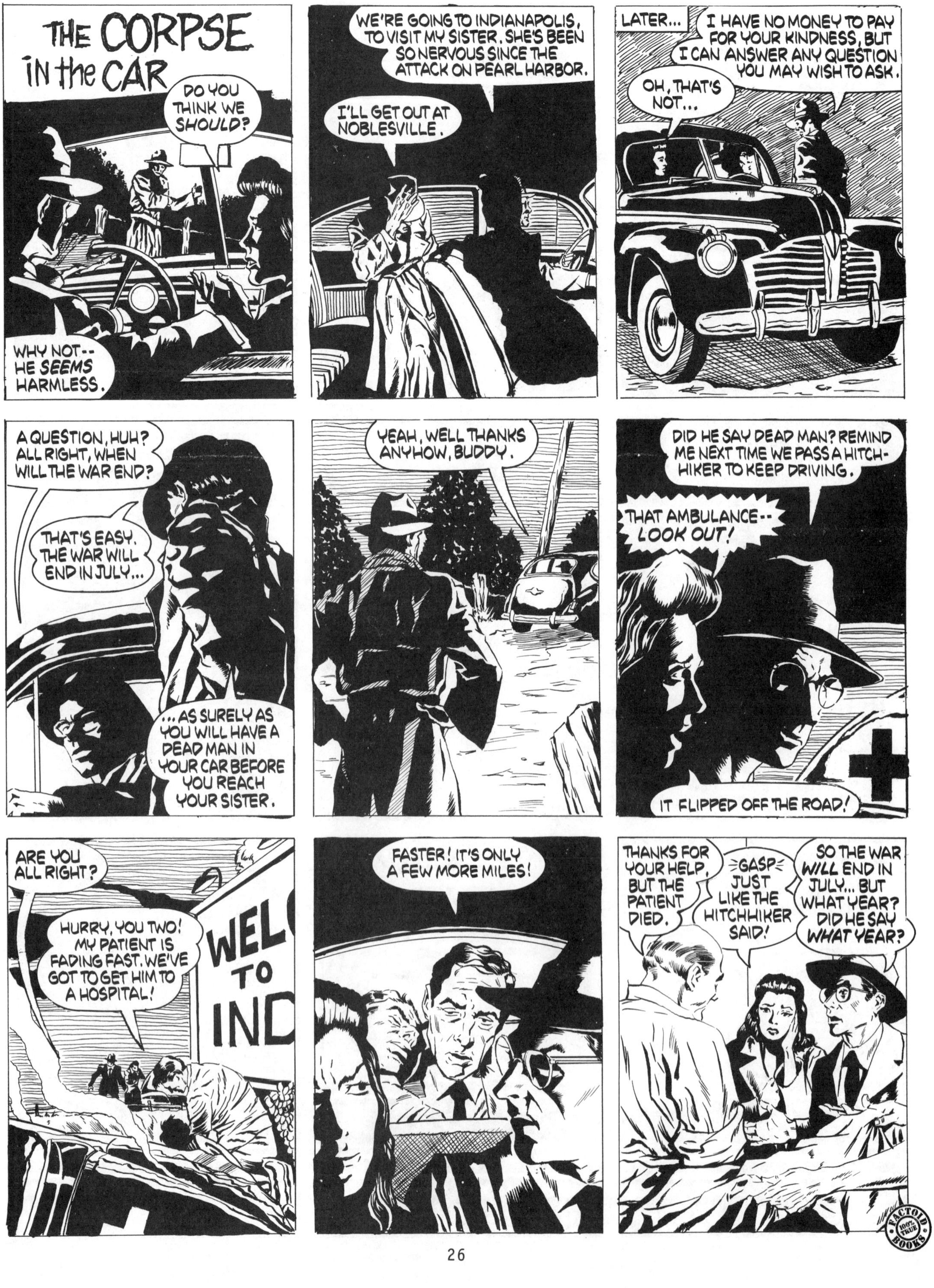
THE CORPSE in the CAR
DO YOU THINK WE SHOULD?
WHY NOT-- HE SEEMS HARMLESS.
WE'RE GOING TO INDIANAPOLIS, TO VISIT MY SISTER. SHE'S BEEN SO NERVOUS SINCE THE ATTACK ON PEARL HARBOR.
I'LL GET OUT AT NOBLESVILLE.
LATER...
I HAVE NO MONEY TO PAY FOR YOUR KINDNESS, BUT I CAN ANSWER ANY QUESTION YOU MAY WISH TO ASK.
OH, THAT'S NOT...
A QUESTION, HUH? ALL RIGHT, WHEN WILL THE WAR END?
THAT'S EASY. THE WAR WILL END IN JULY...
...AS SURELY AS YOU WILL HAVE A DEAD MAN IN YOUR CAR BEFORE YOU REACH YOUR SISTER.
YEAH, WELL THANKS ANYHOW, BUDDY.
DID HE SAY DEAD MAN? REMIND ME NEXT TIME WE PASS A HITCH-HIKER TO KEEP DRIVING.
THAT AMBULANCE-- LOOK OUT!
IT FLIPPED OFF THE ROAD!
ARE YOU ALL RIGHT?
HURRY, YOU TWO! MY PATIENT IS FADING FAST. WE'VE GOT TO GET HIM TO A HOSPITAL!
WEL TO IND
FASTER! IT'S ONLY A FEW MORE MILES!
THANKS FOR YOUR HELP, BUT THE PATIENT DIED.
GASP JUST LIKE THE HITCHHIKER SAID!
SO THE WAR WILL END IN JULY... BUT WHAT YEAR? DID HE SAY WHAT YEAR?
FACTOID BOOKS 100% TRUE

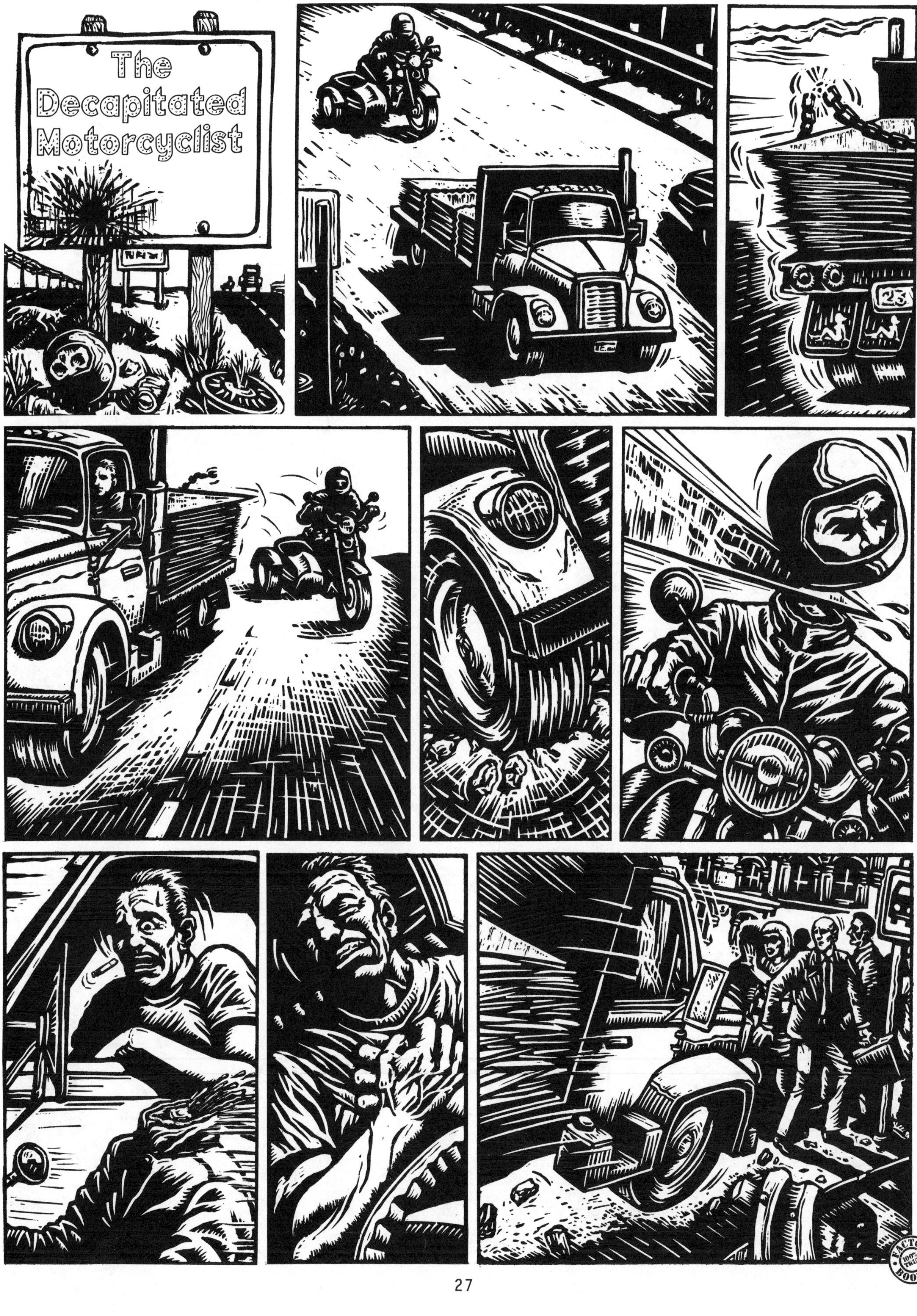
The Decapitated Motorcyclist
23

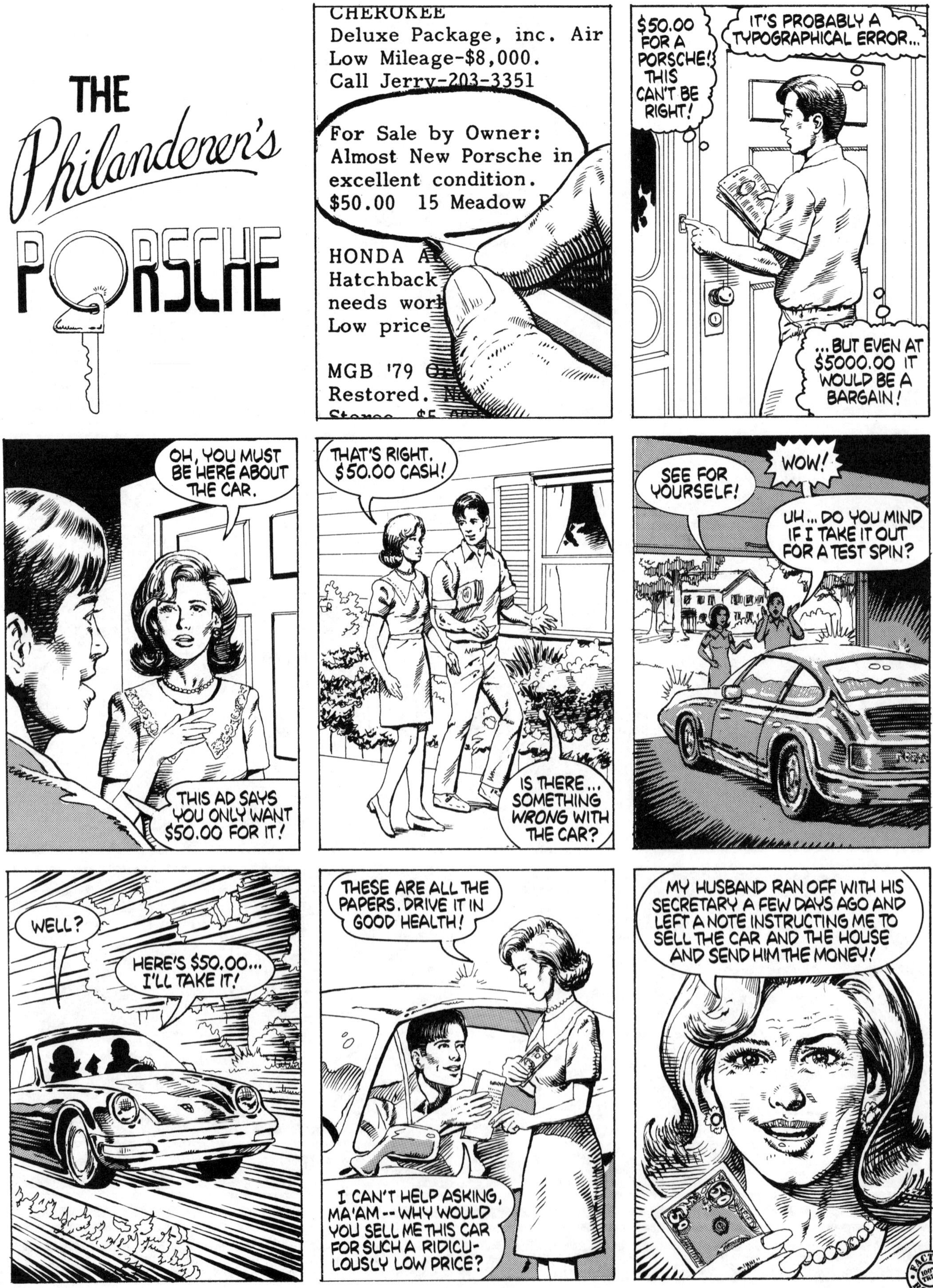
THE
Philanderer's
PORSCHE
CHEROKEE
Deluxe Package, inc. Air
Low Mileage-$8,000.
Call Jerry-203-3351
For Sale by Owner:
Almost New Porsche in
excellent condition.
$50.00 15 Meadow
HONDA
Hatchback
needs work
Low price
MGB '79
Restored.
$50.00 FOR A PORSCHE! THIS CAN'T BE RIGHT!
IT'S PROBABLY A TYPOGRAPHICAL ERROR...
...BUT EVEN AT $5000.00 IT WOULD BE A BARGAIN!
OH, YOU MUST BE HERE ABOUT THE CAR.
THIS AD SAYS YOU ONLY WANT $50.00 FOR IT!
THAT'S RIGHT. $50.00 CASH!
IS THERE... SOMETHING WRONG WITH THE CAR?
SEE FOR YOURSELF!
WOW!
UH... DO YOU MIND IF I TAKE IT OUT FOR A TEST SPIN?
WELL?
HERE'S $50.00... I'LL TAKE IT!
THESE ARE ALL THE PAPERS. DRIVE IT IN GOOD HEALTH!
I CAN'T HELP ASKING, MA'AM -- WHY WOULD YOU SELL ME THIS CAR FOR SUCH A RIDICULOUSLY LOW PRICE?
MY HUSBAND RAN OFF WITH HIS SECRETARY A FEW DAYS AGO AND LEFT A NOTE INSTRUCTING ME TO SELL THE CAR AND THE HOUSE AND SEND HIM THE MONEY!

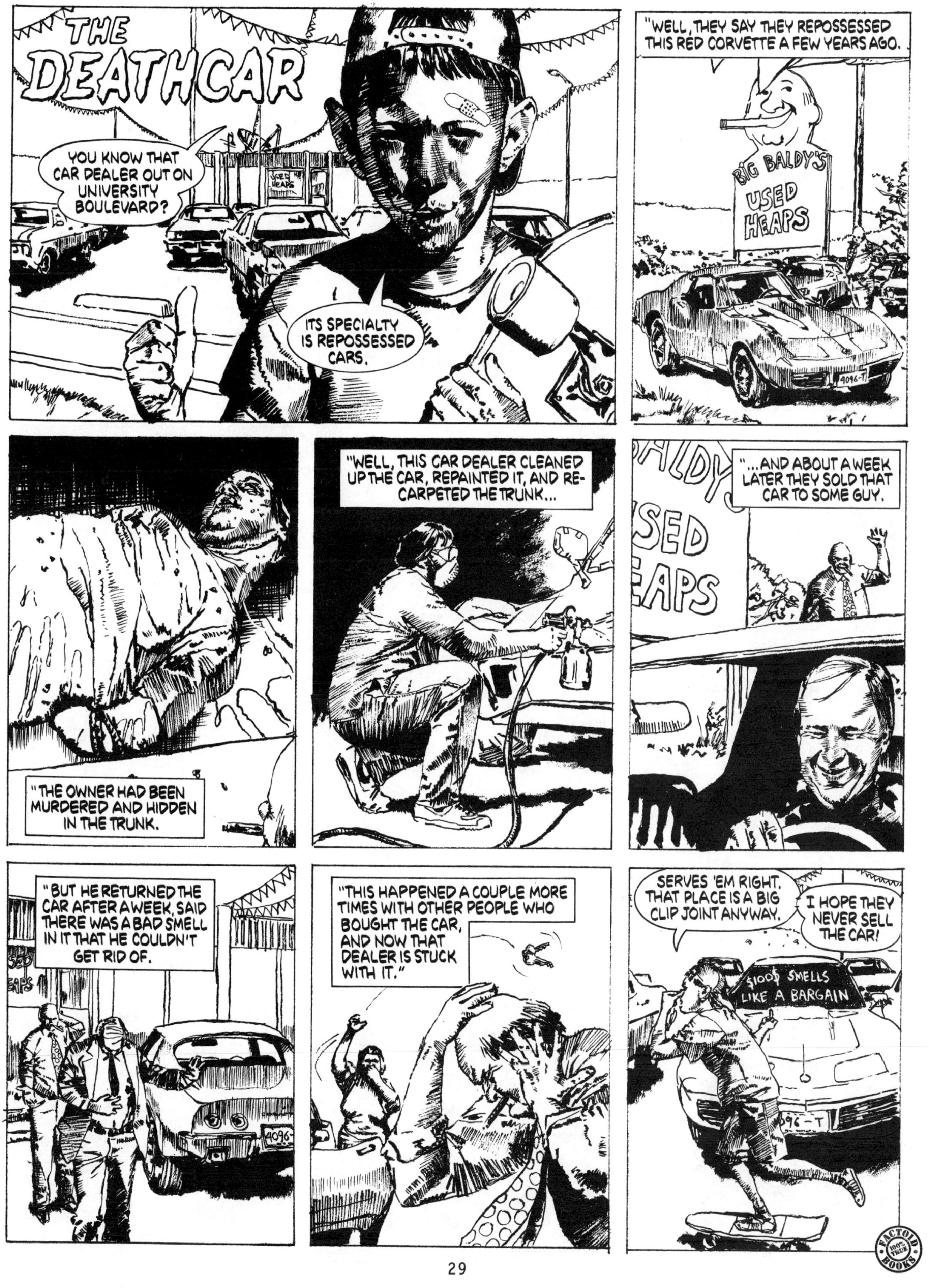
THE DEATHCAR
YOU KNOW THAT CAR DEALER OUT ON UNIVERSITY BOULEVARD?
ITS SPECIALTY IS REPOSSESSED CARS.
"WELL, THEY SAY THEY REPOSSESSED THIS RED CORVETTE A FEW YEARS AGO.
BIG BALDY'S USED HEAPS
"THE OWNER HAD BEEN MURDERED AND HIDDEN IN THE TRUNK.
"WELL, THIS CAR DEALER CLEANED UP THE CAR, REPAINTED IT, AND RE-CARPETED THE TRUNK...
"...AND ABOUT A WEEK LATER THEY SOLD THAT CAR TO SOME GUY.
"BUT HE RETURNED THE CAR AFTER A WEEK, SAID THERE WAS A BAD SMELL IN IT THAT HE COULDN'T GET RID OF.
"THIS HAPPENED A COUPLE MORE TIMES WITH OTHER PEOPLE WHO BOUGHT THE CAR, AND NOW THAT DEALER IS STUCK WITH IT."
SERVES 'EM RIGHT. THAT PLACE IS A BIG CLIP JOINT ANYWAY.
I HOPE THEY NEVER SELL THE CAR!
100 SMELLS LIKE A BARGAIN
FACTOID BOOKS 100% TRUE

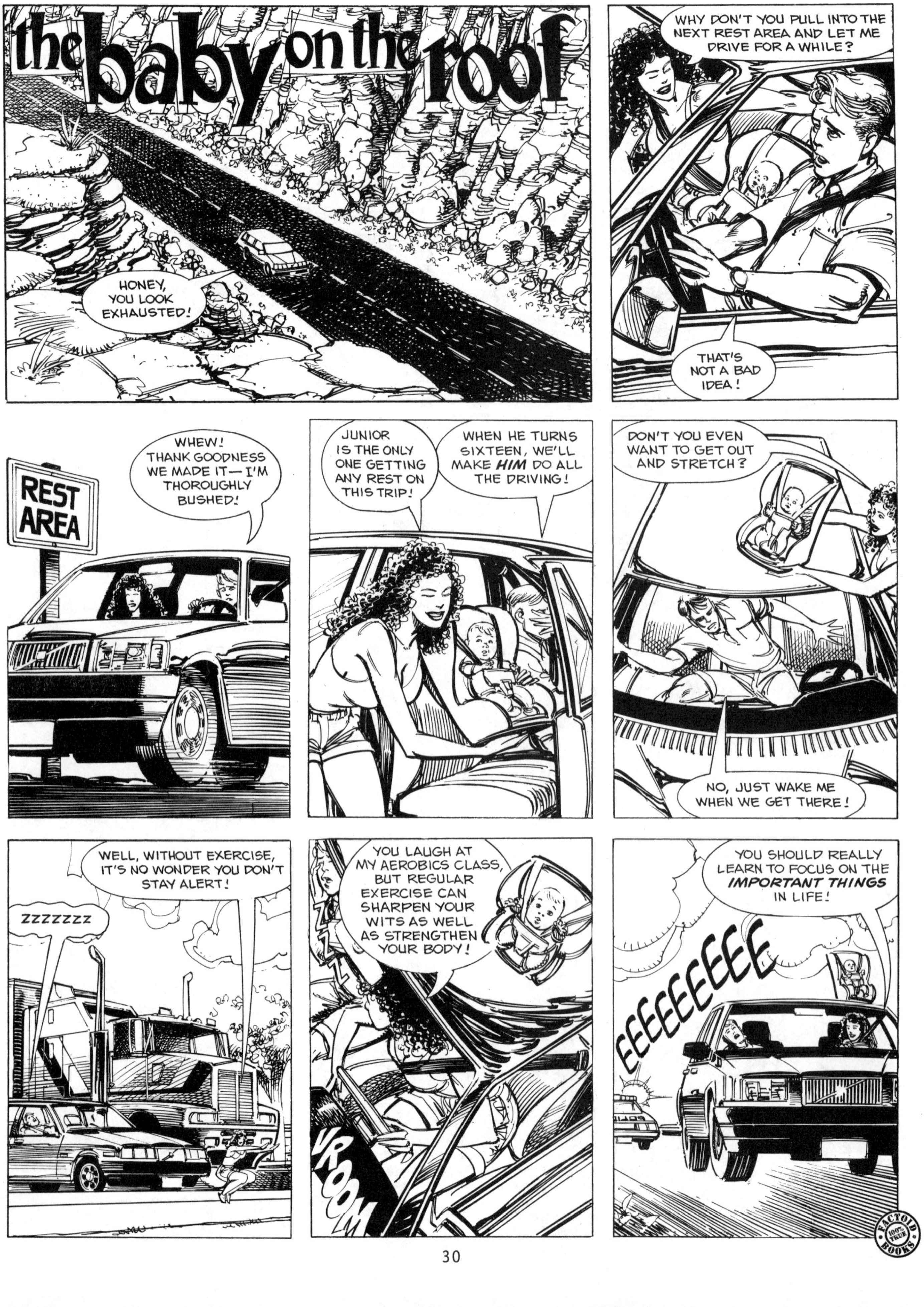
the baby on the roof
HONEY, YOU LOOK EXHAUSTED!
WHY DON'T YOU PULL INTO THE NEXT REST AREA AND LET ME DRIVE FOR A WHILE?
THAT'S NOT A BAD IDEA!
REST AREA
WHEW! THANK GOODNESS WE MADE IT— I'M THOROUGHLY BUSHED!
JUNIOR IS THE ONLY ONE GETTING ANY REST ON THIS TRIP!
WHEN HE TURNS SIXTEEN, WE'LL MAKE HIM DO ALL THE DRIVING!
DON'T YOU EVEN WANT TO GET OUT AND STRETCH?
NO, JUST WAKE ME WHEN WE GET THERE!
WELL, WITHOUT EXERCISE, IT'S NO WONDER YOU DON'T STAY ALERT!
ZZZZZZZ
YOU LAUGH AT MY AEROBICS CLASS, BUT REGULAR EXERCISE CAN SHARPEN YOUR WITS AS WELL AS STRENGTHEN YOUR BODY!
VROOM
YOU SHOULD REALLY LEARN TO FOCUS ON THE IMPORTANT THINGS IN LIFE!
EEEEEEEEEE
FACTOID BOOKS 100% TRUE

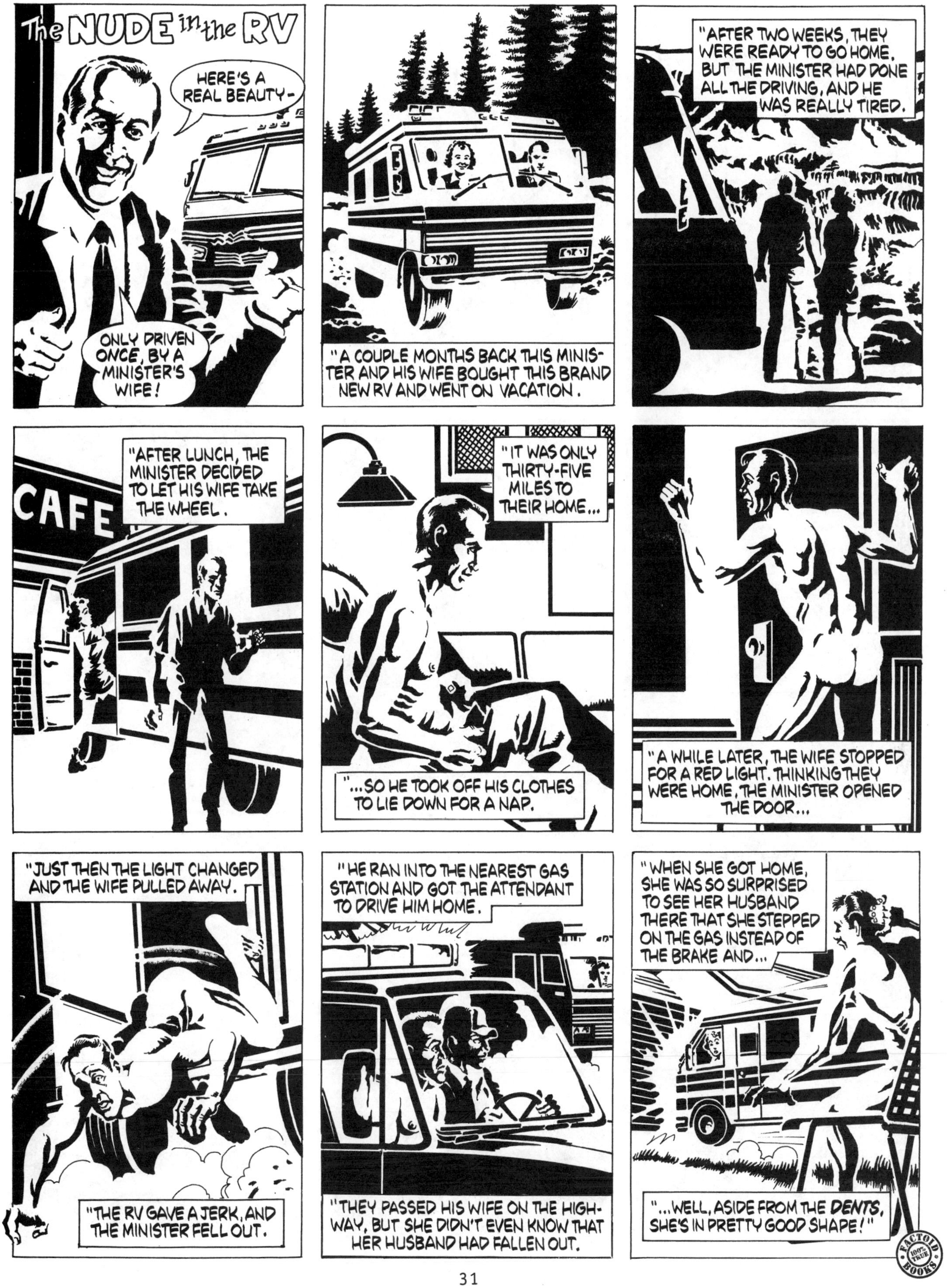
The NUDE in the RV
HERE'S A REAL BEAUTY–
ONLY DRIVEN ONCE, BY A MINISTER'S WIFE!
"A COUPLE MONTHS BACK THIS MINISTER AND HIS WIFE BOUGHT THIS BRAND NEW RV AND WENT ON VACATION.
"AFTER TWO WEEKS, THEY WERE READY TO GO HOME. BUT THE MINISTER HAD DONE ALL THE DRIVING, AND HE WAS REALLY TIRED.
"AFTER LUNCH, THE MINISTER DECIDED TO LET HIS WIFE TAKE THE WHEEL.
CAFE
"IT WAS ONLY THIRTY-FIVE MILES TO THEIR HOME...
"...SO HE TOOK OFF HIS CLOTHES TO LIE DOWN FOR A NAP.
"A WHILE LATER, THE WIFE STOPPED FOR A RED LIGHT. THINKING THEY WERE HOME, THE MINISTER OPENED THE DOOR...
"JUST THEN THE LIGHT CHANGED AND THE WIFE PULLED AWAY.
"THE RV GAVE A JERK, AND THE MINISTER FELL OUT.
"HE RAN INTO THE NEAREST GAS STATION AND GOT THE ATTENDANT TO DRIVE HIM HOME.
"THEY PASSED HIS WIFE ON THE HIGHWAY, BUT SHE DIDN'T EVEN KNOW THAT HER HUSBAND HAD FALLEN OUT.
"WHEN SHE GOT HOME, SHE WAS SO SURPRISED TO SEE HER HUSBAND THERE THAT SHE STEPPED ON THE GAS INSTEAD OF THE BRAKE AND...
"...WELL, ASIDE FROM THE *DENTS*, SHE'S IN PRETTY GOOD SHAPE!"

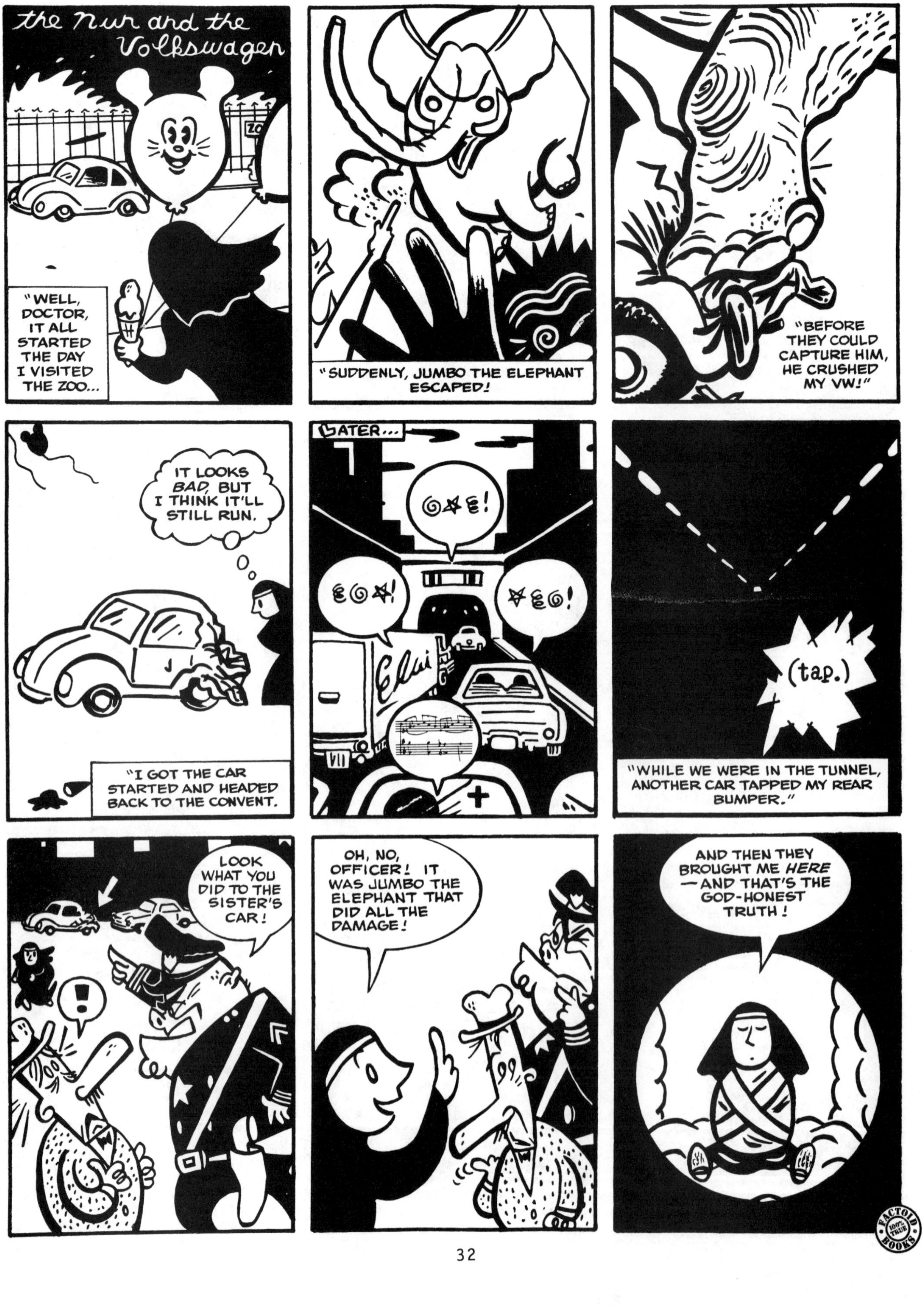
the Nun and the Volkswagen
"WELL, DOCTOR, IT ALL STARTED THE DAY I VISITED THE ZOO...
"SUDDENLY, JUMBO THE ELEPHANT ESCAPED!
"BEFORE THEY COULD CAPTURE HIM, HE CRUSHED MY VW!"
IT LOOKS BAD, BUT I THINK IT'LL STILL RUN.
"I GOT THE CAR STARTED AND HEADED BACK TO THE CONVENT.
LATER...
"WHILE WE WERE IN THE TUNNEL, ANOTHER CAR TAPPED MY REAR BUMPER."
(tap.)
LOOK WHAT YOU DID TO THE SISTER'S CAR!
!
OH, NO, OFFICER! IT WAS JUMBO THE ELEPHANT THAT DID ALL THE DAMAGE!
AND THEN THEY BROUGHT ME HERE —AND THAT'S THE GOD-HONEST TRUTH!
FACTOID BOOKS 100% TRUE

CHAPTER TWO

WILD KINGDOM

Don't read this chapter to your pets; some of these stories could give them nightmares. True, we tend to treat our pets like members of the family, but in urban legends that treatment is more like what you'd love to do to a hated sadistic sibling than to a beloved old grandparent. And even when an animal in a legend occasionally seems to get the upper hand (paw? claw? flipper?), the end results still tend to be tragic for the unlucky beast. Okay, so an occasional rattlesnake, tapeworm, or earwig gets the better of a human, but this isn't exactly a Lassie-type animal character, is it? Poor critters!

ANIMAL LEGENDS

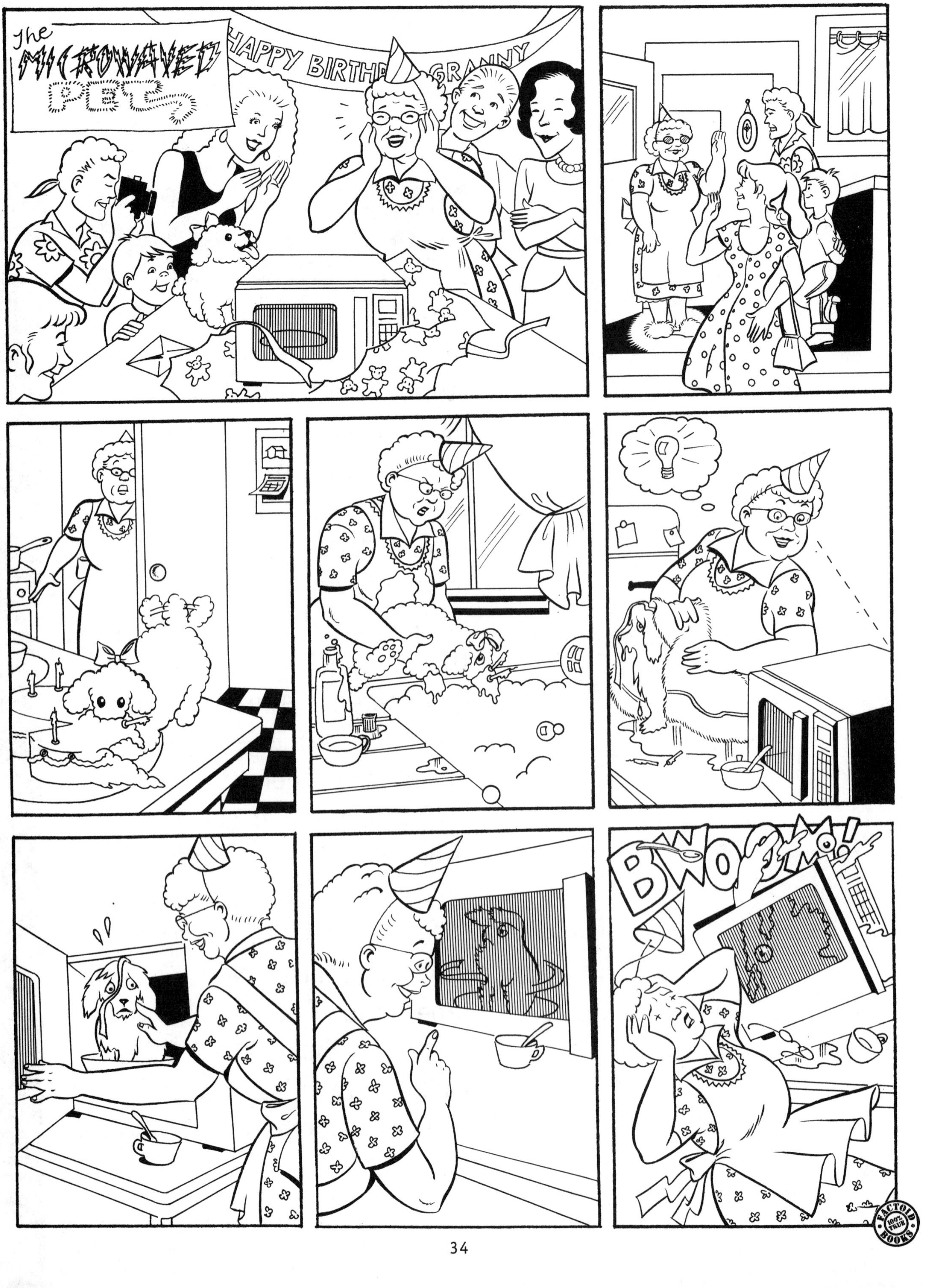

The MICROWAVED PETS
HAPPY BIRTHDAY GRANNY
BWOOM!

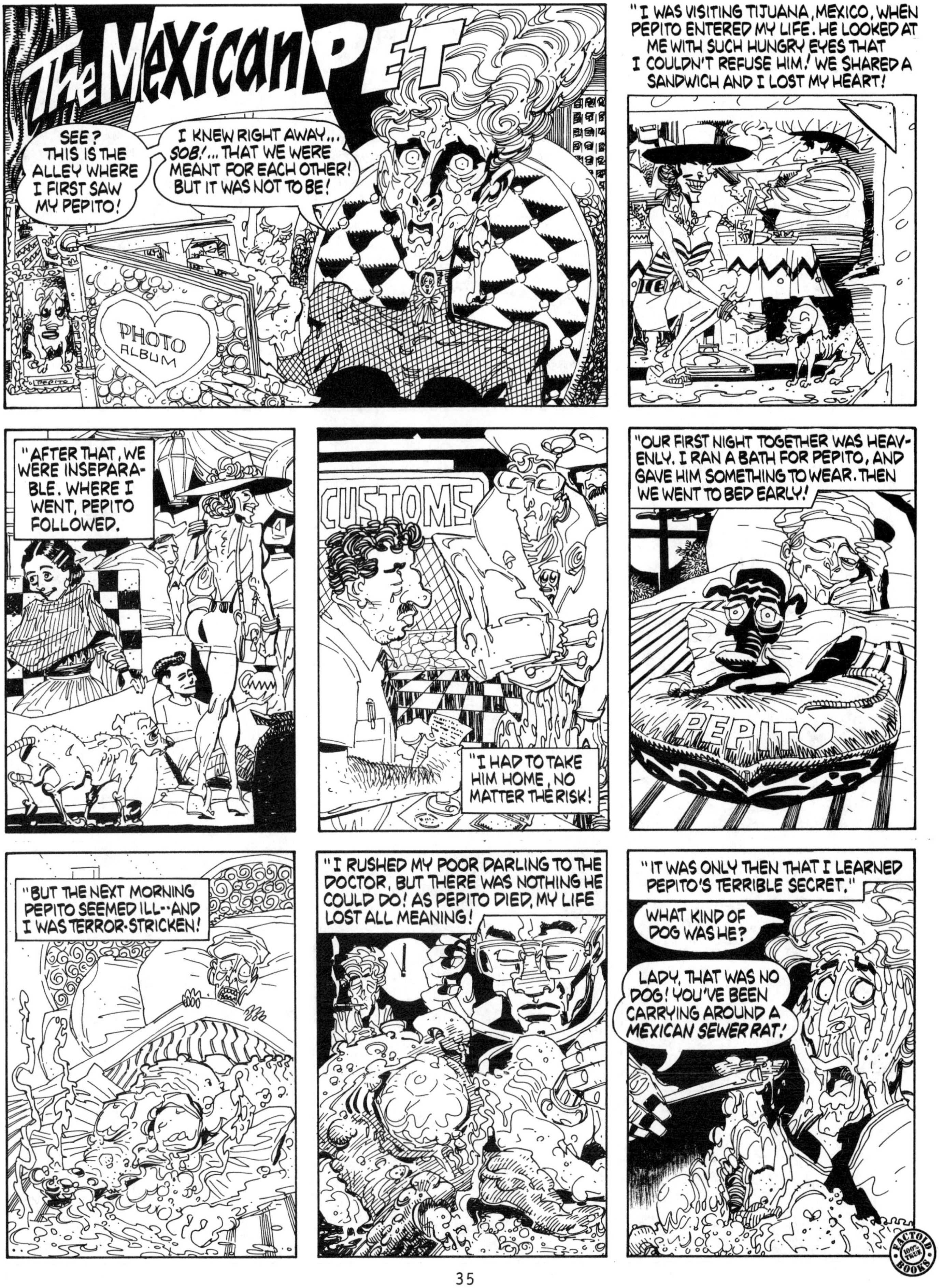
The Mexican PET
"I WAS VISITING TIJUANA, MEXICO, WHEN PEPITO ENTERED MY LIFE. HE LOOKED AT ME WITH SUCH HUNGRY EYES THAT I COULDN'T REFUSE HIM! WE SHARED A SANDWICH AND I LOST MY HEART!
SEE? THIS IS THE ALLEY WHERE I FIRST SAW MY PEPITO!
I KNEW RIGHT AWAY... *SOB!*... THAT WE WERE MEANT FOR EACH OTHER! BUT IT WAS NOT TO BE!
PHOTO ALBUM
"AFTER THAT, WE WERE INSEPARABLE. WHERE I WENT, PEPITO FOLLOWED.
CUSTOMS
"I HAD TO TAKE HIM HOME, NO MATTER THE RISK!
"OUR FIRST NIGHT TOGETHER WAS HEAVENLY. I RAN A BATH FOR PEPITO, AND GAVE HIM SOMETHING TO WEAR. THEN WE WENT TO BED EARLY!
PEPITO
"BUT THE NEXT MORNING PEPITO SEEMED ILL--AND I WAS TERROR-STRICKEN!
"I RUSHED MY POOR DARLING TO THE DOCTOR, BUT THERE WAS NOTHING HE COULD DO! AS PEPITO DIED, MY LIFE LOST ALL MEANING!
!
"IT WAS ONLY THEN THAT I LEARNED PEPITO'S TERRIBLE SECRET."
WHAT KIND OF DOG WAS HE?
LADY, THAT WAS NO DOG! YOU'VE BEEN CARRYING AROUND A *MEXICAN SEWER RAT!*

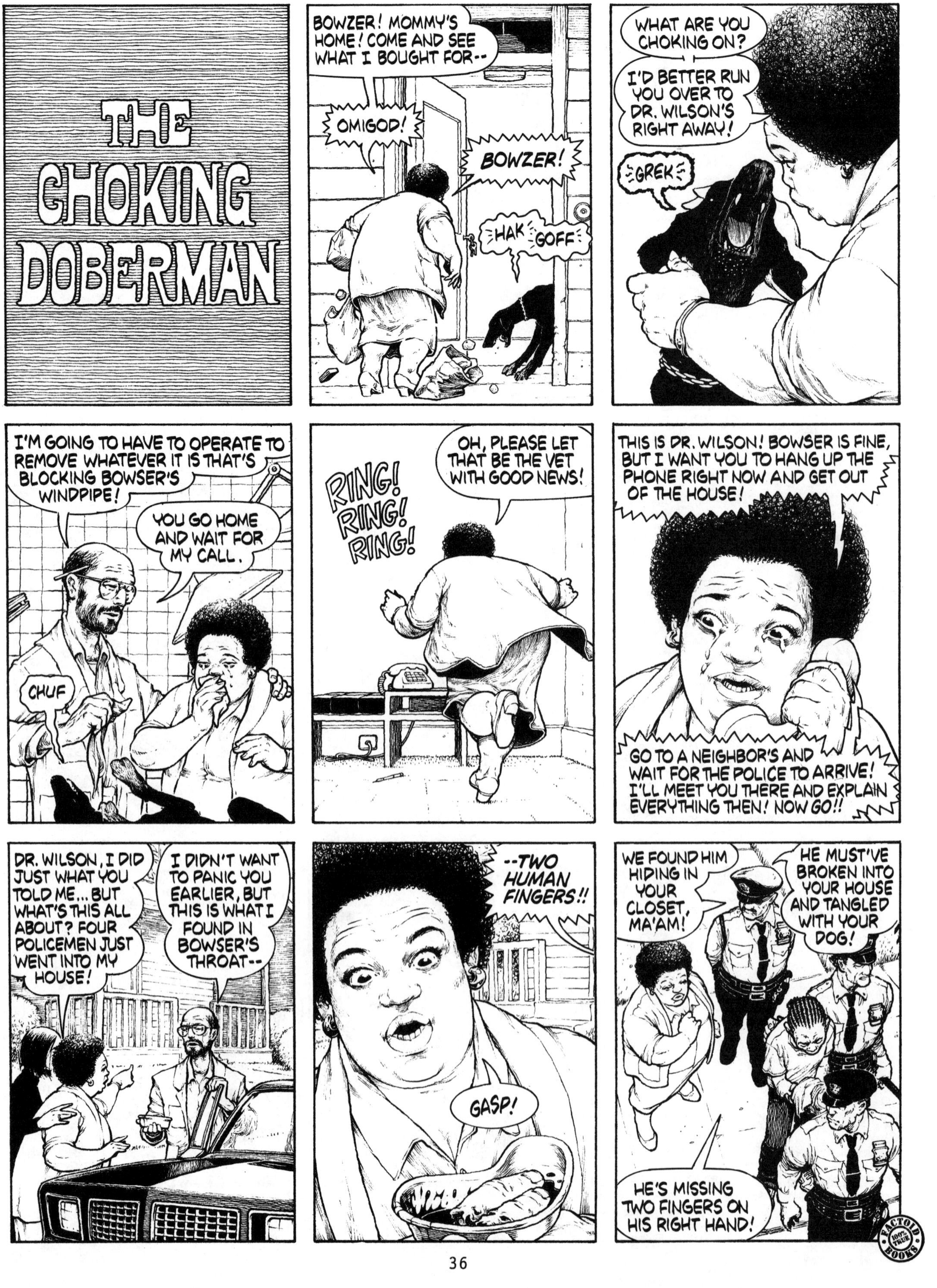
THE CHOKING DOBERMAN
BOWZER! MOMMY'S HOME! COME AND SEE WHAT I BOUGHT FOR--
OMIGOD!
BOWZER!
HAK GOFF
WHAT ARE YOU CHOKING ON?
I'D BETTER RUN YOU OVER TO DR. WILSON'S RIGHT AWAY!
GREK
I'M GOING TO HAVE TO OPERATE TO REMOVE WHATEVER IT IS THAT'S BLOCKING BOWSER'S WINDPIPE!
YOU GO HOME AND WAIT FOR MY CALL.
CHUF
RING! RING! RING!
OH, PLEASE LET THAT BE THE VET WITH GOOD NEWS!
THIS IS DR. WILSON! BOWSER IS FINE, BUT I WANT YOU TO HANG UP THE PHONE RIGHT NOW AND GET OUT OF THE HOUSE!
GO TO A NEIGHBOR'S AND WAIT FOR THE POLICE TO ARRIVE! I'LL MEET YOU THERE AND EXPLAIN EVERYTHING THEN! NOW GO!!
DR. WILSON, I DID JUST WHAT YOU TOLD ME... BUT WHAT'S THIS ALL ABOUT? FOUR POLICEMEN JUST WENT INTO MY HOUSE!
I DIDN'T WANT TO PANIC YOU EARLIER, BUT THIS IS WHAT I FOUND IN BOWSER'S THROAT--
--TWO HUMAN FINGERS!!
GASP!
WE FOUND HIM HIDING IN YOUR CLOSET, MA'AM!
HE MUST'VE BROKEN INTO YOUR HOUSE AND TANGLED WITH YOUR DOG!
HE'S MISSING TWO FINGERS ON HIS RIGHT HAND!
FACTOID BOOKS 100% TRUE

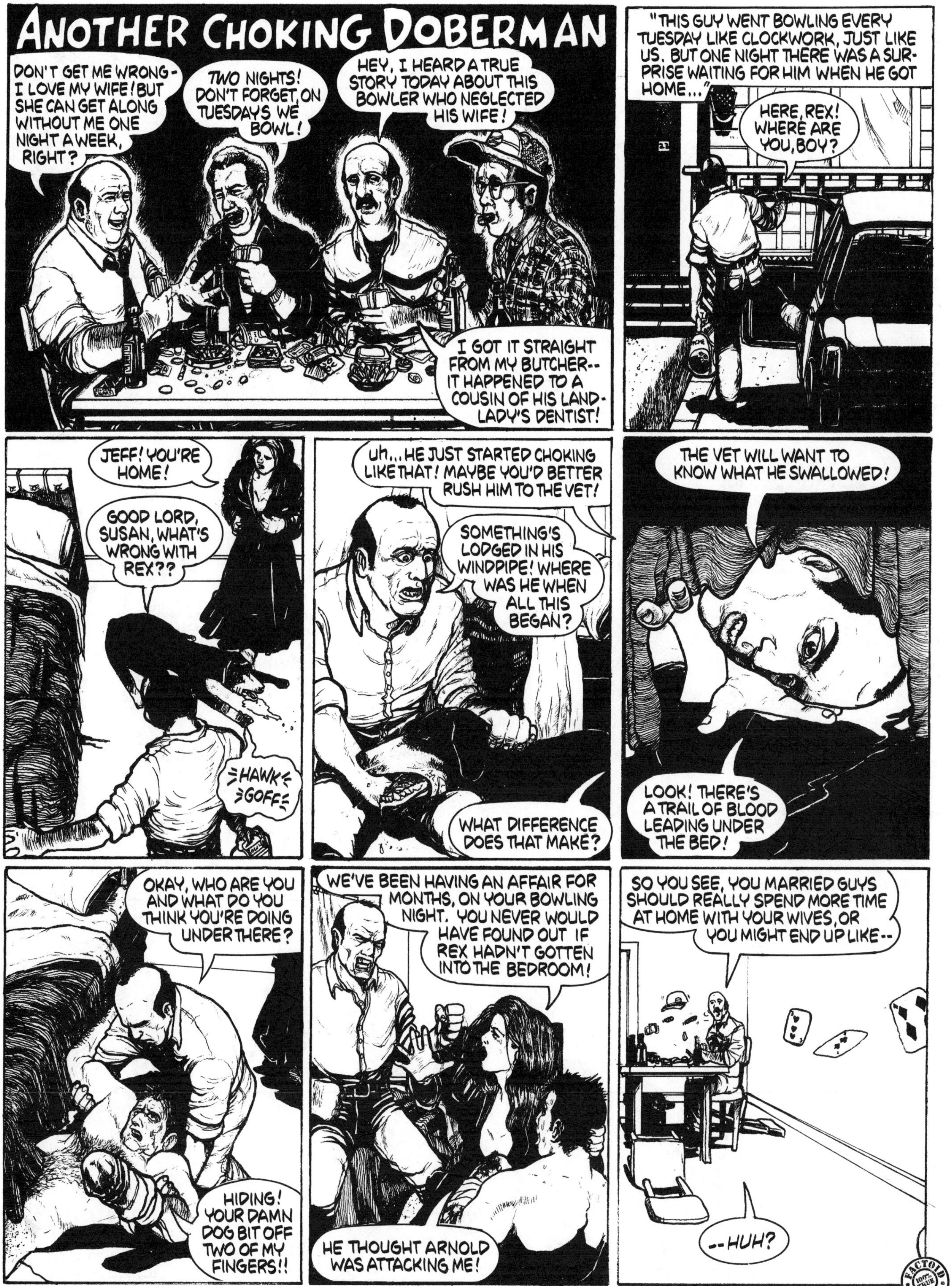
ANOTHER CHOKING DOBERMAN
DON'T GET ME WRONG- I LOVE MY WIFE! BUT SHE CAN GET ALONG WITHOUT ME ONE NIGHT A WEEK, RIGHT?
TWO NIGHTS! DON'T FORGET, ON TUESDAYS WE BOWL!
HEY, I HEARD A TRUE STORY TODAY ABOUT THIS BOWLER WHO NEGLECTED HIS WIFE!
I GOT IT STRAIGHT FROM MY BUTCHER-- IT HAPPENED TO A COUSIN OF HIS LAND-LADY'S DENTIST!
"THIS GUY WENT BOWLING EVERY TUESDAY LIKE CLOCKWORK, JUST LIKE US. BUT ONE NIGHT THERE WAS A SUR-PRISE WAITING FOR HIM WHEN HE GOT HOME..."
HERE, REX! WHERE ARE YOU, BOY?
JEFF! YOU'RE HOME!
GOOD LORD, SUSAN, WHAT'S WRONG WITH REX??
HAWK
GOFF
UH... HE JUST STARTED CHOKING LIKE THAT! MAYBE YOU'D BETTER RUSH HIM TO THE VET!
SOMETHING'S LODGED IN HIS WINDPIPE! WHERE WAS HE WHEN ALL THIS BEGAN?
WHAT DIFFERENCE DOES THAT MAKE?
THE VET WILL WANT TO KNOW WHAT HE SWALLOWED!
LOOK! THERE'S A TRAIL OF BLOOD LEADING UNDER THE BED!
OKAY, WHO ARE YOU AND WHAT DO YOU THINK YOU'RE DOING UNDER THERE?
HIDING! YOUR DAMN DOG BIT OFF TWO OF MY FINGERS!!
WE'VE BEEN HAVING AN AFFAIR FOR MONTHS, ON YOUR BOWLING NIGHT. YOU NEVER WOULD HAVE FOUND OUT IF REX HADN'T GOTTEN INTO THE BEDROOM!
HE THOUGHT ARNOLD WAS ATTACKING ME!
SO YOU SEE, YOU MARRIED GUYS SHOULD REALLY SPEND MORE TIME AT HOME WITH YOUR WIVES, OR YOU MIGHT END UP LIKE--
--HUH?
FACTOID BOOKS 100% TRUE

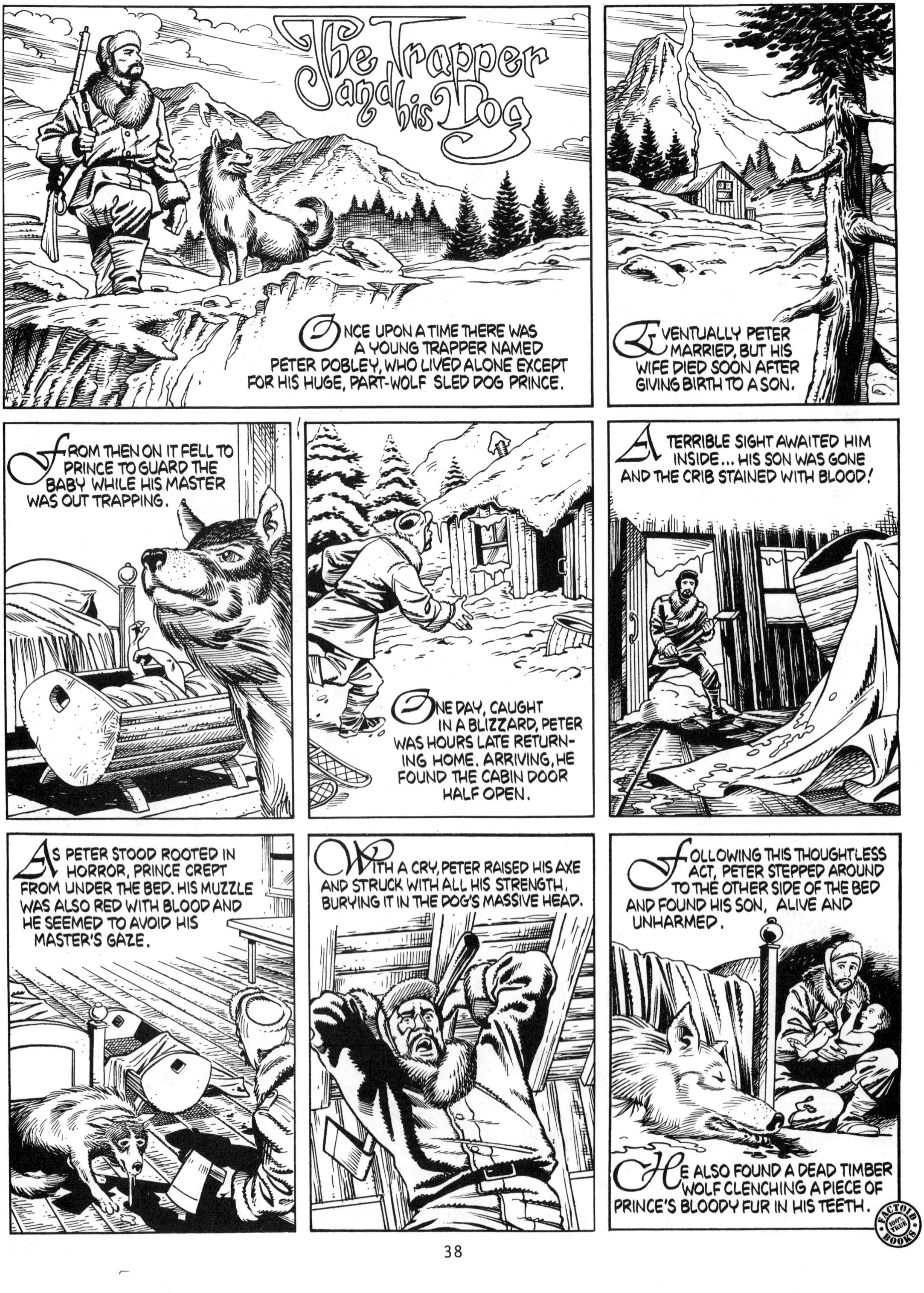
The Trapper and his Dog
ONCE UPON A TIME THERE WAS A YOUNG TRAPPER NAMED PETER DOBLEY, WHO LIVED ALONE EXCEPT FOR HIS HUGE, PART-WOLF SLED DOG PRINCE.
EVENTUALLY PETER MARRIED, BUT HIS WIFE DIED SOON AFTER GIVING BIRTH TO A SON.
FROM THEN ON IT FELL TO PRINCE TO GUARD THE BABY WHILE HIS MASTER WAS OUT TRAPPING.
ONE DAY, CAUGHT IN A BLIZZARD, PETER WAS HOURS LATE RETURNING HOME. ARRIVING, HE FOUND THE CABIN DOOR HALF OPEN.
A TERRIBLE SIGHT AWAITED HIM INSIDE... HIS SON WAS GONE AND THE CRIB STAINED WITH BLOOD!
AS PETER STOOD ROOTED IN HORROR, PRINCE CREPT FROM UNDER THE BED. HIS MUZZLE WAS ALSO RED WITH BLOOD AND HE SEEMED TO AVOID HIS MASTER'S GAZE.
WITH A CRY, PETER RAISED HIS AXE AND STRUCK WITH ALL HIS STRENGTH, BURYING IT IN THE DOG'S MASSIVE HEAD.
FOLLOWING THIS THOUGHTLESS ACT, PETER STEPPED AROUND TO THE OTHER SIDE OF THE BED AND FOUND HIS SON, ALIVE AND UNHARMED.
HE ALSO FOUND A DEAD TIMBER WOLF CLENCHING A PIECE OF PRINCE'S BLOODY FUR IN HIS TEETH.
FACTOID 100% TRUE BOOKS

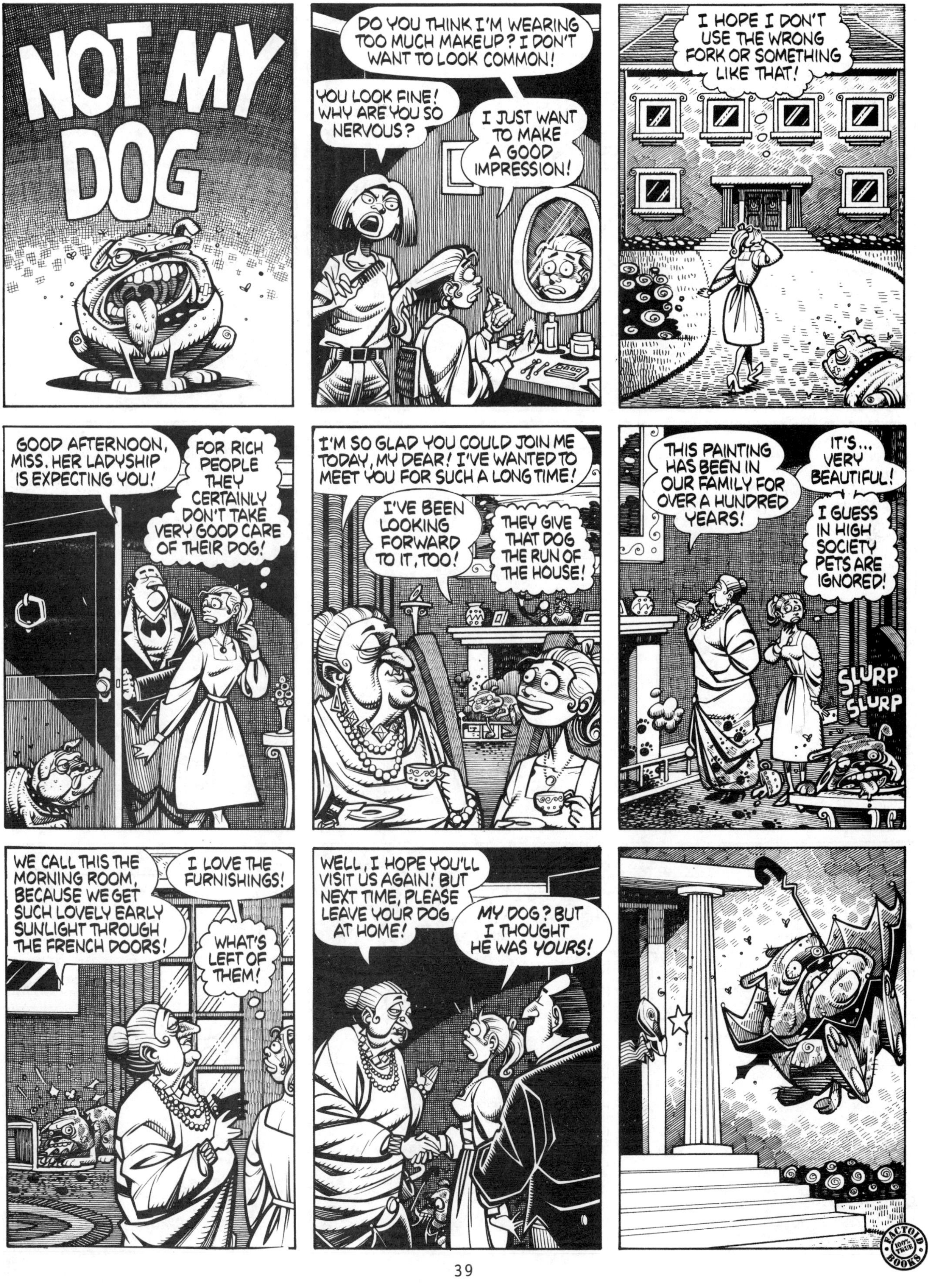
NOT MY DOG
DO YOU THINK I'M WEARING TOO MUCH MAKEUP? I DON'T WANT TO LOOK COMMON!
YOU LOOK FINE! WHY ARE YOU SO NERVOUS?
I JUST WANT TO MAKE A GOOD IMPRESSION!
I HOPE I DON'T USE THE WRONG FORK OR SOMETHING LIKE THAT!
GOOD AFTERNOON, MISS. HER LADYSHIP IS EXPECTING YOU!
FOR RICH PEOPLE THEY CERTAINLY DON'T TAKE VERY GOOD CARE OF THEIR DOG!
I'M SO GLAD YOU COULD JOIN ME TODAY, MY DEAR! I'VE WANTED TO MEET YOU FOR SUCH A LONG TIME!
I'VE BEEN LOOKING FORWARD TO IT, TOO!
THEY GIVE THAT DOG THE RUN OF THE HOUSE!
THIS PAINTING HAS BEEN IN OUR FAMILY FOR OVER A HUNDRED YEARS!
IT'S... VERY BEAUTIFUL!
I GUESS IN HIGH SOCIETY PETS ARE IGNORED!
SLURP SLURP
WE CALL THIS THE MORNING ROOM, BECAUSE WE GET SUCH LOVELY EARLY SUNLIGHT THROUGH THE FRENCH DOORS!
I LOVE THE FURNISHINGS!
WHAT'S LEFT OF THEM!
WELL, I HOPE YOU'LL VISIT US AGAIN! BUT NEXT TIME, PLEASE LEAVE YOUR DOG AT HOME!
MY DOG? BUT I THOUGHT HE WAS *YOURS*!
FACTOID BOOKS 100% TRUE

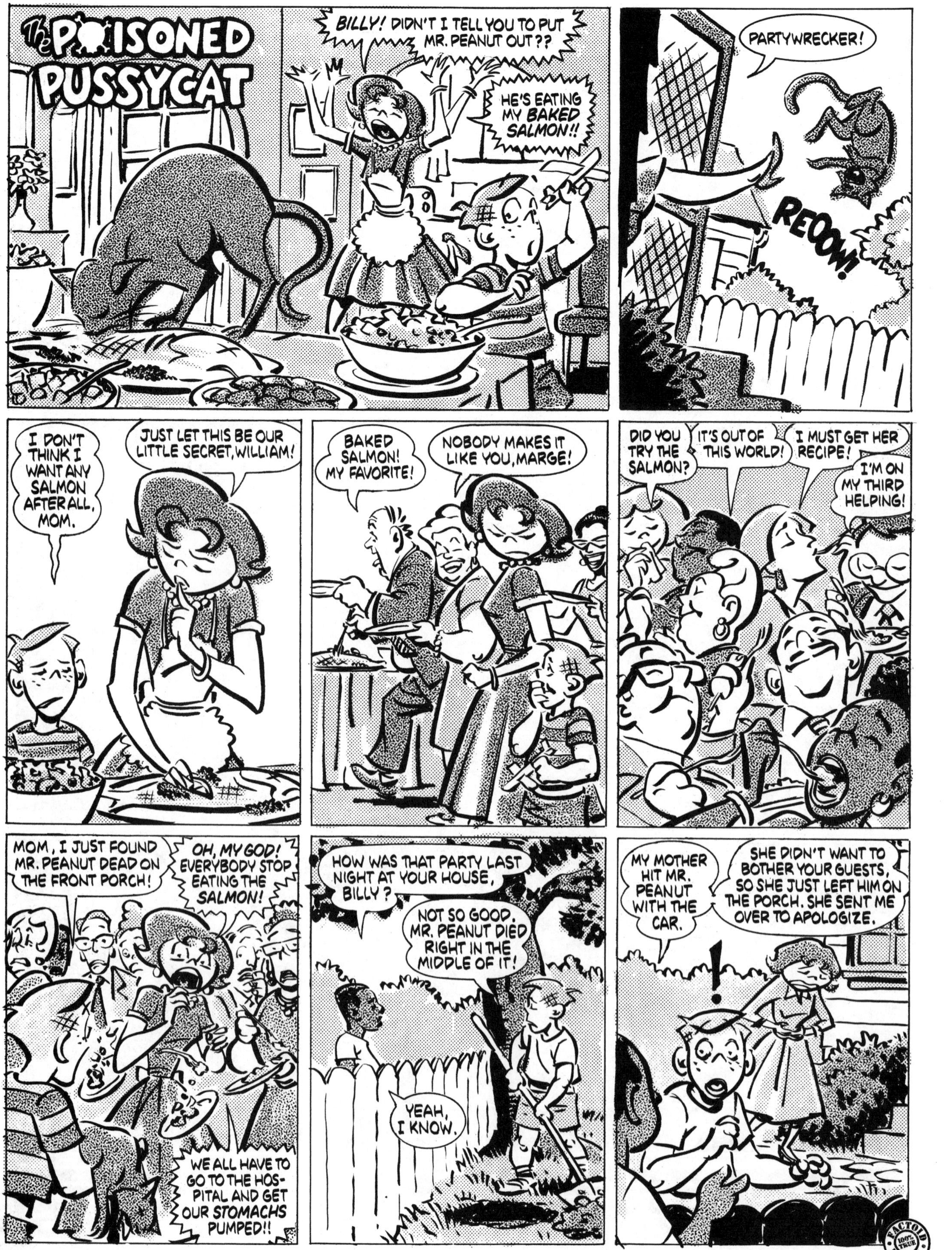
The POISONED PUSSYCAT
BILLY! DIDN'T I TELL YOU TO PUT MR. PEANUT OUT??
HE'S EATING MY BAKED SALMON!!
PARTYWRECKER!
REOOW!
I DON'T THINK I WANT ANY SALMON AFTER ALL, MOM.
JUST LET THIS BE OUR LITTLE SECRET, WILLIAM!
BAKED SALMON! MY FAVORITE!
NOBODY MAKES IT LIKE YOU, MARGE!
DID YOU TRY THE SALMON?
IT'S OUT OF THIS WORLD!
I MUST GET HER RECIPE!
I'M ON MY THIRD HELPING!
MOM, I JUST FOUND MR. PEANUT DEAD ON THE FRONT PORCH!
OH, MY GOD! EVERYBODY STOP EATING THE SALMON!
WE ALL HAVE TO GO TO THE HOS-PITAL AND GET OUR STOMACHS PUMPED!!
HOW WAS THAT PARTY LAST NIGHT AT YOUR HOUSE, BILLY?
NOT SO GOOD. MR. PEANUT DIED RIGHT IN THE MIDDLE OF IT!
YEAH, I KNOW.
MY MOTHER HIT MR. PEANUT WITH THE CAR.
SHE DIDN'T WANT TO BOTHER YOUR GUESTS, SO SHE JUST LEFT HIM ON THE PORCH. SHE SENT ME OVER TO APOLOGIZE.
!
FACTOID BOOKS 100% TRUE

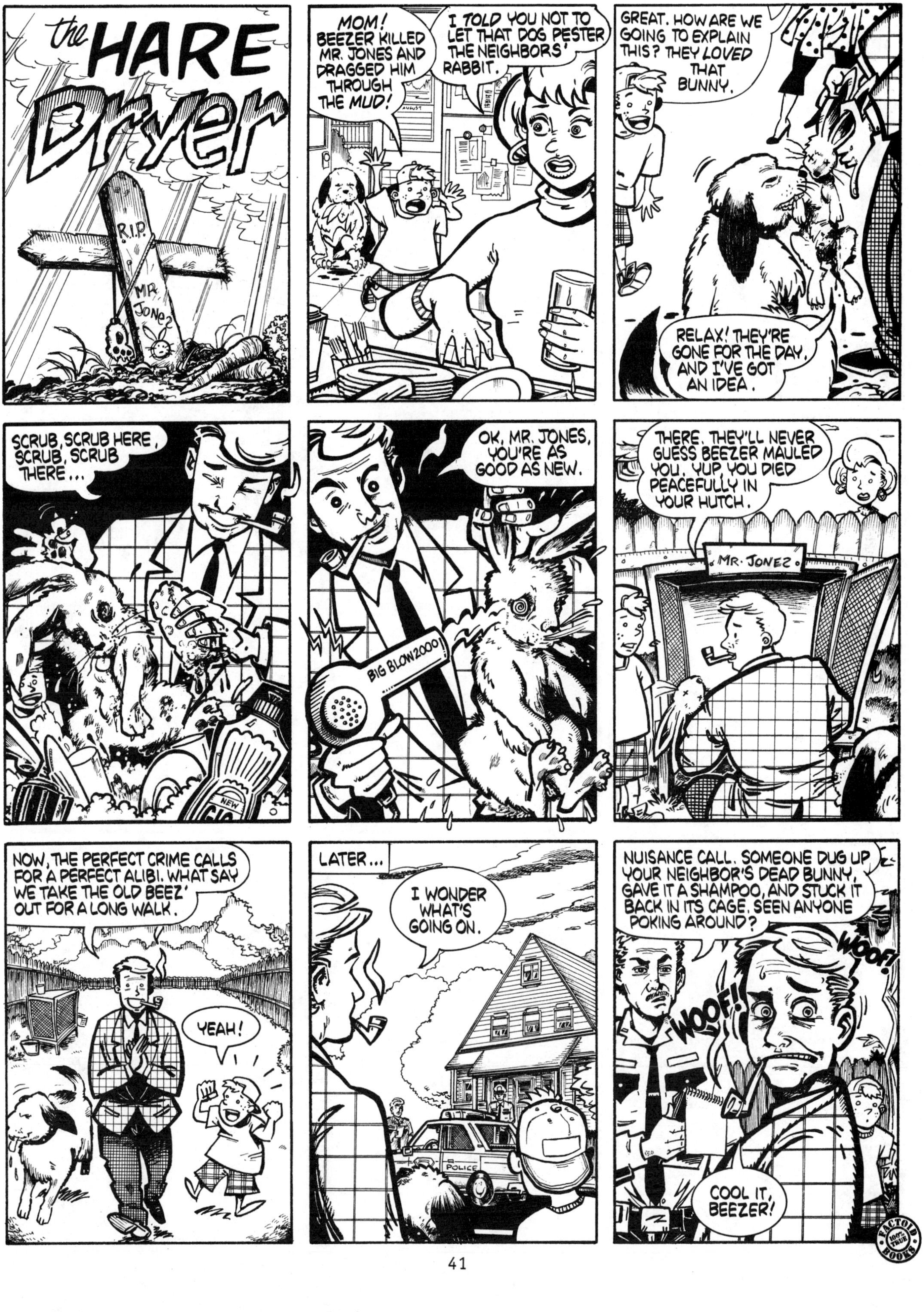
the HARE Dryer
R.I.P. MR. JONEZ
MOM! BEEZER KILLED MR. JONES AND DRAGGED HIM THROUGH THE MUD!
I TOLD YOU NOT TO LET THAT DOG PESTER THE NEIGHBORS' RABBIT.
GREAT. HOW ARE WE GOING TO EXPLAIN THIS? THEY LOVED THAT BUNNY.
RELAX! THEY'RE GONE FOR THE DAY, AND I'VE GOT AN IDEA.
SCRUB, SCRUB HERE, SCRUB, SCRUB THERE...
OK, MR. JONES, YOU'RE AS GOOD AS NEW.
BIG BLOW 2000
THERE. THEY'LL NEVER GUESS BEEZER MAULED YOU. YUP, YOU DIED PEACEFULLY IN YOUR HUTCH.
MR. JONEZ
NOW, THE PERFECT CRIME CALLS FOR A PERFECT ALIBI. WHAT SAY WE TAKE THE OLD BEEZ' OUT FOR A LONG WALK.
YEAH!
LATER...
I WONDER WHAT'S GOING ON.
POLICE
NUISANCE CALL. SOMEONE DUG UP YOUR NEIGHBOR'S DEAD BUNNY, GAVE IT A SHAMPOO, AND STUCK IT BACK IN ITS CAGE. SEEN ANYONE POKING AROUND?
WOOF!
WOOF!!
COOL IT, BEEZER!
FACTOID BOOKS 100% TRUE

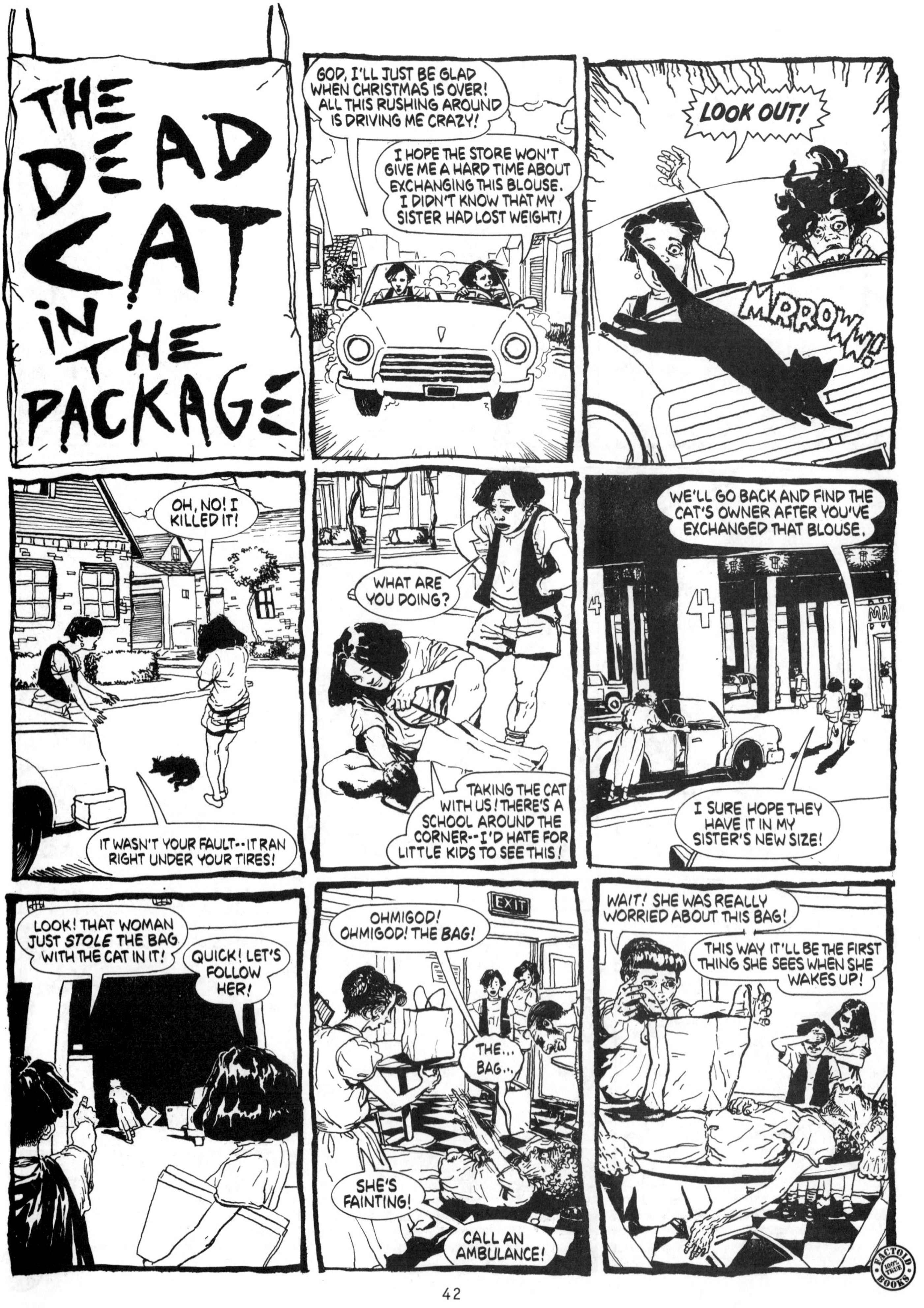
THE DEAD CAT IN THE PACKAGE
GOD, I'LL JUST BE GLAD WHEN CHRISTMAS IS OVER! ALL THIS RUSHING AROUND IS DRIVING ME CRAZY!
I HOPE THE STORE WON'T GIVE ME A HARD TIME ABOUT EXCHANGING THIS BLOUSE. I DIDN'T KNOW THAT MY SISTER HAD LOST WEIGHT!
LOOK OUT!
MRROWW!
OH, NO! I KILLED IT!
IT WASN'T YOUR FAULT--IT RAN RIGHT UNDER YOUR TIRES!
WHAT ARE YOU DOING?
TAKING THE CAT WITH US! THERE'S A SCHOOL AROUND THE CORNER--I'D HATE FOR LITTLE KIDS TO SEE THIS!
WE'LL GO BACK AND FIND THE CAT'S OWNER AFTER YOU'VE EXCHANGED THAT BLOUSE.
I SURE HOPE THEY HAVE IT IN MY SISTER'S NEW SIZE!
LOOK! THAT WOMAN JUST STOLE THE BAG WITH THE CAT IN IT!
QUICK! LET'S FOLLOW HER!
EXIT
OHMIGOD! OHMIGOD! THE BAG!
THE... BAG...
SHE'S FAINTING!
CALL AN AMBULANCE!
WAIT! SHE WAS REALLY WORRIED ABOUT THIS BAG!
THIS WAY IT'LL BE THE FIRST THING SHE SEES WHEN SHE WAKES UP!
FACTOID BOOKS 100% TRUE

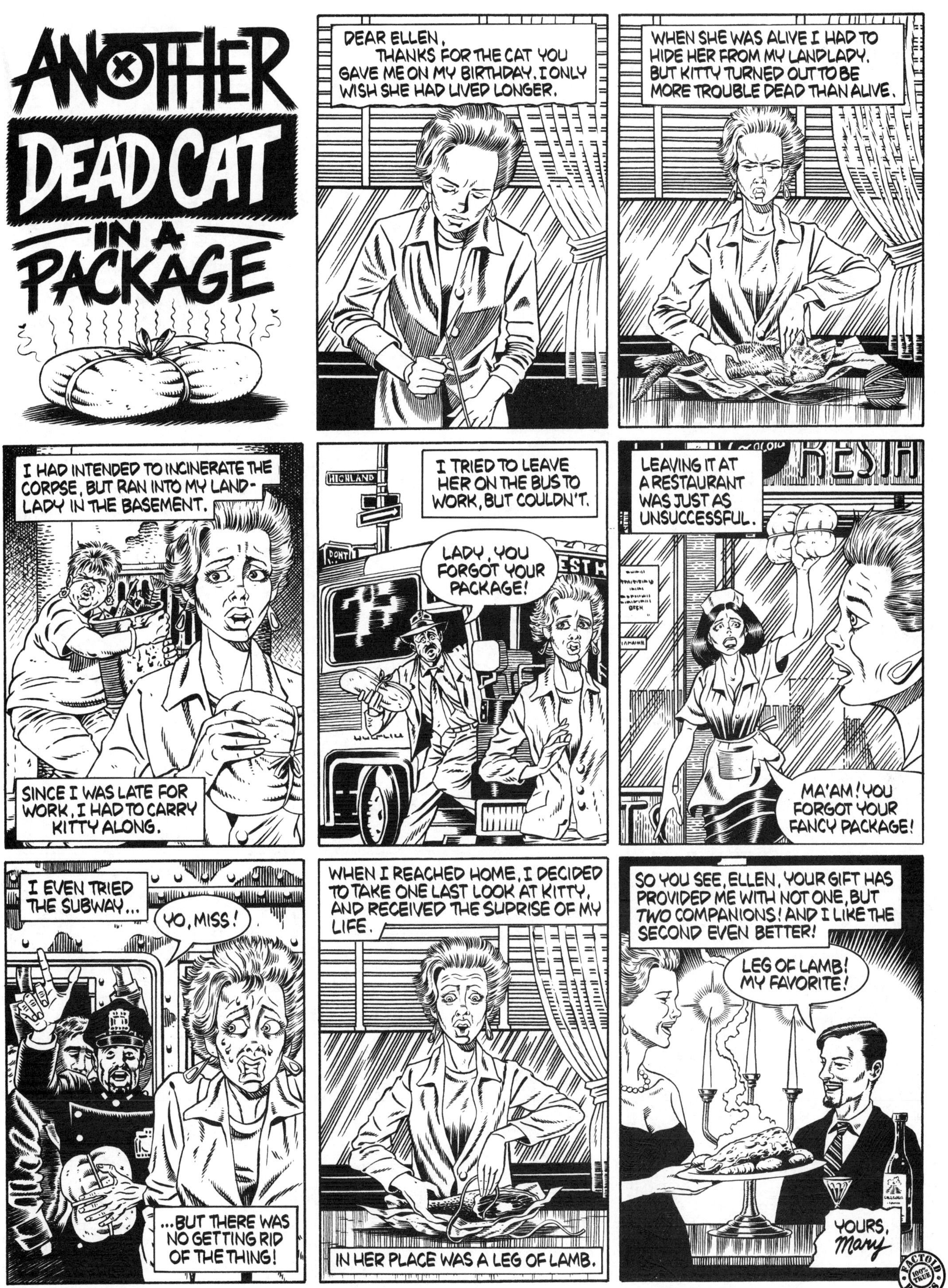
ANOTHER DEAD CAT IN A PACKAGE
DEAR ELLEN, THANKS FOR THE CAT YOU GAVE ME ON MY BIRTHDAY. I ONLY WISH SHE HAD LIVED LONGER.
WHEN SHE WAS ALIVE I HAD TO HIDE HER FROM MY LANDLADY. BUT KITTY TURNED OUT TO BE MORE TROUBLE DEAD THAN ALIVE.
I HAD INTENDED TO INCINERATE THE CORPSE, BUT RAN INTO MY LAND-LADY IN THE BASEMENT.
SINCE I WAS LATE FOR WORK, I HAD TO CARRY KITTY ALONG.
HIGHLAND
I TRIED TO LEAVE HER ON THE BUS TO WORK, BUT COULDN'T.
LADY, YOU FORGOT YOUR PACKAGE!
LEAVING IT AT A RESTAURANT WAS JUST AS UNSUCCESSFUL.
MA'AM! YOU FORGOT YOUR FANCY PACKAGE!
I EVEN TRIED THE SUBWAY...
YO, MISS!
...BUT THERE WAS NO GETTING RID OF THE THING!
WHEN I REACHED HOME, I DECIDED TO TAKE ONE LAST LOOK AT KITTY, AND RECEIVED THE SUPRISE OF MY LIFE.
IN HER PLACE WAS A LEG OF LAMB.
SO YOU SEE, ELLEN, YOUR GIFT HAS PROVIDED ME WITH NOT ONE, BUT TWO COMPANIONS! AND I LIKE THE SECOND EVEN BETTER!
LEG OF LAMB! MY FAVORITE!
YOURS, Mary
FACTOID BOOKS 100% TRUE

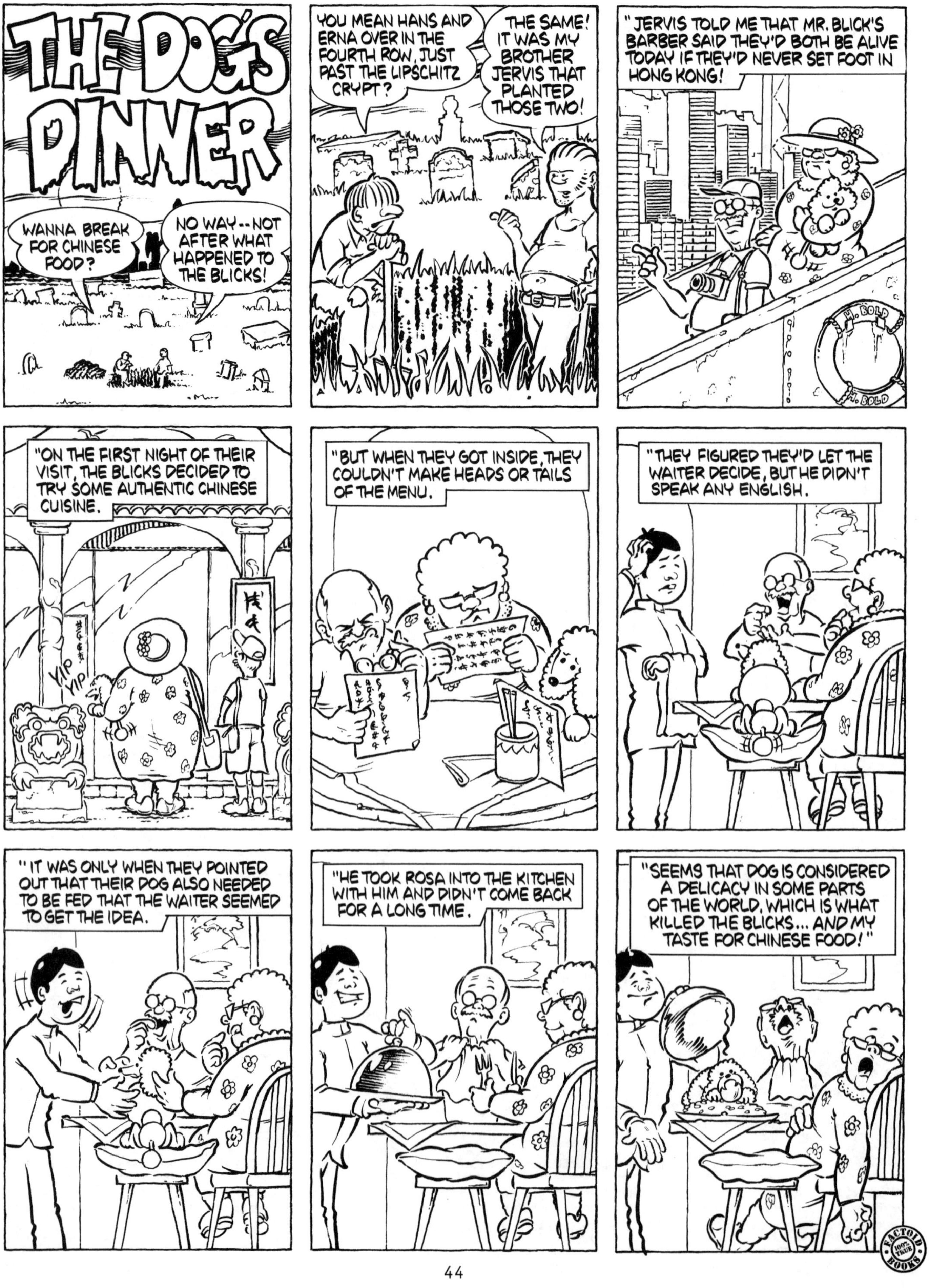
THE DOG'S DINNER
WANNA BREAK FOR CHINESE FOOD?
NO WAY--NOT AFTER WHAT HAPPENED TO THE BLICKS!
YOU MEAN HANS AND ERNA OVER IN THE FOURTH ROW, JUST PAST THE LIPSCHITZ CRYPT?
THE SAME! IT WAS MY BROTHER JERVIS THAT PLANTED THOSE TWO!
"JERVIS TOLD ME THAT MR. BLICK'S BARBER SAID THEY'D BOTH BE ALIVE TODAY IF THEY'D NEVER SET FOOT IN HONG KONG!
H. BOLD
"ON THE FIRST NIGHT OF THEIR VISIT, THE BLICKS DECIDED TO TRY SOME AUTHENTIC CHINESE CUISINE.
YIP YIP
"BUT WHEN THEY GOT INSIDE, THEY COULDN'T MAKE HEADS OR TAILS OF THE MENU.
"THEY FIGURED THEY'D LET THE WAITER DECIDE, BUT HE DIDN'T SPEAK ANY ENGLISH.
"IT WAS ONLY WHEN THEY POINTED OUT THAT THEIR DOG ALSO NEEDED TO BE FED THAT THE WAITER SEEMED TO GET THE IDEA.
"HE TOOK ROSA INTO THE KITCHEN WITH HIM AND DIDN'T COME BACK FOR A LONG TIME.
"SEEMS THAT DOG IS CONSIDERED A DELICACY IN SOME PARTS OF THE WORLD, WHICH IS WHAT KILLED THE BLICKS... AND MY TASTE FOR CHINESE FOOD!"
FACTOID BOOKS 100% TRUE

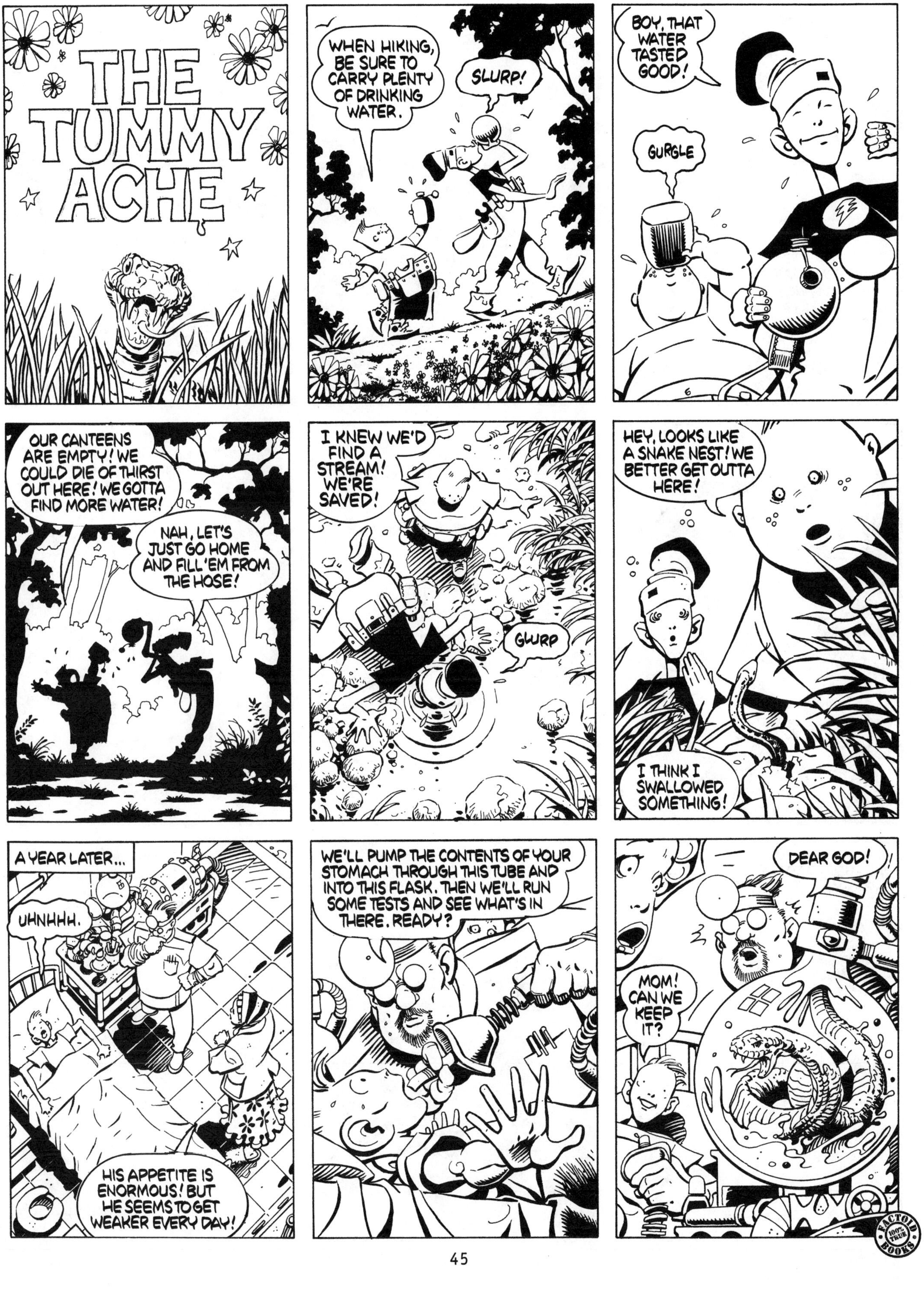
THE TUMMY ACHE
WHEN HIKING, BE SURE TO CARRY PLENTY OF DRINKING WATER.
SLURP!
BOY, THAT WATER TASTED GOOD!
GURGLE
OUR CANTEENS ARE EMPTY! WE COULD DIE OF THIRST OUT HERE! WE GOTTA FIND MORE WATER!
NAH, LET'S JUST GO HOME AND FILL 'EM FROM THE HOSE!
I KNEW WE'D FIND A STREAM! WE'RE SAVED!
GLURP
HEY, LOOKS LIKE A SNAKE NEST! WE BETTER GET OUTTA HERE!
I THINK I SWALLOWED SOMETHING!
A YEAR LATER...
UHNHHH.
HIS APPETITE IS ENORMOUS! BUT HE SEEMS TO GET WEAKER EVERY DAY!
WE'LL PUMP THE CONTENTS OF YOUR STOMACH THROUGH THIS TUBE AND INTO THIS FLASK. THEN WE'LL RUN SOME TESTS AND SEE WHAT'S IN THERE. READY?
DEAR GOD!
MOM! CAN WE KEEP IT?
FACTOID BOOKS 100% TRUE

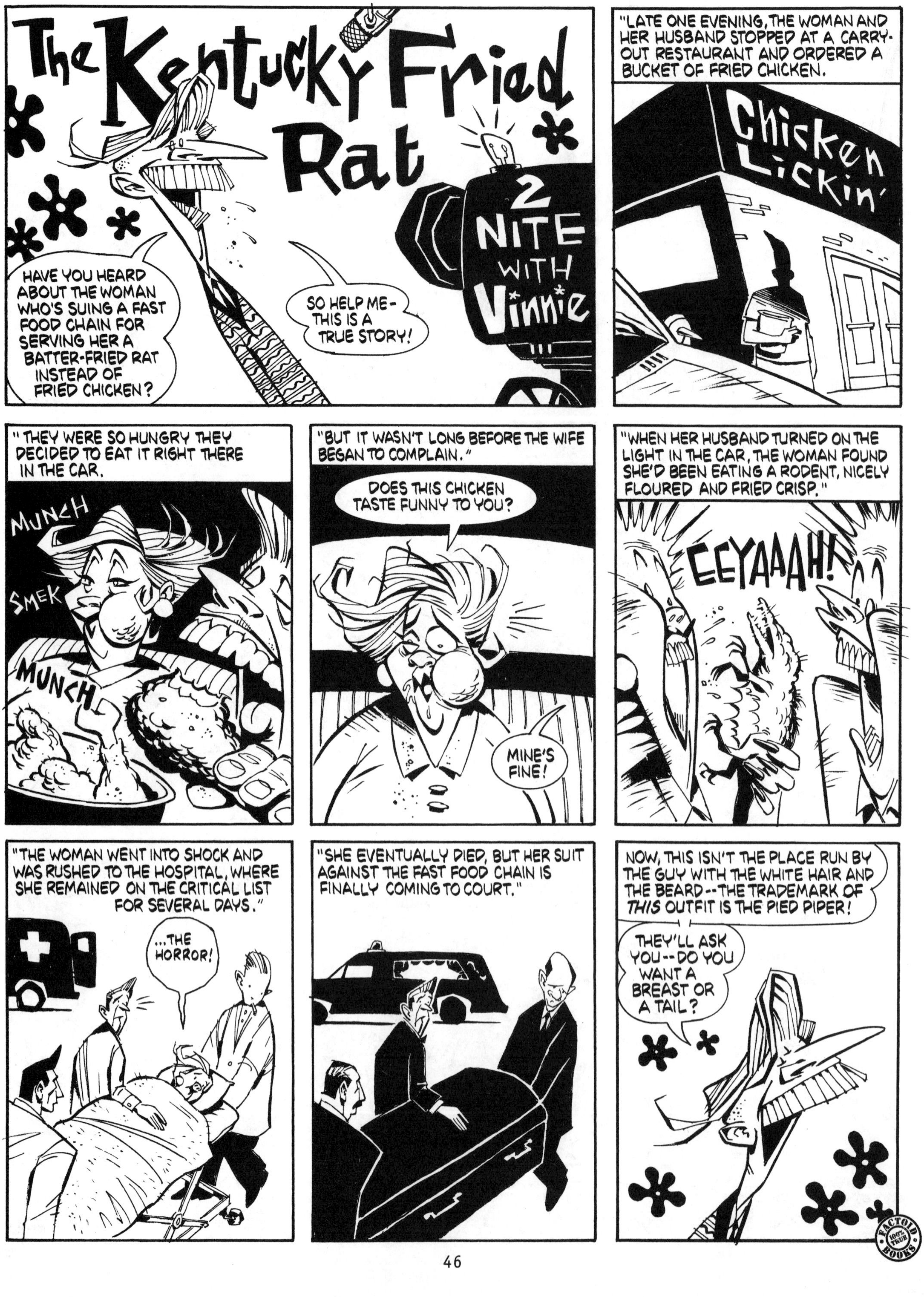
The Kentucky Fried Rat
HAVE YOU HEARD ABOUT THE WOMAN WHO'S SUING A FAST FOOD CHAIN FOR SERVING HER A BATTER-FRIED RAT INSTEAD OF FRIED CHICKEN?
SO HELP ME- THIS IS A TRUE STORY!
2 NITE WITH Vinnie
"LATE ONE EVENING, THE WOMAN AND HER HUSBAND STOPPED AT A CARRY-OUT RESTAURANT AND ORDERED A BUCKET OF FRIED CHICKEN.
Chicken Lickin'
" THEY WERE SO HUNGRY THEY DECIDED TO EAT IT RIGHT THERE IN THE CAR.
MUNCH
SMEK
MUNCH
"BUT IT WASN'T LONG BEFORE THE WIFE BEGAN TO COMPLAIN."
DOES THIS CHICKEN TASTE FUNNY TO YOU?
MINE'S FINE!
"WHEN HER HUSBAND TURNED ON THE LIGHT IN THE CAR, THE WOMAN FOUND SHE'D BEEN EATING A RODENT, NICELY FLOURED AND FRIED CRISP."
EEYAAAH!
"THE WOMAN WENT INTO SHOCK AND WAS RUSHED TO THE HOSPITAL, WHERE SHE REMAINED ON THE CRITICAL LIST FOR SEVERAL DAYS."
...THE HORROR!
"SHE EVENTUALLY DIED, BUT HER SUIT AGAINST THE FAST FOOD CHAIN IS FINALLY COMING TO COURT."
NOW, THIS ISN'T THE PLACE RUN BY THE GUY WITH THE WHITE HAIR AND THE BEARD--THE TRADEMARK OF *THIS* OUTFIT IS THE PIED PIPER!
THEY'LL ASK YOU--DO YOU WANT A BREAST OR A TAIL?
FACTOID BOOKS 100% TRUE

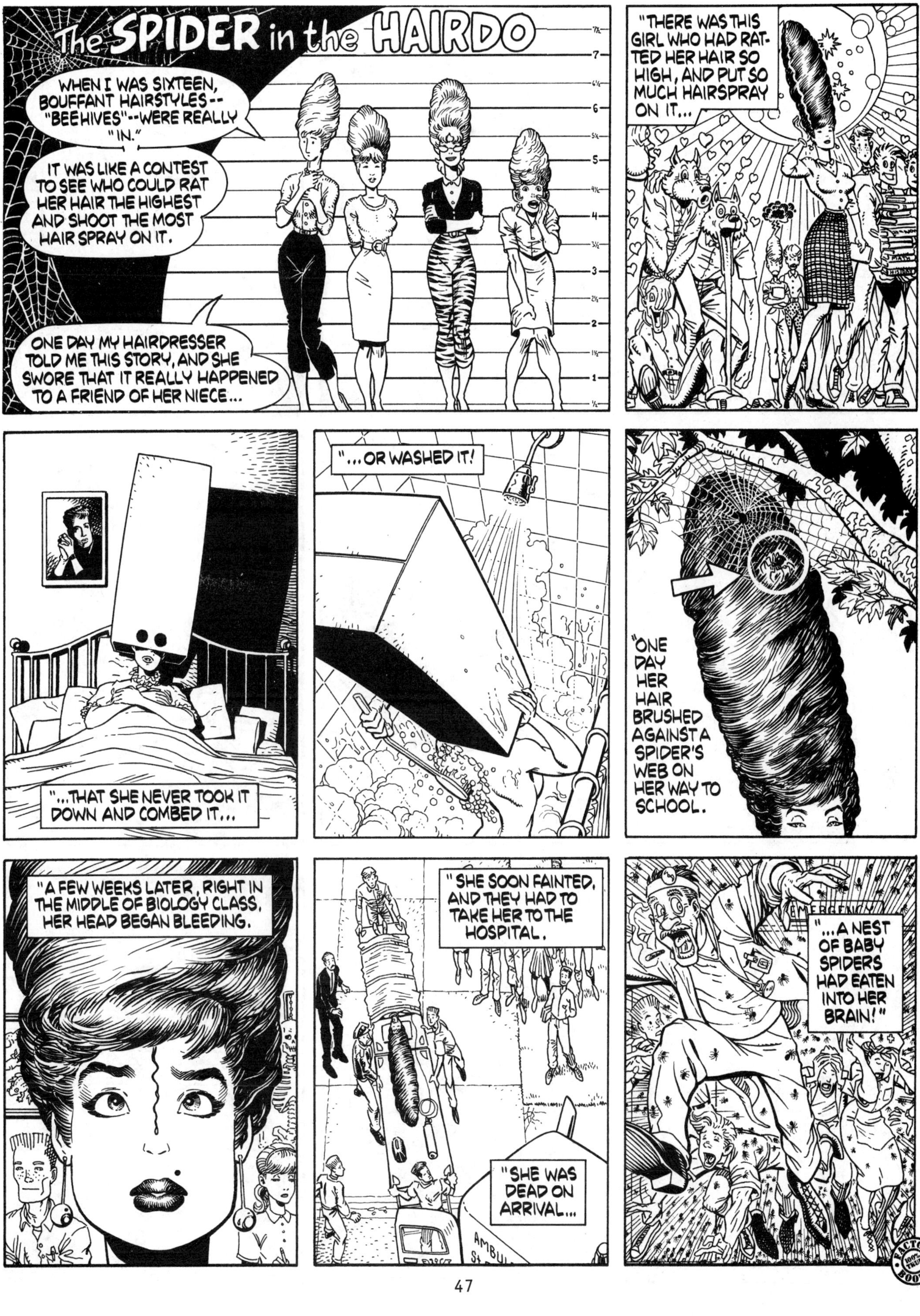
The SPIDER in the HAIRDO
WHEN I WAS SIXTEEN, BOUFFANT HAIRSTYLES -- "BEEHIVES" -- WERE REALLY "IN."
IT WAS LIKE A CONTEST TO SEE WHO COULD RAT HER HAIR THE HIGHEST AND SHOOT THE MOST HAIR SPRAY ON IT.
ONE DAY MY HAIRDRESSER TOLD ME THIS STORY, AND SHE SWORE THAT IT REALLY HAPPENED TO A FRIEND OF HER NIECE...
"THERE WAS THIS GIRL WHO HAD RATTED HER HAIR SO HIGH, AND PUT SO MUCH HAIRSPRAY ON IT...
"...THAT SHE NEVER TOOK IT DOWN AND COMBED IT...
"...OR WASHED IT!
"ONE DAY HER HAIR BRUSHED AGAINST A SPIDER'S WEB ON HER WAY TO SCHOOL.
"A FEW WEEKS LATER, RIGHT IN THE MIDDLE OF BIOLOGY CLASS, HER HEAD BEGAN BLEEDING.
"SHE SOON FAINTED, AND THEY HAD TO TAKE HER TO THE HOSPITAL.
"SHE WAS DEAD ON ARRIVAL...
"...A NEST OF BABY SPIDERS HAD EATEN INTO HER BRAIN!"

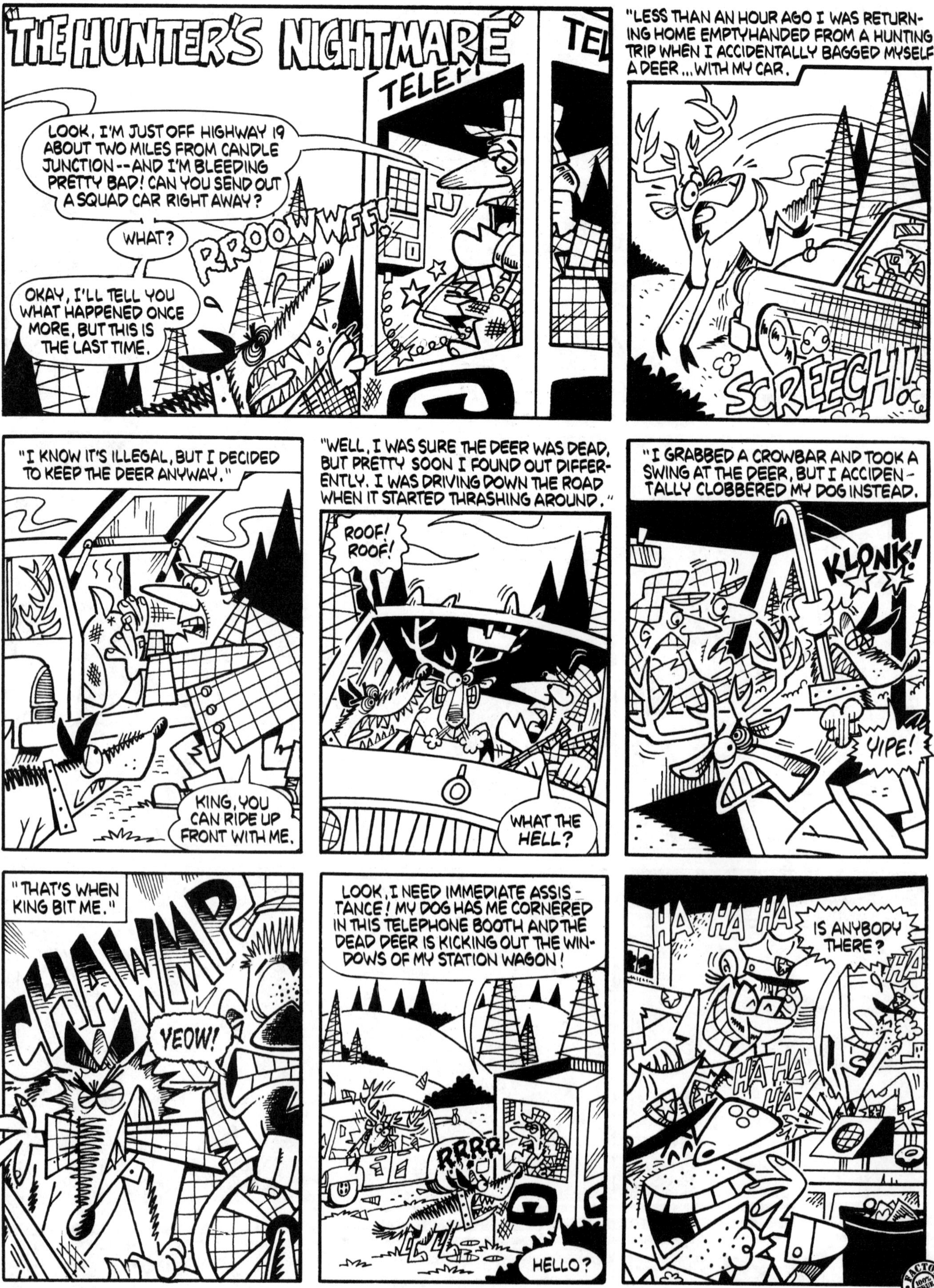
"THE HUNTER'S NIGHTMARE"
LOOK, I'M JUST OFF HIGHWAY 19 ABOUT TWO MILES FROM CANDLE JUNCTION--AND I'M BLEEDING PRETTY BAD! CAN YOU SEND OUT A SQUAD CAR RIGHT AWAY?
WHAT?
RROOWWFF!
OKAY, I'LL TELL YOU WHAT HAPPENED ONCE MORE, BUT THIS IS THE LAST TIME.
"LESS THAN AN HOUR AGO I WAS RETURNING HOME EMPTYHANDED FROM A HUNTING TRIP WHEN I ACCIDENTALLY BAGGED MYSELF A DEER... WITH MY CAR.
SCREECH!
"I KNOW IT'S ILLEGAL, BUT I DECIDED TO KEEP THE DEER ANYWAY."
KING, YOU CAN RIDE UP FRONT WITH ME.
"WELL, I WAS SURE THE DEER WAS DEAD, BUT PRETTY SOON I FOUND OUT DIFFERENTLY. I WAS DRIVING DOWN THE ROAD WHEN IT STARTED THRASHING AROUND."
ROOF! ROOF!
WHAT THE HELL?
"I GRABBED A CROWBAR AND TOOK A SWING AT THE DEER, BUT I ACCIDENTALLY CLOBBERED MY DOG INSTEAD.
KLONK!
YIPE!
"THAT'S WHEN KING BIT ME."
CHAWMP!
YEOW!
LOOK, I NEED IMMEDIATE ASSISTANCE! MY DOG HAS ME CORNERED IN THIS TELEPHONE BOOTH AND THE DEAD DEER IS KICKING OUT THE WINDOWS OF MY STATION WAGON!
RRRR
HELLO?
HA HA HA
IS ANYBODY THERE?
HA
HA HA HA

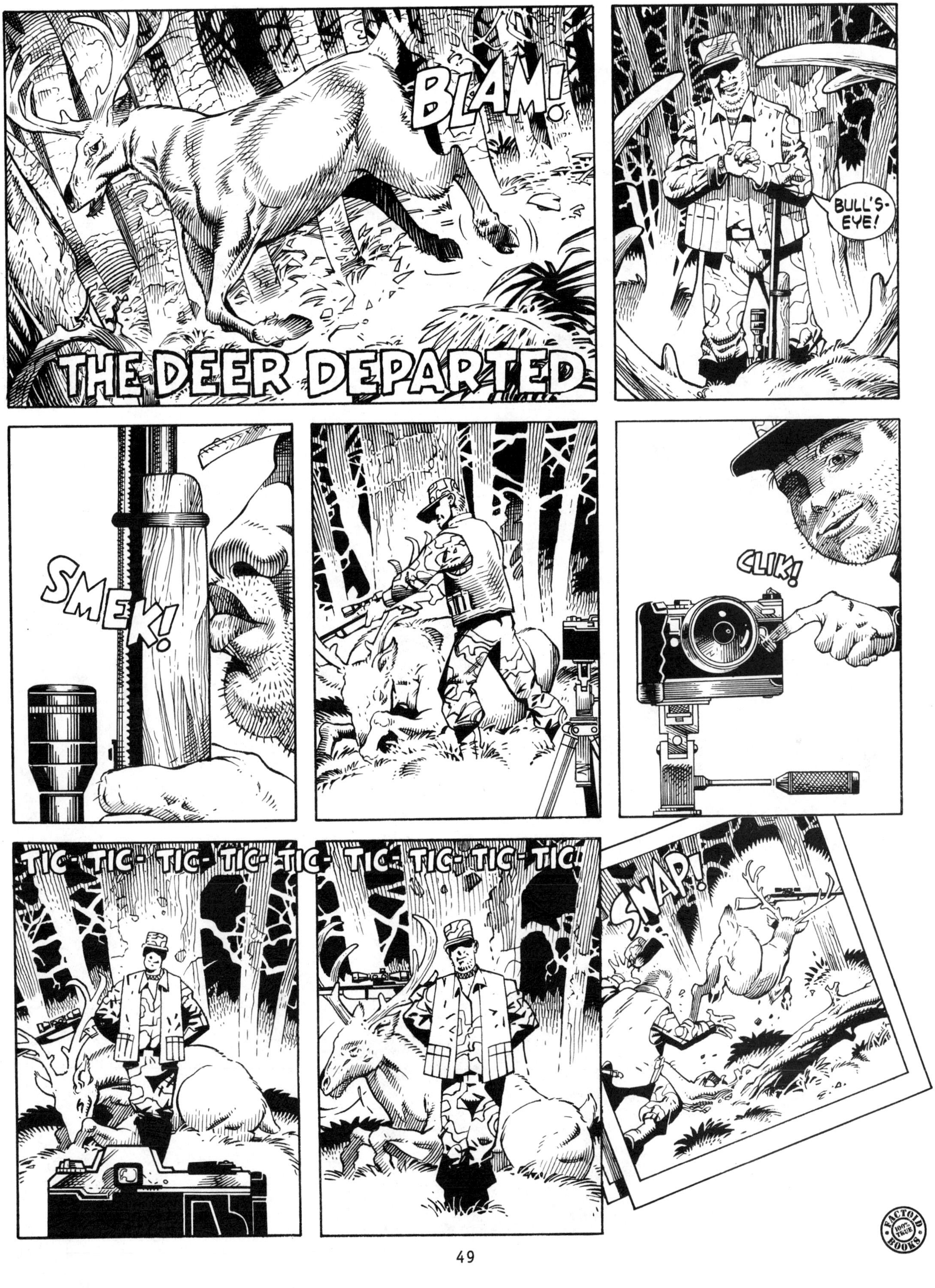
BLAM!
THE DEER DEPARTED
BULL'S-EYE!
SMEK!
CLIK!
TIC-TIC-TIC-TIC-TIC-TIC-TIC-TIC-TIC!
SNAP!
FACTOID BOOKS 100% TRUE

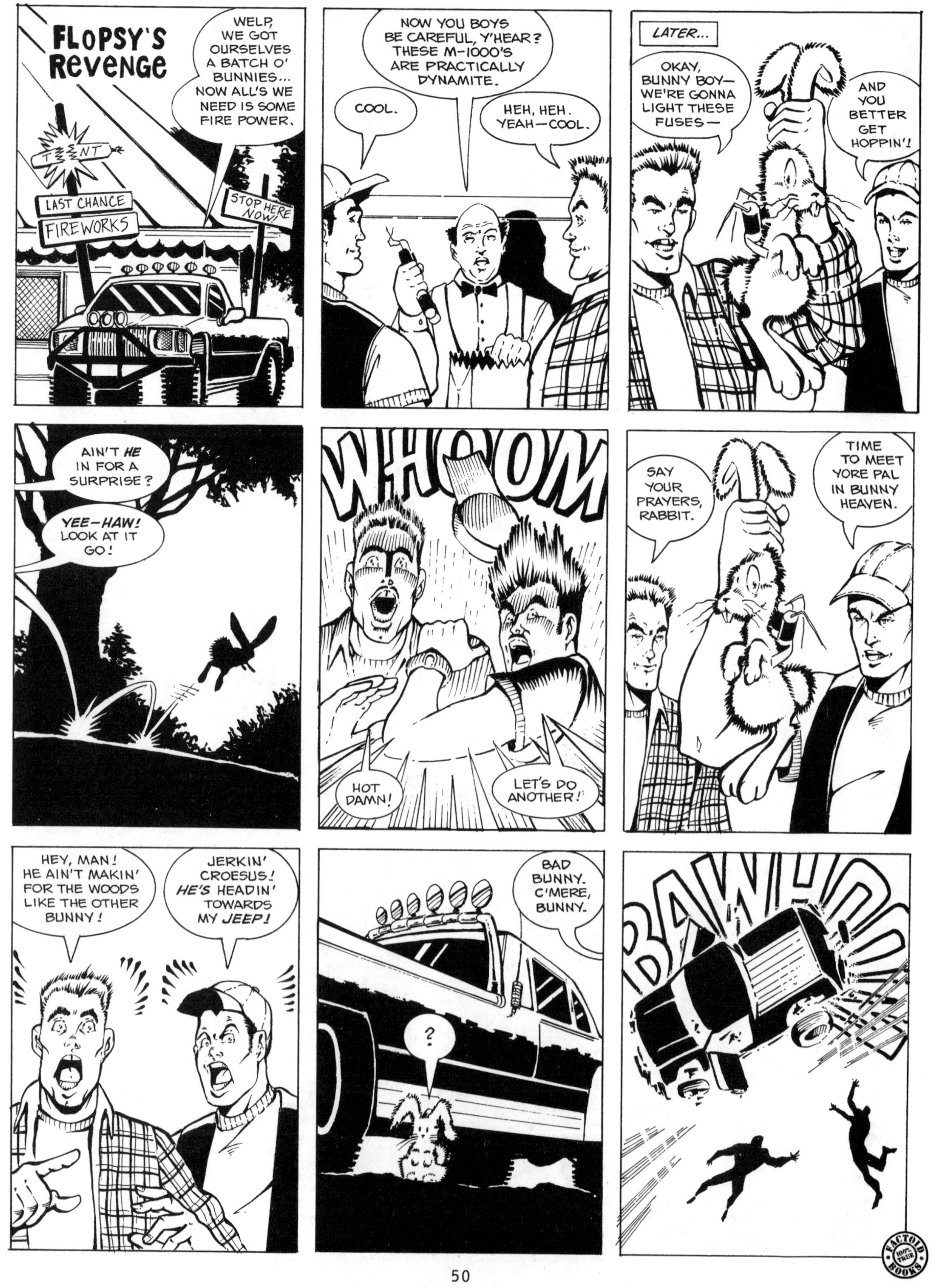
FLOPSY'S Revenge
WELP, WE GOT OURSELVES A BATCH O' BUNNIES... NOW ALL'S WE NEED IS SOME FIRE POWER.
LAST CHANCE
FIREWORKS
STOP HERE NOW!
NOW YOU BOYS BE CAREFUL, Y'HEAR? THESE M-1000'S ARE PRACTICALLY DYNAMITE.
COOL.
HEH, HEH. YEAH—COOL.
LATER...
OKAY, BUNNY BOY— WE'RE GONNA LIGHT THESE FUSES—
AND YOU BETTER GET HOPPIN'!
AIN'T *HE* IN FOR A SURPRISE?
YEE-HAW! LOOK AT IT GO!
WHOOM
HOT DAMN!
LET'S DO ANOTHER!
SAY YOUR PRAYERS, RABBIT.
TIME TO MEET YORE PAL IN BUNNY HEAVEN.
HEY, MAN! HE AIN'T MAKIN' FOR THE WOODS LIKE THE OTHER BUNNY!
JERKIN' CROESUS! *HE'S* HEADIN' TOWARDS MY *JEEP!*
BAD BUNNY. C'MERE, BUNNY.
?

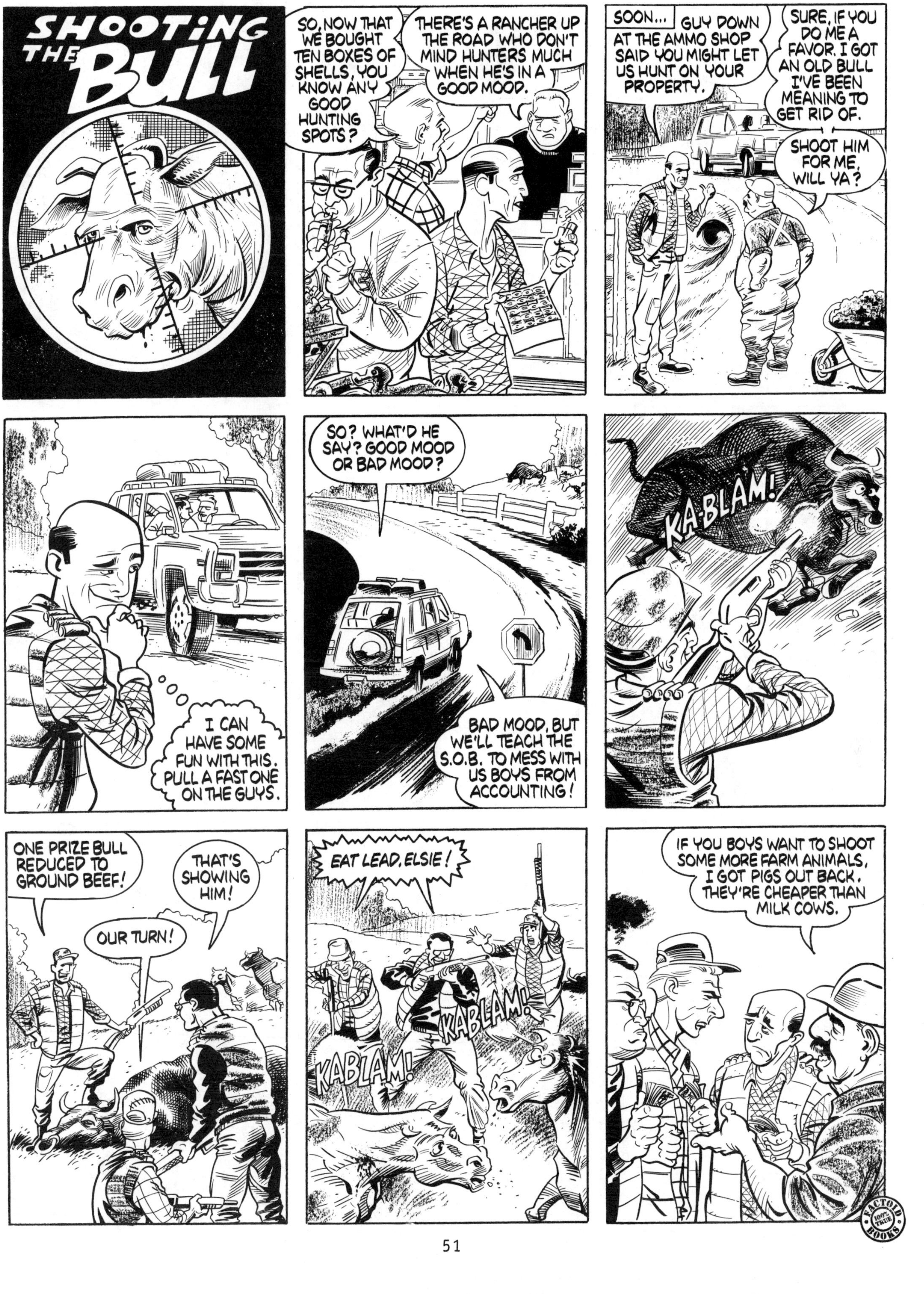
SHOOTING THE BULL
SO, NOW THAT WE BOUGHT TEN BOXES OF SHELLS, YOU KNOW ANY GOOD HUNTING SPOTS?
THERE'S A RANCHER UP THE ROAD WHO DON'T MIND HUNTERS MUCH WHEN HE'S IN A GOOD MOOD.
SOON...
GUY DOWN AT THE AMMO SHOP SAID YOU MIGHT LET US HUNT ON YOUR PROPERTY.
SURE, IF YOU DO ME A FAVOR. I GOT AN OLD BULL I'VE BEEN MEANING TO GET RID OF.
SHOOT HIM FOR ME, WILL YA?
I CAN HAVE SOME FUN WITH THIS. PULL A FAST ONE ON THE GUYS.
SO? WHAT'D HE SAY? GOOD MOOD OR BAD MOOD?
BAD MOOD, BUT WE'LL TEACH THE S.O.B. TO MESS WITH US BOYS FROM ACCOUNTING!
KA-BLAM!
ONE PRIZE BULL REDUCED TO GROUND BEEF!
THAT'S SHOWING HIM!
OUR TURN!
EAT LEAD, ELSIE!
KABLAM!
KABLAM!
IF YOU BOYS WANT TO SHOOT SOME MORE FARM ANIMALS, I GOT PIGS OUT BACK. THEY'RE CHEAPER THAN MILK COWS.
FACTOID BOOKS 100% TRUE

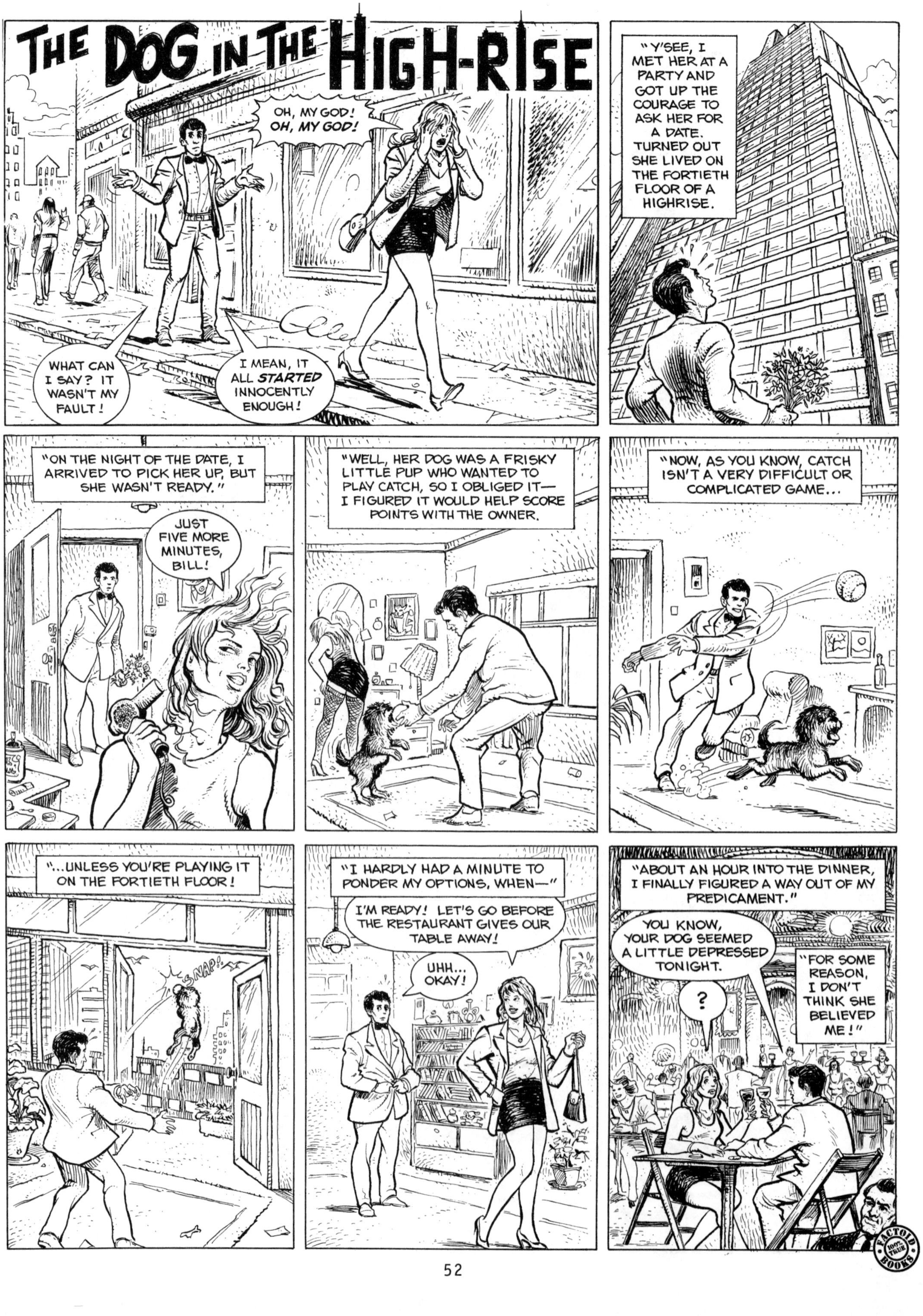
THE DOG IN THE HIGH-RISE
OH, MY GOD! OH, MY GOD!
WHAT CAN I SAY? IT WASN'T MY FAULT!
I MEAN, IT ALL STARTED INNOCENTLY ENOUGH!
"Y'SEE, I MET HER AT A PARTY AND GOT UP THE COURAGE TO ASK HER FOR A DATE. TURNED OUT SHE LIVED ON THE FORTIETH FLOOR OF A HIGHRISE.
"ON THE NIGHT OF THE DATE, I ARRIVED TO PICK HER UP, BUT SHE WASN'T READY."
JUST FIVE MORE MINUTES, BILL!
"WELL, HER DOG WAS A FRISKY LITTLE PUP WHO WANTED TO PLAY CATCH, SO I OBLIGED IT— I FIGURED IT WOULD HELP SCORE POINTS WITH THE OWNER.
"NOW, AS YOU KNOW, CATCH ISN'T A VERY DIFFICULT OR COMPLICATED GAME...
"...UNLESS YOU'RE PLAYING IT ON THE FORTIETH FLOOR!
SNAP!
"I HARDLY HAD A MINUTE TO PONDER MY OPTIONS, WHEN—"
I'M READY! LET'S GO BEFORE THE RESTAURANT GIVES OUR TABLE AWAY!
UHH... OKAY!
"ABOUT AN HOUR INTO THE DINNER, I FINALLY FIGURED A WAY OUT OF MY PREDICAMENT."
YOU KNOW, YOUR DOG SEEMED A LITTLE DEPRESSED TONIGHT.
?
"FOR SOME REASON, I DON'T THINK SHE BELIEVED ME!"
FACTOID BOOKS 100% TRUE

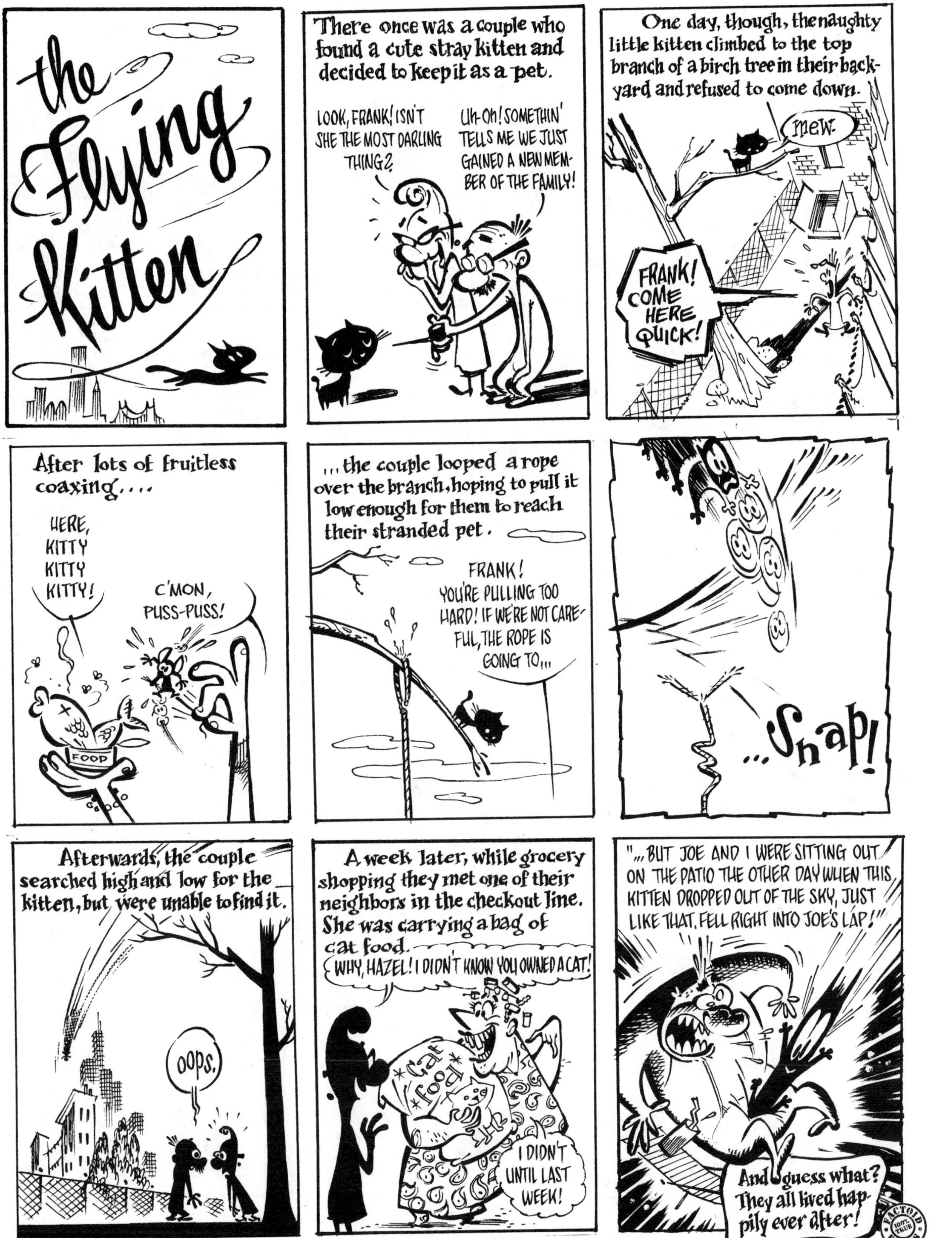
the Flying Kitten
There once was a couple who found a cute stray kitten and decided to keep it as a pet.
LOOK, FRANK! ISN'T SHE THE MOST DARLING THING?
UH-OH! SOMETHIN' TELLS ME WE JUST GAINED A NEW MEMBER OF THE FAMILY!
One day, though, the naughty little kitten climbed to the top branch of a birch tree in their backyard and refused to come down.
mew.
FRANK! COME HERE QUICK!
After lots of fruitless coaxing....
HERE, KITTY KITTY KITTY!
C'MON, PUSS-PUSS!
FOOD
...the couple looped a rope over the branch, hoping to pull it low enough for them to reach their stranded pet.
FRANK! YOU'RE PULLING TOO HARD! IF WE'RE NOT CAREFUL, THE ROPE IS GOING TO...
...Snap!
Afterwards, the couple searched high and low for the kitten, but were unable to find it.
oops.
A week later, while grocery shopping they met one of their neighbors in the checkout line. She was carrying a bag of cat food.
WHY, HAZEL! I DIDN'T KNOW YOU OWNED A CAT!
cat food
I DIDN'T UNTIL LAST WEEK!
"...BUT JOE AND I WERE SITTING OUT ON THE PATIO THE OTHER DAY WHEN THIS KITTEN DROPPED OUT OF THE SKY, JUST LIKE THAT. FELL RIGHT INTO JOE'S LAP!"
And guess what? They all lived happily ever after!
FACTOID BOOKS 100% TRUE

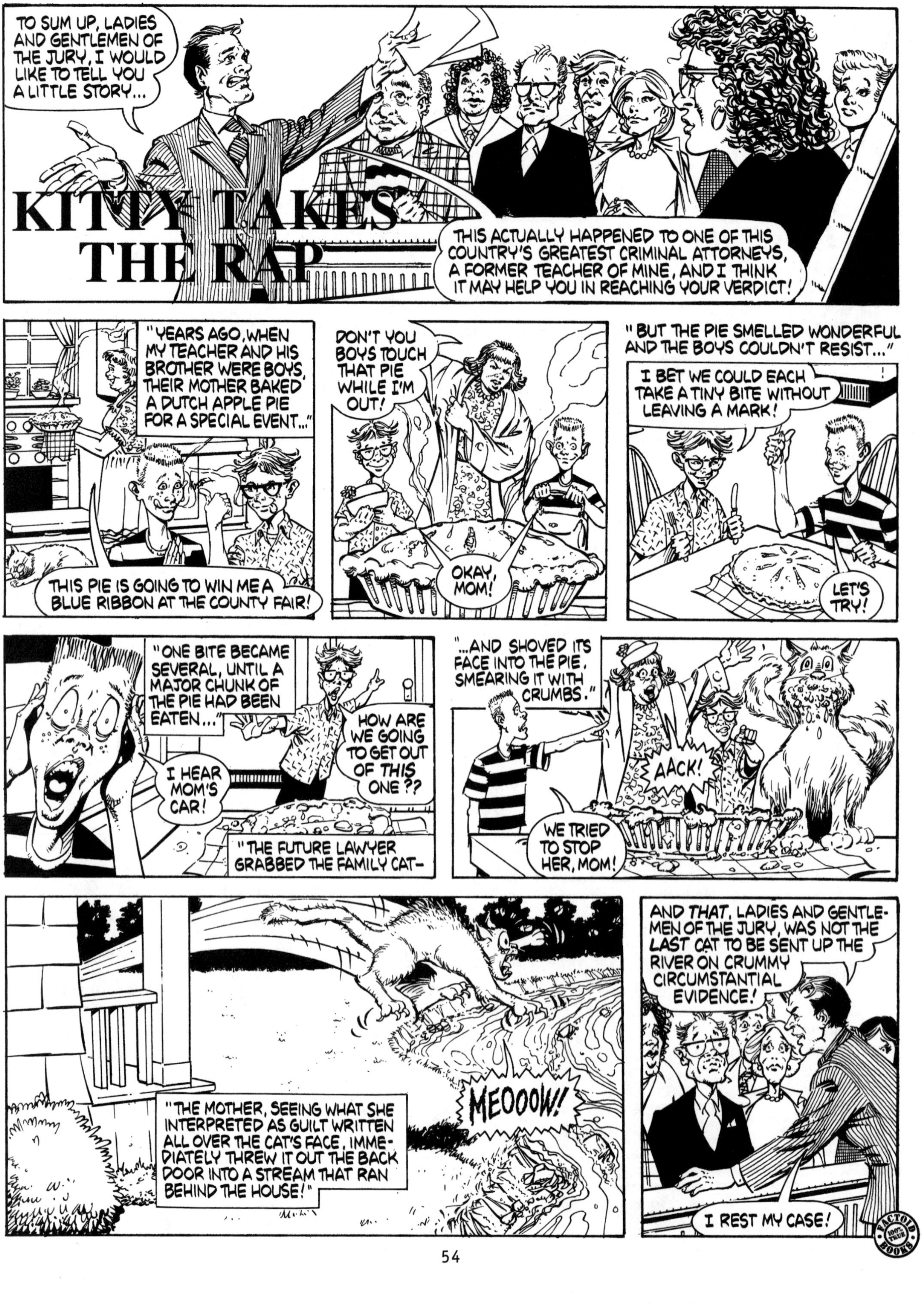
TO SUM UP, LADIES AND GENTLEMEN OF THE JURY, I WOULD LIKE TO TELL YOU A LITTLE STORY...
KITTY TAKES THE RAP
THIS ACTUALLY HAPPENED TO ONE OF THIS COUNTRY'S GREATEST CRIMINAL ATTORNEYS, A FORMER TEACHER OF MINE, AND I THINK IT MAY HELP YOU IN REACHING YOUR VERDICT!
"YEARS AGO, WHEN MY TEACHER AND HIS BROTHER WERE BOYS, THEIR MOTHER BAKED A DUTCH APPLE PIE FOR A SPECIAL EVENT..."
THIS PIE IS GOING TO WIN ME A BLUE RIBBON AT THE COUNTY FAIR!
DON'T YOU BOYS TOUCH THAT PIE WHILE I'M OUT!
OKAY, MOM!
"BUT THE PIE SMELLED WONDERFUL AND THE BOYS COULDN'T RESIST..."
I BET WE COULD EACH TAKE A TINY BITE WITHOUT LEAVING A MARK!
LET'S TRY!
"ONE BITE BECAME SEVERAL, UNTIL A MAJOR CHUNK OF THE PIE HAD BEEN EATEN..."
I HEAR MOM'S CAR!
HOW ARE WE GOING TO GET OUT OF THIS ONE ??
"THE FUTURE LAWYER GRABBED THE FAMILY CAT-
"...AND SHOVED ITS FACE INTO THE PIE, SMEARING IT WITH CRUMBS."
AACK!
WE TRIED TO STOP HER, MOM!
MEOOOW!
"THE MOTHER, SEEING WHAT SHE INTERPRETED AS GUILT WRITTEN ALL OVER THE CAT'S FACE, IMMEDIATELY THREW IT OUT THE BACK DOOR INTO A STREAM THAT RAN BEHIND THE HOUSE!"
AND THAT, LADIES AND GENTLEMEN OF THE JURY, WAS NOT THE LAST CAT TO BE SENT UP THE RIVER ON CRUMMY CIRCUMSTANTIAL EVIDENCE!
I REST MY CASE!
FACTOID BOOKS 100% TRUE

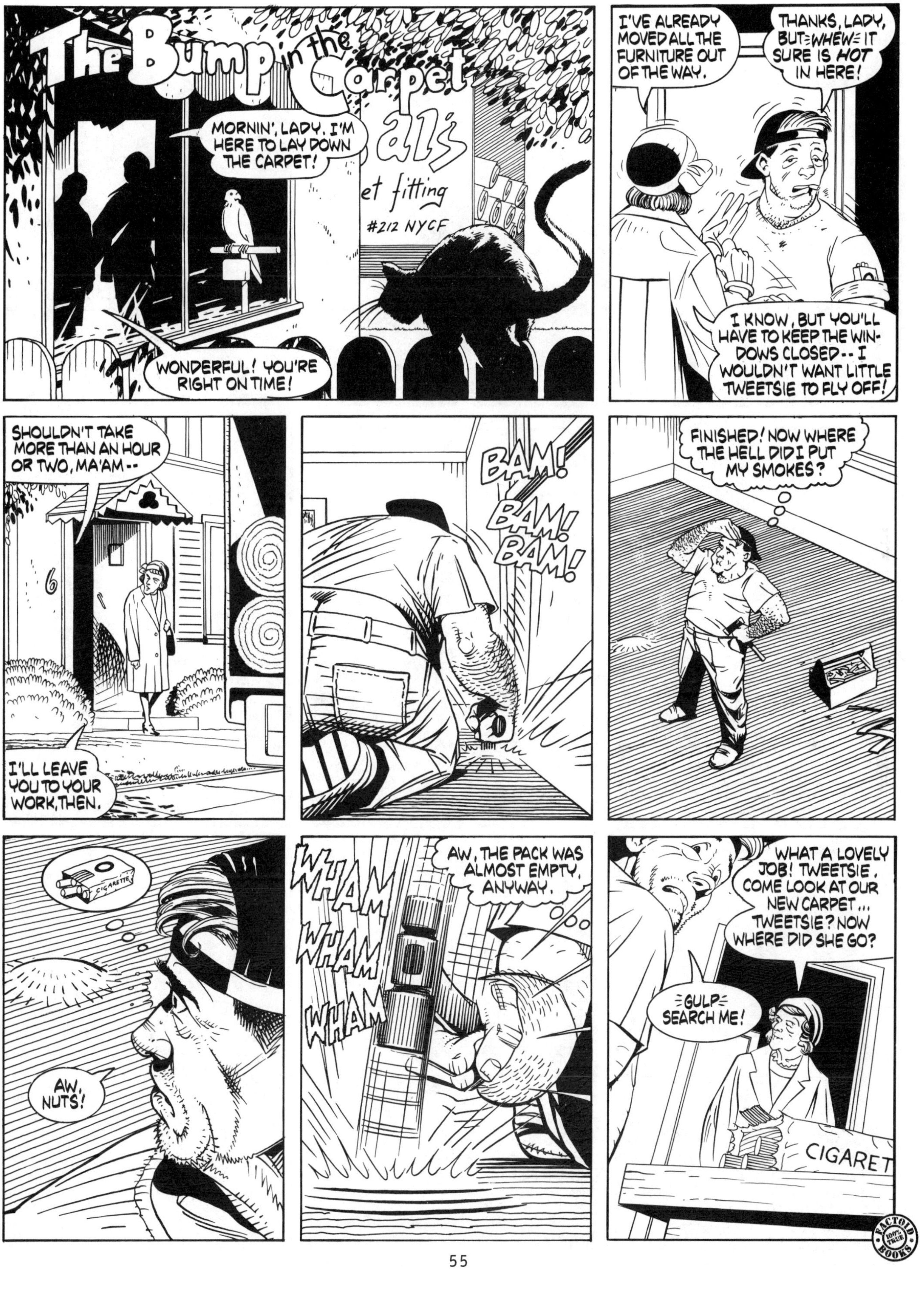
The Bump in the Carpet
MORNIN', LADY. I'M HERE TO LAY DOWN THE CARPET!
WONDERFUL! YOU'RE RIGHT ON TIME!
et fitting
#212 NYCF
I'VE ALREADY MOVED ALL THE FURNITURE OUT OF THE WAY.
THANKS, LADY, BUT WHEW IT SURE IS HOT IN HERE!
I KNOW, BUT YOU'LL HAVE TO KEEP THE WINDOWS CLOSED-- I WOULDN'T WANT LITTLE TWEETSIE TO FLY OFF!
SHOULDN'T TAKE MORE THAN AN HOUR OR TWO, MA'AM--
I'LL LEAVE YOU TO YOUR WORK, THEN.
BAM! BAM! BAM!
FINISHED! NOW WHERE THE HELL DID I PUT MY SMOKES?
CIGARETTE
AW, NUTS!
WHAM WHAM WHAM
AW, THE PACK WAS ALMOST EMPTY, ANYWAY.
WHAT A LOVELY JOB! TWEETSIE, COME LOOK AT OUR NEW CARPET... TWEETSIE? NOW WHERE DID SHE GO?
GULP SEARCH ME!
CIGARET

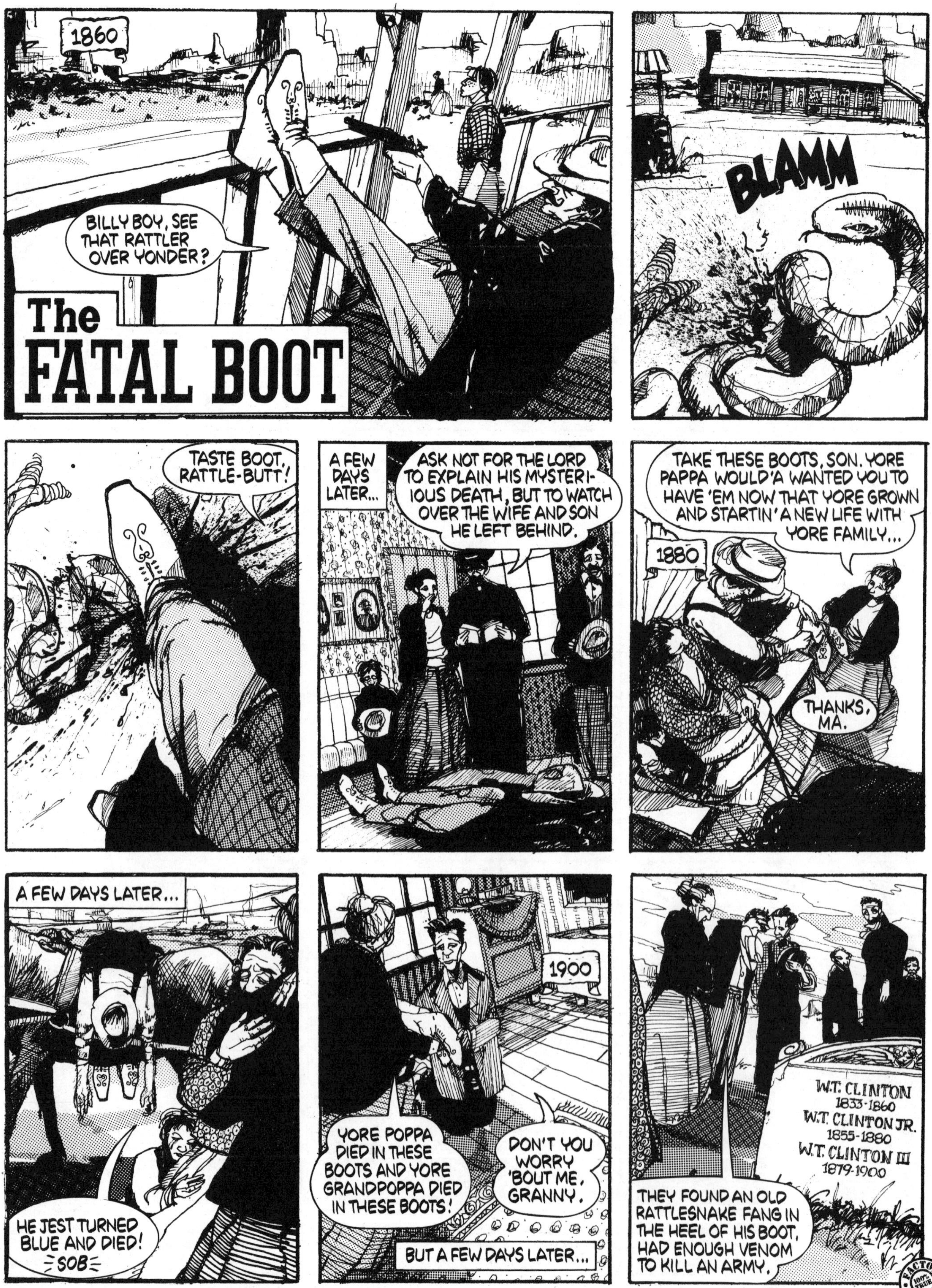
1860
BILLY BOY, SEE THAT RATTLER OVER YONDER?
The FATAL BOOT
BLAMM
TASTE BOOT, RATTLE-BUTT!
A FEW DAYS LATER...
ASK NOT FOR THE LORD TO EXPLAIN HIS MYSTERIIOUS DEATH, BUT TO WATCH OVER THE WIFE AND SON HE LEFT BEHIND.
TAKE THESE BOOTS, SON. YORE PAPPA WOULD'A WANTED YOU TO HAVE 'EM NOW THAT YORE GROWN AND STARTIN' A NEW LIFE WITH YORE FAMILY...
1880
THANKS, MA.
A FEW DAYS LATER...
HE JEST TURNED BLUE AND DIED! SOB
1900
YORE POPPA DIED IN THESE BOOTS AND YORE GRANDPOPPA DIED IN THESE BOOTS!
DON'T YOU WORRY 'BOUT ME, GRANNY.
BUT A FEW DAYS LATER...
W.T. CLINTON 1833-1860
W.T. CLINTON JR. 1855-1880
W.T. CLINTON III 1879-1900
THEY FOUND AN OLD RATTLESNAKE FANG IN THE HEEL OF HIS BOOT, HAD ENOUGH VENOM TO KILL AN ARMY.

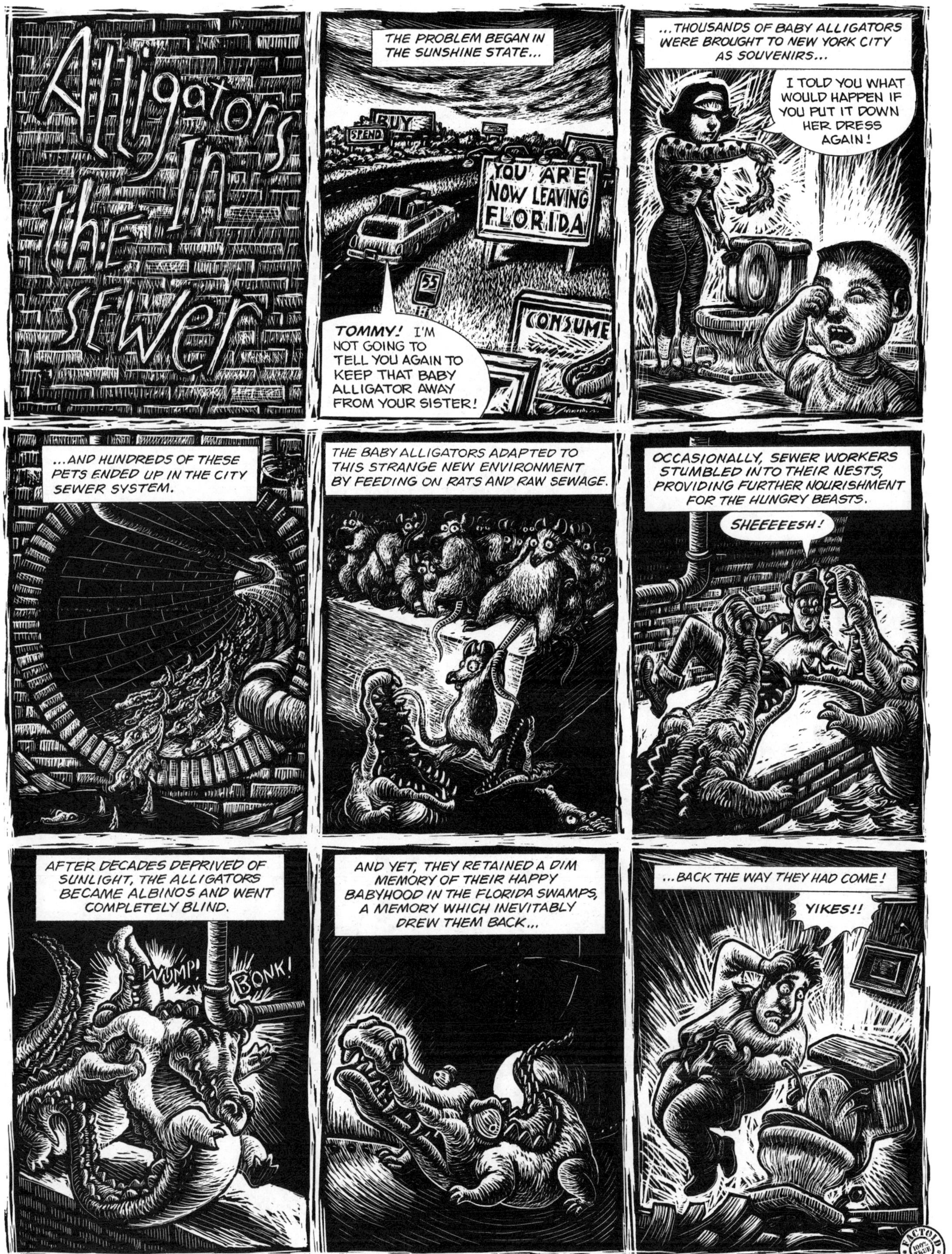
Alligators In the Sewer
THE PROBLEM BEGAN IN THE SUNSHINE STATE...
BUY
SPEND
YOU ARE NOW LEAVING FLORIDA
55
CONSUME
TOMMY! I'M NOT GOING TO TELL YOU AGAIN TO KEEP THAT BABY ALLIGATOR AWAY FROM YOUR SISTER!
...THOUSANDS OF BABY ALLIGATORS WERE BROUGHT TO NEW YORK CITY AS SOUVENIRS...
I TOLD YOU WHAT WOULD HAPPEN IF YOU PUT IT DOWN HER DRESS AGAIN!
...AND HUNDREDS OF THESE PETS ENDED UP IN THE CITY SEWER SYSTEM.
THE BABY ALLIGATORS ADAPTED TO THIS STRANGE NEW ENVIRONMENT BY FEEDING ON RATS AND RAW SEWAGE.
OCCASIONALLY, SEWER WORKERS STUMBLED INTO THEIR NESTS, PROVIDING FURTHER NOURISHMENT FOR THE HUNGRY BEASTS.
SHEEEEESH!
AFTER DECADES DEPRIVED OF SUNLIGHT, THE ALLIGATORS BECAME ALBINOS AND WENT COMPLETELY BLIND.
WUMP!
BONK!
AND YET, THEY RETAINED A DIM MEMORY OF THEIR HAPPY BABYHOOD IN THE FLORIDA SWAMPS, A MEMORY WHICH INEVITABLY DREW THEM BACK...
...BACK THE WAY THEY HAD COME!
YIKES!!
FACTOID BOOKS 100% TRUE

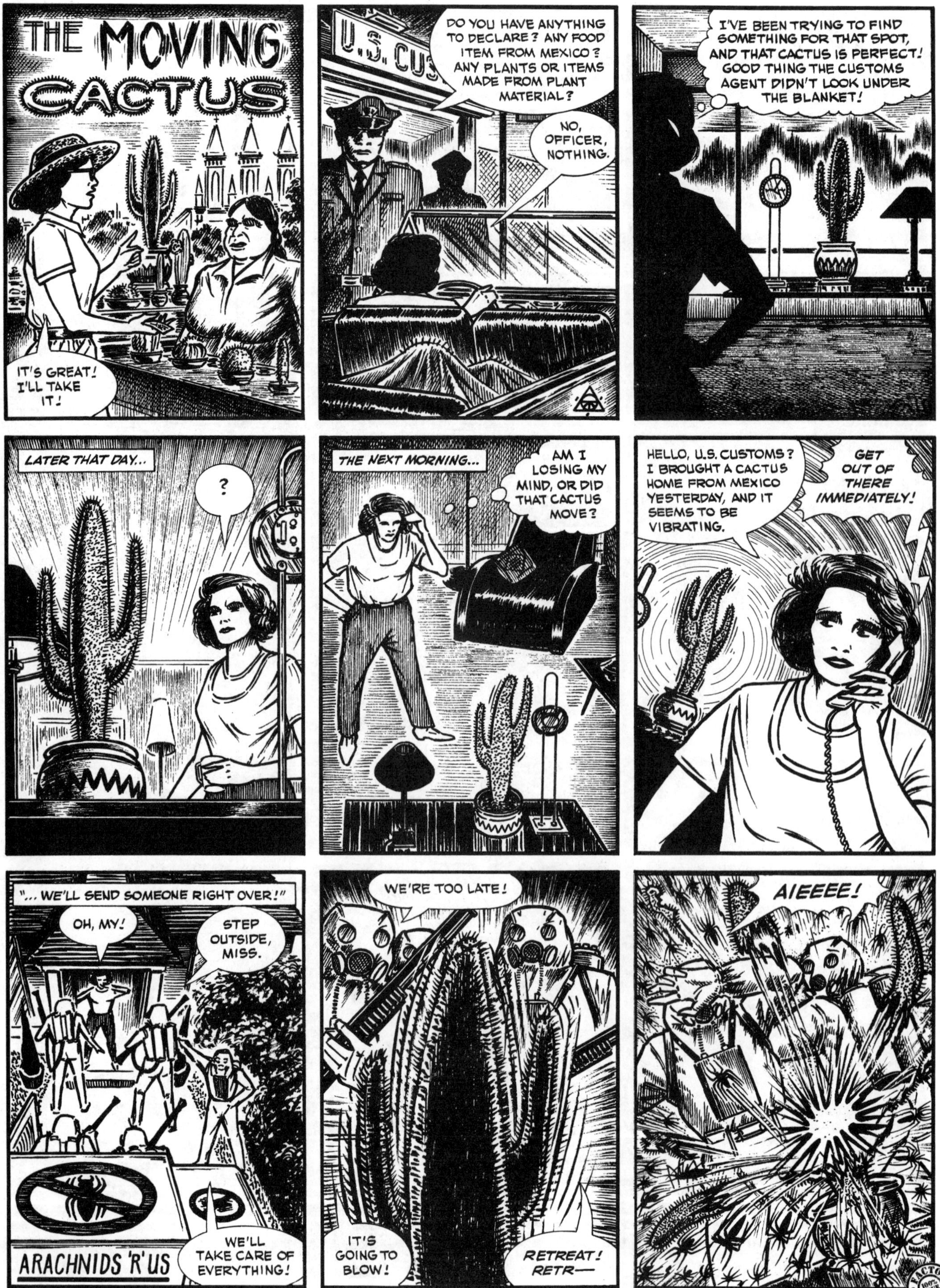
THE MOVING CACTUS
IT'S GREAT! I'LL TAKE IT!
U.S. CUS
DO YOU HAVE ANYTHING TO DECLARE? ANY FOOD ITEM FROM MEXICO? ANY PLANTS OR ITEMS MADE FROM PLANT MATERIAL?
NO, OFFICER, NOTHING.
I'VE BEEN TRYING TO FIND SOMETHING FOR THAT SPOT, AND THAT CACTUS IS PERFECT! GOOD THING THE CUSTOMS AGENT DIDN'T LOOK UNDER THE BLANKET!
LATER THAT DAY...
?
THE NEXT MORNING...
AM I LOSING MY MIND, OR DID THAT CACTUS MOVE?
HELLO, U.S. CUSTOMS? I BROUGHT A CACTUS HOME FROM MEXICO YESTERDAY, AND IT SEEMS TO BE VIBRATING.
GET OUT OF THERE IMMEDIATELY!
"... WE'LL SEND SOMEONE RIGHT OVER!"
OH, MY!
STEP OUTSIDE, MISS.
ARACHNIDS 'R' US
WE'LL TAKE CARE OF EVERYTHING!
WE'RE TOO LATE!
IT'S GOING TO BLOW!
RETREAT! RETR—
AIEEEE!
FACTOID BOOKS 100% TRUE

CHAPTER THREE

HORROR LEGENDS

CAMPFIRE CLASSICS

These are the horror legends traditionally told at slumber parties and summer camps. In a sense, all urban legends are horror stories, though in some the shock is mitigated by humor. ("Ha Ha! They ate their grandmother's ashes!") You be the judge: Is this sort of thing funny-funny, funny-peculiar, or just plain unfunny-horrible? Much of the horror in these legends comes from what the characters in the story do *not* know — The killer is upstairs! The hand was licked by a mad murderer! The smell comes from a decaying body hidden in the hotel room! The nervous *humor,* such as it is, comes mainly from our sense of relief that *we're* not involved in that particular adventure, being (of course) superior in wisdom and insight to the stories' victims.

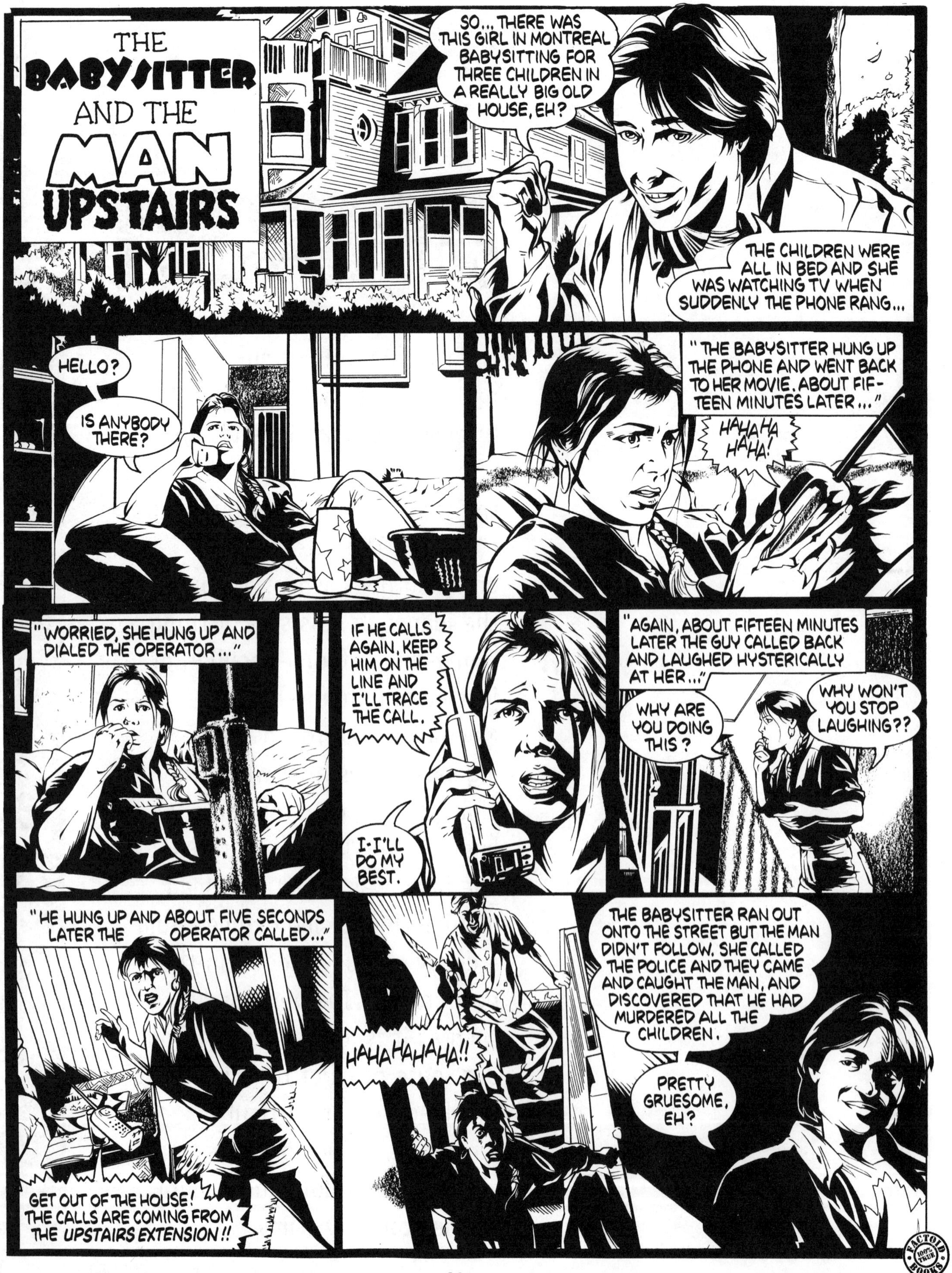

THE BABYSITTER AND THE MAN UPSTAIRS
SO... THERE WAS THIS GIRL IN MONTREAL BABYSITTING FOR THREE CHILDREN IN A REALLY BIG OLD HOUSE, EH?
THE CHILDREN WERE ALL IN BED AND SHE WAS WATCHING TV WHEN SUDDENLY THE PHONE RANG...
HELLO?
IS ANYBODY THERE?
"THE BABYSITTER HUNG UP THE PHONE AND WENT BACK TO HER MOVIE. ABOUT FIF-TEEN MINUTES LATER..."
HAHAHA HAHA!
"WORRIED, SHE HUNG UP AND DIALED THE OPERATOR..."
IF HE CALLS AGAIN, KEEP HIM ON THE LINE AND I'LL TRACE THE CALL.
I-I'LL DO MY BEST.
"AGAIN, ABOUT FIFTEEN MINUTES LATER THE GUY CALLED BACK AND LAUGHED HYSTERICALLY AT HER..."
WHY ARE YOU DOING THIS?
WHY WON'T YOU STOP LAUGHING??
"HE HUNG UP AND ABOUT FIVE SECONDS LATER THE OPERATOR CALLED..."
GET OUT OF THE HOUSE! THE CALLS ARE COMING FROM THE UPSTAIRS EXTENSION!!
HAHAHAHAHA!!
THE BABYSITTER RAN OUT ONTO THE STREET BUT THE MAN DIDN'T FOLLOW. SHE CALLED THE POLICE AND THEY CAME AND CAUGHT THE MAN, AND DISCOVERED THAT HE HAD MURDERED ALL THE CHILDREN.
PRETTY GRUESOME, EH?
FACTOID BOOKS 100% TRUE

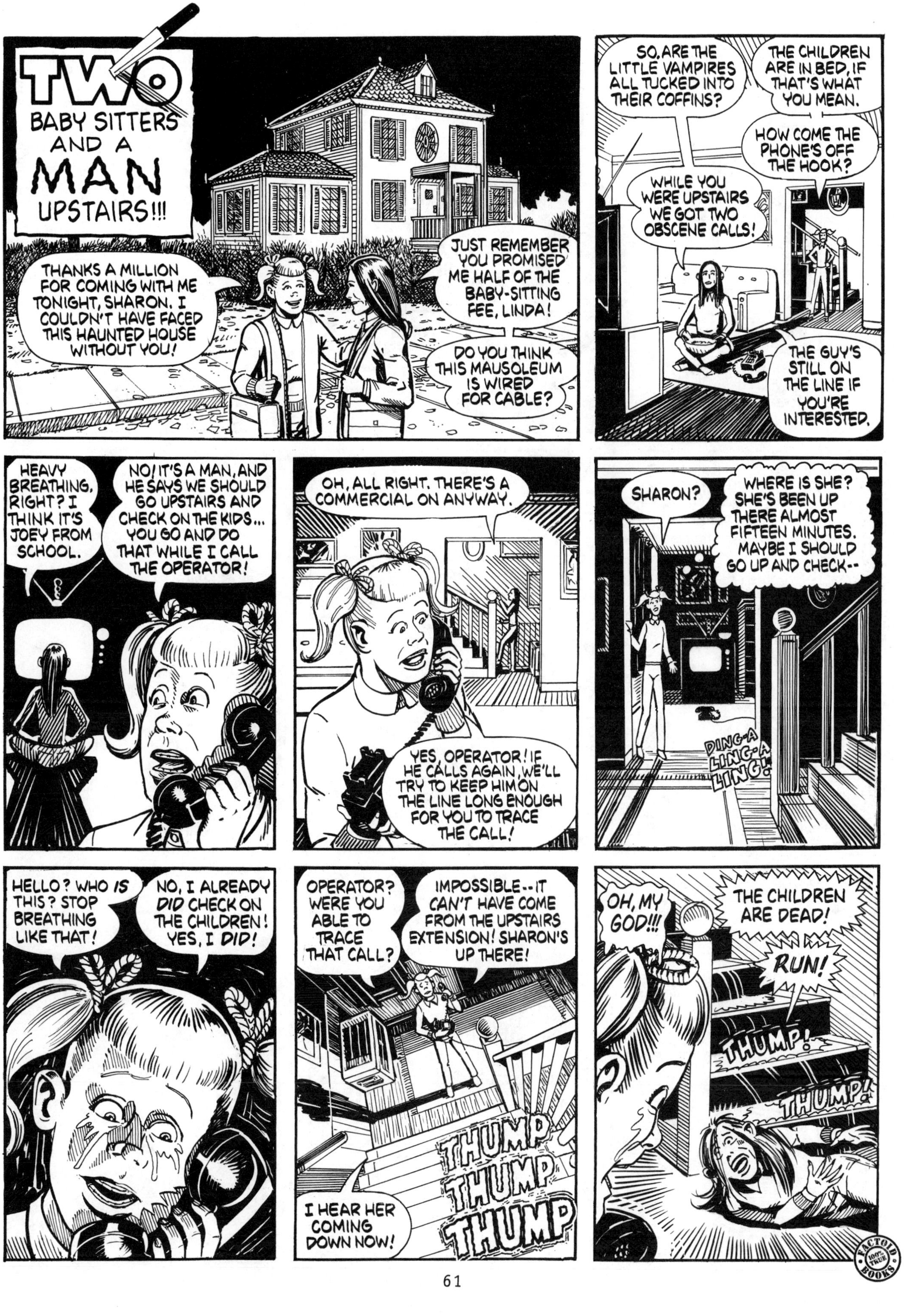
TWO BABY SITTERS AND A MAN UPSTAIRS!!!
THANKS A MILLION FOR COMING WITH ME TONIGHT, SHARON. I COULDN'T HAVE FACED THIS HAUNTED HOUSE WITHOUT YOU!
JUST REMEMBER YOU PROMISED ME HALF OF THE BABY-SITTING FEE, LINDA!
DO YOU THINK THIS MAUSOLEUM IS WIRED FOR CABLE?
SO, ARE THE LITTLE VAMPIRES ALL TUCKED INTO THEIR COFFINS?
THE CHILDREN ARE IN BED, IF THAT'S WHAT YOU MEAN.
HOW COME THE PHONE'S OFF THE HOOK?
WHILE YOU WERE UPSTAIRS WE GOT TWO OBSCENE CALLS!
THE GUY'S STILL ON THE LINE IF YOU'RE INTERESTED.
HEAVY BREATHING, RIGHT? I THINK IT'S JOEY FROM SCHOOL.
NO! IT'S A MAN, AND HE SAYS WE SHOULD GO UPSTAIRS AND CHECK ON THE KIDS... YOU GO AND DO THAT WHILE I CALL THE OPERATOR!
OH, ALL RIGHT. THERE'S A COMMERCIAL ON ANYWAY.
YES, OPERATOR! IF HE CALLS AGAIN, WE'LL TRY TO KEEP HIM ON THE LINE LONG ENOUGH FOR YOU TO TRACE THE CALL!
SHARON?
WHERE IS SHE? SHE'S BEEN UP THERE ALMOST FIFTEEN MINUTES. MAYBE I SHOULD GO UP AND CHECK--
DING-A LING-A LING!
HELLO? WHO IS THIS? STOP BREATHING LIKE THAT!
NO, I ALREADY DID CHECK ON THE CHILDREN! YES, I DID!
OPERATOR? WERE YOU ABLE TO TRACE THAT CALL?
IMPOSSIBLE--IT CAN'T HAVE COME FROM THE UPSTAIRS EXTENSION! SHARON'S UP THERE!
I HEAR HER COMING DOWN NOW!
THUMP THUMP THUMP
OH, MY GOD!!!
THE CHILDREN ARE DEAD!
RUN!
THUMP!
THUMP!
FACTOID BOOKS 100% TRUE

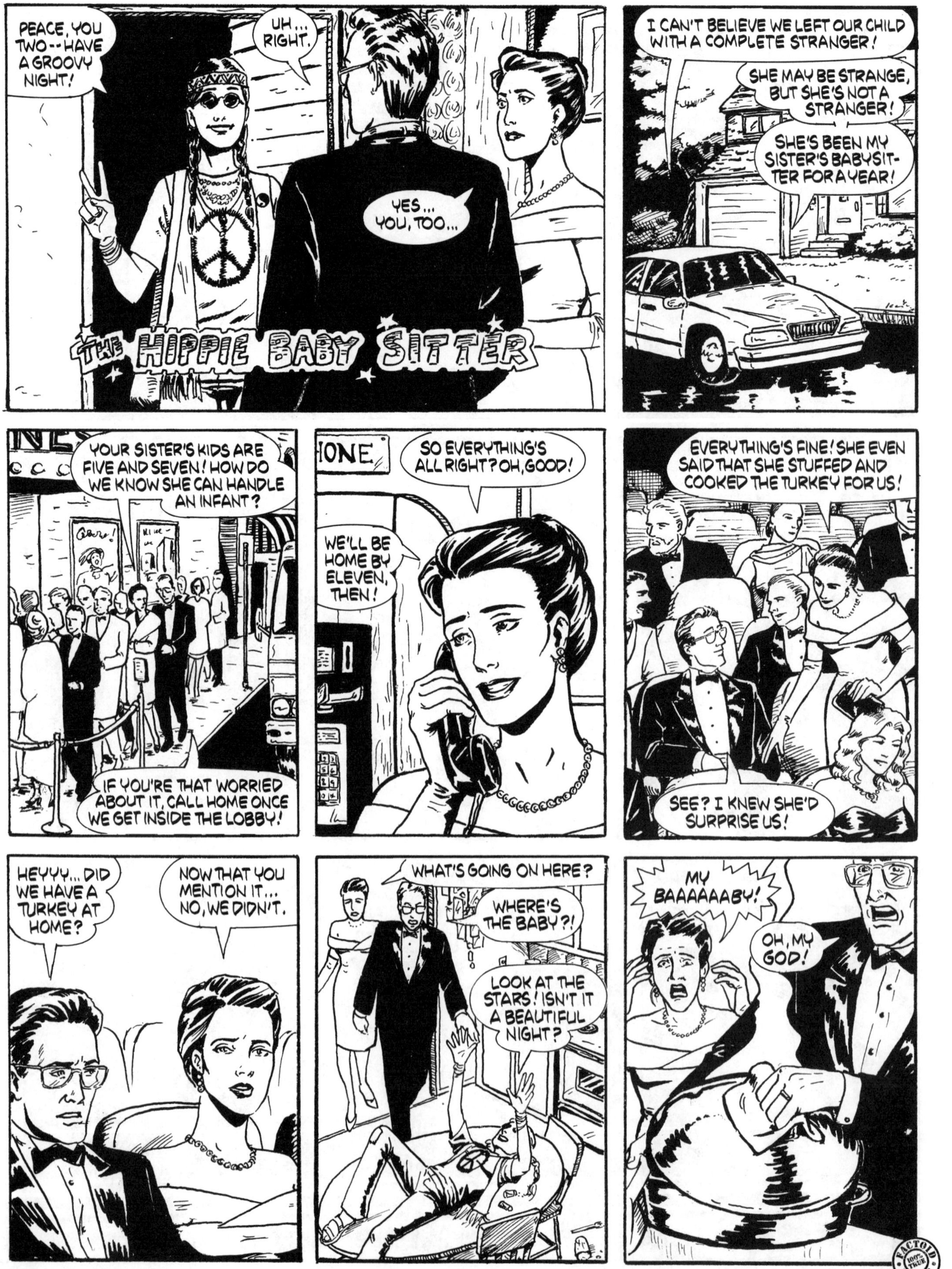
PEACE, YOU TWO--HAVE A GROOVY NIGHT!
UH... RIGHT.
YES... YOU, TOO...
THE HIPPIE BABY SITTER
I CAN'T BELIEVE WE LEFT OUR CHILD WITH A COMPLETE STRANGER!
SHE MAY BE STRANGE, BUT SHE'S NOT A STRANGER!
SHE'S BEEN MY SISTER'S BABYSITTER FOR A YEAR!
YOUR SISTER'S KIDS ARE FIVE AND SEVEN! HOW DO WE KNOW SHE CAN HANDLE AN INFANT?
IF YOU'RE THAT WORRIED ABOUT IT, CALL HOME ONCE WE GET INSIDE THE LOBBY!
SO EVERYTHING'S ALL RIGHT? OH, GOOD!
WE'LL BE HOME BY ELEVEN, THEN!
EVERYTHING'S FINE! SHE EVEN SAID THAT SHE STUFFED AND COOKED THE TURKEY FOR US!
SEE? I KNEW SHE'D SURPRISE US!
HEYYY... DID WE HAVE A TURKEY AT HOME?
NOW THAT YOU MENTION IT... NO, WE DIDN'T.
WHAT'S GOING ON HERE?
WHERE'S THE BABY?!
LOOK AT THE STARS! ISN'T IT A BEAUTIFUL NIGHT?
MY BAAAAAABY!
OH, MY GOD!
FACTOID BOOKS 100% TRUE

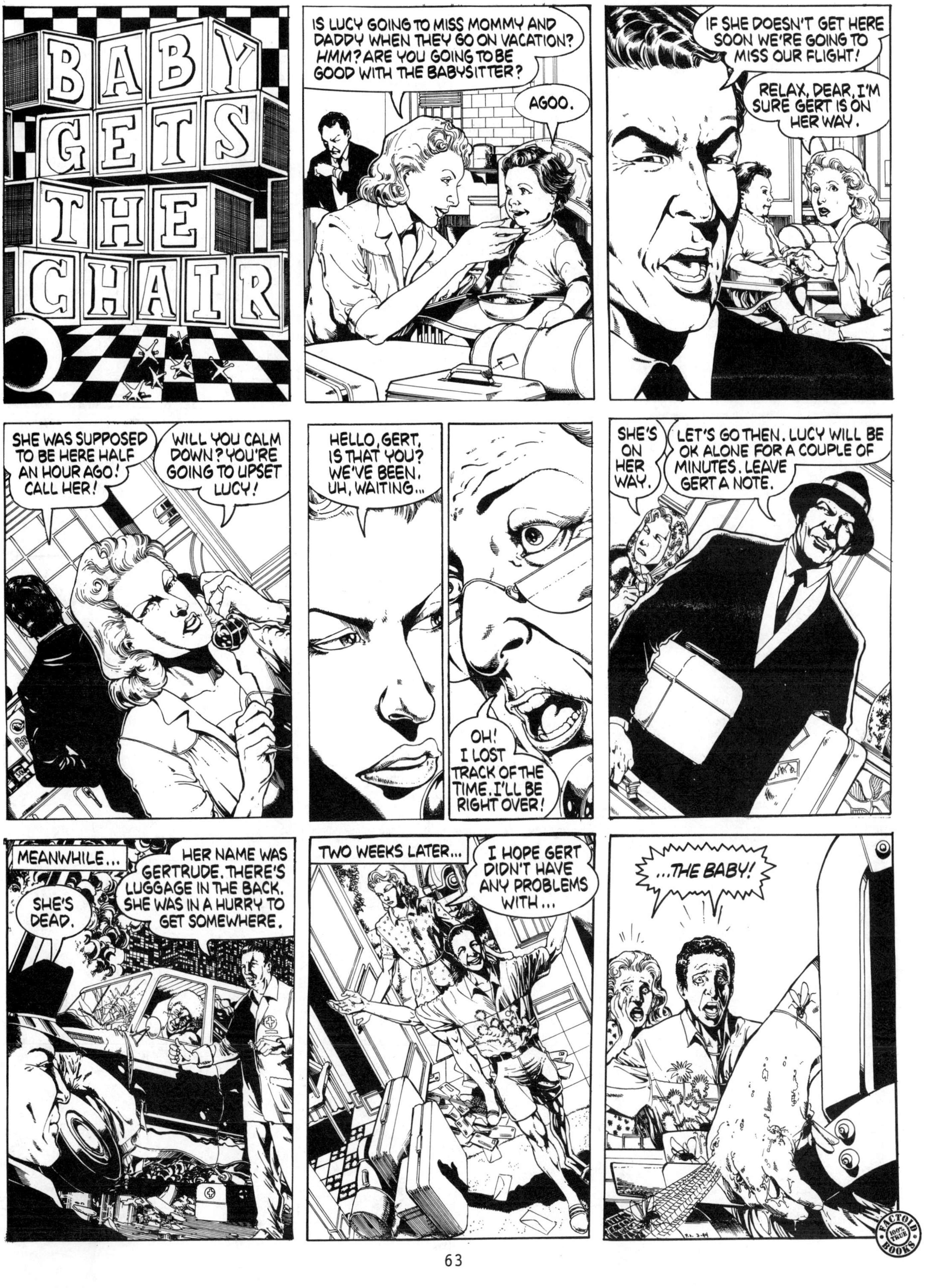

BABY GETS THE CHAIR
IS LUCY GOING TO MISS MOMMY AND DADDY WHEN THEY GO ON VACATION? HMM? ARE YOU GOING TO BE GOOD WITH THE BABYSITTER?
AGOO.
IF SHE DOESN'T GET HERE SOON WE'RE GOING TO MISS OUR FLIGHT!
RELAX, DEAR, I'M SURE GERT IS ON HER WAY.
SHE WAS SUPPOSED TO BE HERE HALF AN HOUR AGO! CALL HER!
WILL YOU CALM DOWN? YOU'RE GOING TO UPSET LUCY!
HELLO, GERT, IS THAT YOU? WE'VE BEEN, UH, WAITING...
OH! I LOST TRACK OF THE TIME. I'LL BE RIGHT OVER!
SHE'S ON HER WAY.
LET'S GO THEN. LUCY WILL BE OK ALONE FOR A COUPLE OF MINUTES. LEAVE GERT A NOTE.
MEANWHILE...
SHE'S DEAD.
HER NAME WAS GERTRUDE. THERE'S LUGGAGE IN THE BACK. SHE WAS IN A HURRY TO GET SOMEWHERE.
TWO WEEKS LATER...
I HOPE GERT DIDN'T HAVE ANY PROBLEMS WITH...
...THE BABY!
FACTOID 100% TRUE BOOKS

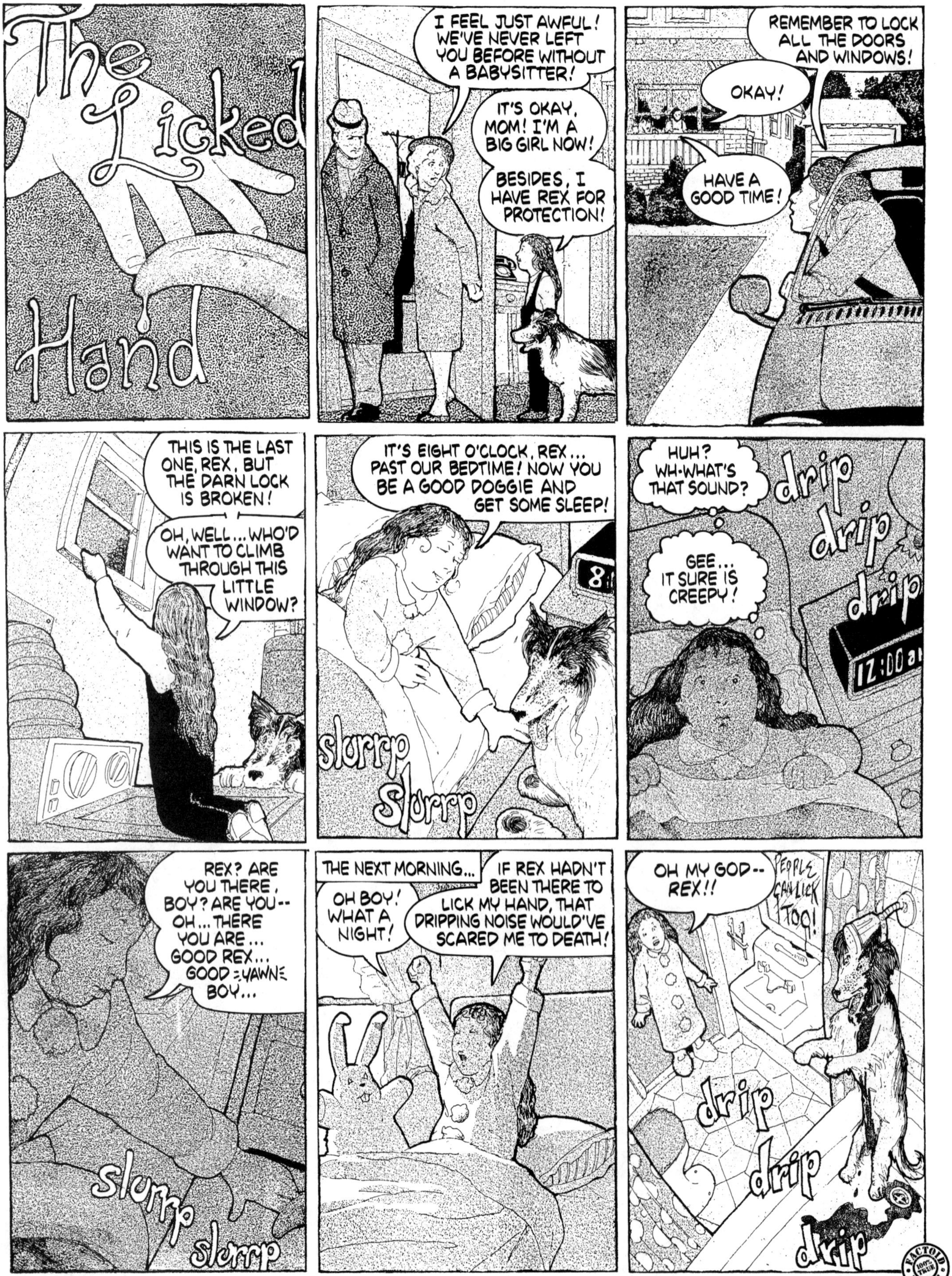
The Licked Hand
I FEEL JUST AWFUL! WE'VE NEVER LEFT YOU BEFORE WITHOUT A BABYSITTER!
IT'S OKAY, MOM! I'M A BIG GIRL NOW!
BESIDES, I HAVE REX FOR PROTECTION!
REMEMBER TO LOCK ALL THE DOORS AND WINDOWS!
OKAY!
HAVE A GOOD TIME!
THIS IS THE LAST ONE, REX, BUT THE DARN LOCK IS BROKEN!
OH, WELL... WHO'D WANT TO CLIMB THROUGH THIS LITTLE WINDOW?
IT'S EIGHT O'CLOCK, REX... PAST OUR BEDTIME! NOW YOU BE A GOOD DOGGIE AND GET SOME SLEEP!
slurrp
slurrp
HUH? WH-WHAT'S THAT SOUND?
GEE... IT SURE IS CREEPY!
drip
drip
drip
REX? ARE YOU THERE, BOY? ARE YOU-- OH... THERE YOU ARE... GOOD REX... GOOD =YAWN= BOY...
slurrp
slurrp
THE NEXT MORNING...
OH BOY! WHAT A NIGHT!
IF REX HADN'T BEEN THERE TO LICK MY HAND, THAT DRIPPING NOISE WOULD'VE SCARED ME TO DEATH!
OH MY GOD-- REX!!
PEOPLE CAN LICK TOO!
drip
drip
drip

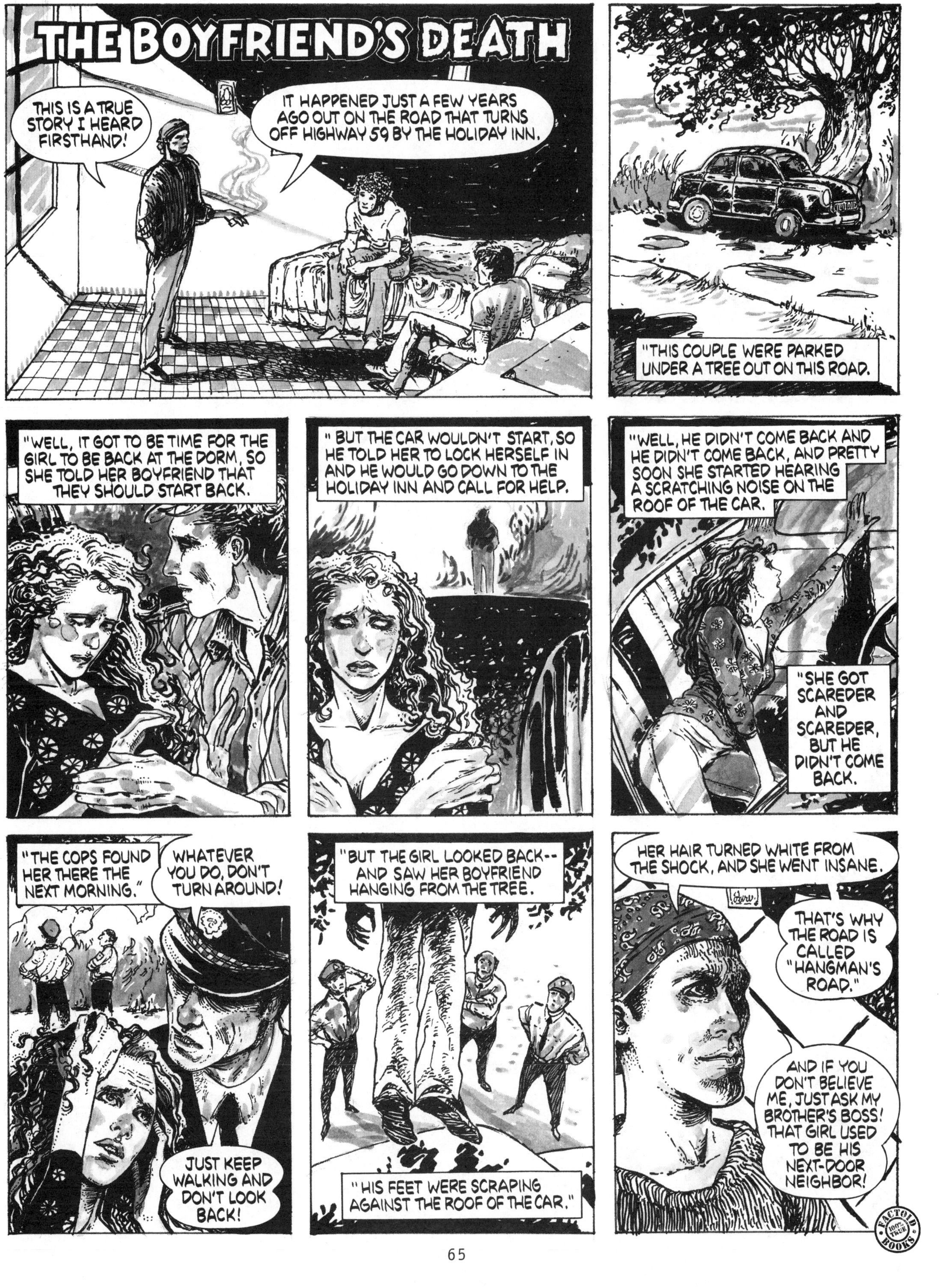
THE BOYFRIEND'S DEATH
THIS IS A TRUE STORY I HEARD FIRSTHAND!
IT HAPPENED JUST A FEW YEARS AGO OUT ON THE ROAD THAT TURNS OFF HIGHWAY 59 BY THE HOLIDAY INN.
"THIS COUPLE WERE PARKED UNDER A TREE OUT ON THIS ROAD.
"WELL, IT GOT TO BE TIME FOR THE GIRL TO BE BACK AT THE DORM, SO SHE TOLD HER BOYFRIEND THAT THEY SHOULD START BACK.
"BUT THE CAR WOULDN'T START, SO HE TOLD HER TO LOCK HERSELF IN AND HE WOULD GO DOWN TO THE HOLIDAY INN AND CALL FOR HELP.
"WELL, HE DIDN'T COME BACK AND HE DIDN'T COME BACK, AND PRETTY SOON SHE STARTED HEARING A SCRATCHING NOISE ON THE ROOF OF THE CAR.
"SHE GOT SCAREDER AND SCAREDER, BUT HE DIDN'T COME BACK.
"THE COPS FOUND HER THERE THE NEXT MORNING."
WHATEVER YOU DO, DON'T TURN AROUND!
JUST KEEP WALKING AND DON'T LOOK BACK!
"BUT THE GIRL LOOKED BACK-- AND SAW HER BOYFRIEND HANGING FROM THE TREE.
"HIS FEET WERE SCRAPING AGAINST THE ROOF OF THE CAR."
HER HAIR TURNED WHITE FROM THE SHOCK, AND SHE WENT INSANE.
THAT'S WHY THE ROAD IS CALLED "HANGMAN'S ROAD."
AND IF YOU DON'T BELIEVE ME, JUST ASK MY BROTHER'S BOSS! THAT GIRL USED TO BE HIS NEXT-DOOR NEIGHBOR!
FACTOID BOOKS 100% TRUE

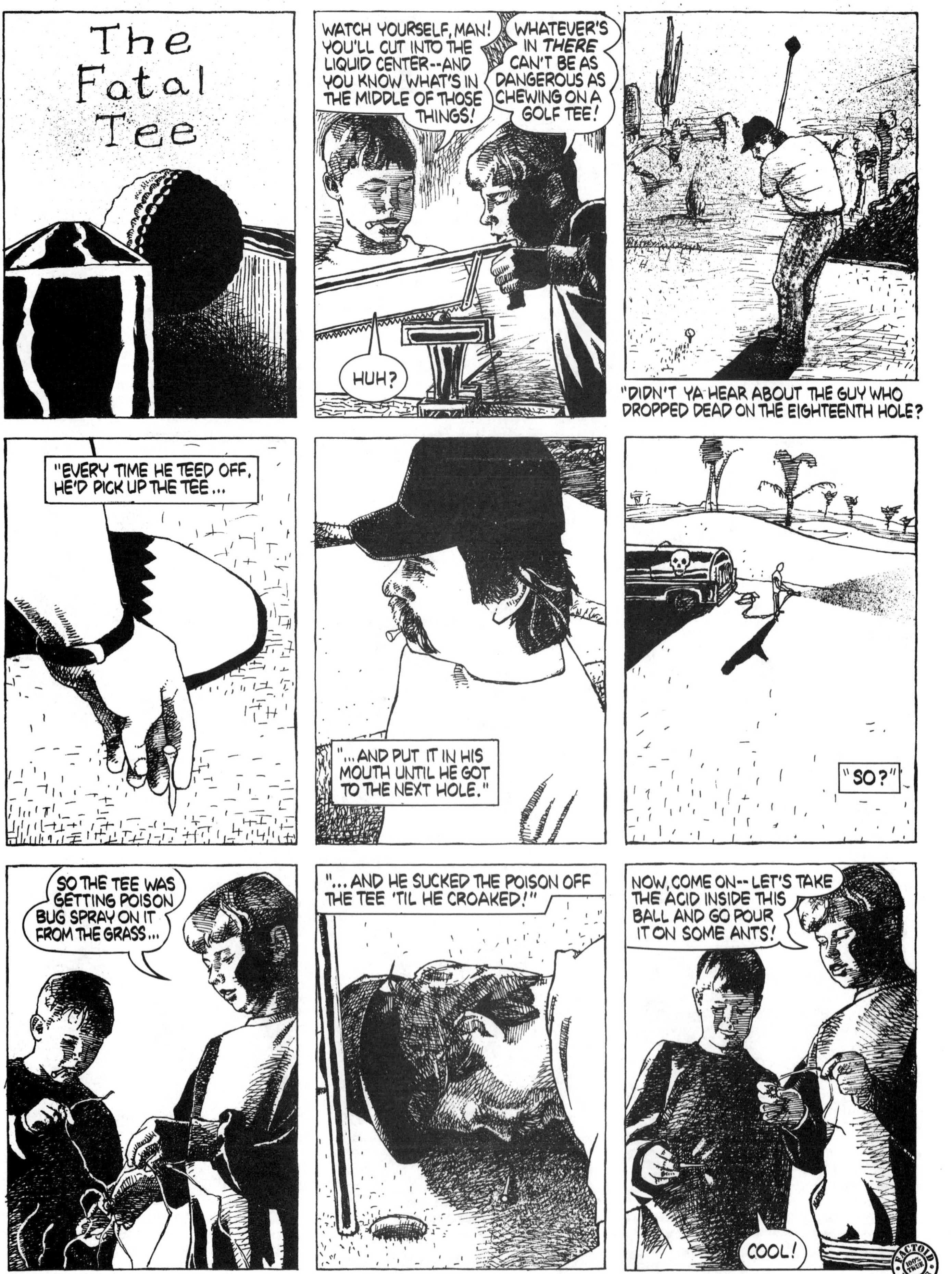
The Fatal Tee
WATCH YOURSELF, MAN! YOU'LL CUT INTO THE LIQUID CENTER--AND YOU KNOW WHAT'S IN THE MIDDLE OF THOSE THINGS!
WHATEVER'S IN THERE CAN'T BE AS DANGEROUS AS CHEWING ON A GOLF TEE!
HUH?
"DIDN'T YA HEAR ABOUT THE GUY WHO DROPPED DEAD ON THE EIGHTEENTH HOLE?
"EVERY TIME HE TEED OFF, HE'D PICK UP THE TEE ...
"... AND PUT IT IN HIS MOUTH UNTIL HE GOT TO THE NEXT HOLE."
"SO?"
SO THE TEE WAS GETTING POISON BUG SPRAY ON IT FROM THE GRASS...
"... AND HE SUCKED THE POISON OFF THE TEE 'TIL HE CROAKED!"
NOW, COME ON-- LET'S TAKE THE ACID INSIDE THIS BALL AND GO POUR IT ON SOME ANTS!
COOL!
FACTOID BOOKS 100% TRUE

OLD MAN BICKFORD WAS BURIED A FEW DAYS AGO, BUT WHAT NO ONE KNOWS IS...

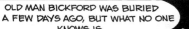
THE GRAVEYARD WAGER

...HE WAS BURIED ALIVE!

BWAH-HA-HA-HA!!

IF YOU GO TO HIS GRAVE, YOU CAN HEAR HIM TRYING TO SCRATCH HIS WAY OUT OF HIS COFFIN.

OH, BROTHER...

NO KIDDIN'! AND IF YOU STICK AROUND LONG ENOUGH, HE GRABS YOU BY THE ANKLE AND PULLS YOU INTO HIS GRAVE!

EMILY, YOU ARE SO FULL OF IT...

THINK SO, JESSIE? WELL, I BET YOU WON'T GO DOWN THERE AND HEAR FOR YOURSELF! I BET YOU'RE CHICKEN!

I BET I'M NOT!

TO PROVE YOU ACTUALLY WENT, YOU HAVE TO DRIVE THIS STAKE INTO THE GROUND OVER OLD MAN BICKFORD'S GRAVE.

THIS IS CREEPY, EVEN IF OLD MAN BICKFORD IS DEAD AS A DOORNAIL.

RRRRIP

AAAAAHHHH! HELP ME! OLD MAN BICKFORD WON'T LET GO!

JESSIE... SHE'S DEAD!

LOOK— SHE TRIED TO STAKE THE GRAVE— BUT STAKED HER OWN NIGHTGOWN TO THE GROUND!

AND WHEN SHE FELL, HER HEAD HIT THE TOMBSTONE!

LOOKS LIKE BICKFORD GOT HER AFTER ALL!

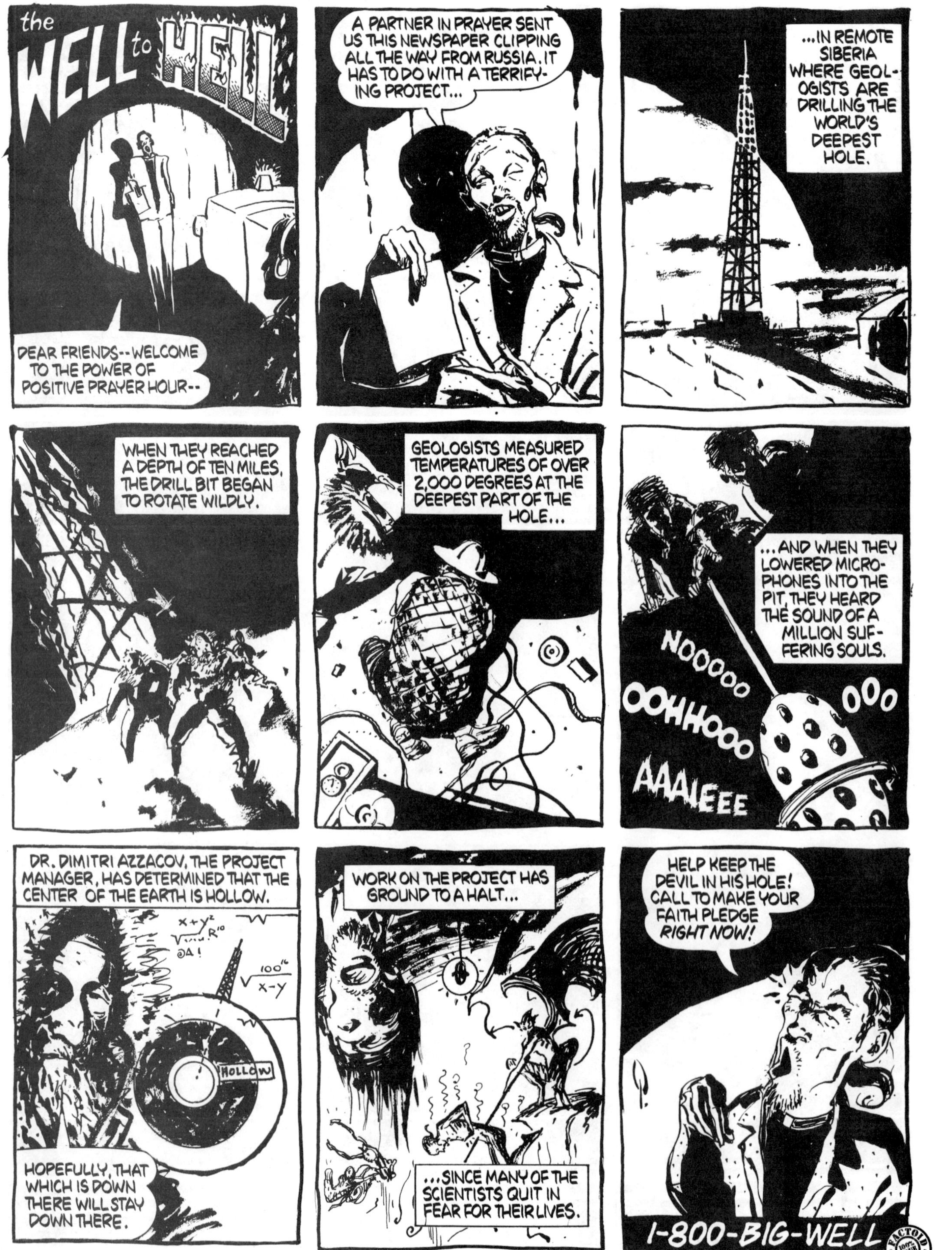
the WELL to HELL
DEAR FRIENDS--WELCOME TO THE POWER OF POSITIVE PRAYER HOUR--
A PARTNER IN PRAYER SENT US THIS NEWSPAPER CLIPPING ALL THE WAY FROM RUSSIA. IT HAS TO DO WITH A TERRIFYING PROJECT...
...IN REMOTE SIBERIA WHERE GEOLOGISTS ARE DRILLING THE WORLD'S DEEPEST HOLE.
WHEN THEY REACHED A DEPTH OF TEN MILES, THE DRILL BIT BEGAN TO ROTATE WILDLY.
GEOLOGISTS MEASURED TEMPERATURES OF OVER 2,000 DEGREES AT THE DEEPEST PART OF THE HOLE...
...AND WHEN THEY LOWERED MICROPHONES INTO THE PIT, THEY HEARD THE SOUND OF A MILLION SUFFERING SOULS.
NOOOOO
OOHHOOO
OOO
AAAIEEE
DR. DIMITRI AZZACOV, THE PROJECT MANAGER, HAS DETERMINED THAT THE CENTER OF THE EARTH IS HOLLOW.
HOLLOW
HOPEFULLY, THAT WHICH IS DOWN THERE WILL STAY DOWN THERE.
WORK ON THE PROJECT HAS GROUND TO A HALT...
...SINCE MANY OF THE SCIENTISTS QUIT IN FEAR FOR THEIR LIVES.
HELP KEEP THE DEVIL IN HIS HOLE! CALL TO MAKE YOUR FAITH PLEDGE RIGHT NOW!
1-800-BIG-WELL

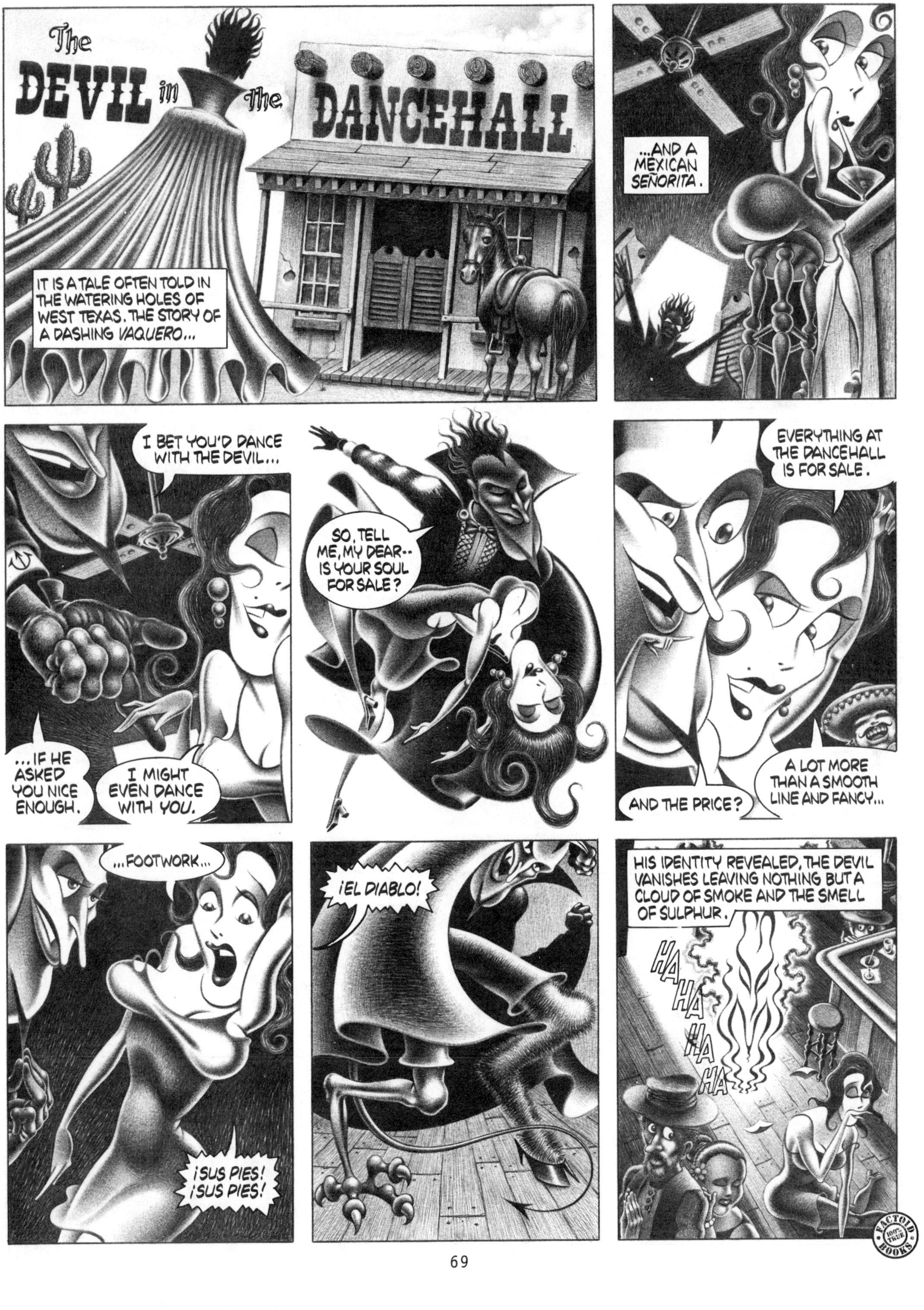
The DEVIL in the DANCEHALL
IT IS A TALE OFTEN TOLD IN THE WATERING HOLES OF WEST TEXAS. THE STORY OF A DASHING VAQUERO...
...AND A MEXICAN SEÑORITA.
I BET YOU'D DANCE WITH THE DEVIL...
...IF HE ASKED YOU NICE ENOUGH.
I MIGHT EVEN DANCE WITH YOU.
SO, TELL ME, MY DEAR-- IS YOUR SOUL FOR SALE?
EVERYTHING AT THE DANCEHALL IS FOR SALE.
AND THE PRICE?
A LOT MORE THAN A SMOOTH LINE AND FANCY...
...FOOTWORK...
¡SUS PIES! ¡SUS PIES!
¡EL DIABLO!
HIS IDENTITY REVEALED, THE DEVIL VANISHES LEAVING NOTHING BUT A CLOUD OF SMOKE AND THE SMELL OF SULPHUR.
HA HA HA HA HA HA
FACTOID 100% TRUE BOOKS

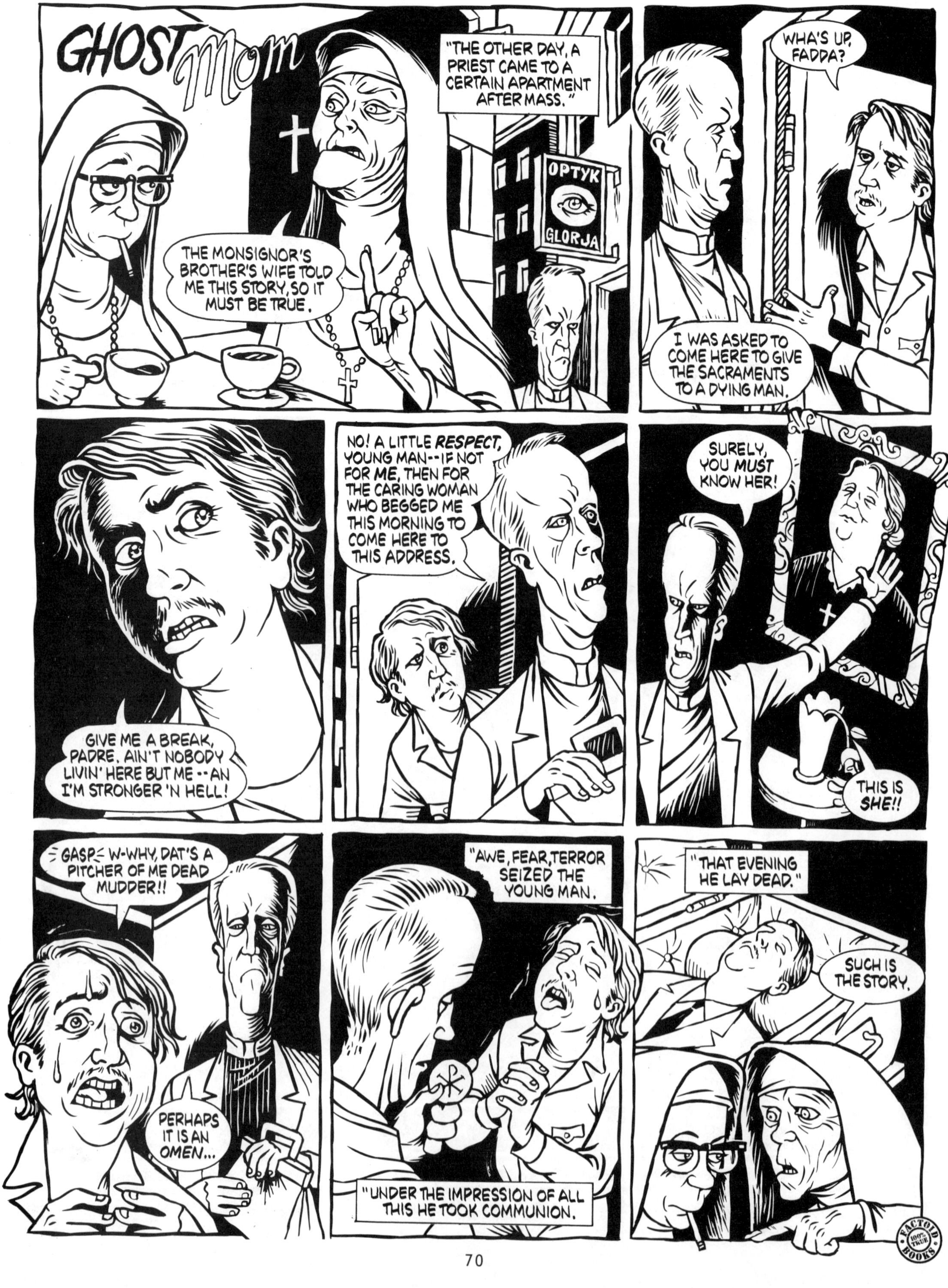
GHOST Mom
THE MONSIGNOR'S BROTHER'S WIFE TOLD ME THIS STORY, SO IT MUST BE TRUE.
"THE OTHER DAY, A PRIEST CAME TO A CERTAIN APARTMENT AFTER MASS."
OPTYK
GLORJA
WHA'S UP, FADDA?
I WAS ASKED TO COME HERE TO GIVE THE SACRAMENTS TO A DYING MAN.
GIVE ME A BREAK, PADRE. AIN'T NOBODY LIVIN' HERE BUT ME -- AN I'M STRONGER 'N HELL!
NO! A LITTLE RESPECT, YOUNG MAN -- IF NOT FOR ME, THEN FOR THE CARING WOMAN WHO BEGGED ME THIS MORNING TO COME HERE TO THIS ADDRESS.
SURELY, YOU MUST KNOW HER!
THIS IS SHE!!
GASP W-WHY, DAT'S A PITCHER OF ME DEAD MUDDER!!
PERHAPS IT IS AN OMEN...
"AWE, FEAR, TERROR SEIZED THE YOUNG MAN.
"UNDER THE IMPRESSION OF ALL THIS HE TOOK COMMUNION.
"THAT EVENING HE LAY DEAD."
SUCH IS THE STORY.
FACTOID BOOKS 100% TRUE

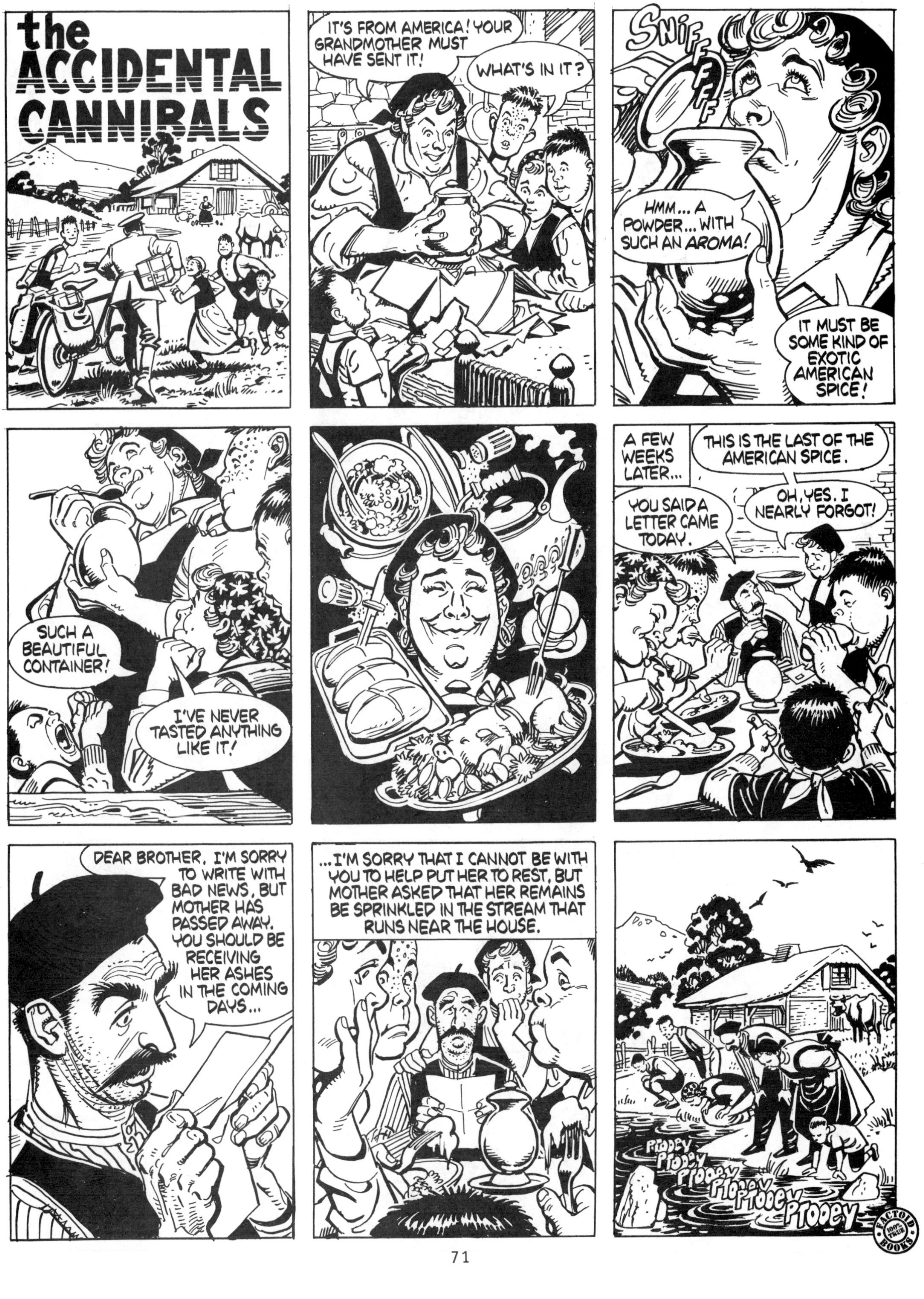
the ACCIDENTAL CANNIBALS
IT'S FROM AMERICA! YOUR GRANDMOTHER MUST HAVE SENT IT!
WHAT'S IN IT?
SNIFFFFF
HMM... A POWDER... WITH SUCH AN AROMA!
IT MUST BE SOME KIND OF EXOTIC AMERICAN SPICE!
SUCH A BEAUTIFUL CONTAINER!
I'VE NEVER TASTED ANYTHING LIKE IT!
A FEW WEEKS LATER...
THIS IS THE LAST OF THE AMERICAN SPICE.
YOU SAID A LETTER CAME TODAY.
OH, YES. I NEARLY FORGOT!
DEAR BROTHER, I'M SORRY TO WRITE WITH BAD NEWS, BUT MOTHER HAS PASSED AWAY. YOU SHOULD BE RECEIVING HER ASHES IN THE COMING DAYS...
...I'M SORRY THAT I CANNOT BE WITH YOU TO HELP PUT HER TO REST, BUT MOTHER ASKED THAT HER REMAINS BE SPRINKLED IN THE STREAM THAT RUNS NEAR THE HOUSE.
PTOOEY PTOOEY PTOOEY PTOOEY PTOOEY PTOOEY PTOOEY
FACTOID BOOKS 100% TRUE

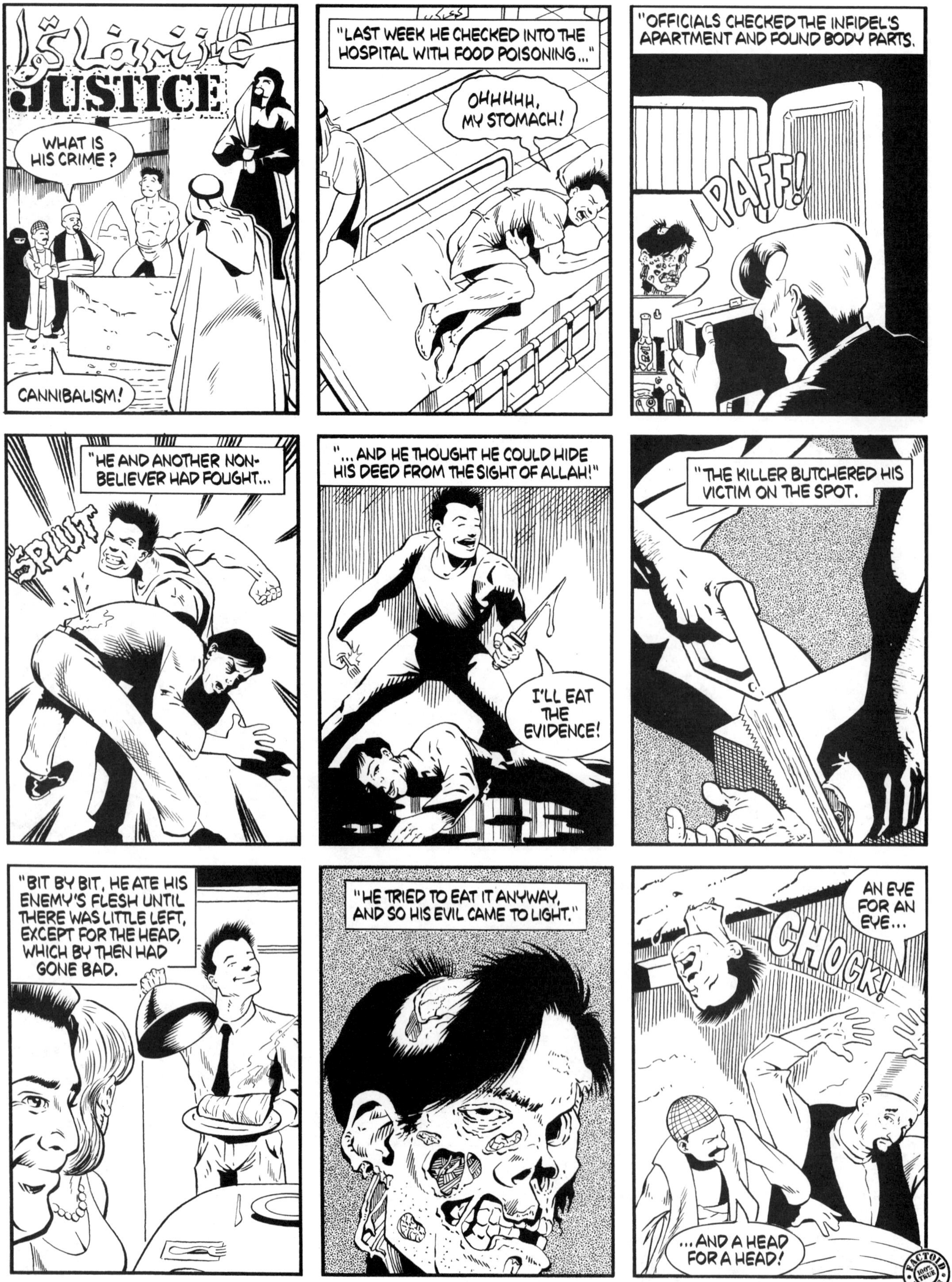
Islamic
JUSTICE
WHAT IS HIS CRIME ?
CANNIBALISM!
"LAST WEEK HE CHECKED INTO THE HOSPITAL WITH FOOD POISONING..."
OHHHHH, MY STOMACH!
"OFFICIALS CHECKED THE INFIDEL'S APARTMENT AND FOUND BODY PARTS.
PAFF!
"HE AND ANOTHER NON-BELIEVER HAD FOUGHT...
SPLUT
"...AND HE THOUGHT HE COULD HIDE HIS DEED FROM THE SIGHT OF ALLAH!"
I'LL EAT THE EVIDENCE!
"THE KILLER BUTCHERED HIS VICTIM ON THE SPOT.
"BIT BY BIT, HE ATE HIS ENEMY'S FLESH UNTIL THERE WAS LITTLE LEFT, EXCEPT FOR THE HEAD, WHICH BY THEN HAD GONE BAD.
"HE TRIED TO EAT IT ANYWAY, AND SO HIS EVIL CAME TO LIGHT."
AN EYE FOR AN EYE...
CHOCK!
...AND A HEAD FOR A HEAD!
FACTOID BOOKS 100% TRUE

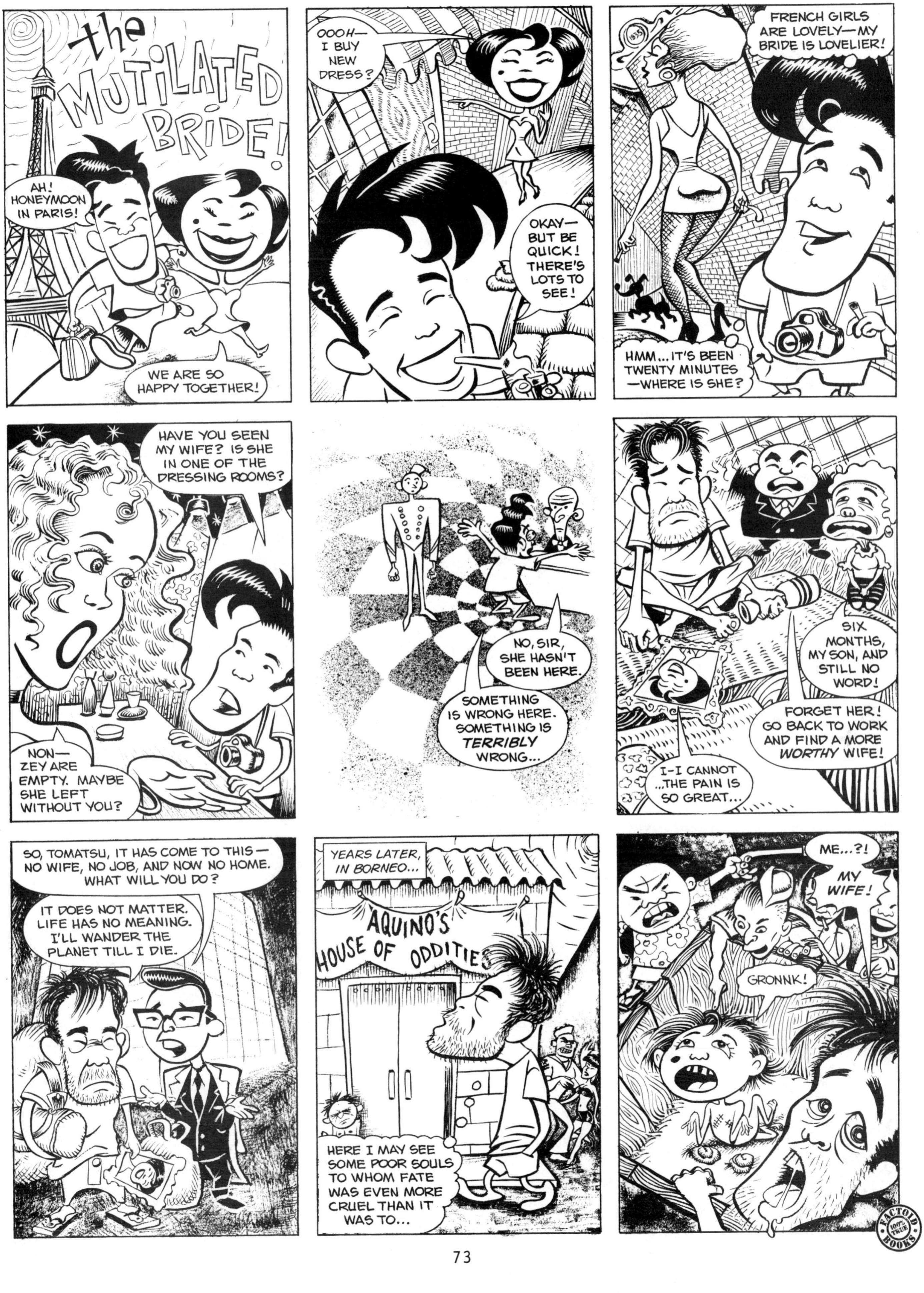
the MUTILATED BRIDE!
AH! HONEYMOON IN PARIS!
WE ARE SO HAPPY TOGETHER!
OOOH— I BUY NEW DRESS?
OKAY— BUT BE QUICK! THERE'S LOTS TO SEE!
FRENCH GIRLS ARE LOVELY—MY BRIDE IS LOVELIER!
HMM... IT'S BEEN TWENTY MINUTES —WHERE IS SHE?
HAVE YOU SEEN MY WIFE? IS SHE IN ONE OF THE DRESSING ROOMS?
NON— ZEY ARE EMPTY. MAYBE SHE LEFT WITHOUT YOU?
NO, SIR, SHE HASN'T BEEN HERE.
SOMETHING IS WRONG HERE. SOMETHING IS *TERRIBLY* WRONG...
SIX MONTHS, MY SON, AND STILL NO WORD!
FORGET HER! GO BACK TO WORK AND FIND A MORE *WORTHY* WIFE!
I-I CANNOT ...THE PAIN IS SO GREAT...
SO, TOMATSU, IT HAS COME TO THIS— NO WIFE, NO JOB, AND NOW NO HOME. WHAT WILL YOU DO?
IT DOES NOT MATTER. LIFE HAS NO MEANING. I'LL WANDER THE PLANET TILL I DIE.
YEARS LATER, IN BORNEO...
AQUINO'S HOUSE OF ODDITIES
HERE I MAY SEE SOME POOR SOULS TO WHOM FATE WAS EVEN MORE CRUEL THAN IT WAS TO...
ME...?!
MY WIFE!
GRONNK!

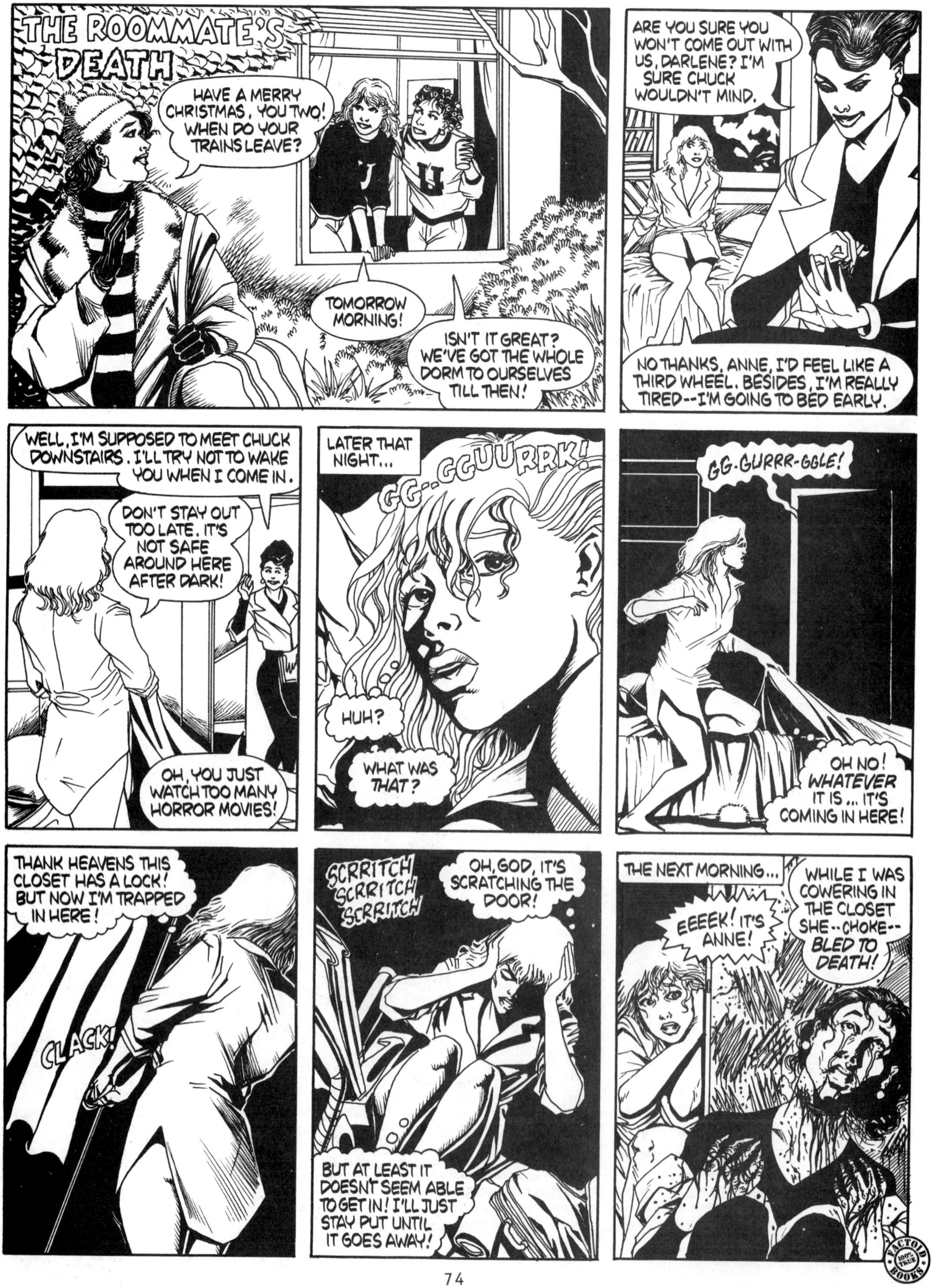

THE ROOMMATE'S DEATH
HAVE A MERRY CHRISTMAS, YOU TWO! WHEN DO YOUR TRAINS LEAVE?
TOMORROW MORNING!
ISN'T IT GREAT? WE'VE GOT THE WHOLE DORM TO OURSELVES TILL THEN!
ARE YOU SURE YOU WON'T COME OUT WITH US, DARLENE? I'M SURE CHUCK WOULDN'T MIND.
NO THANKS, ANNE, I'D FEEL LIKE A THIRD WHEEL. BESIDES, I'M REALLY TIRED--I'M GOING TO BED EARLY.
WELL, I'M SUPPOSED TO MEET CHUCK DOWNSTAIRS. I'LL TRY NOT TO WAKE YOU WHEN I COME IN.
DON'T STAY OUT TOO LATE. IT'S NOT SAFE AROUND HERE AFTER DARK!
OH, YOU JUST WATCH TOO MANY HORROR MOVIES!
LATER THAT NIGHT...
GG--GGUURRRK!
HUH?
WHAT WAS THAT?
GG-GURRR-GGLE!
OH NO! WHATEVER IT IS... IT'S COMING IN HERE!
THANK HEAVENS THIS CLOSET HAS A LOCK! BUT NOW I'M TRAPPED IN HERE!
CLACK!
SCRRITCH SCRRITCH SCRRITCH
OH, GOD, IT'S SCRATCHING THE DOOR!
BUT AT LEAST IT DOESN'T SEEM ABLE TO GET IN! I'LL JUST STAY PUT UNTIL IT GOES AWAY!
THE NEXT MORNING...
EEEEK! IT'S ANNE!
WHILE I WAS COWERING IN THE CLOSET SHE--CHOKE--BLED TO DEATH!
FACTOID BOOKS 100% TRUE

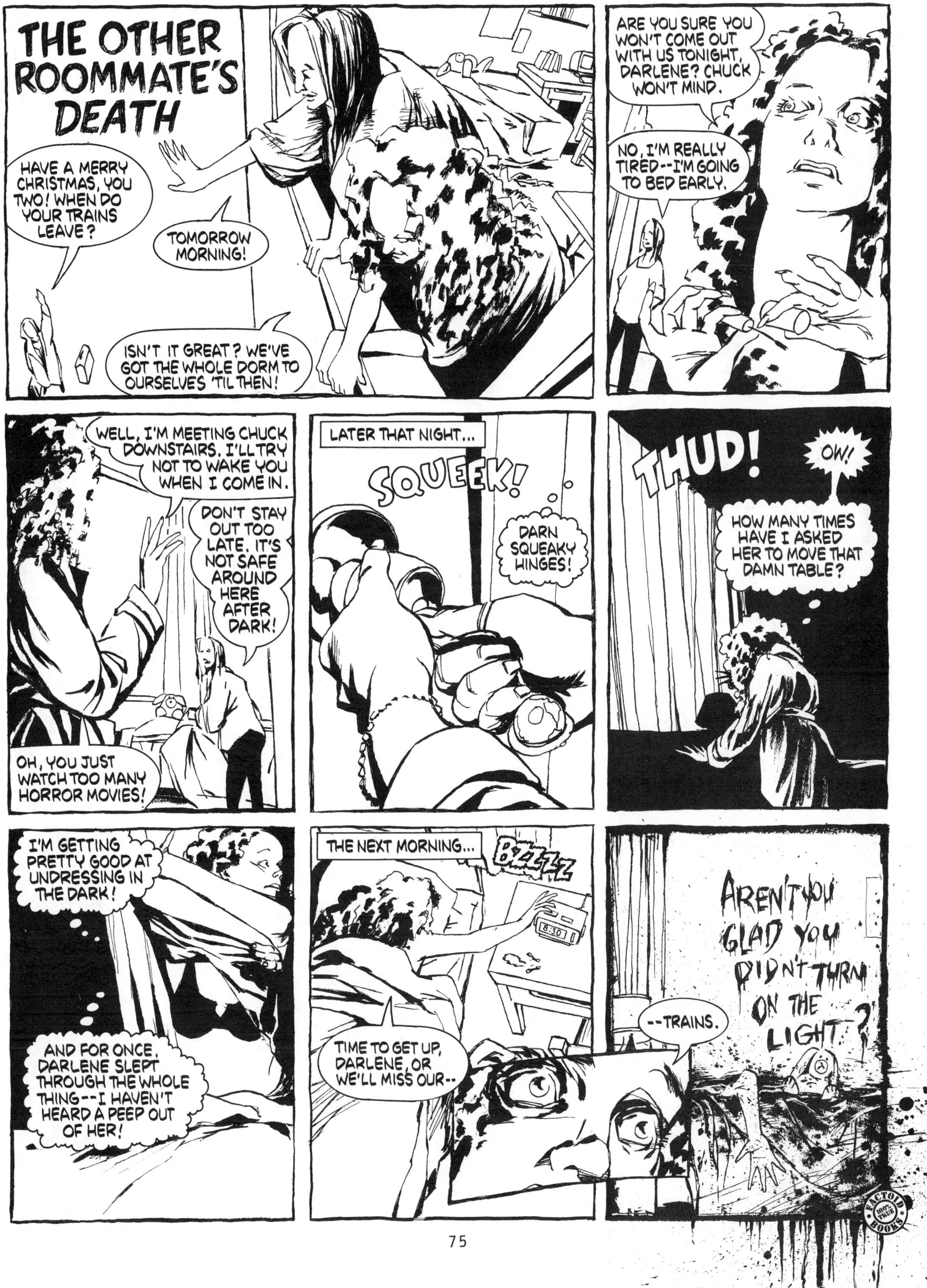

THE OTHER ROOMMATE'S DEATH
HAVE A MERRY CHRISTMAS, YOU TWO! WHEN DO YOUR TRAINS LEAVE?
TOMORROW MORNING!
ISN'T IT GREAT? WE'VE GOT THE WHOLE DORM TO OURSELVES 'TIL THEN!
ARE YOU SURE YOU WON'T COME OUT WITH US TONIGHT, DARLENE? CHUCK WON'T MIND.
NO, I'M REALLY TIRED--I'M GOING TO BED EARLY.
WELL, I'M MEETING CHUCK DOWNSTAIRS. I'LL TRY NOT TO WAKE YOU WHEN I COME IN.
DON'T STAY OUT TOO LATE. IT'S NOT SAFE AROUND HERE AFTER DARK!
OH, YOU JUST WATCH TOO MANY HORROR MOVIES!
LATER THAT NIGHT...
SQUEEK!
DARN SQUEAKY HINGES!
THUD!
OW!
HOW MANY TIMES HAVE I ASKED HER TO MOVE THAT DAMN TABLE?
I'M GETTING PRETTY GOOD AT UNDRESSING IN THE DARK!
AND FOR ONCE, DARLENE SLEPT THROUGH THE WHOLE THING--I HAVEN'T HEARD A PEEP OUT OF HER!
THE NEXT MORNING...
BZZZZZ
8:30
TIME TO GET UP, DARLENE, OR WE'LL MISS OUR--
--TRAINS.
AREN'T YOU GLAD YOU DIDN'T TURN ON THE LIGHT?

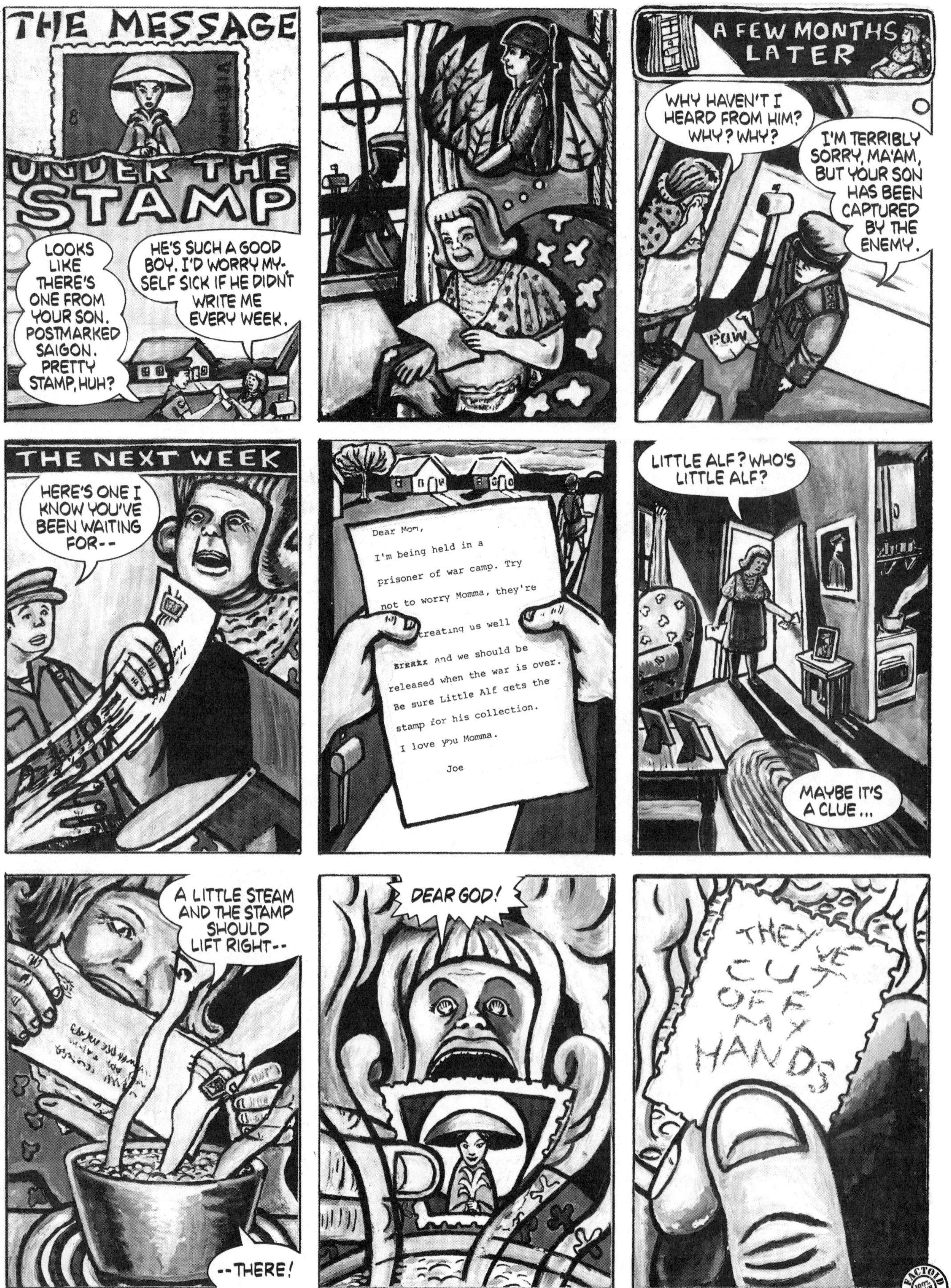

THE MESSAGE
UNDER THE STAMP
LOOKS LIKE THERE'S ONE FROM YOUR SON. POSTMARKED SAIGON. PRETTY STAMP, HUH?
HE'S SUCH A GOOD BOY. I'D WORRY MY-SELF SICK IF HE DIDN'T WRITE ME EVERY WEEK.
A FEW MONTHS LATER
WHY HAVEN'T I HEARD FROM HIM? WHY? WHY?
I'M TERRIBLY SORRY, MA'AM, BUT YOUR SON HAS BEEN CAPTURED BY THE ENEMY.
P.O.W.
THE NEXT WEEK
HERE'S ONE I KNOW YOU'VE BEEN WAITING FOR--
Dear Mom,
I'm being held in a prisoner of war camp. Try not to worry Momma, they're treating us well
and we should be released when the war is over.
Be sure Little Alf gets the stamp for his collection.
I love you Momma.
Joe
LITTLE ALF? WHO'S LITTLE ALF?
MAYBE IT'S A CLUE...
A LITTLE STEAM AND THE STAMP SHOULD LIFT RIGHT--
--THERE!
DEAR GOD!
THEY'VE CUT OFF MY HANDS

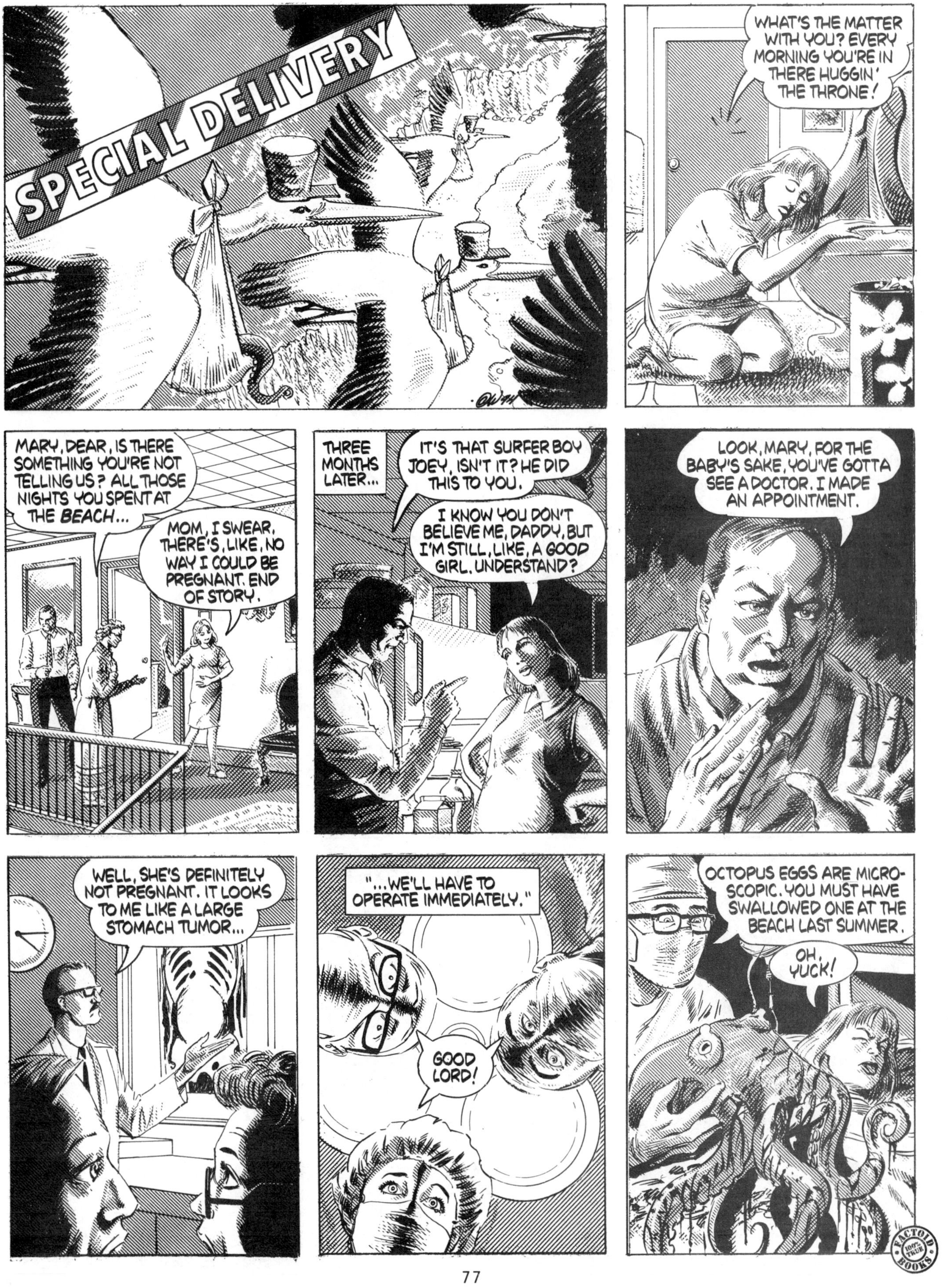
SPECIAL DELIVERY
WHAT'S THE MATTER WITH YOU? EVERY MORNING YOU'RE IN THERE HUGGIN' THE THRONE!
MARY, DEAR, IS THERE SOMETHING YOU'RE NOT TELLING US? ALL THOSE NIGHTS YOU SPENT AT THE BEACH...
MOM, I SWEAR, THERE'S, LIKE, NO WAY I COULD BE PREGNANT. END OF STORY.
THREE MONTHS LATER...
IT'S THAT SURFER BOY JOEY, ISN'T IT? HE DID THIS TO YOU.
I KNOW YOU DON'T BELIEVE ME, DADDY, BUT I'M STILL, LIKE, A GOOD GIRL. UNDERSTAND?
LOOK, MARY, FOR THE BABY'S SAKE, YOU'VE GOTTA SEE A DOCTOR. I MADE AN APPOINTMENT.
WELL, SHE'S DEFINITELY NOT PREGNANT. IT LOOKS TO ME LIKE A LARGE STOMACH TUMOR...
"...WE'LL HAVE TO OPERATE IMMEDIATELY."
GOOD LORD!
OCTOPUS EGGS ARE MICRO-SCOPIC. YOU MUST HAVE SWALLOWED ONE AT THE BEACH LAST SUMMER.
OH, YUCK!
FACTOID BOOKS 100% TRUE

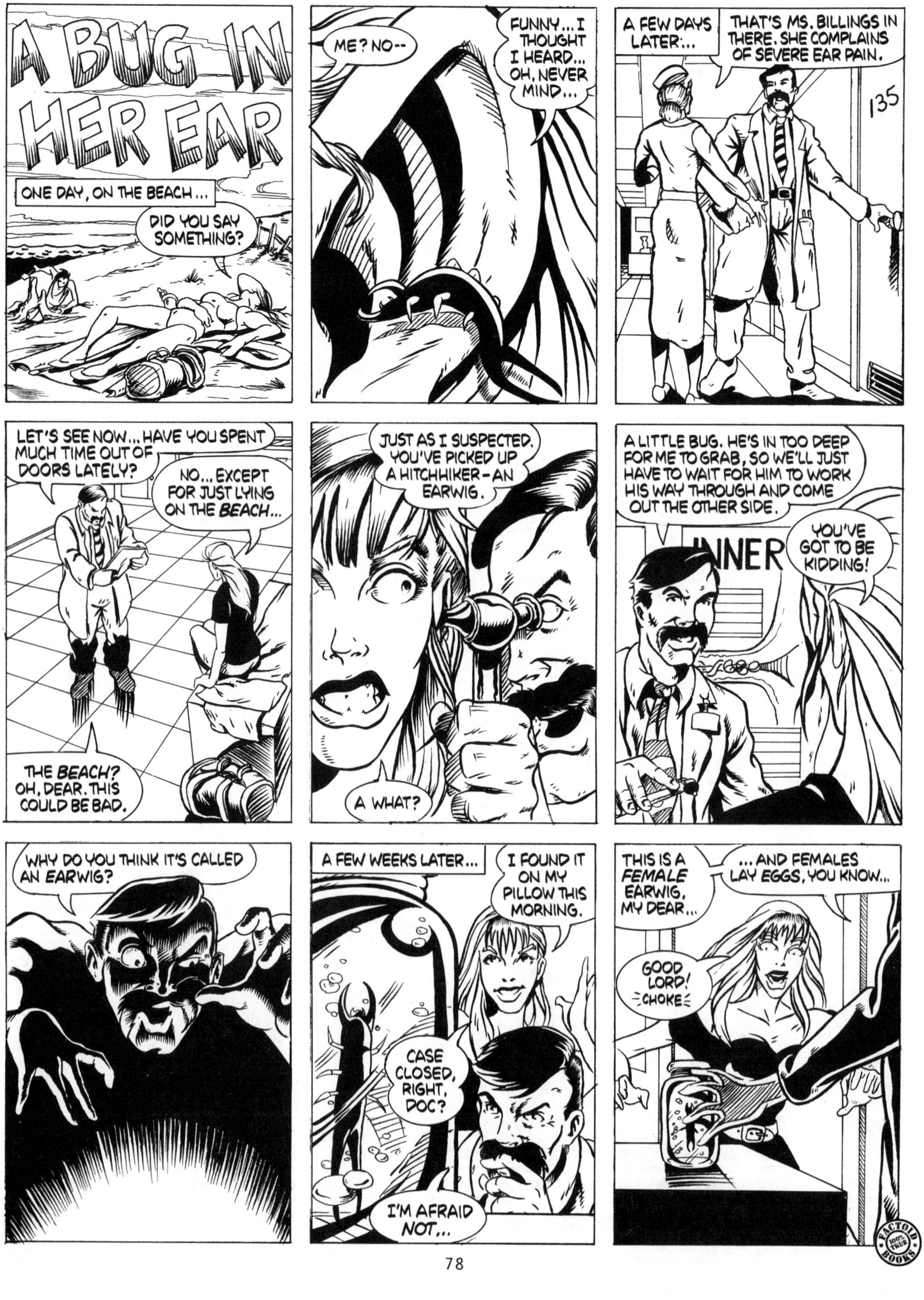
A BUG IN HER EAR
ONE DAY, ON THE BEACH...
DID YOU SAY SOMETHING?
ME? NO--
FUNNY... I THOUGHT I HEARD... OH, NEVER MIND...
A FEW DAYS LATER...
THAT'S MS. BILLINGS IN THERE. SHE COMPLAINS OF SEVERE EAR PAIN.
135
LET'S SEE NOW... HAVE YOU SPENT MUCH TIME OUT OF DOORS LATELY?
NO... EXCEPT FOR JUST LYING ON THE *BEACH*...
THE *BEACH*? OH, DEAR. THIS COULD BE BAD.
JUST AS I SUSPECTED. YOU'VE PICKED UP A HITCHHIKER – AN EARWIG.
A WHAT?
A LITTLE BUG. HE'S IN TOO DEEP FOR ME TO GRAB, SO WE'LL JUST HAVE TO WAIT FOR HIM TO WORK HIS WAY THROUGH AND COME OUT THE OTHER SIDE.
INNER
YOU'VE GOT TO BE KIDDING!
WHY DO YOU THINK IT'S CALLED AN *EARWIG*?
A FEW WEEKS LATER...
I FOUND IT ON MY PILLOW THIS MORNING.
CASE CLOSED, RIGHT, DOC?
I'M AFRAID *NOT*...
THIS IS A *FEMALE* EARWIG, MY DEAR...
...AND FEMALES LAY *EGGS*, YOU KNOW...
GOOD LORD! CHOKE
FACTOID BOOKS 100% TRUE

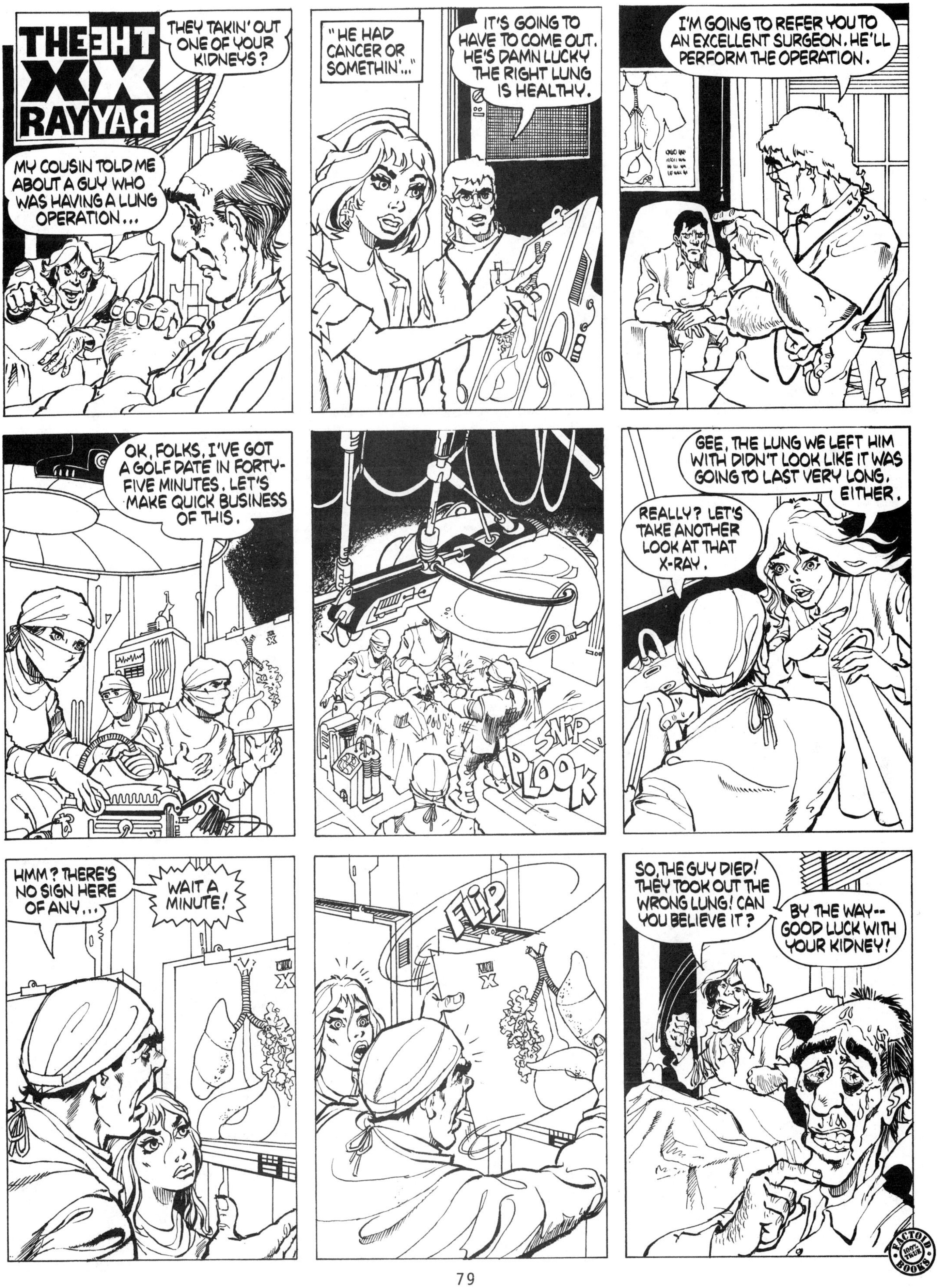
THE X RAY
THEY TAKIN' OUT ONE OF YOUR KIDNEYS?
MY COUSIN TOLD ME ABOUT A GUY WHO WAS HAVING A LUNG OPERATION...
"HE HAD CANCER OR SOMETHIN'..."
IT'S GOING TO HAVE TO COME OUT. HE'S DAMN LUCKY THE RIGHT LUNG IS HEALTHY.
I'M GOING TO REFER YOU TO AN EXCELLENT SURGEON. HE'LL PERFORM THE OPERATION.
OK, FOLKS, I'VE GOT A GOLF DATE IN FORTY-FIVE MINUTES. LET'S MAKE QUICK BUSINESS OF THIS.
SNIP
PLOOK
GEE, THE LUNG WE LEFT HIM WITH DIDN'T LOOK LIKE IT WAS GOING TO LAST VERY LONG, EITHER.
REALLY? LET'S TAKE ANOTHER LOOK AT THAT X-RAY.
HMM? THERE'S NO SIGN HERE OF ANY...
WAIT A MINUTE!
FLIP
SO, THE GUY DIED! THEY TOOK OUT THE WRONG LUNG! CAN YOU BELIEVE IT?
BY THE WAY-- GOOD LUCK WITH YOUR KIDNEY!
FACTOID BOOKS 100% TRUE

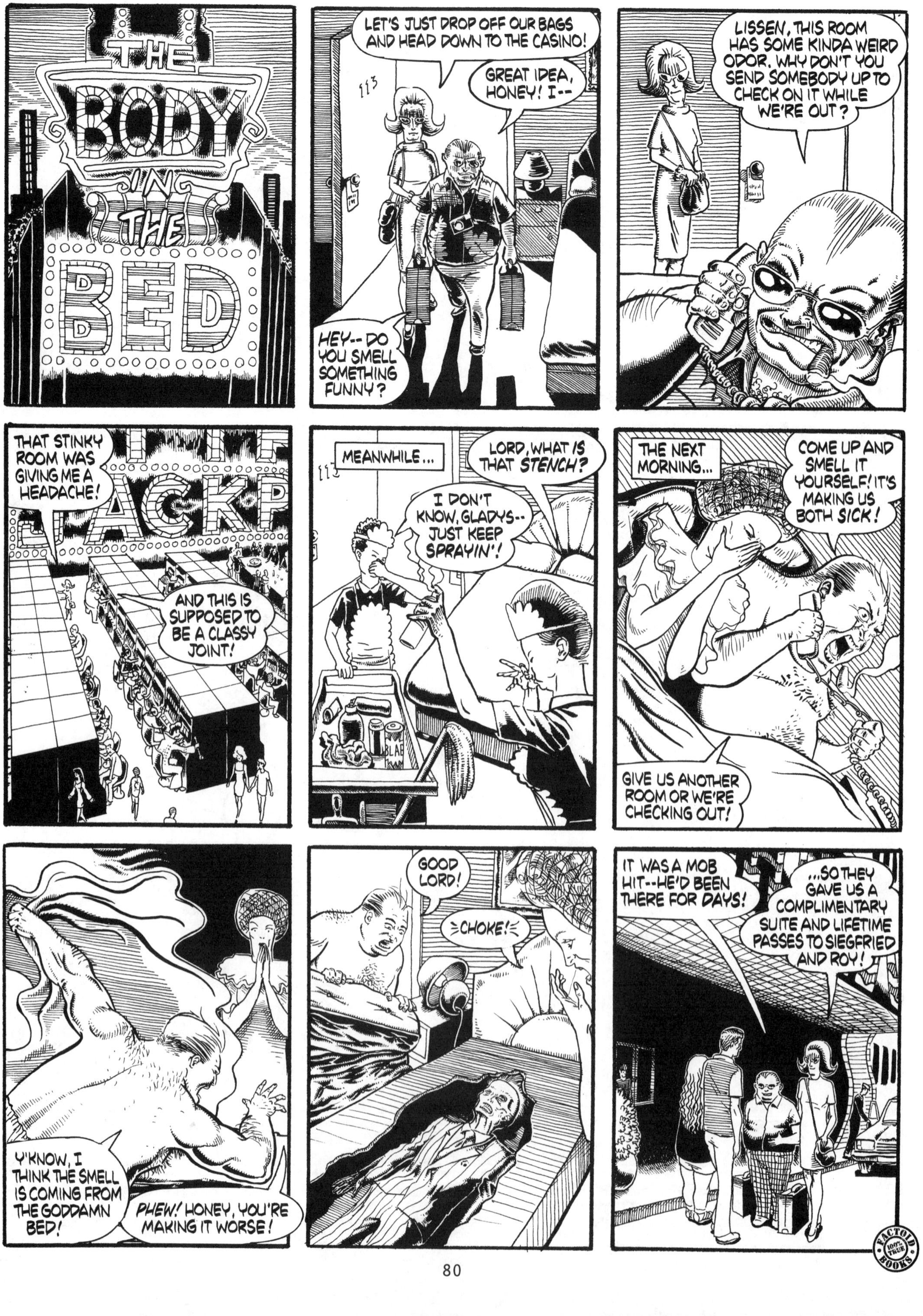
THE BODY IN THE BED
LET'S JUST DROP OFF OUR BAGS AND HEAD DOWN TO THE CASINO!
GREAT IDEA, HONEY! I--
HEY-- DO YOU SMELL SOMETHING FUNNY?
LISSEN, THIS ROOM HAS SOME KINDA WEIRD ODOR. WHY DON'T YOU SEND SOMEBODY UP TO CHECK ON IT WHILE WE'RE OUT?
THAT STINKY ROOM WAS GIVING ME A HEADACHE!
AND THIS IS SUPPOSED TO BE A CLASSY JOINT!
MEANWHILE...
LORD, WHAT IS THAT STENCH?
I DON'T KNOW, GLADYS-- JUST KEEP SPRAYIN'!
THE NEXT MORNING...
COME UP AND SMELL IT YOURSELF! IT'S MAKING US BOTH SICK!
GIVE US ANOTHER ROOM OR WE'RE CHECKING OUT!
Y'KNOW, I THINK THE SMELL IS COMING FROM THE GODDAMN BED!
PHEW! HONEY, YOU'RE MAKING IT WORSE!
GOOD LORD!
CHOKE!
IT WAS A MOB HIT--HE'D BEEN THERE FOR DAYS!
...SO THEY GAVE US A COMPLIMENTARY SUITE AND LIFETIME PASSES TO SIEGFRIED AND ROY!
FACTOID BOOKS 100% TRUE

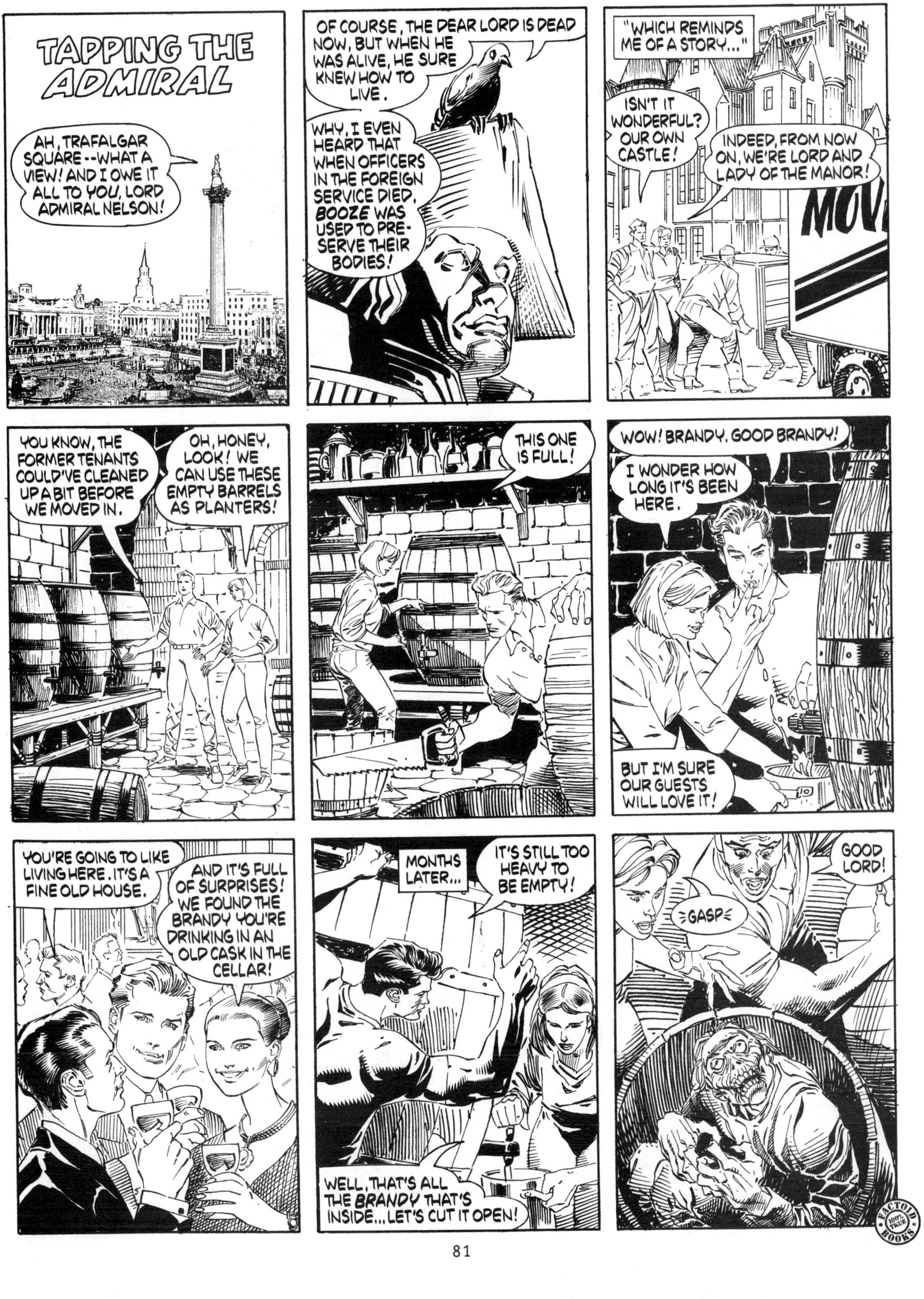
TAPPING THE ADMIRAL
AH, TRAFALGAR SQUARE--WHAT A VIEW! AND I OWE IT ALL TO YOU, LORD ADMIRAL NELSON!
OF COURSE, THE DEAR LORD IS DEAD NOW, BUT WHEN HE WAS ALIVE, HE SURE KNEW HOW TO LIVE.
WHY, I EVEN HEARD THAT WHEN OFFICERS IN THE FOREIGN SERVICE DIED, BOOZE WAS USED TO PRESERVE THEIR BODIES!
"WHICH REMINDS ME OF A STORY..."
ISN'T IT WONDERFUL? OUR OWN CASTLE!
INDEED, FROM NOW ON, WE'RE LORD AND LADY OF THE MANOR!
MOV
YOU KNOW, THE FORMER TENANTS COULD'VE CLEANED UP A BIT BEFORE WE MOVED IN.
OH, HONEY, LOOK! WE CAN USE THESE EMPTY BARRELS AS PLANTERS!
THIS ONE IS FULL!
WOW! BRANDY. GOOD BRANDY!
I WONDER HOW LONG IT'S BEEN HERE.
BUT I'M SURE OUR GUESTS WILL LOVE IT!
YOU'RE GOING TO LIKE LIVING HERE. IT'S A FINE OLD HOUSE.
AND IT'S FULL OF SURPRISES! WE FOUND THE BRANDY YOU'RE DRINKING IN AN OLD CASK IN THE CELLAR!
MONTHS LATER...
IT'S STILL TOO HEAVY TO BE EMPTY!
WELL, THAT'S ALL THE BRANDY THAT'S INSIDE... LET'S CUT IT OPEN!
GOOD LORD!
GASP

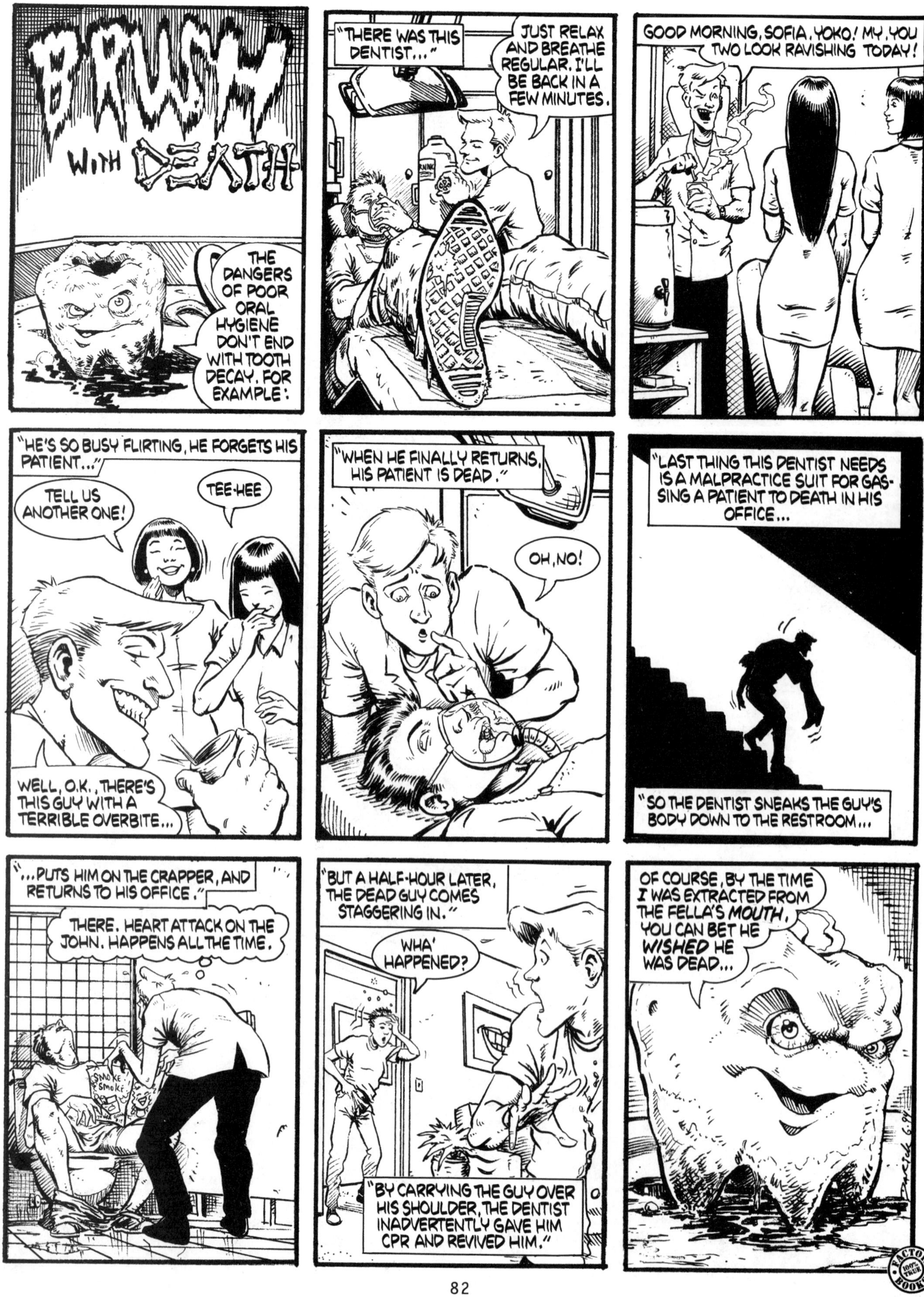
BRUSH WITH DEATH
THE DANGERS OF POOR ORAL HYGIENE DON'T END WITH TOOTH DECAY. FOR EXAMPLE:
"THERE WAS THIS DENTIST..."
JUST RELAX AND BREATHE REGULAR. I'LL BE BACK IN A FEW MINUTES.
GOOD MORNING, SOFIA, YOKO! MY, YOU TWO LOOK RAVISHING TODAY!
"HE'S SO BUSY FLIRTING, HE FORGETS HIS PATIENT..."
TELL US ANOTHER ONE!
TEE-HEE
WELL, O.K., THERE'S THIS GUY WITH A TERRIBLE OVERBITE...
"WHEN HE FINALLY RETURNS, HIS PATIENT IS DEAD."
OH, NO!
"LAST THING THIS DENTIST NEEDS IS A MALPRACTICE SUIT FOR GASSING A PATIENT TO DEATH IN HIS OFFICE...
"SO THE DENTIST SNEAKS THE GUY'S BODY DOWN TO THE RESTROOM...
"...PUTS HIM ON THE CRAPPER, AND RETURNS TO HIS OFFICE."
THERE. HEART ATTACK ON THE JOHN. HAPPENS ALL THE TIME.
"BUT A HALF-HOUR LATER, THE DEAD GUY COMES STAGGERING IN."
WHA' HAPPENED?
"BY CARRYING THE GUY OVER HIS SHOULDER, THE DENTIST INADVERTENTLY GAVE HIM CPR AND REVIVED HIM."
OF COURSE, BY THE TIME *I* WAS EXTRACTED FROM THE FELLA'S *MOUTH*, YOU CAN BET HE *WISHED* HE WAS DEAD...

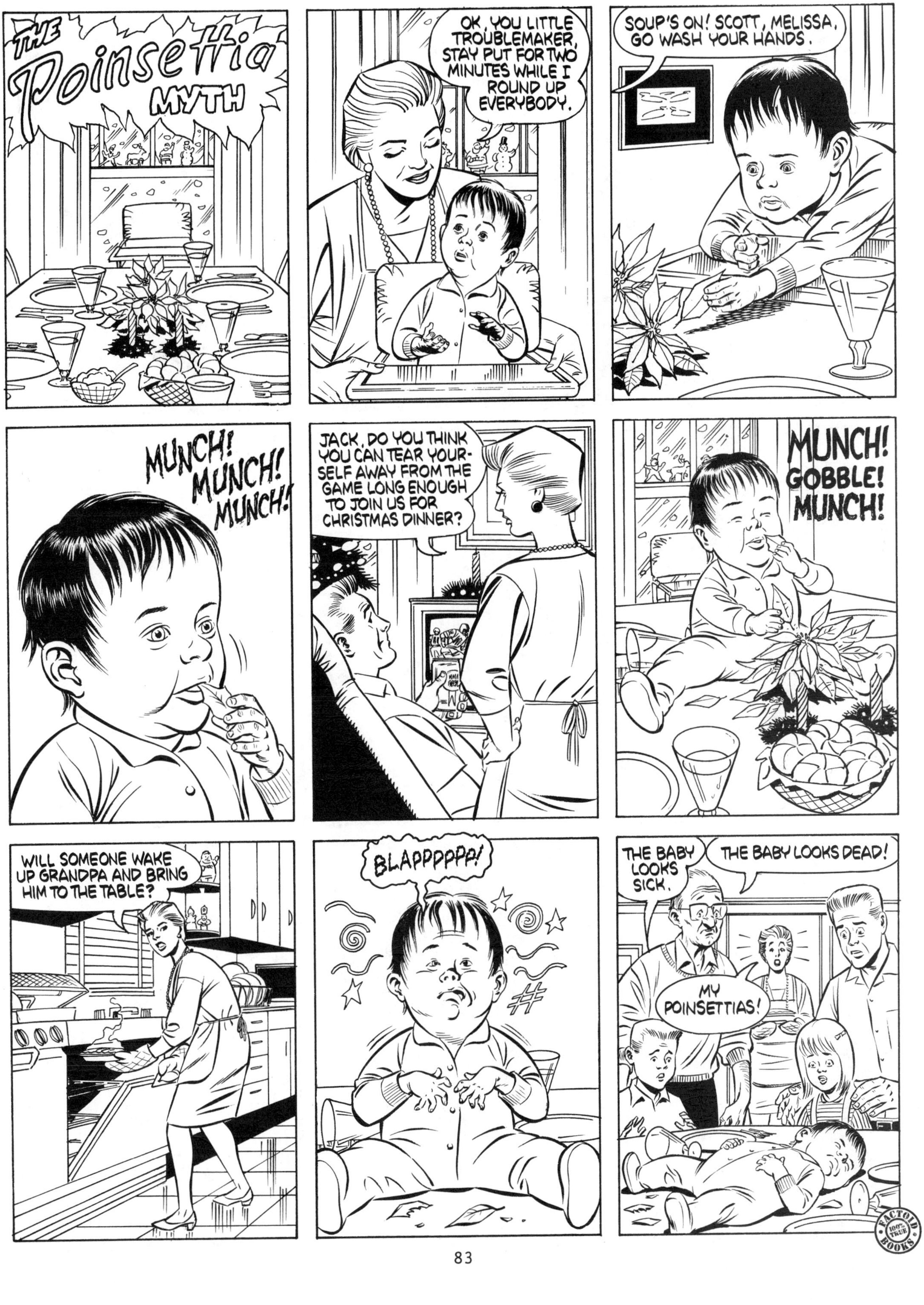
THE Poinsettia MYTH
OK, YOU LITTLE TROUBLEMAKER, STAY PUT FOR TWO MINUTES WHILE I ROUND UP EVERYBODY.
SOUP'S ON! SCOTT, MELISSA, GO WASH YOUR HANDS.
MUNCH! MUNCH! MUNCH!
JACK, DO YOU THINK YOU CAN TEAR YOURSELF AWAY FROM THE GAME LONG ENOUGH TO JOIN US FOR CHRISTMAS DINNER?
MUNCH! GOBBLE! MUNCH!
WILL SOMEONE WAKE UP GRANDPA AND BRING HIM TO THE TABLE?
BLAPPPPPP!
THE BABY LOOKS SICK.
THE BABY LOOKS DEAD!
MY POINSETTIAS!

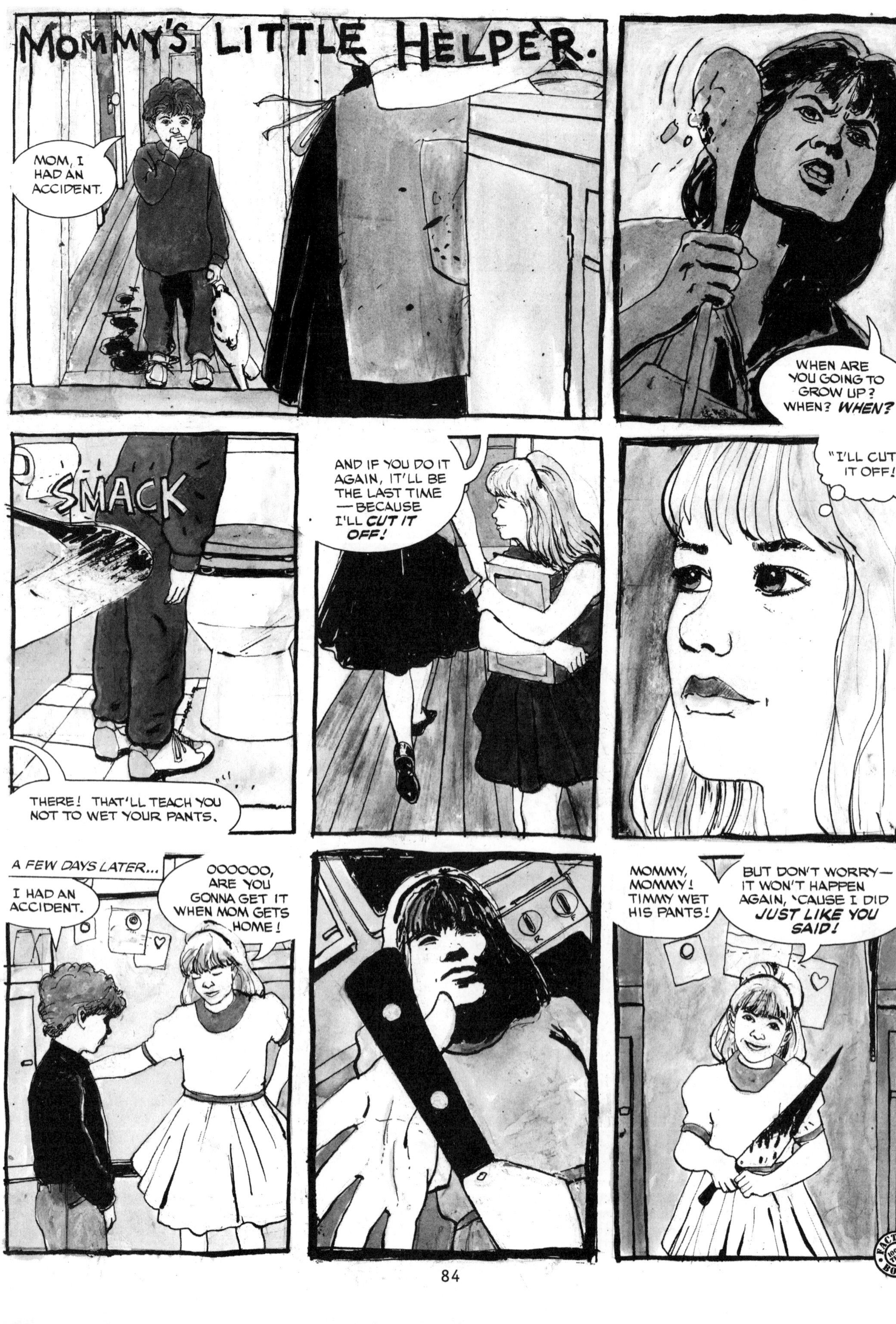

MOMMY'S LITTLE HELPER.
MOM, I HAD AN ACCIDENT.
WHEN ARE YOU GOING TO GROW UP? WHEN? WHEN?
SMACK
THERE! THAT'LL TEACH YOU NOT TO WET YOUR PANTS.
AND IF YOU DO IT AGAIN, IT'LL BE THE LAST TIME —BECAUSE I'LL CUT IT OFF!
"I'LL CUT IT OFF!"
A FEW DAYS LATER...
I HAD AN ACCIDENT.
OOOOOO, ARE YOU GONNA GET IT WHEN MOM GETS HOME!
MOMMY, MOMMY! TIMMY WET HIS PANTS!
BUT DON'T WORRY— IT WON'T HAPPEN AGAIN, 'CAUSE I DID JUST LIKE YOU SAID!

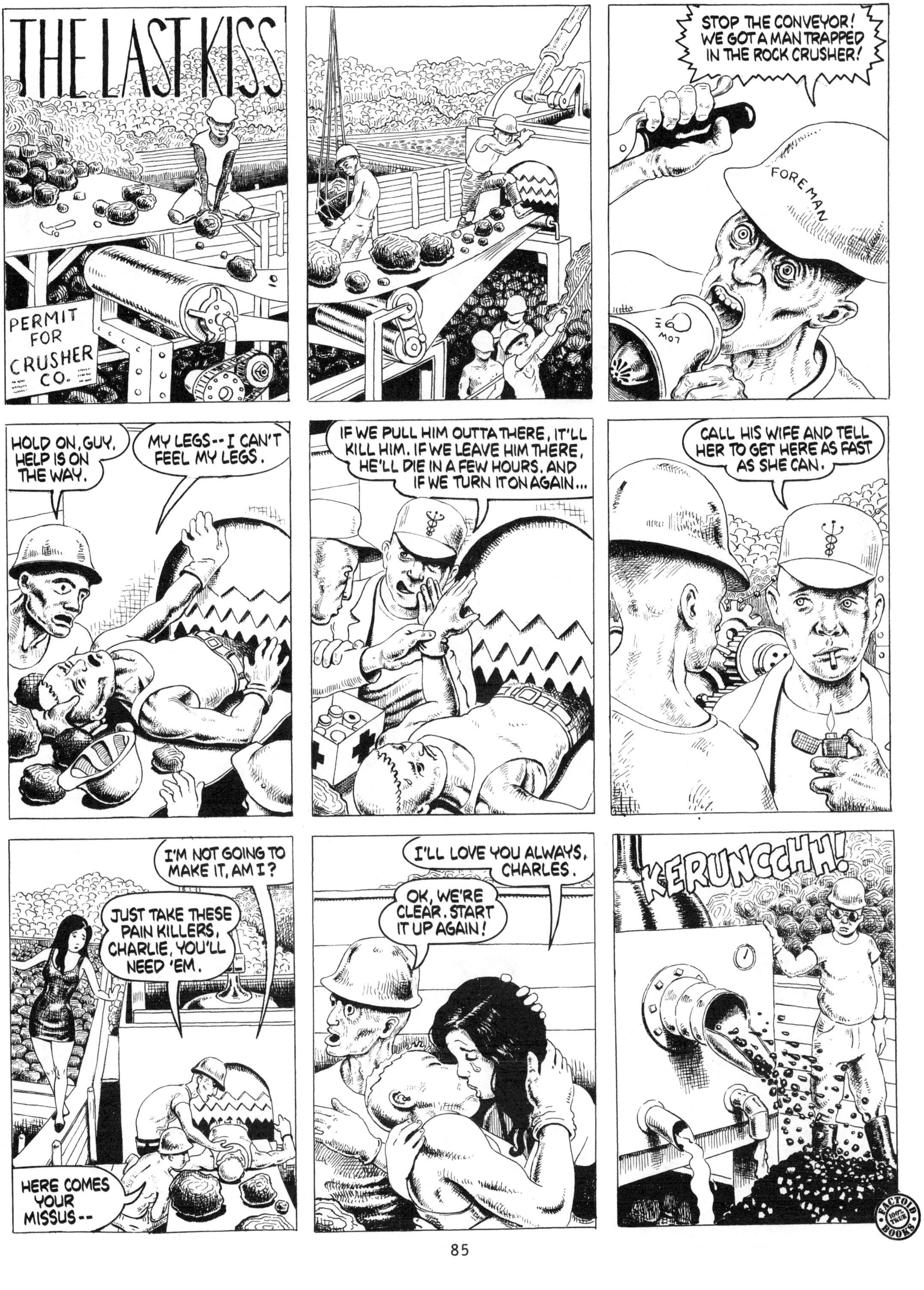
THE LAST KISS
PERMIT FOR CRUSHER CO.
STOP THE CONVEYOR! WE GOT A MAN TRAPPED IN THE ROCK CRUSHER!
FOREMAN
LOW HI
HOLD ON, GUY. HELP IS ON THE WAY.
MY LEGS-- I CAN'T FEEL MY LEGS.
IF WE PULL HIM OUTTA THERE, IT'LL KILL HIM. IF WE LEAVE HIM THERE, HE'LL DIE IN A FEW HOURS. AND IF WE TURN IT ON AGAIN...
CALL HIS WIFE AND TELL HER TO GET HERE AS FAST AS SHE CAN.
I'M NOT GOING TO MAKE IT, AM I?
JUST TAKE THESE PAIN KILLERS, CHARLIE, YOU'LL NEED 'EM.
HERE COMES YOUR MISSUS--
I'LL LOVE YOU ALWAYS, CHARLES.
OK, WE'RE CLEAR. START IT UP AGAIN!
KERUNCCHH!

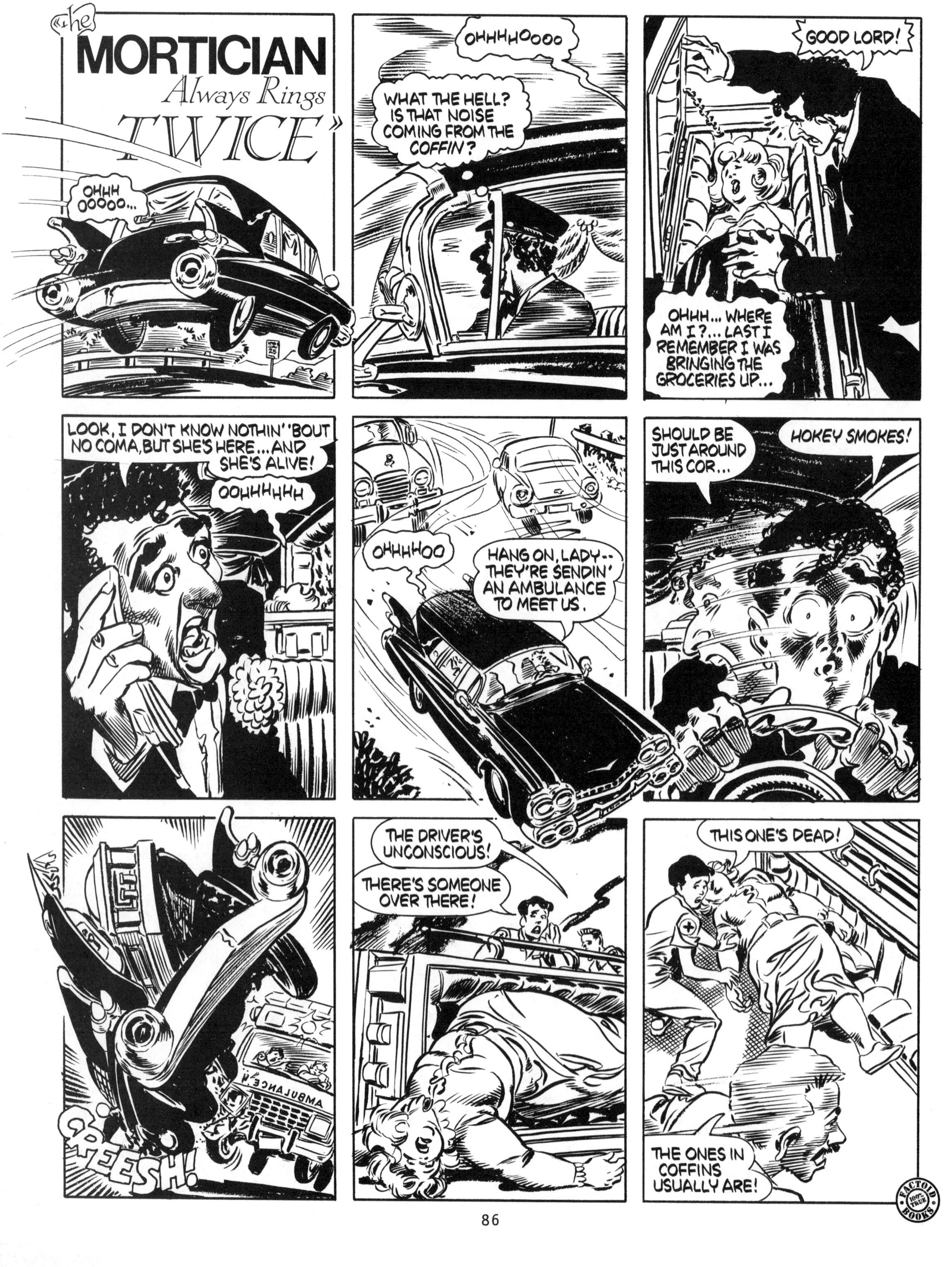
"The MORTICIAN Always Rings TWICE"
OHHH OOOOO...
OHHHHHOOOO
WHAT THE HELL? IS THAT NOISE COMING FROM THE COFFIN?
GOOD LORD!
OHHH... WHERE AM I?... LAST I REMEMBER I WAS BRINGING THE GROCERIES UP...
LOOK, I DON'T KNOW NOTHIN' 'BOUT NO COMA, BUT SHE'S HERE... AND SHE'S ALIVE!
OOHHHHHH
OHHHHOO
HANG ON, LADY-- THEY'RE SENDIN' AN AMBULANCE TO MEET US.
SHOULD BE JUST AROUND THIS COR...
HOKEY SMOKES!
SCREESH!
AMBULANCE
THE DRIVER'S UNCONSCIOUS!
THERE'S SOMEONE OVER THERE!
THIS ONE'S DEAD!
THE ONES IN COFFINS USUALLY ARE!

CHAPTER FOUR

ACCIDENT LEGENDS

There are urban legends about gruesome accidents and hilarious accidents, the distinction being more a matter of how a story is told than of the actual incidents described. The "Barrel of Bricks" *(page 110)*, for example, has been performed as a funny stage routine by several comedians, and it was also turned into a pseudo-folksong ("Dear Boss"); but the slapstick misadventures described, about the poor guy on the construction job, would (as the first panel shows) put him in intensive care for weeks. Then there's "The Ski Accident," my personal favorite *(page 104)*. Murphy's Law rules in this chapter.

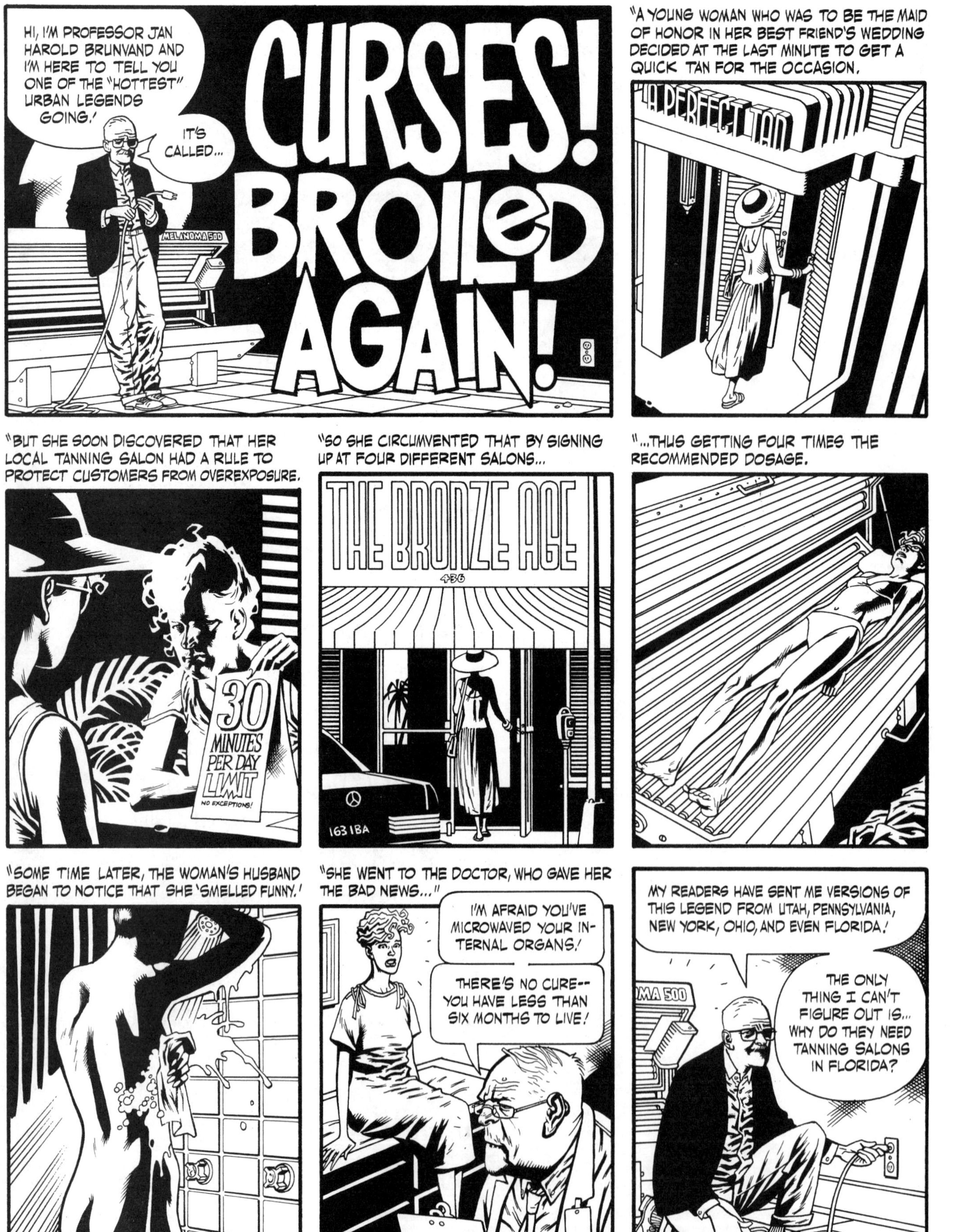
HI, I'M PROFESSOR JAN HAROLD BRUNVAND AND I'M HERE TO TELL YOU ONE OF THE "HOTTEST" URBAN LEGENDS GOING!
IT'S CALLED...
CURSES! BROILED AGAIN!
MELANOMA 500
"A YOUNG WOMAN WHO WAS TO BE THE MAID OF HONOR IN HER BEST FRIEND'S WEDDING DECIDED AT THE LAST MINUTE TO GET A QUICK TAN FOR THE OCCASION.
A PERFECT TAN
"BUT SHE SOON DISCOVERED THAT HER LOCAL TANNING SALON HAD A RULE TO PROTECT CUSTOMERS FROM OVEREXPOSURE.
30 MINUTES PER DAY LIMIT
NO EXCEPTIONS!
"SO SHE CIRCUMVENTED THAT BY SIGNING UP AT FOUR DIFFERENT SALONS...
THE BRONZE AGE
436
163 IBA
"...THUS GETTING FOUR TIMES THE RECOMMENDED DOSAGE.
"SOME TIME LATER, THE WOMAN'S HUSBAND BEGAN TO NOTICE THAT SHE 'SMELLED FUNNY.'
"SHE SHOWERED AND SHOWERED, BUT THE SMELL WOULDN'T GO AWAY.
"SHE WENT TO THE DOCTOR, WHO GAVE HER THE BAD NEWS..."
I'M AFRAID YOU'VE MICROWAVED YOUR INTERNAL ORGANS!
THERE'S NO CURE-- YOU HAVE LESS THAN SIX MONTHS TO LIVE!
MY READERS HAVE SENT ME VERSIONS OF THIS LEGEND FROM UTAH, PENNSYLVANIA, NEW YORK, OHIO, AND EVEN FLORIDA!
OMA 500
THE ONLY THING I CAN'T FIGURE OUT IS... WHY DO THEY NEED TANNING SALONS IN FLORIDA?
FACTOID BOOKS 100% TRUE

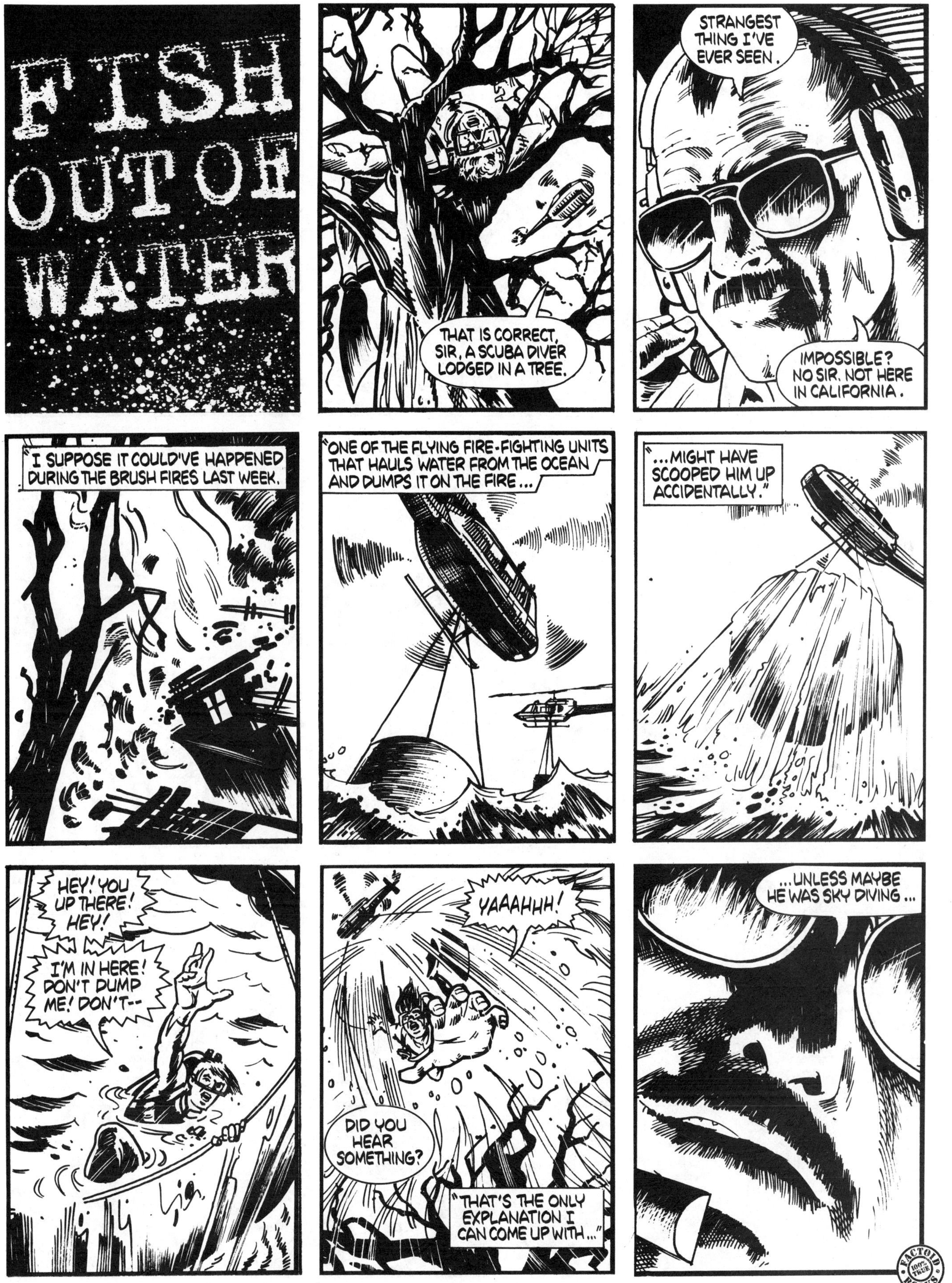
FISH OUT OF WATER
STRANGEST THING I'VE EVER SEEN.
THAT IS CORRECT, SIR, A SCUBA DIVER LODGED IN A TREE.
IMPOSSIBLE? NO SIR. NOT HERE IN CALIFORNIA.
"I SUPPOSE IT COULD'VE HAPPENED DURING THE BRUSH FIRES LAST WEEK.
"ONE OF THE FLYING FIRE-FIGHTING UNITS THAT HAULS WATER FROM THE OCEAN AND DUMPS IT ON THE FIRE...
"...MIGHT HAVE SCOOPED HIM UP ACCIDENTALLY."
HEY! YOU UP THERE! HEY!
I'M IN HERE! DON'T DUMP ME! DON'T--
YAAAHHH!
DID YOU HEAR SOMETHING?
"THAT'S THE ONLY EXPLANATION I CAN COME UP WITH..."
...UNLESS MAYBE HE WAS SKY DIVING...
FACTOID BOOKS 100% TRUE

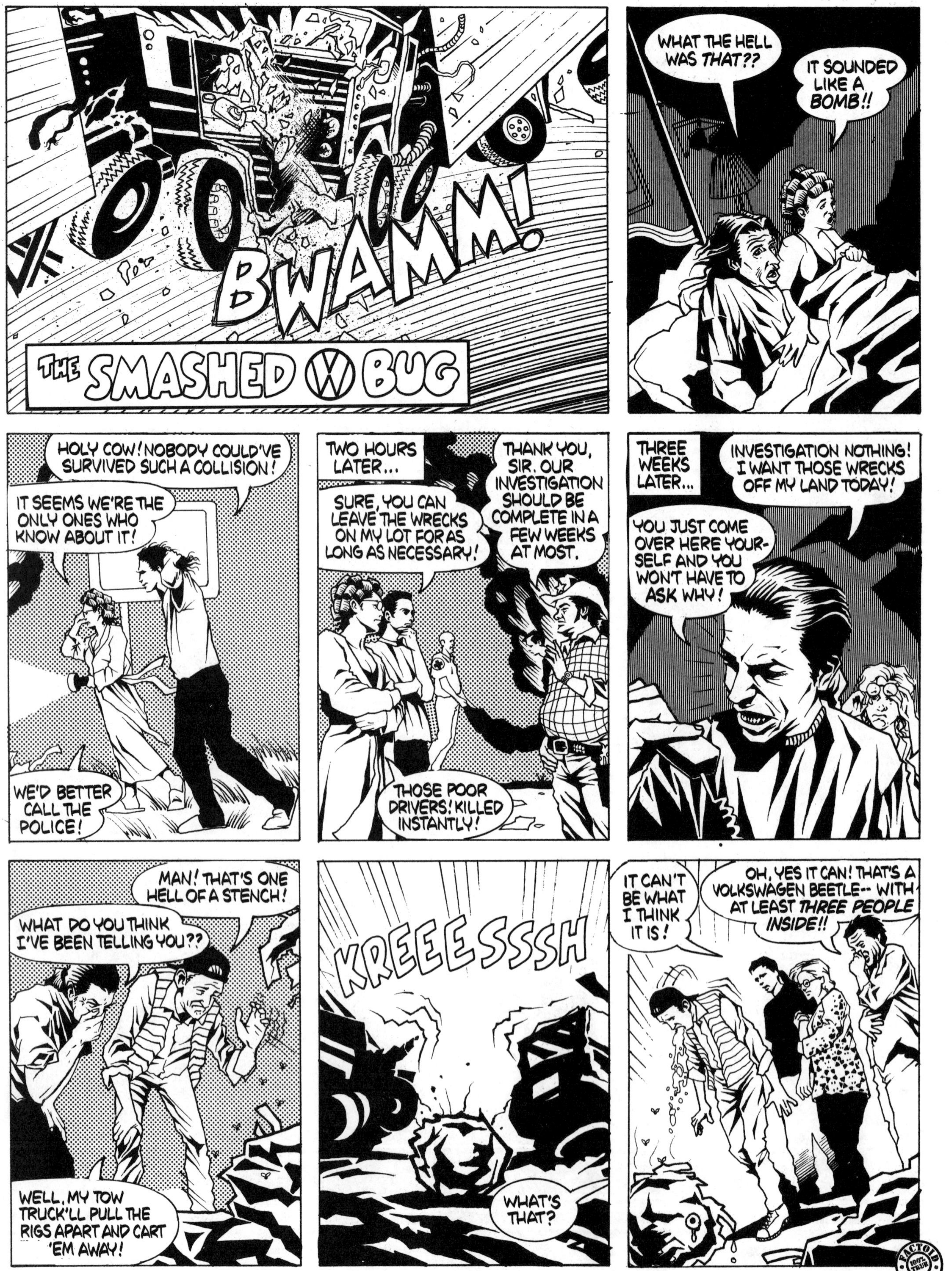
BWAMM!
THE SMASHED VW BUG
WHAT THE HELL WAS THAT??
IT SOUNDED LIKE A BOMB!!
HOLY COW! NOBODY COULD'VE SURVIVED SUCH A COLLISION!
IT SEEMS WE'RE THE ONLY ONES WHO KNOW ABOUT IT!
WE'D BETTER CALL THE POLICE!
TWO HOURS LATER...
SURE, YOU CAN LEAVE THE WRECKS ON MY LOT FOR AS LONG AS NECESSARY!
THANK YOU, SIR. OUR INVESTIGATION SHOULD BE COMPLETE IN A FEW WEEKS AT MOST.
THOSE POOR DRIVERS! KILLED INSTANTLY!
THREE WEEKS LATER...
INVESTIGATION NOTHING! I WANT THOSE WRECKS OFF MY LAND TODAY!
YOU JUST COME OVER HERE YOURSELF AND YOU WON'T HAVE TO ASK WHY!
MAN! THAT'S ONE HELL OF A STENCH!
WHAT DO YOU THINK I'VE BEEN TELLING YOU??
WELL, MY TOW TRUCK'LL PULL THE RIGS APART AND CART 'EM AWAY!
KREEEESSSH
WHAT'S THAT?
IT CAN'T BE WHAT I THINK IT IS!
OH, YES IT CAN! THAT'S A VOLKSWAGEN BEETLE-- WITH AT LEAST THREE PEOPLE INSIDE!!

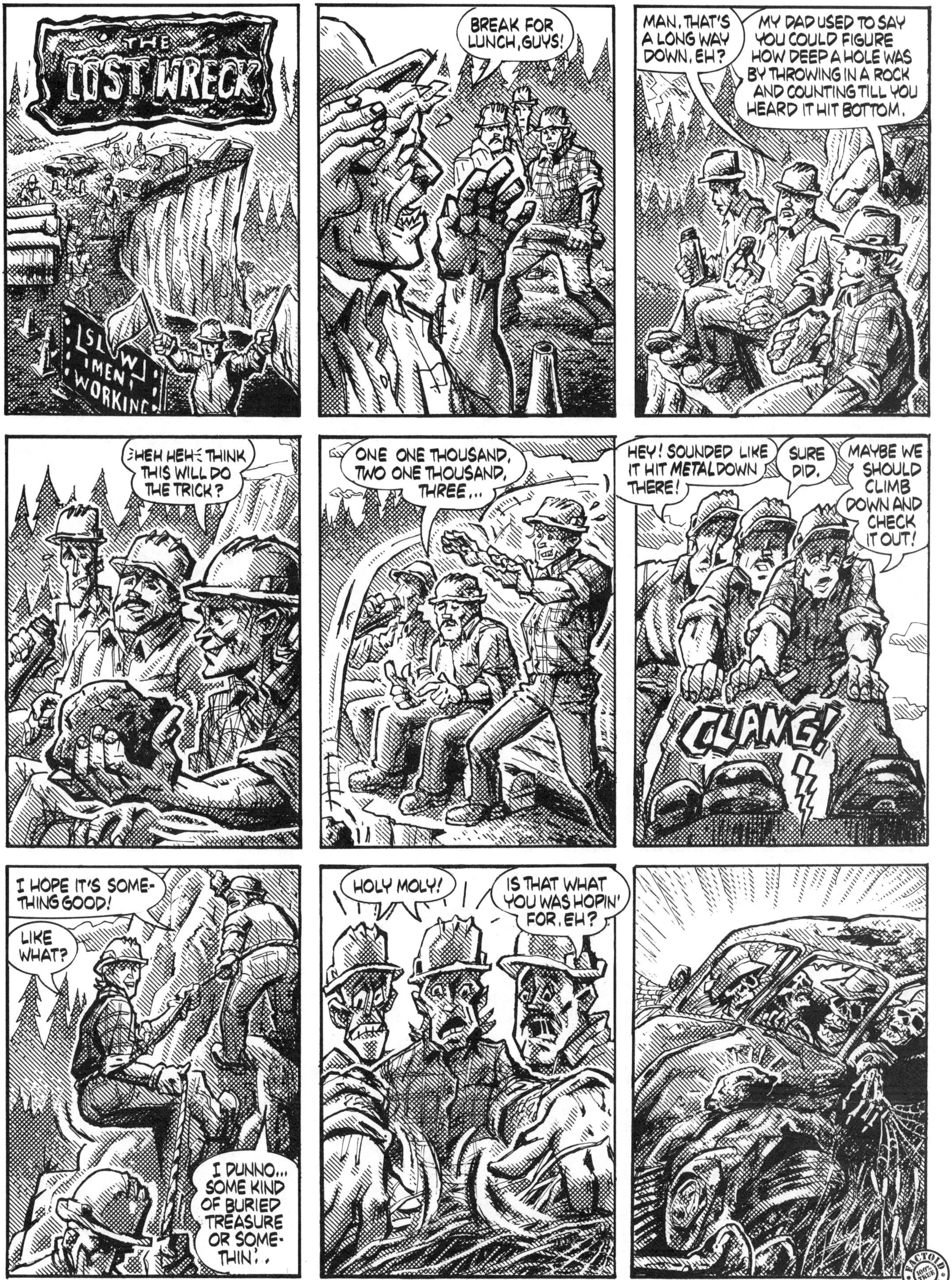
THE LOST WRECK
BREAK FOR LUNCH, GUYS!
MAN, THAT'S A LONG WAY DOWN, EH?
MY DAD USED TO SAY YOU COULD FIGURE HOW DEEP A HOLE WAS BY THROWING IN A ROCK AND COUNTING TILL YOU HEARD IT HIT BOTTOM.
HEH HEH THINK THIS WILL DO THE TRICK?
ONE ONE THOUSAND, TWO ONE THOUSAND, THREE...
HEY! SOUNDED LIKE IT HIT METAL DOWN THERE!
SURE DID.
MAYBE WE SHOULD CLIMB DOWN AND CHECK IT OUT!
CLANG!
I HOPE IT'S SOME-THING GOOD!
LIKE WHAT?
I DUNNO... SOME KIND OF BURIED TREASURE OR SOME-THIN'.
HOLY MOLY!
IS THAT WHAT YOU WAS HOPIN' FOR, EH?

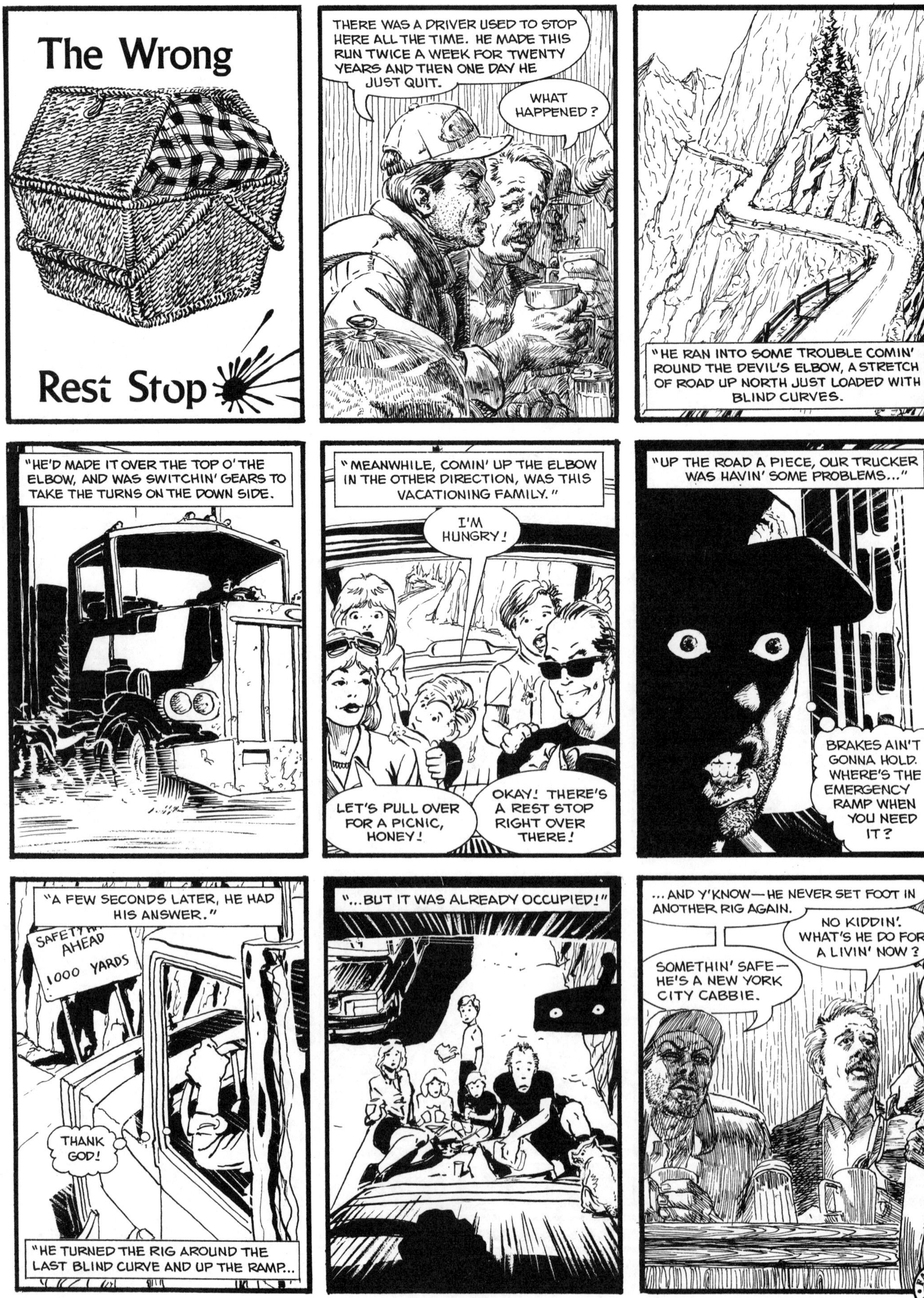
The Wrong
Rest Stop
THERE WAS A DRIVER USED TO STOP HERE ALL THE TIME. HE MADE THIS RUN TWICE A WEEK FOR TWENTY YEARS AND THEN ONE DAY HE JUST QUIT.
WHAT HAPPENED?
"HE RAN INTO SOME TROUBLE COMIN' ROUND THE DEVIL'S ELBOW, A STRETCH OF ROAD UP NORTH JUST LOADED WITH BLIND CURVES.
"HE'D MADE IT OVER THE TOP O' THE ELBOW, AND WAS SWITCHIN' GEARS TO TAKE THE TURNS ON THE DOWN SIDE.
"MEANWHILE, COMIN' UP THE ELBOW IN THE OTHER DIRECTION, WAS THIS VACATIONING FAMILY."
I'M HUNGRY!
LET'S PULL OVER FOR A PICNIC, HONEY!
OKAY! THERE'S A REST STOP RIGHT OVER THERE!
"UP THE ROAD A PIECE, OUR TRUCKER WAS HAVIN' SOME PROBLEMS..."
BRAKES AIN'T GONNA HOLD. WHERE'S THE EMERGENCY RAMP WHEN YOU NEED IT?
"A FEW SECONDS LATER, HE HAD HIS ANSWER."
AHEAD
1000 YARDS
THANK GOD!
"HE TURNED THE RIG AROUND THE LAST BLIND CURVE AND UP THE RAMP...
"...BUT IT WAS ALREADY OCCUPIED!"
...AND Y'KNOW—HE NEVER SET FOOT IN ANOTHER RIG AGAIN.
NO KIDDIN'. WHAT'S HE DO FOR A LIVIN' NOW?
SOMETHIN' SAFE—HE'S A NEW YORK CITY CABBIE.

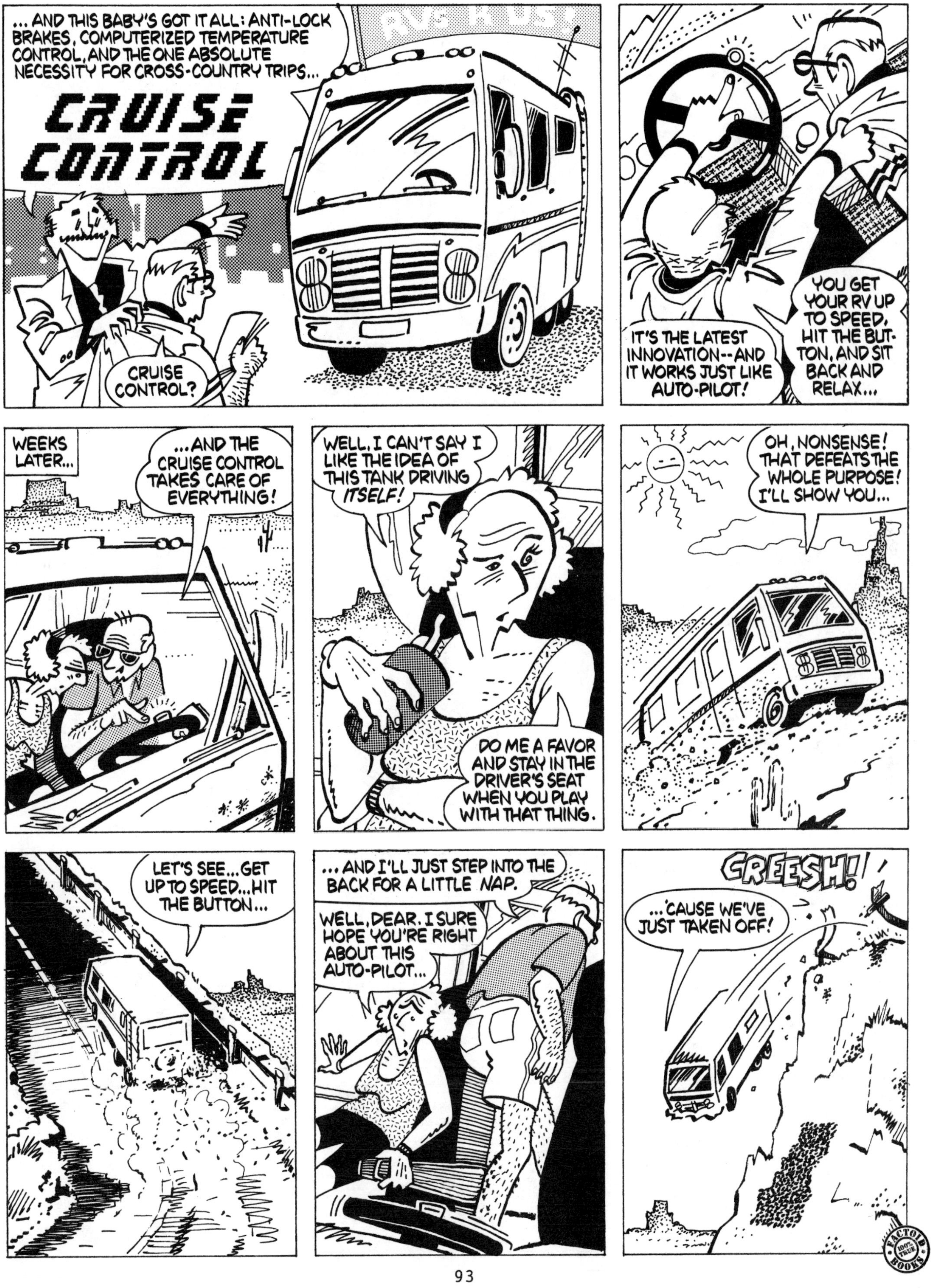
...AND THIS BABY'S GOT IT ALL: ANTI-LOCK BRAKES, COMPUTERIZED TEMPERATURE CONTROL, AND THE ONE ABSOLUTE NECESSITY FOR CROSS-COUNTRY TRIPS...
CRUISE CONTROL
CRUISE CONTROL?
IT'S THE LATEST INNOVATION--AND IT WORKS JUST LIKE AUTO-PILOT!
YOU GET YOUR RV UP TO SPEED, HIT THE BUTTON, AND SIT BACK AND RELAX...
WEEKS LATER...
...AND THE CRUISE CONTROL TAKES CARE OF EVERYTHING!
WELL, I CAN'T SAY I LIKE THE IDEA OF THIS TANK DRIVING *ITSELF*!
DO ME A FAVOR AND STAY IN THE DRIVER'S SEAT WHEN YOU PLAY WITH THAT THING.
OH, NONSENSE! THAT DEFEATS THE WHOLE PURPOSE! I'LL SHOW YOU...
LET'S SEE...GET UP TO SPEED...HIT THE BUTTON...
...AND I'LL JUST STEP INTO THE BACK FOR A LITTLE *NAP*.
WELL, DEAR. I SURE HOPE YOU'RE RIGHT ABOUT THIS AUTO-PILOT...
CREESH!
...'CAUSE WE'VE JUST TAKEN OFF!
FACTOID BOOKS
100% TRUE

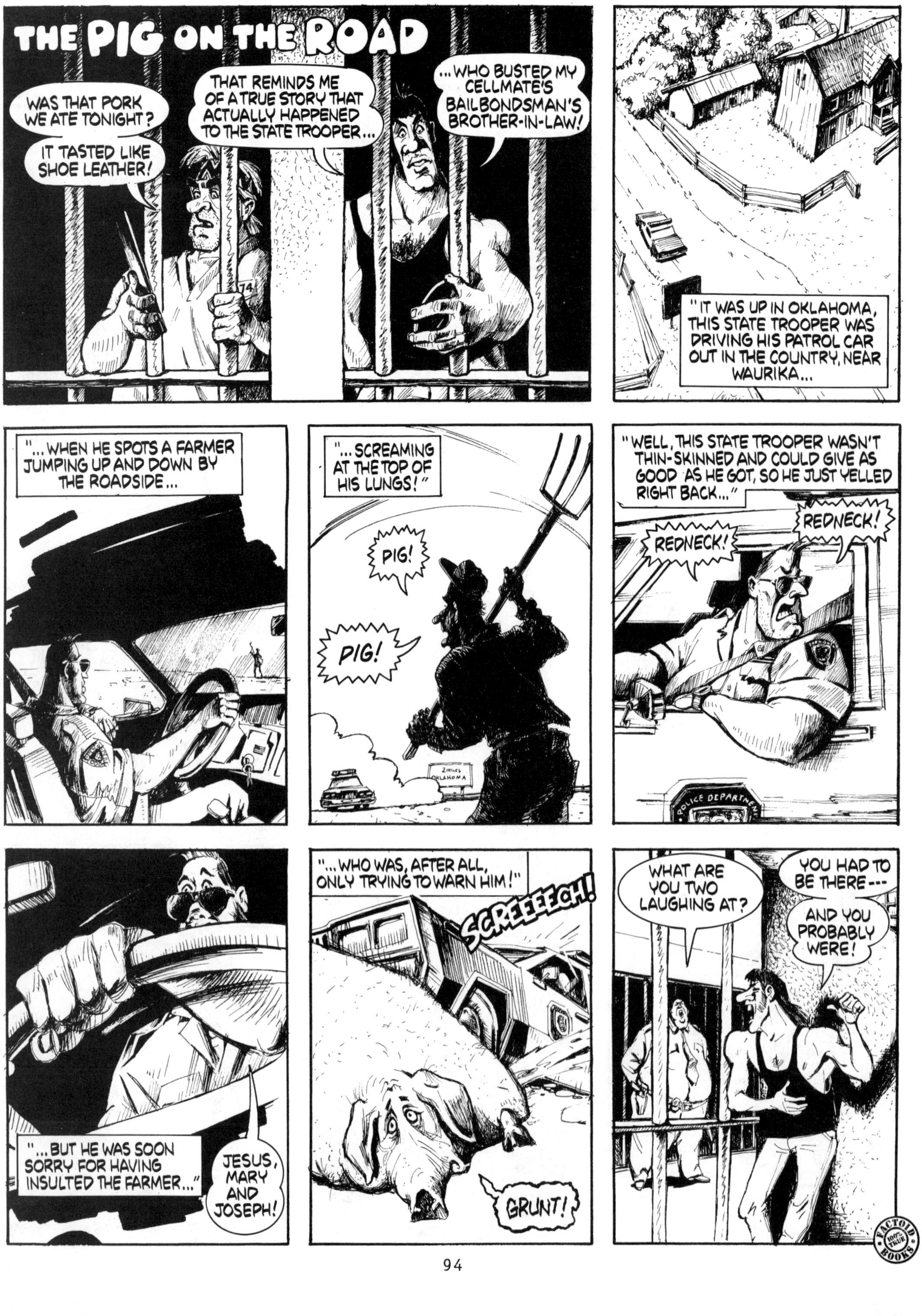
THE PIG ON THE ROAD
WAS THAT PORK WE ATE TONIGHT?
IT TASTED LIKE SHOE LEATHER!
THAT REMINDS ME OF A TRUE STORY THAT ACTUALLY HAPPENED TO THE STATE TROOPER...
...WHO BUSTED MY CELLMATE'S BAILBONDSMAN'S BROTHER-IN-LAW!
74
"IT WAS UP IN OKLAHOMA, THIS STATE TROOPER WAS DRIVING HIS PATROL CAR OUT IN THE COUNTRY, NEAR WAURIKA...
"...WHEN HE SPOTS A FARMER JUMPING UP AND DOWN BY THE ROADSIDE...
"...SCREAMING AT THE TOP OF HIS LUNGS!"
PIG!
PIG!
OKLAHOMA
"WELL, THIS STATE TROOPER WASN'T THIN-SKINNED AND COULD GIVE AS GOOD AS HE GOT, SO HE JUST YELLED RIGHT BACK..."
REDNECK!
REDNECK!
POLICE DEPARTMENT
"...BUT HE WAS SOON SORRY FOR HAVING INSULTED THE FARMER..."
JESUS, MARY AND JOSEPH!
"...WHO WAS, AFTER ALL, ONLY TRYING TO WARN HIM!"
SCREEEECH!
GRUNT!
WHAT ARE YOU TWO LAUGHING AT?
YOU HAD TO BE THERE---
AND YOU PROBABLY WERE!
FACTOID BOOKS 100% TRUE

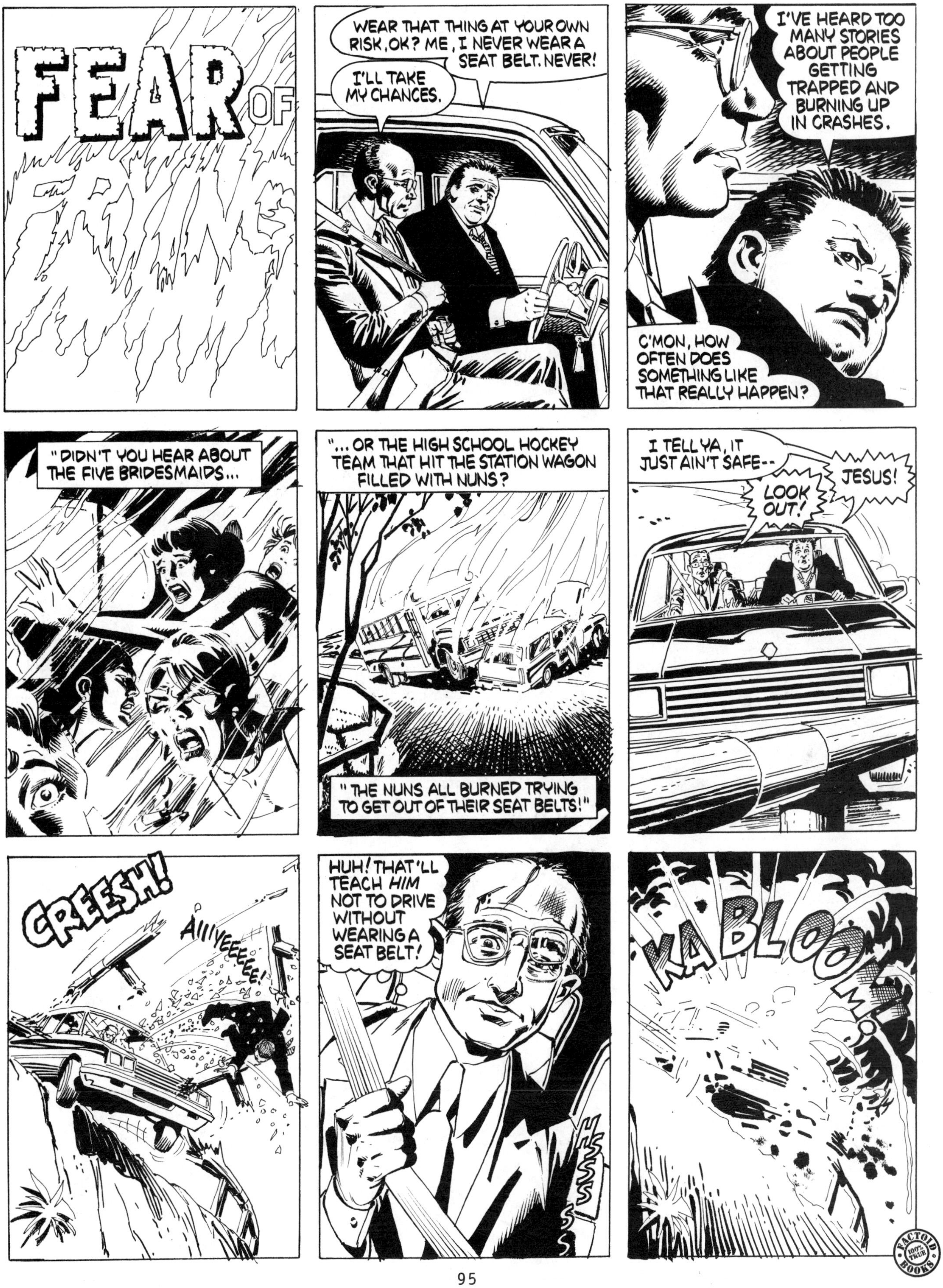
FEAR OF
WEAR THAT THING AT YOUR OWN RISK, OK? ME, I NEVER WEAR A SEAT BELT. NEVER!
I'LL TAKE MY CHANCES.
I'VE HEARD TOO MANY STORIES ABOUT PEOPLE GETTING TRAPPED AND BURNING UP IN CRASHES.
C'MON, HOW OFTEN DOES SOMETHING LIKE THAT REALLY HAPPEN?
"DIDN'T YOU HEAR ABOUT THE FIVE BRIDESMAIDS...
"...OR THE HIGH SCHOOL HOCKEY TEAM THAT HIT THE STATION WAGON FILLED WITH NUNS?
"THE NUNS ALL BURNED TRYING TO GET OUT OF THEIR SEAT BELTS!"
I TELL YA, IT JUST AIN'T SAFE--
LOOK OUT!
JESUS!
CREESH!
AIIIYEEEEEE!
HUH! THAT'LL TEACH HIM NOT TO DRIVE WITHOUT WEARING A SEAT BELT!
HSSSSSS
KA BLOOOM!
FACTOID BOOKS 100% TRUE

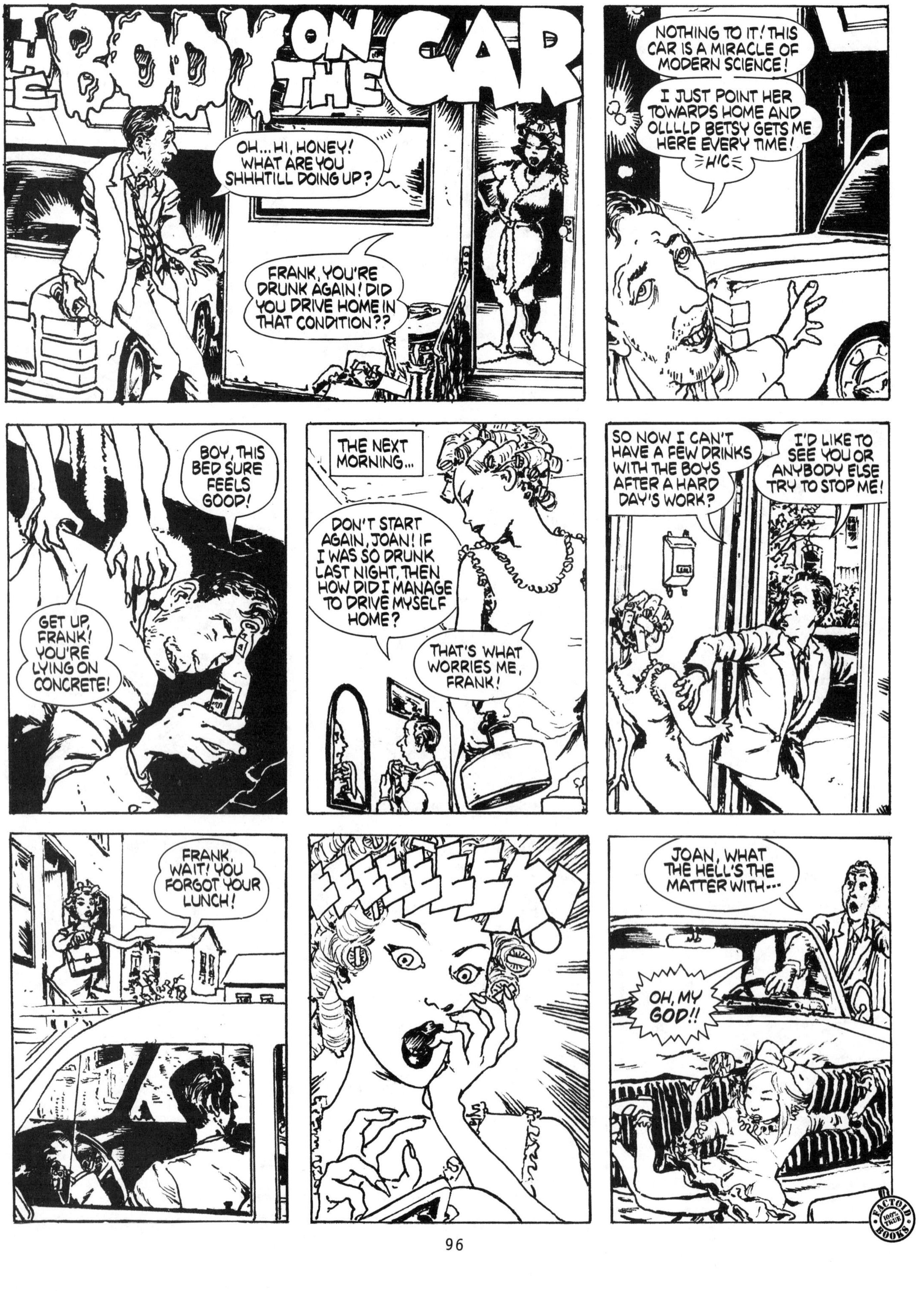
THE BODY ON THE CAR
OH... HI, HONEY! WHAT ARE YOU SHHHTILL DOING UP?
FRANK, YOU'RE DRUNK AGAIN! DID YOU DRIVE HOME IN THAT CONDITION??
NOTHING TO IT! THIS CAR IS A MIRACLE OF MODERN SCIENCE!
I JUST POINT HER TOWARDS HOME AND OLLLLD BETSY GETS ME HERE EVERY TIME!
HIC
BOY, THIS BED SURE FEELS GOOD!
GET UP, FRANK! YOU'RE LYING ON CONCRETE!
THE NEXT MORNING...
DON'T START AGAIN, JOAN! IF I WAS SO DRUNK LAST NIGHT, THEN HOW DID I MANAGE TO DRIVE MYSELF HOME?
THAT'S WHAT WORRIES ME, FRANK!
SO NOW I CAN'T HAVE A FEW DRINKS WITH THE BOYS AFTER A HARD DAY'S WORK?
I'D LIKE TO SEE YOU OR ANYBODY ELSE TRY TO STOP ME!
FRANK, WAIT! YOU FORGOT YOUR LUNCH!
EEEEEEEK!
JOAN, WHAT THE HELL'S THE MATTER WITH...
OH, MY GOD!!
FACTOID BOOKS 100% TRUE

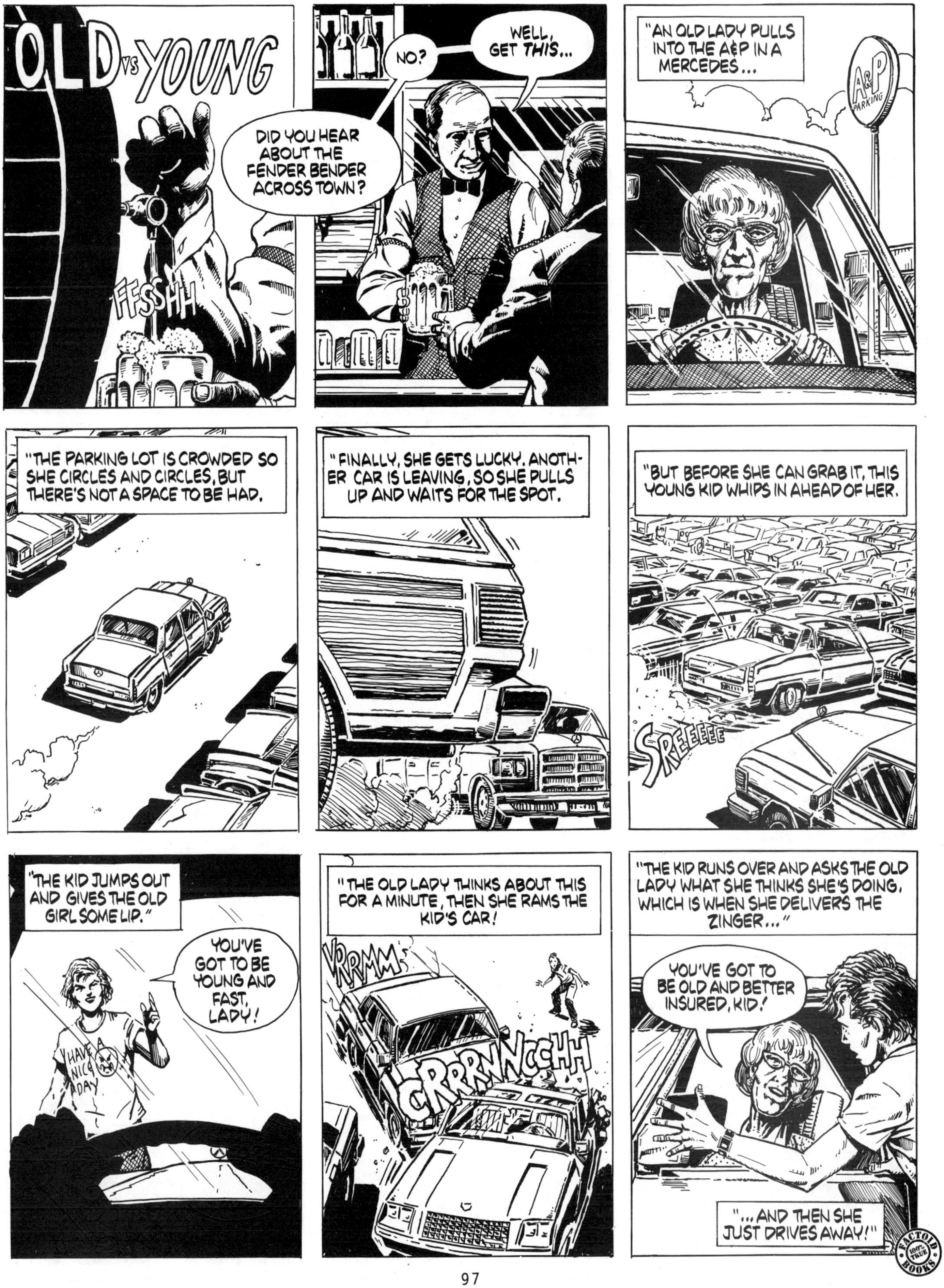
OLD vs YOUNG
FFSSHH
DID YOU HEAR ABOUT THE FENDER BENDER ACROSS TOWN?
NO?
WELL, GET THIS...
"AN OLD LADY PULLS INTO THE A&P IN A MERCEDES...
A&P PARKING
"THE PARKING LOT IS CROWDED SO SHE CIRCLES AND CIRCLES, BUT THERE'S NOT A SPACE TO BE HAD.
"FINALLY, SHE GETS LUCKY. ANOTHER CAR IS LEAVING, SO SHE PULLS UP AND WAITS FOR THE SPOT.
"BUT BEFORE SHE CAN GRAB IT, THIS YOUNG KID WHIPS IN AHEAD OF HER.
SREEEEE
"THE KID JUMPS OUT AND GIVES THE OLD GIRL SOME LIP."
YOU'VE GOT TO BE YOUNG AND FAST, LADY!
HAVE A NICE DAY
"THE OLD LADY THINKS ABOUT THIS FOR A MINUTE, THEN SHE RAMS THE KID'S CAR!
VRRMM
CRRRNNCCHH
"THE KID RUNS OVER AND ASKS THE OLD LADY WHAT SHE THINKS SHE'S DOING, WHICH IS WHEN SHE DELIVERS THE ZINGER..."
YOU'VE GOT TO BE OLD AND BETTER INSURED, KID!
"...AND THEN SHE JUST DRIVES AWAY!"
FACTOID BOOKS 100% TRUE

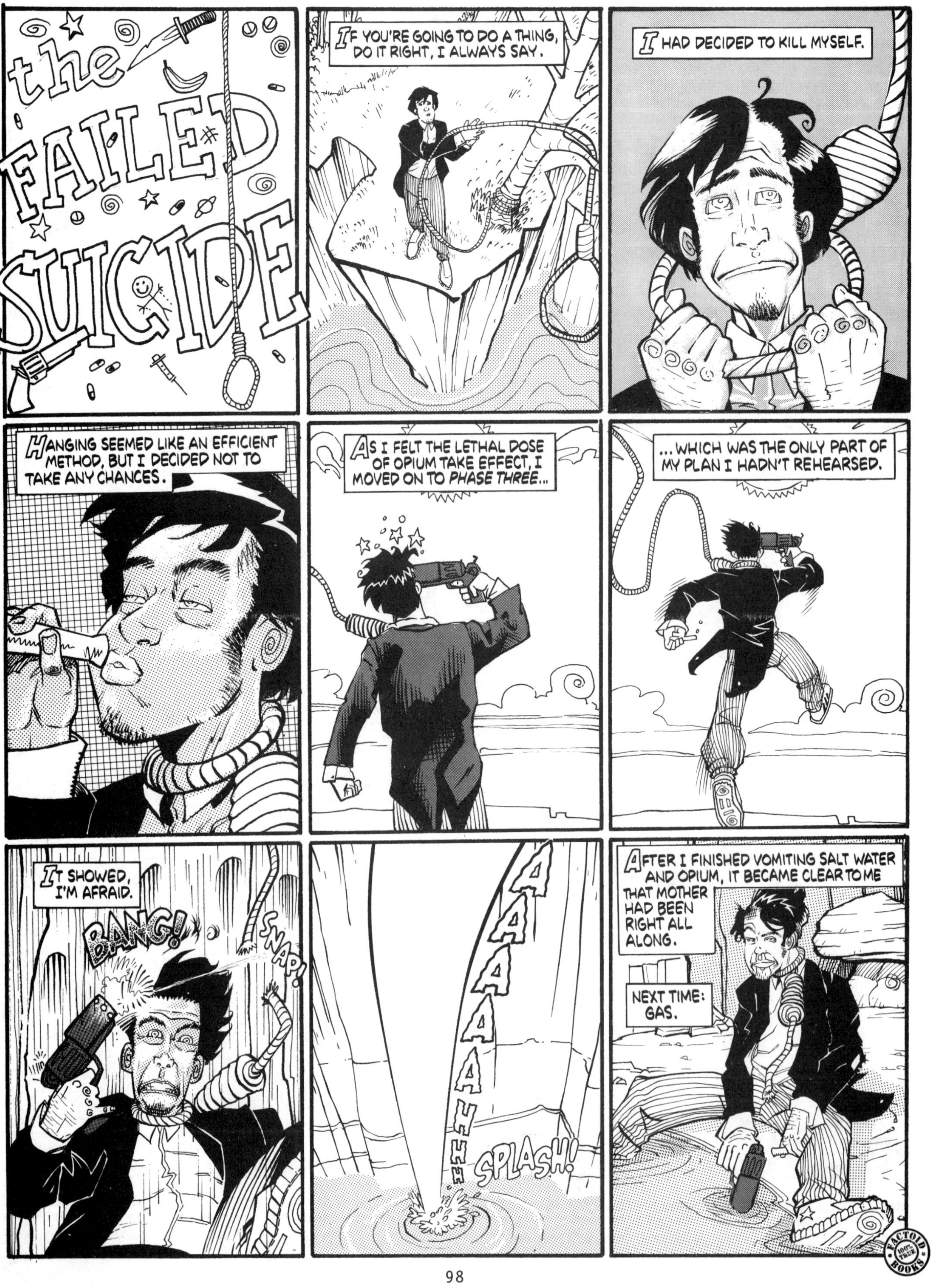

the FAILED SUICIDE
IF YOU'RE GOING TO DO A THING, DO IT RIGHT, I ALWAYS SAY.
I HAD DECIDED TO KILL MYSELF.
HANGING SEEMED LIKE AN EFFICIENT METHOD, BUT I DECIDED NOT TO TAKE ANY CHANCES.
AS I FELT THE LETHAL DOSE OF OPIUM TAKE EFFECT, I MOVED ON TO PHASE THREE...
...WHICH WAS THE ONLY PART OF MY PLAN I HADN'T REHEARSED.
IT SHOWED, I'M AFRAID.
BANG!
SNAP!
AAAAAAAAHHHH
SPLASH!
AFTER I FINISHED VOMITING SALT WATER AND OPIUM, IT BECAME CLEAR TO ME
THAT MOTHER HAD BEEN RIGHT ALL ALONG.
NEXT TIME: GAS.

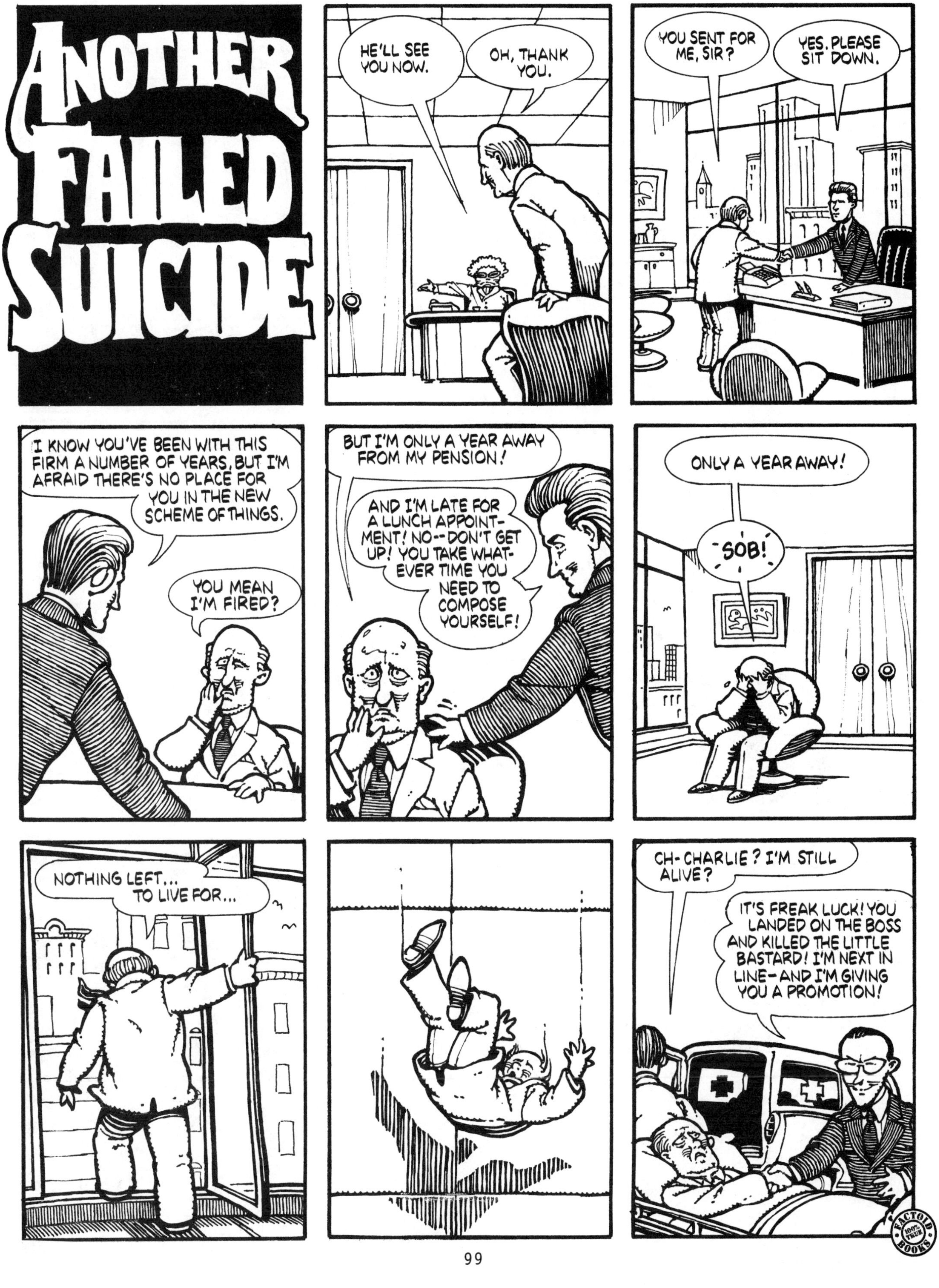
ANOTHER FAILED SUICIDE
HE'LL SEE YOU NOW.
OH, THANK YOU.
YOU SENT FOR ME, SIR?
YES. PLEASE SIT DOWN.
I KNOW YOU'VE BEEN WITH THIS FIRM A NUMBER OF YEARS, BUT I'M AFRAID THERE'S NO PLACE FOR YOU IN THE NEW SCHEME OF THINGS.
YOU MEAN I'M FIRED?
BUT I'M ONLY A YEAR AWAY FROM MY PENSION!
AND I'M LATE FOR A LUNCH APPOINTMENT! NO--DON'T GET UP! YOU TAKE WHATEVER TIME YOU NEED TO COMPOSE YOURSELF!
ONLY A YEAR AWAY!
SOB!
NOTHING LEFT... TO LIVE FOR...
CH-CHARLIE? I'M STILL ALIVE?
IT'S FREAK LUCK! YOU LANDED ON THE BOSS AND KILLED THE LITTLE BASTARD! I'M NEXT IN LINE—AND I'M GIVING YOU A PROMOTION!
FACTOID BOOKS 100% TRUE

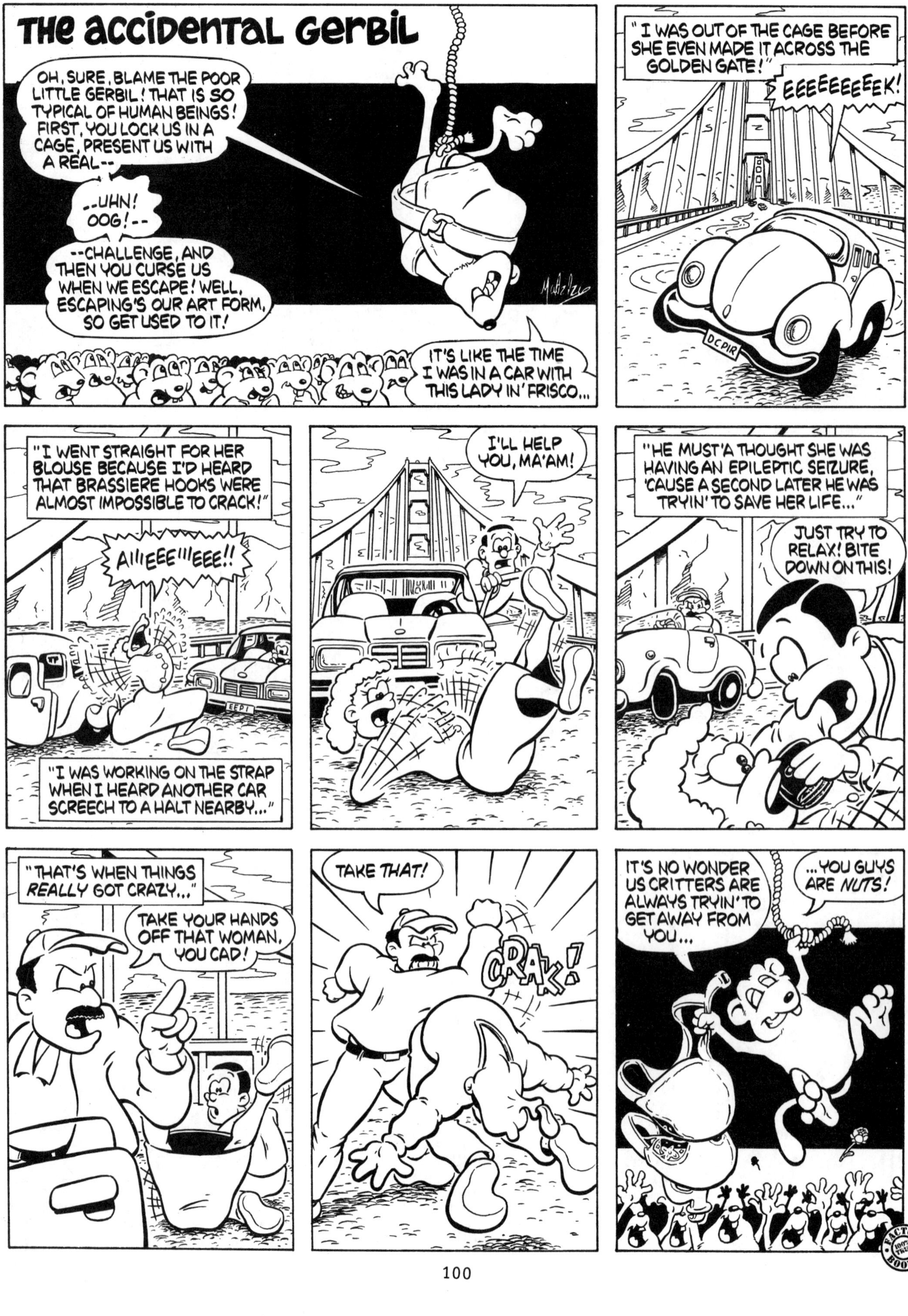
THE ACCIDENTAL GERBIL
OH, SURE, BLAME THE POOR LITTLE GERBIL! THAT IS SO TYPICAL OF HUMAN BEINGS! FIRST, YOU LOCK US IN A CAGE, PRESENT US WITH A REAL--
--UHN! OOG!--
--CHALLENGE, AND THEN YOU CURSE US WHEN WE ESCAPE! WELL, ESCAPING'S OUR ART FORM, SO GET USED TO IT!
IT'S LIKE THE TIME I WAS IN A CAR WITH THIS LADY IN' FRISCO...
"I WAS OUT OF THE CAGE BEFORE SHE EVEN MADE IT ACROSS THE GOLDEN GATE!"
EEEEEEEEEK!
DCPIR
"I WENT STRAIGHT FOR HER BLOUSE BECAUSE I'D HEARD THAT BRASSIERE HOOKS WERE ALMOST IMPOSSIBLE TO CRACK!"
AIIIEEEIIIEEE!!
EEPI
"I WAS WORKING ON THE STRAP WHEN I HEARD ANOTHER CAR SCREECH TO A HALT NEARBY..."
I'LL HELP YOU, MA'AM!
"HE MUST'A THOUGHT SHE WAS HAVING AN EPILEPTIC SEIZURE, 'CAUSE A SECOND LATER HE WAS TRYIN' TO SAVE HER LIFE..."
JUST TRY TO RELAX! BITE DOWN ON THIS!
"THAT'S WHEN THINGS *REALLY* GOT CRAZY..."
TAKE YOUR HANDS OFF THAT WOMAN, YOU CAD!
TAKE *THAT*!
CRAK!
IT'S NO WONDER US CRITTERS ARE ALWAYS TRYIN' TO GET AWAY FROM YOU...
...YOU GUYS ARE *NUTS*!

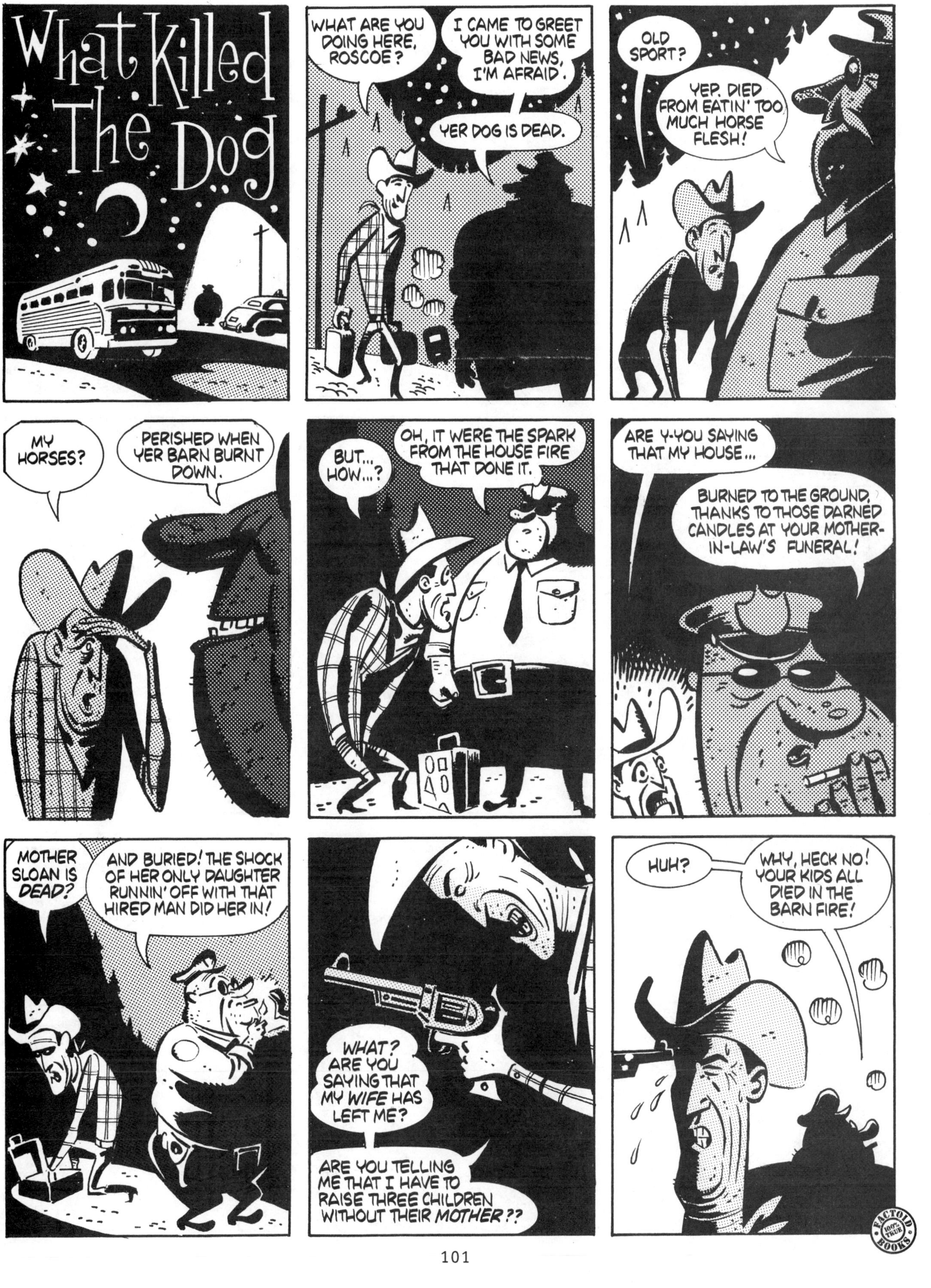
What Killed The Dog
WHAT ARE YOU DOING HERE, ROSCOE?
I CAME TO GREET YOU WITH SOME BAD NEWS, I'M AFRAID.
YER DOG IS DEAD.
OLD SPORT?
YEP. DIED FROM EATIN' TOO MUCH HORSE FLESH!
MY HORSES?
PERISHED WHEN YER BARN BURNT DOWN.
BUT... HOW...?
OH, IT WERE THE SPARK FROM THE HOUSE FIRE THAT DONE IT.
ARE Y-YOU SAYING THAT MY HOUSE...
BURNED TO THE GROUND, THANKS TO THOSE DARNED CANDLES AT YOUR MOTHER-IN-LAW'S FUNERAL!
MOTHER SLOAN IS *DEAD?*
AND BURIED! THE SHOCK OF HER ONLY DAUGHTER RUNNIN' OFF WITH THAT HIRED MAN DID HER IN!
WHAT? ARE YOU SAYING THAT MY *WIFE* HAS LEFT ME?
ARE YOU TELLING ME THAT I HAVE TO RAISE THREE CHILDREN WITHOUT THEIR *MOTHER??*
HUH?
WHY, HECK NO! YOUR KIDS ALL DIED IN THE BARN FIRE!
FACTOID 100% TRUE BOOKS

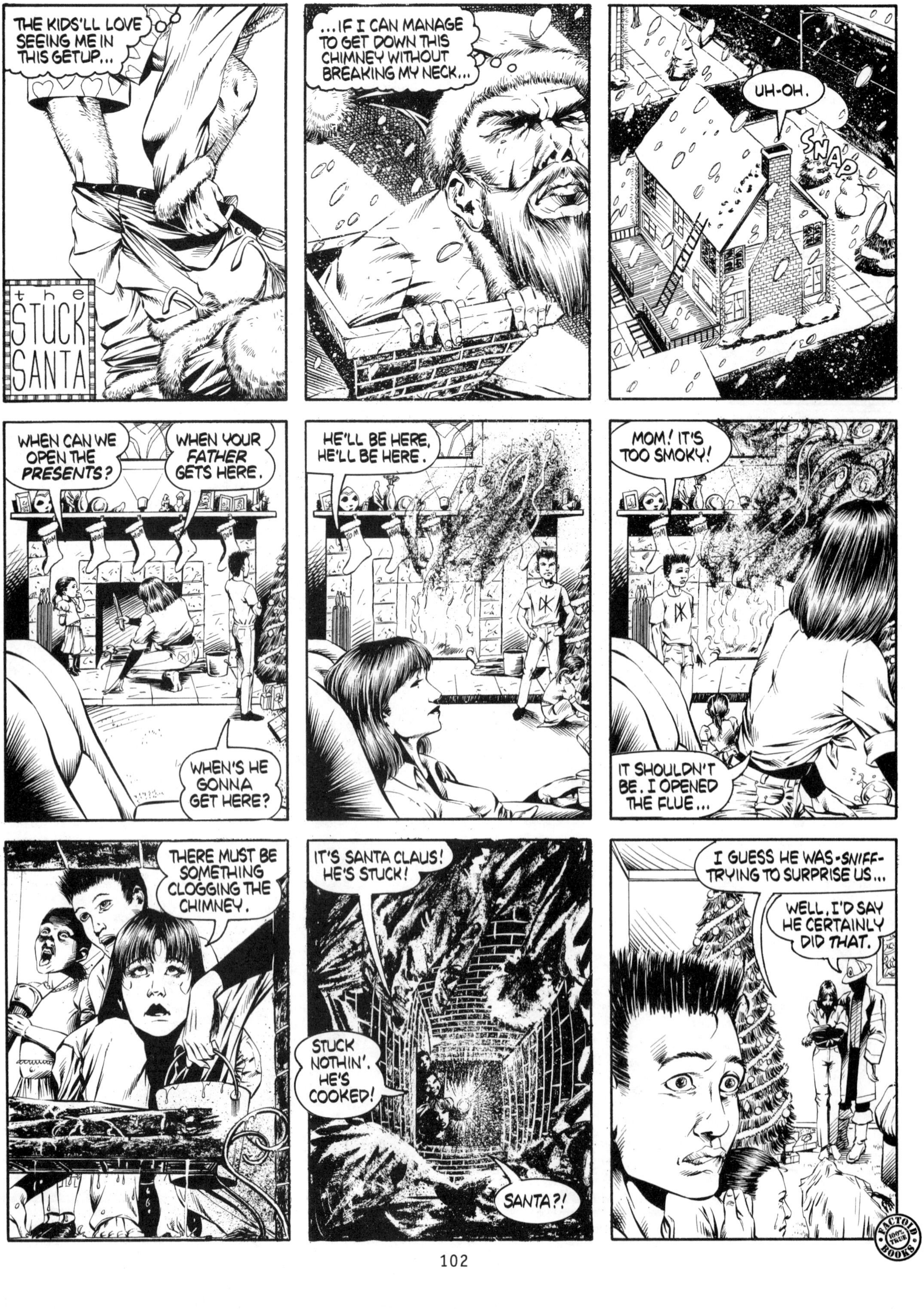
THE KIDS'LL LOVE SEEING ME IN THIS GETUP...
the STUCK SANTA
...IF I CAN MANAGE TO GET DOWN THIS CHIMNEY WITHOUT BREAKING MY NECK...
UH-OH.
SNAP
WHEN CAN WE OPEN THE PRESENTS?
WHEN YOUR FATHER GETS HERE.
WHEN'S HE GONNA GET HERE?
HE'LL BE HERE, HE'LL BE HERE.
MOM! IT'S TOO SMOKY!
IT SHOULDN'T BE. I OPENED THE FLUE...
THERE MUST BE SOMETHING CLOGGING THE CHIMNEY.
IT'S SANTA CLAUS! HE'S STUCK!
STUCK NOTHIN'. HE'S COOKED!
SANTA?!
I GUESS HE WAS-SNIFF-TRYING TO SURPRISE US...
WELL, I'D SAY HE CERTAINLY DID THAT.
FACTOID BOOKS 100% TRUE

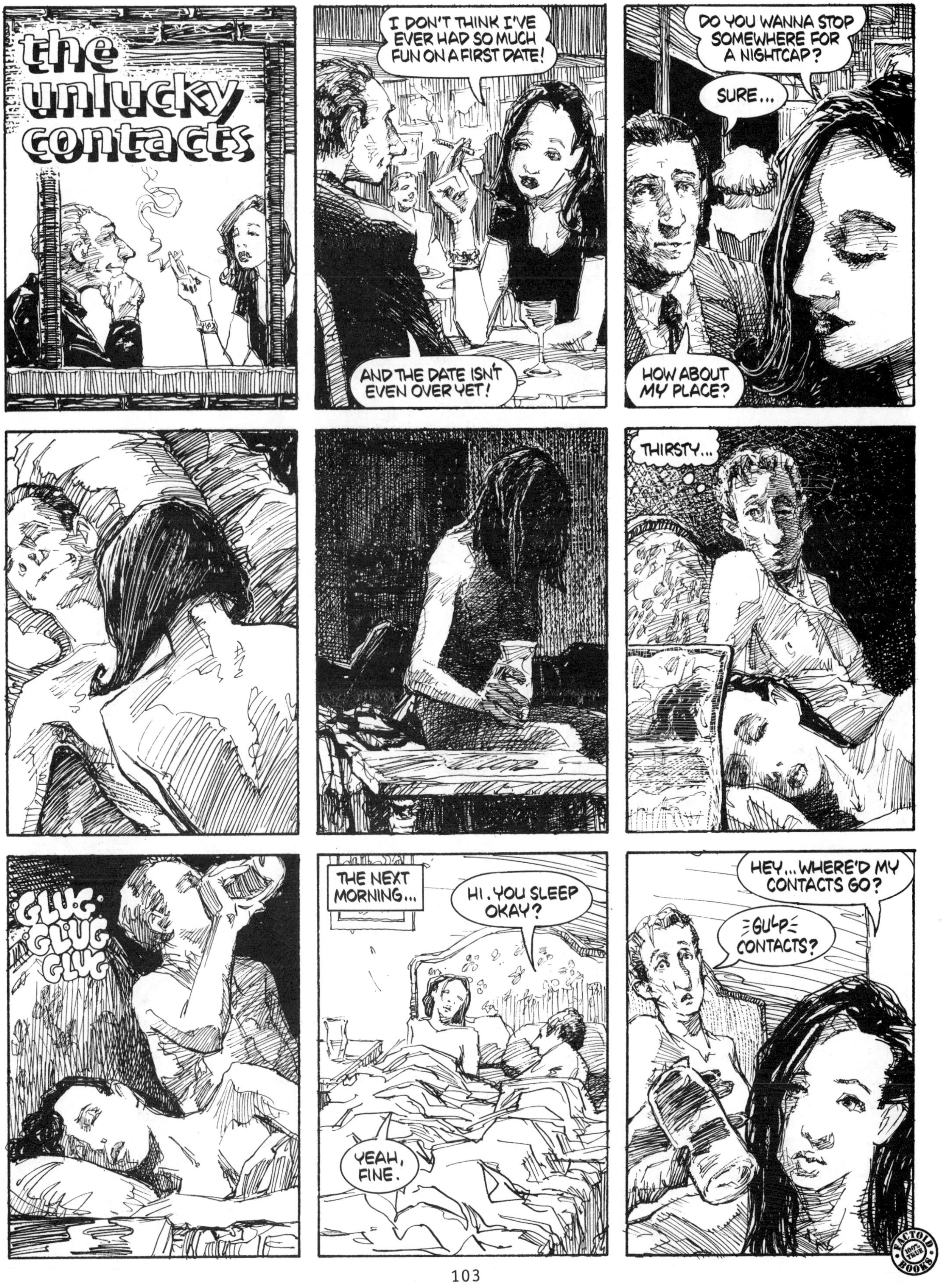
the unlucky contacts
I DON'T THINK I'VE EVER HAD SO MUCH FUN ON A FIRST DATE!
AND THE DATE ISN'T EVEN OVER YET!
DO YOU WANNA STOP SOMEWHERE FOR A NIGHTCAP?
SURE...
HOW ABOUT MY PLACE?
THIRSTY...
GLUG GLUG GLUG
THE NEXT MORNING...
HI. YOU SLEEP OKAY?
YEAH, FINE.
HEY... WHERE'D MY CONTACTS GO?
GULP
CONTACTS?

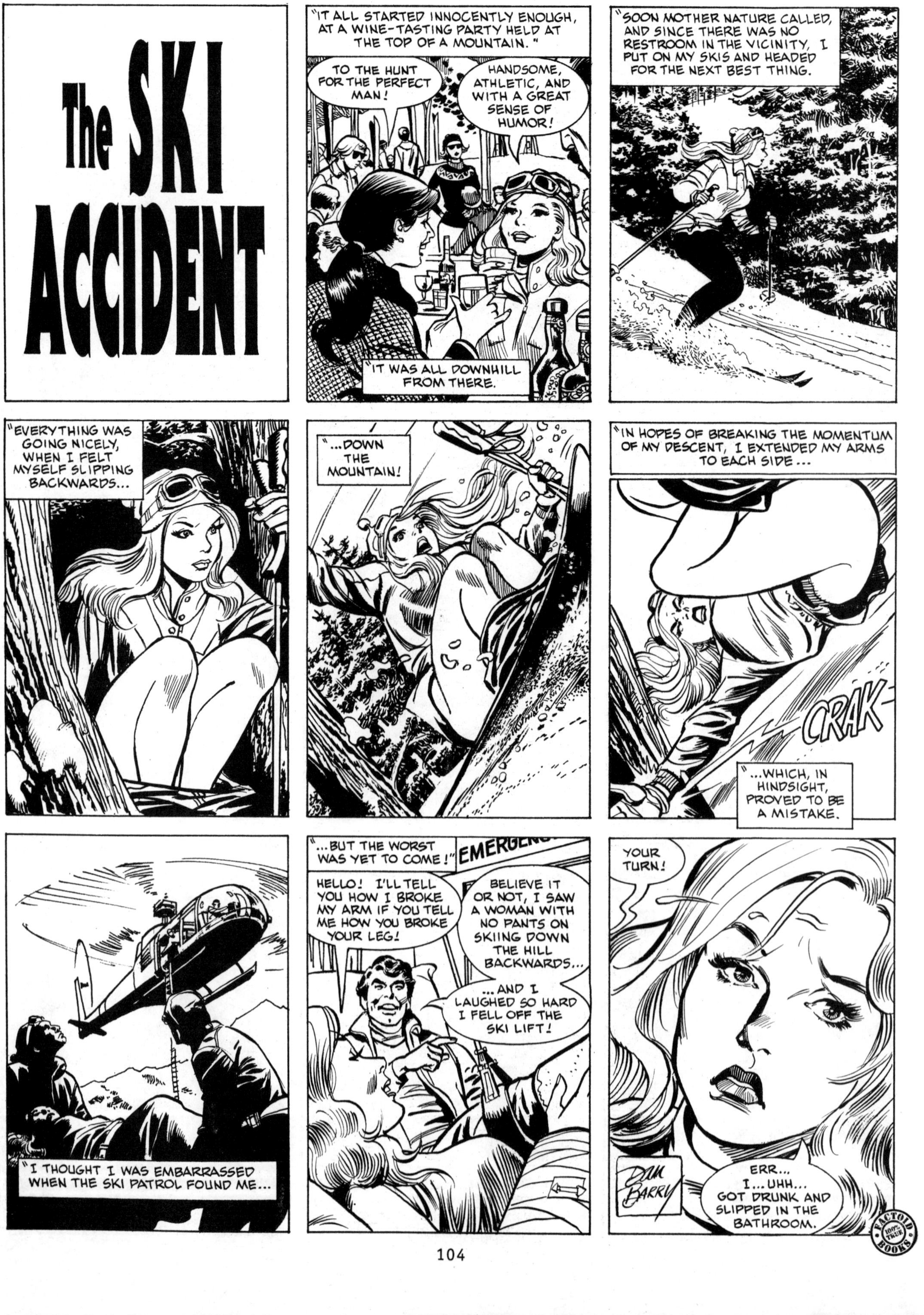
The SKI ACCIDENT
"IT ALL STARTED INNOCENTLY ENOUGH, AT A WINE-TASTING PARTY HELD AT THE TOP OF A MOUNTAIN."
TO THE HUNT FOR THE PERFECT MAN!
HANDSOME, ATHLETIC, AND WITH A GREAT SENSE OF HUMOR!
"IT WAS ALL DOWNHILL FROM THERE.
"SOON MOTHER NATURE CALLED, AND SINCE THERE WAS NO RESTROOM IN THE VICINITY, I PUT ON MY SKIS AND HEADED FOR THE NEXT BEST THING.
"EVERYTHING WAS GOING NICELY, WHEN I FELT MYSELF SLIPPING BACKWARDS...
"...DOWN THE MOUNTAIN!
"IN HOPES OF BREAKING THE MOMENTUM OF MY DESCENT, I EXTENDED MY ARMS TO EACH SIDE...
CRAK
"...WHICH, IN HINDSIGHT, PROVED TO BE A MISTAKE.
"I THOUGHT I WAS EMBARRASSED WHEN THE SKI PATROL FOUND ME...
"...BUT THE WORST WAS YET TO COME!"
HELLO! I'LL TELL YOU HOW I BROKE MY ARM IF YOU TELL ME HOW YOU BROKE YOUR LEG!
BELIEVE IT OR NOT, I SAW A WOMAN WITH NO PANTS ON SKIING DOWN THE HILL BACKWARDS...
...AND I LAUGHED SO HARD I FELL OFF THE SKI LIFT!
YOUR TURN!
ERR... I...UHH... GOT DRUNK AND SLIPPED IN THE BATHROOM.
DAN BARRY
FACTOID BOOKS 100% TRUE

THE HEEL IN THE GRATE
MY SHOE IS CAUGHT IN SOMETHING!
LEAVE IT BEHIND.
THE BRIDESMAID LOST HER SHOE!
IT'S STUCK!
BETTER TAKE THE WHOLE THING OR SOMEONE ELSE IN THE WEDDING PARTY MIGHT TRIP OVER IT!
?!
WHUD!
LATER...
YOU MAY KISS THE BRIDE.
SMEK!

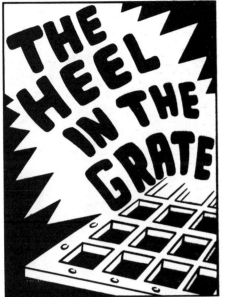

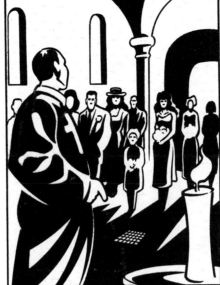

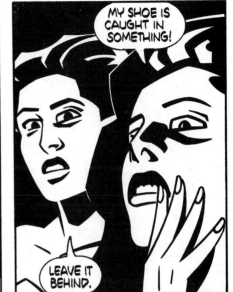

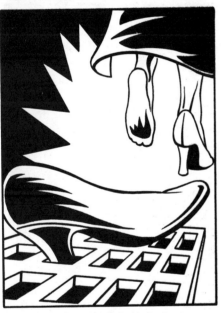

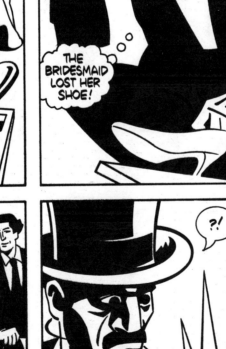

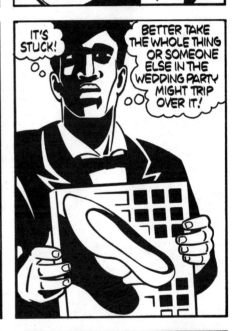

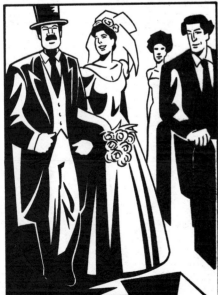

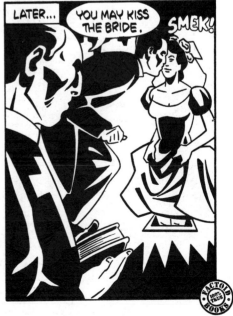

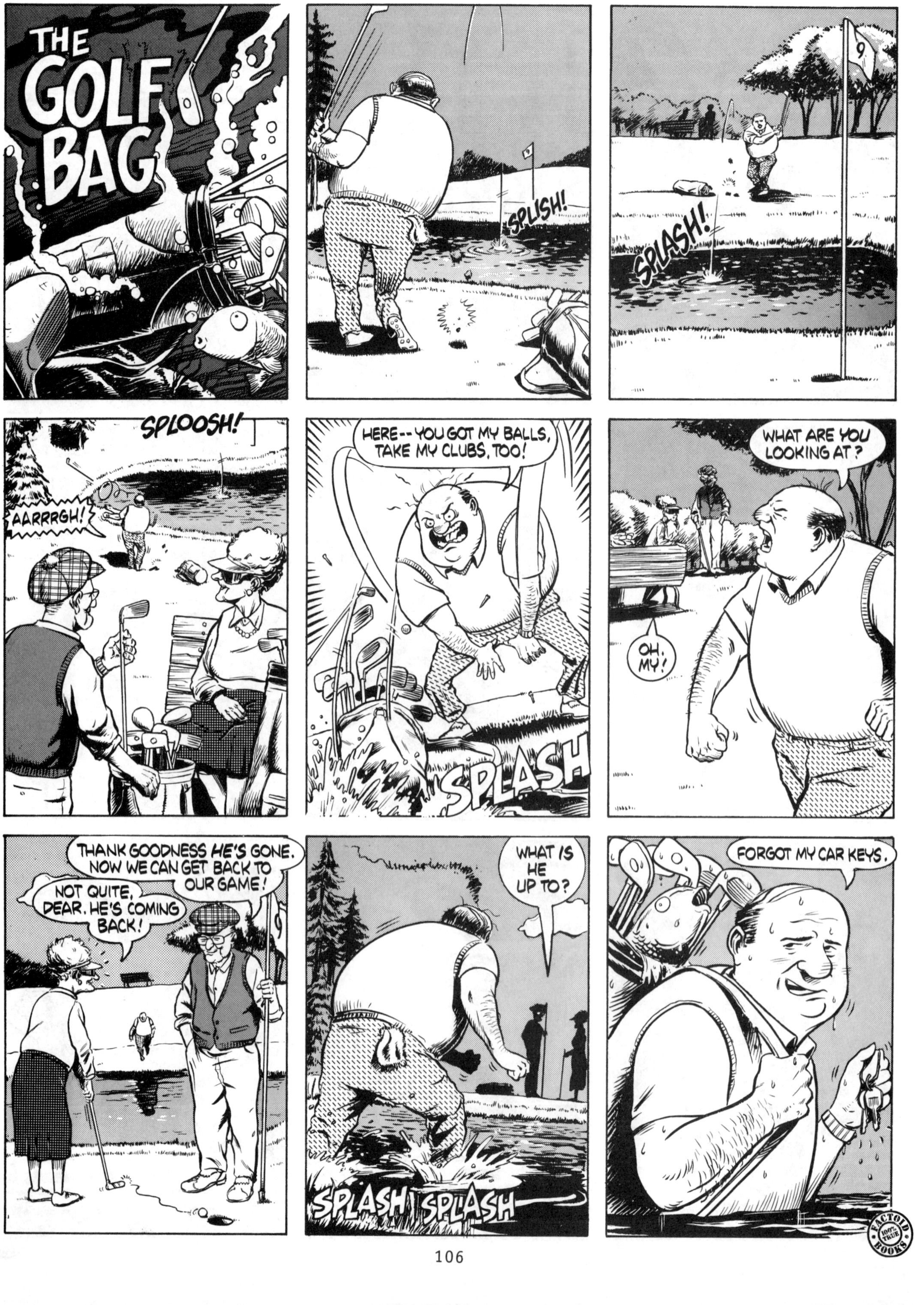
THE GOLF BAG
SPLISH!
SPLASH!
SPLOOSH!
AARRRGH!
HERE-- YOU GOT MY BALLS, TAKE MY CLUBS, TOO!
SPLASH
WHAT ARE YOU LOOKING AT?
OH, MY!
THANK GOODNESS HE'S GONE. NOW WE CAN GET BACK TO OUR GAME!
NOT QUITE, DEAR. HE'S COMING BACK!
WHAT IS HE UP TO?
SPLASH SPLASH
FORGOT MY CAR KEYS.
FACTOID BOOKS 100% TRUE

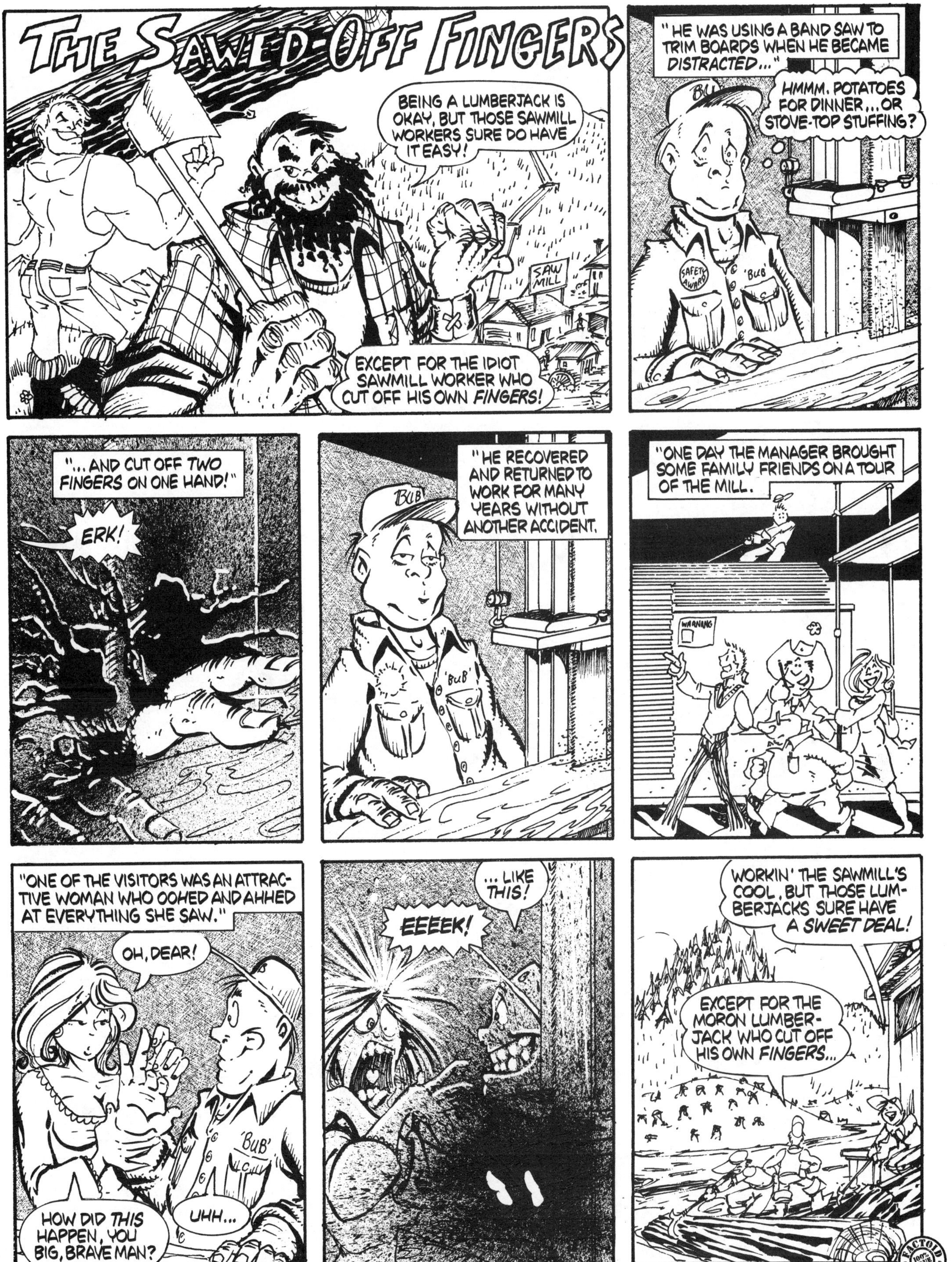
THE SAWED-OFF FINGERS
BEING A LUMBERJACK IS OKAY, BUT THOSE SAWMILL WORKERS SURE DO HAVE IT EASY!
SAW MILL
EXCEPT FOR THE IDIOT SAWMILL WORKER WHO CUT OFF HIS OWN FINGERS!
"HE WAS USING A BAND SAW TO TRIM BOARDS WHEN HE BECAME DISTRACTED..."
HMMM. POTATOES FOR DINNER, ...OR STOVE-TOP STUFFING?
'BUB
"...AND CUT OFF TWO FINGERS ON ONE HAND!"
ERK!
"HE RECOVERED AND RETURNED TO WORK FOR MANY YEARS WITHOUT ANOTHER ACCIDENT.
BUB
'BUB'
"ONE DAY THE MANAGER BROUGHT SOME FAMILY FRIENDS ON A TOUR OF THE MILL.
WARNING
"ONE OF THE VISITORS WAS AN ATTRACTIVE WOMAN WHO OOHED AND AHHED AT EVERYTHING SHE SAW."
OH, DEAR!
'BUB'
HOW DID THIS HAPPEN, YOU BIG, BRAVE MAN?
UHH...
...LIKE THIS!
EEEEK!
WORKIN' THE SAWMILL'S COOL, BUT THOSE LUMBERJACKS SURE HAVE A SWEET DEAL!
EXCEPT FOR THE MORON LUMBERJACK WHO CUT OFF HIS OWN FINGERS...
FACTOID BOOKS 100% TRUE

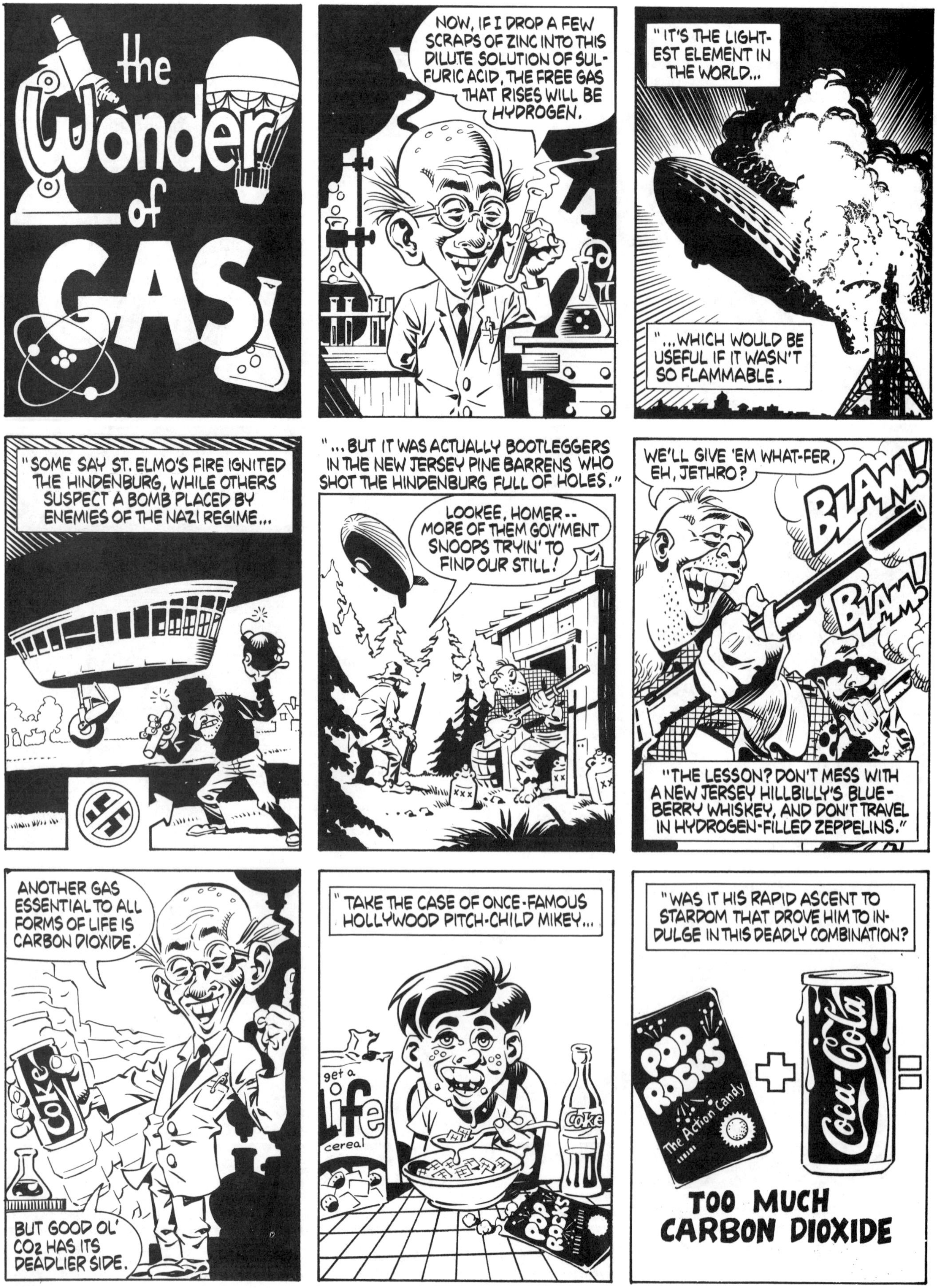
the Wonder of GAS
NOW, IF I DROP A FEW SCRAPS OF ZINC INTO THIS DILUTE SOLUTION OF SULFURIC ACID, THE FREE GAS THAT RISES WILL BE HYDROGEN.
"IT'S THE LIGHTEST ELEMENT IN THE WORLD...
"...WHICH WOULD BE USEFUL IF IT WASN'T SO FLAMMABLE.
"SOME SAY ST. ELMO'S FIRE IGNITED THE HINDENBURG, WHILE OTHERS SUSPECT A BOMB PLACED BY ENEMIES OF THE NAZI REGIME...
"...BUT IT WAS ACTUALLY BOOTLEGGERS IN THE NEW JERSEY PINE BARRENS WHO SHOT THE HINDENBURG FULL OF HOLES."
LOOKEE, HOMER -- MORE OF THEM GOV'MENT SNOOPS TRYIN' TO FIND OUR STILL!
XXX
WE'LL GIVE 'EM WHAT-FER, EH, JETHRO?
BLAM!
BLAM!
"THE LESSON? DON'T MESS WITH A NEW JERSEY HILLBILLY'S BLUEBERRY WHISKEY, AND DON'T TRAVEL IN HYDROGEN-FILLED ZEPPELINS."
ANOTHER GAS ESSENTIAL TO ALL FORMS OF LIFE IS CARBON DIOXIDE.
Coke
BUT GOOD OL' CO_2 HAS ITS DEADLIER SIDE.
"TAKE THE CASE OF ONCE-FAMOUS HOLLYWOOD PITCH-CHILD MIKEY...
get a life cereal
Coke
POP ROCKS
"WAS IT HIS RAPID ASCENT TO STARDOM THAT DROVE HIM TO INDULGE IN THIS DEADLY COMBINATION?
POP ROCKS The Action Candy
Coca-Cola
TOO MUCH CARBON DIOXIDE

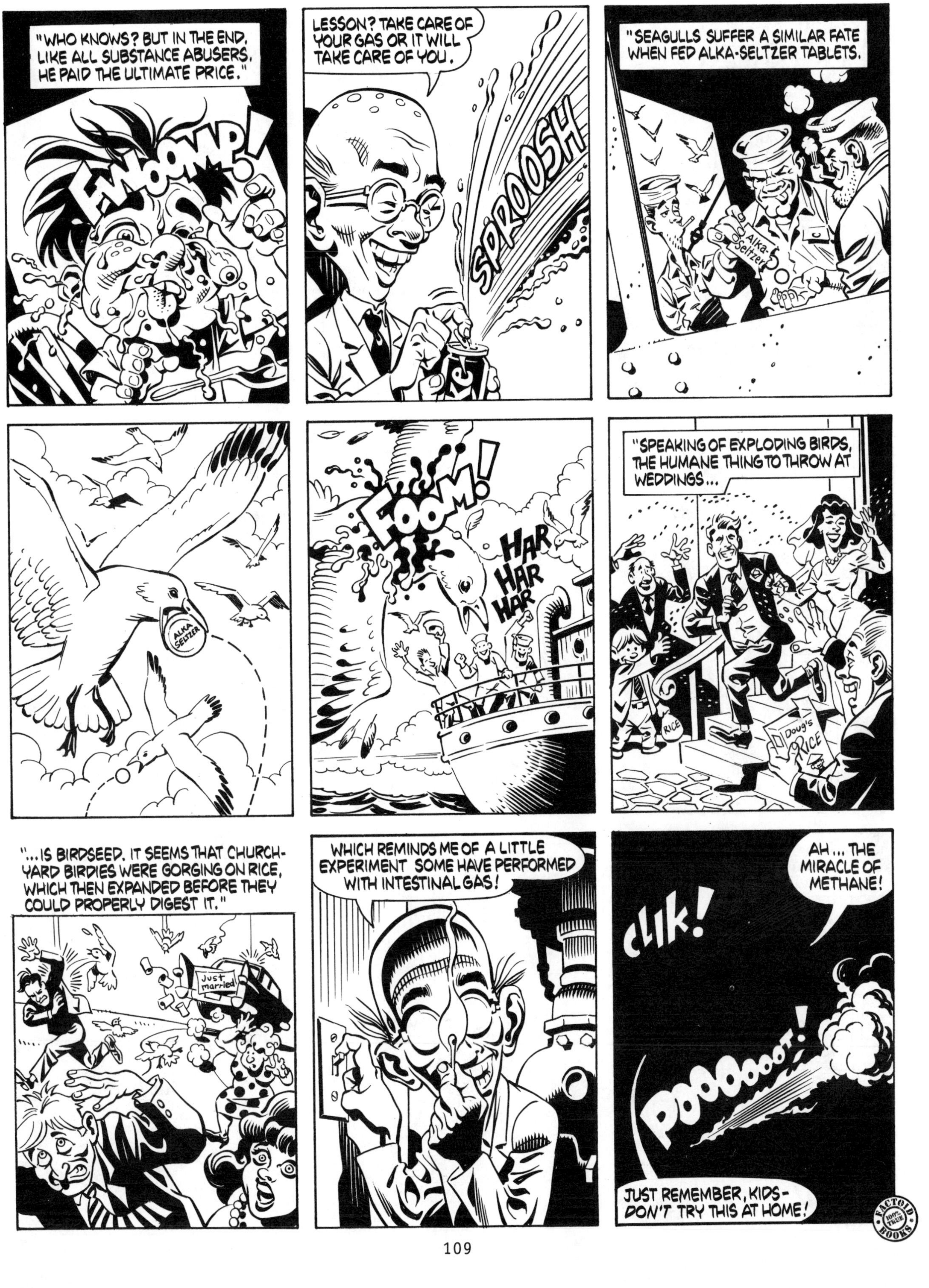
"WHO KNOWS? BUT IN THE END, LIKE ALL SUBSTANCE ABUSERS, HE PAID THE ULTIMATE PRICE."
FWOOMP!
LESSON? TAKE CARE OF YOUR GAS OR IT WILL TAKE CARE OF YOU.
SPROOSH
"SEAGULLS SUFFER A SIMILAR FATE WHEN FED ALKA-SELTZER TABLETS.
Alka-Seltzer
ALKA SELTZER
FOOM!
HAR HAR HAR
"SPEAKING OF EXPLODING BIRDS, THE HUMANE THING TO THROW AT WEDDINGS...
RICE
Doug's RICE
"...IS BIRDSEED. IT SEEMS THAT CHURCH-YARD BIRDIES WERE GORGING ON RICE, WHICH THEN EXPANDED BEFORE THEY COULD PROPERLY DIGEST IT."
Just married
WHICH REMINDS ME OF A LITTLE EXPERIMENT SOME HAVE PERFORMED WITH INTESTINAL GAS!
AH... THE MIRACLE OF METHANE!
CLIK!
POOOoooT!
JUST REMEMBER, KIDS-DON'T TRY THIS AT HOME!
FACTOID 100% TRUE BOOKS

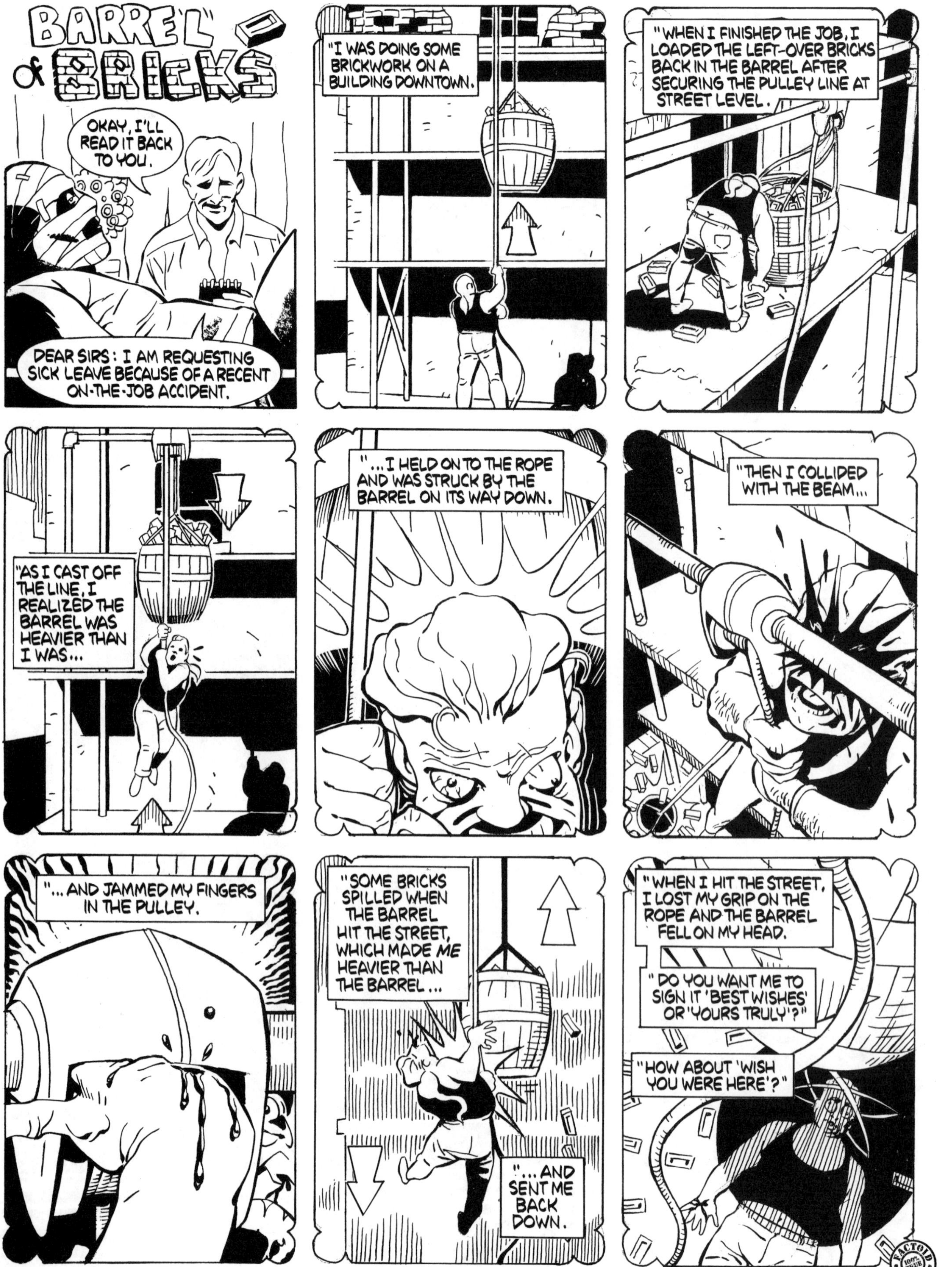
BARREL OF BRICKS
OKAY, I'LL READ IT BACK TO YOU.
DEAR SIRS: I AM REQUESTING SICK LEAVE BECAUSE OF A RECENT ON-THE-JOB ACCIDENT.
"I WAS DOING SOME BRICKWORK ON A BUILDING DOWNTOWN.
"WHEN I FINISHED THE JOB, I LOADED THE LEFT-OVER BRICKS BACK IN THE BARREL AFTER SECURING THE PULLEY LINE AT STREET LEVEL.
"AS I CAST OFF THE LINE, I REALIZED THE BARREL WAS HEAVIER THAN I WAS...
"...I HELD ON TO THE ROPE AND WAS STRUCK BY THE BARREL ON ITS WAY DOWN.
"THEN I COLLIDED WITH THE BEAM...
"...AND JAMMED MY FINGERS IN THE PULLEY.
"SOME BRICKS SPILLED WHEN THE BARREL HIT THE STREET, WHICH MADE ME HEAVIER THAN THE BARREL...
"...AND SENT ME BACK DOWN.
"WHEN I HIT THE STREET, I LOST MY GRIP ON THE ROPE AND THE BARREL FELL ON MY HEAD.
" DO YOU WANT ME TO SIGN IT 'BEST WISHES' OR 'YOURS TRULY'?"
"HOW ABOUT 'WISH YOU WERE HERE'?"
FACTOID BOOKS 100% TRUE

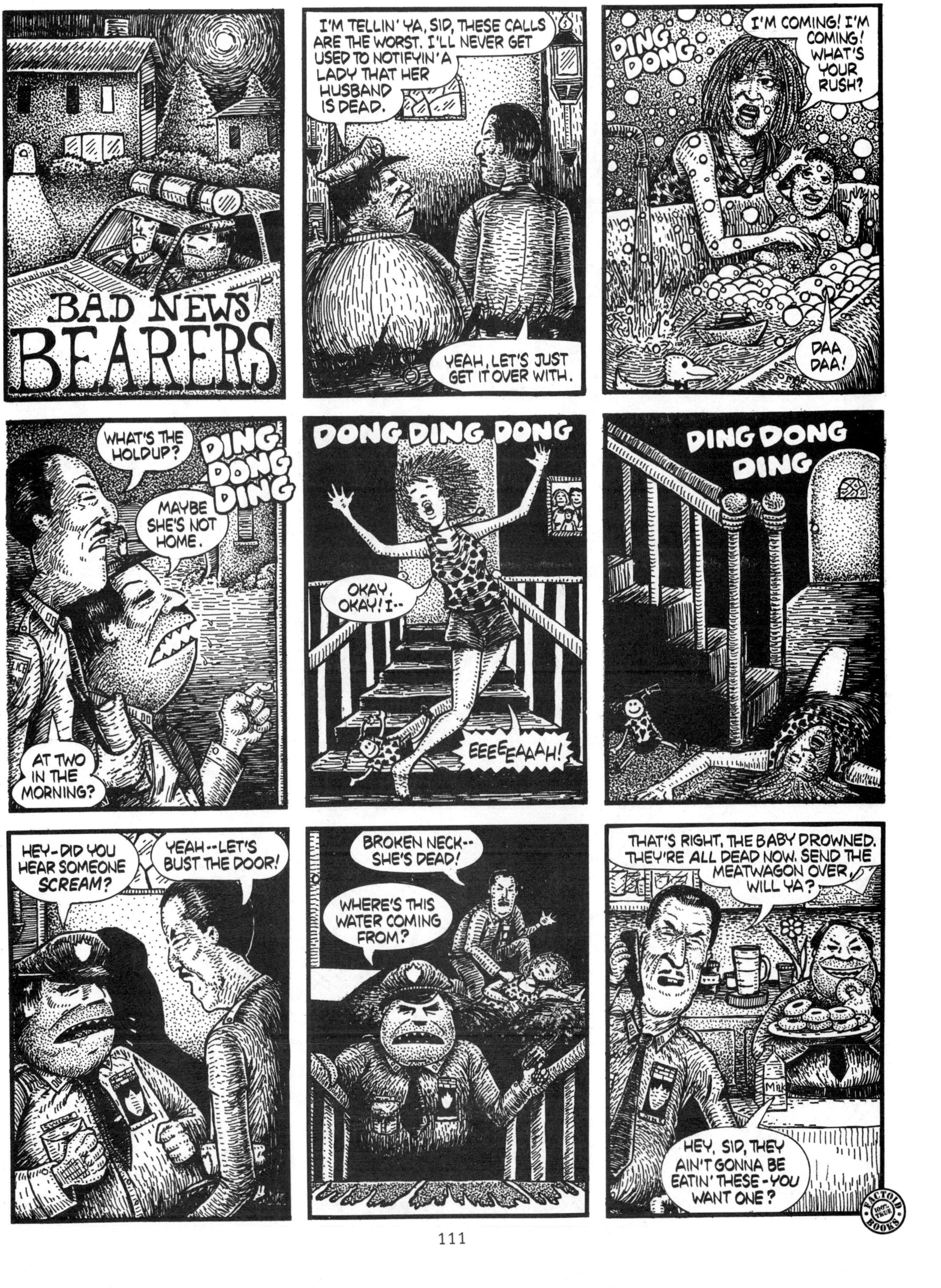
BAD NEWS BEARERS
I'M TELLIN' YA, SID, THESE CALLS ARE THE WORST. I'LL NEVER GET USED TO NOTIFYIN' A LADY THAT HER HUSBAND IS DEAD.
YEAH, LET'S JUST GET IT OVER WITH.
DING DONG
I'M COMING! I'M COMING! WHAT'S YOUR RUSH?
DAA DAA!
WHAT'S THE HOLDUP?
DING DONG DING
MAYBE SHE'S NOT HOME.
AT TWO IN THE MORNING?
DONG DING DONG
OKAY, OKAY! I--
EEEEEAAAH!
DING DONG DING
HEY- DID YOU HEAR SOMEONE SCREAM?
YEAH --LET'S BUST THE DOOR!
BROKEN NECK-- SHE'S DEAD!
WHERE'S THIS WATER COMING FROM?
THAT'S RIGHT, THE BABY DROWNED. THEY'RE ALL DEAD NOW. SEND THE MEATWAGON OVER, WILL YA?
HEY, SID, THEY AIN'T GONNA BE EATIN' THESE - YOU WANT ONE?
FACTOID 100% TRUE BOOKS

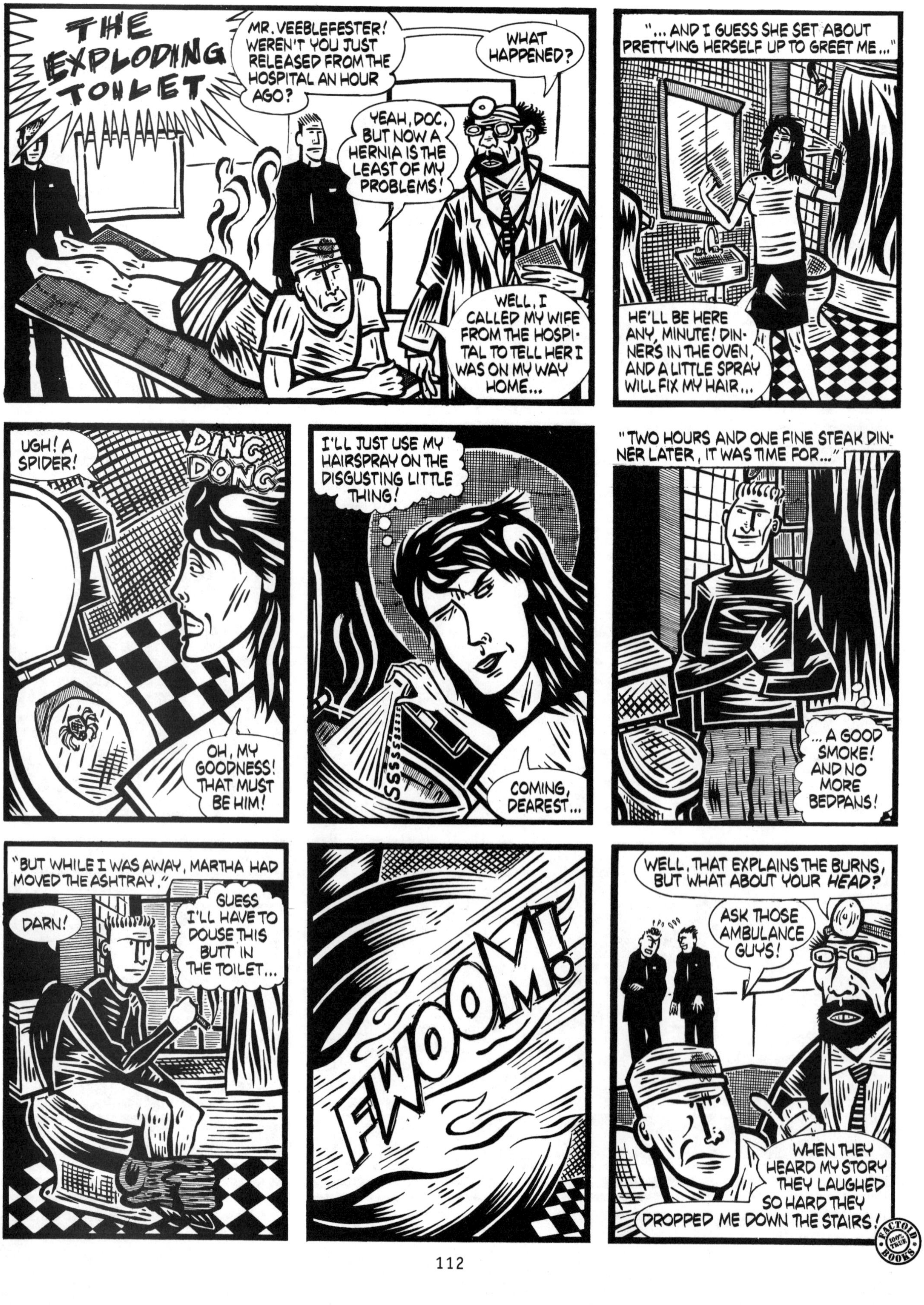
THE EXPLODING TOILET
AAAAAAAAAAH
MR. VEEBLEFESTER! WEREN'T YOU JUST RELEASED FROM THE HOSPITAL AN HOUR AGO?
WHAT HAPPENED?
YEAH, DOC, BUT NOW A HERNIA IS THE LEAST OF MY PROBLEMS!
WELL, I CALLED MY WIFE FROM THE HOSPITAL TO TELL HER I WAS ON MY WAY HOME...
"... AND I GUESS SHE SET ABOUT PRETTYING HERSELF UP TO GREET ME..."
HE'LL BE HERE ANY, MINUTE! DINNER'S IN THE OVEN, AND A LITTLE SPRAY WILL FIX MY HAIR...
UGH! A SPIDER!
DING DONG
OH, MY GOODNESS! THAT MUST BE HIM!
I'LL JUST USE MY HAIRSPRAY ON THE DISGUSTING LITTLE THING!
SSSSSSSSS
COMING, DEAREST...
"TWO HOURS AND ONE FINE STEAK DINNER LATER, IT WAS TIME FOR..."
...A GOOD SMOKE! AND NO MORE BEDPANS!
"BUT WHILE I WAS AWAY, MARTHA HAD MOVED THE ASHTRAY."
DARN!
GUESS I'LL HAVE TO DOUSE THIS BUTT IN THE TOILET...
FWOOM!
WELL, THAT EXPLAINS THE BURNS, BUT WHAT ABOUT YOUR HEAD?
ASK THOSE AMBULANCE GUYS!
WHEN THEY HEARD MY STORY THEY LAUGHED SO HARD THEY DROPPED ME DOWN THE STAIRS!
FACTOID 100% TRUE BOOKS

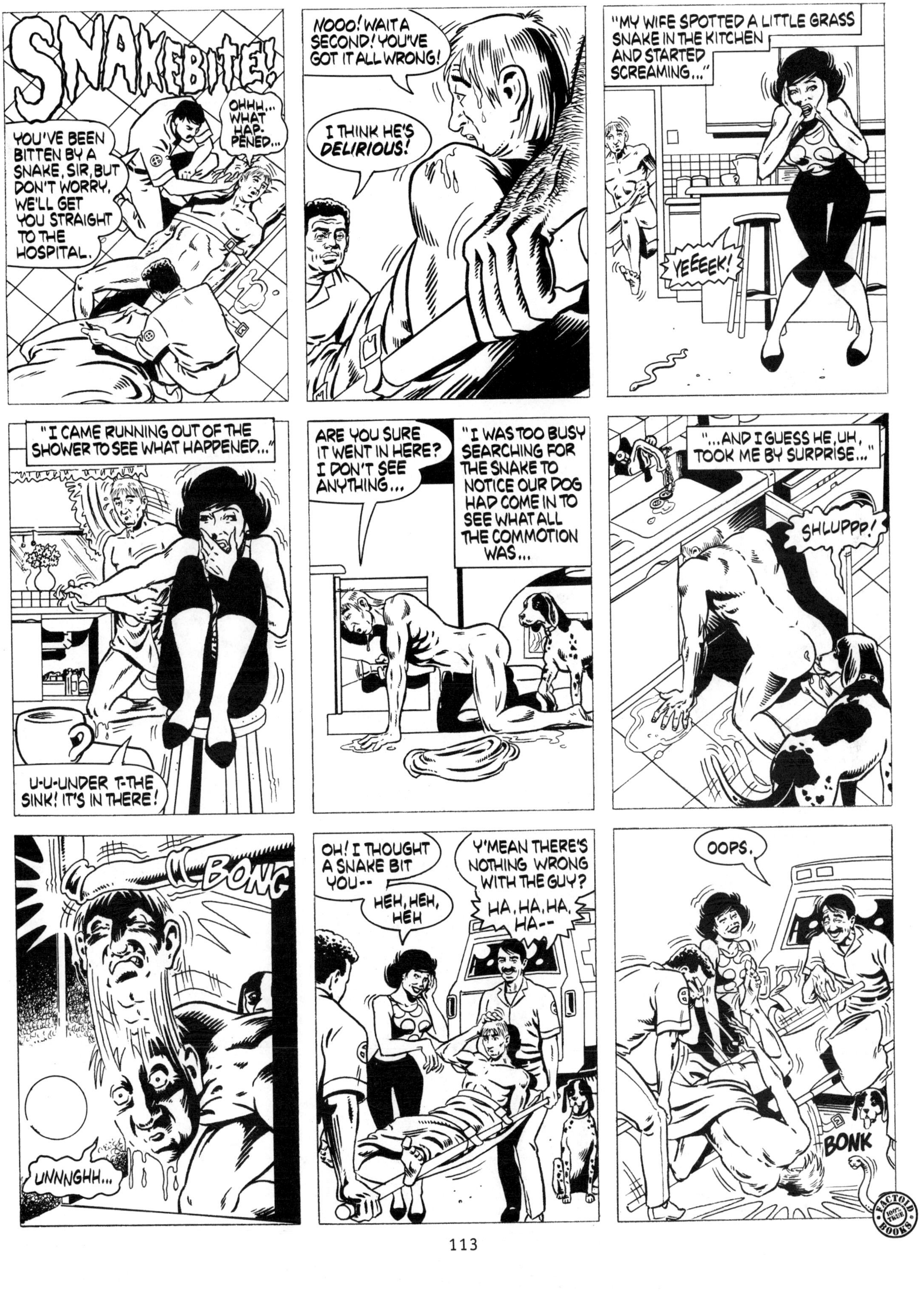
SNAKEBITE!
OHHH... WHAT HAP-PENED...
YOU'VE BEEN BITTEN BY A SNAKE, SIR, BUT DON'T WORRY, WE'LL GET YOU STRAIGHT TO THE HOSPITAL.
NOOO! WAIT A SECOND! YOU'VE GOT IT ALL WRONG!
I THINK HE'S DELIRIOUS!
"MY WIFE SPOTTED A LITTLE GRASS SNAKE IN THE KITCHEN AND STARTED SCREAMING..."
YEEEEK!
"I CAME RUNNING OUT OF THE SHOWER TO SEE WHAT HAPPENED..."
U-U-UNDER T-THE SINK! IT'S IN THERE!
ARE YOU SURE IT WENT IN HERE? I DON'T SEE ANYTHING...
"I WAS TOO BUSY SEARCHING FOR THE SNAKE TO NOTICE OUR DOG HAD COME IN TO SEE WHAT ALL THE COMMOTION WAS...
"...AND I GUESS HE, UH, TOOK ME BY SURPRISE..."
SHLUPPP!
BONG
UNNNGHH...
OH! I THOUGHT A SNAKE BIT YOU--
HEH, HEH, HEH
Y'MEAN THERE'S NOTHING WRONG WITH THE GUY?
HA, HA, HA, HA--
OOPS.
BONK
FACTOID BOOKS 100% TRUE

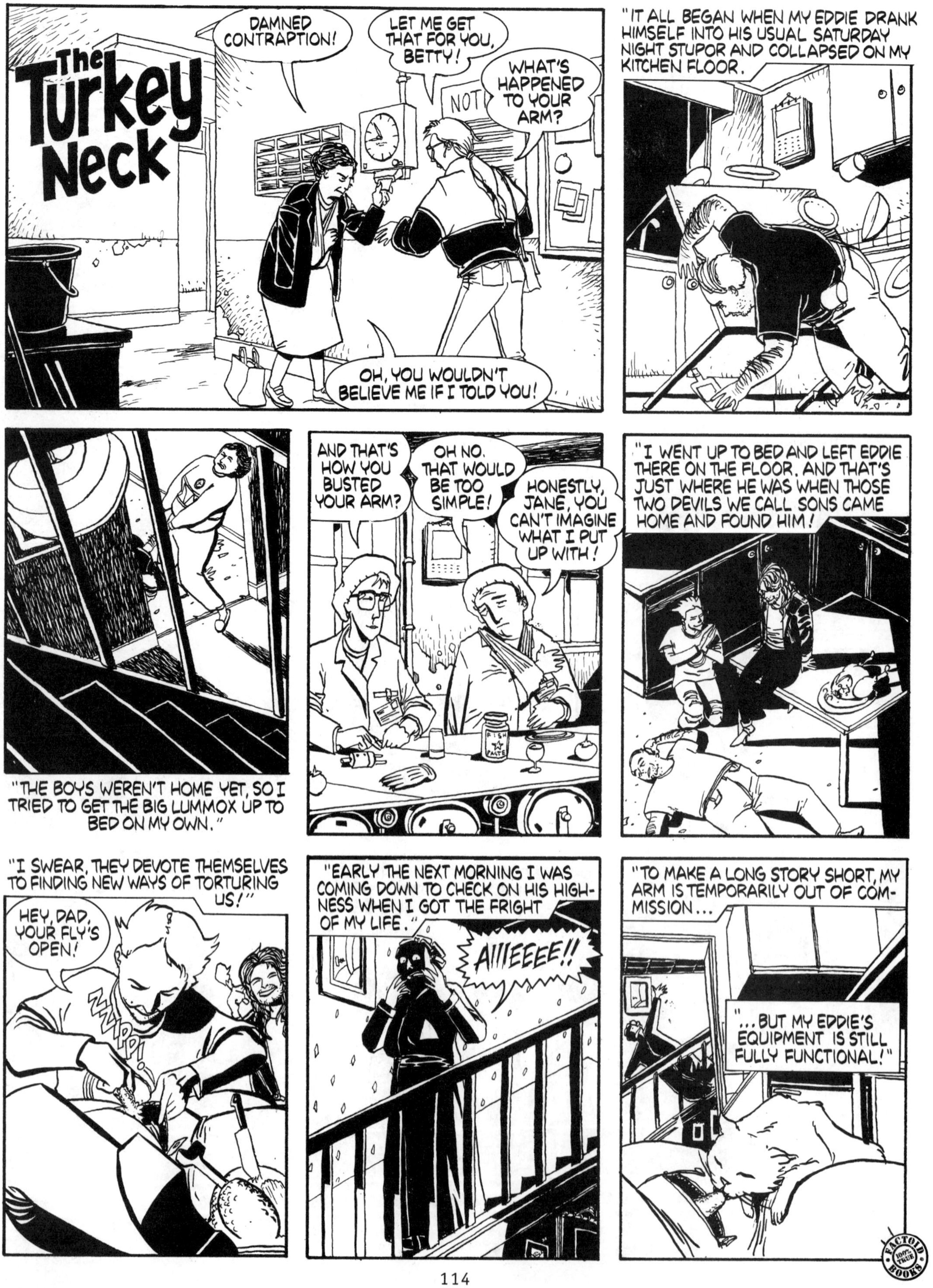
The Turkey Neck
DAMNED CONTRAPTION!
LET ME GET THAT FOR YOU, BETTY!
WHAT'S HAPPENED TO YOUR ARM?
OH, YOU WOULDN'T BELIEVE ME IF I TOLD YOU!
"IT ALL BEGAN WHEN MY EDDIE DRANK HIMSELF INTO HIS USUAL SATURDAY NIGHT STUPOR AND COLLAPSED ON MY KITCHEN FLOOR.
"THE BOYS WEREN'T HOME YET, SO I TRIED TO GET THE BIG LUMMOX UP TO BED ON MY OWN."
AND THAT'S HOW YOU BUSTED YOUR ARM?
OH NO. THAT WOULD BE TOO SIMPLE!
HONESTLY, JANE, YOU CAN'T IMAGINE WHAT I PUT UP WITH!
FISH PASTE
"I WENT UP TO BED AND LEFT EDDIE THERE ON THE FLOOR. AND THAT'S JUST WHERE HE WAS WHEN THOSE TWO DEVILS WE CALL SONS CAME HOME AND FOUND HIM!
"I SWEAR, THEY DEVOTE THEMSELVES TO FINDING NEW WAYS OF TORTURING US!"
HEY, DAD, YOUR FLY'S OPEN!
ZZZIPP!
"EARLY THE NEXT MORNING I WAS COMING DOWN TO CHECK ON HIS HIGH-NESS WHEN I GOT THE FRIGHT OF MY LIFE."
AIIIEEEE!!
"TO MAKE A LONG STORY SHORT, MY ARM IS TEMPORARILY OUT OF COM-MISSION...
"...BUT MY EDDIE'S EQUIPMENT IS STILL FULLY FUNCTIONAL!"
FACTOID BOOKS 100% TRUE

CHAPTER FIVE

SEX AND SCANDAL LEGENDS

CAUGHT IN THE ACT

In her May 1, 1994 column, Ann Landers published a letter from a reader in Van Nuys, California, who claimed that "The Blind Date" *(page 121)* incident had really happened to him. When I wrote to Ann and explained how old and widespread — not to mention *outdated* — the story is, she replied that dozens of readers had told her the same thing, and she signed herself "Red-Faced in Chicago." She ought to be embarrassed, since her column reprints "The Nude Housewife" *(page 139)* as a true tale about once a year. But who can blame her? These are great stories of sex and scandal, as long as they happen to a FOAF and not to ourselves.

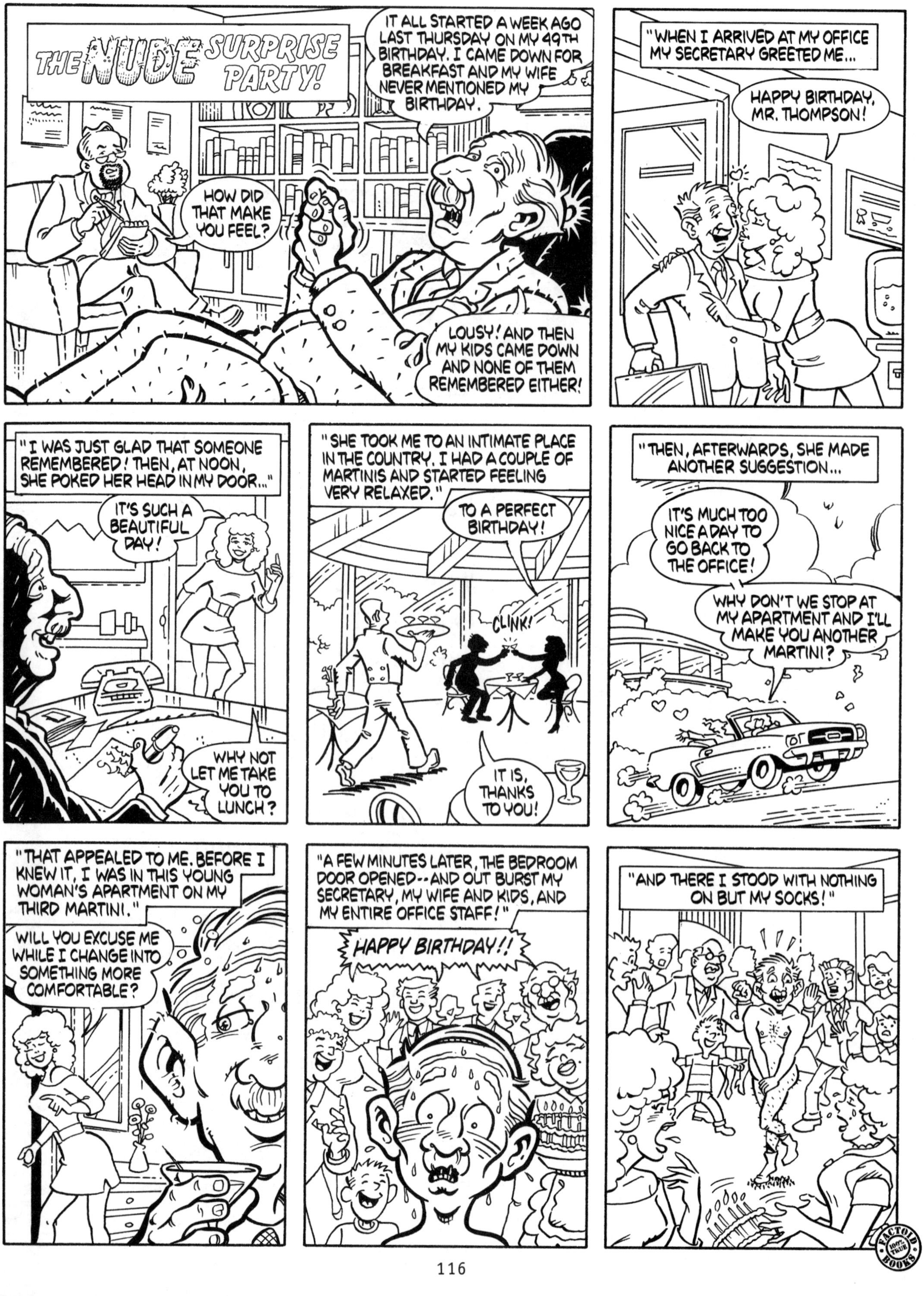
THE NUDE SURPRISE PARTY!
IT ALL STARTED A WEEK AGO LAST THURSDAY ON MY 49TH BIRTHDAY. I CAME DOWN FOR BREAKFAST AND MY WIFE NEVER MENTIONED MY BIRTHDAY.
HOW DID THAT MAKE YOU FEEL?
LOUSY! AND THEN MY KIDS CAME DOWN AND NONE OF THEM REMEMBERED EITHER!
"WHEN I ARRIVED AT MY OFFICE MY SECRETARY GREETED ME...
HAPPY BIRTHDAY, MR. THOMPSON!
"I WAS JUST GLAD THAT SOMEONE REMEMBERED! THEN, AT NOON, SHE POKED HER HEAD IN MY DOOR..."
IT'S SUCH A BEAUTIFUL DAY!
WHY NOT LET ME TAKE YOU TO LUNCH?
"SHE TOOK ME TO AN INTIMATE PLACE IN THE COUNTRY. I HAD A COUPLE OF MARTINIS AND STARTED FEELING VERY RELAXED."
TO A PERFECT BIRTHDAY!
CLINK!
IT IS, THANKS TO YOU!
"THEN, AFTERWARDS, SHE MADE ANOTHER SUGGESTION...
IT'S MUCH TOO NICE A DAY TO GO BACK TO THE OFFICE!
WHY DON'T WE STOP AT MY APARTMENT AND I'LL MAKE YOU ANOTHER MARTINI?
"THAT APPEALED TO ME. BEFORE I KNEW IT, I WAS IN THIS YOUNG WOMAN'S APARTMENT ON MY THIRD MARTINI."
WILL YOU EXCUSE ME WHILE I CHANGE INTO SOMETHING MORE COMFORTABLE?
"A FEW MINUTES LATER, THE BEDROOM DOOR OPENED--AND OUT BURST MY SECRETARY, MY WIFE AND KIDS, AND MY ENTIRE OFFICE STAFF!"
HAPPY BIRTHDAY!!
"AND THERE I STOOD WITH NOTHING ON BUT MY SOCKS!"
FACTOID BOOKS 100% TRUE

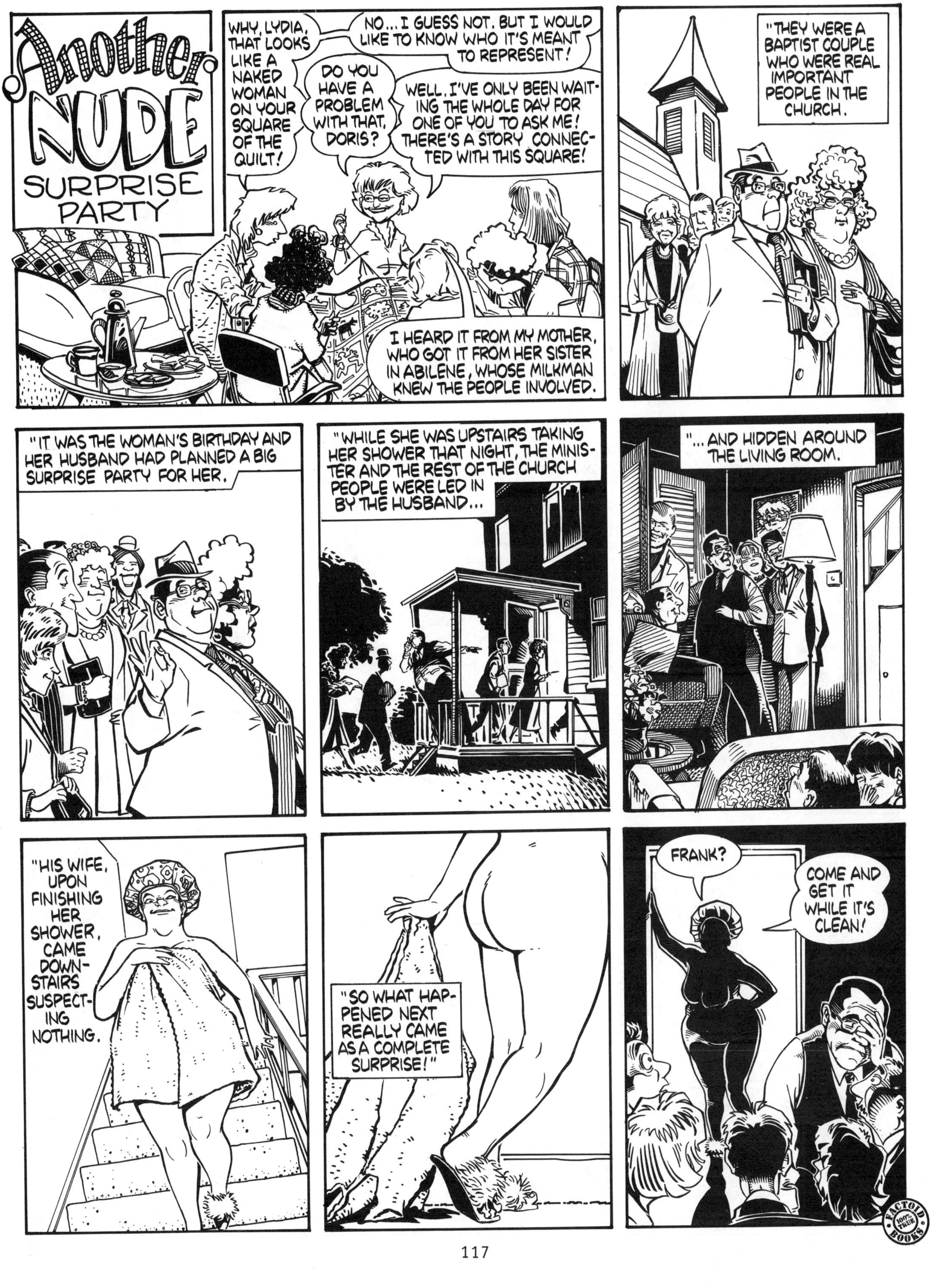
Another NUDE SURPRISE PARTY
WHY, LYDIA, THAT LOOKS LIKE A NAKED WOMAN ON YOUR SQUARE OF THE QUILT!
NO... I GUESS NOT. BUT I WOULD LIKE TO KNOW WHO IT'S MEANT TO REPRESENT!
DO YOU HAVE A PROBLEM WITH THAT, DORIS?
WELL, I'VE ONLY BEEN WAITING THE WHOLE DAY FOR ONE OF YOU TO ASK ME! THERE'S A STORY CONNECTED WITH THIS SQUARE!
I HEARD IT FROM MY MOTHER, WHO GOT IT FROM HER SISTER IN ABILENE, WHOSE MILKMAN KNEW THE PEOPLE INVOLVED.
"THEY WERE A BAPTIST COUPLE WHO WERE REAL IMPORTANT PEOPLE IN THE CHURCH.
"IT WAS THE WOMAN'S BIRTHDAY AND HER HUSBAND HAD PLANNED A BIG SURPRISE PARTY FOR HER.
"WHILE SHE WAS UPSTAIRS TAKING HER SHOWER THAT NIGHT, THE MINISTER AND THE REST OF THE CHURCH PEOPLE WERE LED IN BY THE HUSBAND...
"...AND HIDDEN AROUND THE LIVING ROOM.
"HIS WIFE, UPON FINISHING HER SHOWER, CAME DOWNSTAIRS SUSPECTING NOTHING.
"SO WHAT HAPPENED NEXT REALLY CAME AS A COMPLETE SURPRISE!"
FRANK?
COME AND GET IT WHILE IT'S CLEAN!
FACTOID BOOKS 100% TRUE

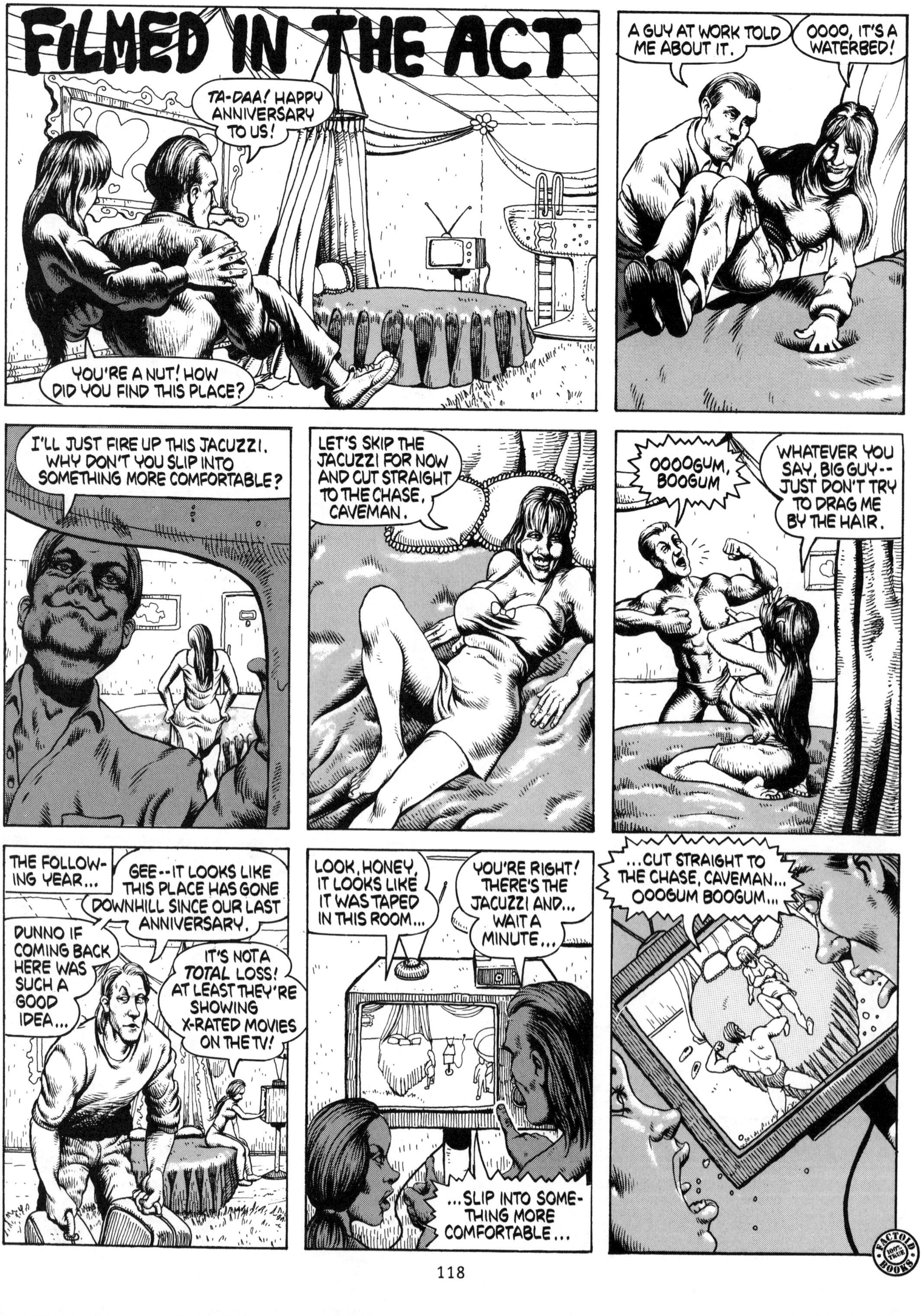
FILMED IN THE ACT
TA-DAA! HAPPY ANNIVERSARY TO US!
YOU'RE A NUT! HOW DID YOU FIND THIS PLACE?
A GUY AT WORK TOLD ME ABOUT IT.
OOOO, IT'S A WATERBED!
I'LL JUST FIRE UP THIS JACUZZI. WHY DON'T YOU SLIP INTO SOMETHING MORE COMFORTABLE?
LET'S SKIP THE JACUZZI FOR NOW AND CUT STRAIGHT TO THE CHASE, CAVEMAN.
OOOOGUM, BOOGUM
WHATEVER YOU SAY, BIG GUY-- JUST DON'T TRY TO DRAG ME BY THE HAIR.
THE FOLLOWING YEAR...
GEE--IT LOOKS LIKE THIS PLACE HAS GONE DOWNHILL SINCE OUR LAST ANNIVERSARY.
DUNNO IF COMING BACK HERE WAS SUCH A GOOD IDEA...
IT'S NOT A TOTAL LOSS! AT LEAST THEY'RE SHOWING X-RATED MOVIES ON THE TV!
LOOK, HONEY, IT LOOKS LIKE IT WAS TAPED IN THIS ROOM...
YOU'RE RIGHT! THERE'S THE JACUZZI AND... WAIT A MINUTE...
...SLIP INTO SOMETHING MORE COMFORTABLE...
...CUT STRAIGHT TO THE CHASE, CAVEMAN... OOOGUM BOOGUM...
FACTOID BOOKS 100% TRUE

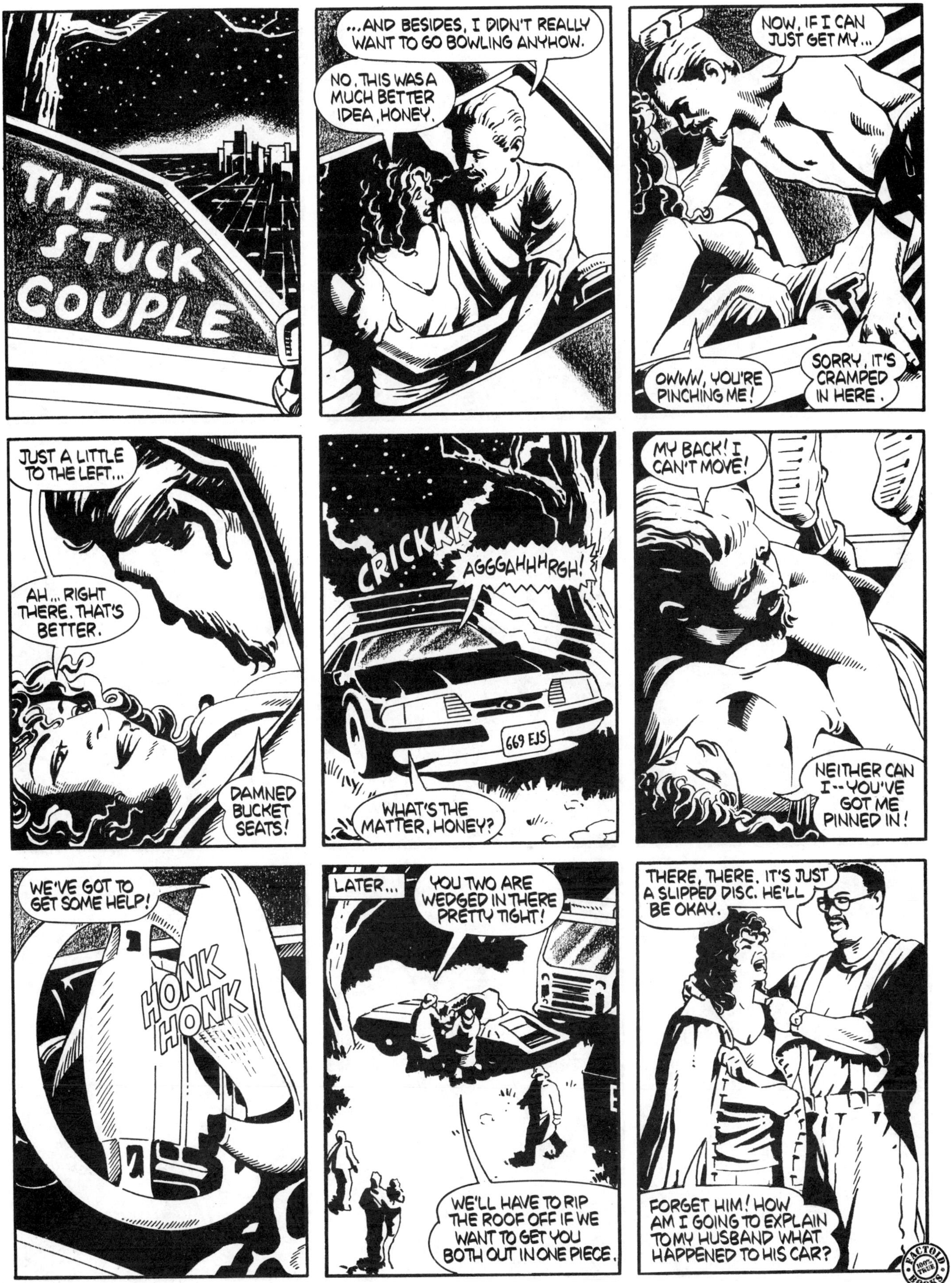
THE STUCK COUPLE
...AND BESIDES, I DIDN'T REALLY WANT TO GO BOWLING ANYHOW.
NO, THIS WAS A MUCH BETTER IDEA, HONEY.
NOW, IF I CAN JUST GET MY...
OWWW, YOU'RE PINCHING ME!
SORRY, IT'S CRAMPED IN HERE.
JUST A LITTLE TO THE LEFT...
AH... RIGHT THERE. THAT'S BETTER.
DAMNED BUCKET SEATS!
CRICKKK
AGGGAHHHRGH!
669 EJS
WHAT'S THE MATTER, HONEY?
MY BACK! I CAN'T MOVE!
NEITHER CAN I--YOU'VE GOT ME PINNED IN!
WE'VE GOT TO GET SOME HELP!
HONK HONK
LATER...
YOU TWO ARE WEDGED IN THERE PRETTY TIGHT!
WE'LL HAVE TO RIP THE ROOF OFF IF WE WANT TO GET YOU BOTH OUT IN ONE PIECE.
THERE, THERE. IT'S JUST A SLIPPED DISC. HE'LL BE OKAY.
FORGET HIM! HOW AM I GOING TO EXPLAIN TO MY HUSBAND WHAT HAPPENED TO HIS CAR?

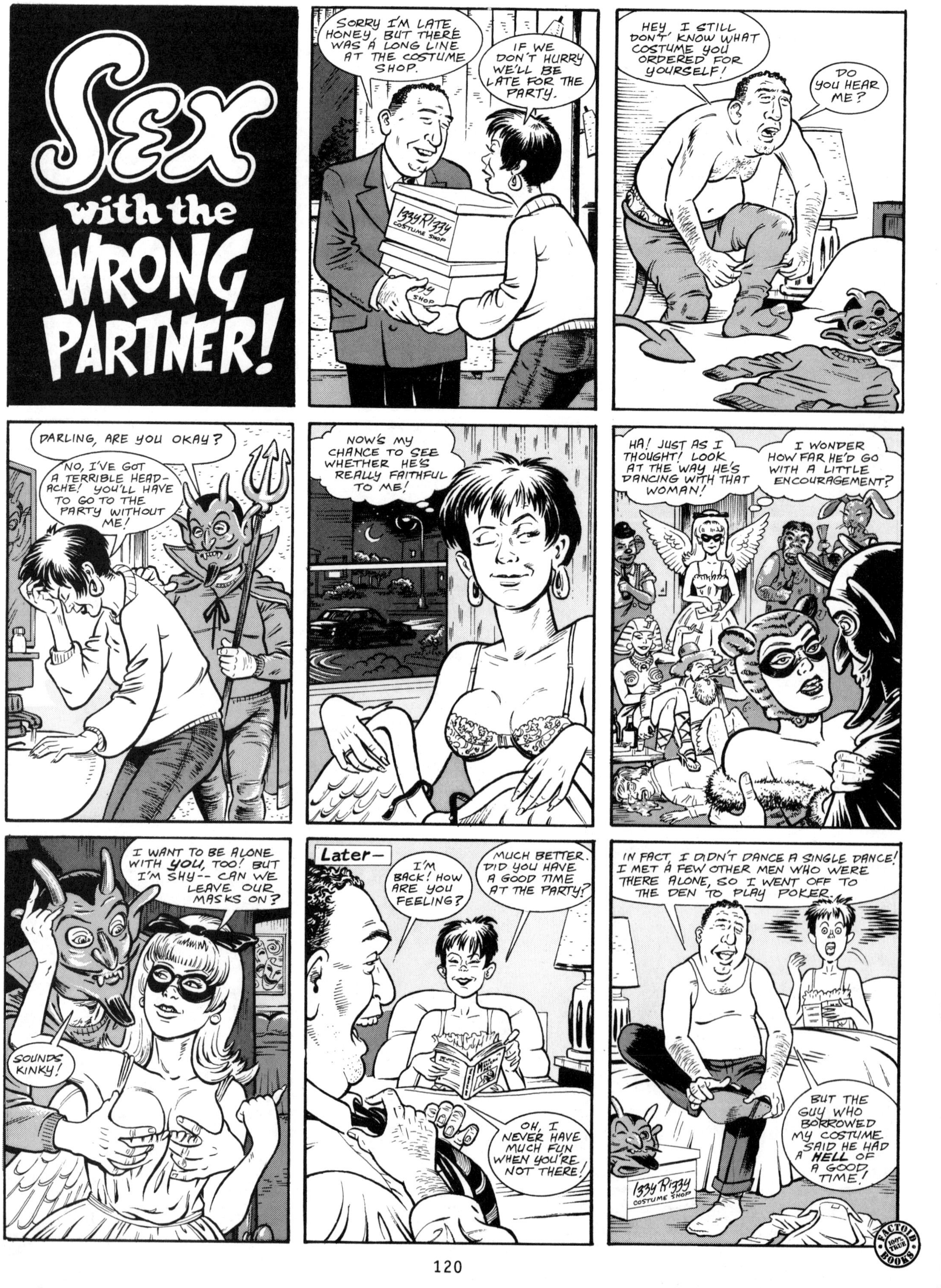
SEX with the WRONG PARTNER!
SORRY I'M LATE HONEY, BUT THERE WAS A LONG LINE AT THE COSTUME SHOP.
IF WE DON'T HURRY WE'LL BE LATE FOR THE PARTY.
IZZY RIZZY COSTUME SHOP
HEY, I STILL DON'T KNOW WHAT COSTUME YOU ORDERED FOR YOURSELF!
DO YOU HEAR ME?
DARLING, ARE YOU OKAY?
NO, I'VE GOT A TERRIBLE HEADACHE! YOU'LL HAVE TO GO TO THE PARTY WITHOUT ME!
NOW'S MY CHANCE TO SEE WHETHER HE'S REALLY FAITHFUL TO ME!
HA! JUST AS I THOUGHT! LOOK AT THE WAY HE'S DANCING WITH THAT WOMAN!
I WONDER HOW FAR HE'D GO WITH A LITTLE ENCOURAGEMENT?
I WANT TO BE ALONE WITH YOU, TOO! BUT I'M SHY-- CAN WE LEAVE OUR MASKS ON?
SOUNDS KINKY!
Later—
I'M BACK! HOW ARE YOU FEELING?
MUCH BETTER. DID YOU HAVE A GOOD TIME AT THE PARTY?
OH, I NEVER HAVE MUCH FUN WHEN YOU'RE NOT THERE!
IN FACT, I DIDN'T DANCE A SINGLE DANCE! I MET A FEW OTHER MEN WHO WERE THERE ALONE, SO I WENT OFF TO THE DEN TO PLAY POKER.
BUT THE GUY WHO BORROWED MY COSTUME SAID HE HAD A HELL OF A GOOD TIME!
IZZY RIZZY COSTUME SHOP
FACTOID BOOKS 100% TRUE

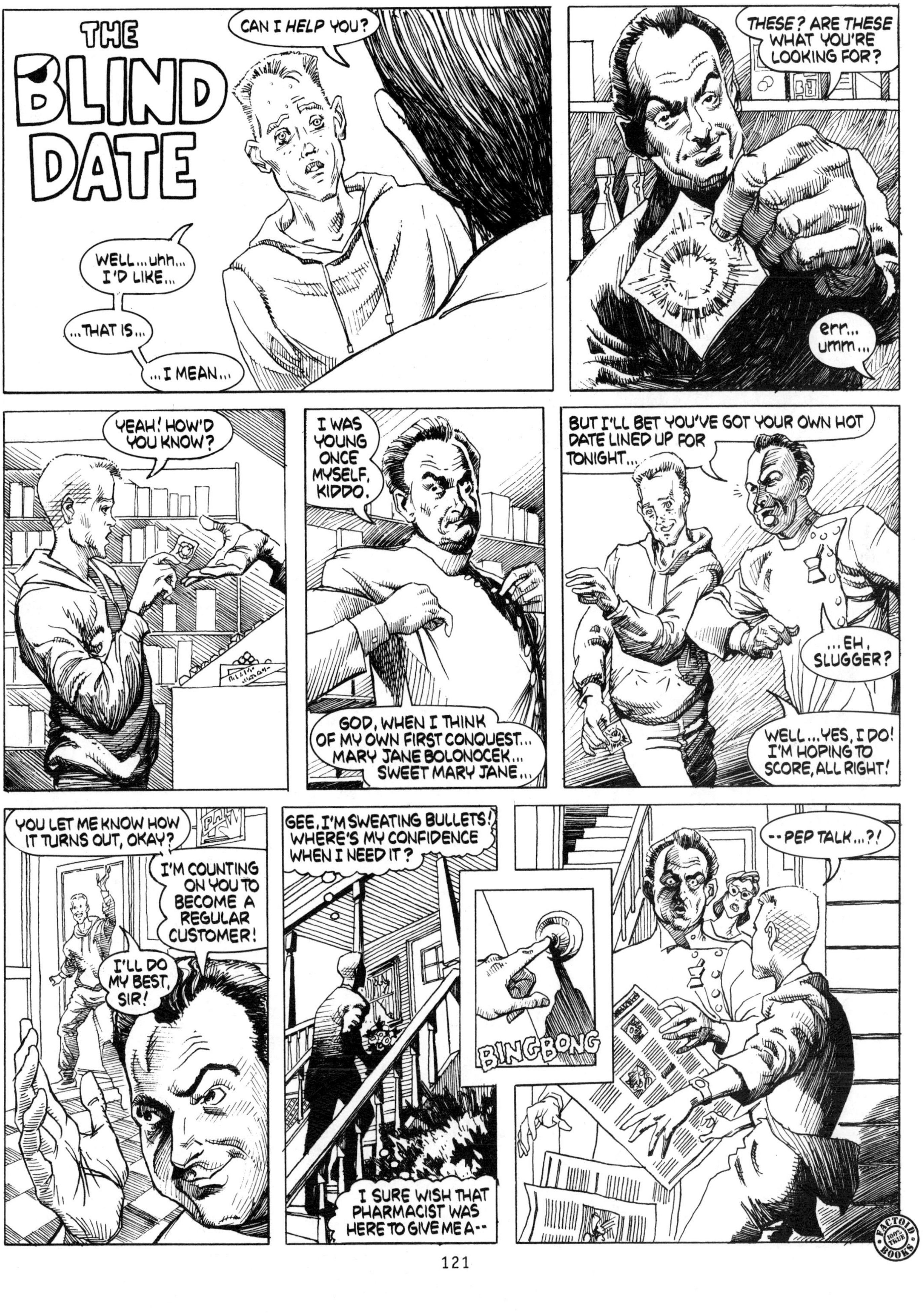
THE BLIND DATE
CAN I HELP YOU?
WELL...uhh... I'D LIKE...
...THAT IS...
...I MEAN...
THESE? ARE THESE WHAT YOU'RE LOOKING FOR?
err... umm...
YEAH! HOW'D YOU KNOW?
I WAS YOUNG ONCE MYSELF, KIDDO.
GOD, WHEN I THINK OF MY OWN FIRST CONQUEST... MARY JANE BOLONOCEK... SWEET MARY JANE...
BUT I'LL BET YOU'VE GOT YOUR OWN HOT DATE LINED UP FOR TONIGHT...
...EH, SLUGGER?
WELL...YES, I DO! I'M HOPING TO SCORE, ALL RIGHT!
YOU LET ME KNOW HOW IT TURNS OUT, OKAY?
I'M COUNTING ON YOU TO BECOME A REGULAR CUSTOMER!
I'LL DO MY BEST, SIR!
GEE, I'M SWEATING BULLETS! WHERE'S MY CONFIDENCE WHEN I NEED IT?
I SURE WISH THAT PHARMACIST WAS HERE TO GIVE ME A--
BINGBONG
--PEP TALK...?!
FACTOID BOOKS 100% TRUE

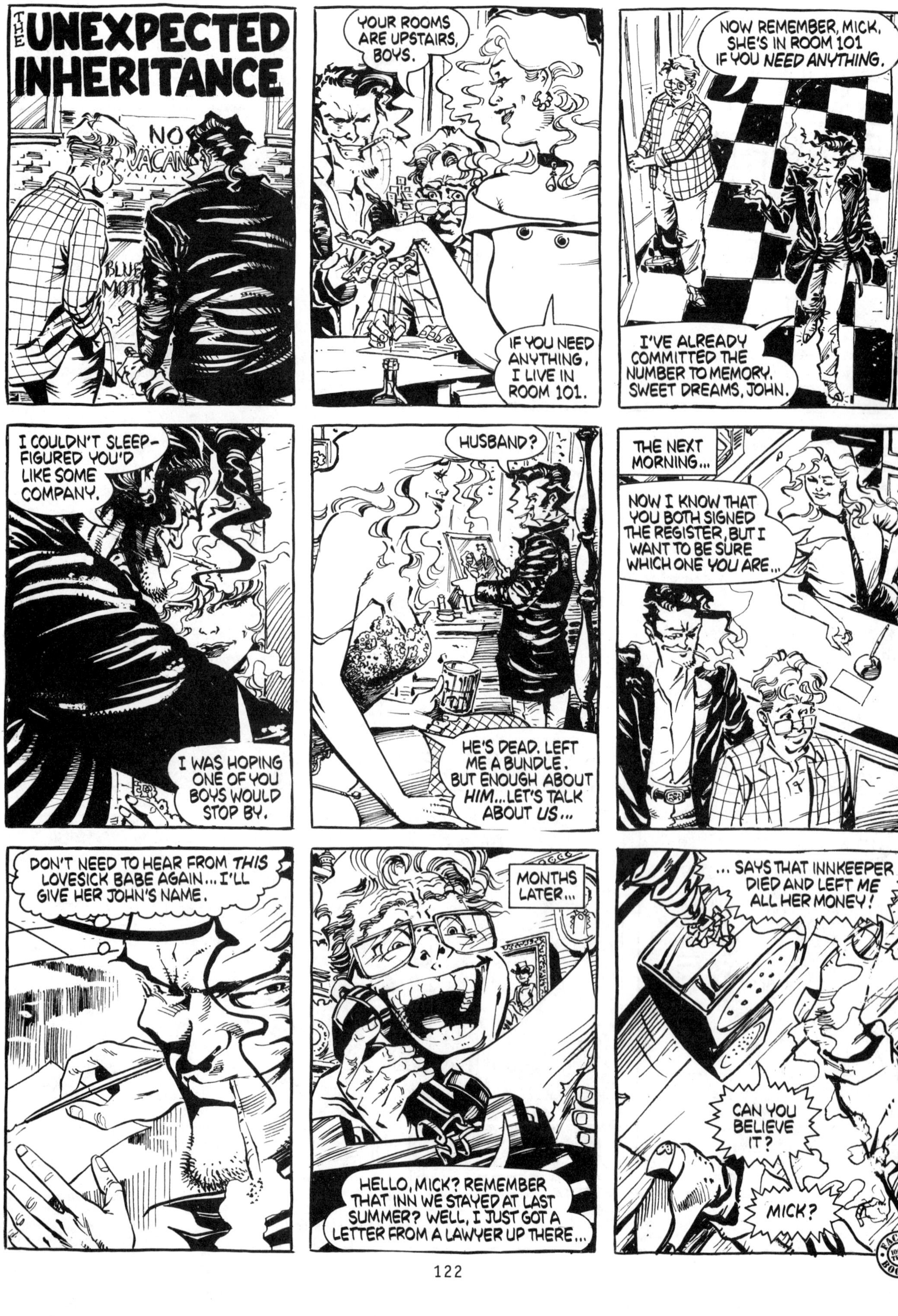
THE UNEXPECTED INHERITANCE
NO VACAN
BLUE MOT
YOUR ROOMS ARE UPSTAIRS, BOYS.
IF YOU NEED ANYTHING, I LIVE IN ROOM 101.
NOW REMEMBER, MICK, SHE'S IN ROOM 101 IF YOU NEED ANYTHING.
I'VE ALREADY COMMITTED THE NUMBER TO MEMORY. SWEET DREAMS, JOHN.
I COULDN'T SLEEP-FIGURED YOU'D LIKE SOME COMPANY.
I WAS HOPING ONE OF YOU BOYS WOULD STOP BY.
HUSBAND?
HE'S DEAD. LEFT ME A BUNDLE. BUT ENOUGH ABOUT HIM...LET'S TALK ABOUT US...
THE NEXT MORNING...
NOW I KNOW THAT YOU BOTH SIGNED THE REGISTER, BUT I WANT TO BE SURE WHICH ONE YOU ARE...
DON'T NEED TO HEAR FROM THIS LOVESICK BABE AGAIN... I'LL GIVE HER JOHN'S NAME.
MONTHS LATER...
HELLO, MICK? REMEMBER THAT INN WE STAYED AT LAST SUMMER? WELL, I JUST GOT A LETTER FROM A LAWYER UP THERE...
... SAYS THAT INNKEEPER DIED AND LEFT ME ALL HER MONEY!
CAN YOU BELIEVE IT?
MICK?
FACTOID BOOKS 100% TRUE

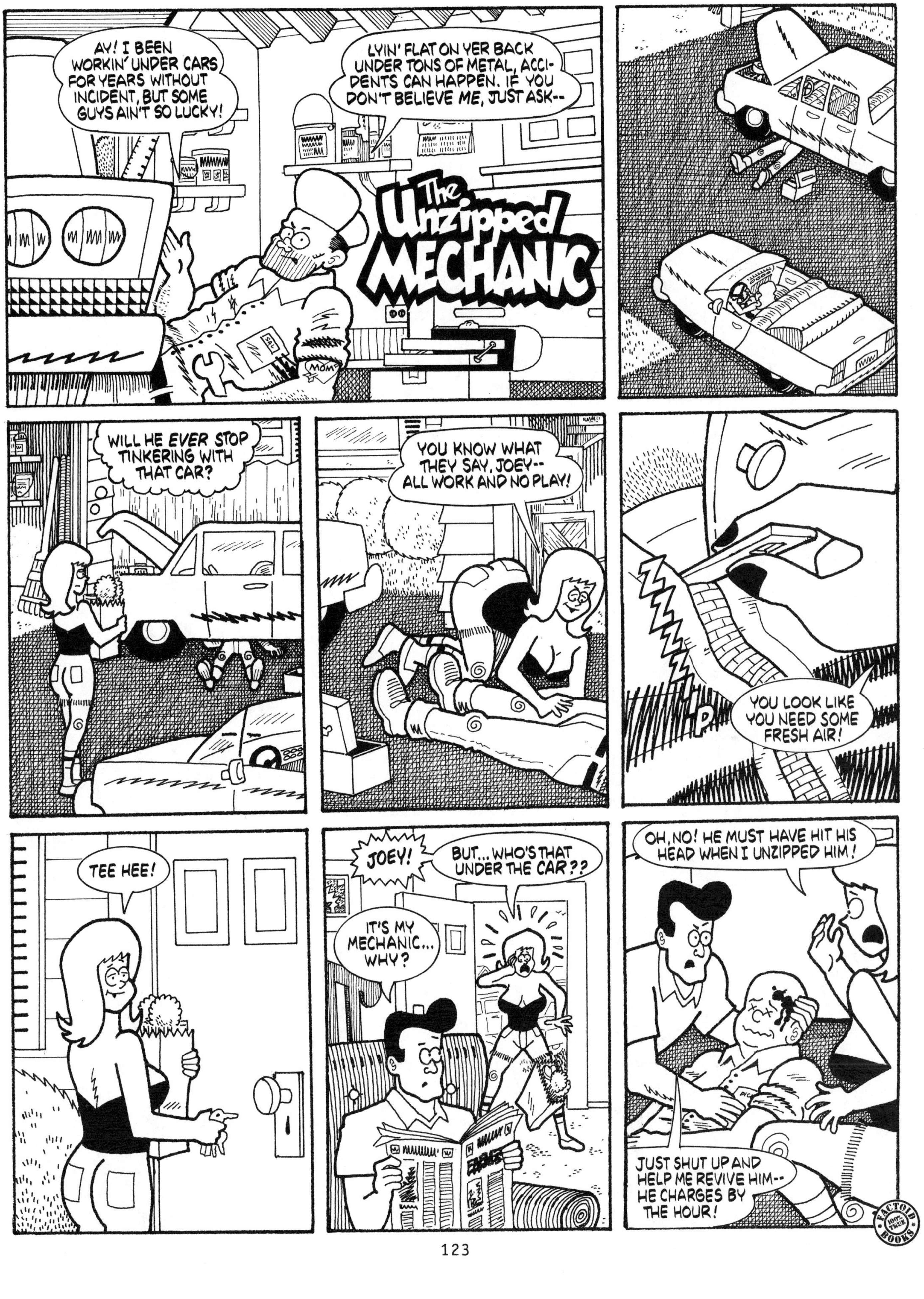
AY! I BEEN WORKIN' UNDER CARS FOR YEARS WITHOUT INCIDENT, BUT SOME GUYS AIN'T SO LUCKY!
LYIN' FLAT ON YER BACK UNDER TONS OF METAL, ACCI-DENTS CAN HAPPEN. IF YOU DON'T BELIEVE ME, JUST ASK--
The Unzipped MECHANIC
MOM
WILL HE EVER STOP TINKERING WITH THAT CAR?
YOU KNOW WHAT THEY SAY, JOEY-- ALL WORK AND NO PLAY!
ZZZZZIP
YOU LOOK LIKE YOU NEED SOME FRESH AIR!
TEE HEE!
JOEY!
BUT... WHO'S THAT UNDER THE CAR??
IT'S MY MECHANIC... WHY?
OH, NO! HE MUST HAVE HIT HIS HEAD WHEN I UNZIPPED HIM!
JUST SHUT UP AND HELP ME REVIVE HIM-- HE CHARGES BY THE HOUR!
FACTOID BOOKS 100% TRUE

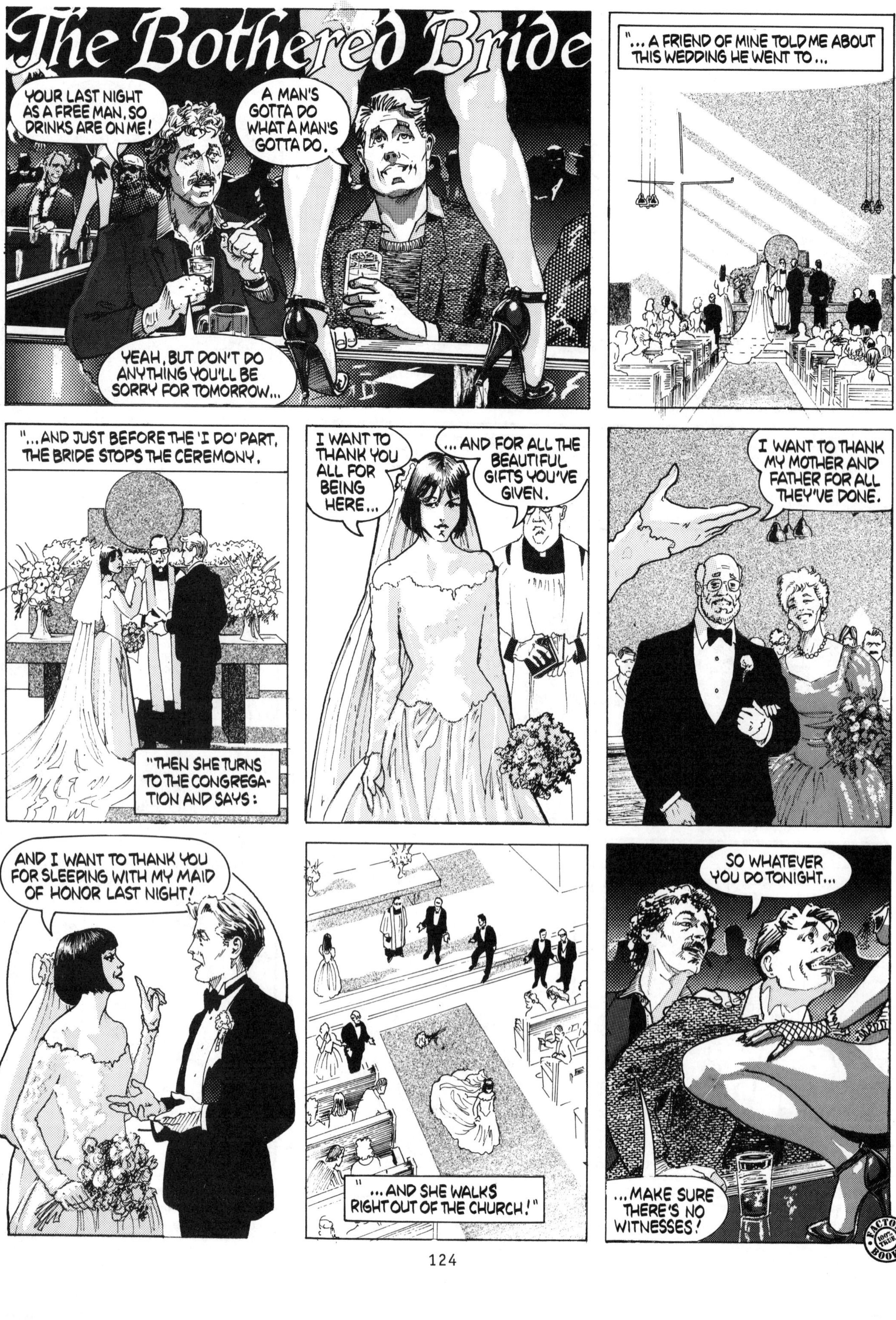
The Bothered Bride
YOUR LAST NIGHT AS A FREE MAN, SO DRINKS ARE ON ME!
A MAN'S GOTTA DO WHAT A MAN'S GOTTA DO.
YEAH, BUT DON'T DO ANYTHING YOU'LL BE SORRY FOR TOMORROW...
"... A FRIEND OF MINE TOLD ME ABOUT THIS WEDDING HE WENT TO...
"... AND JUST BEFORE THE 'I DO' PART, THE BRIDE STOPS THE CEREMONY.
"THEN SHE TURNS TO THE CONGREGATION AND SAYS:
I WANT TO THANK YOU ALL FOR BEING HERE...
... AND FOR ALL THE BEAUTIFUL GIFTS YOU'VE GIVEN.
I WANT TO THANK MY MOTHER AND FATHER FOR ALL THEY'VE DONE.
AND I WANT TO THANK YOU FOR SLEEPING WITH MY MAID OF HONOR LAST NIGHT!
"... AND SHE WALKS RIGHT OUT OF THE CHURCH!"
SO WHATEVER YOU DO TONIGHT...
... MAKE SURE THERE'S NO WITNESSES!
FACTOID 100% TRUE BOOKS

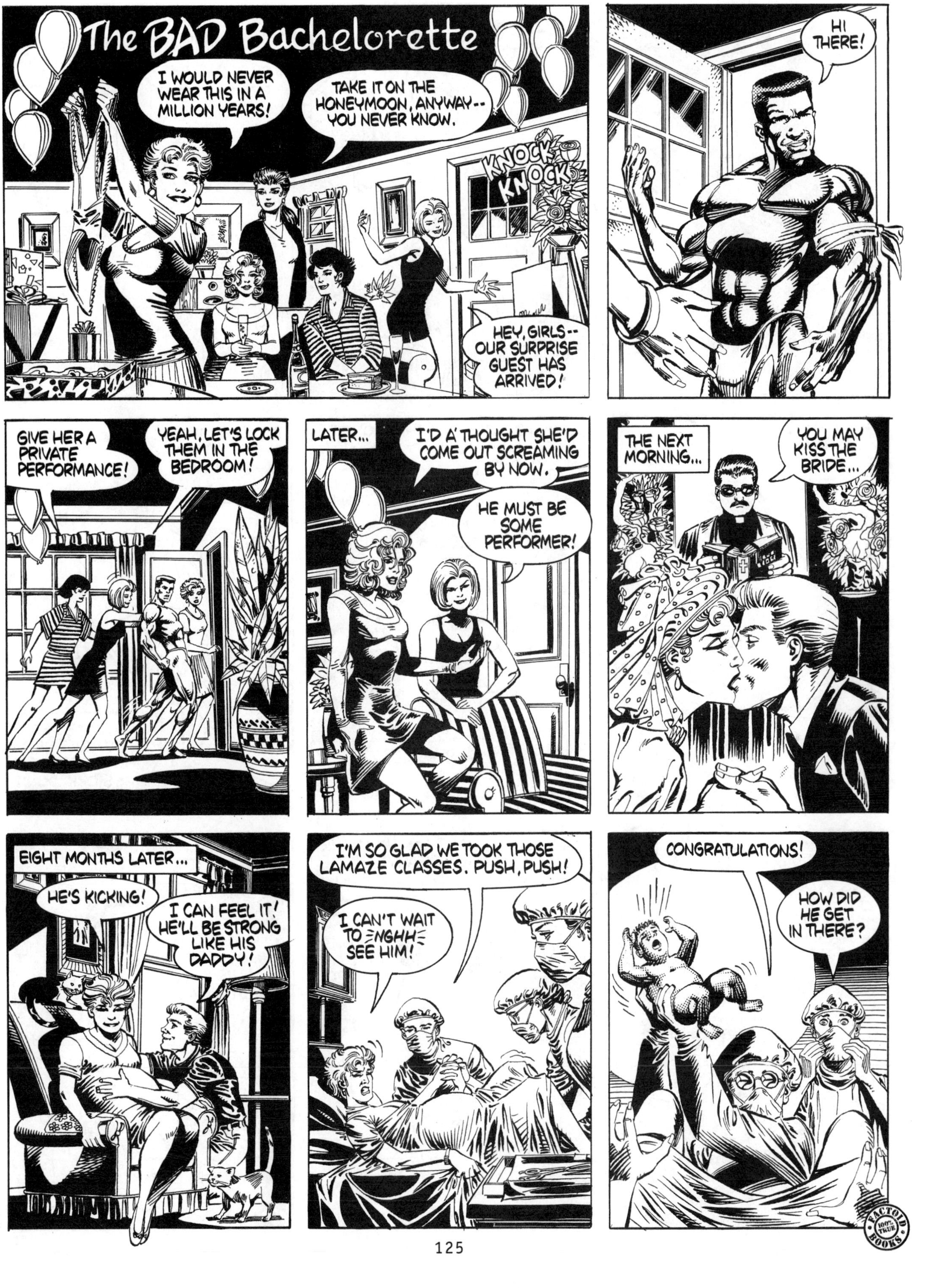
The BAD Bachelorette
I WOULD NEVER WEAR THIS IN A MILLION YEARS!
TAKE IT ON THE HONEYMOON, ANYWAY-- YOU NEVER KNOW.
KNOCK KNOCK
HEY, GIRLS-- OUR SURPRISE GUEST HAS ARRIVED!
HI THERE!
GIVE HER A PRIVATE PERFORMANCE!
YEAH, LET'S LOCK THEM IN THE BEDROOM!
LATER...
I'D A' THOUGHT SHE'D COME OUT SCREAMING BY NOW.
HE MUST BE SOME PERFORMER!
THE NEXT MORNING...
YOU MAY KISS THE BRIDE...
EIGHT MONTHS LATER...
HE'S KICKING!
I CAN FEEL IT! HE'LL BE STRONG LIKE HIS DADDY!
I'M SO GLAD WE TOOK THOSE LAMAZE CLASSES. PUSH, PUSH!
I CAN'T WAIT TO NGHH SEE HIM!
CONGRATULATIONS!
HOW DID HE GET IN THERE?
FACTOID BOOKS 100% TRUE

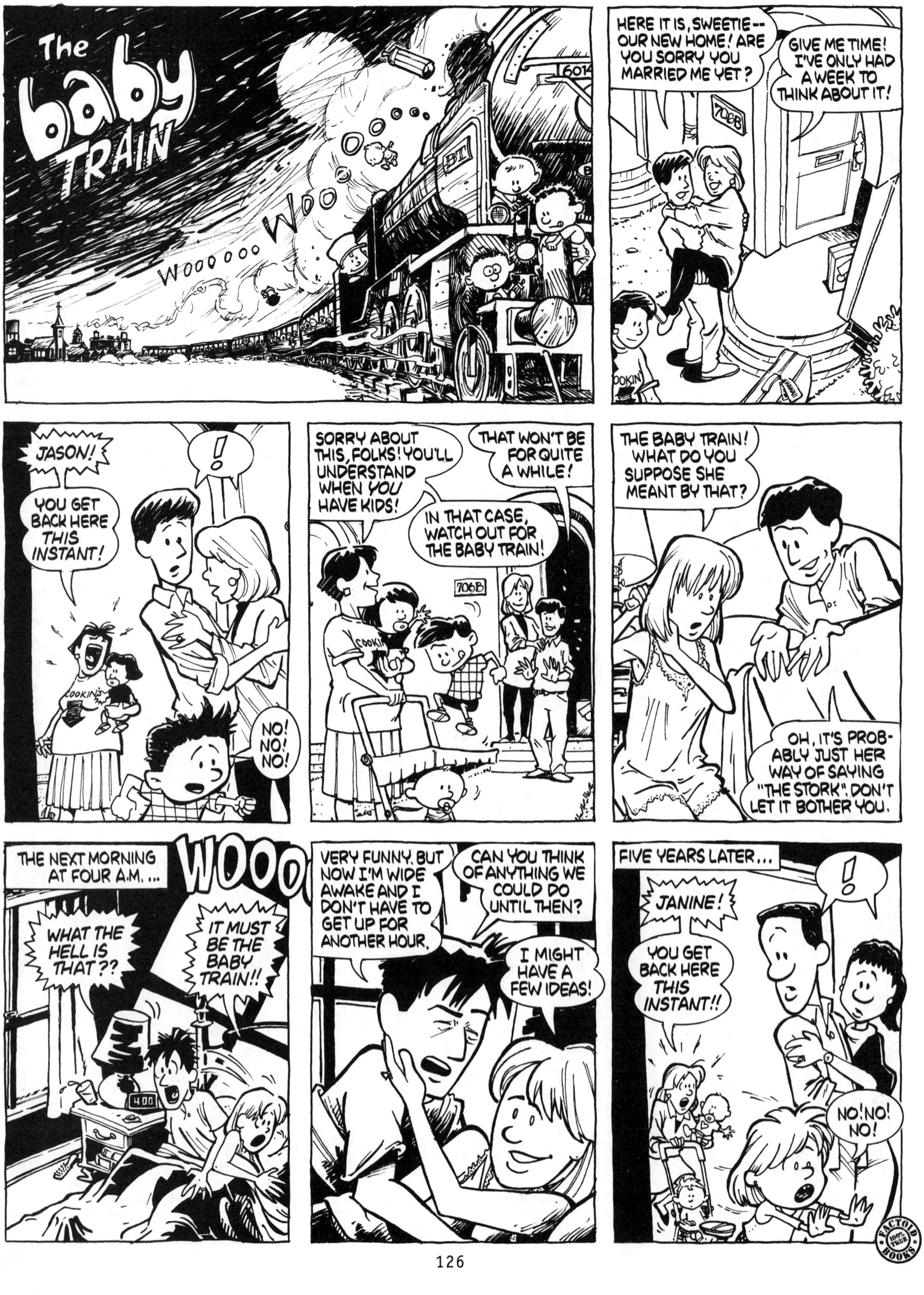
The baby TRAIN
WOOOOOO WOO OOOO
HERE IT IS, SWEETIE-- OUR NEW HOME! ARE YOU SORRY YOU MARRIED ME YET?
GIVE ME TIME! I'VE ONLY HAD A WEEK TO THINK ABOUT IT!
JASON!
YOU GET BACK HERE THIS INSTANT!
!
NO! NO! NO!
SORRY ABOUT THIS, FOLKS! YOU'LL UNDERSTAND WHEN YOU HAVE KIDS!
THAT WON'T BE FOR QUITE A WHILE!
IN THAT CASE, WATCH OUT FOR THE BABY TRAIN!
THE BABY TRAIN! WHAT DO YOU SUPPOSE SHE MEANT BY THAT?
OH, IT'S PROBABLY JUST HER WAY OF SAYING "THE STORK". DON'T LET IT BOTHER YOU.
THE NEXT MORNING AT FOUR A.M. ...
WOOO
WHAT THE HELL IS THAT??
IT MUST BE THE BABY TRAIN!!
VERY FUNNY, BUT NOW I'M WIDE AWAKE AND I DON'T HAVE TO GET UP FOR ANOTHER HOUR.
CAN YOU THINK OF ANYTHING WE COULD DO UNTIL THEN?
I MIGHT HAVE A FEW IDEAS!
FIVE YEARS LATER...
!
JANINE!
YOU GET BACK HERE THIS INSTANT!!
NO! NO! NO!
FACTOID BOOKS 100% TRUE

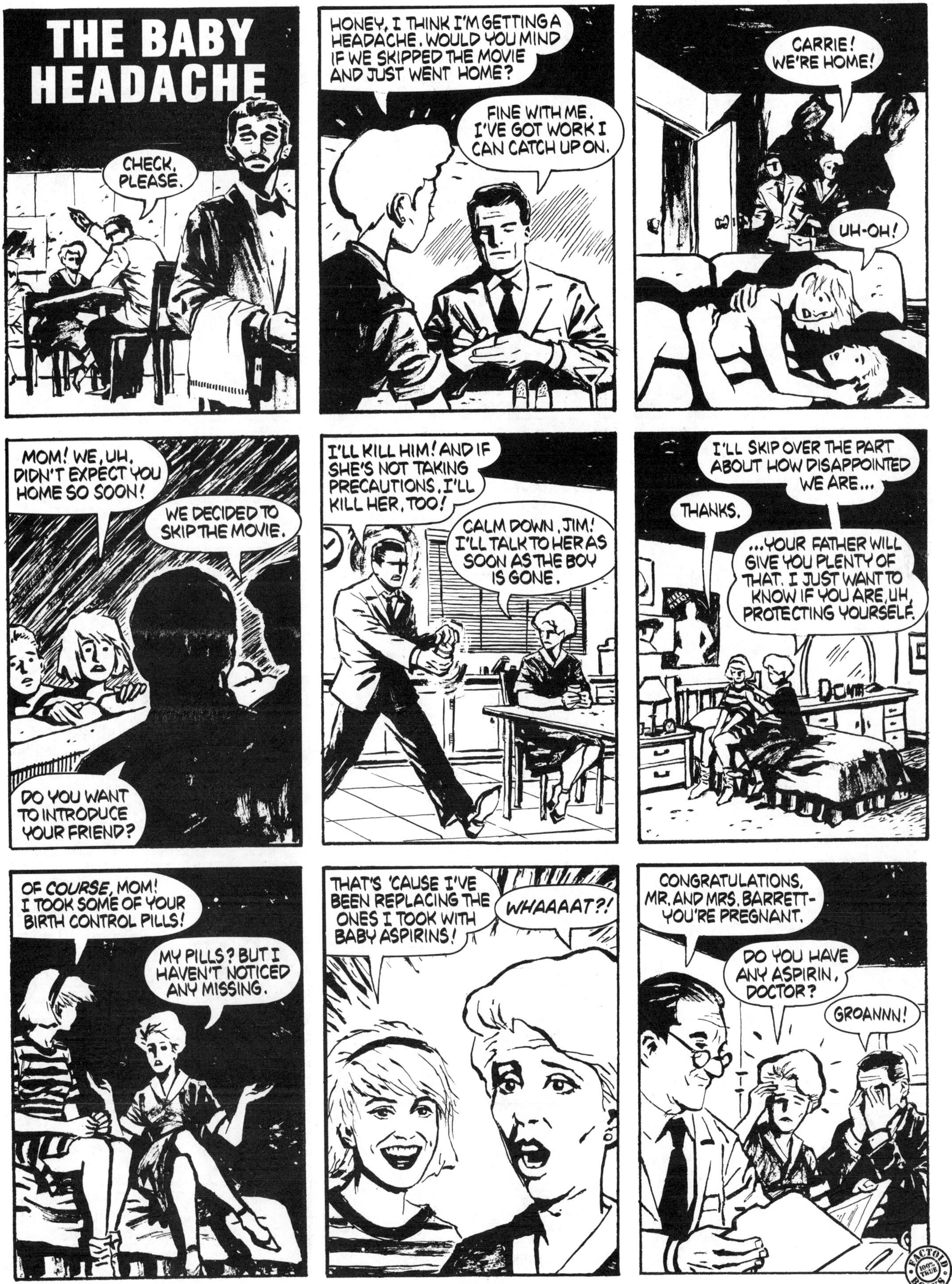
THE BABY HEADACHE
CHECK, PLEASE.
HONEY, I THINK I'M GETTING A HEADACHE. WOULD YOU MIND IF WE SKIPPED THE MOVIE AND JUST WENT HOME?
FINE WITH ME. I'VE GOT WORK I CAN CATCH UP ON.
CARRIE! WE'RE HOME!
UH-OH!
MOM! WE, UH, DIDN'T EXPECT YOU HOME SO SOON!
WE DECIDED TO SKIP THE MOVIE.
DO YOU WANT TO INTRODUCE YOUR FRIEND?
I'LL KILL HIM! AND IF SHE'S NOT TAKING PRECAUTIONS, I'LL KILL HER, TOO!
CALM DOWN, JIM! I'LL TALK TO HER AS SOON AS THE BOY IS GONE.
I'LL SKIP OVER THE PART ABOUT HOW DISAPPOINTED WE ARE...
THANKS.
...YOUR FATHER WILL GIVE YOU PLENTY OF THAT. I JUST WANT TO KNOW IF YOU ARE, UH, PROTECTING YOURSELF.
OF COURSE, MOM! I TOOK SOME OF YOUR BIRTH CONTROL PILLS!
MY PILLS? BUT I HAVEN'T NOTICED ANY MISSING.
THAT'S 'CAUSE I'VE BEEN REPLACING THE ONES I TOOK WITH BABY ASPIRINS!
WHAAAAT?!
CONGRATULATIONS, MR. AND MRS. BARRETT- YOU'RE PREGNANT.
DO YOU HAVE ANY ASPIRIN, DOCTOR?
GROANNN!
FACTOID BOOKS 100% TRUE

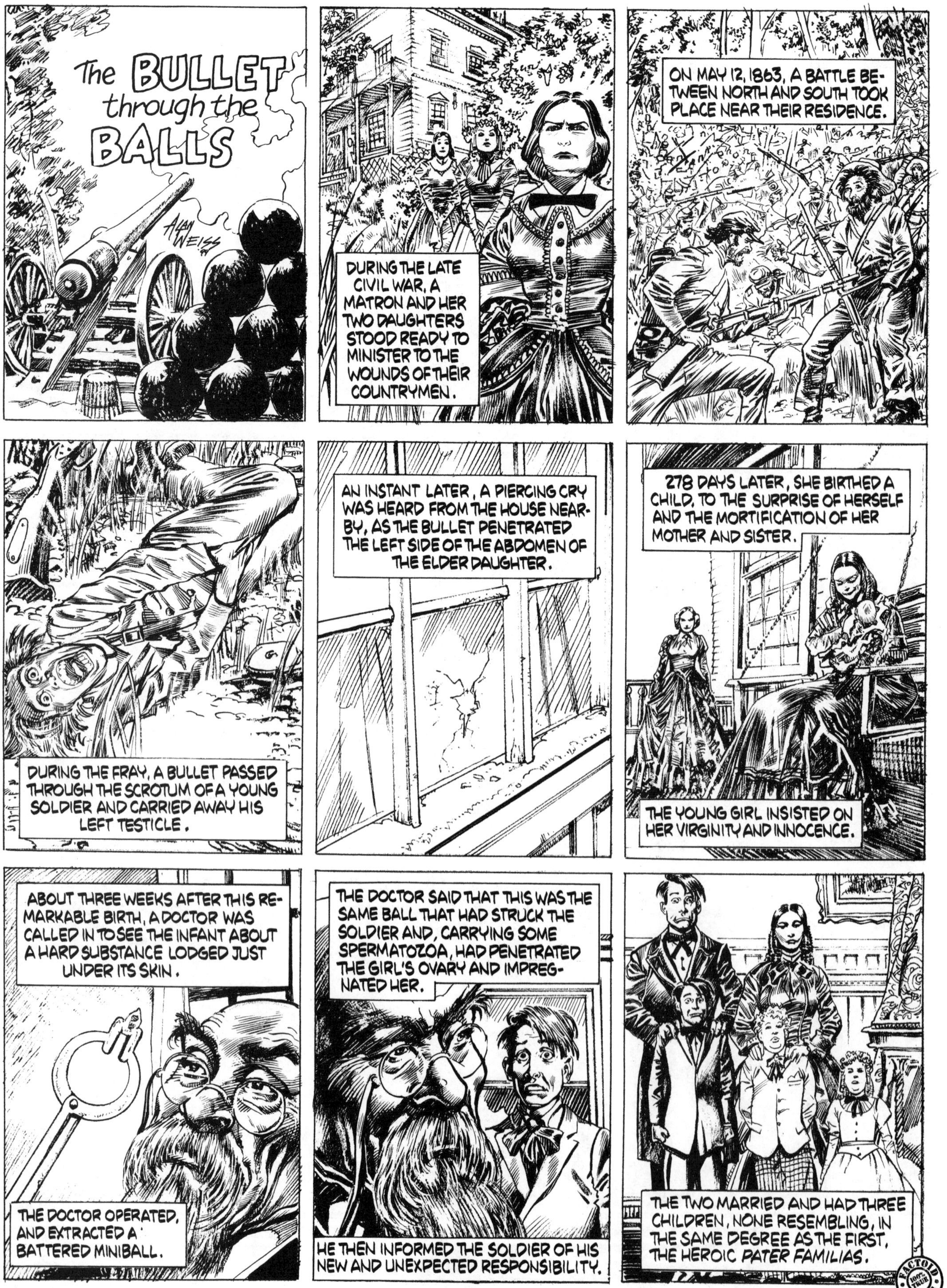
The BULLET through the BALLS
ALAN WEISS
DURING THE LATE CIVIL WAR, A MATRON AND HER TWO DAUGHTERS STOOD READY TO MINISTER TO THE WOUNDS OF THEIR COUNTRYMEN.
ON MAY 12, 1863, A BATTLE BETWEEN NORTH AND SOUTH TOOK PLACE NEAR THEIR RESIDENCE.
DURING THE FRAY, A BULLET PASSED THROUGH THE SCROTUM OF A YOUNG SOLDIER AND CARRIED AWAY HIS LEFT TESTICLE.
AN INSTANT LATER, A PIERCING CRY WAS HEARD FROM THE HOUSE NEARBY, AS THE BULLET PENETRATED THE LEFT SIDE OF THE ABDOMEN OF THE ELDER DAUGHTER.
278 DAYS LATER, SHE BIRTHED A CHILD, TO THE SURPRISE OF HERSELF AND THE MORTIFICATION OF HER MOTHER AND SISTER.
THE YOUNG GIRL INSISTED ON HER VIRGINITY AND INNOCENCE.
ABOUT THREE WEEKS AFTER THIS REMARKABLE BIRTH, A DOCTOR WAS CALLED IN TO SEE THE INFANT ABOUT A HARD SUBSTANCE LODGED JUST UNDER ITS SKIN.
THE DOCTOR OPERATED, AND EXTRACTED A BATTERED MINIBALL.
THE DOCTOR SAID THAT THIS WAS THE SAME BALL THAT HAD STRUCK THE SOLDIER AND, CARRYING SOME SPERMATOZOA, HAD PENETRATED THE GIRL'S OVARY AND IMPREGNATED HER.
HE THEN INFORMED THE SOLDIER OF HIS NEW AND UNEXPECTED RESPONSIBILITY.
THE TWO MARRIED AND HAD THREE CHILDREN, NONE RESEMBLING, IN THE SAME DEGREE AS THE FIRST, THE HEROIC PATER FAMILIAS.
FACTOID BOOKS 100% TRUE

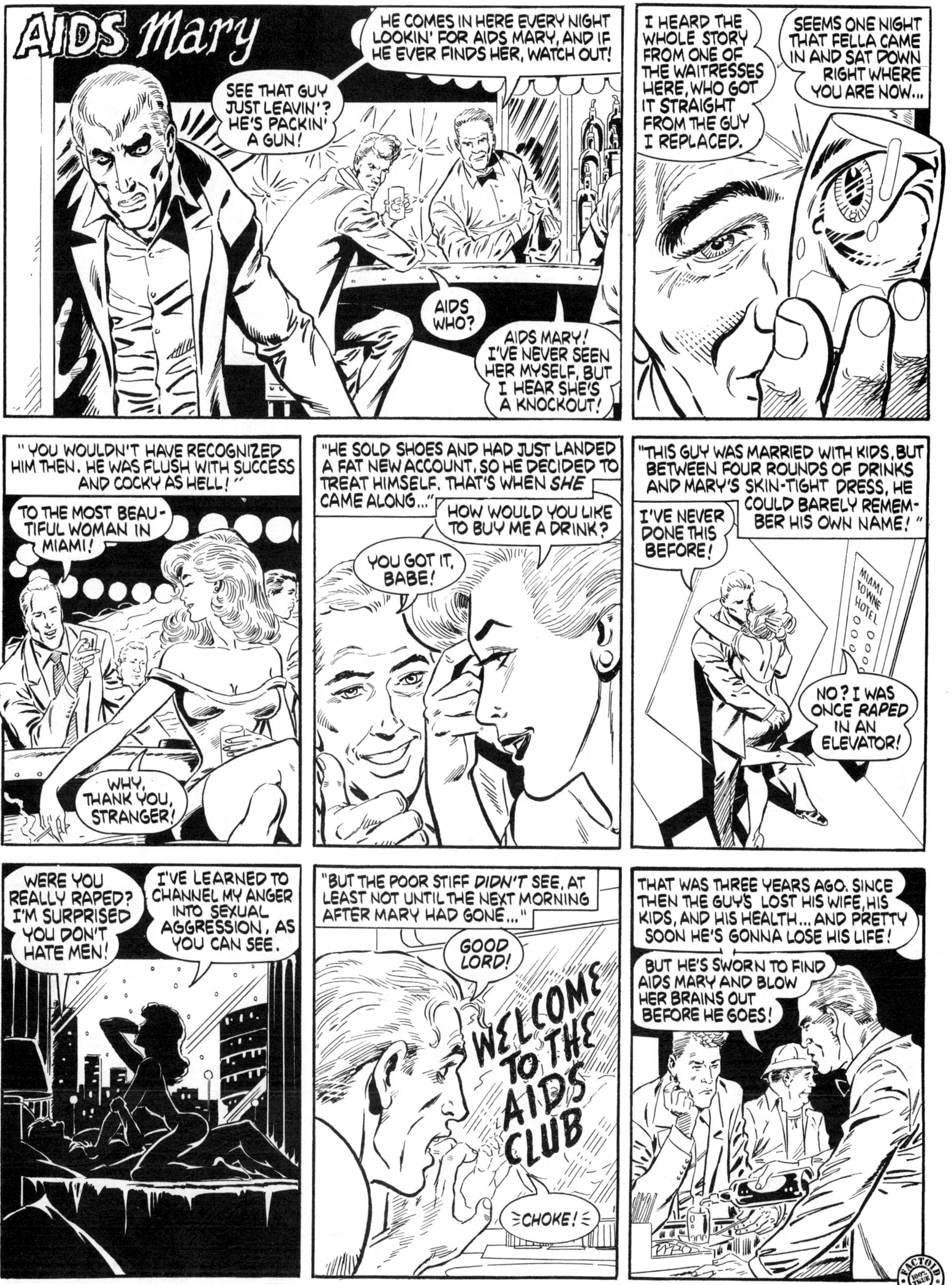
AIDS Mary
SEE THAT GUY JUST LEAVIN'? HE'S PACKIN' A GUN!
HE COMES IN HERE EVERY NIGHT LOOKIN' FOR AIDS MARY, AND IF HE EVER FINDS HER, WATCH OUT!
AIDS WHO?
AIDS MARY! I'VE NEVER SEEN HER MYSELF, BUT I HEAR SHE'S A KNOCKOUT!
I HEARD THE WHOLE STORY FROM ONE OF THE WAITRESSES HERE, WHO GOT IT STRAIGHT FROM THE GUY I REPLACED.
SEEMS ONE NIGHT THAT FELLA CAME IN AND SAT DOWN RIGHT WHERE YOU ARE NOW...
"YOU WOULDN'T HAVE RECOGNIZED HIM THEN. HE WAS FLUSH WITH SUCCESS AND COCKY AS HELL!"
TO THE MOST BEAUTIFUL WOMAN IN MIAMI!
WHY, THANK YOU, STRANGER!
"HE SOLD SHOES AND HAD JUST LANDED A FAT NEW ACCOUNT, SO HE DECIDED TO TREAT HIMSELF. THAT'S WHEN SHE CAME ALONG..."
HOW WOULD YOU LIKE TO BUY ME A DRINK?
YOU GOT IT, BABE!
"THIS GUY WAS MARRIED WITH KIDS, BUT BETWEEN FOUR ROUNDS OF DRINKS AND MARY'S SKIN-TIGHT DRESS, HE COULD BARELY REMEMBER HIS OWN NAME!"
I'VE NEVER DONE THIS BEFORE!
MIAMI TOWNE HOTEL
NO? I WAS ONCE RAPED IN AN ELEVATOR!
WERE YOU REALLY RAPED? I'M SURPRISED YOU DON'T HATE MEN!
I'VE LEARNED TO CHANNEL MY ANGER INTO SEXUAL AGGRESSION, AS YOU CAN SEE.
"BUT THE POOR STIFF DIDN'T SEE, AT LEAST NOT UNTIL THE NEXT MORNING AFTER MARY HAD GONE..."
GOOD LORD!
WELCOME TO THE AIDS CLUB
CHOKE!
THAT WAS THREE YEARS AGO. SINCE THEN THE GUY'S LOST HIS WIFE, HIS KIDS, AND HIS HEALTH... AND PRETTY SOON HE'S GONNA LOSE HIS LIFE!
BUT HE'S SWORN TO FIND AIDS MARY AND BLOW HER BRAINS OUT BEFORE HE GOES!
FACTOID BOOKS 100% TRUE

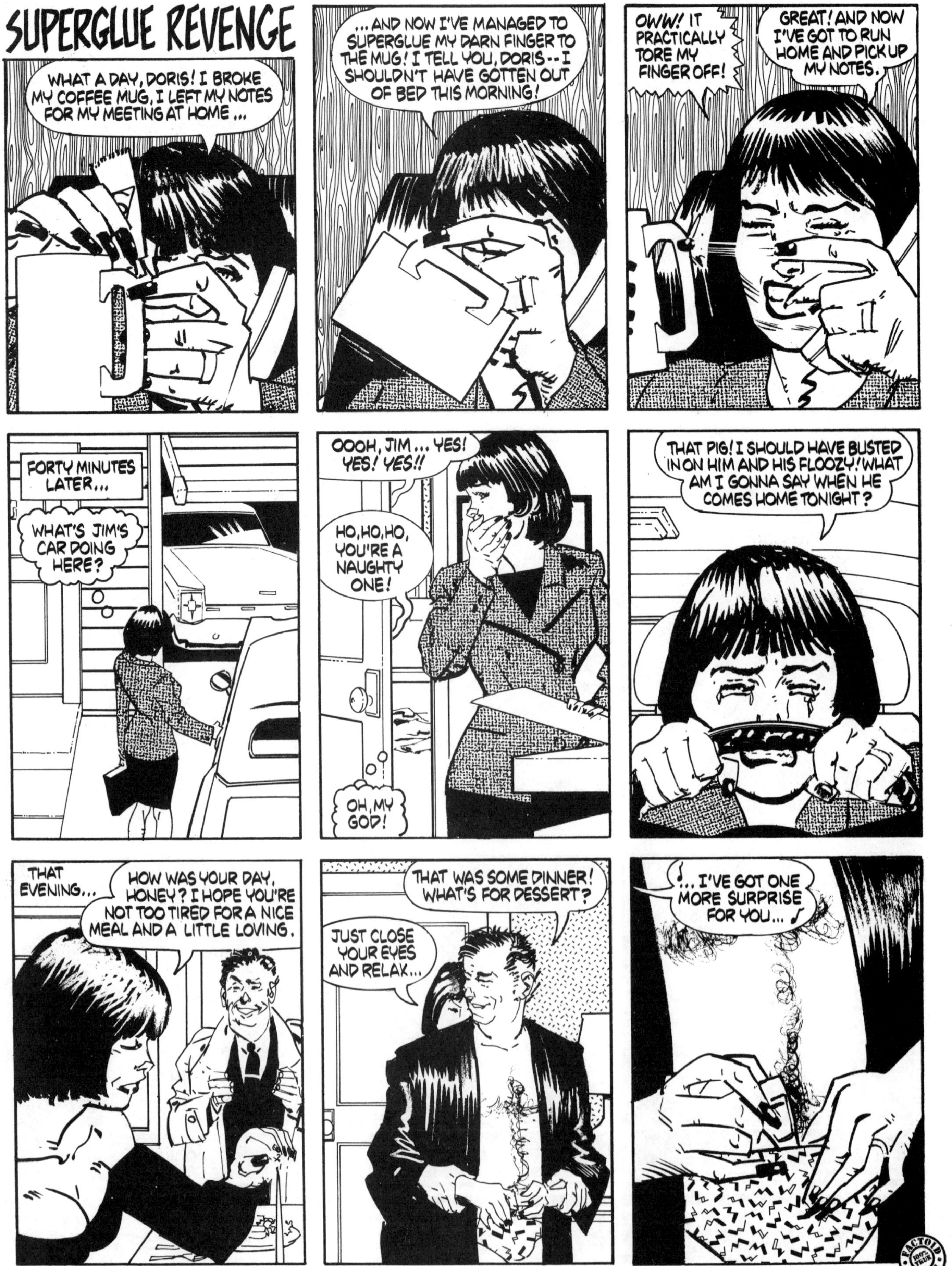
SUPERGLUE REVENGE
WHAT A DAY, DORIS! I BROKE MY COFFEE MUG, I LEFT MY NOTES FOR MY MEETING AT HOME ...
... AND NOW I'VE MANAGED TO SUPERGLUE MY DARN FINGER TO THE MUG! I TELL YOU, DORIS -- I SHOULDN'T HAVE GOTTEN OUT OF BED THIS MORNING!
OWW! IT PRACTICALLY TORE MY FINGER OFF!
GREAT! AND NOW I'VE GOT TO RUN HOME AND PICK UP MY NOTES.
FORTY MINUTES LATER...
WHAT'S JIM'S CAR DOING HERE?
OOOH, JIM ... YES! YES! YES!!
HO, HO, HO, YOU'RE A NAUGHTY ONE!
OH, MY GOD!
THAT PIG! I SHOULD HAVE BUSTED IN ON HIM AND HIS FLOOZY! WHAT AM I GONNA SAY WHEN HE COMES HOME TONIGHT?
THAT EVENING...
HOW WAS YOUR DAY, HONEY? I HOPE YOU'RE NOT TOO TIRED FOR A NICE MEAL AND A LITTLE LOVING.
THAT WAS SOME DINNER! WHAT'S FOR DESSERT?
JUST CLOSE YOUR EYES AND RELAX...
♪.. I'VE GOT ONE MORE SURPRISE FOR YOU... ♪
FACTOID BOOKS

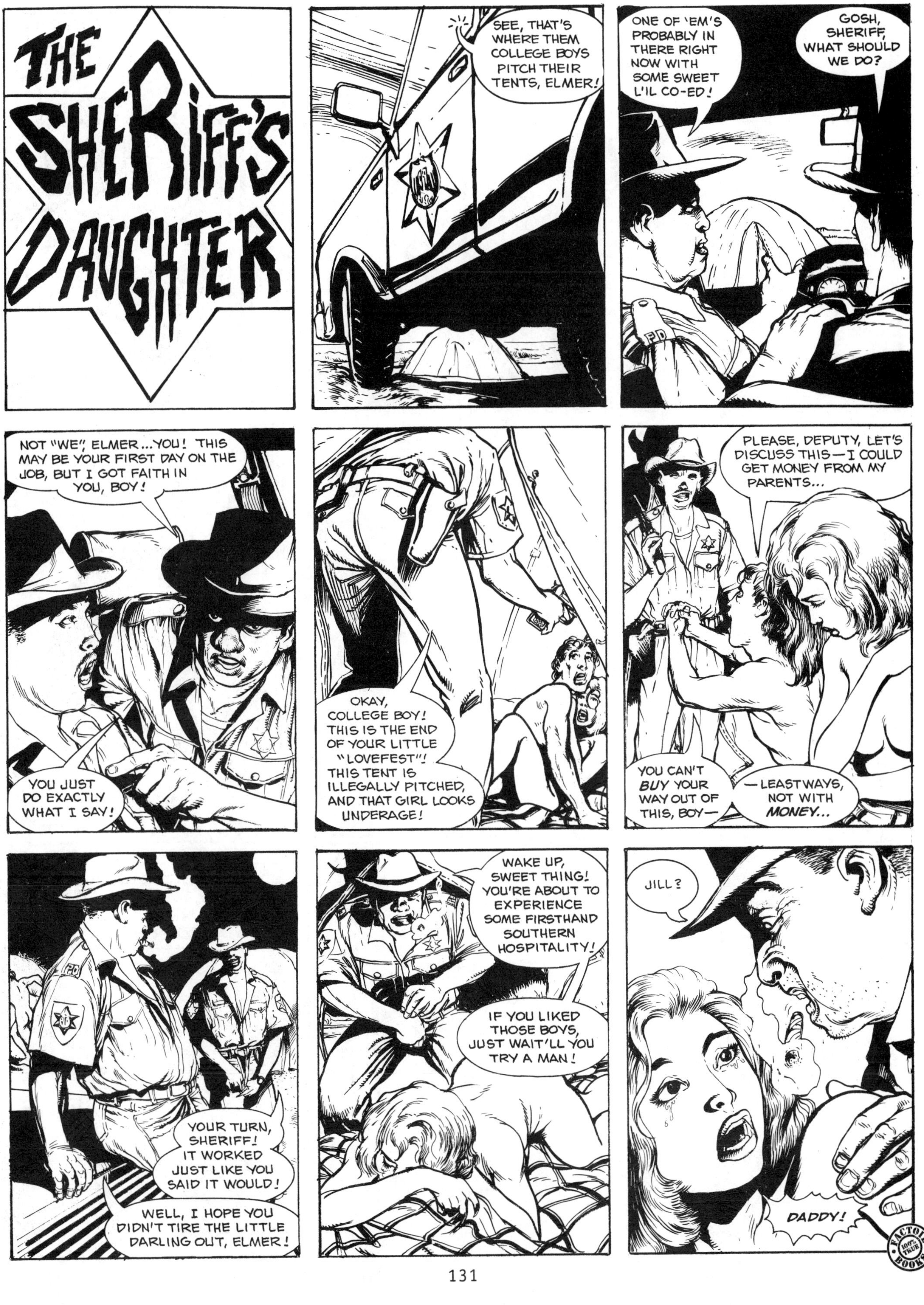
THE SHERIFF'S DAUGHTER
SEE, THAT'S WHERE THEM COLLEGE BOYS PITCH THEIR TENTS, ELMER!
ONE OF 'EM'S PROBABLY IN THERE RIGHT NOW WITH SOME SWEET L'IL CO-ED!
GOSH, SHERIFF, WHAT SHOULD WE DO?
NOT "WE," ELMER...YOU! THIS MAY BE YOUR FIRST DAY ON THE JOB, BUT I GOT FAITH IN YOU, BOY!
YOU JUST DO EXACTLY WHAT I SAY!
OKAY, COLLEGE BOY! THIS IS THE END OF YOUR LITTLE "LOVEFEST"! THIS TENT IS ILLEGALLY PITCHED, AND THAT GIRL LOOKS UNDERAGE!
PLEASE, DEPUTY, LET'S DISCUSS THIS—I COULD GET MONEY FROM MY PARENTS...
YOU CAN'T *BUY* YOUR WAY OUT OF THIS, BOY—
—LEASTWAYS, NOT WITH ***MONEY...***
YOUR TURN, SHERIFF! IT WORKED JUST LIKE YOU SAID IT WOULD!
WELL, I HOPE YOU DIDN'T TIRE THE LITTLE DARLING OUT, ELMER!
WAKE UP, SWEET THING! YOU'RE ABOUT TO EXPERIENCE SOME FIRSTHAND SOUTHERN HOSPITALITY!
IF YOU LIKED THOSE BOYS, JUST WAIT'LL YOU TRY A MAN!
JILL?
DADDY!

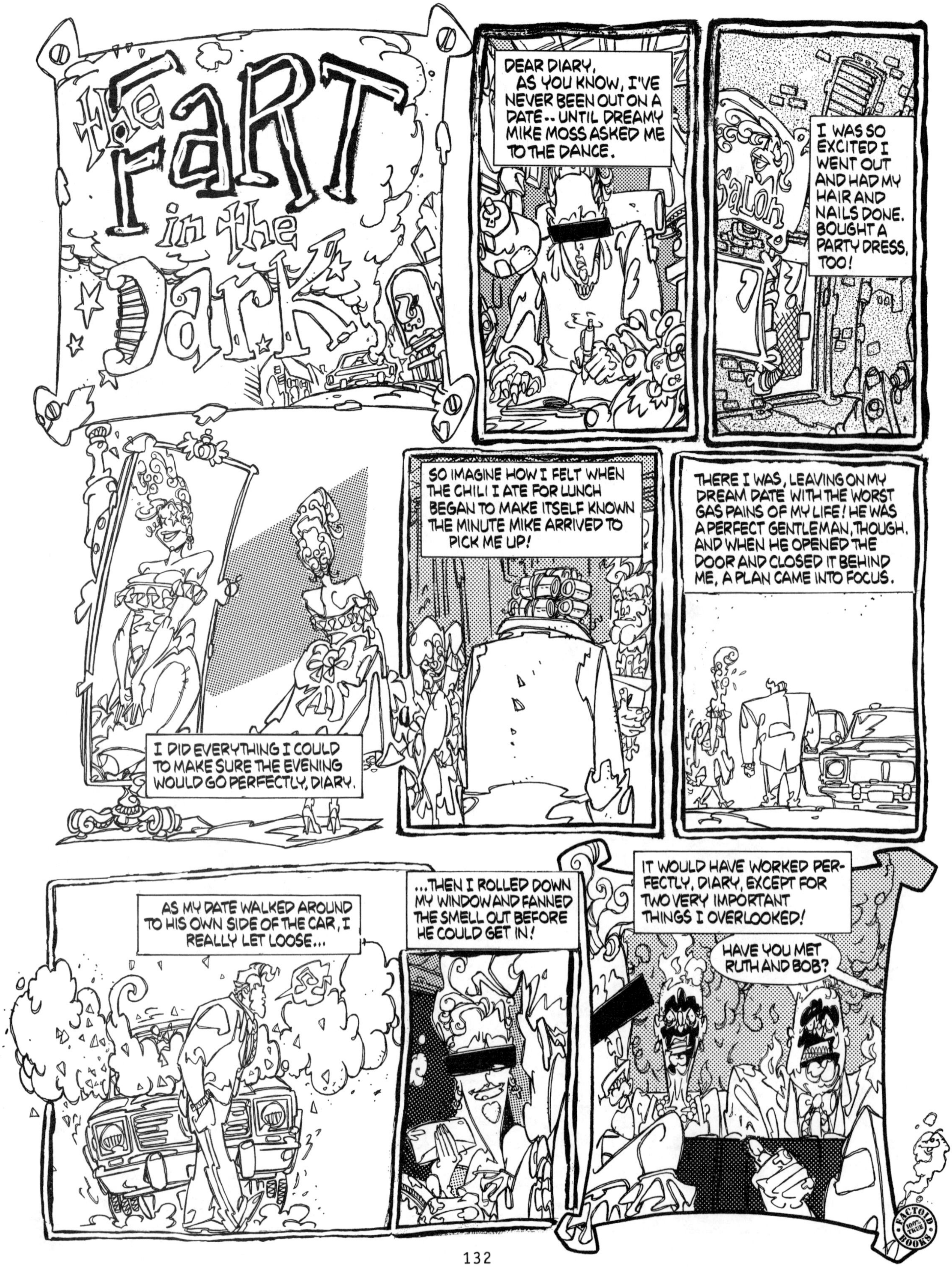
The Fart in the Dark
DEAR DIARY, AS YOU KNOW, I'VE NEVER BEEN OUT ON A DATE -- UNTIL DREAMY MIKE MOSS ASKED ME TO THE DANCE.
I WAS SO EXCITED I WENT OUT AND HAD MY HAIR AND NAILS DONE. BOUGHT A PARTY DRESS, TOO!
SALON
I DID EVERYTHING I COULD TO MAKE SURE THE EVENING WOULD GO PERFECTLY, DIARY.
SO IMAGINE HOW I FELT WHEN THE CHILI I ATE FOR LUNCH BEGAN TO MAKE ITSELF KNOWN THE MINUTE MIKE ARRIVED TO PICK ME UP!
THERE I WAS, LEAVING ON MY DREAM DATE WITH THE WORST GAS PAINS OF MY LIFE! HE WAS A PERFECT GENTLEMAN, THOUGH. AND WHEN HE OPENED THE DOOR AND CLOSED IT BEHIND ME, A PLAN CAME INTO FOCUS.
AS MY DATE WALKED AROUND TO HIS OWN SIDE OF THE CAR, I REALLY LET LOOSE...
...THEN I ROLLED DOWN MY WINDOW AND FANNED THE SMELL OUT BEFORE HE COULD GET IN!
IT WOULD HAVE WORKED PERFECTLY, DIARY, EXCEPT FOR TWO VERY IMPORTANT THINGS I OVERLOOKED!
HAVE YOU MET RUTH AND BOB?
FACTOID BOOKS

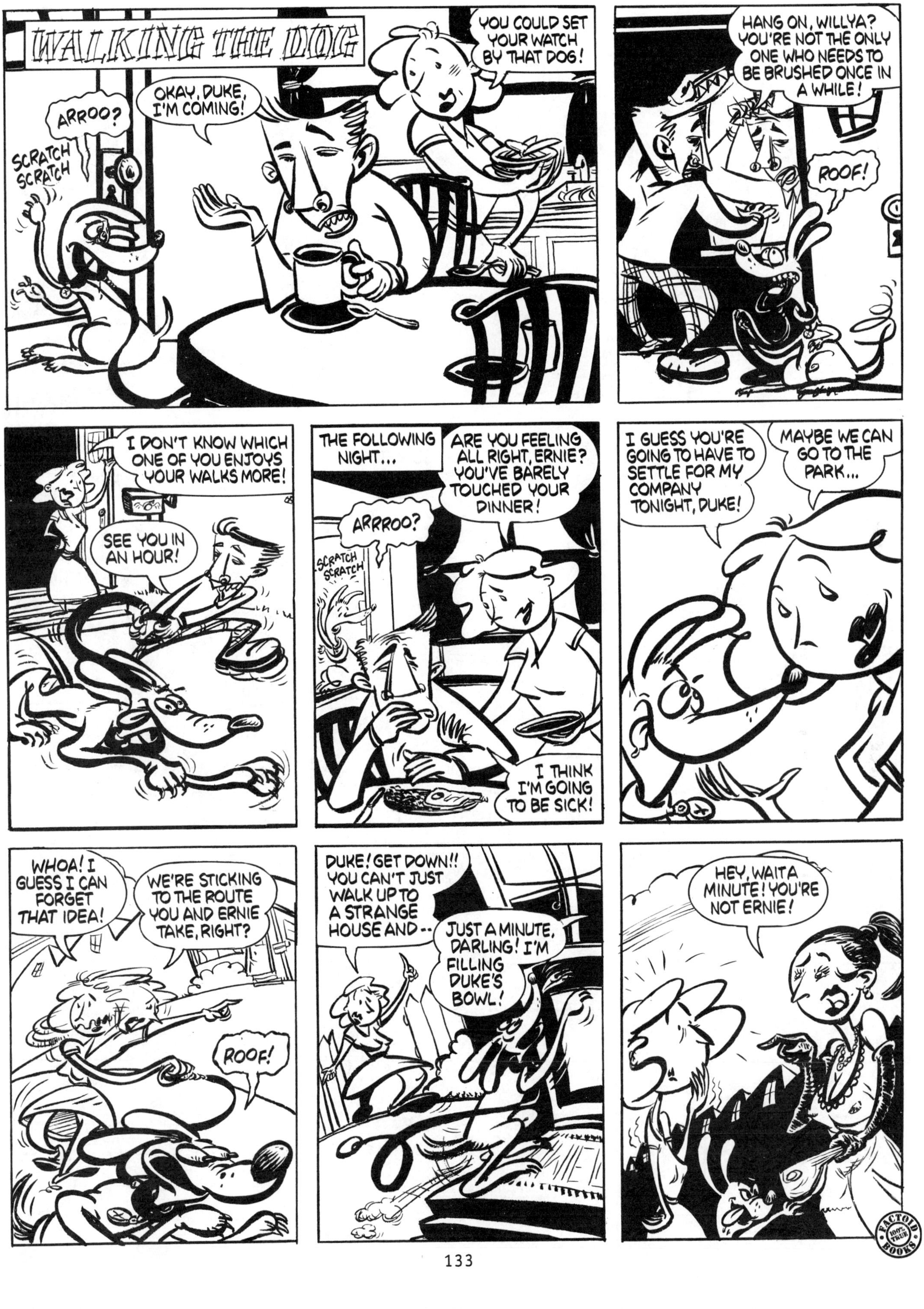
WALKING THE DOG
YOU COULD SET YOUR WATCH BY THAT DOG!
OKAY, DUKE, I'M COMING!
ARROO?
SCRATCH SCRATCH
HANG ON, WILLYA? YOU'RE NOT THE ONLY ONE WHO NEEDS TO BE BRUSHED ONCE IN A WHILE!
ROOF!
I DON'T KNOW WHICH ONE OF YOU ENJOYS YOUR WALKS MORE!
SEE YOU IN AN HOUR!
THE FOLLOWING NIGHT...
ARE YOU FEELING ALL RIGHT, ERNIE? YOU'VE BARELY TOUCHED YOUR DINNER!
ARRROO?
SCRATCH SCRATCH
I THINK I'M GOING TO BE SICK!
I GUESS YOU'RE GOING TO HAVE TO SETTLE FOR MY COMPANY TONIGHT, DUKE!
MAYBE WE CAN GO TO THE PARK...
WHOA! I GUESS I CAN FORGET THAT IDEA!
WE'RE STICKING TO THE ROUTE YOU AND ERNIE TAKE, RIGHT?
ROOF!
DUKE! GET DOWN!! YOU CAN'T JUST WALK UP TO A STRANGE HOUSE AND--
JUST A MINUTE, DARLING! I'M FILLING DUKE'S BOWL!
HEY, WAIT A MINUTE! YOU'RE NOT ERNIE!
FACTOID BOOKS 100% TRUE

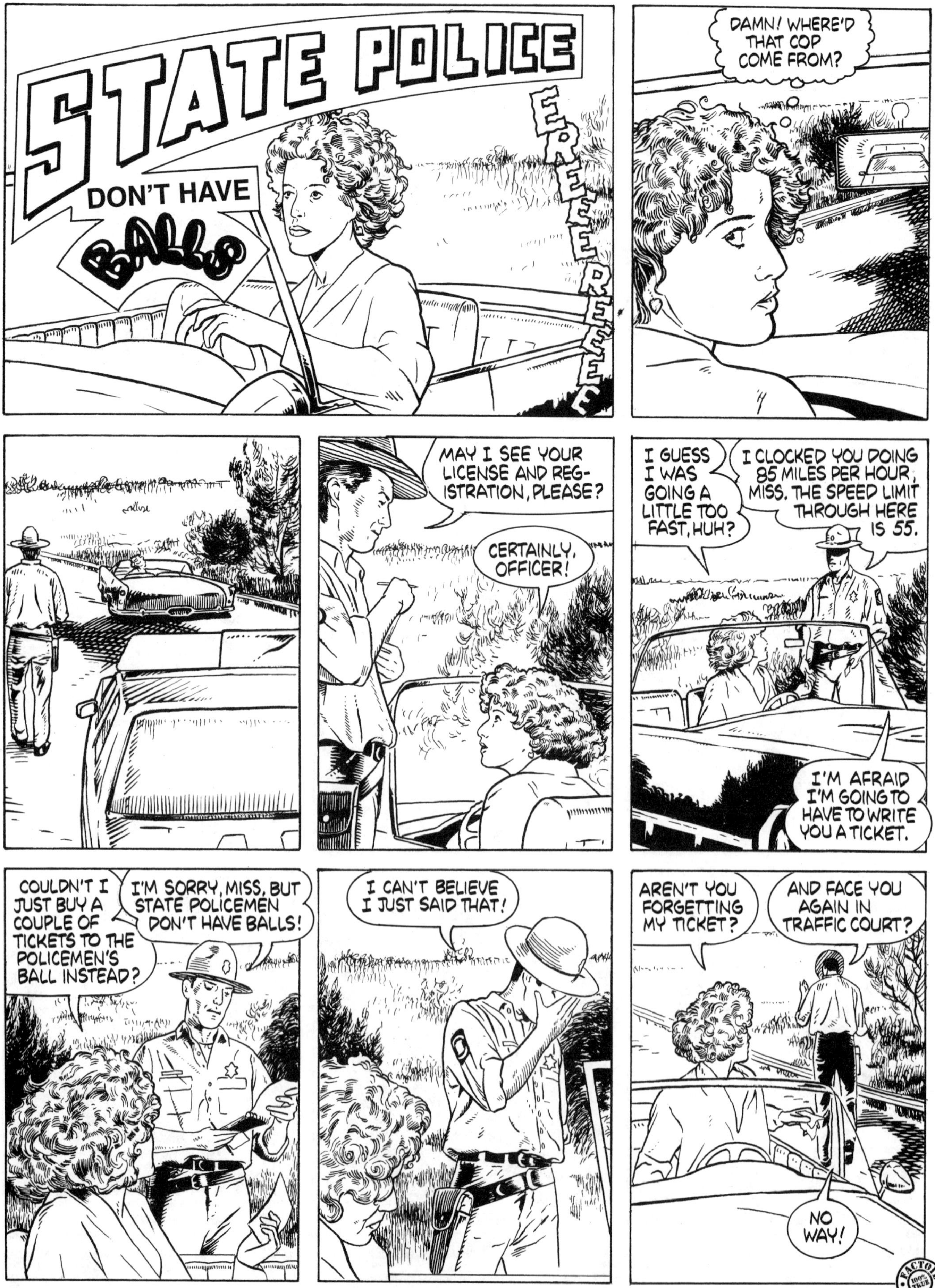
STATE POLICE
DON'T HAVE
BALLS
DAMN! WHERE'D THAT COP COME FROM?
MAY I SEE YOUR LICENSE AND REG-ISTRATION, PLEASE?
CERTAINLY, OFFICER!
I GUESS I WAS GOING A LITTLE TOO FAST, HUH?
I CLOCKED YOU DOING 85 MILES PER HOUR, MISS. THE SPEED LIMIT THROUGH HERE IS 55.
I'M AFRAID I'M GOING TO HAVE TO WRITE YOU A TICKET.
COULDN'T I JUST BUY A COUPLE OF TICKETS TO THE POLICEMEN'S BALL INSTEAD?
I'M SORRY, MISS, BUT STATE POLICEMEN DON'T HAVE BALLS!
I CAN'T BELIEVE I JUST SAID THAT!
AREN'T YOU FORGETTING MY TICKET?
AND FACE YOU AGAIN IN TRAFFIC COURT?
NO WAY!

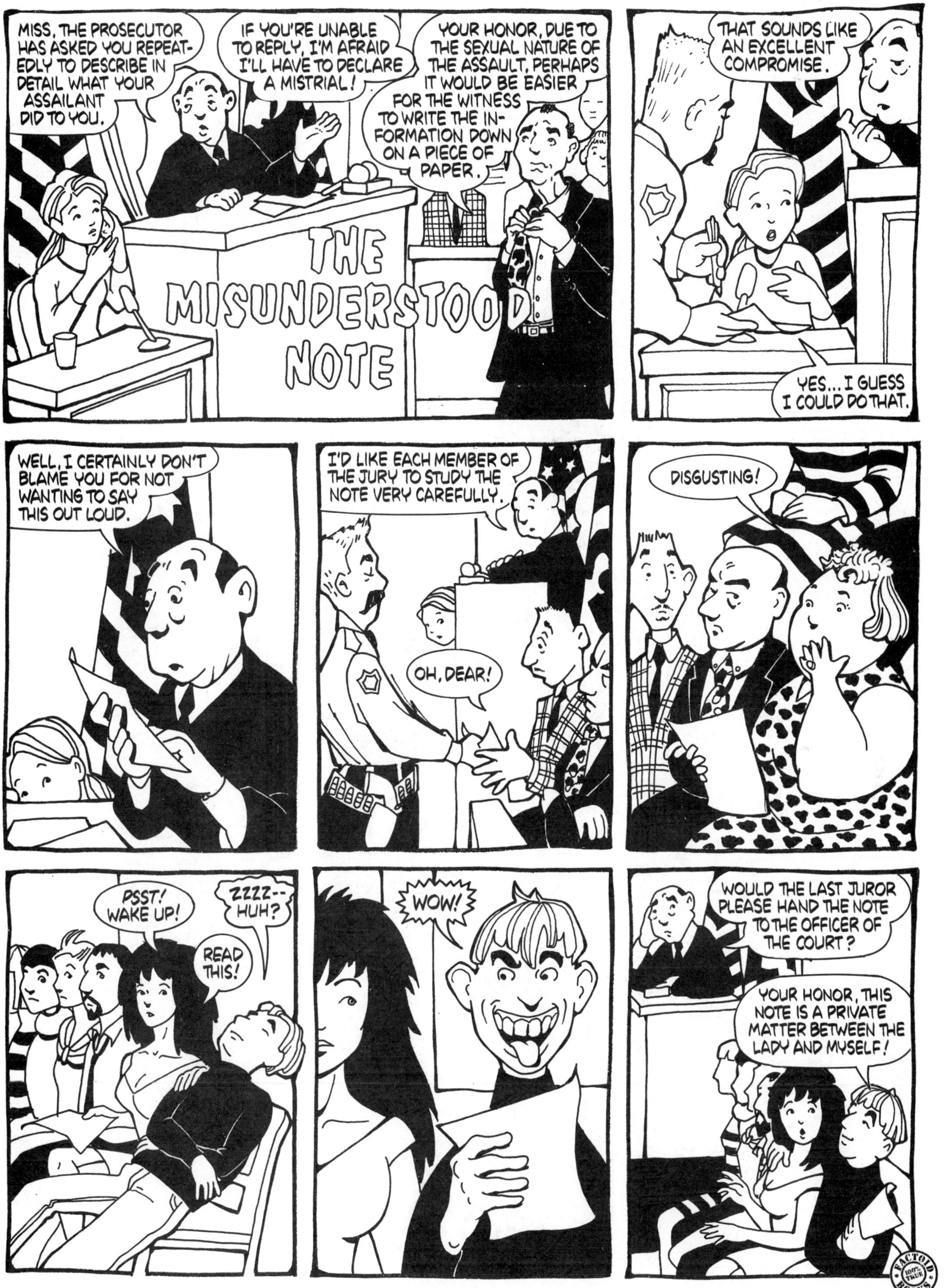
MISS, THE PROSECUTOR HAS ASKED YOU REPEATEDLY TO DESCRIBE IN DETAIL WHAT YOUR ASSAILANT DID TO YOU.
IF YOU'RE UNABLE TO REPLY, I'M AFRAID I'LL HAVE TO DECLARE A MISTRIAL!
YOUR HONOR, DUE TO THE SEXUAL NATURE OF THE ASSAULT, PERHAPS IT WOULD BE EASIER FOR THE WITNESS TO WRITE THE INFORMATION DOWN ON A PIECE OF PAPER.
THE MISUNDERSTOOD NOTE
THAT SOUNDS LIKE AN EXCELLENT COMPROMISE.
YES... I GUESS I COULD DO THAT.
WELL, I CERTAINLY DON'T BLAME YOU FOR NOT WANTING TO SAY THIS OUT LOUD.
I'D LIKE EACH MEMBER OF THE JURY TO STUDY THE NOTE VERY CAREFULLY.
OH, DEAR!
DISGUSTING!
PSST! WAKE UP!
ZZZZ--HUH?
READ THIS!
WOW!
WOULD THE LAST JUROR PLEASE HAND THE NOTE TO THE OFFICER OF THE COURT?
YOUR HONOR, THIS NOTE IS A PRIVATE MATTER BETWEEN THE LADY AND MYSELF!
FACTOID 100% TRUE BOOKS

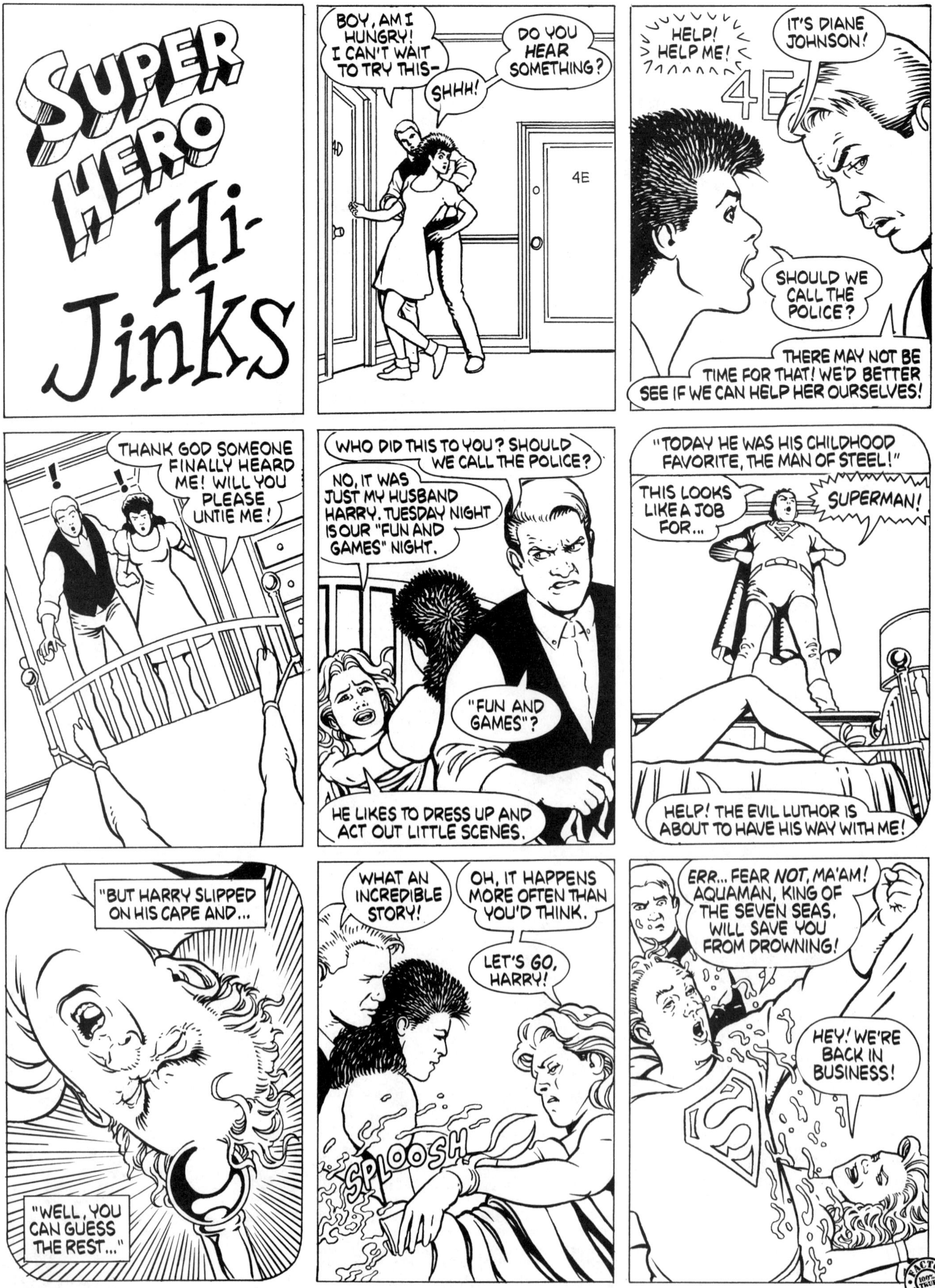
SUPER HERO Hi-Jinks
BOY, AM I HUNGRY! I CAN'T WAIT TO TRY THIS-
SHHH!
DO YOU HEAR SOMETHING?
4D
4E
HELP! HELP ME!
IT'S DIANE JOHNSON!
4E
SHOULD WE CALL THE POLICE?
THERE MAY NOT BE TIME FOR THAT! WE'D BETTER SEE IF WE CAN HELP HER OURSELVES!
THANK GOD SOMEONE FINALLY HEARD ME! WILL YOU PLEASE UNTIE ME!
WHO DID THIS TO YOU? SHOULD WE CALL THE POLICE?
NO, IT WAS JUST MY HUSBAND HARRY. TUESDAY NIGHT IS OUR "FUN AND GAMES" NIGHT.
"FUN AND GAMES"?
HE LIKES TO DRESS UP AND ACT OUT LITTLE SCENES.
"TODAY HE WAS HIS CHILDHOOD FAVORITE, THE MAN OF STEEL!"
THIS LOOKS LIKE A JOB FOR...
SUPERMAN!
HELP! THE EVIL LUTHOR IS ABOUT TO HAVE HIS WAY WITH ME!
"BUT HARRY SLIPPED ON HIS CAPE AND...
"WELL, YOU CAN GUESS THE REST..."
WHAT AN INCREDIBLE STORY!
OH, IT HAPPENS MORE OFTEN THAN YOU'D THINK.
LET'S GO, HARRY!
SPLOOSH
ERR... FEAR NOT, MA'AM! AQUAMAN, KING OF THE SEVEN SEAS, WILL SAVE YOU FROM DROWNING!
HEY! WE'RE BACK IN BUSINESS!

FACTOID BOOKS 100% TRUE

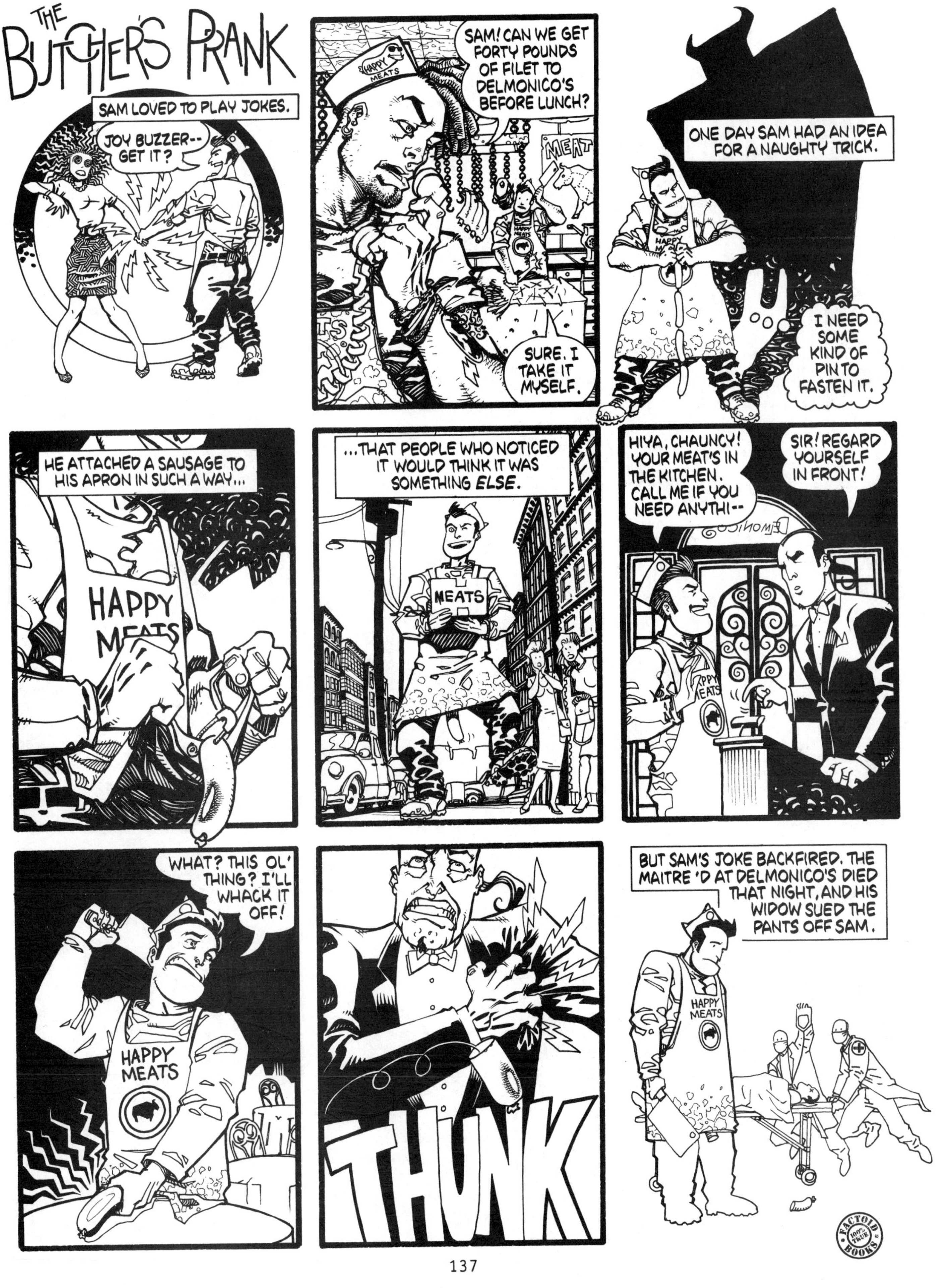
THE BUTCHER'S PRANK
SAM LOVED TO PLAY JOKES.
JOY BUZZER-- GET IT?
SAM! CAN WE GET FORTY POUNDS OF FILET TO DELMONICO'S BEFORE LUNCH?
HAPPY MEATS
MEAT
SURE. I TAKE IT MYSELF.
ONE DAY SAM HAD AN IDEA FOR A NAUGHTY TRICK.
I NEED SOME KIND OF PIN TO FASTEN IT.
HE ATTACHED A SAUSAGE TO HIS APRON IN SUCH A WAY...
HAPPY MEATS
...THAT PEOPLE WHO NOTICED IT WOULD THINK IT WAS SOMETHING ELSE.
MEATS
HIYA, CHAUNCY! YOUR MEAT'S IN THE KITCHEN. CALL ME IF YOU NEED ANYTHI--
SIR! REGARD YOURSELF IN FRONT!
WHAT? THIS OL' THING? I'LL WHACK IT OFF!
HAPPY MEATS
THUNK
BUT SAM'S JOKE BACKFIRED. THE MAITRE 'D AT DELMONICO'S DIED THAT NIGHT, AND HIS WIDOW SUED THE PANTS OFF SAM.
HAPPY MEATS
FACTOID 100% TRUE BOOKS

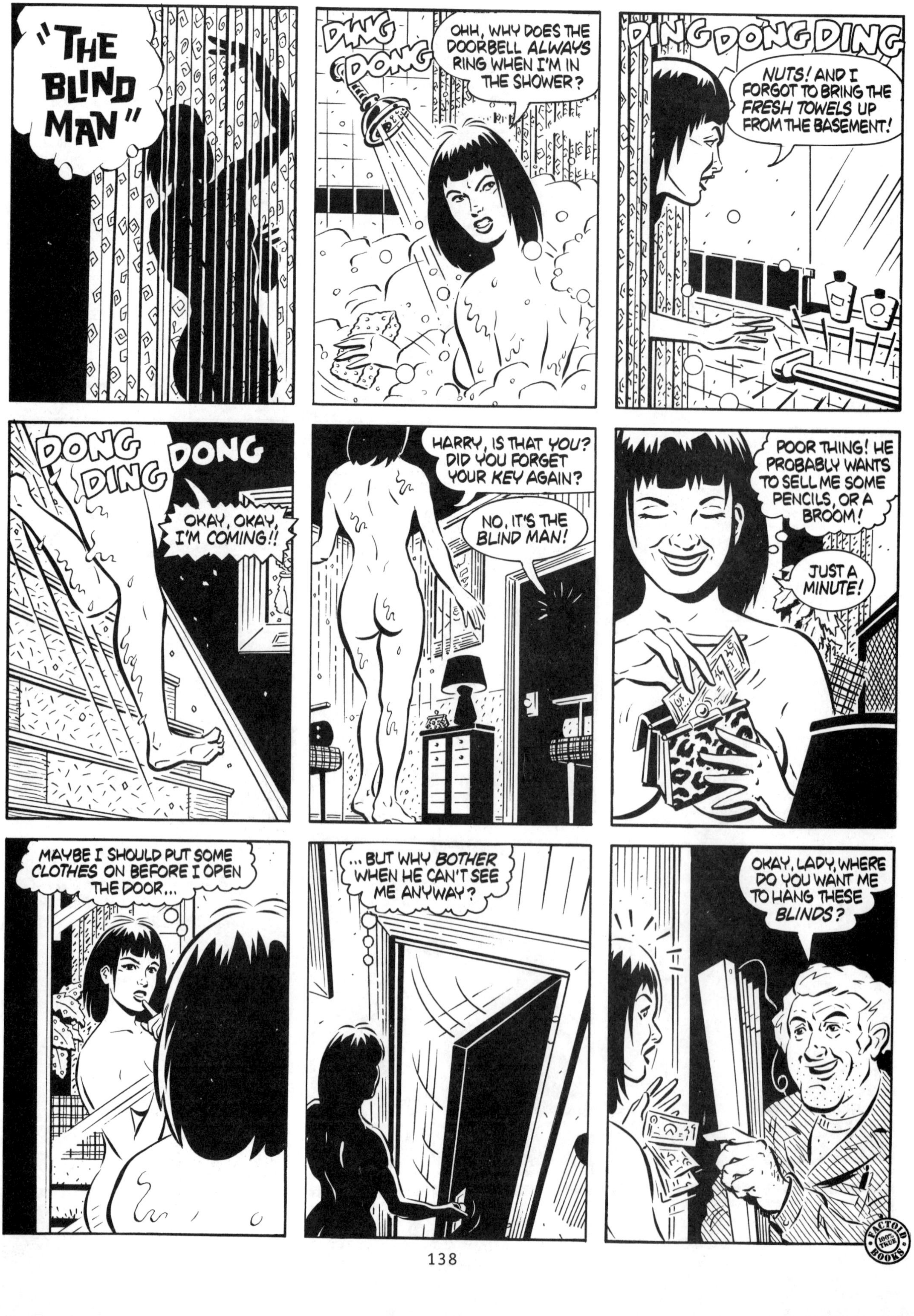
"THE BLIND MAN"
DING DONG
OHH, WHY DOES THE DOORBELL ALWAYS RING WHEN I'M IN THE SHOWER?
DING DONG DING
NUTS! AND I FORGOT TO BRING THE FRESH TOWELS UP FROM THE BASEMENT!
DONG DING DONG
OKAY, OKAY, I'M COMING!!
HARRY, IS THAT YOU? DID YOU FORGET YOUR KEY AGAIN?
NO, IT'S THE BLIND MAN!
POOR THING! HE PROBABLY WANTS TO SELL ME SOME PENCILS, OR A BROOM!
JUST A MINUTE!
MAYBE I SHOULD PUT SOME CLOTHES ON BEFORE I OPEN THE DOOR...
...BUT WHY BOTHER WHEN HE CAN'T SEE ME ANYWAY?
OKAY, LADY, WHERE DO YOU WANT ME TO HANG THESE BLINDS?
FACTOID 100% TRUE BOOKS

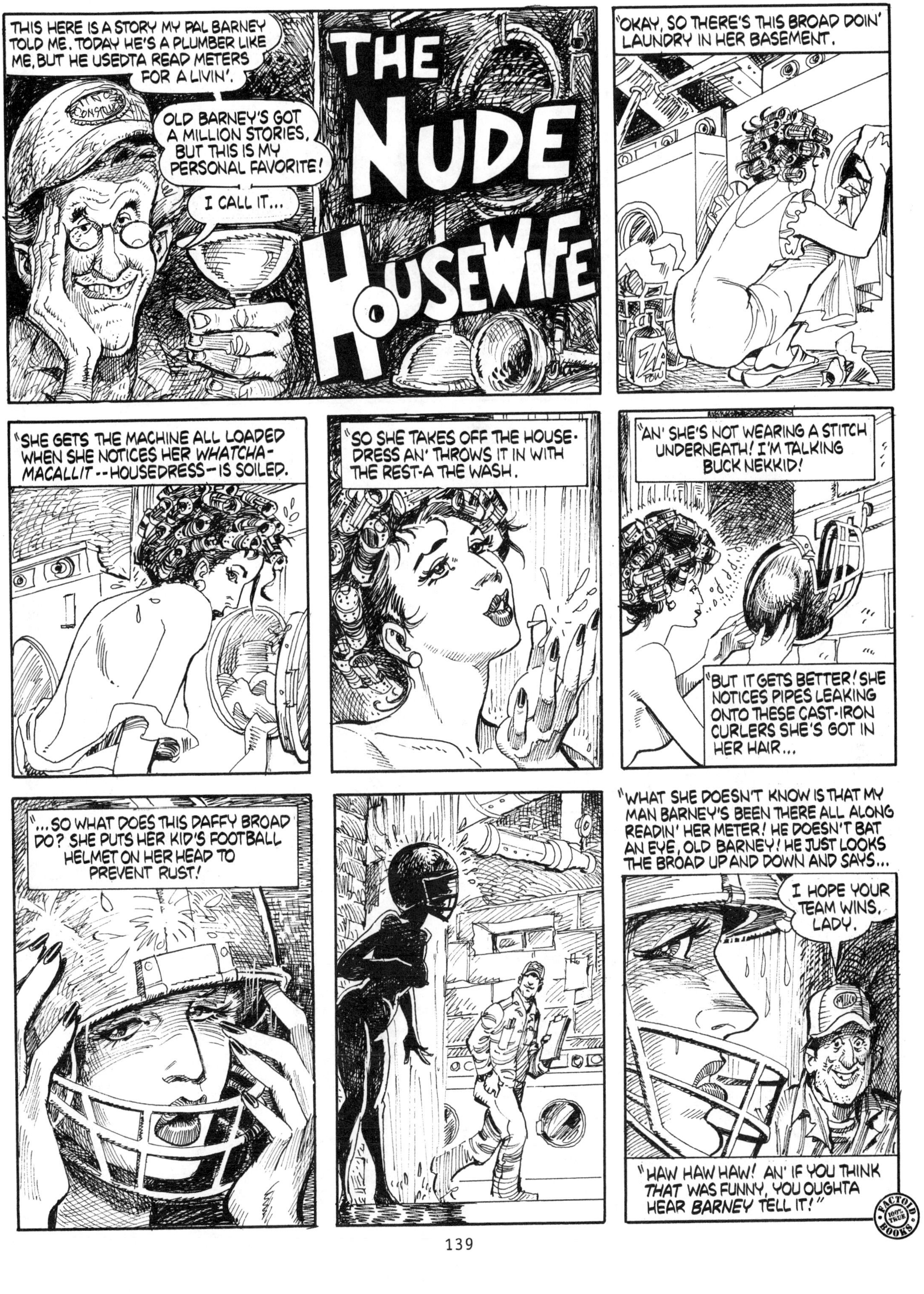
THIS HERE IS A STORY MY PAL BARNEY TOLD ME. TODAY HE'S A PLUMBER LIKE ME, BUT HE USEDTA READ METERS FOR A LIVIN'.
OLD BARNEY'S GOT A MILLION STORIES, BUT THIS IS MY PERSONAL FAVORITE!
I CALL IT...
THE NUDE HOUSEWIFE
"OKAY, SO THERE'S THIS BROAD DOIN' LAUNDRY IN HER BASEMENT.
"SHE GETS THE MACHINE ALL LOADED WHEN SHE NOTICES HER *WHATCHA-MACALLIT* -- HOUSEDRESS -- IS SOILED.
"SO SHE TAKES OFF THE HOUSE-DRESS AN' THROWS IT IN WITH THE REST-A THE WASH.
"AN' SHE'S NOT WEARING A STITCH UNDERNEATH! I'M TALKING BUCK NEKKID!
"BUT IT GETS BETTER! SHE NOTICES PIPES LEAKING ONTO THESE CAST-IRON CURLERS SHE'S GOT IN HER HAIR...
"...SO WHAT DOES THIS DAFFY BROAD DO? SHE PUTS HER KID'S FOOTBALL HELMET ON HER HEAD TO PREVENT RUST!
"WHAT SHE DOESN'T KNOW IS THAT MY MAN BARNEY'S BEEN THERE ALL ALONG READIN' HER METER! HE DOESN'T BAT AN EYE, OLD BARNEY! HE JUST LOOKS THE BROAD UP AND DOWN AND SAYS...
I HOPE YOUR TEAM WINS, LADY.
"HAW HAW HAW! AN' IF YOU THINK *THAT* WAS FUNNY, YOU OUGHTA HEAR *BARNEY* TELL IT!"
FACTOID BOOKS 100% TRUE

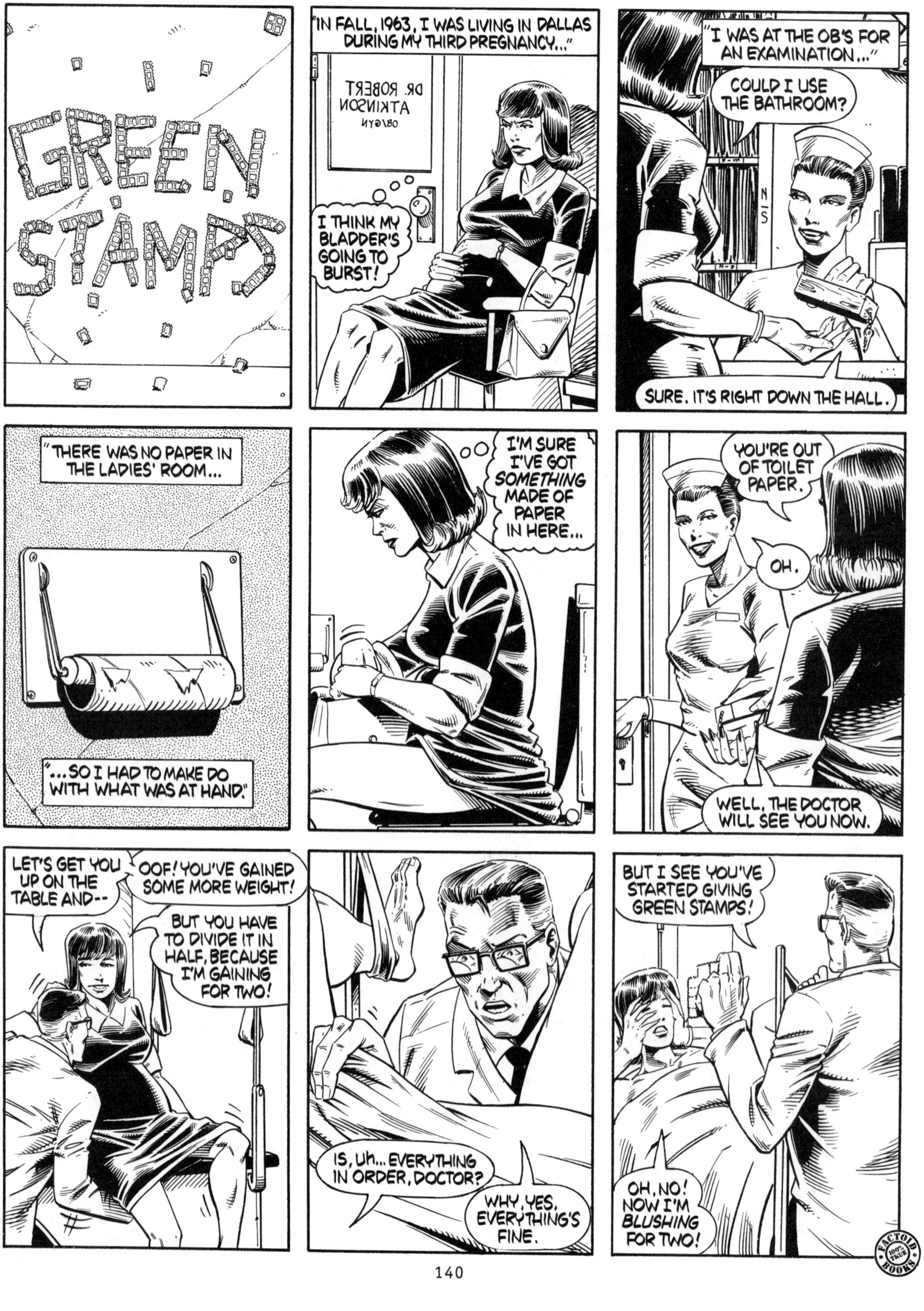
GREEN STAMPS
"IN FALL, 1963, I WAS LIVING IN DALLAS DURING MY THIRD PREGNANCY..."
DR. ROBERT ATKINSON OB/GYN
I THINK MY BLADDER'S GOING TO BURST!
"I WAS AT THE OB'S FOR AN EXAMINATION..."
COULD I USE THE BATHROOM?
SURE. IT'S RIGHT DOWN THE HALL.
"THERE WAS NO PAPER IN THE LADIES' ROOM...
"...SO I HAD TO MAKE DO WITH WHAT WAS AT HAND."
I'M SURE I'VE GOT SOMETHING MADE OF PAPER IN HERE...
YOU'RE OUT OF TOILET PAPER.
OH.
WELL, THE DOCTOR WILL SEE YOU NOW.
LET'S GET YOU UP ON THE TABLE AND--
OOF! YOU'VE GAINED SOME MORE WEIGHT!
BUT YOU HAVE TO DIVIDE IT IN HALF, BECAUSE I'M GAINING FOR TWO!
IS, UH... EVERYTHING IN ORDER, DOCTOR?
WHY, YES, EVERYTHING'S FINE.
BUT I SEE YOU'VE STARTED GIVING GREEN STAMPS!
OH, NO! NOW I'M BLUSHING FOR TWO!
FACTOID BOOKS 100% TRUE

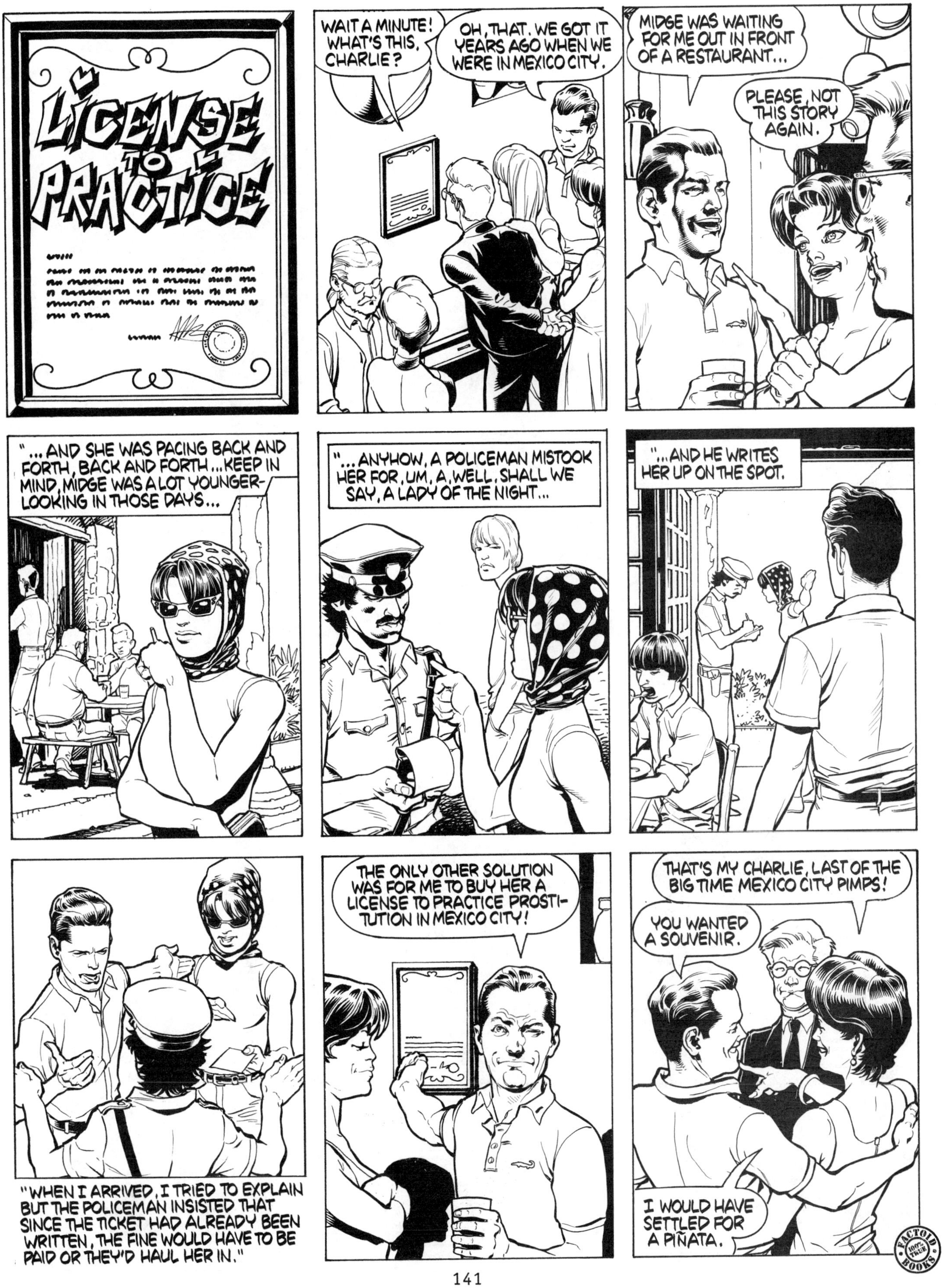
LICENSE TO PRACTICE
WAIT A MINUTE! WHAT'S THIS, CHARLIE?
OH, THAT. WE GOT IT YEARS AGO WHEN WE WERE IN MEXICO CITY.
MIDGE WAS WAITING FOR ME OUT IN FRONT OF A RESTAURANT...
PLEASE, NOT THIS STORY AGAIN.
"...AND SHE WAS PACING BACK AND FORTH, BACK AND FORTH...KEEP IN MIND, MIDGE WAS A LOT YOUNGER-LOOKING IN THOSE DAYS...
"...ANYHOW, A POLICEMAN MISTOOK HER FOR, UM, A, WELL, SHALL WE SAY, A LADY OF THE NIGHT...
"...AND HE WRITES HER UP ON THE SPOT.
"WHEN I ARRIVED, I TRIED TO EXPLAIN BUT THE POLICEMAN INSISTED THAT SINCE THE TICKET HAD ALREADY BEEN WRITTEN, THE FINE WOULD HAVE TO BE PAID OR THEY'D HAUL HER IN."
THE ONLY OTHER SOLUTION WAS FOR ME TO BUY HER A LICENSE TO PRACTICE PROSTITUTION IN MEXICO CITY!
THAT'S MY CHARLIE, LAST OF THE BIG TIME MEXICO CITY PIMPS!
YOU WANTED A SOUVENIR.
I WOULD HAVE SETTLED FOR A PIÑATA.

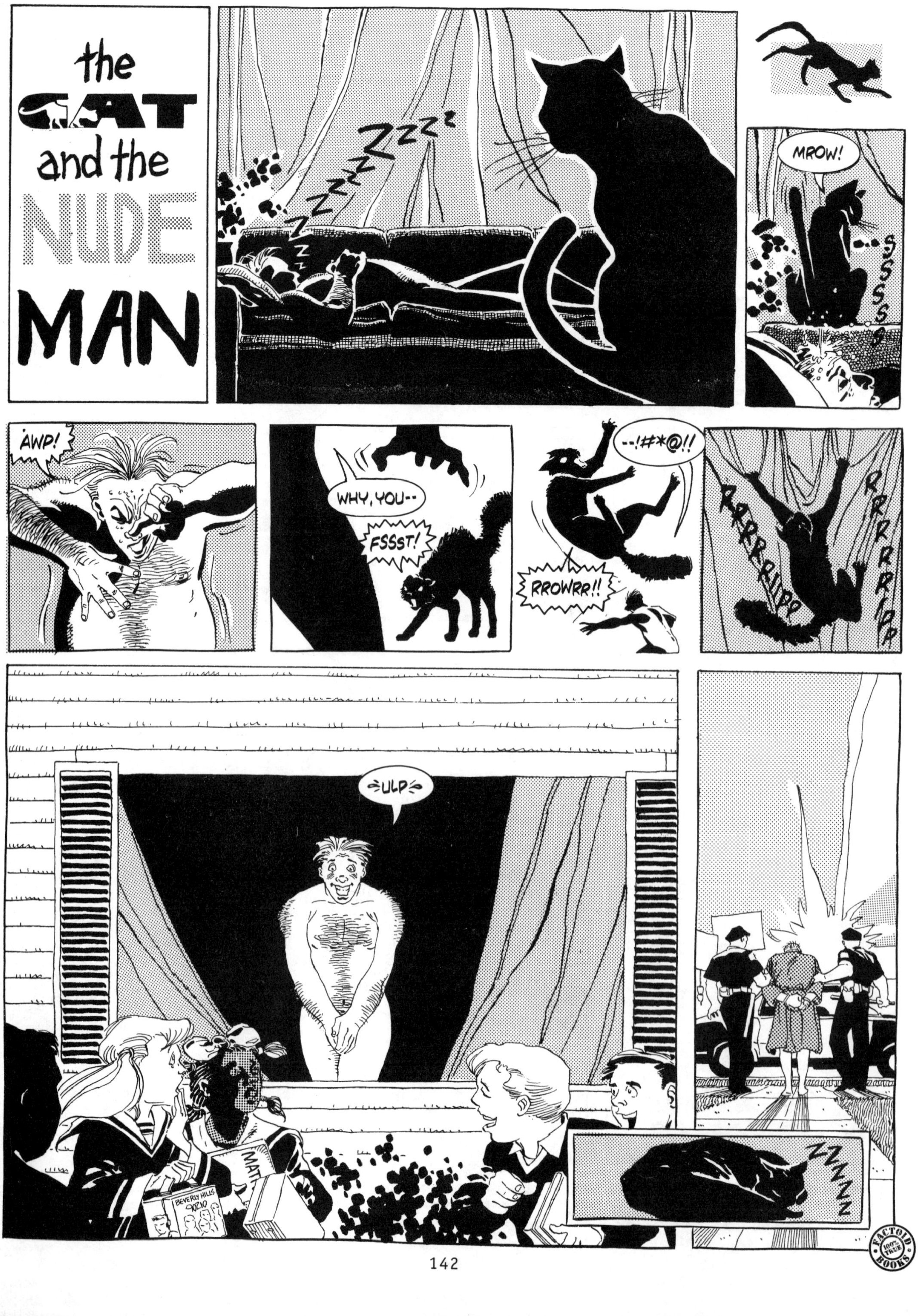
the
CAT
and the
NUDE
MAN
ZZZZZZZZZZ
MROW!
SSSSS
AWP!
WHY, YOU--
FSSST!
--!#*@!!
RROWRR!!
RRRRRIPP
RRRRRRIPP
ULP
BEVERLY HILLS 90210
ZZZZZ
FACTOID BOOKS 100% TRUE

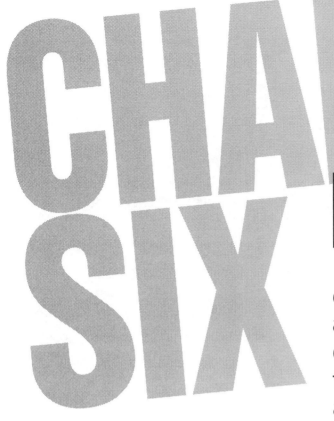

CHAPTER SIX

CRIME LEGENDS

CRIMES AND MISDEMEANORS

In real life, many everyday crimes are just predictable and depressing incidents — a dismal series of muggings, car thefts, holdups, shopliftings and the like. Most of us, thankfully, have little experience with the likes of murders, jewel thefts, terrorism, or international spying, except in mystery novels and other media products. The perspective on crime that urban legends provide is of rather ordinary criminal acts that lead up to an unexpected and often ironic and humorous plot twist. The most common legend-crime is theft, involving anything from a cookie *(page 159)* to a kidney *(page 154)*.

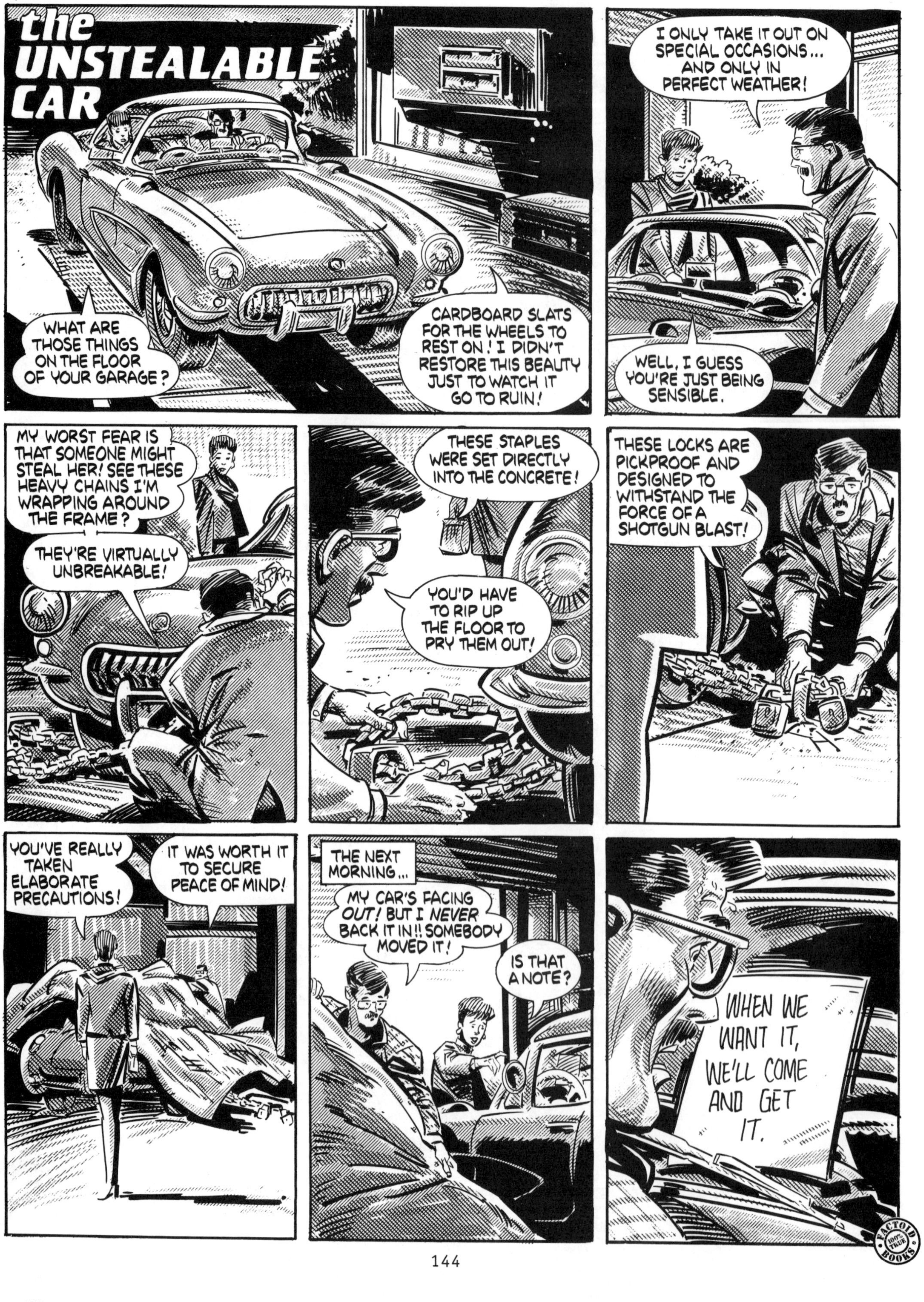
the UNSTEALABLE CAR
WHAT ARE THOSE THINGS ON THE FLOOR OF YOUR GARAGE?
CARDBOARD SLATS FOR THE WHEELS TO REST ON! I DIDN'T RESTORE THIS BEAUTY JUST TO WATCH IT GO TO RUIN!
I ONLY TAKE IT OUT ON SPECIAL OCCASIONS... AND ONLY IN PERFECT WEATHER!
WELL, I GUESS YOU'RE JUST BEING SENSIBLE.
MY WORST FEAR IS THAT SOMEONE MIGHT STEAL HER! SEE THESE HEAVY CHAINS I'M WRAPPING AROUND THE FRAME?
THEY'RE VIRTUALLY UNBREAKABLE!
THESE STAPLES WERE SET DIRECTLY INTO THE CONCRETE!
YOU'D HAVE TO RIP UP THE FLOOR TO PRY THEM OUT!
THESE LOCKS ARE PICKPROOF AND DESIGNED TO WITHSTAND THE FORCE OF A SHOTGUN BLAST!
YOU'VE REALLY TAKEN ELABORATE PRECAUTIONS!
IT WAS WORTH IT TO SECURE PEACE OF MIND!
THE NEXT MORNING...
MY CAR'S FACING OUT! BUT I NEVER BACK IT IN!! SOMEBODY MOVED IT!
IS THAT A NOTE?
WHEN WE WANT IT, WE'LL COME AND GET IT.
FACTOID BOOKS 100% TRUE

THE DOUBLE THEFT

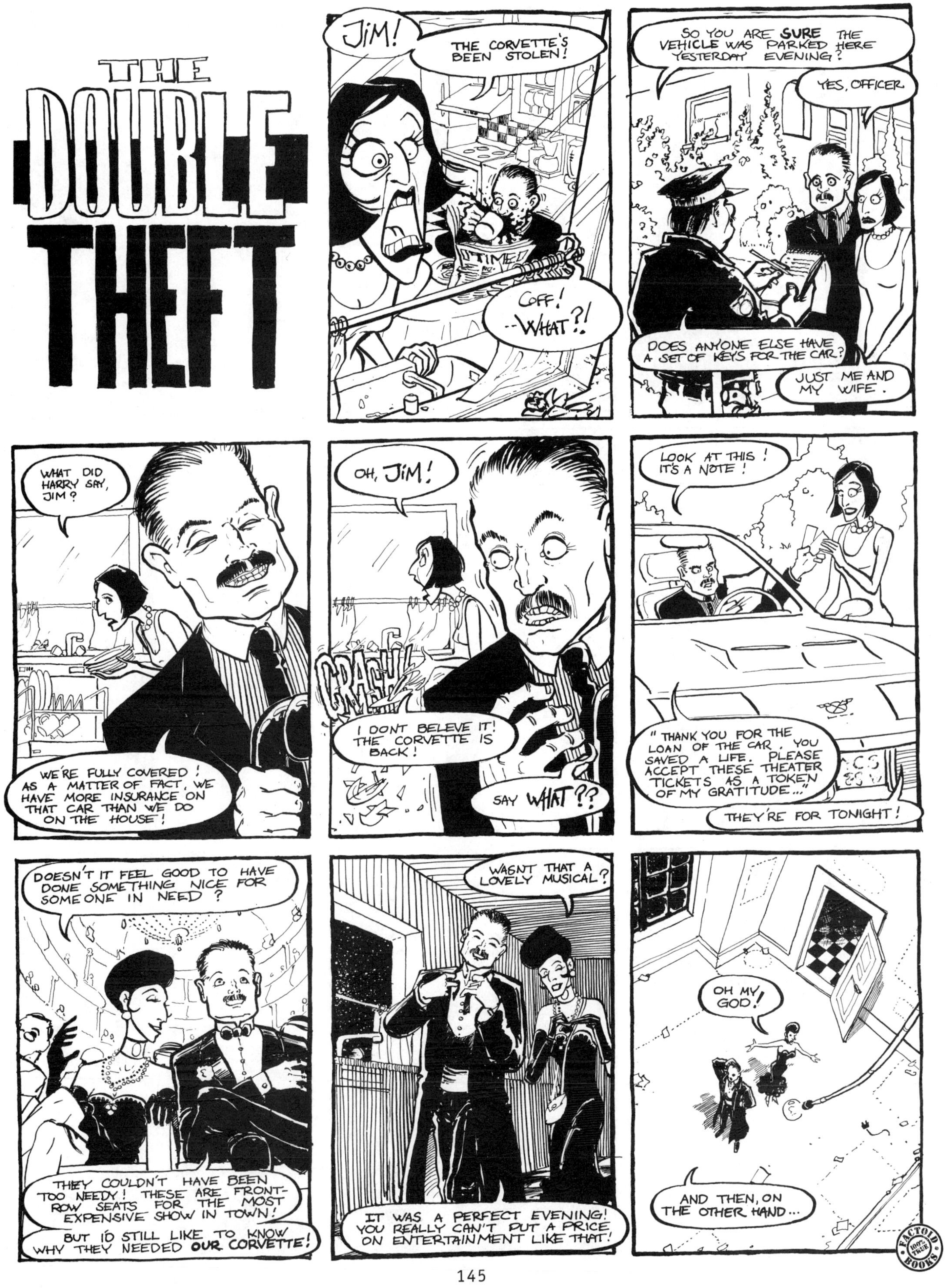

JIM!
THE CORVETTE'S BEEN STOLEN!
COFF! --WHAT?!
SO YOU ARE **SURE** THE VEHICLE WAS PARKED HERE YESTERDAY EVENING?
YES, OFFICER.
DOES ANYONE ELSE HAVE A SET OF KEYS FOR THE CAR?
JUST ME AND MY WIFE.
WHAT DID HARRY SAY, JIM?
WE'RE FULLY COVERED! AS A MATTER OF FACT, WE HAVE MORE INSURANCE ON THAT CAR THAN WE DO ON THE HOUSE!
OH, JIM!
CRASH!
I DONT BELEVE IT! THE CORVETTE IS BACK!
SAY WHAT??
LOOK AT THIS! IT'S A NOTE!
"THANK YOU FOR THE LOAN OF THE CAR. YOU SAVED A LIFE. PLEASE ACCEPT THESE THEATER TICKETS AS A TOKEN OF MY GRATITUDE..."
THEY'RE FOR TONIGHT!
DOESN'T IT FEEL GOOD TO HAVE DONE SOMETHING NICE FOR SOMEONE IN NEED?
THEY COULDN'T HAVE BEEN TOO NEEDY! THESE ARE FRONT-ROW SEATS FOR THE MOST EXPENSIVE SHOW IN TOWN!
BUT I'D STILL LIKE TO KNOW WHY THEY NEEDED **OUR CORVETTE**!
WASNT THAT A LOVELY MUSICAL?
IT WAS A PERFECT EVENING! YOU REALLY CAN'T PUT A PRICE ON ENTERTAINMENT LIKE THAT!
OH MY GOD!
AND THEN, ON THE OTHER HAND...
FACTOID BOOKS 100% TRUE

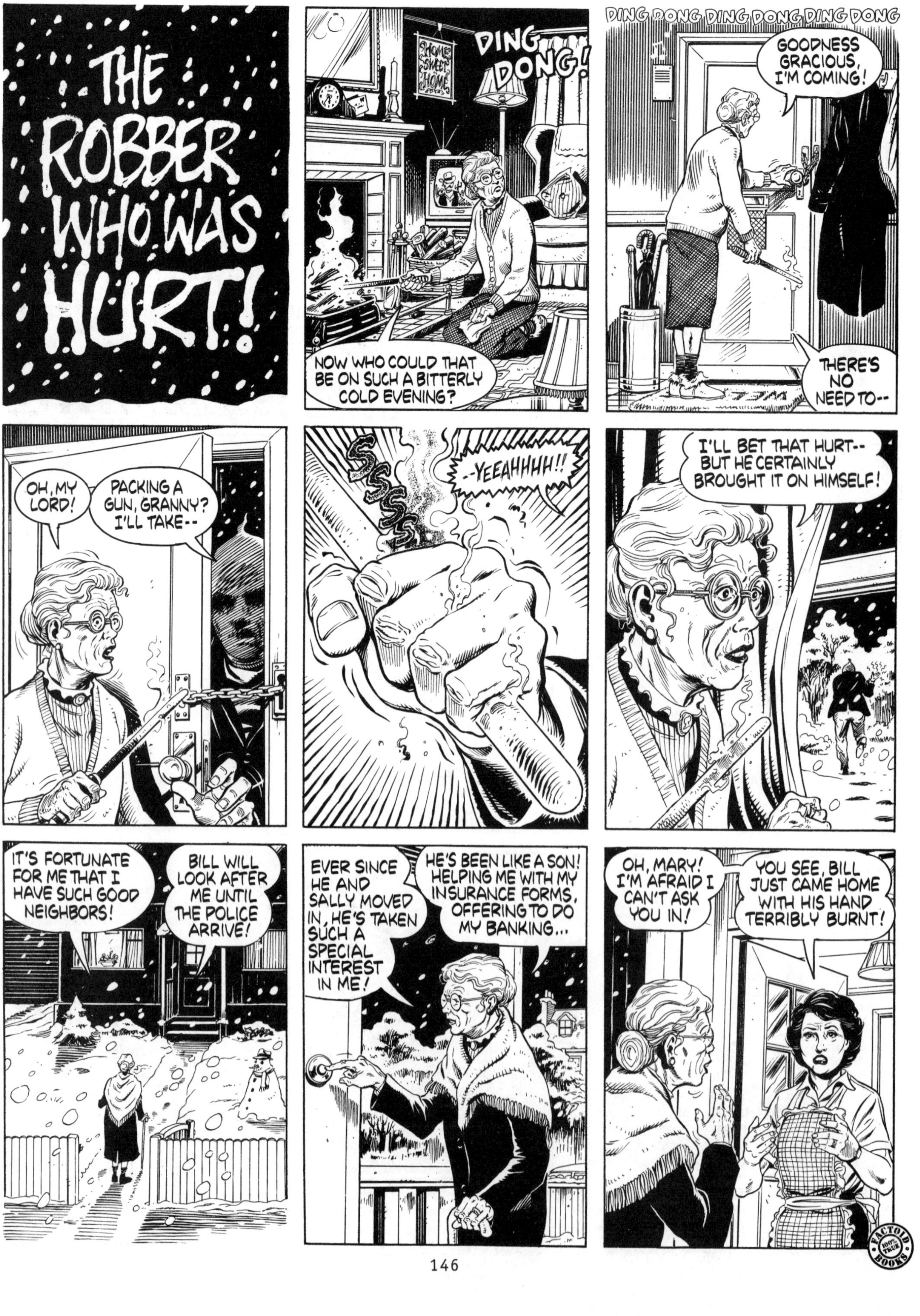
THE ROBBER WHO WAS HURT!
DING DONG!
NOW WHO COULD THAT BE ON SUCH A BITTERLY COLD EVENING?
DING DONG DING DONG DING DONG
GOODNESS GRACIOUS, I'M COMING!
THERE'S NO NEED TO--
OH, MY LORD!
PACKING A GUN, GRANNY? I'LL TAKE--
SSSSS
--YEEAHHHH!!
I'LL BET THAT HURT-- BUT HE CERTAINLY BROUGHT IT ON HIMSELF!
IT'S FORTUNATE FOR ME THAT I HAVE SUCH GOOD NEIGHBORS!
BILL WILL LOOK AFTER ME UNTIL THE POLICE ARRIVE!
EVER SINCE HE AND SALLY MOVED IN, HE'S TAKEN SUCH A SPECIAL INTEREST IN ME!
HE'S BEEN LIKE A SON! HELPING ME WITH MY INSURANCE FORMS, OFFERING TO DO MY BANKING...
OH, MARY! I'M AFRAID I CAN'T ASK YOU IN!
YOU SEE, BILL JUST CAME HOME WITH HIS HAND TERRIBLY BURNT!
FACTOID BOOKS 100% TRUE

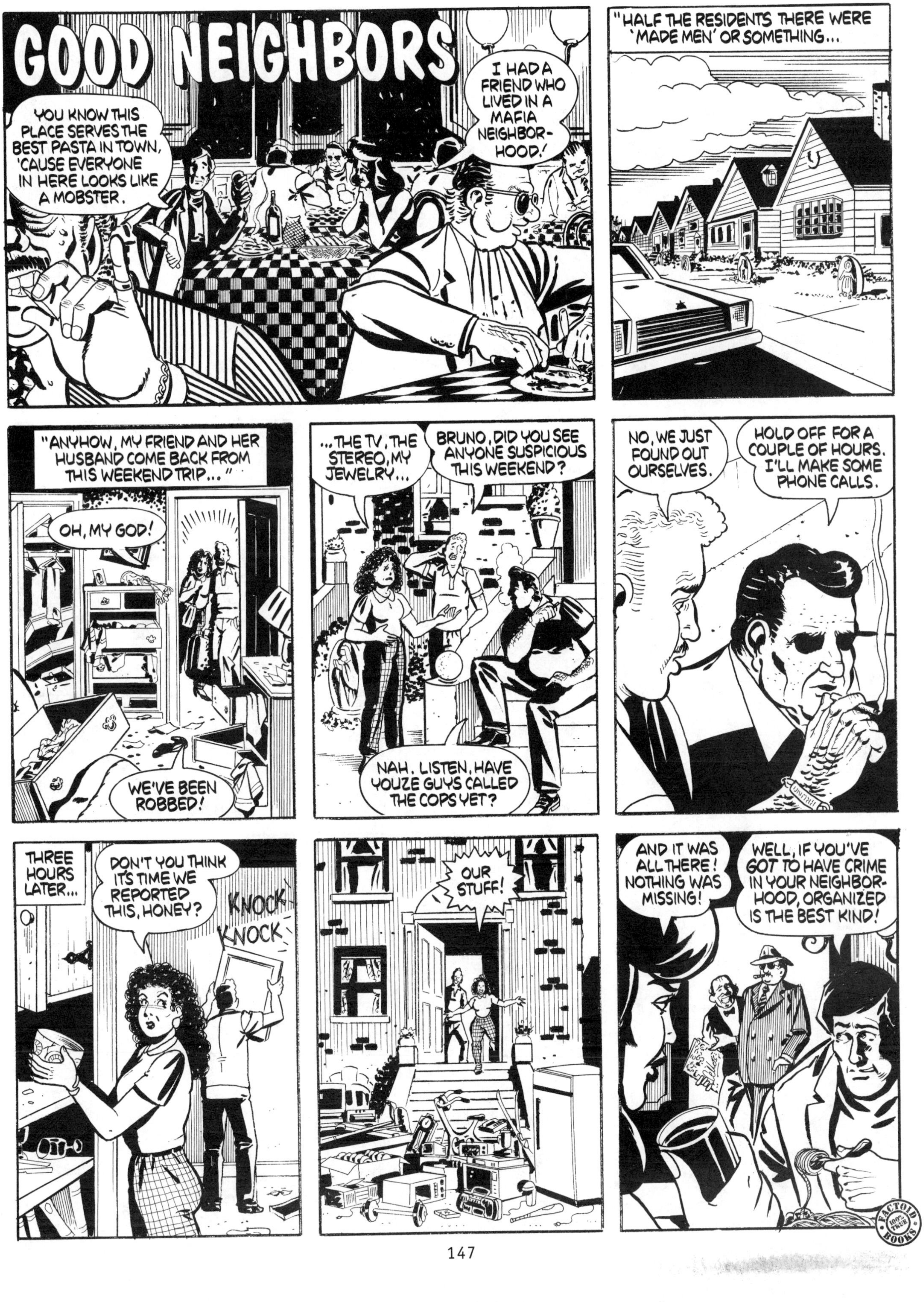
GOOD NEIGHBORS
YOU KNOW THIS PLACE SERVES THE BEST PASTA IN TOWN, 'CAUSE EVERYONE IN HERE LOOKS LIKE A MOBSTER.
I HAD A FRIEND WHO LIVED IN A MAFIA NEIGHBOR-HOOD!
"HALF THE RESIDENTS THERE WERE 'MADE MEN' OR SOMETHING...
"ANYHOW, MY FRIEND AND HER HUSBAND COME BACK FROM THIS WEEKEND TRIP..."
OH, MY GOD!
WE'VE BEEN ROBBED!
...THE TV, THE STEREO, MY JEWELRY...
BRUNO, DID YOU SEE ANYONE SUSPICIOUS THIS WEEKEND?
NAH. LISTEN, HAVE YOUZE GUYS CALLED THE COPS YET?
NO, WE JUST FOUND OUT OURSELVES.
HOLD OFF FOR A COUPLE OF HOURS. I'LL MAKE SOME PHONE CALLS.
THREE HOURS LATER...
DON'T YOU THINK IT'S TIME WE REPORTED THIS, HONEY?
KNOCK KNOCK
OUR STUFF!
AND IT WAS ALL THERE! NOTHING WAS MISSING!
WELL, IF YOU'VE *GOT* TO HAVE CRIME IN YOUR NEIGHBOR-HOOD, ORGANIZED IS THE BEST KIND!

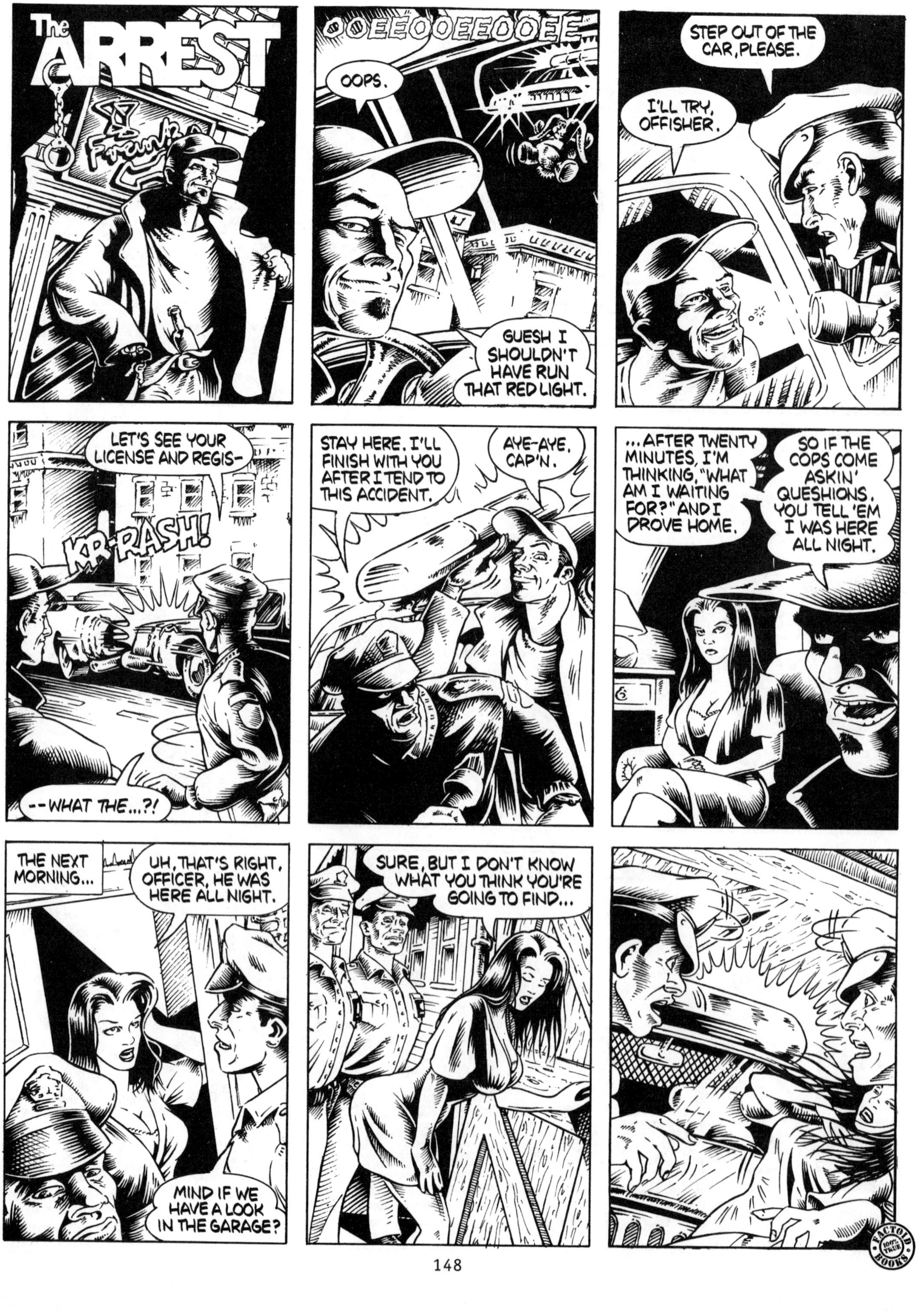
The ARREST
OOEEEOOEEEOOEE
OOPS.
GUESH I SHOULDN'T HAVE RUN THAT RED LIGHT.
STEP OUT OF THE CAR, PLEASE.
I'LL TRY, OFFISHER.
LET'S SEE YOUR LICENSE AND REGIS-
KR-RASH!
--WHAT THE...?!
STAY HERE. I'LL FINISH WITH YOU AFTER I TEND TO THIS ACCIDENT.
AYE-AYE, CAP'N.
...AFTER TWENTY MINUTES, I'M THINKING, "WHAT AM I WAITING FOR?" AND I DROVE HOME.
SO IF THE COPS COME ASKIN' QUESHIONS, YOU TELL 'EM I WAS HERE ALL NIGHT.
THE NEXT MORNING...
UH, THAT'S RIGHT, OFFICER, HE WAS HERE ALL NIGHT.
MIND IF WE HAVE A LOOK IN THE GARAGE?
SURE, BUT I DON'T KNOW WHAT YOU THINK YOU'RE GOING TO FIND...

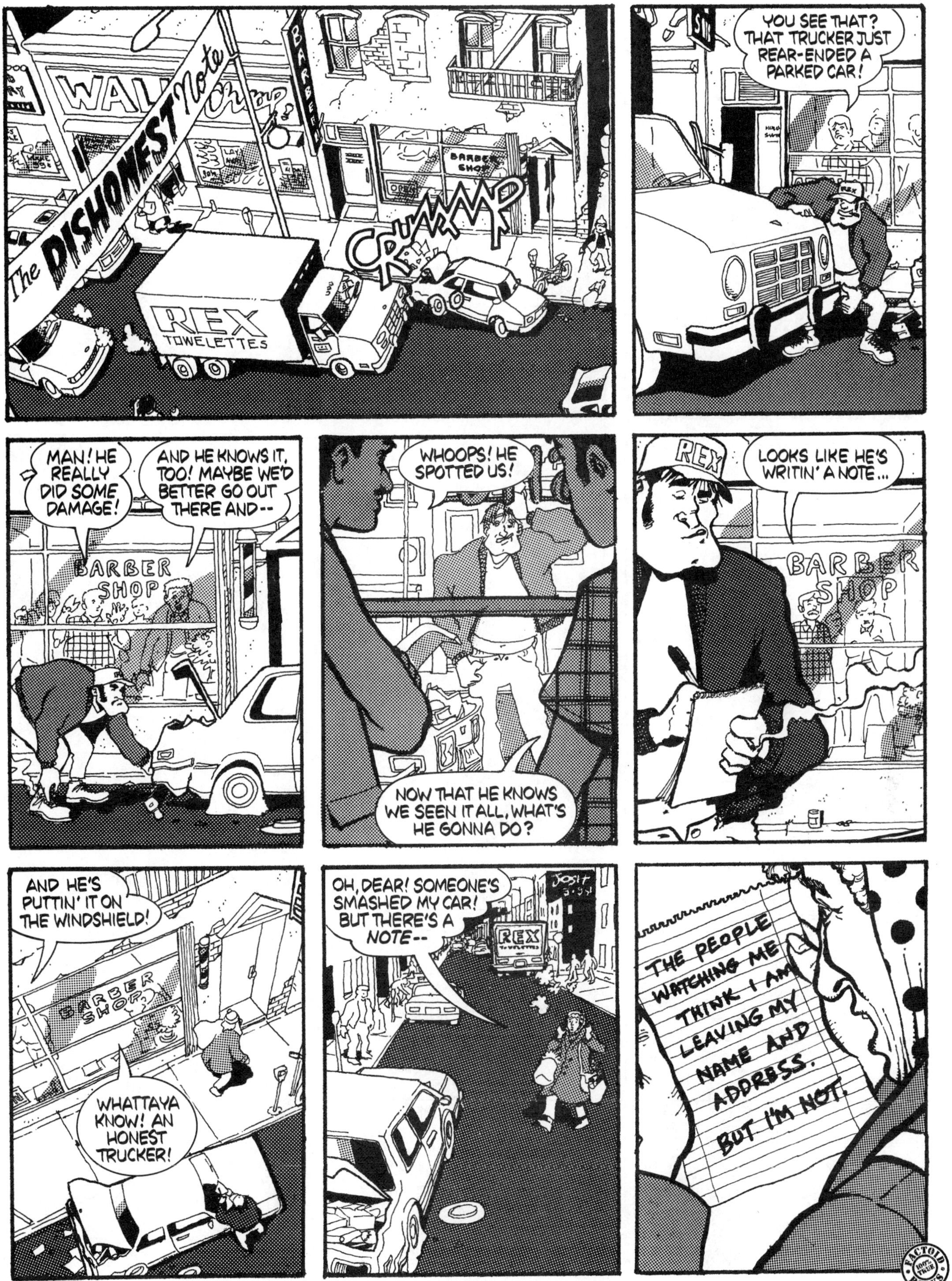

The DISHONEST Note
BARBER
BARBER SHOP
REX TOWELETTES
CRUNNNCH
YOU SEE THAT? THAT TRUCKER JUST REAR-ENDED A PARKED CAR!
MAN! HE REALLY DID SOME DAMAGE!
AND HE KNOWS IT, TOO! MAYBE WE'D BETTER GO OUT THERE AND--
BARBER SHOP
WHOOPS! HE SPOTTED US!
NOW THAT HE KNOWS WE SEEN IT ALL, WHAT'S HE GONNA DO?
REX
LOOKS LIKE HE'S WRITIN' A NOTE...
BARBER SHOP
AND HE'S PUTTIN' IT ON THE WINDSHIELD!
BARBER SHOP
WHATTAYA KNOW! AN HONEST TRUCKER!
OH, DEAR! SOMEONE'S SMASHED MY CAR! BUT THERE'S A *NOTE*--
REX TOWELETTES
THE PEOPLE WATCHING ME THINK I AM LEAVING MY NAME AND ADDRESS. BUT I'M NOT.
FACTOID BOOKS 100% TRUE

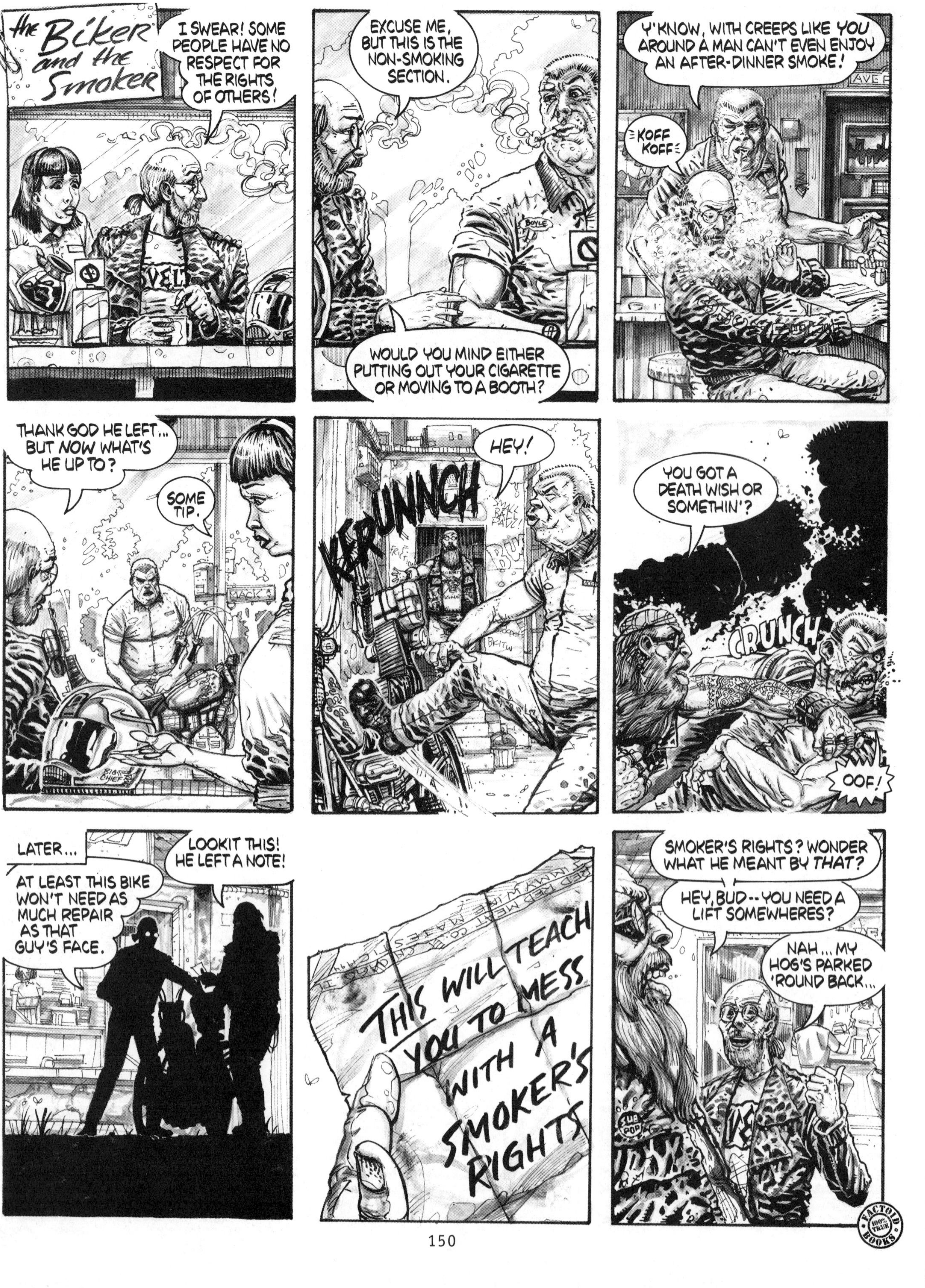
The Biker and the Smoker
I SWEAR! SOME PEOPLE HAVE NO RESPECT FOR THE RIGHTS OF OTHERS!
EXCUSE ME, BUT THIS IS THE NON-SMOKING SECTION.
WOULD YOU MIND EITHER PUTTING OUT YOUR CIGARETTE OR MOVING TO A BOOTH?
Y'KNOW, WITH CREEPS LIKE YOU AROUND A MAN CAN'T EVEN ENJOY AN AFTER-DINNER SMOKE!
KOFF KOFF
THANK GOD HE LEFT... BUT NOW WHAT'S HE UP TO?
SOME TIP.
HEY!
KERUNNCH
YOU GOT A DEATH WISH OR SOMETHIN'?
CRUNCH
OOF!
LATER...
LOOKIT THIS! HE LEFT A NOTE!
AT LEAST THIS BIKE WON'T NEED AS MUCH REPAIR AS THAT GUY'S FACE.
THIS WILL TEACH YOU TO MESS WITH A SMOKER'S RIGHTS
SMOKER'S RIGHTS? WONDER WHAT HE MEANT BY THAT?
HEY, BUD-- YOU NEED A LIFT SOMEWHERES?
NAH... MY HOG'S PARKED 'ROUND BACK...
FACTOID BOOKS 100% TRUE

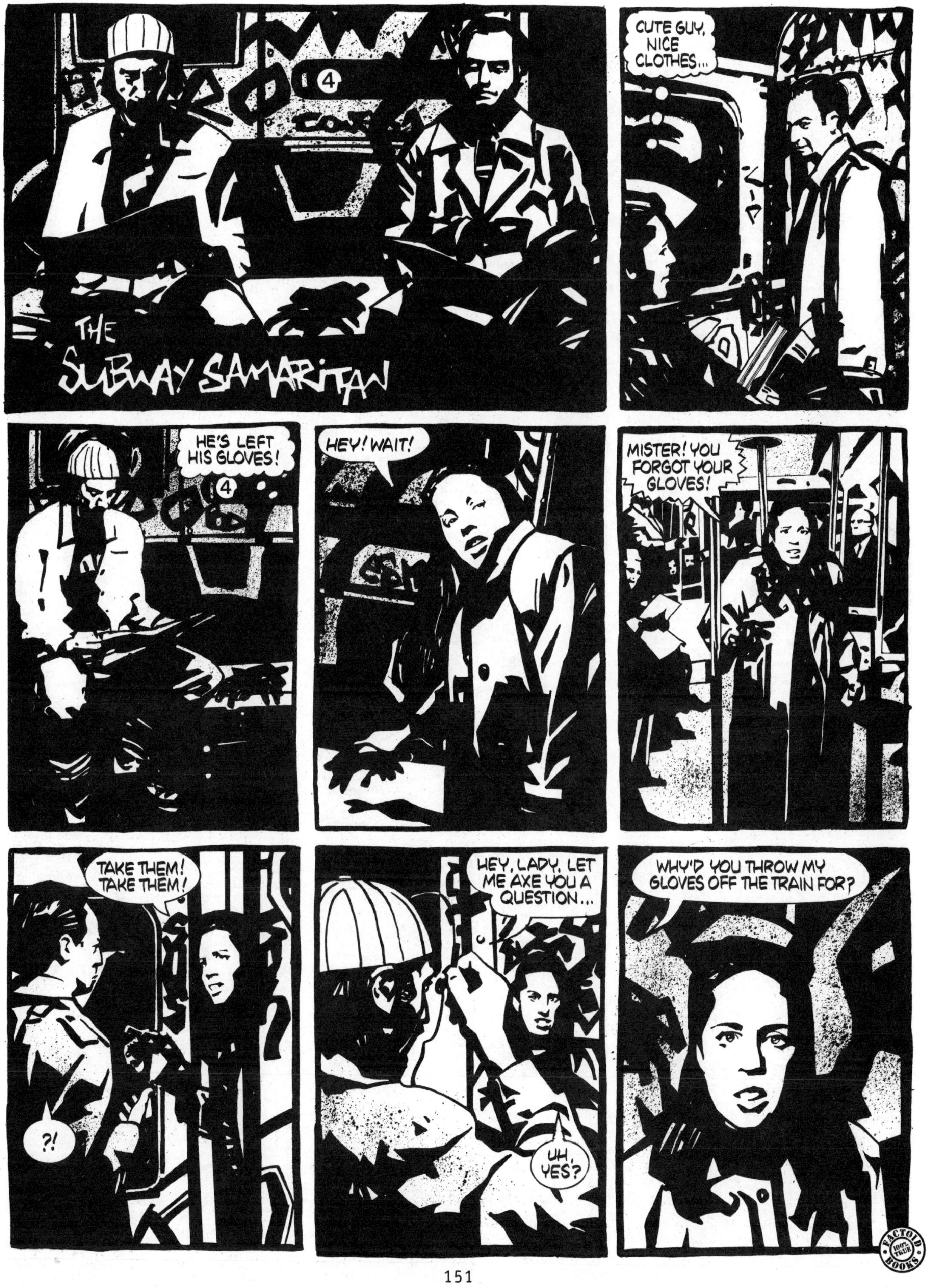
THE SUBWAY SAMARITAN
CUTE GUY, NICE CLOTHES...
HE'S LEFT HIS GLOVES!
HEY! WAIT!
MISTER! YOU FORGOT YOUR GLOVES!
TAKE THEM! TAKE THEM!
?!
HEY, LADY, LET ME AXE YOU A QUESTION...
UH, YES?
WHY'D YOU THROW MY GLOVES OFF THE TRAIN FOR?
FACTOID BOOKS 100% TRUE

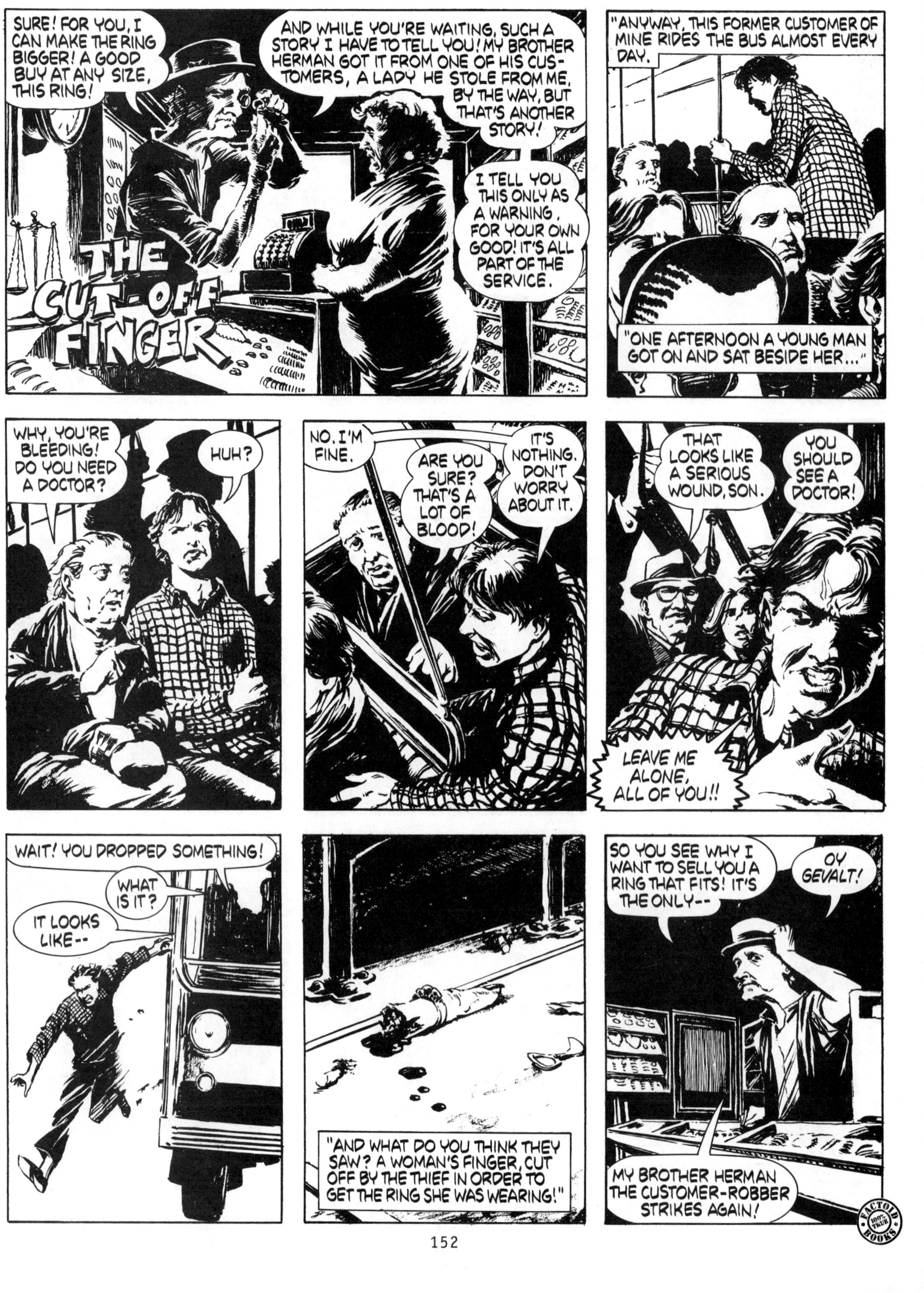
THE CUT-OFF FINGER
SURE! FOR YOU, I CAN MAKE THE RING BIGGER! A GOOD BUY AT ANY SIZE, THIS RING!
AND WHILE YOU'RE WAITING, SUCH A STORY I HAVE TO TELL YOU! MY BROTHER HERMAN GOT IT FROM ONE OF HIS CUSTOMERS, A LADY HE STOLE FROM ME, BY THE WAY, BUT THAT'S ANOTHER STORY!
I TELL YOU THIS ONLY AS A WARNING, FOR YOUR OWN GOOD! IT'S ALL PART OF THE SERVICE.
"ANYWAY, THIS FORMER CUSTOMER OF MINE RIDES THE BUS ALMOST EVERY DAY.
"ONE AFTERNOON A YOUNG MAN GOT ON AND SAT BESIDE HER..."
WHY, YOU'RE BLEEDING! DO YOU NEED A DOCTOR?
HUH?
NO. I'M FINE.
ARE YOU SURE? THAT'S A LOT OF BLOOD!
IT'S NOTHING. DON'T WORRY ABOUT IT.
THAT LOOKS LIKE A SERIOUS WOUND, SON.
YOU SHOULD SEE A DOCTOR!
LEAVE ME ALONE, ALL OF YOU!!
WAIT! YOU DROPPED SOMETHING!
WHAT IS IT?
IT LOOKS LIKE--
"AND WHAT DO YOU THINK THEY SAW? A WOMAN'S FINGER, CUT OFF BY THE THIEF IN ORDER TO GET THE RING SHE WAS WEARING!"
SO YOU SEE WHY I WANT TO SELL YOU A RING THAT FITS! IT'S THE ONLY--
OY GEVALT!
MY BROTHER HERMAN THE CUSTOMER-ROBBER STRIKES AGAIN!
FACTOID BOOKS 100% TRUE

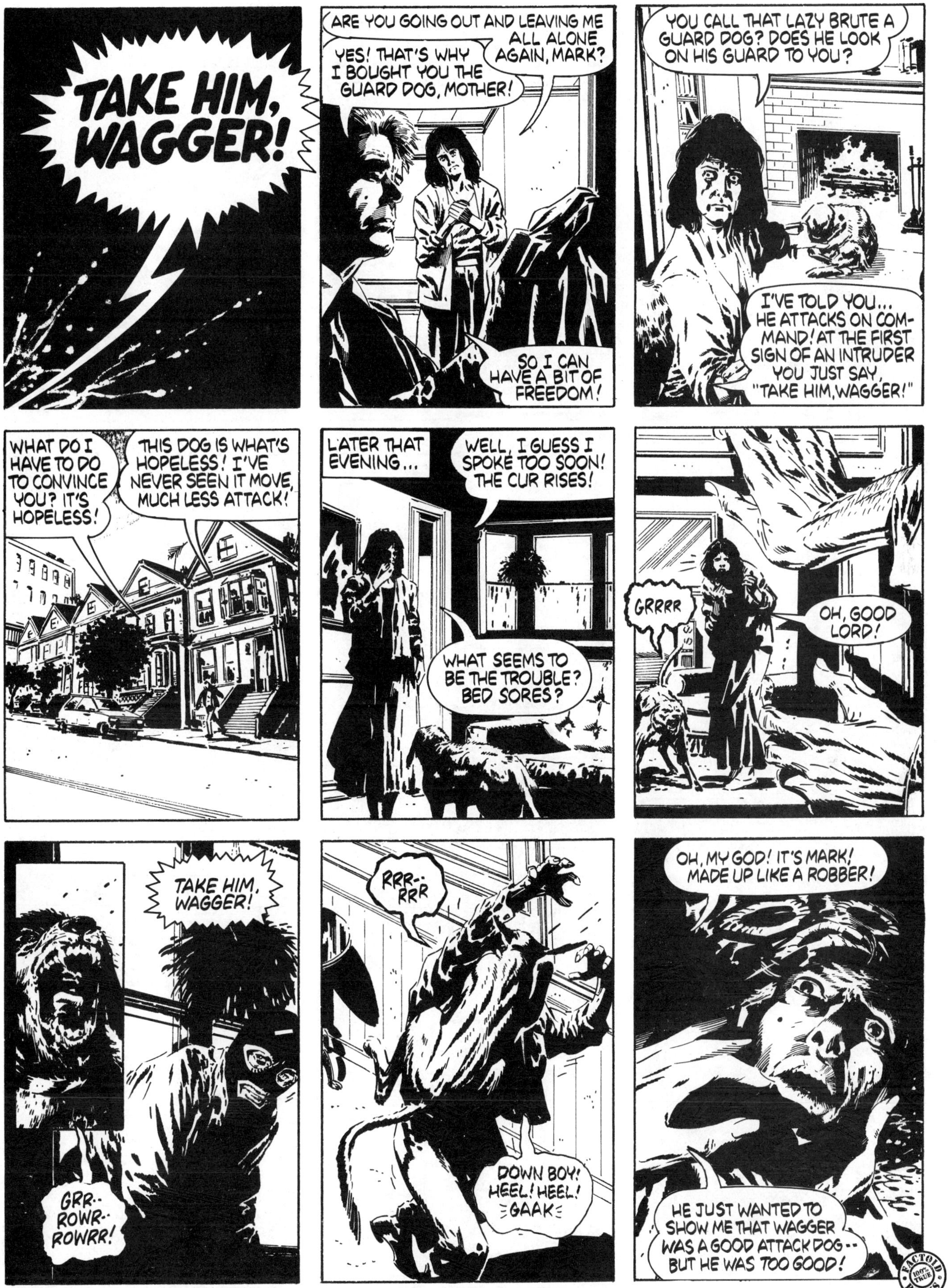
TAKE HIM, WAGGER!
ARE YOU GOING OUT AND LEAVING ME ALL ALONE AGAIN, MARK?
YES! THAT'S WHY I BOUGHT YOU THE GUARD DOG, MOTHER!
SO I CAN HAVE A BIT OF FREEDOM!
YOU CALL THAT LAZY BRUTE A GUARD DOG? DOES HE LOOK ON HIS GUARD TO YOU?
I'VE TOLD YOU... HE ATTACKS ON COMMAND! AT THE FIRST SIGN OF AN INTRUDER YOU JUST SAY, "TAKE HIM, WAGGER!"
WHAT DO I HAVE TO DO TO CONVINCE YOU? IT'S HOPELESS!
THIS DOG IS WHAT'S HOPELESS! I'VE NEVER SEEN IT MOVE, MUCH LESS ATTACK!
LATER THAT EVENING...
WELL, I GUESS I SPOKE TOO SOON! THE CUR RISES!
WHAT SEEMS TO BE THE TROUBLE? BED SORES?
GRRRR
OH, GOOD LORD!
TAKE HIM, WAGGER!
GRR.. ROWR.. ROWRR!
RRR.. RRR
DOWN BOY! HEEL! HEEL! GAAK
OH, MY GOD! IT'S MARK! MADE UP LIKE A ROBBER!
HE JUST WANTED TO SHOW ME THAT WAGGER WAS A GOOD ATTACK DOG-- BUT HE WAS TOO GOOD!
FACTOID BOOKS 100% TRUE

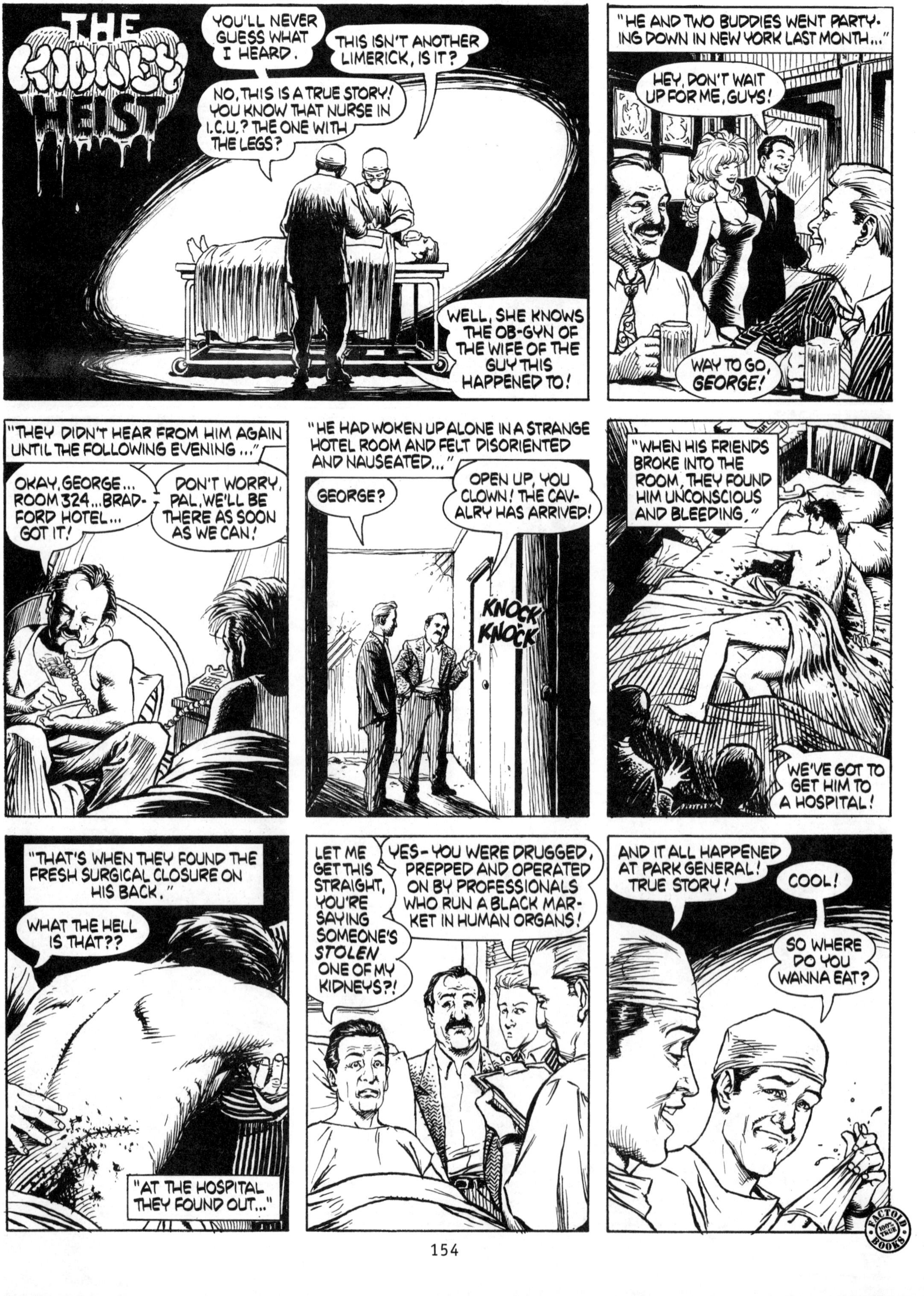
THE KIDNEY HEIST
YOU'LL NEVER GUESS WHAT I HEARD.
THIS ISN'T ANOTHER LIMERICK, IS IT?
NO, THIS IS A TRUE STORY! YOU KNOW THAT NURSE IN I.C.U.? THE ONE WITH THE LEGS?
WELL, SHE KNOWS THE OB-GYN OF THE WIFE OF THE GUY THIS HAPPENED TO!
"HE AND TWO BUDDIES WENT PARTYING DOWN IN NEW YORK LAST MONTH..."
HEY, DON'T WAIT UP FOR ME, GUYS!
WAY TO GO, GEORGE!
"THEY DIDN'T HEAR FROM HIM AGAIN UNTIL THE FOLLOWING EVENING..."
OKAY, GEORGE... ROOM 324... BRADFORD HOTEL... GOT IT!
DON'T WORRY, PAL, WE'LL BE THERE AS SOON AS WE CAN!
"HE HAD WOKEN UP ALONE IN A STRANGE HOTEL ROOM AND FELT DISORIENTED AND NAUSEATED..."
GEORGE?
OPEN UP, YOU CLOWN! THE CAVALRY HAS ARRIVED!
KNOCK KNOCK
"WHEN HIS FRIENDS BROKE INTO THE ROOM, THEY FOUND HIM UNCONSCIOUS AND BLEEDING."
WE'VE GOT TO GET HIM TO A HOSPITAL!
"THAT'S WHEN THEY FOUND THE FRESH SURGICAL CLOSURE ON HIS BACK."
WHAT THE HELL IS THAT??
"AT THE HOSPITAL THEY FOUND OUT..."
LET ME GET THIS STRAIGHT, YOU'RE SAYING SOMEONE'S STOLEN ONE OF MY KIDNEYS?!
YES - YOU WERE DRUGGED, PREPPED AND OPERATED ON BY PROFESSIONALS WHO RUN A BLACK MARKET IN HUMAN ORGANS!
AND IT ALL HAPPENED AT PARK GENERAL! TRUE STORY!
COOL!
SO WHERE DO YOU WANNA EAT?
FACTOID BOOKS 100% TRUE

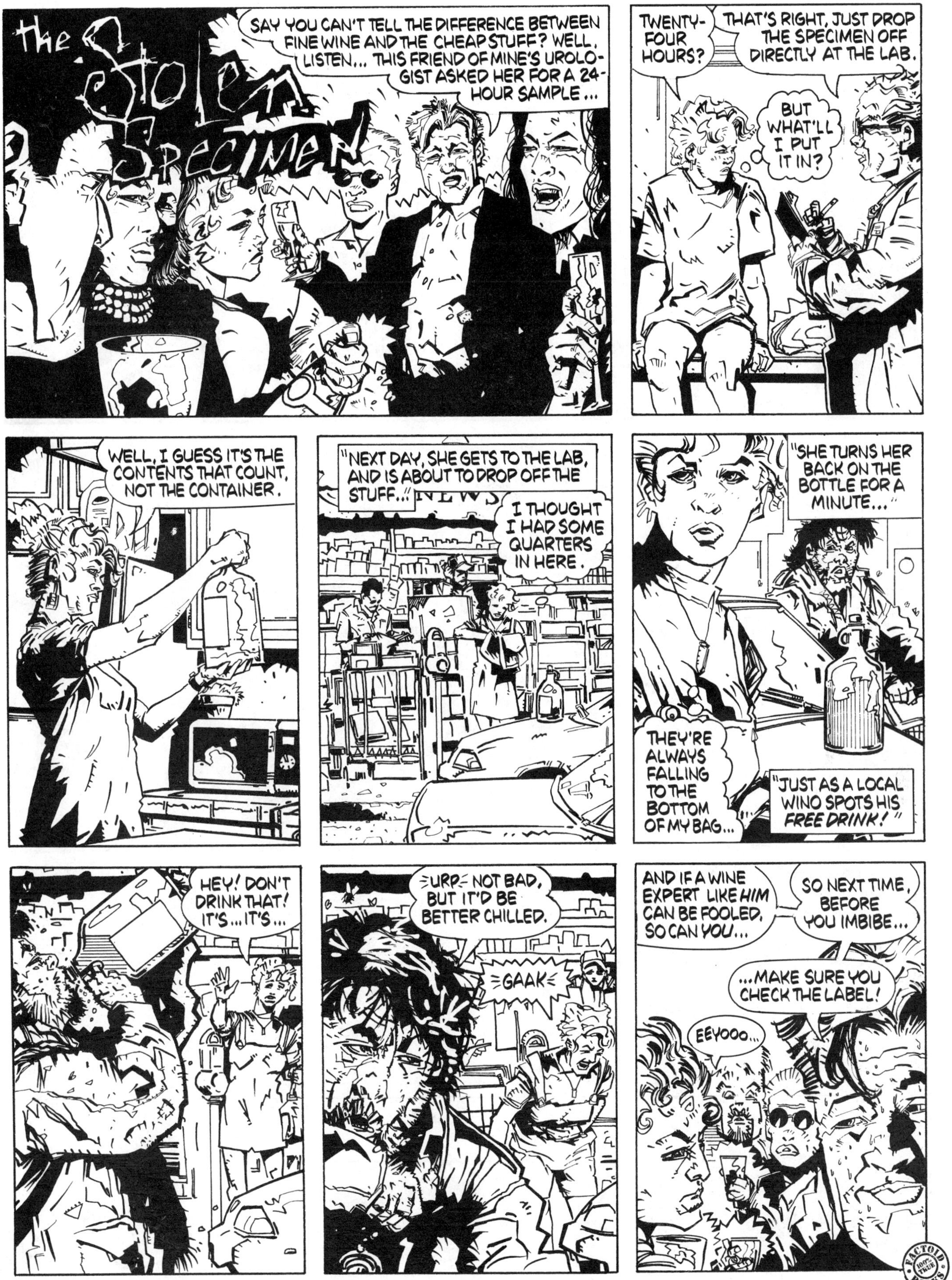
The Stolen Specimen!
SAY YOU CAN'T TELL THE DIFFERENCE BETWEEN FINE WINE AND THE CHEAP STUFF? WELL, LISTEN... THIS FRIEND OF MINE'S UROLOGIST ASKED HER FOR A 24-HOUR SAMPLE...
TWENTY-FOUR HOURS?
THAT'S RIGHT, JUST DROP THE SPECIMEN OFF DIRECTLY AT THE LAB.
BUT WHAT'LL I PUT IT IN?
WELL, I GUESS IT'S THE CONTENTS THAT COUNT, NOT THE CONTAINER.
"NEXT DAY, SHE GETS TO THE LAB, AND IS ABOUT TO DROP OFF THE STUFF..."
NEWS
I THOUGHT I HAD SOME QUARTERS IN HERE.
"SHE TURNS HER BACK ON THE BOTTLE FOR A MINUTE..."
THEY'RE ALWAYS FALLING TO THE BOTTOM OF MY BAG...
"JUST AS A LOCAL WINO SPOTS HIS *FREE DRINK!*"
HEY! DON'T DRINK THAT! IT'S... IT'S...
URP NOT BAD, BUT IT'D BE BETTER CHILLED.
GAAK
AND IF A WINE EXPERT LIKE *HIM* CAN BE FOOLED, SO CAN *YOU*...
SO NEXT TIME, BEFORE YOU IMBIBE...
...MAKE SURE YOU CHECK THE LABEL!
EEYOOO...
FACTOID BOOKS 100% TRUE

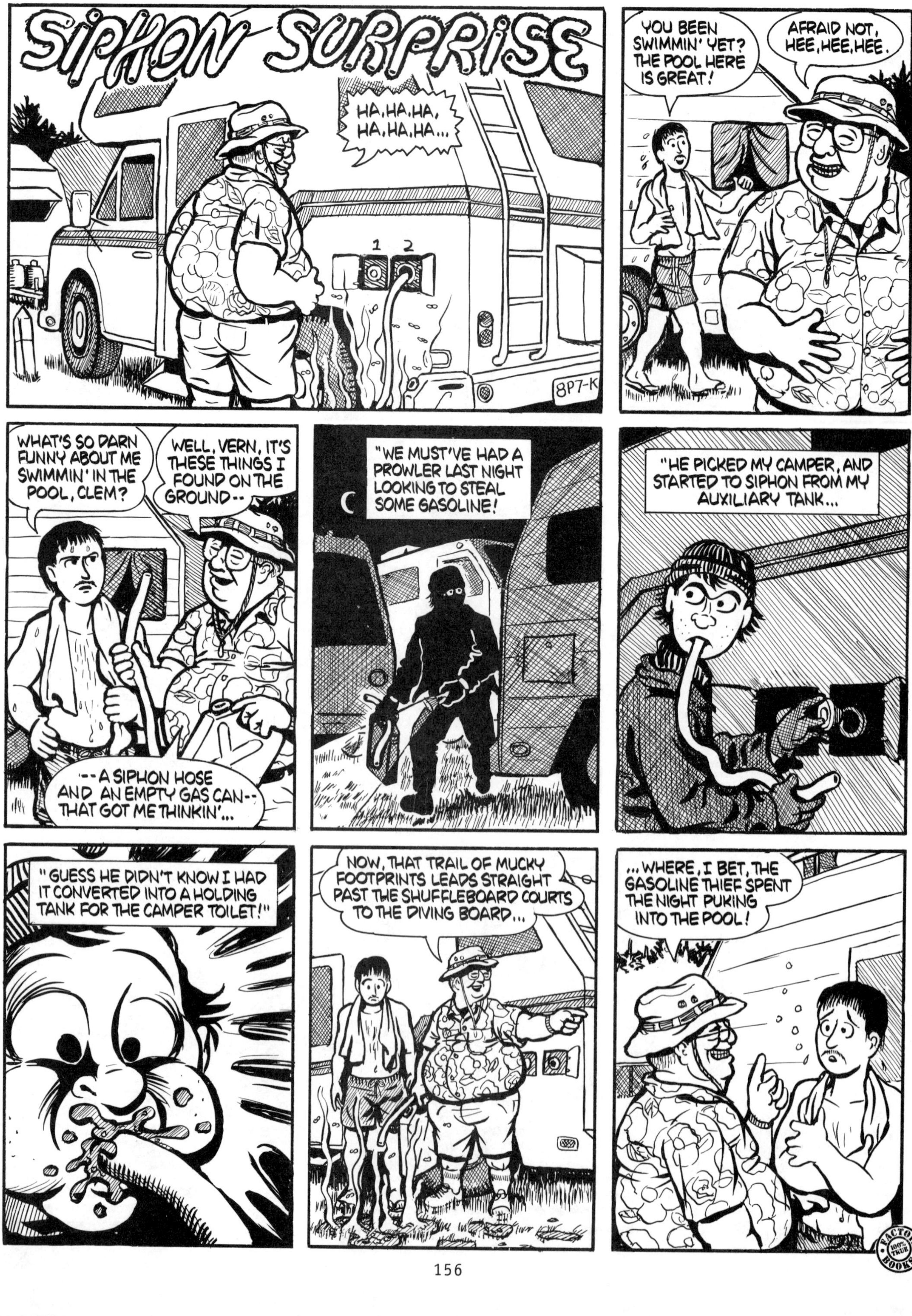
SIPHON SURPRISE
HA,HA,HA, HA,HA,HA...
1 2
8P7-K
YOU BEEN SWIMMIN' YET? THE POOL HERE IS GREAT!
AFRAID NOT, HEE,HEE,HEE.
WHAT'S SO DARN FUNNY ABOUT ME SWIMMIN' IN THE POOL, CLEM?
WELL, VERN, IT'S THESE THINGS I FOUND ON THE GROUND--
--A SIPHON HOSE AND AN EMPTY GAS CAN--THAT GOT ME THINKIN'...
"WE MUST'VE HAD A PROWLER LAST NIGHT LOOKING TO STEAL SOME GASOLINE!
"HE PICKED MY CAMPER, AND STARTED TO SIPHON FROM MY AUXILIARY TANK...
"GUESS HE DIDN'T KNOW I HAD IT CONVERTED INTO A HOLDING TANK FOR THE CAMPER TOILET!"
NOW, THAT TRAIL OF MUCKY FOOTPRINTS LEADS STRAIGHT PAST THE SHUFFLEBOARD COURTS TO THE DIVING BOARD...
...WHERE, I BET, THE GASOLINE THIEF SPENT THE NIGHT PUKING INTO THE POOL!
FACTOID 100% TRUE BOOKS

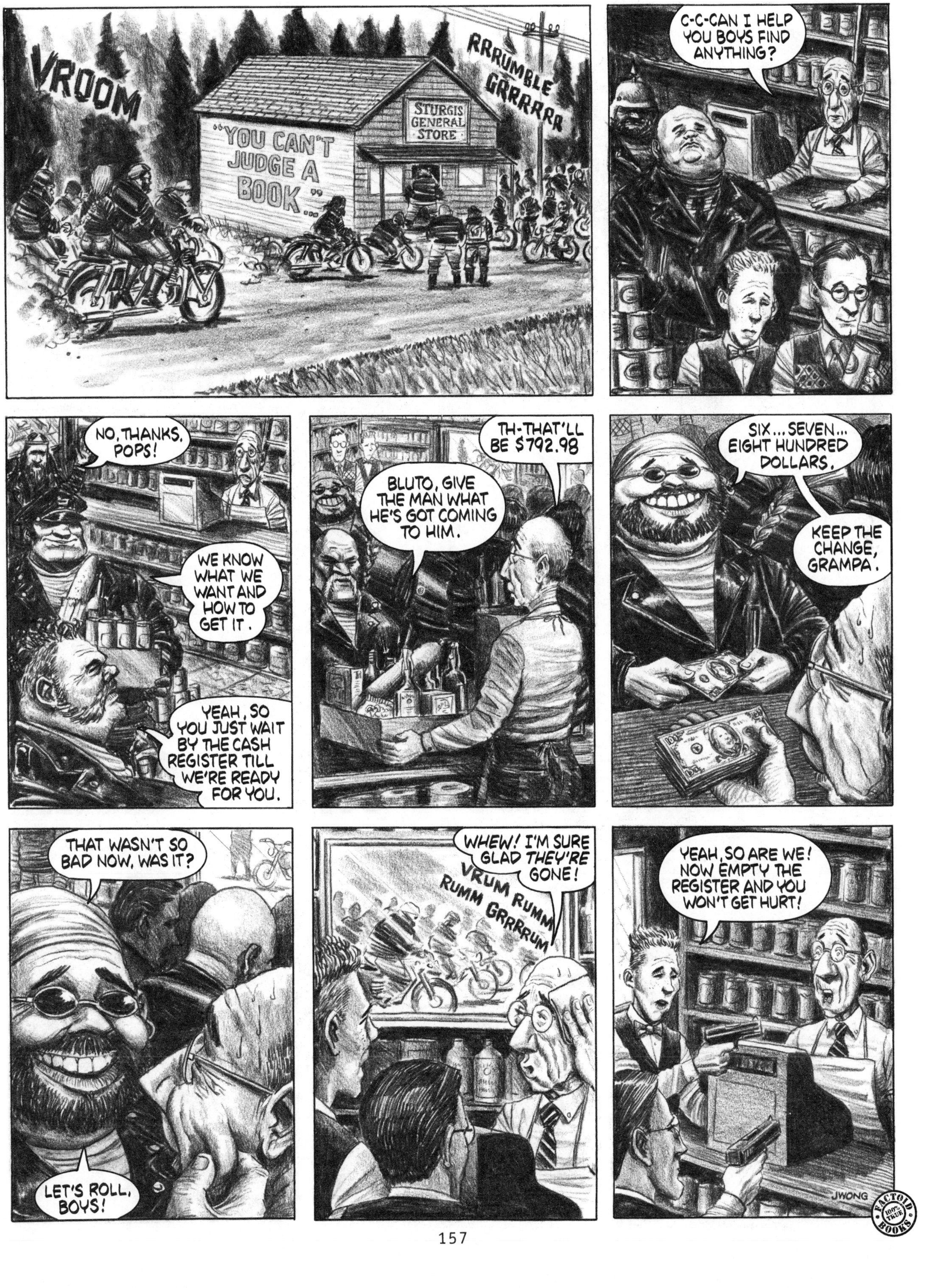
VROOM
RRRUMBLE GRRRRRR
STURGIS GENERAL STORE
"YOU CAN'T JUDGE A BOOK..."
C-C-CAN I HELP YOU BOYS FIND ANYTHING?
NO, THANKS, POPS!
WE KNOW WHAT WE WANT AND HOW TO GET IT.
YEAH, SO YOU JUST WAIT BY THE CASH REGISTER TILL WE'RE READY FOR YOU.
TH-THAT'LL BE $792.98
BLUTO, GIVE THE MAN WHAT HE'S GOT COMING TO HIM.
SIX... SEVEN... EIGHT HUNDRED DOLLARS.
KEEP THE CHANGE, GRAMPA.
THAT WASN'T SO BAD NOW, WAS IT?
LET'S ROLL, BOYS!
WHEW! I'M SURE GLAD THEY'RE GONE!
VRUM RUMM RUMM GRRRRUM
YEAH, SO ARE WE! NOW EMPTY THE REGISTER AND YOU WON'T GET HURT!
JWONG
FACTOID BOOKS 100% TRUE

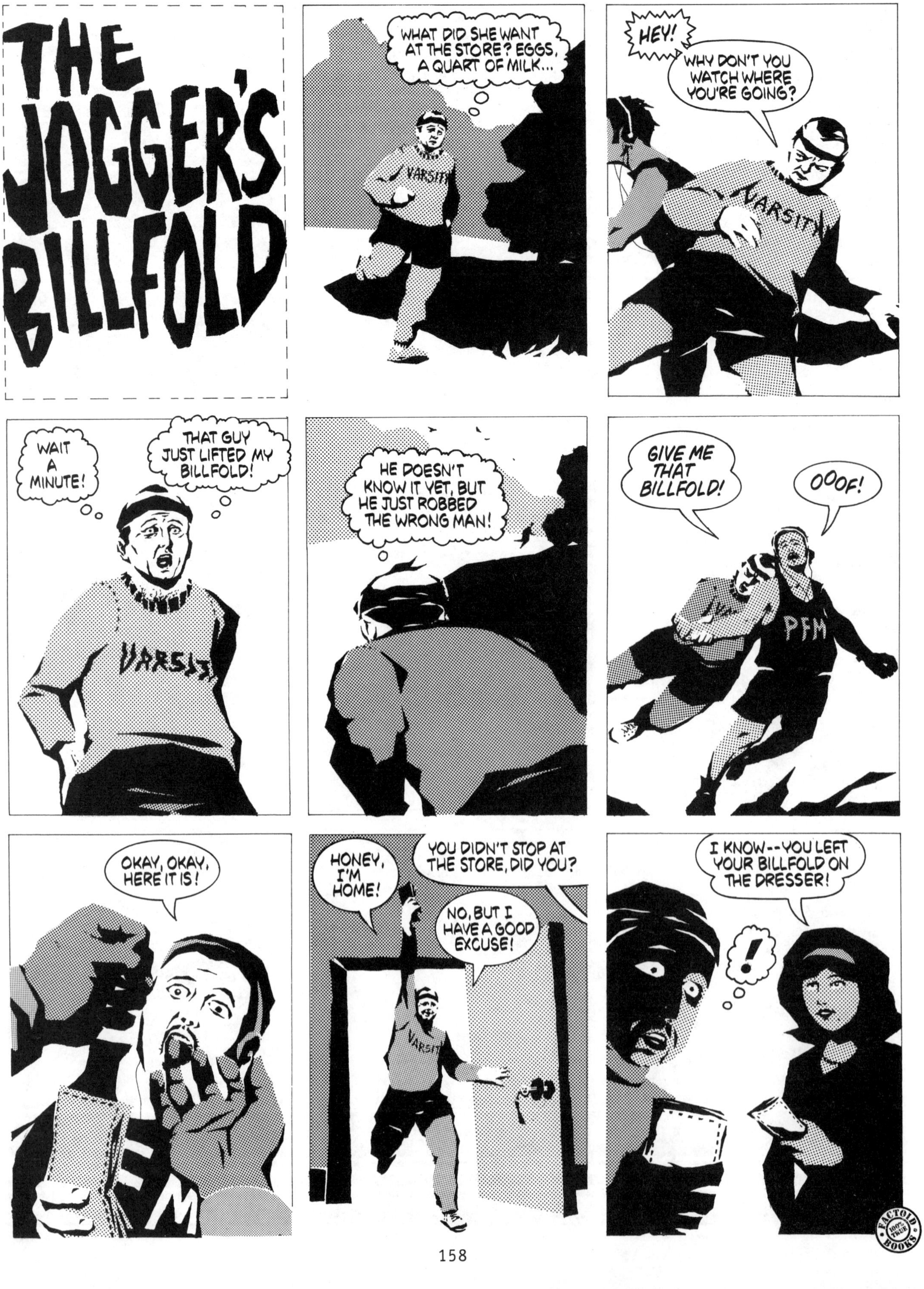
THE JOGGER'S BILLFOLD
WHAT DID SHE WANT AT THE STORE? EGGS, A QUART OF MILK...
VARSITY
HEY!
WHY DON'T YOU WATCH WHERE YOU'RE GOING?
VARSITY
WAIT A MINUTE!
THAT GUY JUST LIFTED MY BILLFOLD!
VARSITY
HE DOESN'T KNOW IT YET, BUT HE JUST ROBBED THE WRONG MAN!
GIVE ME THAT BILLFOLD!
OOOF!
PFM
OKAY, OKAY, HERE IT IS!
HONEY, I'M HOME!
YOU DIDN'T STOP AT THE STORE, DID YOU?
NO, BUT I HAVE A GOOD EXCUSE!
VARSITY
I KNOW--YOU LEFT YOUR BILLFOLD ON THE DRESSER!
!

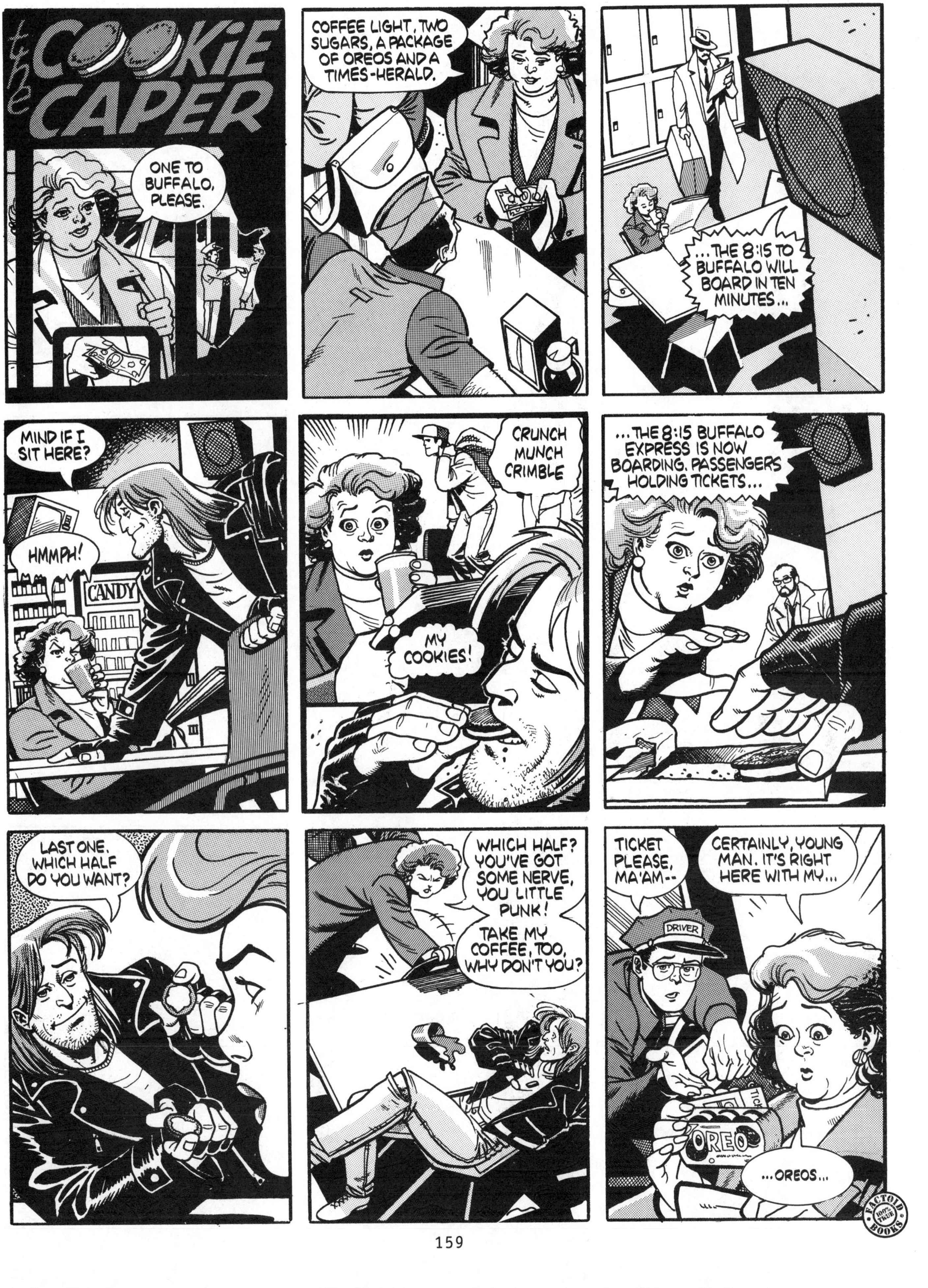
the COOKiE CAPER
ONE TO BUFFALO, PLEASE.
COFFEE LIGHT, TWO SUGARS, A PACKAGE OF OREOS AND A TIMES-HERALD.
...THE 8:15 TO BUFFALO WILL BOARD IN TEN MINUTES...
MIND IF I SIT HERE?
HMMPH!
CANDY
CRUNCH MUNCH CRIMBLE
MY COOKIES!
...THE 8:15 BUFFALO EXPRESS IS NOW BOARDING. PASSENGERS HOLDING TICKETS...
LAST ONE. WHICH HALF DO YOU WANT?
WHICH HALF? YOU'VE GOT SOME NERVE, YOU LITTLE PUNK!
TAKE MY COFFEE, TOO, WHY DON'T YOU?
TICKET PLEASE, MA'AM--
CERTAINLY, YOUNG MAN. IT'S RIGHT HERE WITH MY...
DRIVER
OREO
...OREOS...
FACTOID BOOKS
100% TRUE

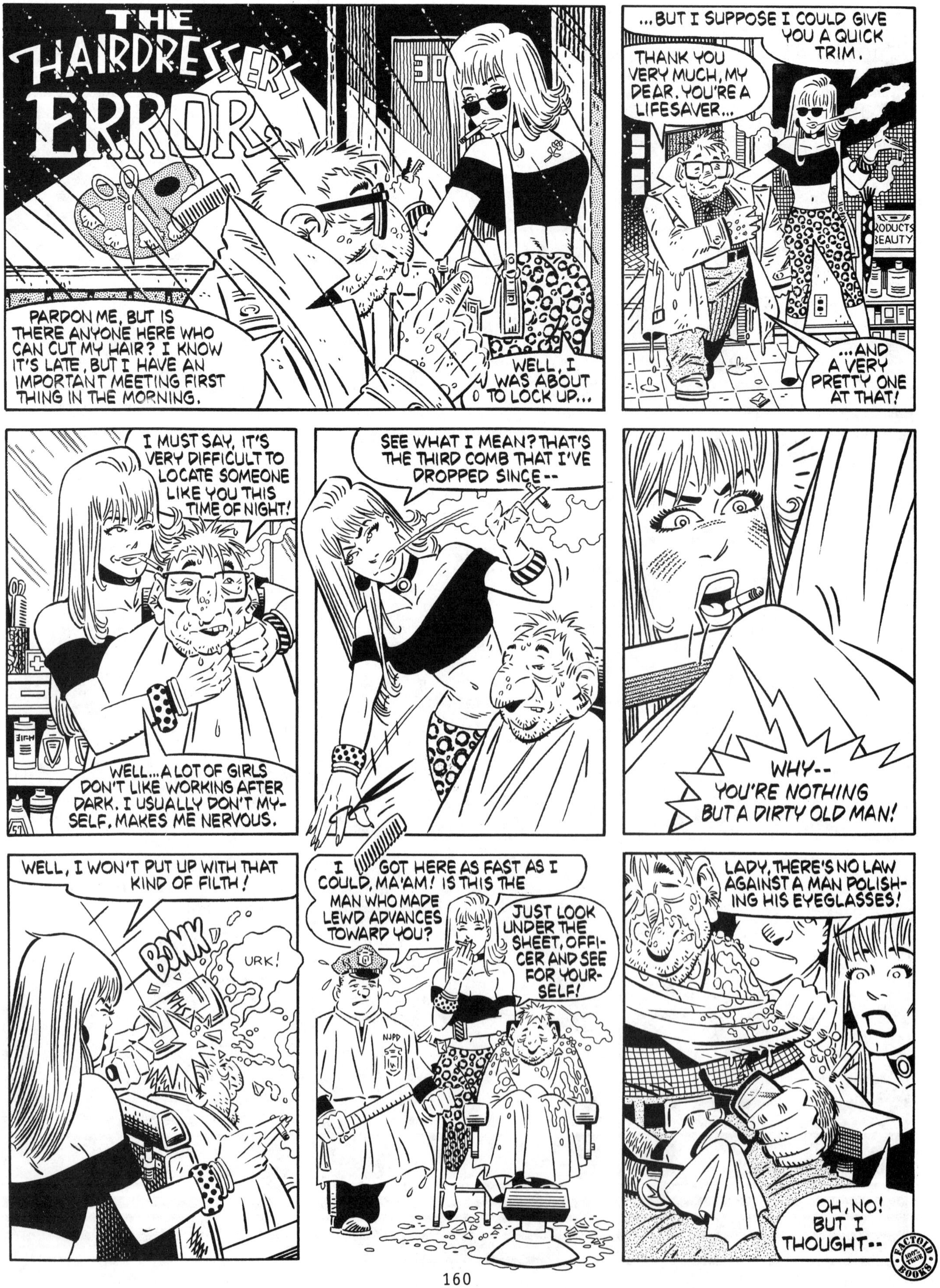
THE HAIRDRESSER'S ERROR
PARDON ME, BUT IS THERE ANYONE HERE WHO CAN CUT MY HAIR? I KNOW IT'S LATE, BUT I HAVE AN IMPORTANT MEETING FIRST THING IN THE MORNING.
WELL, I WAS ABOUT TO LOCK UP...
...BUT I SUPPOSE I COULD GIVE YOU A QUICK TRIM.
THANK YOU VERY MUCH, MY DEAR. YOU'RE A LIFESAVER...
...AND A VERY PRETTY ONE AT THAT!
PRODUCTS BEAUTY
I MUST SAY, IT'S VERY DIFFICULT TO LOCATE SOMEONE LIKE YOU THIS TIME OF NIGHT!
WELL... A LOT OF GIRLS DON'T LIKE WORKING AFTER DARK. I USUALLY DON'T MYSELF. MAKES ME NERVOUS.
SEE WHAT I MEAN? THAT'S THE THIRD COMB THAT I'VE DROPPED SINCE--
WHY-- YOU'RE NOTHING BUT A DIRTY OLD MAN!
WELL, I WON'T PUT UP WITH THAT KIND OF FILTH!
BONK!
URK!
I GOT HERE AS FAST AS I COULD, MA'AM! IS THIS THE MAN WHO MADE LEWD ADVANCES TOWARD YOU?
JUST LOOK UNDER THE SHEET, OFFICER AND SEE FOR YOURSELF!
NJPD
LADY, THERE'S NO LAW AGAINST A MAN POLISHING HIS EYEGLASSES!
OH, NO! BUT I THOUGHT--
FACTOID BOOKS 100% TRUE

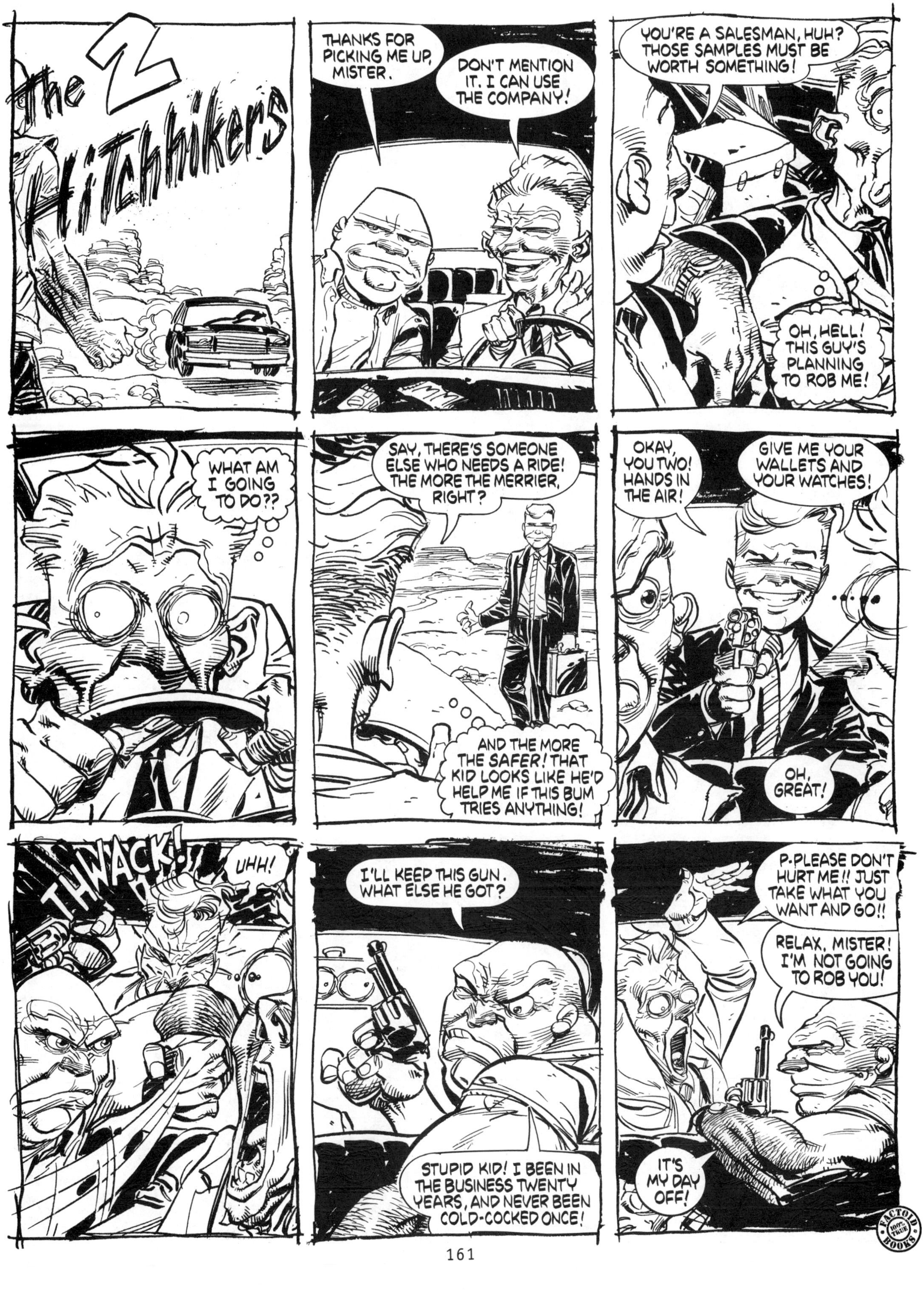
The 2 Hitchhikers
THANKS FOR PICKING ME UP, MISTER.
DON'T MENTION IT. I CAN USE THE COMPANY!
YOU'RE A SALESMAN, HUH? THOSE SAMPLES MUST BE WORTH SOMETHING!
OH, HELL! THIS GUY'S PLANNING TO ROB ME!
WHAT AM I GOING TO DO??
SAY, THERE'S SOMEONE ELSE WHO NEEDS A RIDE! THE MORE THE MERRIER, RIGHT?
AND THE MORE THE SAFER! THAT KID LOOKS LIKE HE'D HELP ME IF THIS BUM TRIES ANYTHING!
OKAY, YOU TWO! HANDS IN THE AIR!
GIVE ME YOUR WALLETS AND YOUR WATCHES!
OH, GREAT!
THWACK!
UHH!
I'LL KEEP THIS GUN. WHAT ELSE HE GOT?
STUPID KID! I BEEN IN THE BUSINESS TWENTY YEARS, AND NEVER BEEN COLD-COCKED ONCE!
P-PLEASE DON'T HURT ME!! JUST TAKE WHAT YOU WANT AND GO!!
RELAX, MISTER! I'M NOT GOING TO ROB YOU!
IT'S MY DAY OFF!
FACTOID BOOKS 100% TRUE

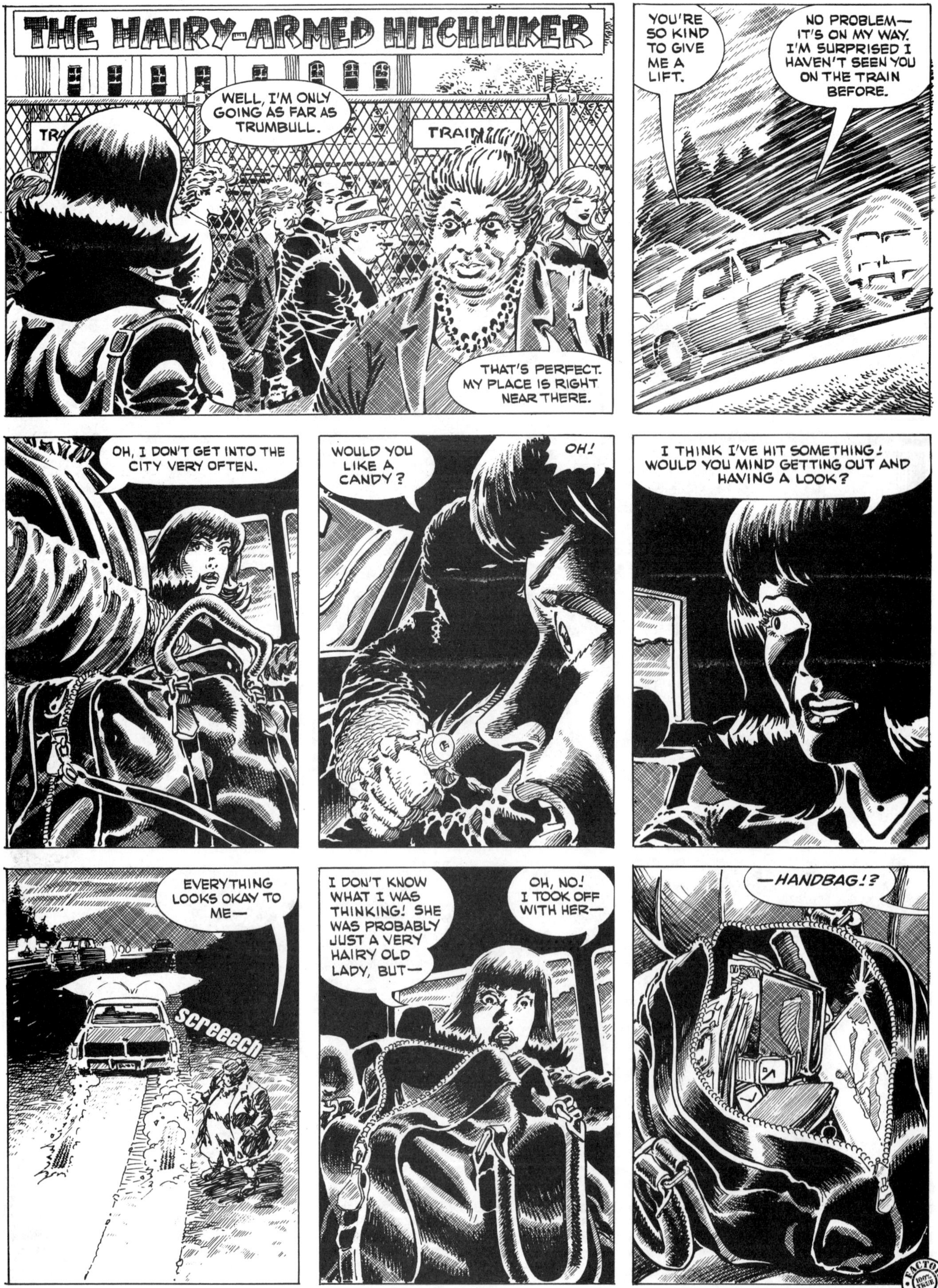
THE HAIRY-ARMED HITCHHIKER
WELL, I'M ONLY GOING AS FAR AS TRUMBULL.
THAT'S PERFECT. MY PLACE IS RIGHT NEAR THERE.
YOU'RE SO KIND TO GIVE ME A LIFT.
NO PROBLEM— IT'S ON MY WAY. I'M SURPRISED I HAVEN'T SEEN YOU ON THE TRAIN BEFORE.
OH, I DON'T GET INTO THE CITY VERY OFTEN.
WOULD YOU LIKE A CANDY?
OH!
I THINK I'VE HIT SOMETHING! WOULD YOU MIND GETTING OUT AND HAVING A LOOK?
EVERYTHING LOOKS OKAY TO ME—
SCREEECH
I DON'T KNOW WHAT I WAS THINKING! SHE WAS PROBABLY JUST A VERY HAIRY OLD LADY, BUT—
OH, NO! I TOOK OFF WITH HER—
—HANDBAG!?

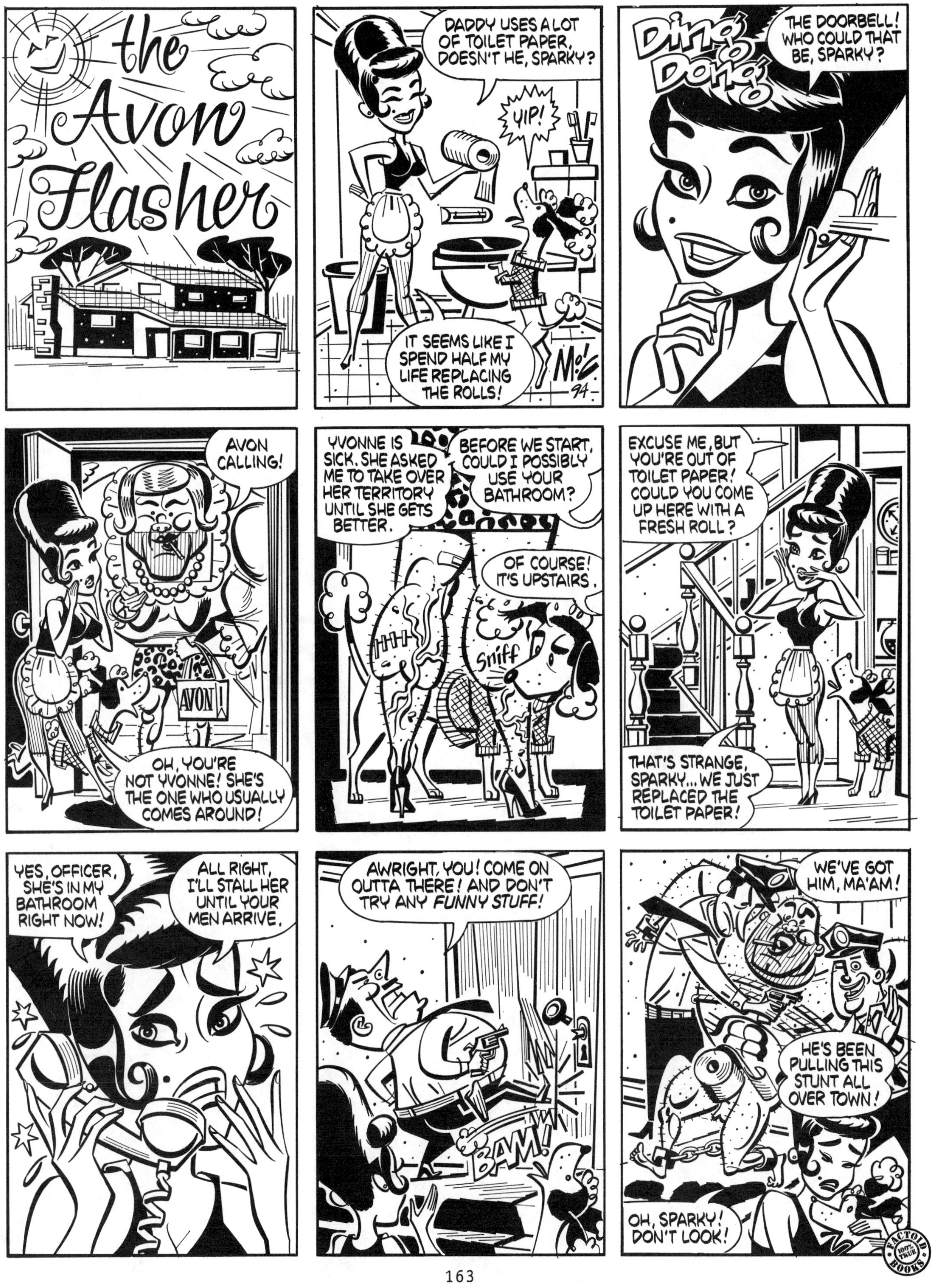
the Avon Flasher
DADDY USES A LOT OF TOILET PAPER, DOESN'T HE, SPARKY?
YIP!
IT SEEMS LIKE I SPEND HALF MY LIFE REPLACING THE ROLLS!
Ding Dong
THE DOORBELL! WHO COULD THAT BE, SPARKY?
AVON CALLING!
OH, YOU'RE NOT YVONNE! SHE'S THE ONE WHO USUALLY COMES AROUND!
AVON
YVONNE IS SICK. SHE ASKED ME TO TAKE OVER HER TERRITORY UNTIL SHE GETS BETTER.
BEFORE WE START, COULD I POSSIBLY USE YOUR BATHROOM?
OF COURSE! IT'S UPSTAIRS.
Sniff
EXCUSE ME, BUT YOU'RE OUT OF TOILET PAPER! COULD YOU COME UP HERE WITH A FRESH ROLL?
THAT'S STRANGE, SPARKY... WE JUST REPLACED THE TOILET PAPER!
YES, OFFICER, SHE'S IN MY BATHROOM RIGHT NOW!
ALL RIGHT, I'LL STALL HER UNTIL YOUR MEN ARRIVE.
AWRIGHT, YOU! COME ON OUTTA THERE! AND DON'T TRY ANY FUNNY STUFF!
BAM!
WE'VE GOT HIM, MA'AM!
HE'S BEEN PULLING THIS STUNT ALL OVER TOWN!
OH, SPARKY! DON'T LOOK!
FACTOID BOOKS 100% TRUE

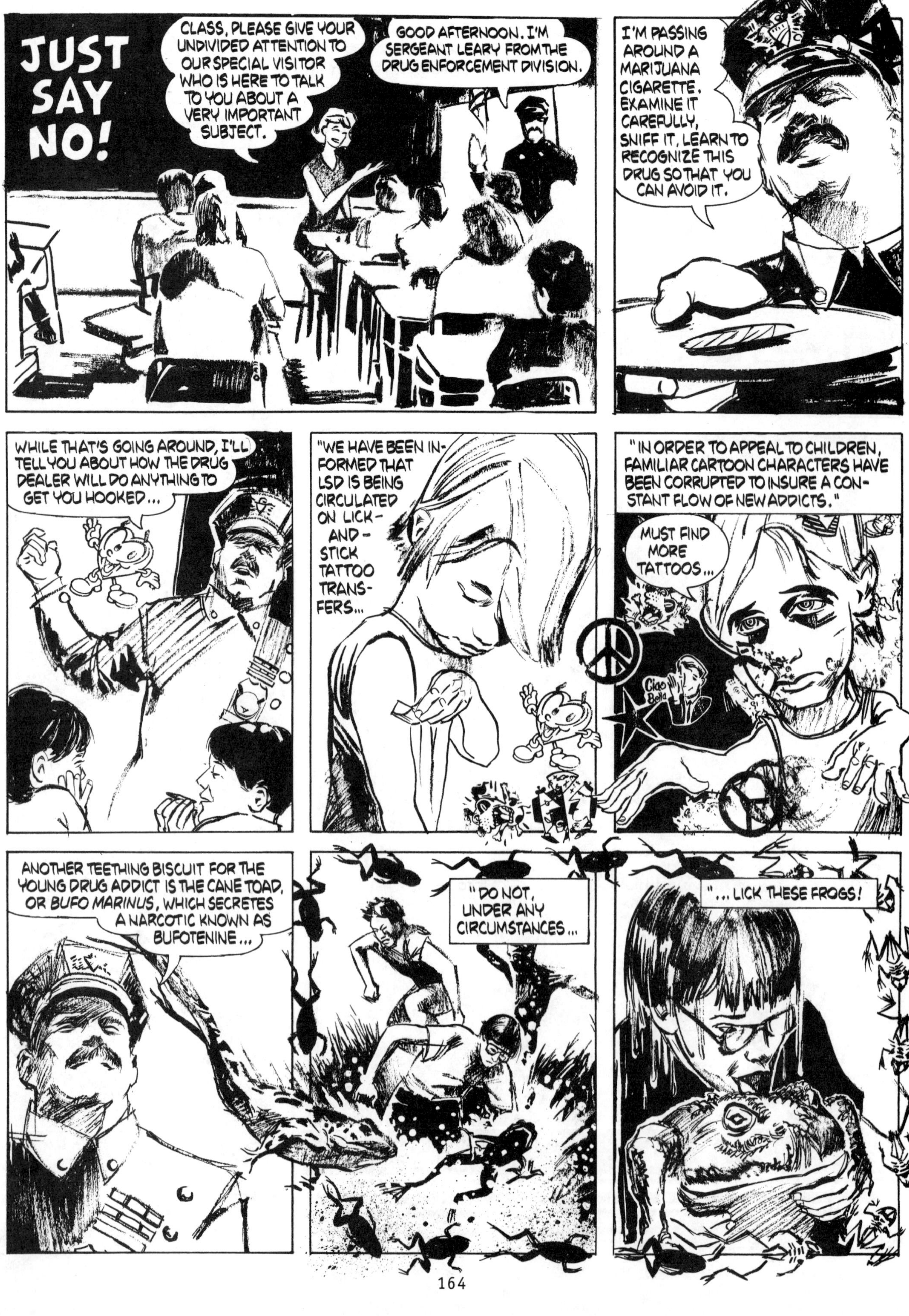
JUST SAY NO!
CLASS, PLEASE GIVE YOUR UNDIVIDED ATTENTION TO OUR SPECIAL VISITOR WHO IS HERE TO TALK TO YOU ABOUT A VERY IMPORTANT SUBJECT.
GOOD AFTERNOON. I'M SERGEANT LEARY FROM THE DRUG ENFORCEMENT DIVISION.
I'M PASSING AROUND A MARIJUANA CIGARETTE. EXAMINE IT CAREFULLY, SNIFF IT, LEARN TO RECOGNIZE THIS DRUG SO THAT YOU CAN AVOID IT.
WHILE THAT'S GOING AROUND, I'LL TELL YOU ABOUT HOW THE DRUG DEALER WILL DO ANYTHING TO GET YOU HOOKED...
"WE HAVE BEEN INFORMED THAT LSD IS BEING CIRCULATED ON LICK-AND-STICK TATTOO TRANSFERS...
"IN ORDER TO APPEAL TO CHILDREN, FAMILIAR CARTOON CHARACTERS HAVE BEEN CORRUPTED TO INSURE A CONSTANT FLOW OF NEW ADDICTS."
MUST FIND MORE TATTOOS...
Ciao Bella
ANOTHER TEETHING BISCUIT FOR THE YOUNG DRUG ADDICT IS THE CANE TOAD, OR BUFO MARINUS, WHICH SECRETES A NARCOTIC KNOWN AS BUFOTENINE...
"DO NOT, UNDER ANY CIRCUMSTANCES...
"... LICK THESE FROGS!

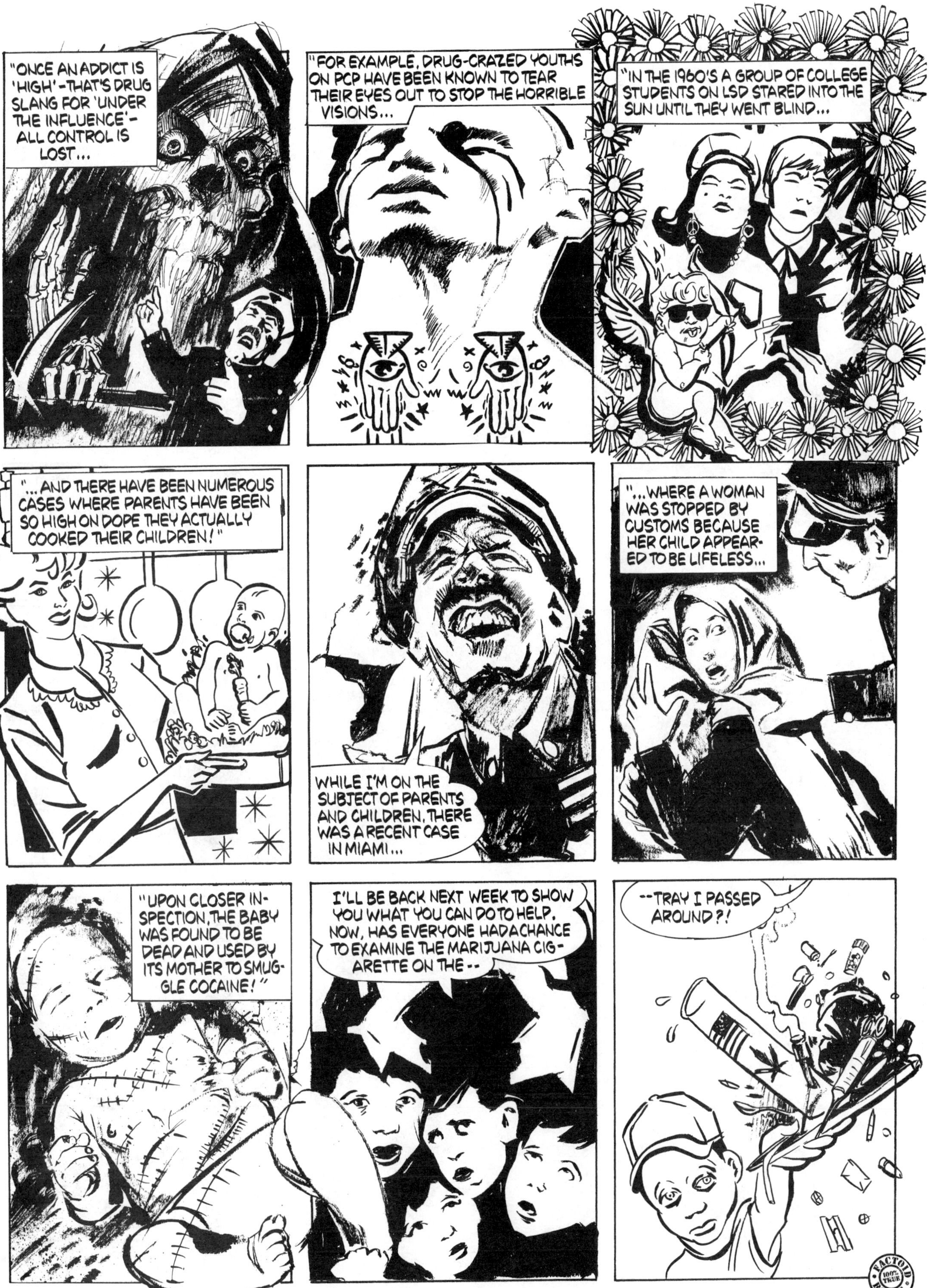
"ONCE AN ADDICT IS 'HIGH' - THAT'S DRUG SLANG FOR 'UNDER THE INFLUENCE' - ALL CONTROL IS LOST...
"FOR EXAMPLE, DRUG-CRAZED YOUTHS ON PCP HAVE BEEN KNOWN TO TEAR THEIR EYES OUT TO STOP THE HORRIBLE VISIONS...
"IN THE 1960'S A GROUP OF COLLEGE STUDENTS ON LSD STARED INTO THE SUN UNTIL THEY WENT BLIND...
"...AND THERE HAVE BEEN NUMEROUS CASES WHERE PARENTS HAVE BEEN SO HIGH ON DOPE THEY ACTUALLY COOKED THEIR CHILDREN!"
WHILE I'M ON THE SUBJECT OF PARENTS AND CHILDREN, THERE WAS A RECENT CASE IN MIAMI...
"...WHERE A WOMAN WAS STOPPED BY CUSTOMS BECAUSE HER CHILD APPEARED TO BE LIFELESS...
"UPON CLOSER INSPECTION, THE BABY WAS FOUND TO BE DEAD AND USED BY ITS MOTHER TO SMUGGLE COCAINE!"
I'LL BE BACK NEXT WEEK TO SHOW YOU WHAT YOU CAN DO TO HELP. NOW, HAS EVERYONE HAD A CHANCE TO EXAMINE THE MARIJUANA CIGARETTE ON THE --
--TRAY I PASSED AROUND?!
FACTOID BOOKS 100% TRUE

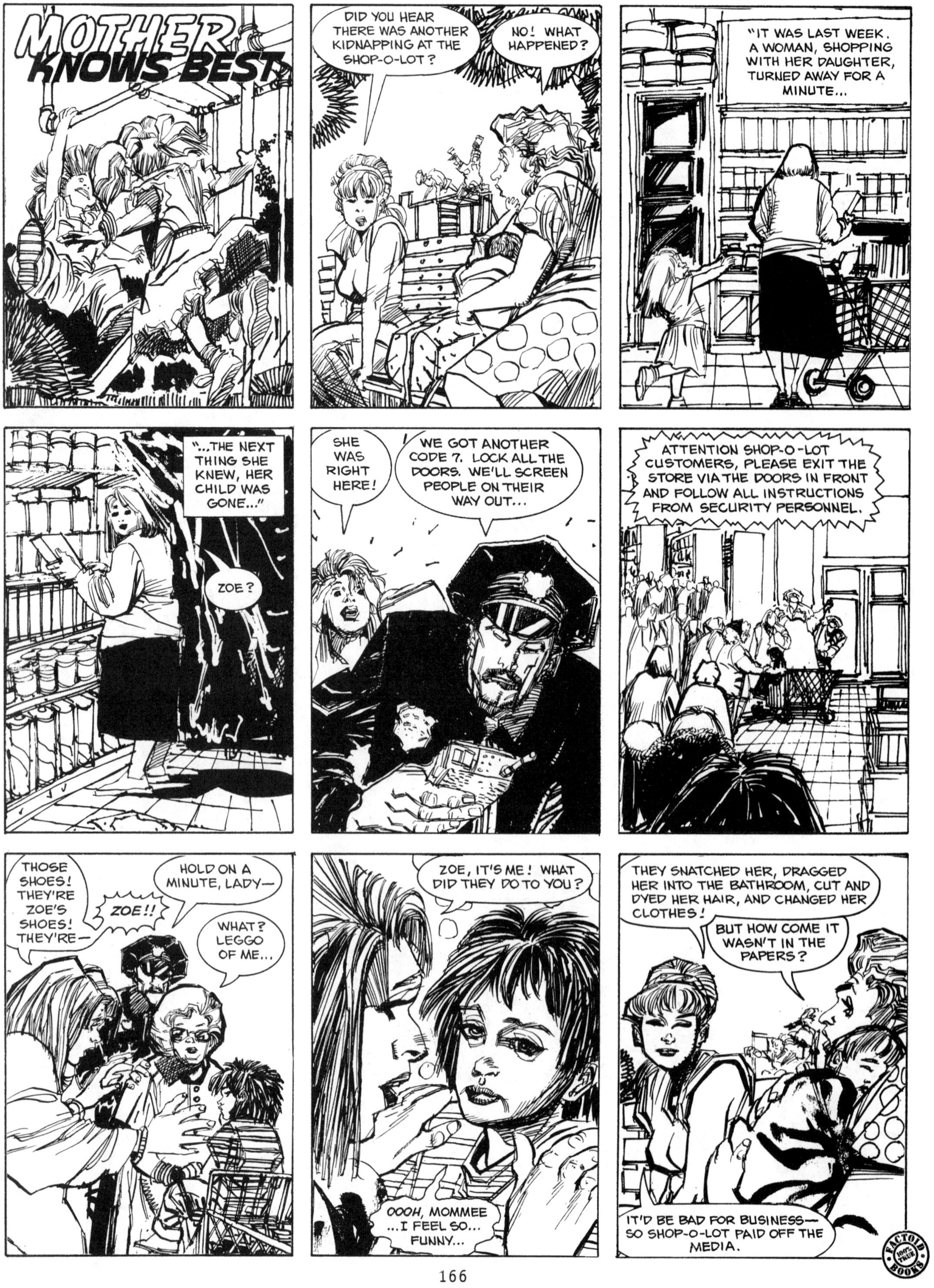
MOTHER KNOWS BEST
DID YOU HEAR THERE WAS ANOTHER KIDNAPPING AT THE SHOP-O-LOT?
NO! WHAT HAPPENED?
"IT WAS LAST WEEK. A WOMAN, SHOPPING WITH HER DAUGHTER, TURNED AWAY FOR A MINUTE...
"...THE NEXT THING SHE KNEW, HER CHILD WAS GONE..."
ZOE?
SHE WAS RIGHT HERE!
WE GOT ANOTHER CODE 7. LOCK ALL THE DOORS. WE'LL SCREEN PEOPLE ON THEIR WAY OUT...
ATTENTION SHOP-O-LOT CUSTOMERS, PLEASE EXIT THE STORE VIA THE DOORS IN FRONT AND FOLLOW ALL INSTRUCTIONS FROM SECURITY PERSONNEL.
THOSE SHOES! THEY'RE ZOE'S SHOES! THEY'RE—
ZOE!!
HOLD ON A MINUTE, LADY—
WHAT? LEGGO OF ME...
ZOE, IT'S ME! WHAT DID THEY DO TO YOU?
OOOH, MOMMEE ...I FEEL SO... FUNNY...
THEY SNATCHED HER, DRAGGED HER INTO THE BATHROOM, CUT AND DYED HER HAIR, AND CHANGED HER CLOTHES!
BUT HOW COME IT WASN'T IN THE PAPERS?
IT'D BE BAD FOR BUSINESS— SO SHOP-O-LOT PAID OFF THE MEDIA.
FACTOID BOOKS 100% TRUE

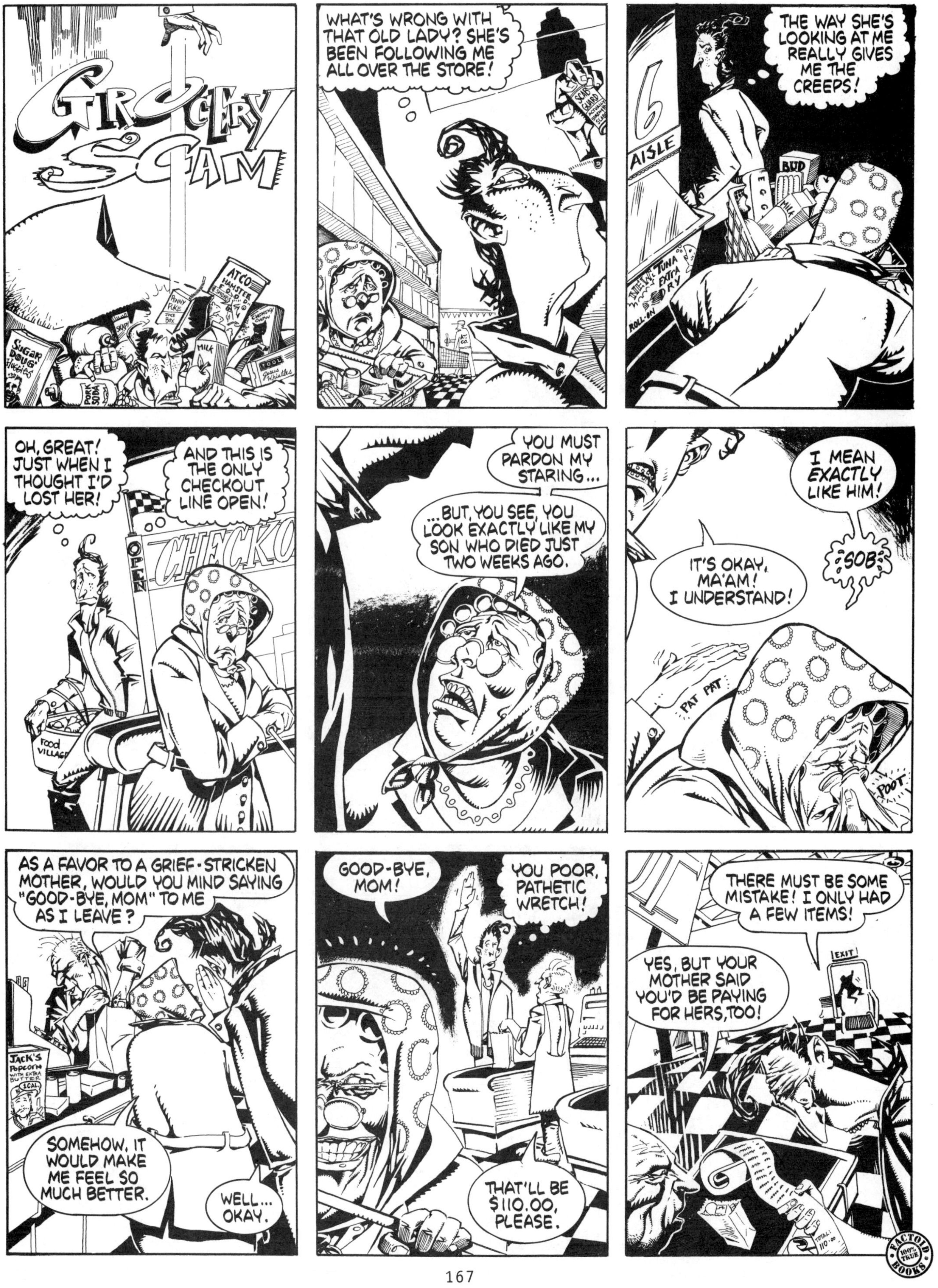
THE GROCERY SCAM
WHAT'S WRONG WITH THAT OLD LADY? SHE'S BEEN FOLLOWING ME ALL OVER THE STORE!
THE WAY SHE'S LOOKING AT ME REALLY GIVES ME THE CREEPS!
AISLE 6
OH, GREAT! JUST WHEN I THOUGHT I'D LOST HER!
AND THIS IS THE ONLY CHECKOUT LINE OPEN!
OPEN
YOU MUST PARDON MY STARING...
...BUT, YOU SEE, YOU LOOK EXACTLY LIKE MY SON WHO DIED JUST TWO WEEKS AGO.
I MEAN EXACTLY LIKE HIM!
SOB
IT'S OKAY, MA'AM! I UNDERSTAND!
PAT PAT
POOT
AS A FAVOR TO A GRIEF-STRICKEN MOTHER, WOULD YOU MIND SAYING "GOOD-BYE, MOM" TO ME AS I LEAVE?
SOMEHOW, IT WOULD MAKE ME FEEL SO MUCH BETTER.
WELL... OKAY.
GOOD-BYE, MOM!
YOU POOR, PATHETIC WRETCH!
THAT'LL BE $110.00, PLEASE.
THERE MUST BE SOME MISTAKE! I ONLY HAD A FEW ITEMS!
YES, BUT YOUR MOTHER SAID YOU'D BE PAYING FOR HERS, TOO!
EXIT
FACTOID BOOKS 100% TRUE

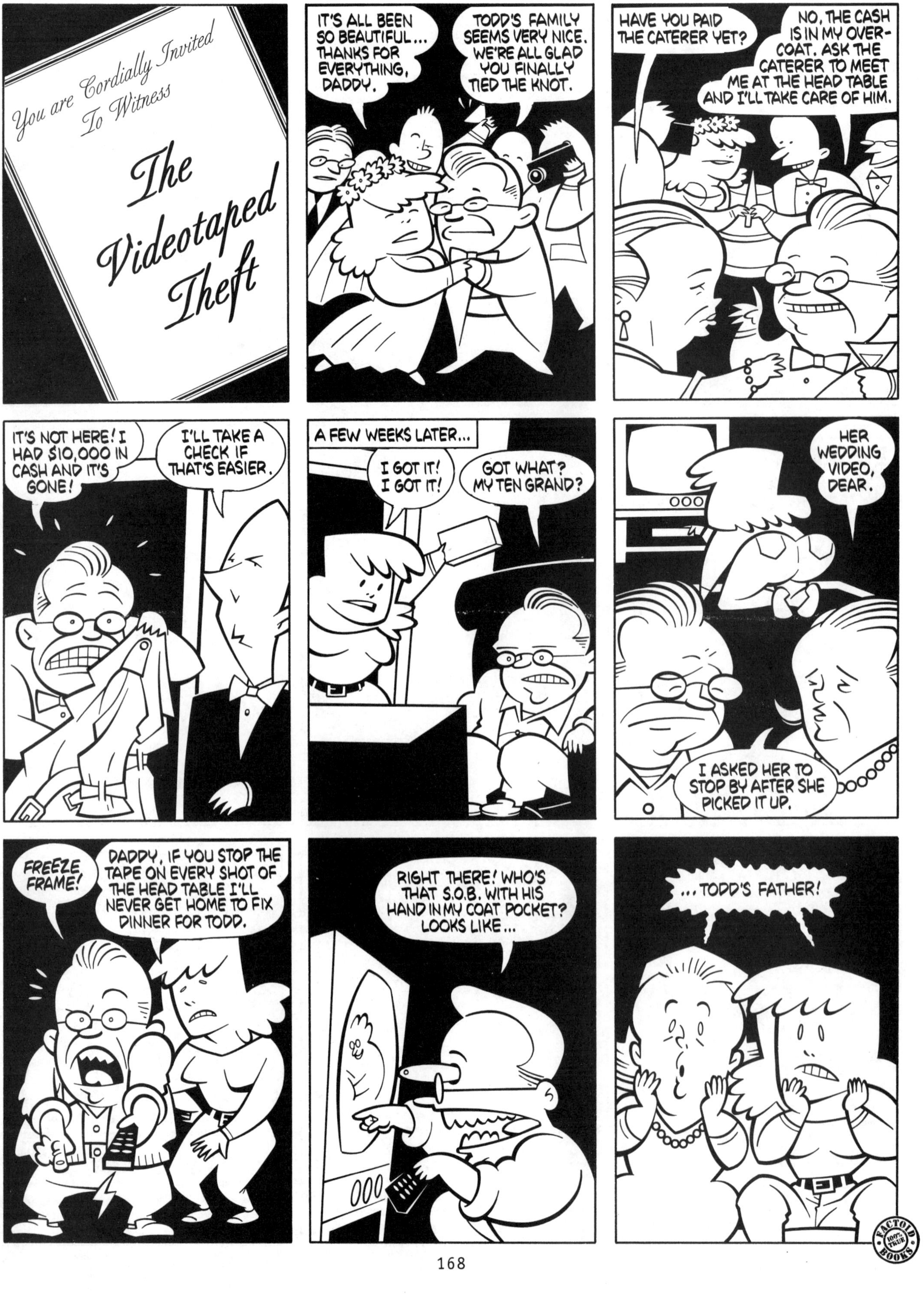
You are Cordially Invited To Witness
The Videotaped Theft
IT'S ALL BEEN SO BEAUTIFUL... THANKS FOR EVERYTHING, DADDY.
TODD'S FAMILY SEEMS VERY NICE. WE'RE ALL GLAD YOU FINALLY TIED THE KNOT.
HAVE YOU PAID THE CATERER YET?
NO, THE CASH IS IN MY OVER-COAT. ASK THE CATERER TO MEET ME AT THE HEAD TABLE AND I'LL TAKE CARE OF HIM.
IT'S NOT HERE! I HAD $10,000 IN CASH AND IT'S GONE!
I'LL TAKE A CHECK IF THAT'S EASIER.
A FEW WEEKS LATER...
I GOT IT! I GOT IT!
GOT WHAT? MY TEN GRAND?
HER WEDDING VIDEO, DEAR.
I ASKED HER TO STOP BY AFTER SHE PICKED IT UP.
FREEZE FRAME!
DADDY, IF YOU STOP THE TAPE ON EVERY SHOT OF THE HEAD TABLE I'LL NEVER GET HOME TO FIX DINNER FOR TODD.
RIGHT THERE! WHO'S THAT S.O.B. WITH HIS HAND IN MY COAT POCKET? LOOKS LIKE...
...TODD'S FATHER!

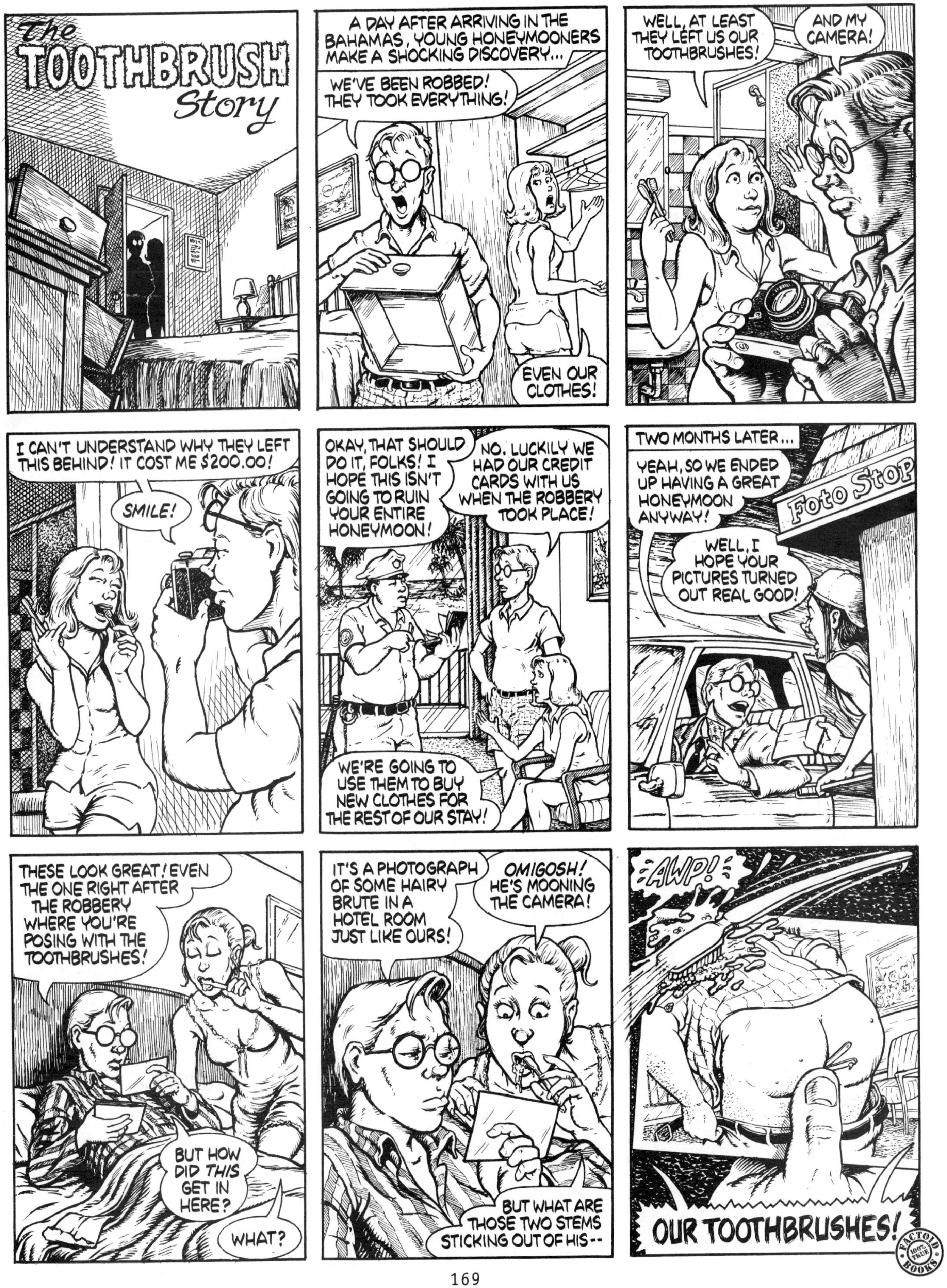
The TOOTHBRUSH Story
A DAY AFTER ARRIVING IN THE BAHAMAS, YOUNG HONEYMOONERS MAKE A SHOCKING DISCOVERY...
WE'VE BEEN ROBBED! THEY TOOK EVERYTHING!
EVEN OUR CLOTHES!
WELL, AT LEAST THEY LEFT US OUR TOOTHBRUSHES!
AND MY CAMERA!
I CAN'T UNDERSTAND WHY THEY LEFT THIS BEHIND! IT COST ME $200.00!
SMILE!
OKAY, THAT SHOULD DO IT, FOLKS! I HOPE THIS ISN'T GOING TO RUIN YOUR ENTIRE HONEYMOON!
NO. LUCKILY WE HAD OUR CREDIT CARDS WITH US WHEN THE ROBBERY TOOK PLACE!
WE'RE GOING TO USE THEM TO BUY NEW CLOTHES FOR THE REST OF OUR STAY!
TWO MONTHS LATER...
YEAH, SO WE ENDED UP HAVING A GREAT HONEYMOON ANYWAY!
Foto Stop
WELL, I HOPE YOUR PICTURES TURNED OUT REAL GOOD!
THESE LOOK GREAT! EVEN THE ONE RIGHT AFTER THE ROBBERY WHERE YOU'RE POSING WITH THE TOOTHBRUSHES!
BUT HOW DID THIS GET IN HERE?
WHAT?
IT'S A PHOTOGRAPH OF SOME HAIRY BRUTE IN A HOTEL ROOM JUST LIKE OURS!
OMIGOSH! HE'S MOONING THE CAMERA!
BUT WHAT ARE THOSE TWO STEMS STICKING OUT OF HIS--
AWP!
OUR TOOTHBRUSHES!
FACTOID 100% TRUE BOOKS

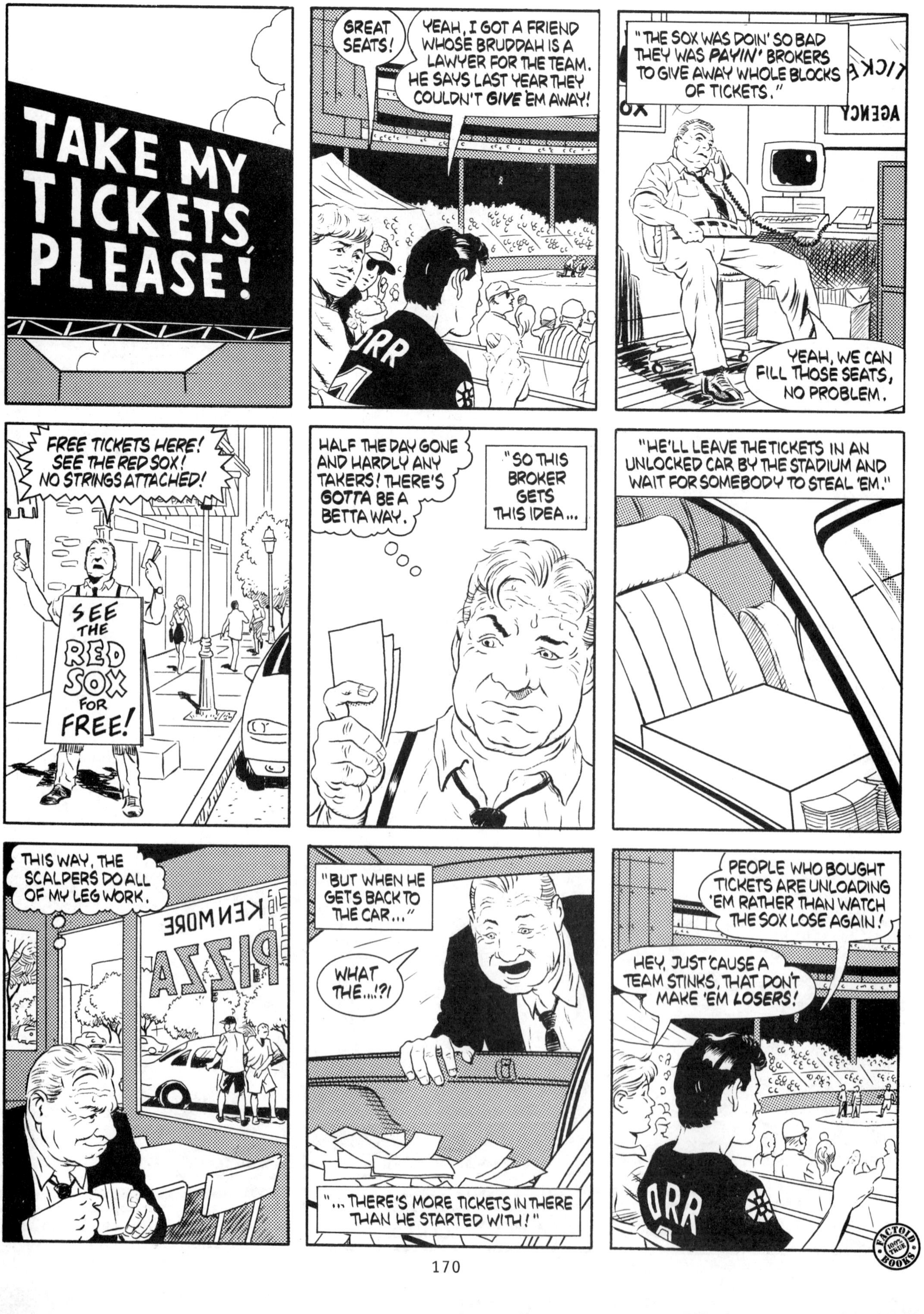
TAKE MY TICKETS, PLEASE!
GREAT SEATS!
YEAH, I GOT A FRIEND WHOSE BRUDDAH IS A LAWYER FOR THE TEAM. HE SAYS LAST YEAR THEY COULDN'T GIVE 'EM AWAY!
ORR
"THE SOX WAS DOIN' SO BAD THEY WAS PAYIN' BROKERS TO GIVE AWAY WHOLE BLOCKS OF TICKETS."
YEAH, WE CAN FILL THOSE SEATS, NO PROBLEM.
FREE TICKETS HERE! SEE THE RED SOX! NO STRINGS ATTACHED!
SEE THE RED SOX FOR FREE!
HALF THE DAY GONE AND HARDLY ANY TAKERS! THERE'S GOTTA BE A BETTA WAY.
"SO THIS BROKER GETS THIS IDEA...
"HE'LL LEAVE THE TICKETS IN AN UNLOCKED CAR BY THE STADIUM AND WAIT FOR SOMEBODY TO STEAL 'EM."
THIS WAY, THE SCALPERS DO ALL OF MY LEG WORK.
"BUT WHEN HE GETS BACK TO THE CAR..."
WHAT THE...!?!
"...THERE'S MORE TICKETS IN THERE THAN HE STARTED WITH!"
PEOPLE WHO BOUGHT TICKETS ARE UNLOADING 'EM RATHER THAN WATCH THE SOX LOSE AGAIN!
HEY, JUST 'CAUSE A TEAM STINKS, THAT DON'T MAKE 'EM LOSERS!
ORR
FACTOID 100% TRUE BOOKS

CHAPTER SEVEN

BUSINESS, PROFESSIONAL AND GOVERNMENT LEGENDS

OCCUPATIONAL HAZARDS

The world of work, products, and services has its legends too, often stories based on misunderstandings concerning how things function. Beyond problems involving contamination of processed foods such as candy *(page 173)* and soda *(page 175)*, the organizationally-oriented legends also describe problems with things like the 911 emergency telephone system, and computerized space-travel navigation systems *(pages 191-192)*. Still, some old non-technical favorites continue to circulate, notably the expensive cake-recipe story *(page 180)* and the one about the bedbugs in the Pullman car *(page 177)*.

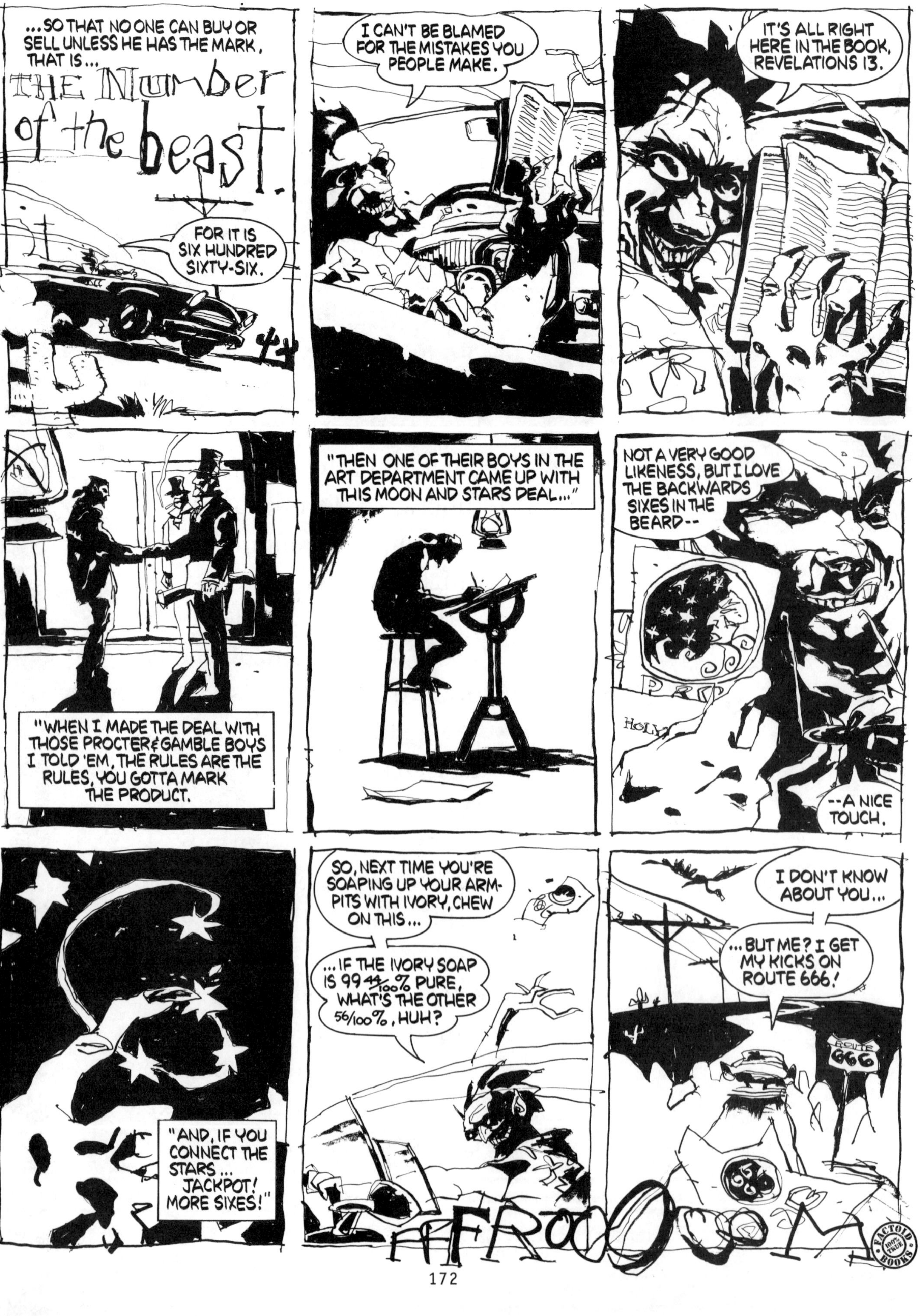

...SO THAT NO ONE CAN BUY OR SELL UNLESS HE HAS THE MARK, THAT IS...
THE NUMBER of the beast.
FOR IT IS SIX HUNDRED SIXTY-SIX.
I CAN'T BE BLAMED FOR THE MISTAKES YOU PEOPLE MAKE.
IT'S ALL RIGHT HERE IN THE BOOK, REVELATIONS 13.
"WHEN I MADE THE DEAL WITH THOSE PROCTER & GAMBLE BOYS I TOLD 'EM, THE RULES ARE THE RULES, YOU GOTTA MARK THE PRODUCT.
"THEN ONE OF THEIR BOYS IN THE ART DEPARTMENT CAME UP WITH THIS MOON AND STARS DEAL..."
NOT A VERY GOOD LIKENESS, BUT I LOVE THE BACKWARDS SIXES IN THE BEARD--
HOLY
--A NICE TOUCH.
"AND, IF YOU CONNECT THE STARS... JACKPOT! MORE SIXES!"
SO, NEXT TIME YOU'RE SOAPING UP YOUR ARMPITS WITH IVORY, CHEW ON THIS...
...IF THE IVORY SOAP IS 99 44/100% PURE, WHAT'S THE OTHER 56/100%, HUH?
I DON'T KNOW ABOUT YOU...
...BUT ME? I GET MY KICKS ON ROUTE 666!
ROUTE 666
AFROOOOOM
FACTOID BOOKS 100% TRUE

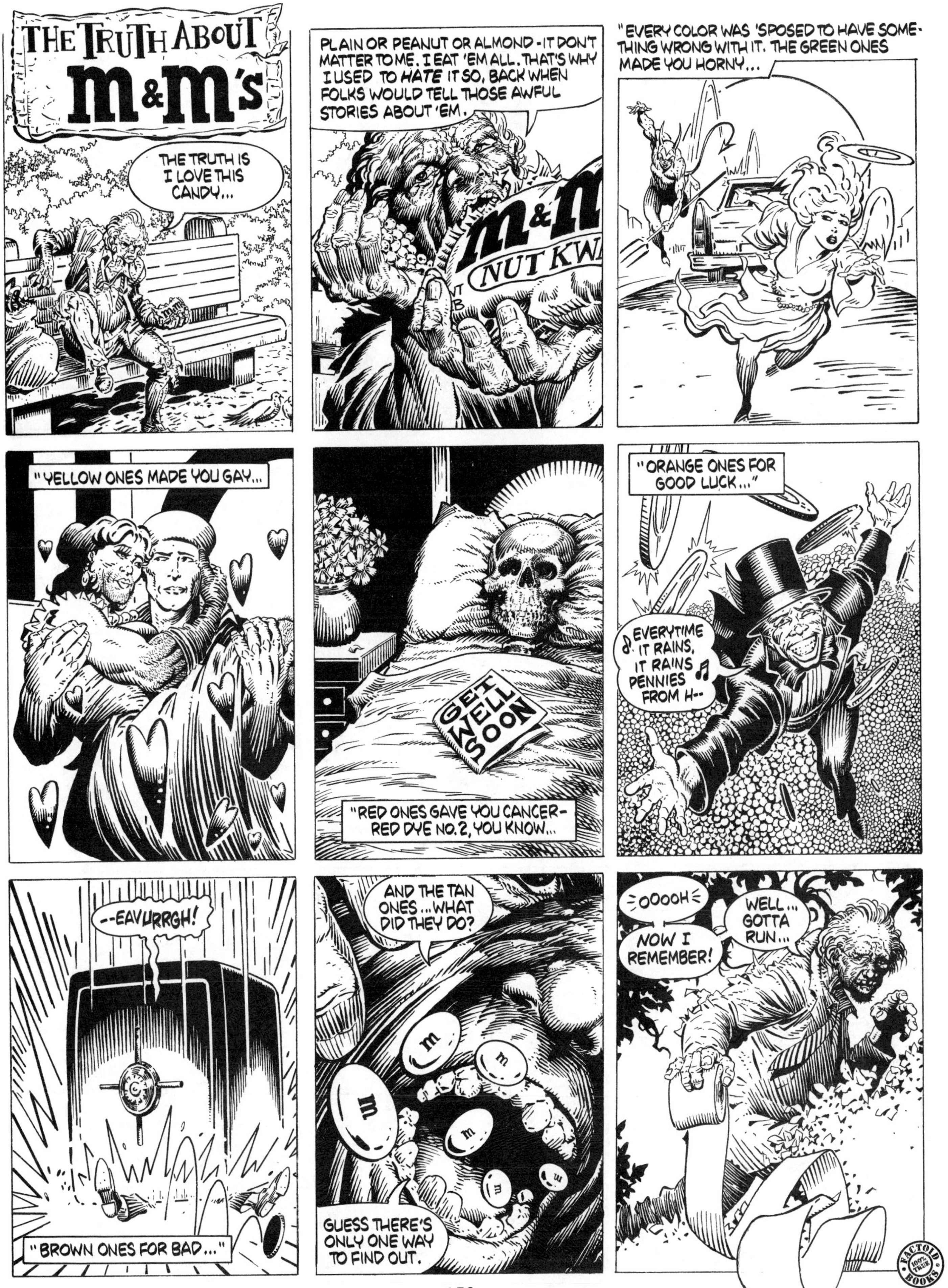
THE TRUTH ABOUT m&m's
THE TRUTH IS I LOVE THIS CANDY...
PLAIN OR PEANUT OR ALMOND - IT DON'T MATTER TO ME. I EAT 'EM ALL. THAT'S WHY I USED TO HATE IT SO, BACK WHEN FOLKS WOULD TELL THOSE AWFUL STORIES ABOUT 'EM.
m&m NUT KW
"EVERY COLOR WAS 'SPOSED TO HAVE SOMETHING WRONG WITH IT. THE GREEN ONES MADE YOU HORNY...
"YELLOW ONES MADE YOU GAY...
GET WELL SOON
"RED ONES GAVE YOU CANCER- RED DYE NO. 2, YOU KNOW...
"ORANGE ONES FOR GOOD LUCK..."
EVERYTIME IT RAINS, IT RAINS PENNIES FROM H--
--EAVURRGH!
"BROWN ONES FOR BAD..."
AND THE TAN ONES...WHAT DID THEY DO?
GUESS THERE'S ONLY ONE WAY TO FIND OUT.
OOOOH
NOW I REMEMBER!
WELL... GOTTA RUN...
FACTOID BOOKS 100% TRUE

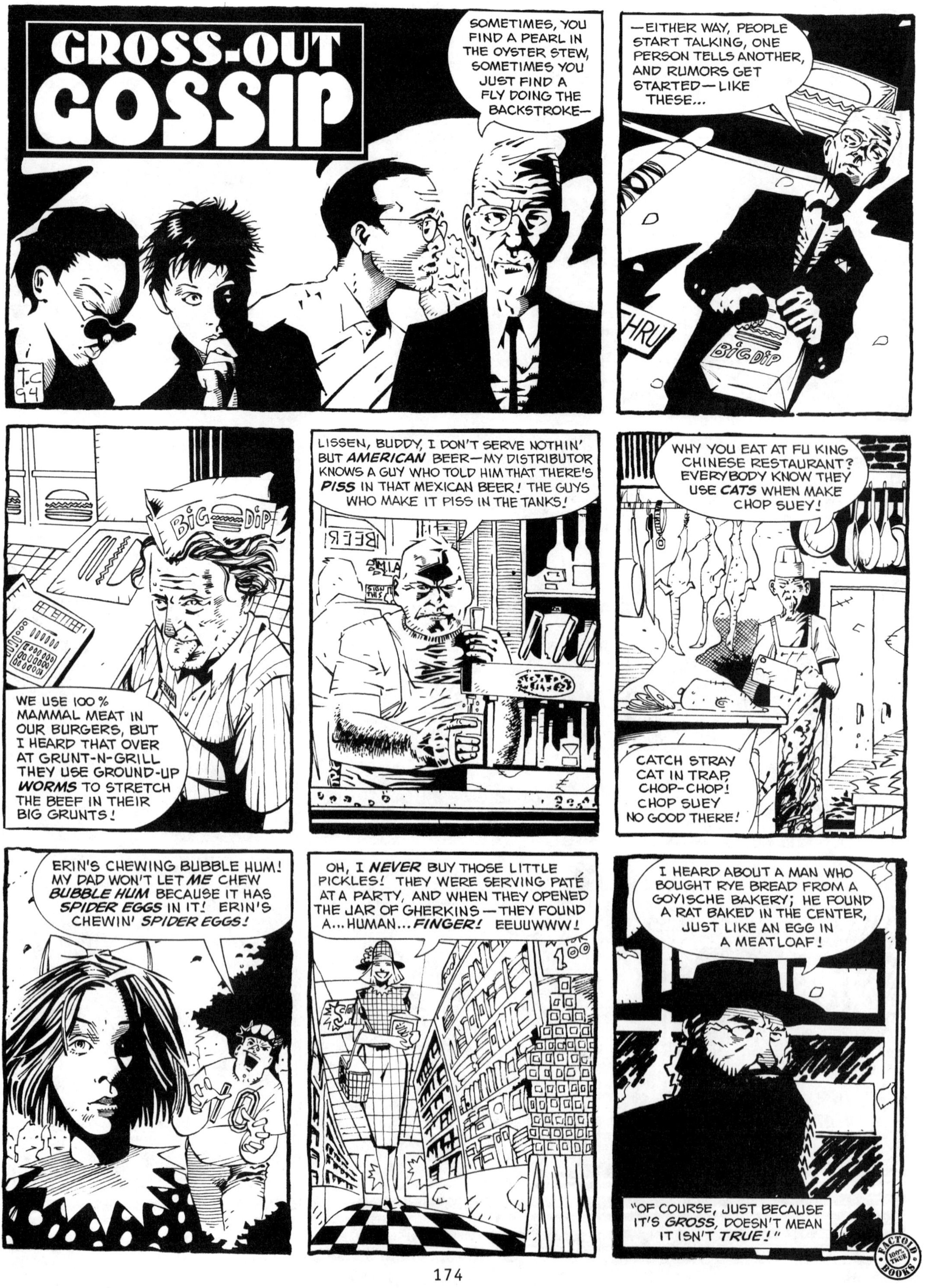
GROSS-OUT GOSSIP
SOMETIMES, YOU FIND A PEARL IN THE OYSTER STEW, SOMETIMES YOU JUST FIND A FLY DOING THE BACKSTROKE—
T.C 94
—EITHER WAY, PEOPLE START TALKING, ONE PERSON TELLS ANOTHER, AND RUMORS GET STARTED—LIKE THESE...
THRU
BIG DIP
BIG DIP
WE USE 100% MAMMAL MEAT IN OUR BURGERS, BUT I HEARD THAT OVER AT GRUNT-N-GRILL THEY USE GROUND-UP WORMS TO STRETCH THE BEEF IN THEIR BIG GRUNTS!
LISSEN, BUDDY, I DON'T SERVE NOTHIN' BUT AMERICAN BEER—MY DISTRIBUTOR KNOWS A GUY WHO TOLD HIM THAT THERE'S PISS IN THAT MEXICAN BEER! THE GUYS WHO MAKE IT PISS IN THE TANKS!
BEER
WHY YOU EAT AT FU KING CHINESE RESTAURANT? EVERYBODY KNOW THEY USE CATS WHEN MAKE CHOP SUEY!
CATCH STRAY CAT IN TRAP, CHOP-CHOP! CHOP SUEY NO GOOD THERE!
ERIN'S CHEWING BUBBLE HUM! MY DAD WON'T LET ME CHEW BUBBLE HUM BECAUSE IT HAS SPIDER EGGS IN IT! ERIN'S CHEWIN' SPIDER EGGS!
OH, I NEVER BUY THOSE LITTLE PICKLES! THEY WERE SERVING PATÉ AT A PARTY, AND WHEN THEY OPENED THE JAR OF GHERKINS—THEY FOUND A...HUMAN...FINGER! EEUUWWW!
1.00
I HEARD ABOUT A MAN WHO BOUGHT RYE BREAD FROM A GOYISCHE BAKERY; HE FOUND A RAT BAKED IN THE CENTER, JUST LIKE AN EGG IN A MEATLOAF!
"OF COURSE, JUST BECAUSE IT'S GROSS, DOESN'T MEAN IT ISN'T TRUE!"
FACTOID BOOKS 100% TRUE

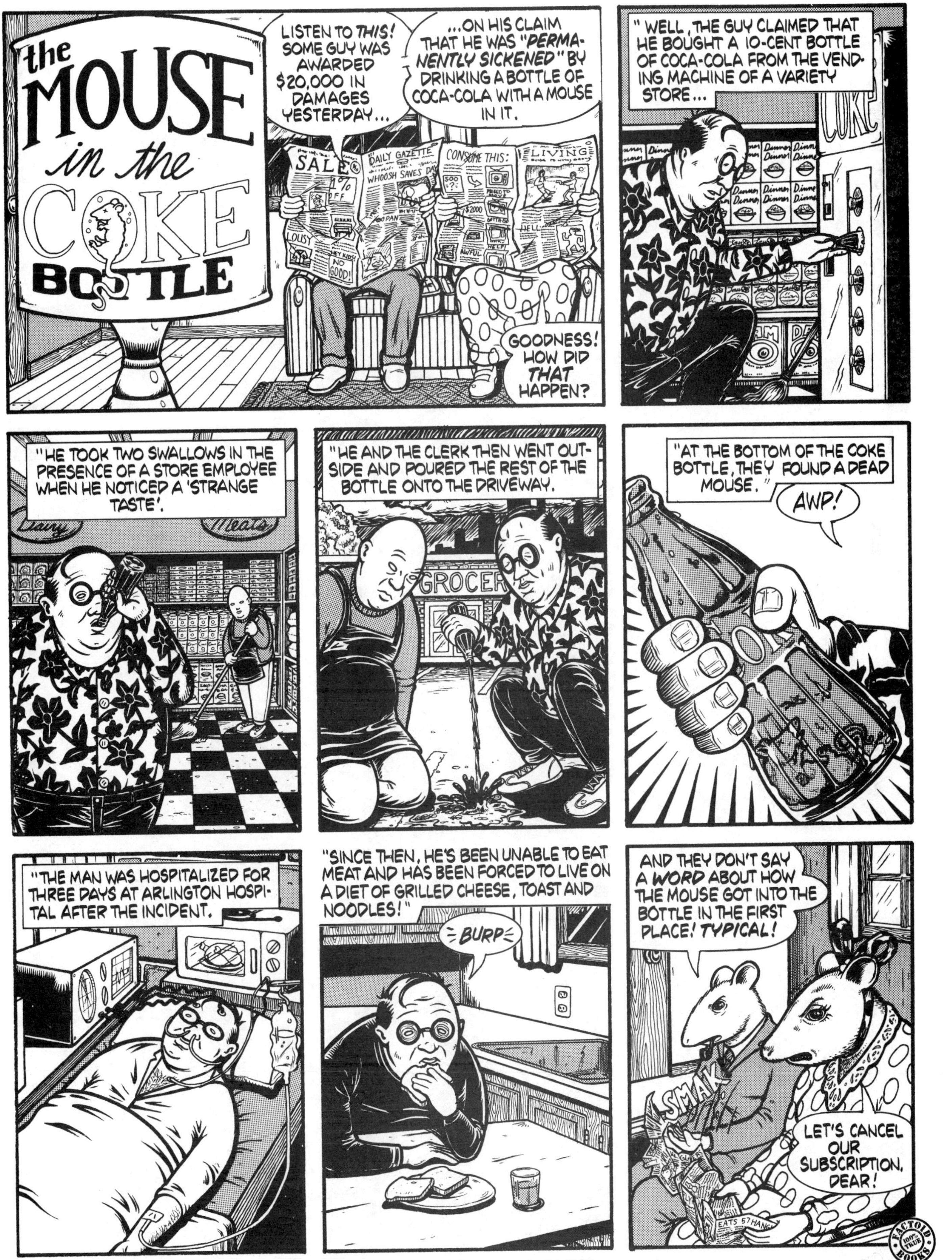

the MOUSE in the COKE BOTTLE
LISTEN TO THIS! SOME GUY WAS AWARDED $20,000 IN DAMAGES YESTERDAY...
...ON HIS CLAIM THAT HE WAS "PERMANENTLY SICKENED" BY DRINKING A BOTTLE OF COCA-COLA WITH A MOUSE IN IT.
DAILY GAZETTE
WHOOSH SAVES' DAY
SALE
CONSUME THIS:
LIVING
LOUSY
AWFUL
HELL
NO GOOD!
GOODNESS! HOW DID THAT HAPPEN?
" WELL, THE GUY CLAIMED THAT HE BOUGHT A 10-CENT BOTTLE OF COCA-COLA FROM THE VENDING MACHINE OF A VARIETY STORE...
COKE
"HE TOOK TWO SWALLOWS IN THE PRESENCE OF A STORE EMPLOYEE WHEN HE NOTICED A 'STRANGE TASTE'.
"HE AND THE CLERK THEN WENT OUTSIDE AND POURED THE REST OF THE BOTTLE ONTO THE DRIVEWAY.
GROCER
"AT THE BOTTOM OF THE COKE BOTTLE, THEY FOUND A DEAD MOUSE."
AWP!
"THE MAN WAS HOSPITALIZED FOR THREE DAYS AT ARLINGTON HOSPITAL AFTER THE INCIDENT.
"SINCE THEN, HE'S BEEN UNABLE TO EAT MEAT AND HAS BEEN FORCED TO LIVE ON A DIET OF GRILLED CHEESE, TOAST AND NOODLES!"
BURP
AND THEY DON'T SAY A WORD ABOUT HOW THE MOUSE GOT INTO THE BOTTLE IN THE FIRST PLACE! TYPICAL!
SMAK
LET'S CANCEL OUR SUBSCRIPTION, DEAR!
EATS 57 HANG
FACTOID BOOKS 100% TRUE

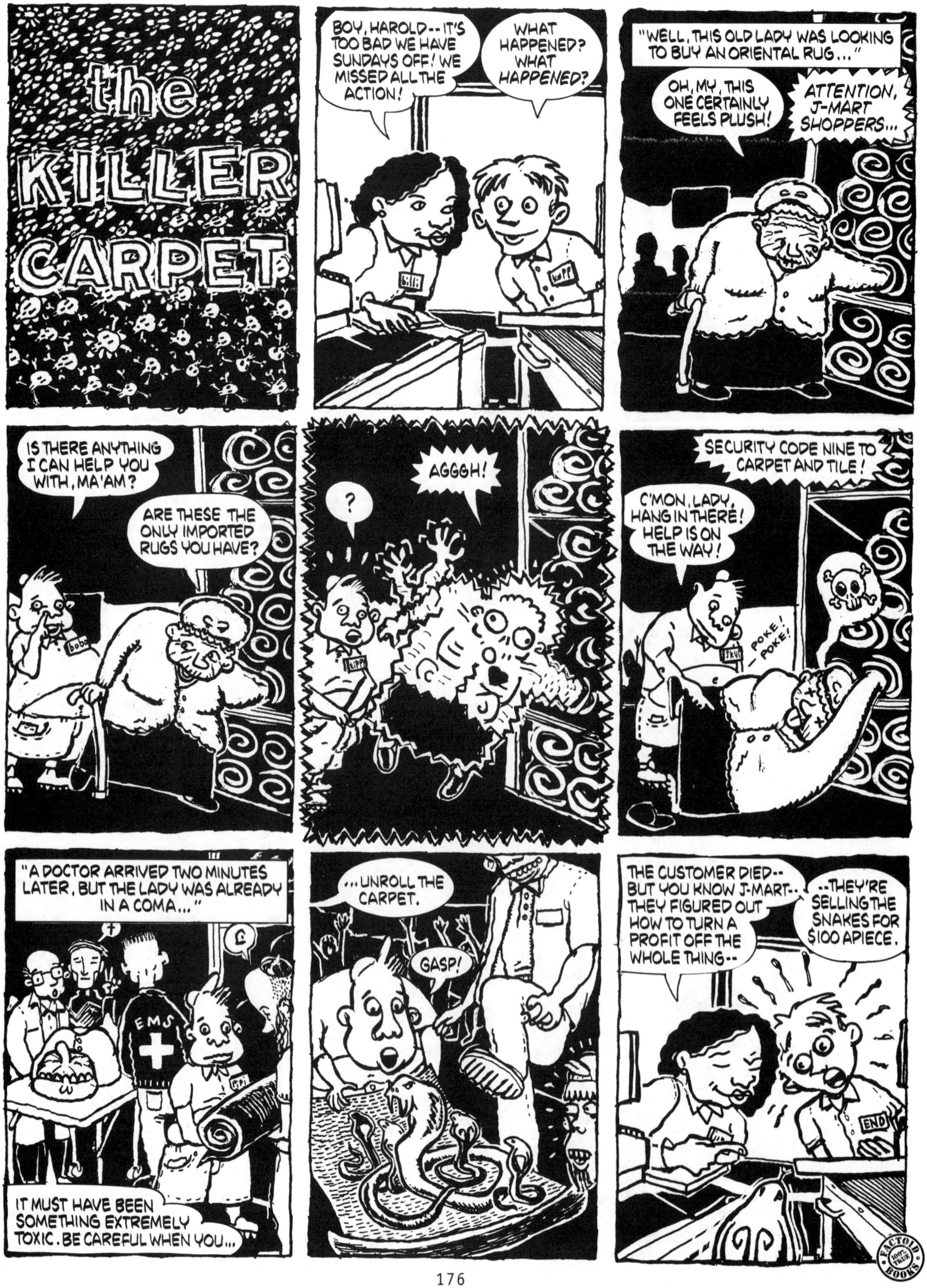
the KILLER CARPET
BOY, HAROLD-- IT'S TOO BAD WE HAVE SUNDAYS OFF! WE MISSED ALL THE ACTION!
WHAT HAPPENED? WHAT HAPPENED?
"WELL, THIS OLD LADY WAS LOOKING TO BUY AN ORIENTAL RUG..."
OH, MY, THIS ONE CERTAINLY FEELS PLUSH!
ATTENTION, J-MART SHOPPERS...
IS THERE ANYTHING I CAN HELP YOU WITH, MA'AM?
ARE THESE THE ONLY IMPORTED RUGS YOU HAVE?
?
AGGGH!
SECURITY CODE NINE TO CARPET AND TILE!
C'MON, LADY, HANG IN THERE! HELP IS ON THE WAY!
POKE! POKE!
"A DOCTOR ARRIVED TWO MINUTES LATER, BUT THE LADY WAS ALREADY IN A COMA..."
EMS
IT MUST HAVE BEEN SOMETHING EXTREMELY TOXIC. BE CAREFUL WHEN YOU...
...UNROLL THE CARPET.
GASP!
THE CUSTOMER DIED-- BUT YOU KNOW J-MART-- THEY FIGURED OUT HOW TO TURN A PROFIT OFF THE WHOLE THING--
--THEY'RE SELLING THE SNAKES FOR $100 APIECE.
END

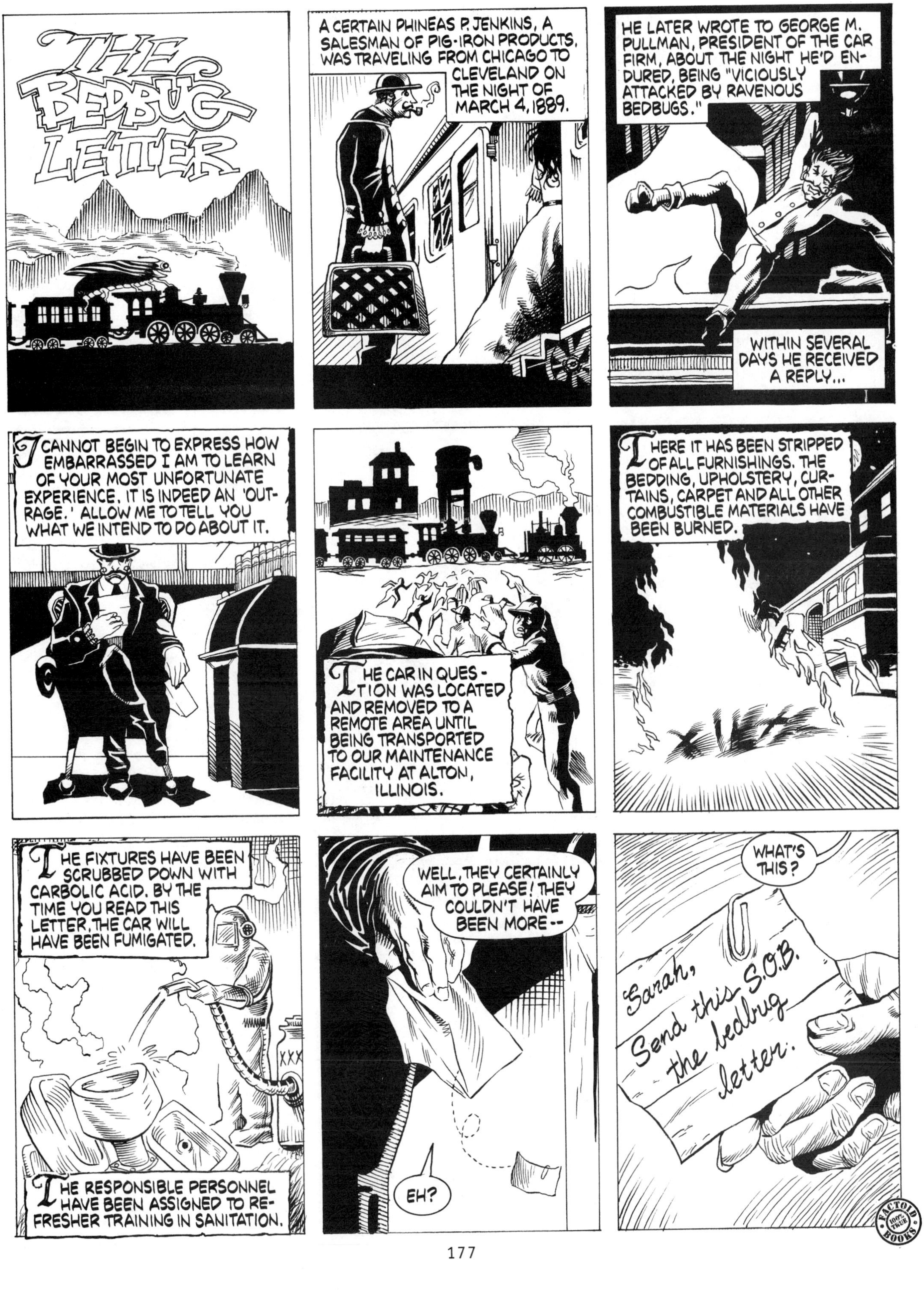
THE BEDBUG LETTER
A CERTAIN PHINEAS P. JENKINS, A SALESMAN OF PIG-IRON PRODUCTS, WAS TRAVELING FROM CHICAGO TO CLEVELAND ON THE NIGHT OF MARCH 4, 1889.
HE LATER WROTE TO GEORGE M. PULLMAN, PRESIDENT OF THE CAR FIRM, ABOUT THE NIGHT HE'D ENDURED, BEING "VICIOUSLY ATTACKED BY RAVENOUS BEDBUGS."
WITHIN SEVERAL DAYS HE RECEIVED A REPLY...
I CANNOT BEGIN TO EXPRESS HOW EMBARRASSED I AM TO LEARN OF YOUR MOST UNFORTUNATE EXPERIENCE. IT IS INDEED AN 'OUTRAGE.' ALLOW ME TO TELL YOU WHAT WE INTEND TO DO ABOUT IT.
THE CAR IN QUESTION WAS LOCATED AND REMOVED TO A REMOTE AREA UNTIL BEING TRANSPORTED TO OUR MAINTENANCE FACILITY AT ALTON, ILLINOIS.
THERE IT HAS BEEN STRIPPED OF ALL FURNISHINGS. THE BEDDING, UPHOLSTERY, CURTAINS, CARPET AND ALL OTHER COMBUSTIBLE MATERIALS HAVE BEEN BURNED.
THE FIXTURES HAVE BEEN SCRUBBED DOWN WITH CARBOLIC ACID. BY THE TIME YOU READ THIS LETTER, THE CAR WILL HAVE BEEN FUMIGATED.
XXX
THE RESPONSIBLE PERSONNEL HAVE BEEN ASSIGNED TO REFRESHER TRAINING IN SANITATION.
WELL, THEY CERTAINLY AIM TO PLEASE! THEY COULDN'T HAVE BEEN MORE --
EH?
WHAT'S THIS?
Sarah, Send this S.O.B. the bedbug letter.
FACTOID BOOKS 100% TRUE

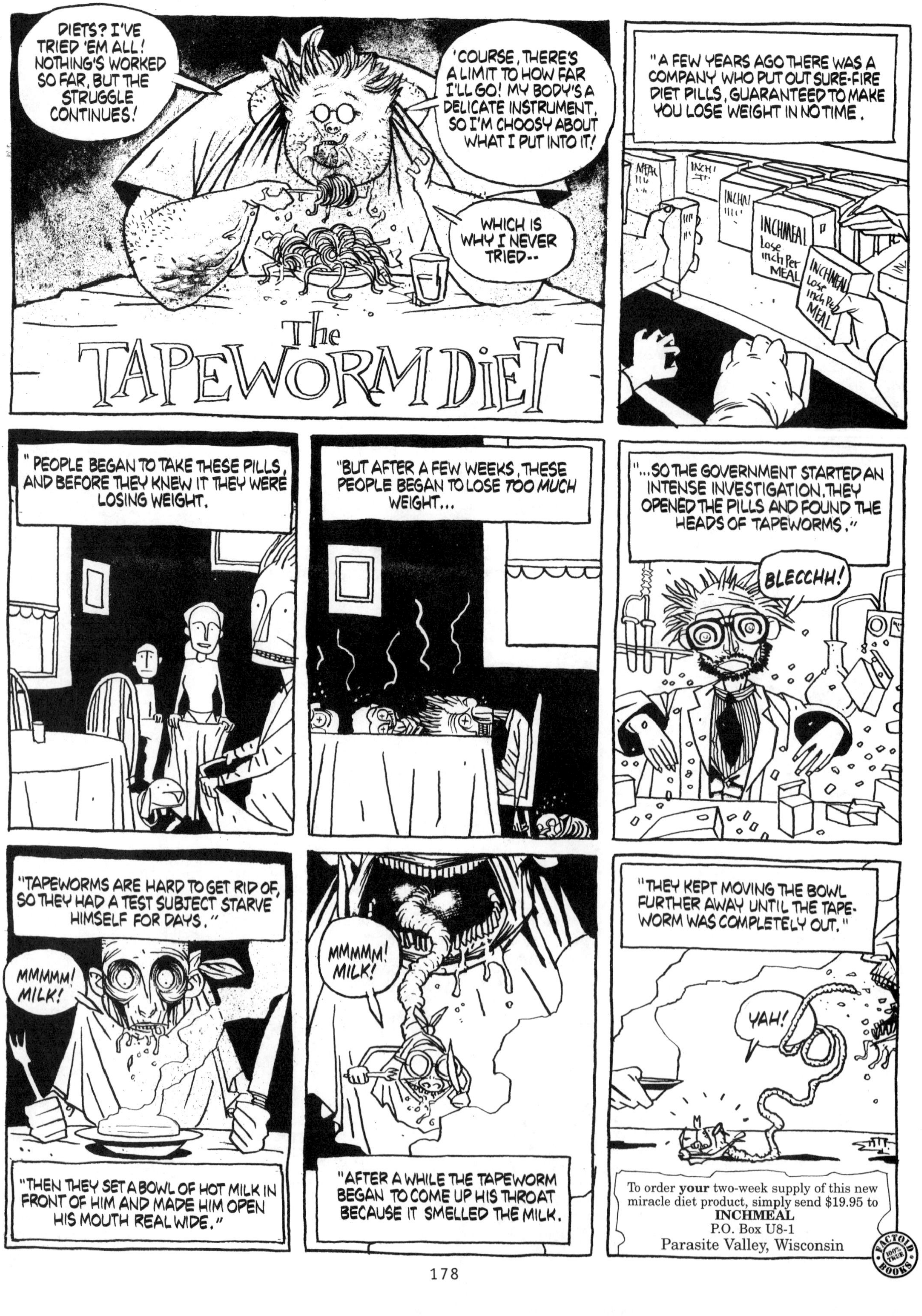
DIETS? I'VE TRIED 'EM ALL! NOTHING'S WORKED SO FAR, BUT THE STRUGGLE CONTINUES!
'COURSE, THERE'S A LIMIT TO HOW FAR I'LL GO! MY BODY'S A DELICATE INSTRUMENT, SO I'M CHOOSY ABOUT WHAT I PUT INTO IT!
WHICH IS WHY I NEVER TRIED--
The TAPEWORM DIET
"A FEW YEARS AGO THERE WAS A COMPANY WHO PUT OUT SURE-FIRE DIET PILLS, GUARANTEED TO MAKE YOU LOSE WEIGHT IN NO TIME.
INCHMEAL Lose inch Per MEAL
"PEOPLE BEGAN TO TAKE THESE PILLS, AND BEFORE THEY KNEW IT THEY WERE LOSING WEIGHT.
"BUT AFTER A FEW WEEKS, THESE PEOPLE BEGAN TO LOSE TOO MUCH WEIGHT...
"...SO THE GOVERNMENT STARTED AN INTENSE INVESTIGATION. THEY OPENED THE PILLS AND FOUND THE HEADS OF TAPEWORMS."
BLECCHH!
"TAPEWORMS ARE HARD TO GET RID OF, SO THEY HAD A TEST SUBJECT STARVE HIMSELF FOR DAYS."
MMMMM! MILK!
"THEN THEY SET A BOWL OF HOT MILK IN FRONT OF HIM AND MADE HIM OPEN HIS MOUTH REAL WIDE."
MMMMM! MILK!
"AFTER A WHILE THE TAPEWORM BEGAN TO COME UP HIS THROAT BECAUSE IT SMELLED THE MILK.
"THEY KEPT MOVING THE BOWL FURTHER AWAY UNTIL THE TAPE-WORM WAS COMPLETELY OUT."
YAH!
To order your two-week supply of this new miracle diet product, simply send $19.95 to
INCHMEAL
P.O. Box U8-1
Parasite Valley, Wisconsin
FACTOID BOOKS 100% TRUE

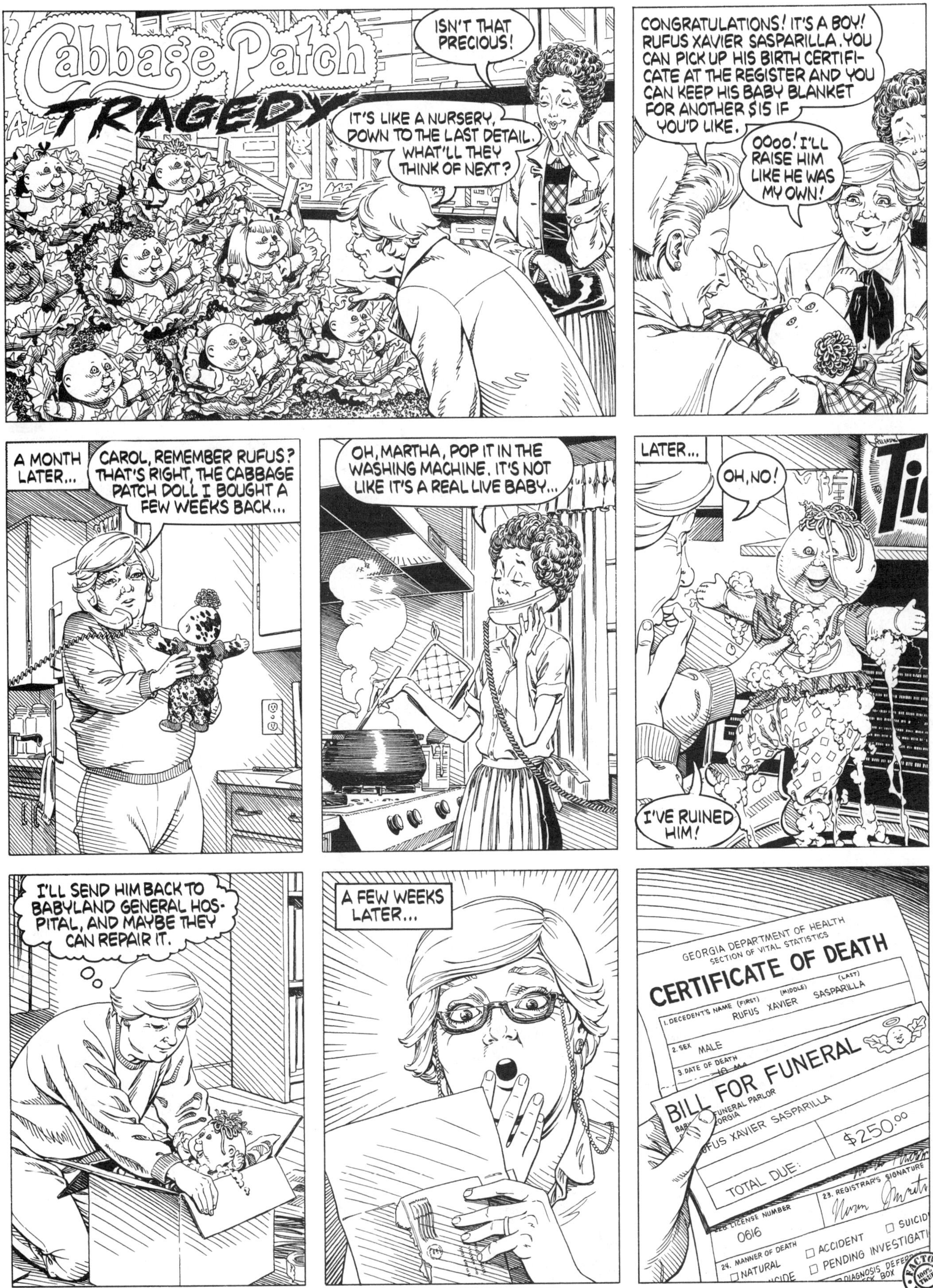
Cabbage Patch
TRAGEDY
ISN'T THAT PRECIOUS!
IT'S LIKE A NURSERY, DOWN TO THE LAST DETAIL. WHAT'LL THEY THINK OF NEXT?
CONGRATULATIONS! IT'S A BOY! RUFUS XAVIER SASPARILLA. YOU CAN PICK UP HIS BIRTH CERTIFICATE AT THE REGISTER AND YOU CAN KEEP HIS BABY BLANKET FOR ANOTHER $15 IF YOU'D LIKE.
OOoo! I'LL RAISE HIM LIKE HE WAS MY OWN!
A MONTH LATER...
CAROL, REMEMBER RUFUS? THAT'S RIGHT, THE CABBAGE PATCH DOLL I BOUGHT A FEW WEEKS BACK...
OH, MARTHA, POP IT IN THE WASHING MACHINE. IT'S NOT LIKE IT'S A REAL LIVE BABY...
LATER...
OH, NO!
I'VE RUINED HIM!
I'LL SEND HIM BACK TO BABYLAND GENERAL HOSPITAL, AND MAYBE THEY CAN REPAIR IT.
A FEW WEEKS LATER...
GEORGIA DEPARTMENT OF HEALTH
SECTION OF VITAL STATISTICS
CERTIFICATE OF DEATH
1. DECEDENT'S NAME (FIRST) (MIDDLE) (LAST)
RUFUS XAVIER SASPARILLA
2. SEX MALE
3. DATE OF DEATH
BILL FOR FUNERAL
FUNERAL PARLOR
GEORGIA
RUFUS XAVIER SASPARILLA
$250.00
TOTAL DUE:
23. REGISTRAR'S SIGNATURE
LICENSE NUMBER
0616
24. MANNER OF DEATH
NATURAL
ACCIDENT
PENDING INVESTIGATI
SUICID

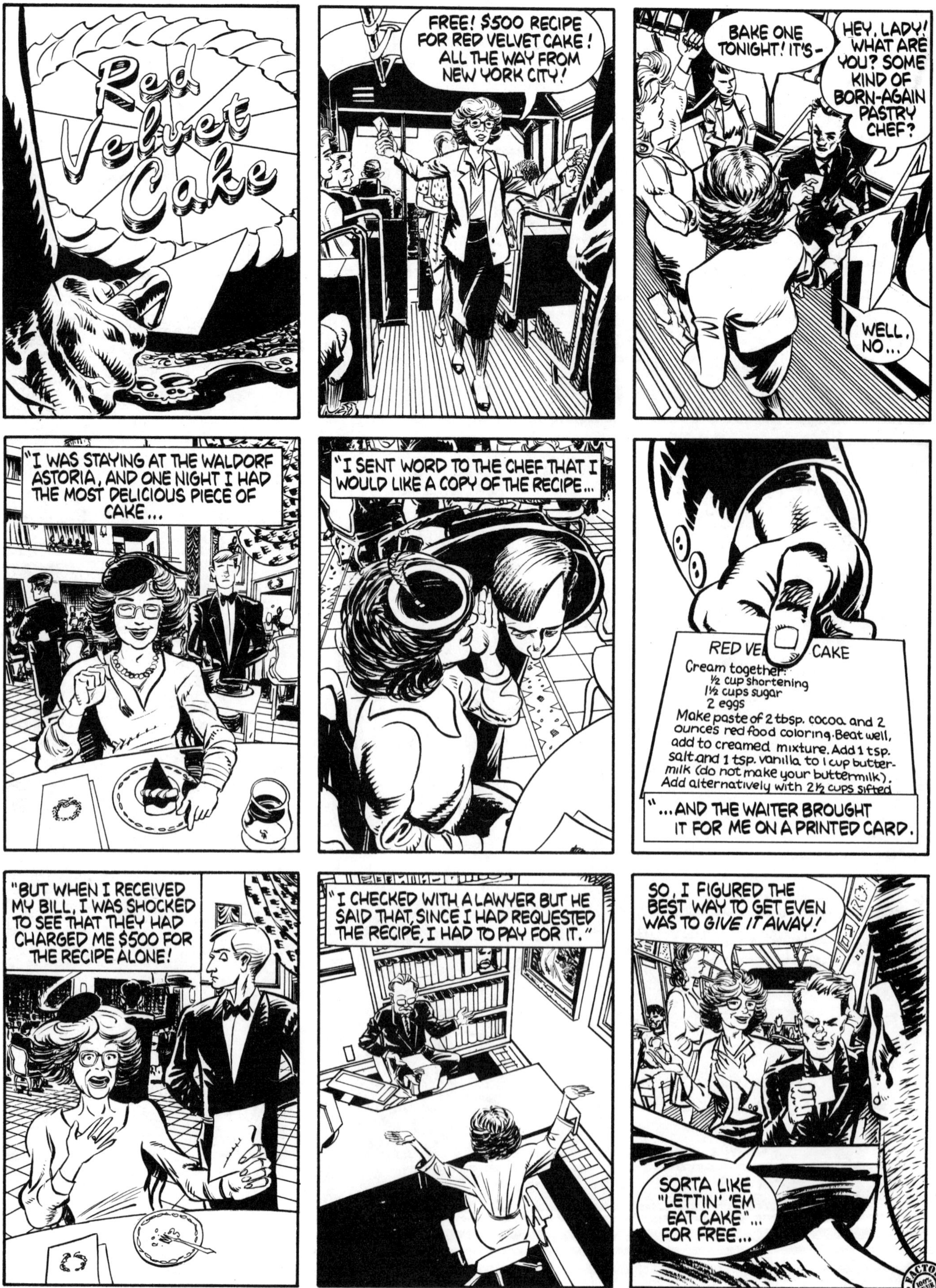
Red Velvet Cake
FREE! $500 RECIPE FOR RED VELVET CAKE! ALL THE WAY FROM NEW YORK CITY!
BAKE ONE TONIGHT! IT'S -
HEY, LADY! WHAT ARE YOU? SOME KIND OF BORN-AGAIN PASTRY CHEF?
WELL, NO...
"I WAS STAYING AT THE WALDORF ASTORIA, AND ONE NIGHT I HAD THE MOST DELICIOUS PIECE OF CAKE...
"I SENT WORD TO THE CHEF THAT I WOULD LIKE A COPY OF THE RECIPE...
RED VEL CAKE
Cream together:
½ cup shortening
1½ cups sugar
2 eggs
Make paste of 2 tbsp. cocoa and 2 ounces red food coloring. Beat well, add to creamed mixture. Add 1 tsp. salt and 1 tsp. vanilla to 1 cup buttermilk (do not make your buttermilk). Add alternatively with 2½ cups sifted
"...AND THE WAITER BROUGHT IT FOR ME ON A PRINTED CARD.
"BUT WHEN I RECEIVED MY BILL, I WAS SHOCKED TO SEE THAT THEY HAD CHARGED ME $500 FOR THE RECIPE ALONE!
"I CHECKED WITH A LAWYER BUT HE SAID THAT, SINCE I HAD REQUESTED THE RECIPE, I HAD TO PAY FOR IT."
SO, I FIGURED THE BEST WAY TO GET EVEN WAS TO GIVE IT AWAY!
SORTA LIKE "LETTIN' 'EM EAT CAKE"... FOR FREE...

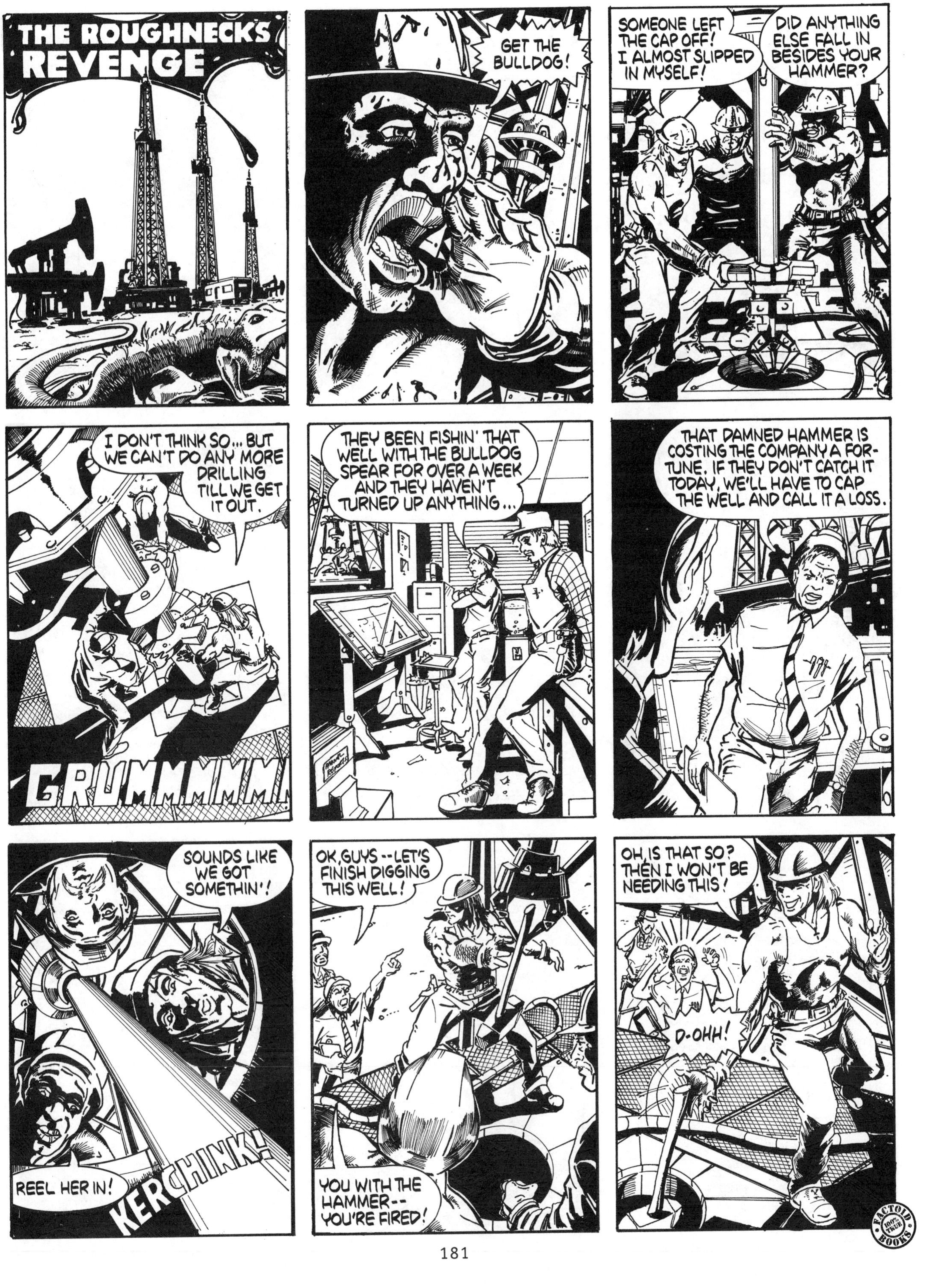
THE ROUGHNECK'S REVENGE
GET THE BULLDOG!
SOMEONE LEFT THE CAP OFF! I ALMOST SLIPPED IN MYSELF!
DID ANYTHING ELSE FALL IN BESIDES YOUR HAMMER?
I DON'T THINK SO... BUT WE CAN'T DO ANY MORE DRILLING TILL WE GET IT OUT.
GRUMMMMM
THEY BEEN FISHIN' THAT WELL WITH THE BULLDOG SPEAR FOR OVER A WEEK AND THEY HAVEN'T TURNED UP ANYTHING...
THAT DAMNED HAMMER IS COSTING THE COMPANY A FORTUNE. IF THEY DON'T CATCH IT TODAY, WE'LL HAVE TO CAP THE WELL AND CALL IT A LOSS.
SOUNDS LIKE WE GOT SOMETHIN'!
REEL HER IN!
KERCHINK!
OK, GUYS --LET'S FINISH DIGGING THIS WELL!
YOU WITH THE HAMMER-- YOU'RE FIRED!
OH, IS THAT SO? THEN I WON'T BE NEEDING THIS!
D-OHH!

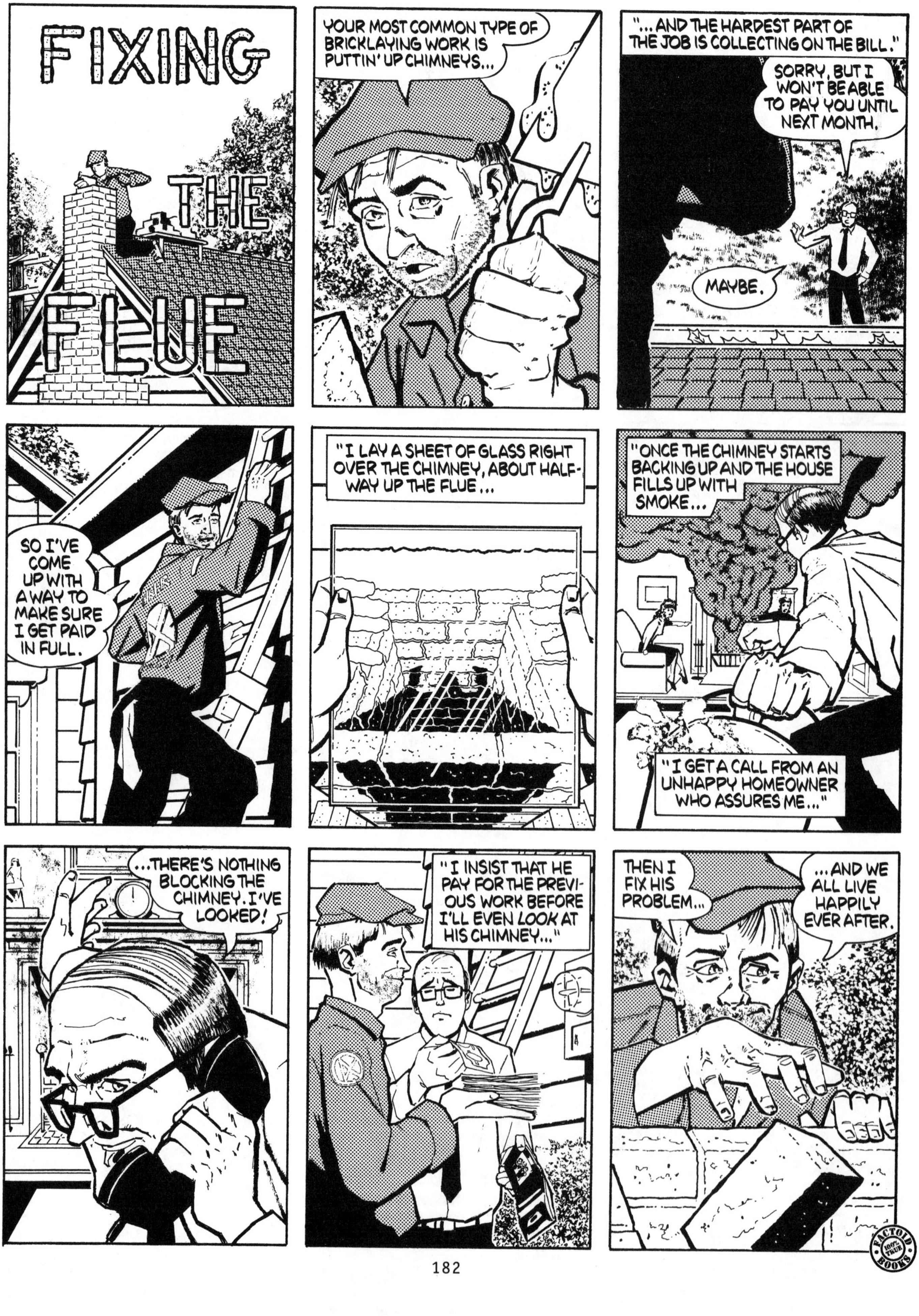
FIXING THE FLUE
YOUR MOST COMMON TYPE OF BRICKLAYING WORK IS PUTTIN' UP CHIMNEYS...
"... AND THE HARDEST PART OF THE JOB IS COLLECTING ON THE BILL."
SORRY, BUT I WON'T BE ABLE TO PAY YOU UNTIL NEXT MONTH.
MAYBE.
SO I'VE COME UP WITH A WAY TO MAKE SURE I GET PAID IN FULL.
"I LAY A SHEET OF GLASS RIGHT OVER THE CHIMNEY, ABOUT HALF-WAY UP THE FLUE...
"ONCE THE CHIMNEY STARTS BACKING UP AND THE HOUSE FILLS UP WITH SMOKE...
"I GET A CALL FROM AN UNHAPPY HOMEOWNER WHO ASSURES ME..."
...THERE'S NOTHING BLOCKING THE CHIMNEY. I'VE LOOKED!
"I INSIST THAT HE PAY FOR THE PREVIOUS WORK BEFORE I'LL EVEN LOOK AT HIS CHIMNEY..."
THEN I FIX HIS PROBLEM...
...AND WE ALL LIVE HAPPILY EVER AFTER.
FACTOID BOOKS 100% TRUE

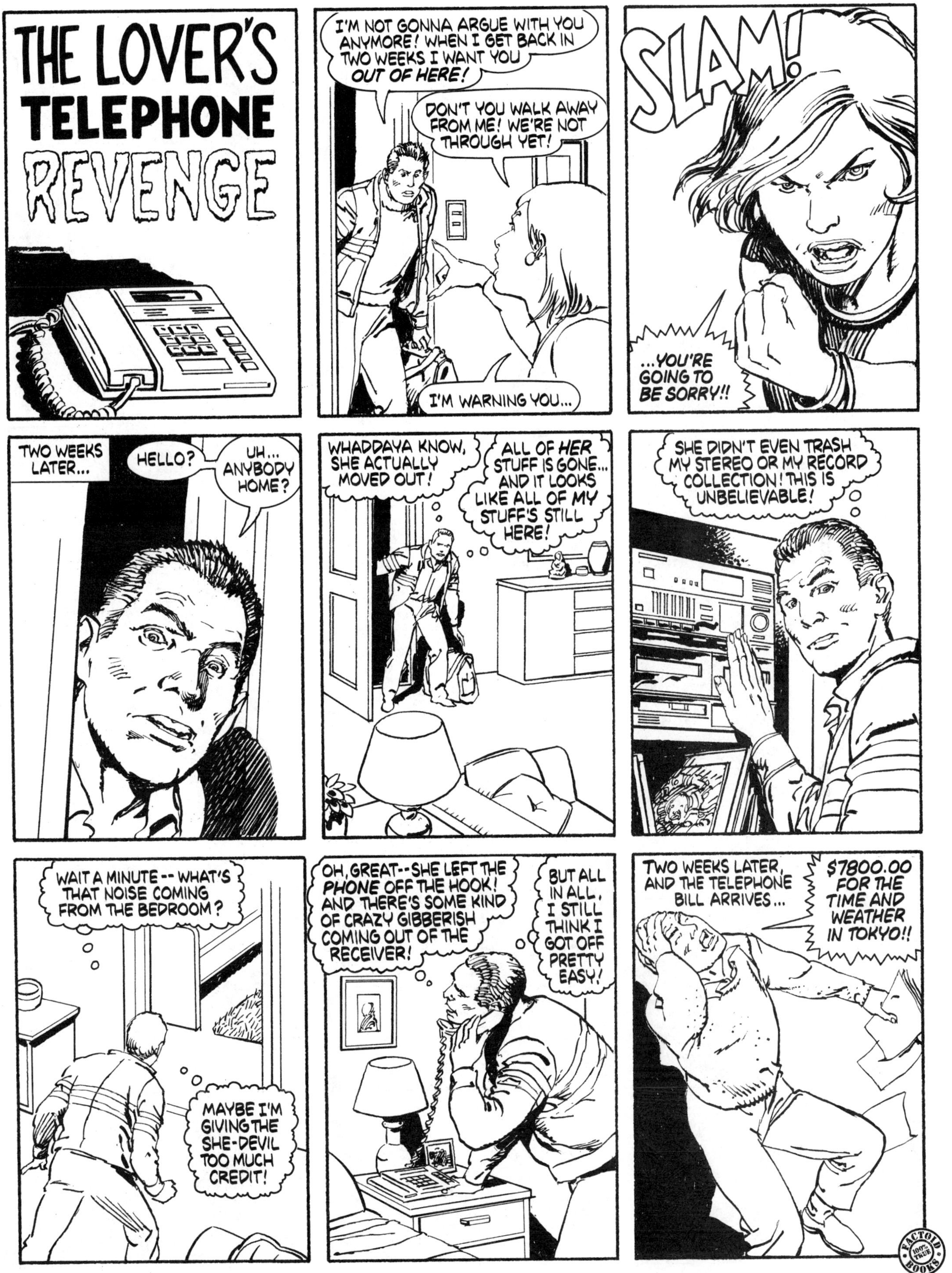
THE LOVER'S TELEPHONE REVENGE
I'M NOT GONNA ARGUE WITH YOU ANYMORE! WHEN I GET BACK IN TWO WEEKS I WANT YOU OUT OF HERE!
DON'T YOU WALK AWAY FROM ME! WE'RE NOT THROUGH YET!
I'M WARNING YOU...
SLAM!
...YOU'RE GOING TO BE SORRY!!
TWO WEEKS LATER...
HELLO?
UH... ANYBODY HOME?
WHADDAYA KNOW, SHE ACTUALLY MOVED OUT!
ALL OF HER STUFF IS GONE... AND IT LOOKS LIKE ALL OF MY STUFF'S STILL HERE!
SHE DIDN'T EVEN TRASH MY STEREO OR MY RECORD COLLECTION! THIS IS UNBELIEVABLE!
WAIT A MINUTE -- WHAT'S THAT NOISE COMING FROM THE BEDROOM?
MAYBE I'M GIVING THE SHE-DEVIL TOO MUCH CREDIT!
OH, GREAT--SHE LEFT THE PHONE OFF THE HOOK! AND THERE'S SOME KIND OF CRAZY GIBBERISH COMING OUT OF THE RECEIVER!
BUT ALL IN ALL, I STILL THINK I GOT OFF PRETTY EASY!
TWO WEEKS LATER, AND THE TELEPHONE BILL ARRIVES...
$7800.00 FOR THE TIME AND WEATHER IN TOKYO!!

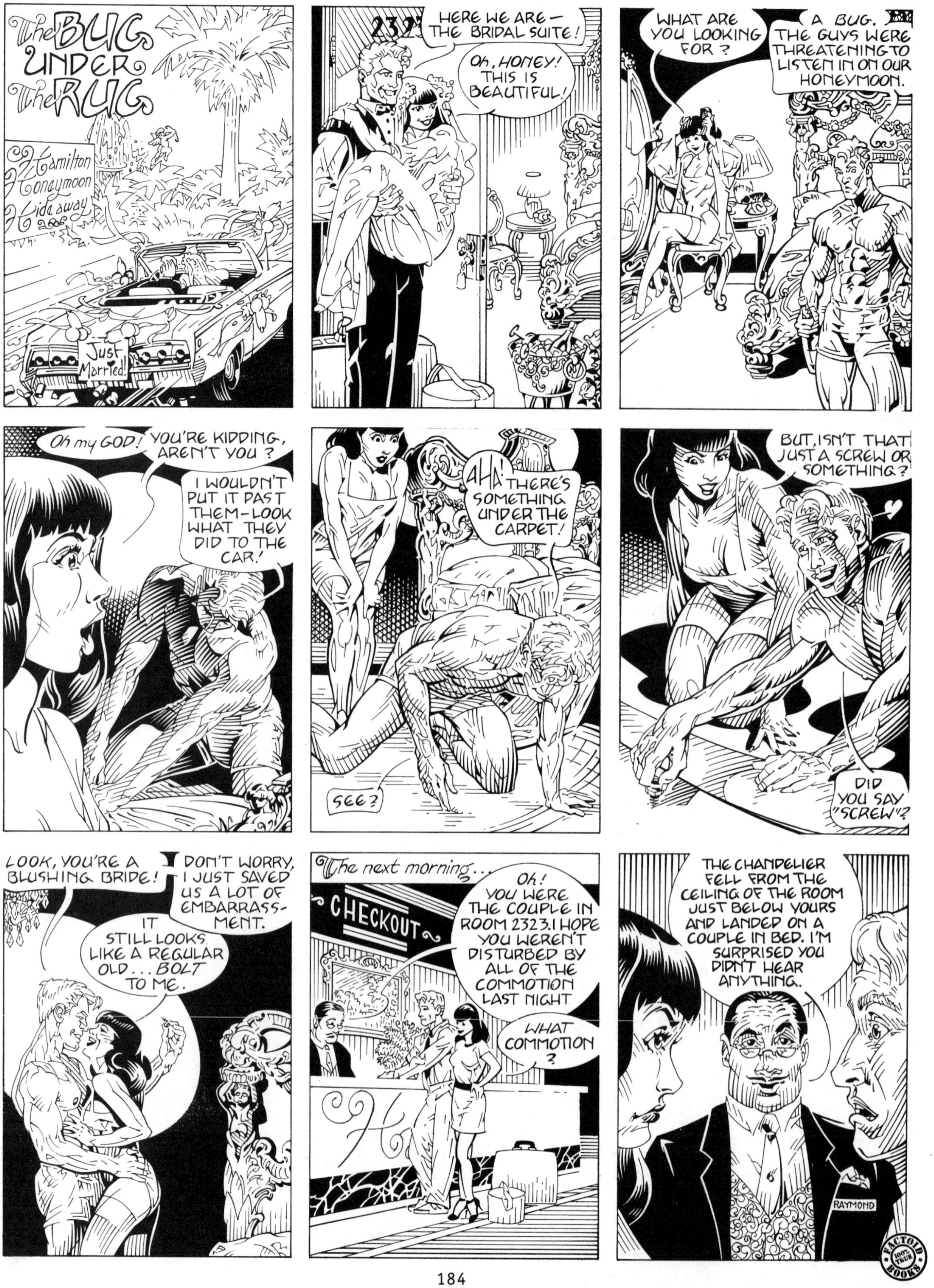
The BUG UNDER The RUG
Hamilton Honeymoon Hideaway
Just Married!
2323
HERE WE ARE — THE BRIDAL SUITE!
OH, HONEY! THIS IS BEAUTIFUL!
WHAT ARE YOU LOOKING FOR ?
A BUG. THE GUYS WERE THREATENING TO LISTEN IN ON OUR HONEYMOON.
Oh my GOD!
YOU'RE KIDDING, AREN'T YOU ?
I WOULDN'T PUT IT PAST THEM—LOOK WHAT THEY DID TO THE CAR!
AHA! THERE'S SOMETHING UNDER THE CARPET!
SEE?
BUT, ISN'T THAT JUST A SCREW OR SOMETHING?
DID YOU SAY "SCREW"?
LOOK, YOU'RE A BLUSHING BRIDE!
I DON'T WORRY, I JUST SAVED US A LOT OF EMBARRASS-MENT.
IT STILL LOOKS LIKE A REGULAR OLD... BOLT TO ME.
The next morning...
CHECKOUT
OH! YOU WERE THE COUPLE IN ROOM 2323. I HOPE YOU WEREN'T DISTURBED BY ALL OF THE COMMOTION LAST NIGHT.
WHAT COMMOTION ?
THE CHANDELIER FELL FROM THE CEILING OF THE ROOM JUST BELOW YOURS AND LANDED ON A COUPLE IN BED. I'M SURPRISED YOU DIDN'T HEAR ANYTHING.
RAYMOND
FACTOID 100% TRUE BOOKS

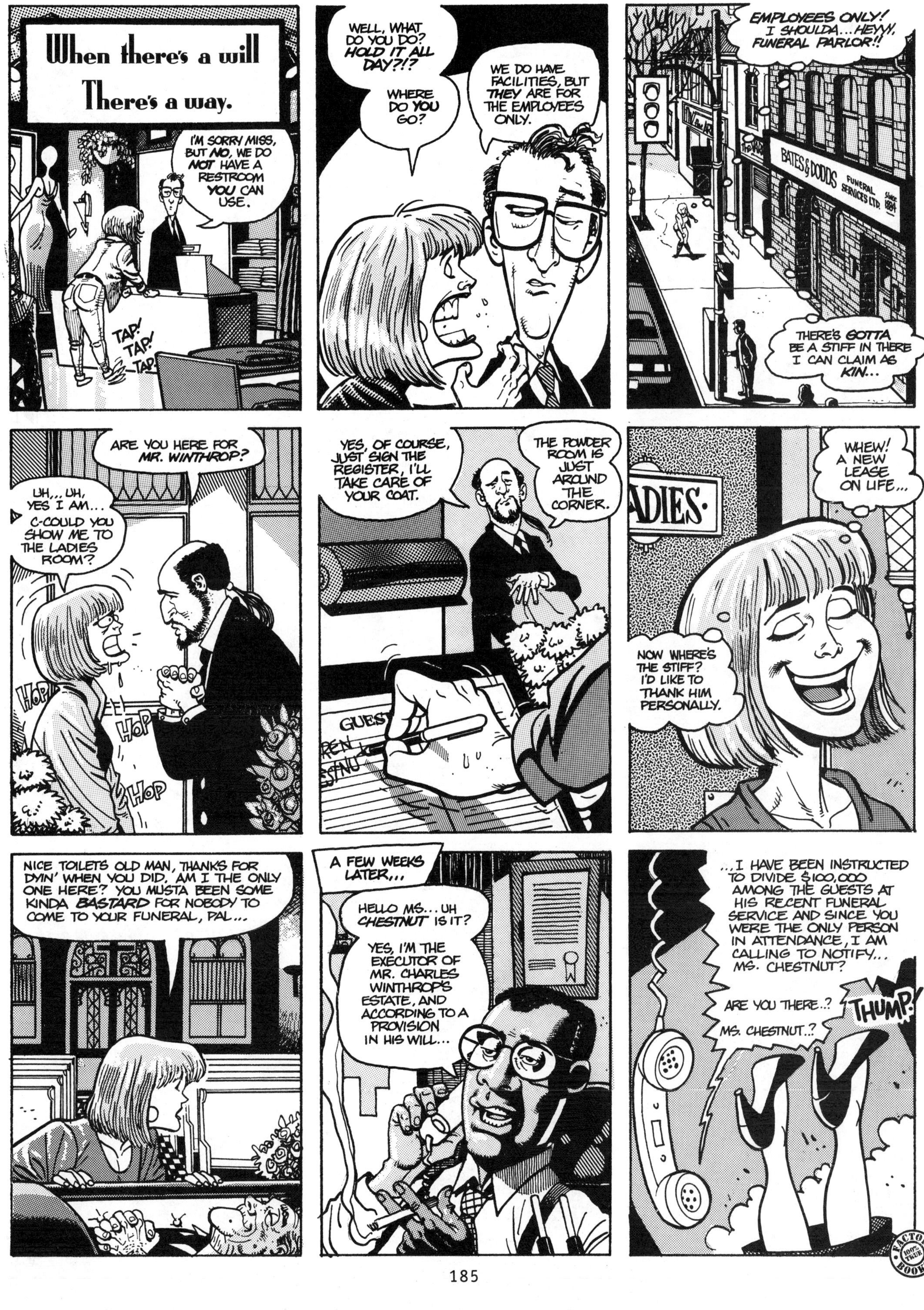
When there's a will
There's a way.
I'M SORRY MISS, BUT NO, WE DO NOT HAVE A RESTROOM YOU CAN USE.
TAP! TAP! TAP!
WELL, WHAT DO YOU DO? HOLD IT ALL DAY?!?
WHERE DO YOU GO?
WE DO HAVE FACILITIES, BUT THEY ARE FOR THE EMPLOYEES ONLY.
EMPLOYEES ONLY! I SHOULDA... HEYYY, FUNERAL PARLOR!!
BATES & DODDS FUNERAL SERVICES LTD. SINCE 1884
THERE'S GOTTA BE A STIFF IN THERE I CAN CLAIM AS KIN...
ARE YOU HERE FOR MR. WINTHROP?
UH,.. UH, YES I AM... C-COULD YOU SHOW ME TO THE LADIES ROOM?
HOP HOP HOP
YES, OF COURSE, JUST SIGN THE REGISTER, I'LL TAKE CARE OF YOUR COAT.
THE POWDER ROOM IS JUST AROUND THE CORNER.
GUEST
WHEW! A NEW LEASE ON LIFE...
NOW WHERE'S THE STIFF? I'D LIKE TO THANK HIM PERSONALLY.
NICE TOILETS OLD MAN, THANKS FOR DYIN' WHEN YOU DID, AM I THE ONLY ONE HERE? YOU MUSTA BEEN SOME KINDA BASTARD FOR NOBODY TO COME TO YOUR FUNERAL, PAL...
A FEW WEEKS LATER...
HELLO MS... UH CHESTNUT IS IT?
YES, I'M THE EXECUTOR OF MR. CHARLES WINTHROP'S ESTATE, AND ACCORDING TO A PROVISION IN HIS WILL...
...I HAVE BEEN INSTRUCTED TO DIVIDE $100,000 AMONG THE GUESTS AT HIS RECENT FUNERAL SERVICE AND SINCE YOU WERE THE ONLY PERSON IN ATTENDANCE, I AM CALLING TO NOTIFY... MS. CHESTNUT?
ARE YOU THERE..?
MS. CHESTNUT..?
THUMP!
FACTOID BOOKS 100% TRUE

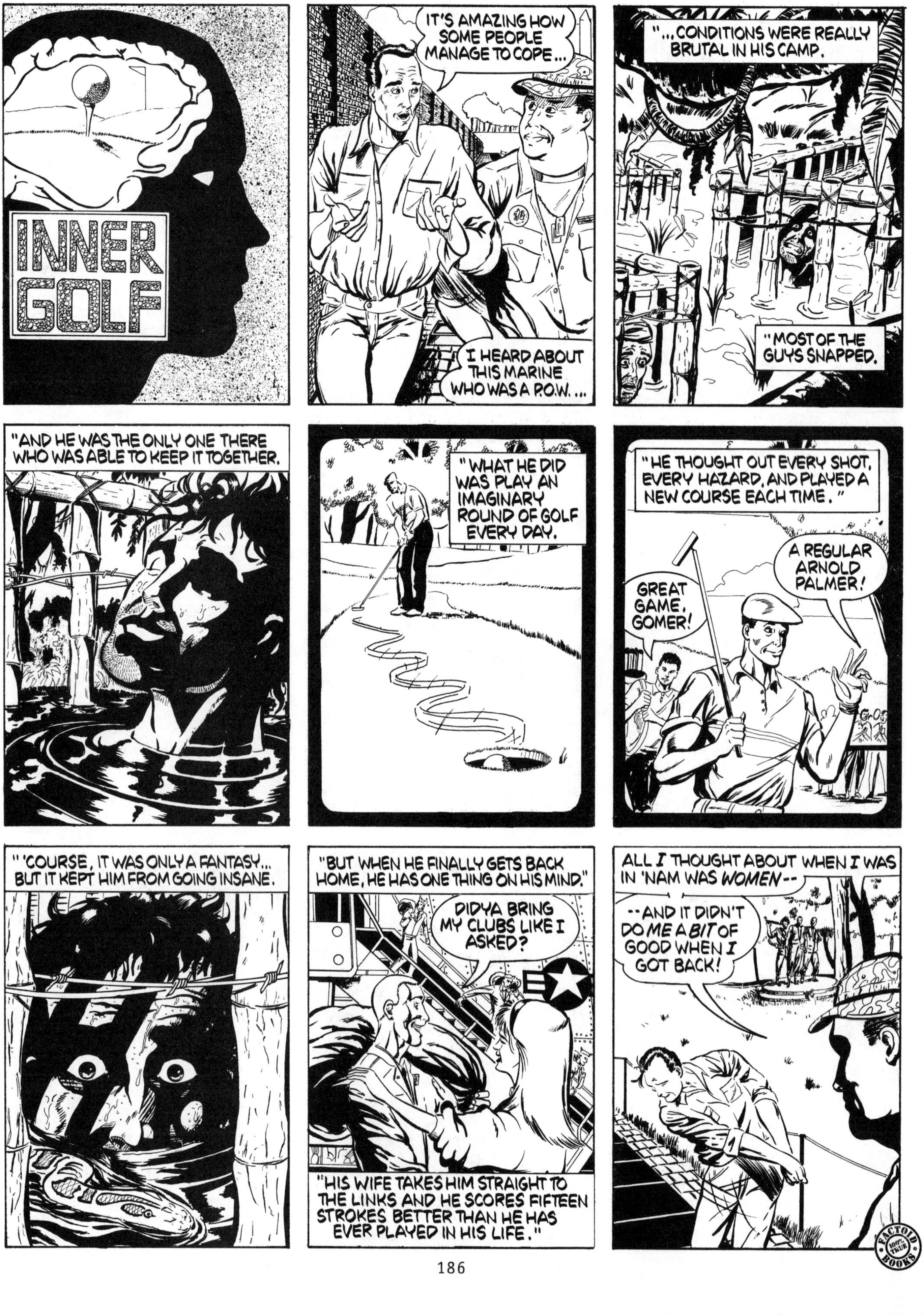
INNER GOLF
IT'S AMAZING HOW SOME PEOPLE MANAGE TO COPE...
I HEARD ABOUT THIS MARINE WHO WAS A P.O.W. ...
"...CONDITIONS WERE REALLY BRUTAL IN HIS CAMP.
"MOST OF THE GUYS SNAPPED.
"AND HE WAS THE ONLY ONE THERE WHO WAS ABLE TO KEEP IT TOGETHER.
"WHAT HE DID WAS PLAY AN IMAGINARY ROUND OF GOLF EVERY DAY.
"HE THOUGHT OUT EVERY SHOT, EVERY HAZARD, AND PLAYED A NEW COURSE EACH TIME."
GREAT GAME, GOMER!
A REGULAR ARNOLD PALMER!
"'COURSE, IT WAS ONLY A FANTASY... BUT IT KEPT HIM FROM GOING INSANE.
"BUT WHEN HE FINALLY GETS BACK HOME, HE HAS ONE THING ON HIS MIND."
DIDYA BRING MY CLUBS LIKE I ASKED?
"HIS WIFE TAKES HIM STRAIGHT TO THE LINKS AND HE SCORES FIFTEEN STROKES BETTER THAN HE HAS EVER PLAYED IN HIS LIFE."
ALL *I* THOUGHT ABOUT WHEN *I* WAS IN 'NAM WAS *WOMEN*--
--AND IT DIDN'T DO *ME* A *BIT* OF GOOD WHEN *I* GOT BACK!
FACTOID BOOKS 100% TRUE

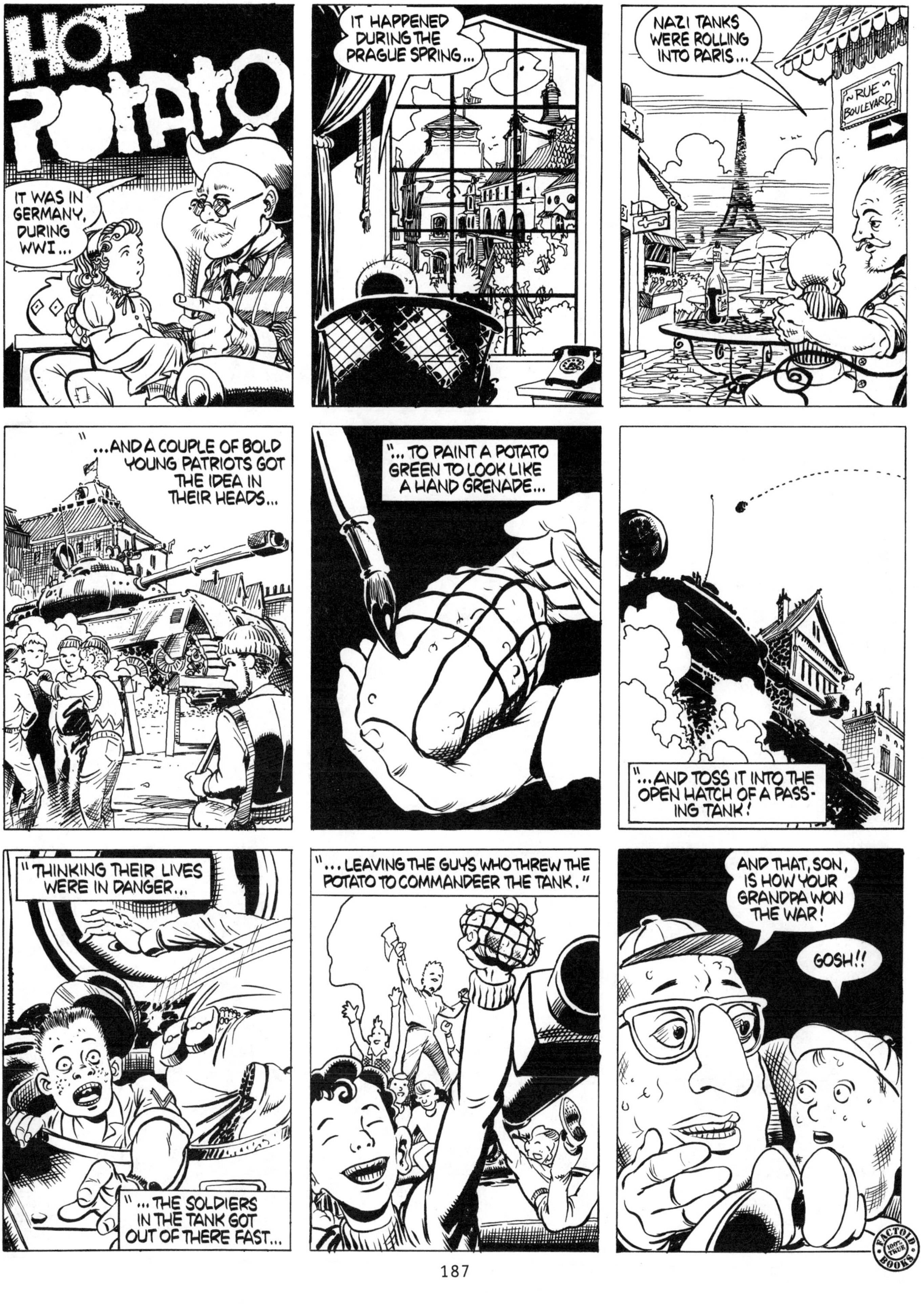
HOT POTATO
IT WAS IN GERMANY, DURING WWI...
IT HAPPENED DURING THE PRAGUE SPRING...
NAZI TANKS WERE ROLLING INTO PARIS...
RUE BOULEVARD
"...AND A COUPLE OF BOLD YOUNG PATRIOTS GOT THE IDEA IN THEIR HEADS...
"...TO PAINT A POTATO GREEN TO LOOK LIKE A HAND GRENADE...
"...AND TOSS IT INTO THE OPEN HATCH OF A PASSING TANK!
"THINKING THEIR LIVES WERE IN DANGER...
"...THE SOLDIERS IN THE TANK GOT OUT OF THERE FAST...
"...LEAVING THE GUYS WHO THREW THE POTATO TO COMMANDEER THE TANK."
AND THAT, SON, IS HOW YOUR GRANDPA WON THE WAR!
GOSH!!
FACTOID BOOKS 100% TRUE

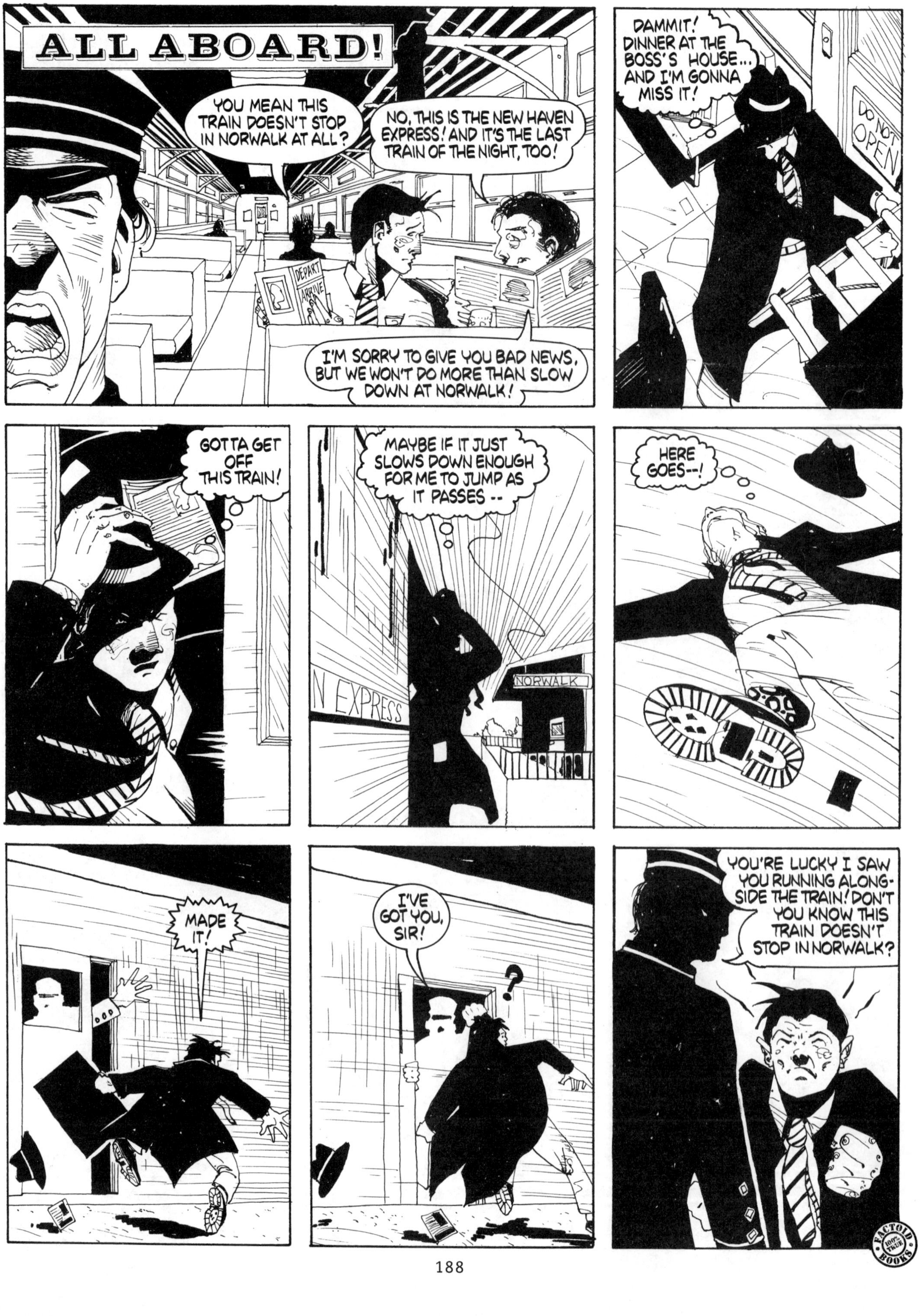
ALL ABOARD!
YOU MEAN THIS TRAIN DOESN'T STOP IN NORWALK AT ALL?
NO, THIS IS THE NEW HAVEN EXPRESS! AND IT'S THE LAST TRAIN OF THE NIGHT, TOO!
DEPART
ARRIVE
I'M SORRY TO GIVE YOU BAD NEWS, BUT WE WON'T DO MORE THAN SLOW DOWN AT NORWALK!
DAMMIT! DINNER AT THE BOSS'S HOUSE... AND I'M GONNA MISS IT!
DO NOT OPEN
GOTTA GET OFF THIS TRAIN!
MAYBE IF IT JUST SLOWS DOWN ENOUGH FOR ME TO JUMP AS IT PASSES --
N EXPRESS
NORWALK
HERE GOES--!
MADE IT!
I'VE GOT YOU, SIR!
?
YOU'RE LUCKY I SAW YOU RUNNING ALONG-SIDE THE TRAIN! DON'T YOU KNOW THIS TRAIN DOESN'T STOP IN NORWALK?

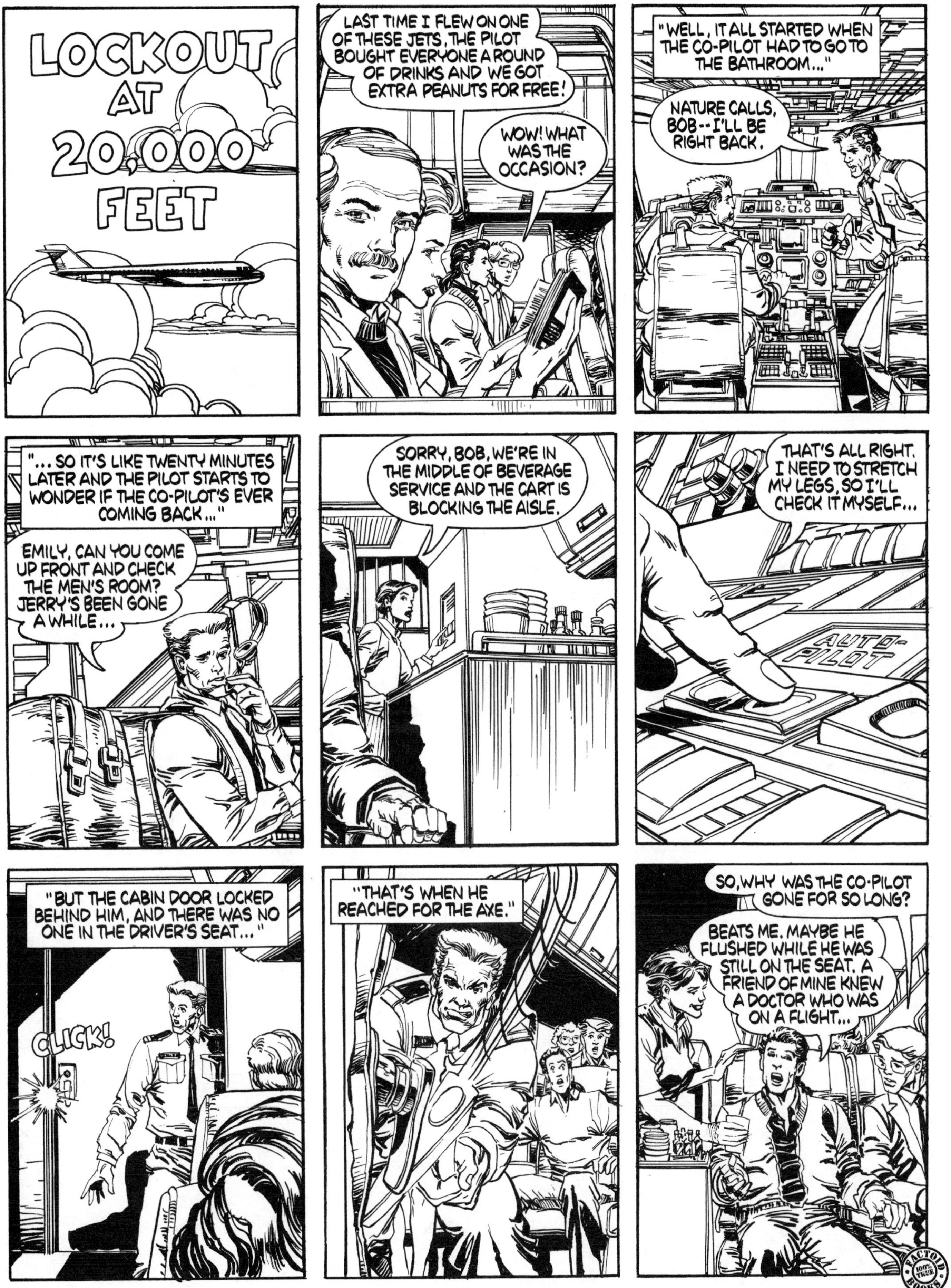
LOCKOUT AT 20,000 FEET
LAST TIME I FLEW ON ONE OF THESE JETS, THE PILOT BOUGHT EVERYONE A ROUND OF DRINKS AND WE GOT EXTRA PEANUTS FOR FREE!
WOW! WHAT WAS THE OCCASION?
"WELL, IT ALL STARTED WHEN THE CO-PILOT HAD TO GO TO THE BATHROOM..."
NATURE CALLS, BOB--I'LL BE RIGHT BACK.
"... SO IT'S LIKE TWENTY MINUTES LATER AND THE PILOT STARTS TO WONDER IF THE CO-PILOT'S EVER COMING BACK..."
EMILY, CAN YOU COME UP FRONT AND CHECK THE MEN'S ROOM? JERRY'S BEEN GONE A WHILE...
SORRY, BOB, WE'RE IN THE MIDDLE OF BEVERAGE SERVICE AND THE CART IS BLOCKING THE AISLE.
THAT'S ALL RIGHT. I NEED TO STRETCH MY LEGS, SO I'LL CHECK IT MYSELF...
AUTO-PILOT
"BUT THE CABIN DOOR LOCKED BEHIND HIM, AND THERE WAS NO ONE IN THE DRIVER'S SEAT..."
CLICK!
"THAT'S WHEN HE REACHED FOR THE AXE."
SO, WHY WAS THE CO-PILOT GONE FOR SO LONG?
BEATS ME. MAYBE HE FLUSHED WHILE HE WAS STILL ON THE SEAT. A FRIEND OF MINE KNEW A DOCTOR WHO WAS ON A FLIGHT...

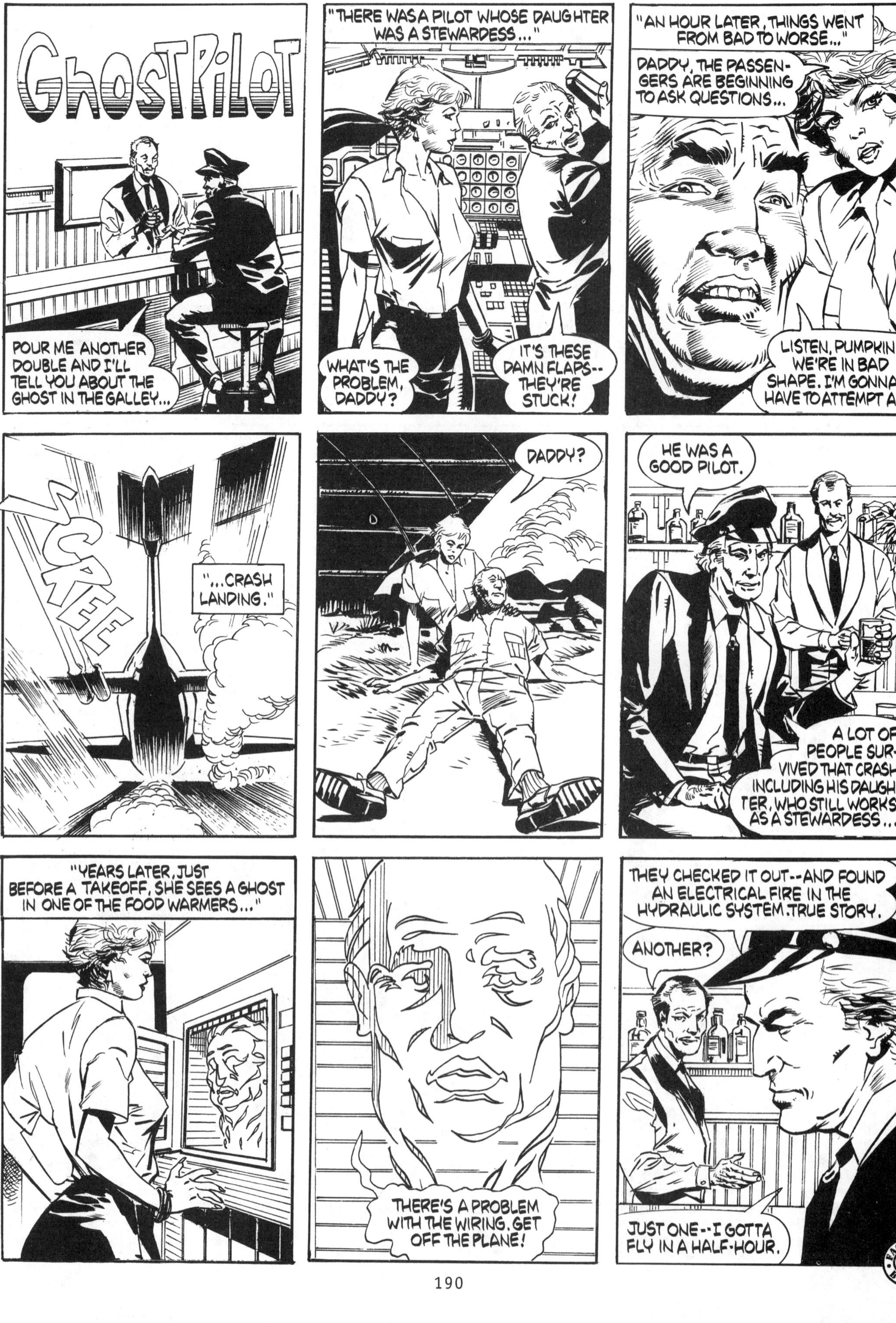
GHOST PILOT
POUR ME ANOTHER DOUBLE AND I'LL TELL YOU ABOUT THE GHOST IN THE GALLEY...
"THERE WAS A PILOT WHOSE DAUGHTER WAS A STEWARDESS..."
WHAT'S THE PROBLEM, DADDY?
IT'S THESE DAMN FLAPS-- THEY'RE STUCK!
"AN HOUR LATER, THINGS WENT FROM BAD TO WORSE..."
DADDY, THE PASSENGERS ARE BEGINNING TO ASK QUESTIONS...
LISTEN, PUMPKIN, WE'RE IN BAD SHAPE. I'M GONNA HAVE TO ATTEMPT A...
SCREEE
"...CRASH LANDING."
DADDY?
HE WAS A GOOD PILOT.
A LOT OF PEOPLE SURVIVED THAT CRASH INCLUDING HIS DAUGHTER, WHO STILL WORKS AS A STEWARDESS...
"YEARS LATER, JUST BEFORE A TAKEOFF, SHE SEES A GHOST IN ONE OF THE FOOD WARMERS..."
THERE'S A PROBLEM WITH THE WIRING. GET OFF THE PLANE!
THEY CHECKED IT OUT--AND FOUND AN ELECTRICAL FIRE IN THE HYDRAULIC SYSTEM. TRUE STORY.
ANOTHER?
JUST ONE--I GOTTA FLY IN A HALF-HOUR.
FACTOID BOOKS 100% TRUE

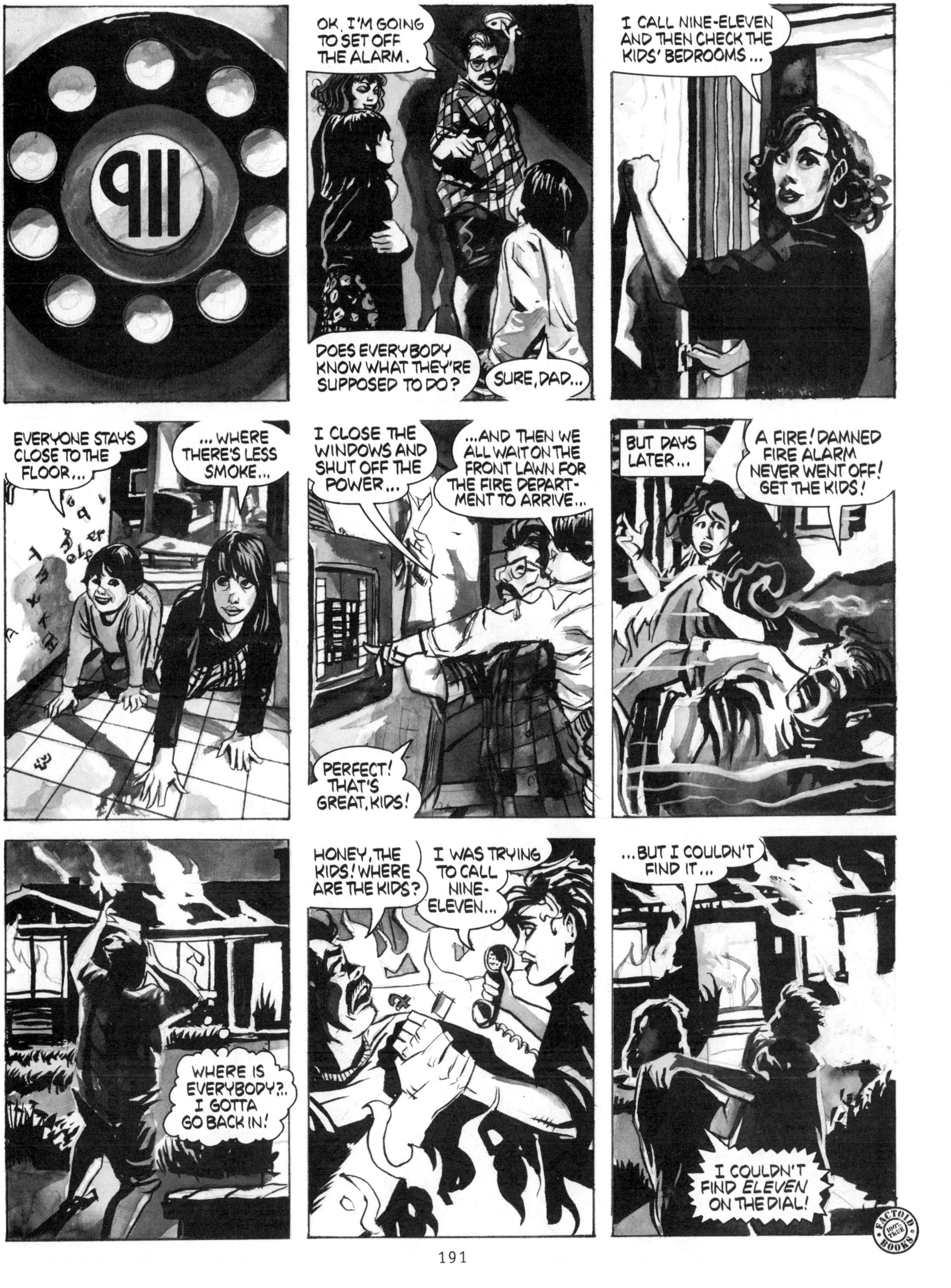
911
OK, I'M GOING TO SET OFF THE ALARM.
DOES EVERYBODY KNOW WHAT THEY'RE SUPPOSED TO DO?
SURE, DAD...
I CALL NINE-ELEVEN AND THEN CHECK THE KIDS' BEDROOMS...
EVERYONE STAYS CLOSE TO THE FLOOR...
...WHERE THERE'S LESS SMOKE...
I CLOSE THE WINDOWS AND SHUT OFF THE POWER...
...AND THEN WE ALL WAIT ON THE FRONT LAWN FOR THE FIRE DEPARTMENT TO ARRIVE...
PERFECT! THAT'S GREAT, KIDS!
BUT DAYS LATER...
A FIRE! DAMNED FIRE ALARM NEVER WENT OFF! GET THE KIDS!
WHERE IS EVERYBODY?.. I GOTTA GO BACK IN!
HONEY, THE KIDS! WHERE ARE THE KIDS?
I WAS TRYING TO CALL NINE-ELEVEN...
...BUT I COULDN'T FIND IT...
I COULDN'T FIND *ELEVEN* ON THE DIAL!
FACTOID BOOKS 100% TRUE

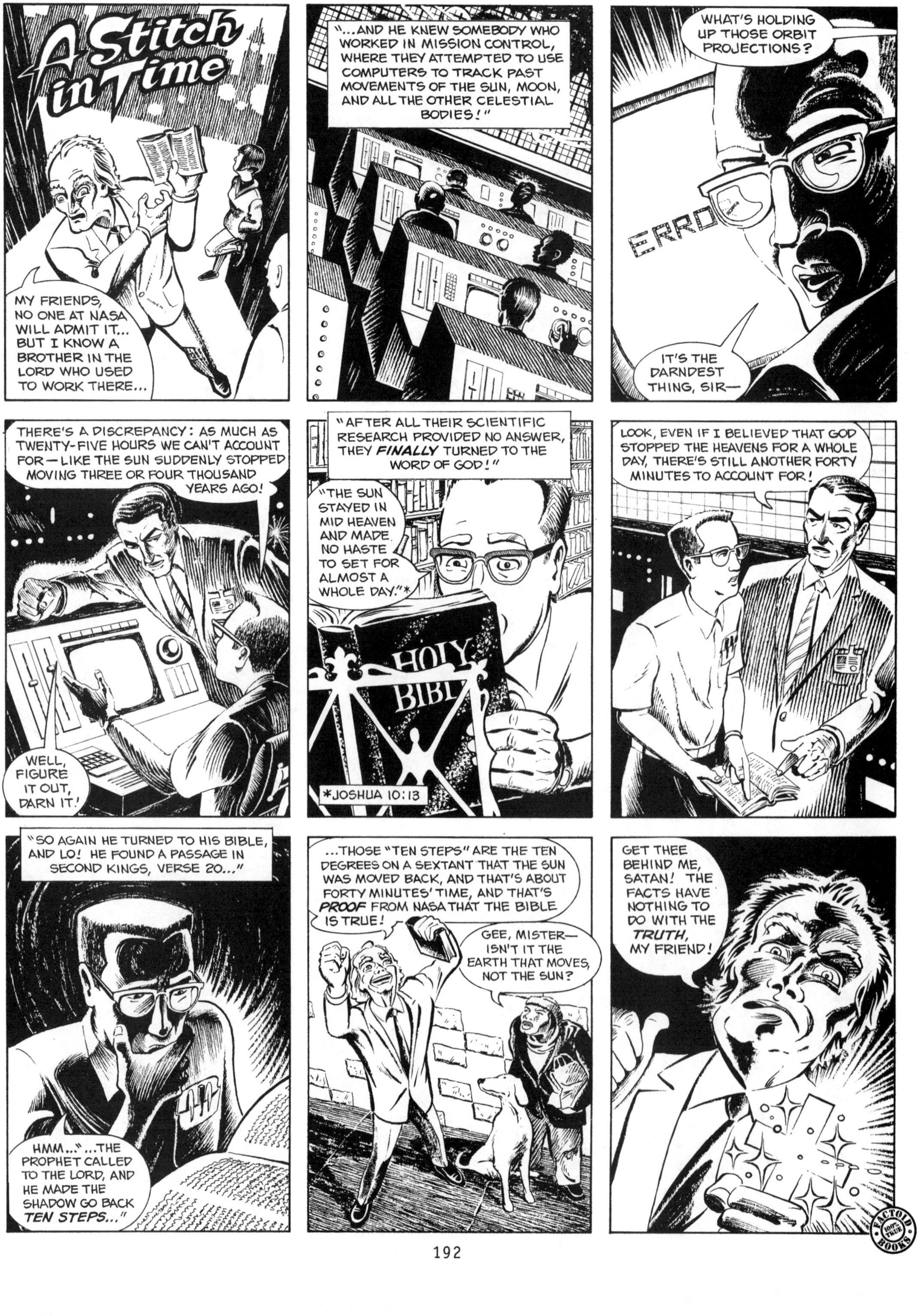
A Stitch in Time
MY FRIENDS, NO ONE AT NASA WILL ADMIT IT... BUT I KNOW A BROTHER IN THE LORD WHO USED TO WORK THERE...
"...AND HE KNEW SOMEBODY WHO WORKED IN MISSION CONTROL, WHERE THEY ATTEMPTED TO USE COMPUTERS TO TRACK PAST MOVEMENTS OF THE SUN, MOON, AND ALL THE OTHER CELESTIAL BODIES!"
WHAT'S HOLDING UP THOSE ORBIT PROJECTIONS?
ERRO
IT'S THE DARNDEST THING, SIR—
THERE'S A DISCREPANCY: AS MUCH AS TWENTY-FIVE HOURS WE CAN'T ACCOUNT FOR—LIKE THE SUN SUDDENLY STOPPED MOVING THREE OR FOUR THOUSAND YEARS AGO!
WELL, FIGURE IT OUT, DARN IT!
"AFTER ALL THEIR SCIENTIFIC RESEARCH PROVIDED NO ANSWER, THEY FINALLY TURNED TO THE WORD OF GOD!"
"THE SUN STAYED IN MID HEAVEN AND MADE NO HASTE TO SET FOR ALMOST A WHOLE DAY."*
HOLY BIBLE
*JOSHUA 10:13
LOOK, EVEN IF I BELIEVED THAT GOD STOPPED THE HEAVENS FOR A WHOLE DAY, THERE'S STILL ANOTHER FORTY MINUTES TO ACCOUNT FOR!
"SO AGAIN HE TURNED TO HIS BIBLE, AND LO! HE FOUND A PASSAGE IN SECOND KINGS, VERSE 20..."
HMM..." ...THE PROPHET CALLED TO THE LORD, AND HE MADE THE SHADOW GO BACK TEN STEPS..."
...THOSE "TEN STEPS" ARE THE TEN DEGREES ON A SEXTANT THAT THE SUN WAS MOVED BACK, AND THAT'S ABOUT FORTY MINUTES' TIME, AND THAT'S PROOF FROM NASA THAT THE BIBLE IS TRUE!
GEE, MISTER— ISN'T IT THE EARTH THAT MOVES, NOT THE SUN?
GET THEE BEHIND ME, SATAN! THE FACTS HAVE NOTHING TO DO WITH THE TRUTH, MY FRIEND!
FACTOID 100% TRUE BOOKS

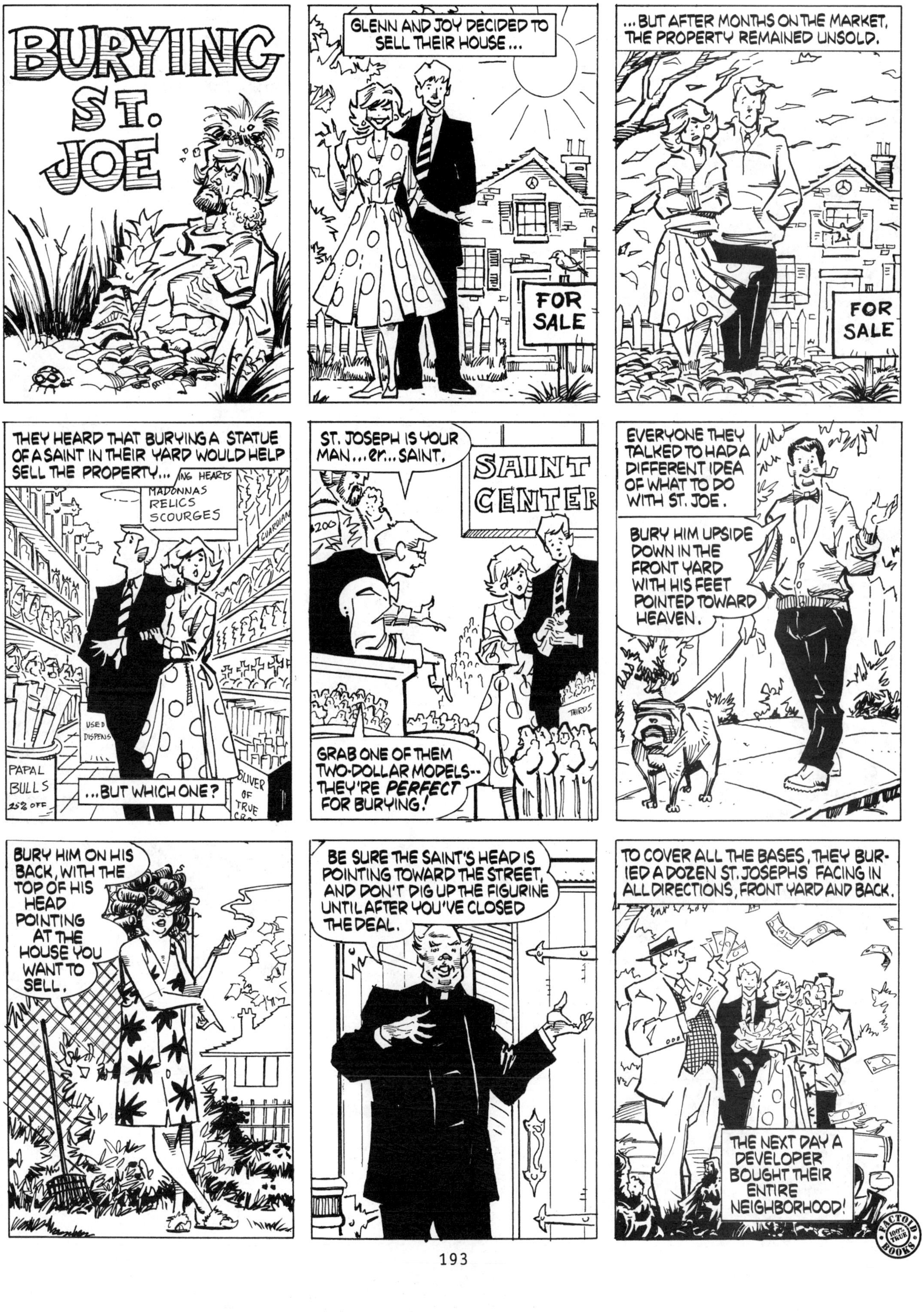
BURYING ST. JOE
GLENN AND JOY DECIDED TO SELL THEIR HOUSE...
FOR SALE
...BUT AFTER MONTHS ON THE MARKET, THE PROPERTY REMAINED UNSOLD.
FOR SALE
THEY HEARD THAT BURYING A STATUE OF A SAINT IN THEIR YARD WOULD HELP SELL THE PROPERTY...
MADONNAS
RELICS
SCOURGES
PAPAL BULLS 25% OFF
...BUT WHICH ONE?
ST. JOSEPH IS YOUR MAN...er...SAINT.
SAINT CENTER
GRAB ONE OF THEM TWO-DOLLAR MODELS-- THEY'RE *PERFECT* FOR BURYING!
EVERYONE THEY TALKED TO HAD A DIFFERENT IDEA OF WHAT TO DO WITH ST. JOE.
BURY HIM UPSIDE DOWN IN THE FRONT YARD WITH HIS FEET POINTED TOWARD HEAVEN.
BURY HIM ON HIS BACK, WITH THE TOP OF HIS HEAD POINTING AT THE HOUSE YOU WANT TO SELL.
BE SURE THE SAINT'S HEAD IS POINTING TOWARD THE STREET, AND DON'T DIG UP THE FIGURINE UNTIL AFTER YOU'VE CLOSED THE DEAL.
TO COVER ALL THE BASES, THEY BURIED A DOZEN ST. JOSEPHS FACING IN ALL DIRECTIONS, FRONT YARD AND BACK.
THE NEXT DAY A DEVELOPER BOUGHT THEIR ENTIRE NEIGHBORHOOD!
FACTOID BOOKS 100% TRUE

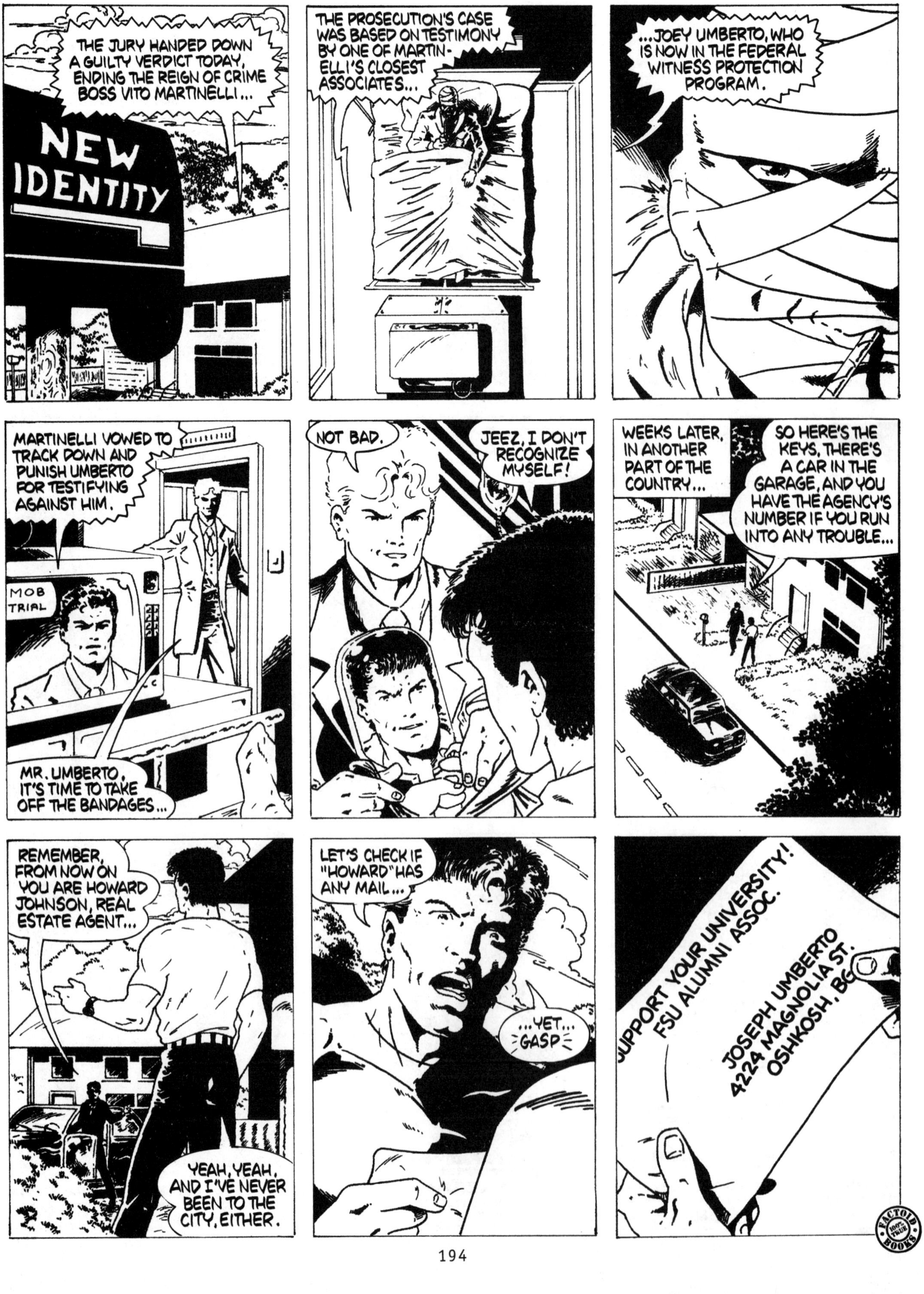
THE JURY HANDED DOWN A GUILTY VERDICT TODAY, ENDING THE REIGN OF CRIME BOSS VITO MARTINELLI...
NEW IDENTITY
THE PROSECUTION'S CASE WAS BASED ON TESTIMONY BY ONE OF MARTINELLI'S CLOSEST ASSOCIATES...
...JOEY UMBERTO, WHO IS NOW IN THE FEDERAL WITNESS PROTECTION PROGRAM.
MARTINELLI VOWED TO TRACK DOWN AND PUNISH UMBERTO FOR TESTIFYING AGAINST HIM.
MOB TRIAL
MR. UMBERTO, IT'S TIME TO TAKE OFF THE BANDAGES...
NOT BAD.
JEEZ, I DON'T RECOGNIZE MYSELF!
WEEKS LATER, IN ANOTHER PART OF THE COUNTRY...
SO HERE'S THE KEYS, THERE'S A CAR IN THE GARAGE, AND YOU HAVE THE AGENCY'S NUMBER IF YOU RUN INTO ANY TROUBLE...
REMEMBER, FROM NOW ON YOU ARE HOWARD JOHNSON, REAL ESTATE AGENT...
YEAH, YEAH, AND I'VE NEVER BEEN TO THE CITY, EITHER.
LET'S CHECK IF "HOWARD" HAS ANY MAIL...
...YET... GASP
SUPPORT YOUR UNIVERSITY! FSU ALUMNI ASSOC.
JOSEPH UMBERTO
4224 MAGNOLIA ST.
OSHKOSH, BG
FACTOID BOOKS 100% TRUE

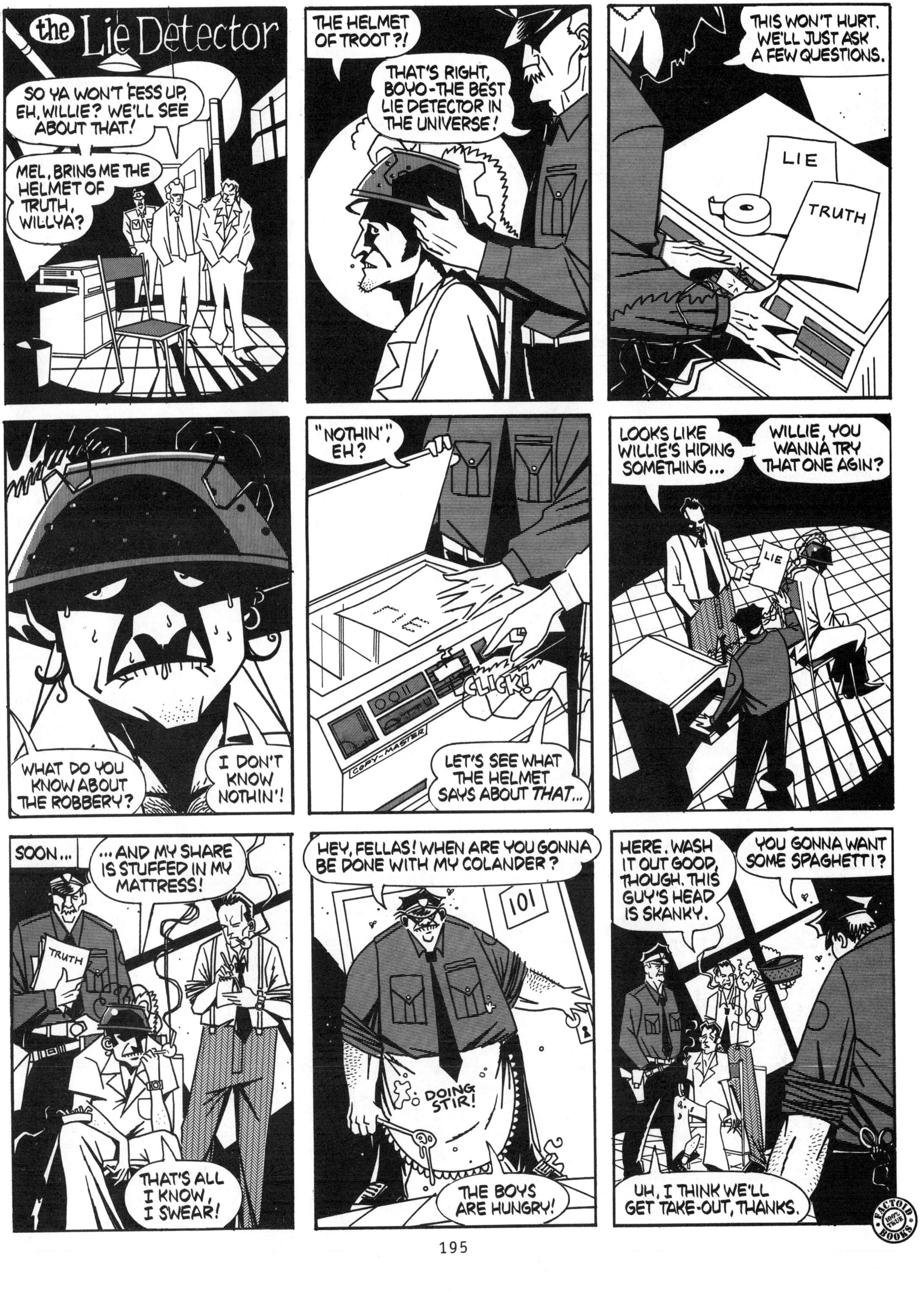
the Lie Detector
SO YA WON'T 'FESS UP, EH, WILLIE? WE'LL SEE ABOUT THAT!
MEL, BRING ME THE HELMET OF TRUTH, WILLYA?
THE HELMET OF TROOT?!
THAT'S RIGHT, BOYO-THE BEST LIE DETECTOR IN THE UNIVERSE!
THIS WON'T HURT. WE'LL JUST ASK A FEW QUESTIONS.
LIE
TRUTH
WHAT DO YOU KNOW ABOUT THE ROBBERY?
I DON'T KNOW NOTHIN'!
"NOTHIN'", EH?
LIE
CLICK!
COPY-MASTER
LET'S SEE WHAT THE HELMET SAYS ABOUT THAT...
LOOKS LIKE WILLIE'S HIDING SOMETHING...
WILLIE, YOU WANNA TRY THAT ONE AGIN?
LIE
SOON...
...AND MY SHARE IS STUFFED IN MY MATTRESS!
TRUTH
THAT'S ALL I KNOW, I SWEAR!
HEY, FELLAS! WHEN ARE YOU GONNA BE DONE WITH MY COLANDER?
101
DOING STIR!
THE BOYS ARE HUNGRY!
HERE. WASH IT OUT GOOD, THOUGH. THIS GUY'S HEAD IS SKANKY.
YOU GONNA WANT SOME SPAGHETTI?
UH, I THINK WE'LL GET TAKE-OUT, THANKS.
FACTOID BOOKS 100% TRUE

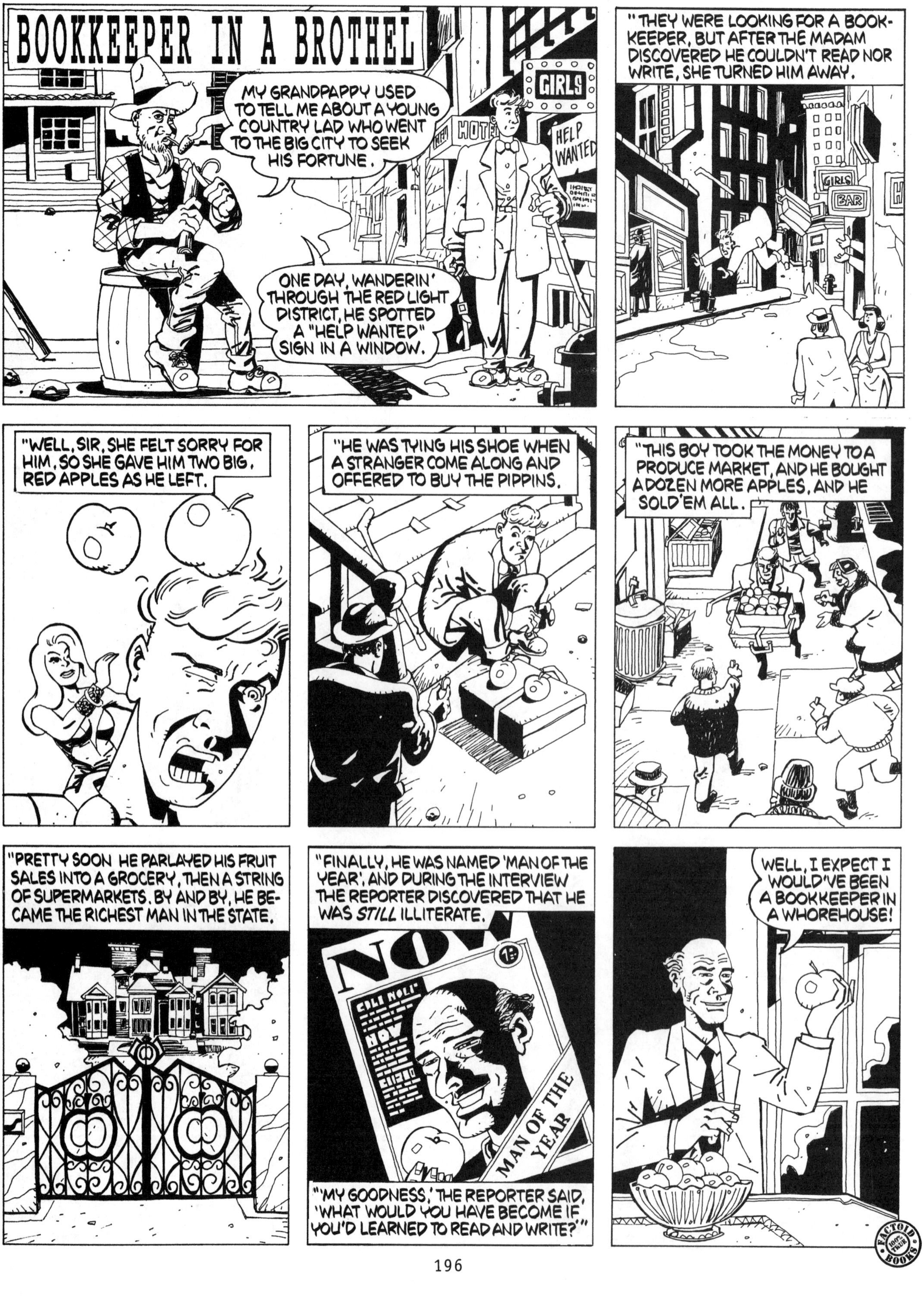
BOOKKEEPER IN A BROTHEL
MY GRANDPAPPY USED TO TELL ME ABOUT A YOUNG COUNTRY LAD WHO WENT TO THE BIG CITY TO SEEK HIS FORTUNE.
GIRLS
HOTEL
HELP WANTED
ONE DAY, WANDERIN' THROUGH THE RED LIGHT DISTRICT, HE SPOTTED A "HELP WANTED" SIGN IN A WINDOW.
"THEY WERE LOOKING FOR A BOOK-KEEPER, BUT AFTER THE MADAM DISCOVERED HE COULDN'T READ NOR WRITE, SHE TURNED HIM AWAY.
GIRLS
BAR
"WELL, SIR, SHE FELT SORRY FOR HIM, SO SHE GAVE HIM TWO BIG, RED APPLES AS HE LEFT.
"HE WAS TYING HIS SHOE WHEN A STRANGER COME ALONG AND OFFERED TO BUY THE PIPPINS.
"THIS BOY TOOK THE MONEY TO A PRODUCE MARKET, AND HE BOUGHT A DOZEN MORE APPLES, AND HE SOLD 'EM ALL.
"PRETTY SOON HE PARLAYED HIS FRUIT SALES INTO A GROCERY, THEN A STRING OF SUPERMARKETS. BY AND BY, HE BECAME THE RICHEST MAN IN THE STATE.
"FINALLY, HE WAS NAMED 'MAN OF THE YEAR', AND DURING THE INTERVIEW THE REPORTER DISCOVERED THAT HE WAS STILL ILLITERATE.
NOW
MAN OF THE YEAR
"MY GOODNESS,' THE REPORTER SAID, 'WHAT WOULD YOU HAVE BECOME IF YOU'D LEARNED TO READ AND WRITE?'"
WELL, I EXPECT I WOULD'VE BEEN A BOOKKEEPER IN A WHOREHOUSE!
FACTOID BOOKS 100% TRUE

CHAPTER EIGHT

CELEBRITY RUMORS, ACADEMIA LEGENDS AND MISCELLANEOUS

FOAF-A-RAMA

It seems like every classification system must have a final "Miscellaneous" category, and so this is mine. I flatter myself, probably, by grouping academic legends with those about celebrities, or dare I say about "other celebrities"? On the other hand, here are professors and students sharing the section with the likes of Bozo the Clown *(page 199)*, not to mention Richard Nixon *(page 202)*. And what's Jesus doing here? He's obviously involved in one legend here as just another variation of "The Vanishing Hitchhiker." This is where I came in! (See Chapter 1.)

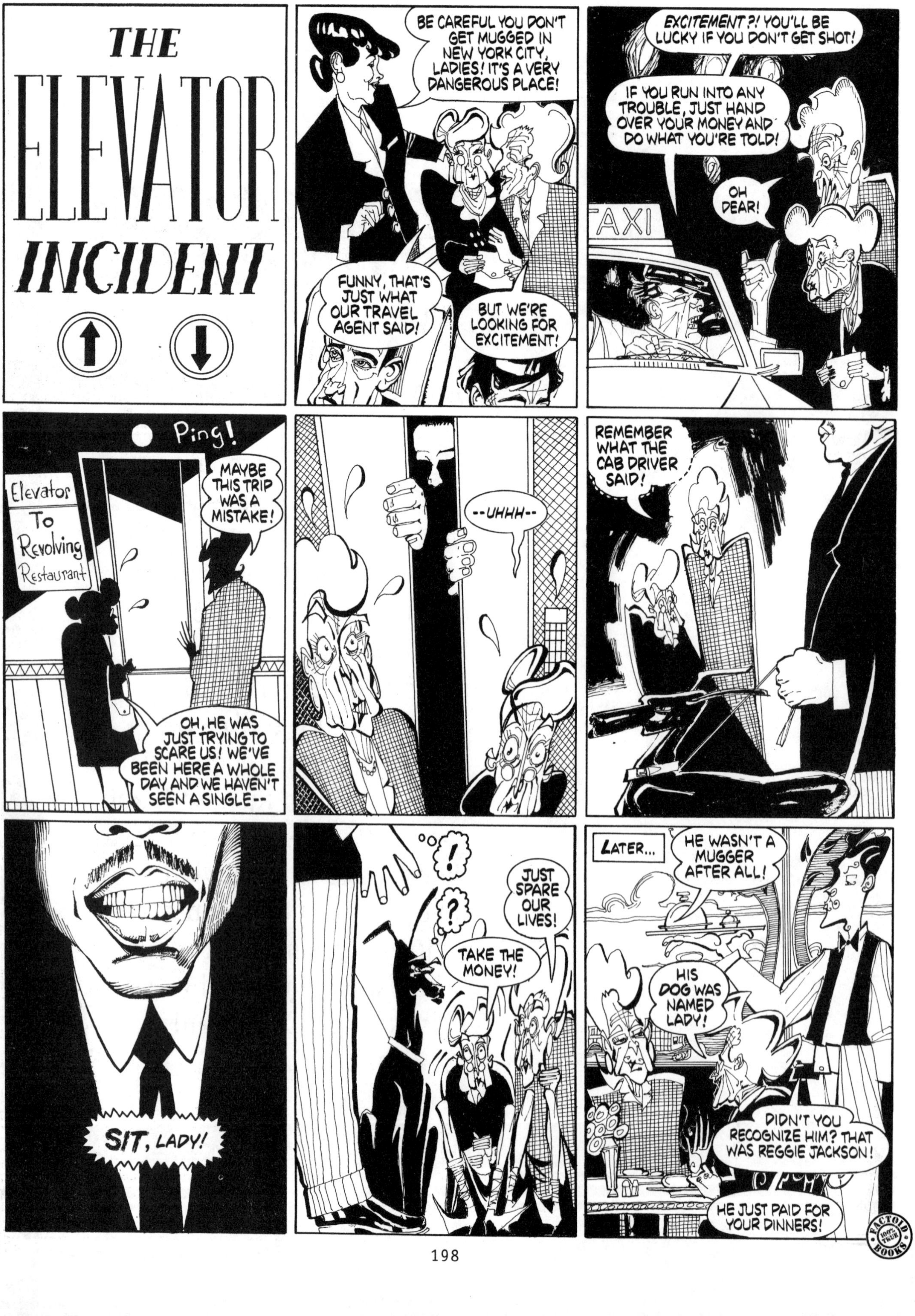
THE ELEVATOR INCIDENT
BE CAREFUL YOU DON'T GET MUGGED IN NEW YORK CITY, LADIES! IT'S A VERY DANGEROUS PLACE!
FUNNY, THAT'S JUST WHAT OUR TRAVEL AGENT SAID!
BUT WE'RE LOOKING FOR EXCITEMENT!
EXCITEMENT?! YOU'LL BE LUCKY IF YOU DON'T GET SHOT!
IF YOU RUN INTO ANY TROUBLE, JUST HAND OVER YOUR MONEY AND DO WHAT YOU'RE TOLD!
OH DEAR!
TAXI
Ping!
Elevator To Revolving Restaurant
MAYBE THIS TRIP WAS A MISTAKE!
OH, HE WAS JUST TRYING TO SCARE US! WE'VE BEEN HERE A WHOLE DAY AND WE HAVEN'T SEEN A SINGLE--
--UHHH--
REMEMBER WHAT THE CAB DRIVER SAID!
SIT, LADY!
!
?
JUST SPARE OUR LIVES!
TAKE THE MONEY!
LATER...
HE WASN'T A MUGGER AFTER ALL!
HIS DOG WAS NAMED LADY!
DIDN'T YOU RECOGNIZE HIM? THAT WAS REGGIE JACKSON!
HE JUST PAID FOR YOUR DINNERS!
FACTOID BOOKS 100% TRUE

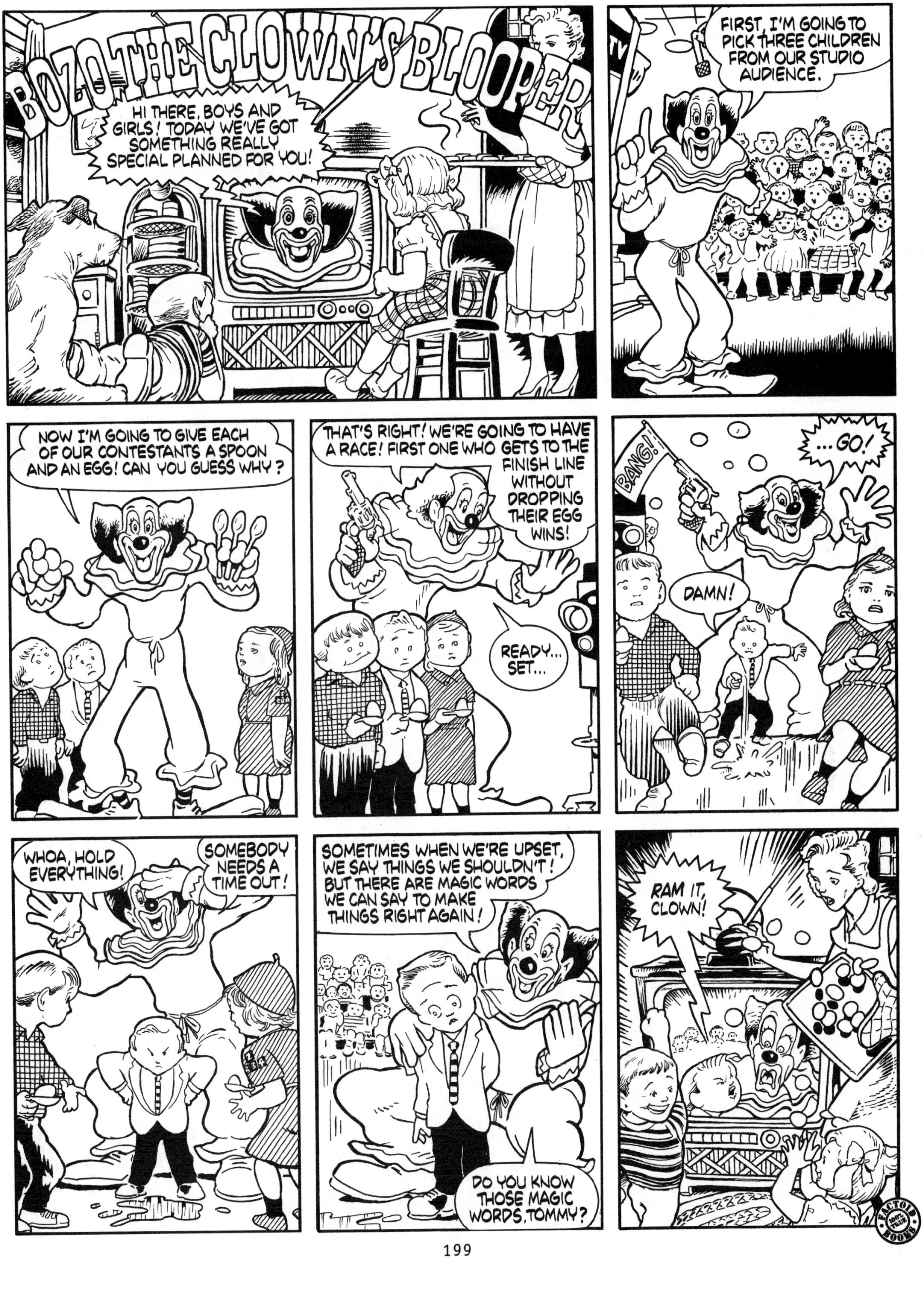

BOZO THE CLOWN'S BLOOPER
HI THERE, BOYS AND GIRLS! TODAY WE'VE GOT SOMETHING REALLY SPECIAL PLANNED FOR YOU!
FIRST, I'M GOING TO PICK THREE CHILDREN FROM OUR STUDIO AUDIENCE.
TV
NOW I'M GOING TO GIVE EACH OF OUR CONTESTANTS A SPOON AND AN EGG! CAN YOU GUESS WHY?
THAT'S RIGHT! WE'RE GOING TO HAVE A RACE! FIRST ONE WHO GETS TO THE FINISH LINE WITHOUT DROPPING THEIR EGG WINS!
READY... SET...
BANG!
...GO!
DAMN!
WHOA, HOLD EVERYTHING!
SOMEBODY NEEDS A TIME OUT!
SOMETIMES WHEN WE'RE UPSET, WE SAY THINGS WE SHOULDN'T! BUT THERE ARE MAGIC WORDS WE CAN SAY TO MAKE THINGS RIGHT AGAIN!
DO YOU KNOW THOSE MAGIC WORDS, TOMMY?
RAM IT, CLOWN!

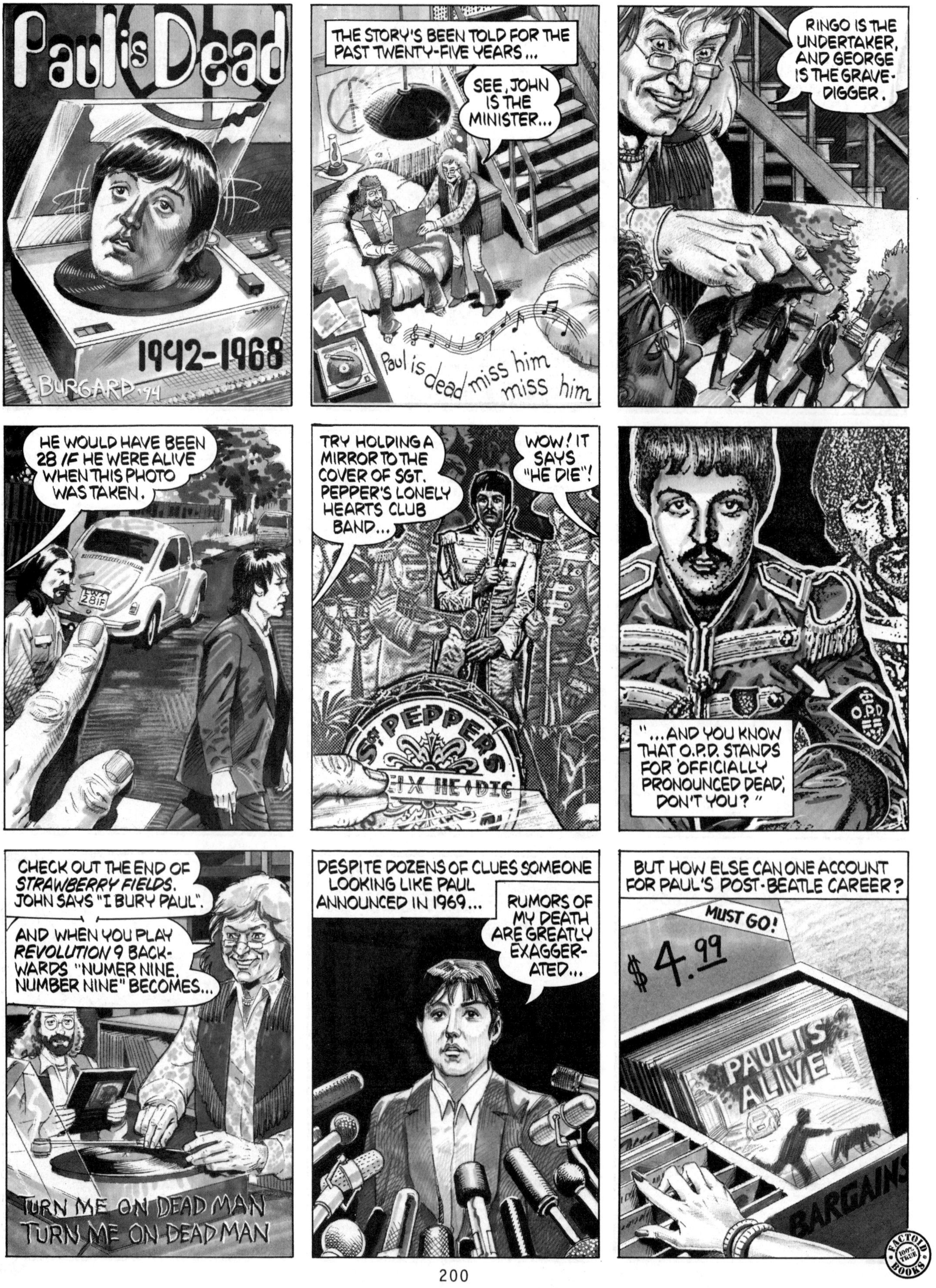
Paul is Dead
1942-1968
BURGARD '94
THE STORY'S BEEN TOLD FOR THE PAST TWENTY-FIVE YEARS...
SEE, JOHN IS THE MINISTER...
Paul is dead miss him miss him
RINGO IS THE UNDERTAKER, AND GEORGE IS THE GRAVE-DIGGER.
HE WOULD HAVE BEEN 28 IF HE WERE ALIVE WHEN THIS PHOTO WAS TAKEN.
28IF
TRY HOLDING A MIRROR TO THE COVER OF SGT. PEPPER'S LONELY HEARTS CLUB BAND...
WOW! IT SAYS "HE DIE"!
SGT PEPPERS
"...AND YOU KNOW THAT O.P.D. STANDS FOR 'OFFICIALLY PRONOUNCED DEAD', DON'T YOU?"
O.P.D.
CHECK OUT THE END OF STRAWBERRY FIELDS. JOHN SAYS "I BURY PAUL".
AND WHEN YOU PLAY REVOLUTION 9 BACKWARDS "NUMER NINE, NUMBER NINE" BECOMES...
TURN ME ON DEAD MAN
TURN ME ON DEAD MAN
DESPITE DOZENS OF CLUES SOMEONE LOOKING LIKE PAUL ANNOUNCED IN 1969...
RUMORS OF MY DEATH ARE GREATLY EXAGGERATED...
BUT HOW ELSE CAN ONE ACCOUNT FOR PAUL'S POST-BEATLE CAREER?
MUST GO!
$4.99
PAUL IS ALIVE
BARGAINS

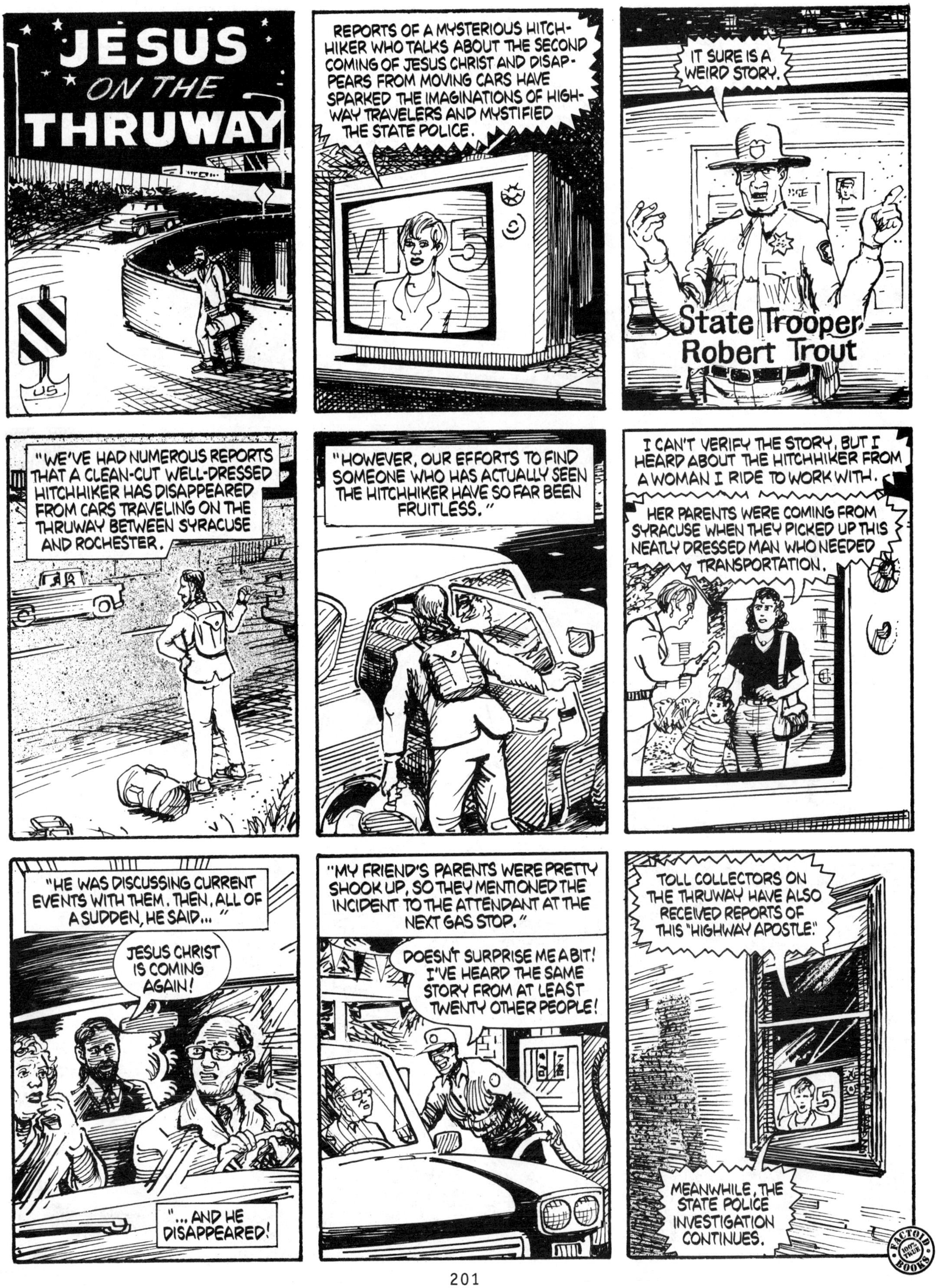
JESUS
ON THE
THRUWAY
US
REPORTS OF A MYSTERIOUS HITCH-HIKER WHO TALKS ABOUT THE SECOND COMING OF JESUS CHRIST AND DISAPPEARS FROM MOVING CARS HAVE SPARKED THE IMAGINATIONS OF HIGHWAY TRAVELERS AND MYSTIFIED THE STATE POLICE.
IT SURE IS A WEIRD STORY.
State Trooper Robert Trout
"WE'VE HAD NUMEROUS REPORTS THAT A CLEAN-CUT WELL-DRESSED HITCHHIKER HAS DISAPPEARED FROM CARS TRAVELING ON THE THRUWAY BETWEEN SYRACUSE AND ROCHESTER.
"HOWEVER, OUR EFFORTS TO FIND SOMEONE WHO HAS ACTUALLY SEEN THE HITCHHIKER HAVE SO FAR BEEN FRUITLESS."
I CAN'T VERIFY THE STORY, BUT I HEARD ABOUT THE HITCHHIKER FROM A WOMAN I RIDE TO WORK WITH.
HER PARENTS WERE COMING FROM SYRACUSE WHEN THEY PICKED UP THIS NEATLY DRESSED MAN WHO NEEDED TRANSPORTATION.
"HE WAS DISCUSSING CURRENT EVENTS WITH THEM. THEN, ALL OF A SUDDEN, HE SAID..."
JESUS CHRIST IS COMING AGAIN!
"...AND HE DISAPPEARED!
"MY FRIEND'S PARENTS WERE PRETTY SHOOK UP, SO THEY MENTIONED THE INCIDENT TO THE ATTENDANT AT THE NEXT GAS STOP."
DOESN'T SURPRISE ME A BIT! I'VE HEARD THE SAME STORY FROM AT LEAST TWENTY OTHER PEOPLE!
TOLL COLLECTORS ON THE THRUWAY HAVE ALSO RECEIVED REPORTS OF THIS "HIGHWAY APOSTLE."
MEANWHILE, THE STATE POLICE INVESTIGATION CONTINUES.
FACTOID BOOKS 100% TRUE

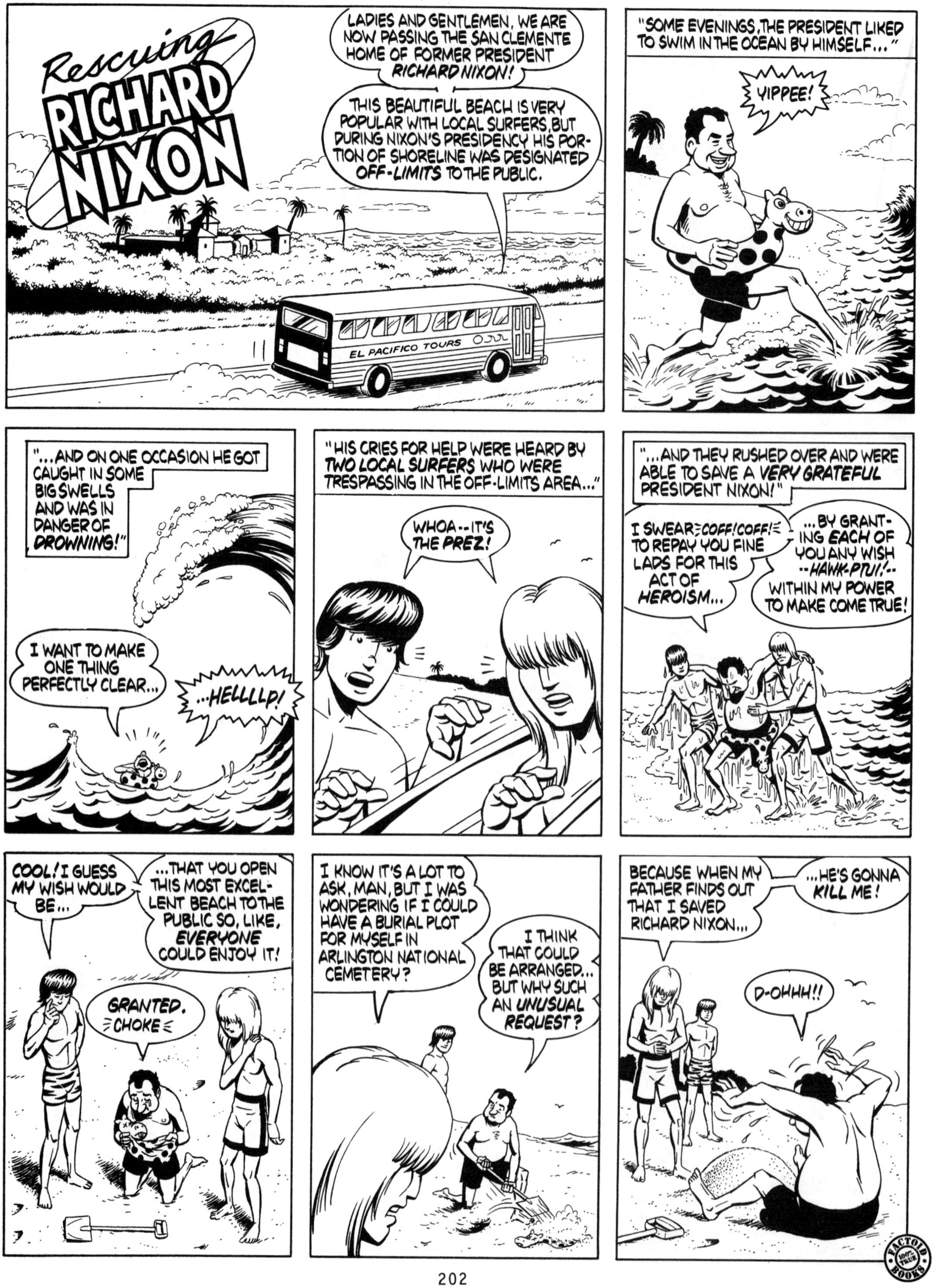
Rescuing RICHARD NIXON
LADIES AND GENTLEMEN, WE ARE NOW PASSING THE SAN CLEMENTE HOME OF FORMER PRESIDENT RICHARD NIXON!
THIS BEAUTIFUL BEACH IS VERY POPULAR WITH LOCAL SURFERS, BUT DURING NIXON'S PRESIDENCY HIS PORTION OF SHORELINE WAS DESIGNATED OFF-LIMITS TO THE PUBLIC.
EL PACIFICO TOURS
"SOME EVENINGS, THE PRESIDENT LIKED TO SWIM IN THE OCEAN BY HIMSELF..."
YIPPEE!
"...AND ON ONE OCCASION HE GOT CAUGHT IN SOME BIG SWELLS AND WAS IN DANGER OF DROWNING!"
I WANT TO MAKE ONE THING PERFECTLY CLEAR...
...HELLLLP!
"HIS CRIES FOR HELP WERE HEARD BY TWO LOCAL SURFERS WHO WERE TRESPASSING IN THE OFF-LIMITS AREA..."
WHOA--IT'S THE PREZ!
"...AND THEY RUSHED OVER AND WERE ABLE TO SAVE A VERY GRATEFUL PRESIDENT NIXON!"
I SWEAR COFF! COFF! TO REPAY YOU FINE LADS FOR THIS ACT OF HEROISM...
...BY GRANTING EACH OF YOU ANY WISH --HAWK-PTUI!-- WITHIN MY POWER TO MAKE COME TRUE!
COOL! I GUESS MY WISH WOULD BE...
...THAT YOU OPEN THIS MOST EXCELLENT BEACH TO THE PUBLIC SO, LIKE, EVERYONE COULD ENJOY IT!
GRANTED. CHOKE
I KNOW IT'S A LOT TO ASK, MAN, BUT I WAS WONDERING IF I COULD HAVE A BURIAL PLOT FOR MYSELF IN ARLINGTON NATIONAL CEMETERY?
I THINK THAT COULD BE ARRANGED... BUT WHY SUCH AN UNUSUAL REQUEST?
BECAUSE WHEN MY FATHER FINDS OUT THAT I SAVED RICHARD NIXON...
...HE'S GONNA KILL ME!
D-OHHH!!
FACTOID 100% TRUE BOOKS

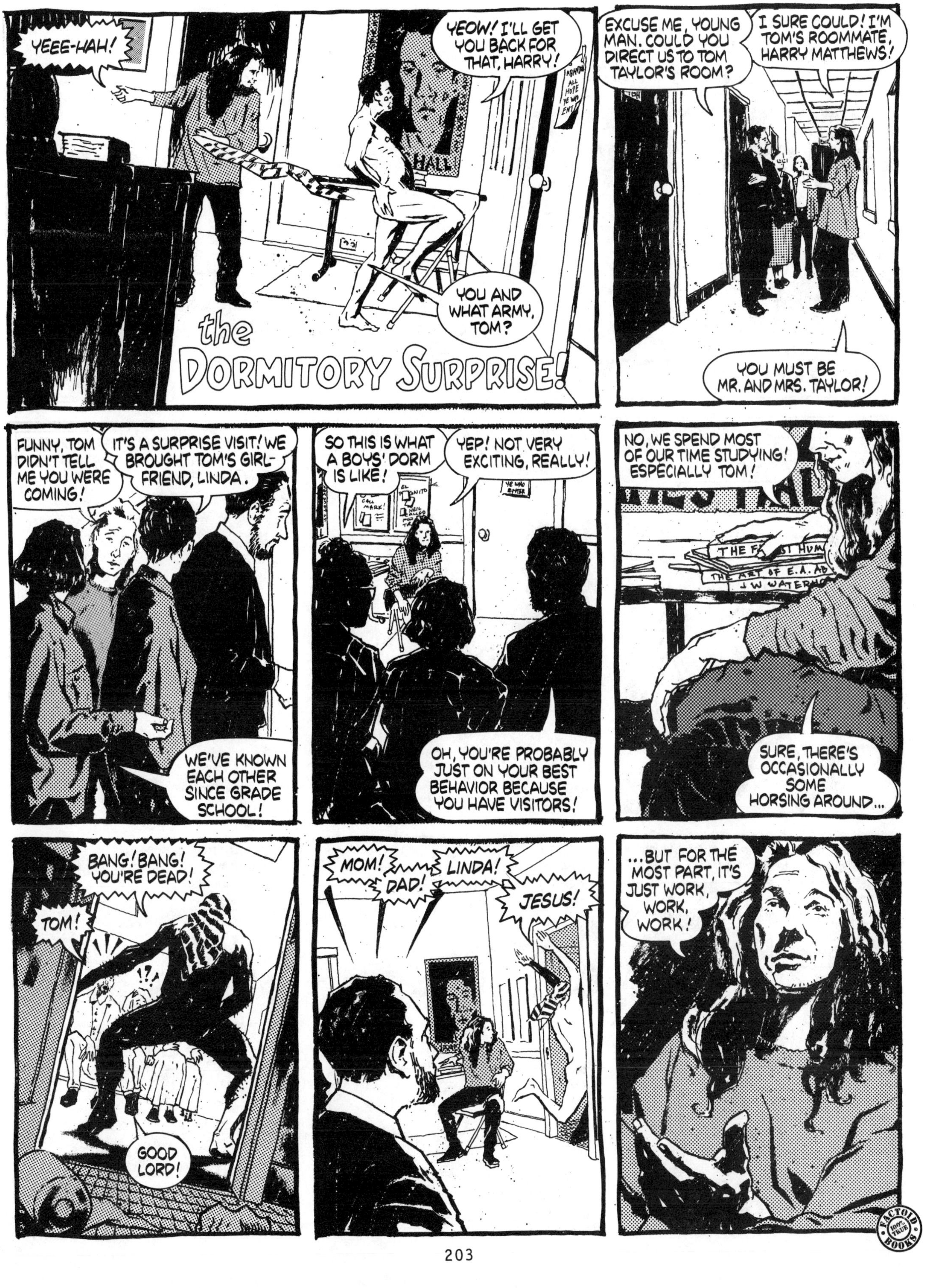
YEEE-HAH!
YEOW! I'LL GET YOU BACK FOR THAT, HARRY!
YOU AND WHAT ARMY, TOM?
the DORMITORY SURPRISE!
EXCUSE ME, YOUNG MAN. COULD YOU DIRECT US TO TOM TAYLOR'S ROOM?
I SURE COULD! I'M TOM'S ROOMMATE, HARRY MATTHEWS!
YOU MUST BE MR. AND MRS. TAYLOR!
FUNNY, TOM DIDN'T TELL ME YOU WERE COMING!
IT'S A SURPRISE VISIT! WE BROUGHT TOM'S GIRL-FRIEND, LINDA.
WE'VE KNOWN EACH OTHER SINCE GRADE SCHOOL!
SO THIS IS WHAT A BOYS' DORM IS LIKE!
YEP! NOT VERY EXCITING, REALLY!
OH, YOU'RE PROBABLY JUST ON YOUR BEST BEHAVIOR BECAUSE YOU HAVE VISITORS!
NO, WE SPEND MOST OF OUR TIME STUDYING! ESPECIALLY TOM!
SURE, THERE'S OCCASIONALLY SOME HORSING AROUND...
BANG! BANG! YOU'RE DEAD!
TOM!
!?!
GOOD LORD!
MOM!
DAD!
LINDA!
JESUS!
...BUT FOR THE MOST PART, IT'S JUST WORK, WORK, WORK!
FACTOID BOOKS
100% TRUE

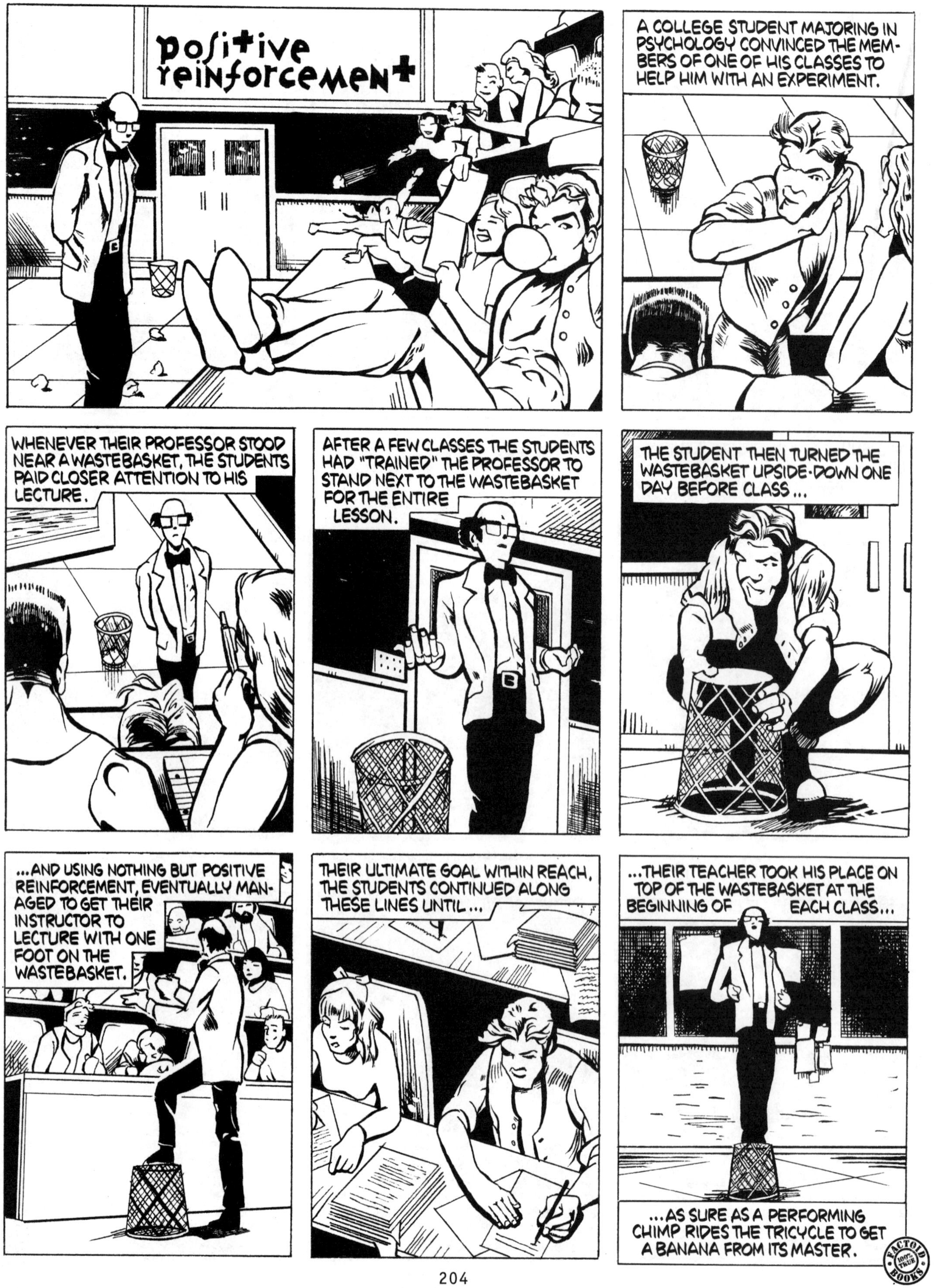
positive reinforcement
A COLLEGE STUDENT MAJORING IN PSYCHOLOGY CONVINCED THE MEMBERS OF ONE OF HIS CLASSES TO HELP HIM WITH AN EXPERIMENT.
WHENEVER THEIR PROFESSOR STOOD NEAR A WASTEBASKET, THE STUDENTS PAID CLOSER ATTENTION TO HIS LECTURE.
AFTER A FEW CLASSES THE STUDENTS HAD "TRAINED" THE PROFESSOR TO STAND NEXT TO THE WASTEBASKET FOR THE ENTIRE LESSON.
THE STUDENT THEN TURNED THE WASTEBASKET UPSIDE-DOWN ONE DAY BEFORE CLASS...
...AND USING NOTHING BUT POSITIVE REINFORCEMENT, EVENTUALLY MANAGED TO GET THEIR INSTRUCTOR TO LECTURE WITH ONE FOOT ON THE WASTEBASKET.
THEIR ULTIMATE GOAL WITHIN REACH, THE STUDENTS CONTINUED ALONG THESE LINES UNTIL...
...THEIR TEACHER TOOK HIS PLACE ON TOP OF THE WASTEBASKET AT THE BEGINNING OF EACH CLASS...
...AS SURE AS A PERFORMING CHIMP RIDES THE TRICYCLE TO GET A BANANA FROM ITS MASTER.
FACTOID 100% TRUE BOOKS

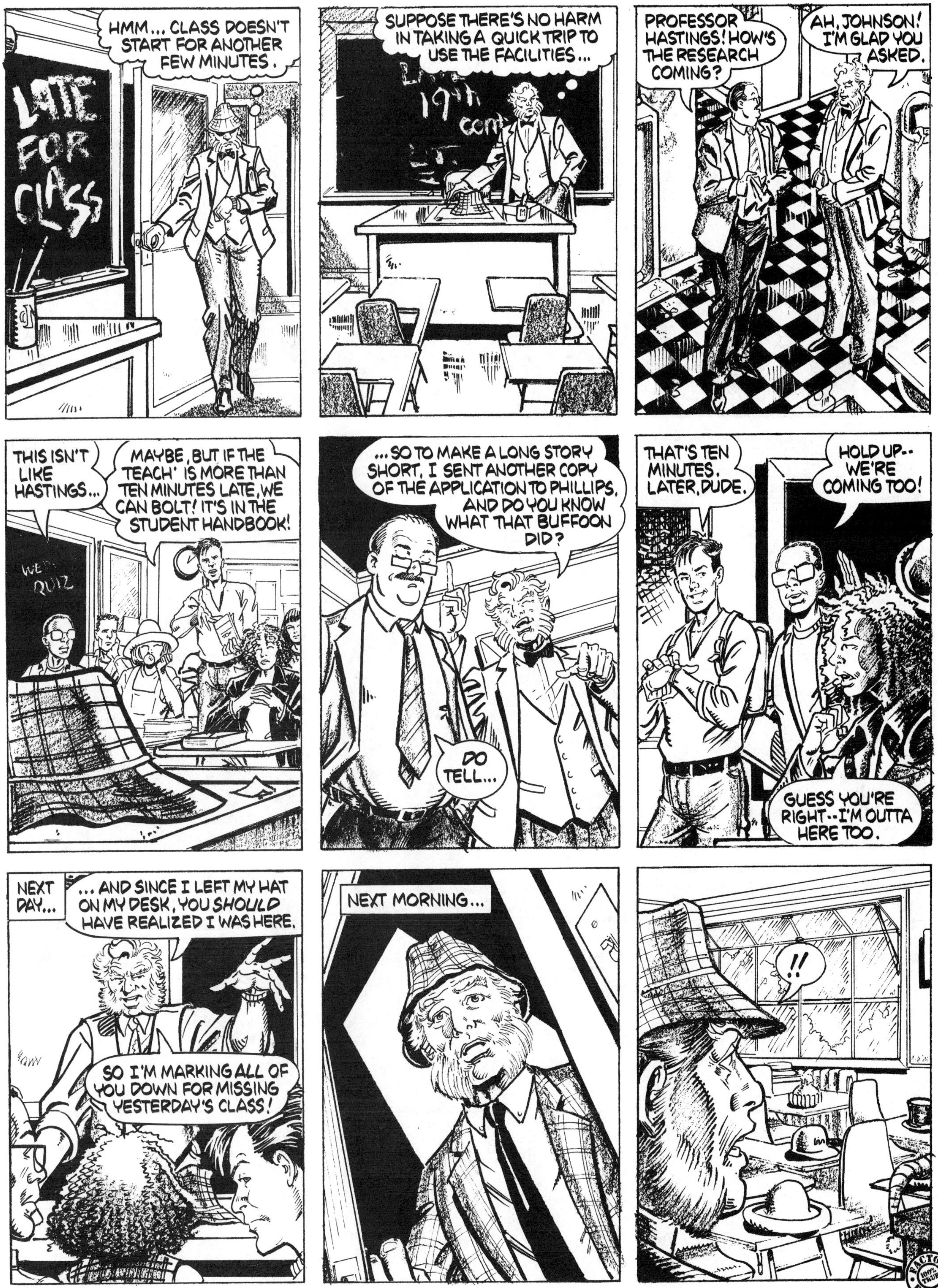
HMM... CLASS DOESN'T START FOR ANOTHER FEW MINUTES.
LATE FOR CLASS
SUPPOSE THERE'S NO HARM IN TAKING A QUICK TRIP TO USE THE FACILITIES...
PROFESSOR HASTINGS! HOW'S THE RESEARCH COMING?
AH, JOHNSON! I'M GLAD YOU ASKED.
THIS ISN'T LIKE HASTINGS...
MAYBE, BUT IF THE TEACH' IS MORE THAN TEN MINUTES LATE, WE CAN BOLT! IT'S IN THE STUDENT HANDBOOK!
...SO TO MAKE A LONG STORY SHORT, I SENT ANOTHER COPY OF THE APPLICATION TO PHILLIPS. AND DO YOU KNOW WHAT THAT BUFFOON DID?
DO TELL...
THAT'S TEN MINUTES. LATER, DUDE.
HOLD UP-- WE'RE COMING TOO!
GUESS YOU'RE RIGHT--I'M OUTTA HERE TOO.
NEXT DAY...
...AND SINCE I LEFT MY HAT ON MY DESK, YOU SHOULD HAVE REALIZED I WAS HERE.
SO I'M MARKING ALL OF YOU DOWN FOR MISSING YESTERDAY'S CLASS!
NEXT MORNING...
!!

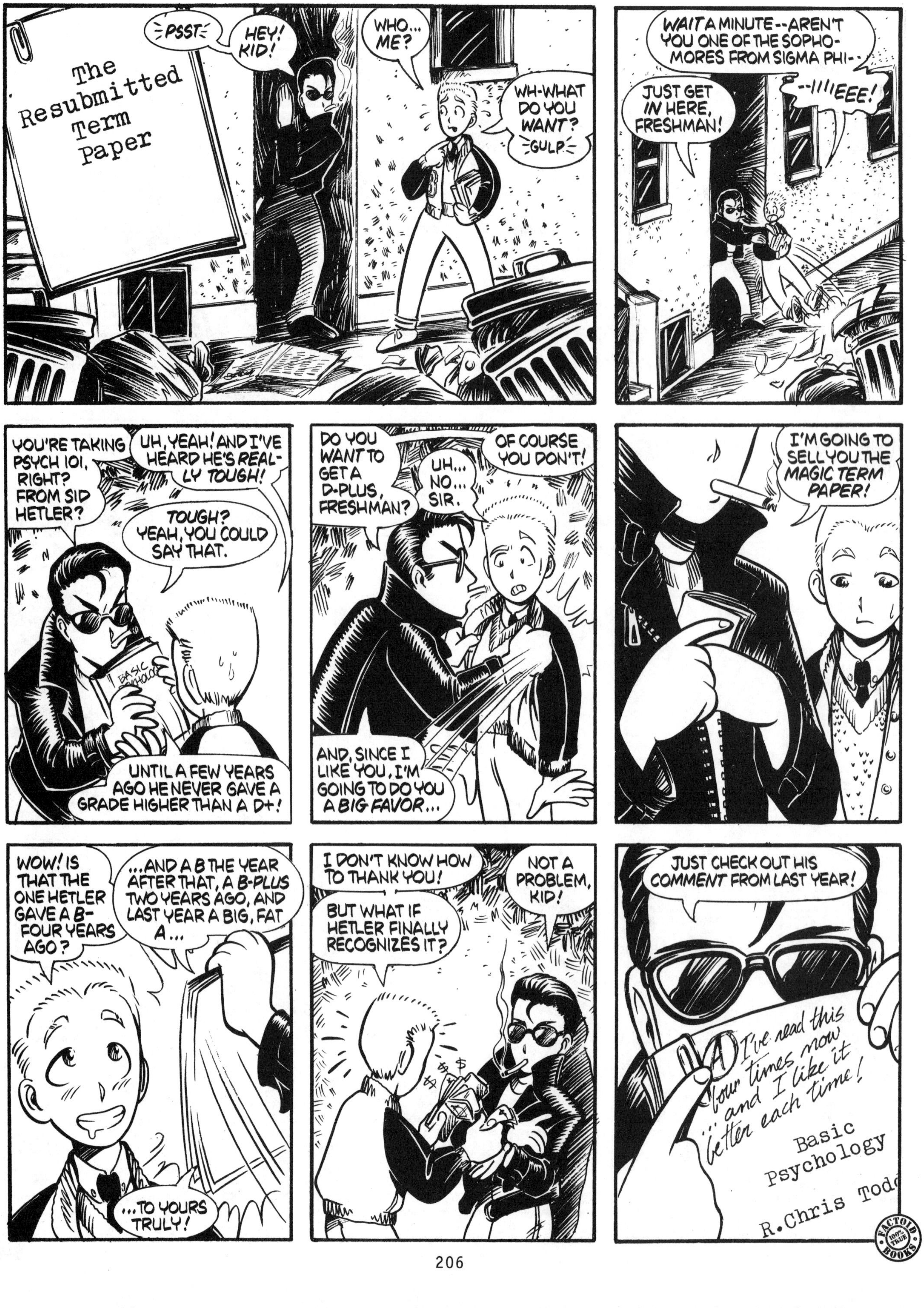
The Resubmitted Term Paper
PSST
HEY! KID!
WHO... ME?
WH-WHAT DO YOU WANT? GULP
WAIT A MINUTE--AREN'T YOU ONE OF THE SOPHOMORES FROM SIGMA PHI--
JUST GET IN HERE, FRESHMAN!
--IIIEEE!
YOU'RE TAKING PSYCH 101, RIGHT? FROM SID HETLER?
UH, YEAH! AND I'VE HEARD HE'S REALLY TOUGH!
TOUGH? YEAH, YOU COULD SAY THAT.
UNTIL A FEW YEARS AGO HE NEVER GAVE A GRADE HIGHER THAN A D+!
DO YOU WANT TO GET A D-PLUS, FRESHMAN?
UH... NO... SIR.
OF COURSE YOU DON'T!
AND, SINCE I LIKE YOU, I'M GOING TO DO YOU A BIG FAVOR...
I'M GOING TO SELL YOU THE MAGIC TERM PAPER!
WOW! IS THAT THE ONE HETLER GAVE A B- FOUR YEARS AGO?
...AND A B THE YEAR AFTER THAT, A B-PLUS TWO YEARS AGO, AND LAST YEAR A BIG, FAT A...
...TO YOURS TRULY!
I DON'T KNOW HOW TO THANK YOU!
BUT WHAT IF HETLER FINALLY RECOGNIZES IT?
NOT A PROBLEM, KID!
JUST CHECK OUT HIS COMMENT FROM LAST YEAR!
A I've read this four times now ... and I like it better each time!
Basic Psychology
R.Chris Tod

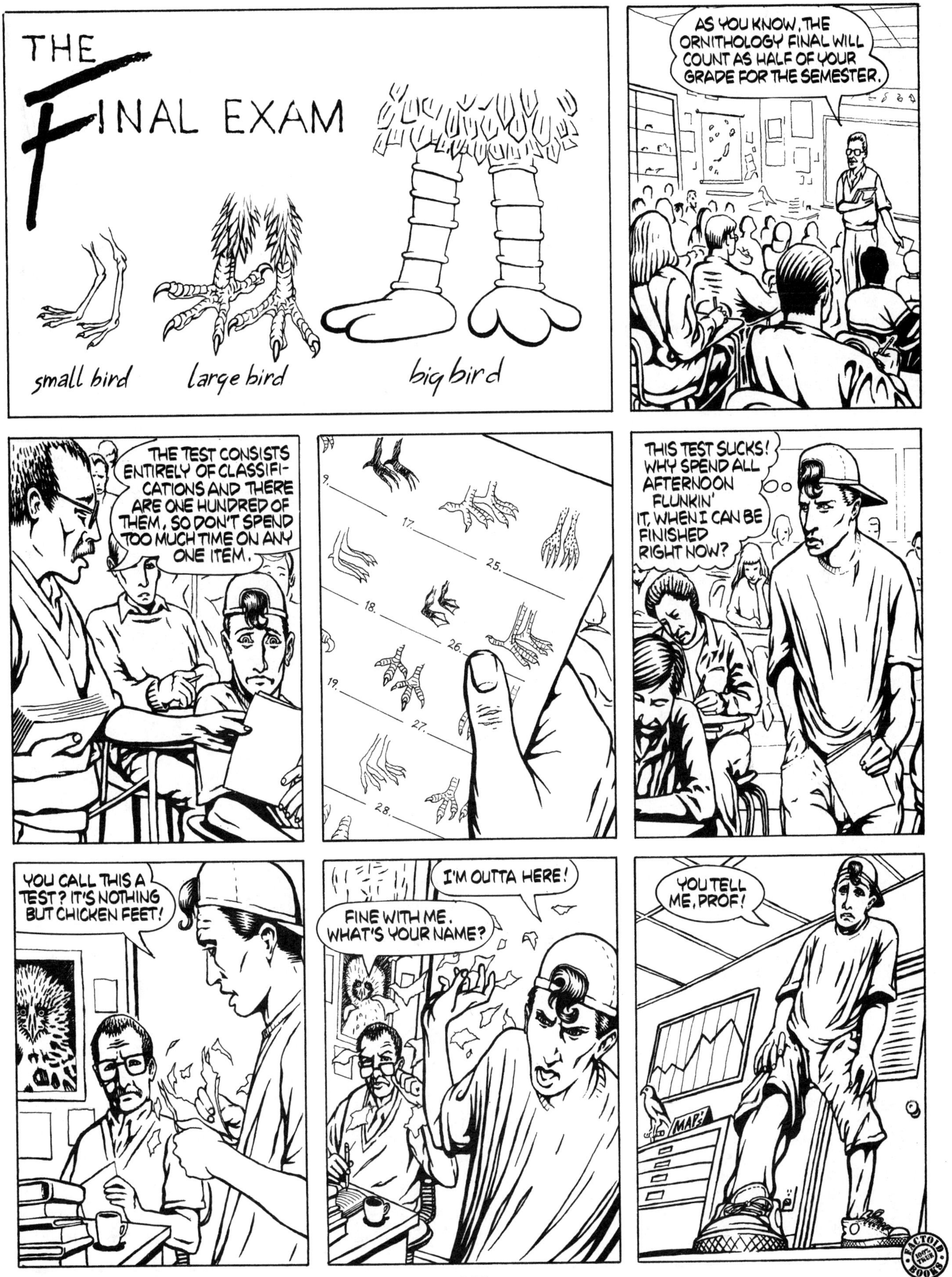
THE FINAL EXAM
small bird
large bird
big bird
AS YOU KNOW, THE ORNITHOLOGY FINAL WILL COUNT AS HALF OF YOUR GRADE FOR THE SEMESTER.
THE TEST CONSISTS ENTIRELY OF CLASSIFI-CATIONS AND THERE ARE ONE HUNDRED OF THEM, SO DON'T SPEND TOO MUCH TIME ON ANY ONE ITEM.
9.
17.
25.
18.
26.
19.
27.
28.
THIS TEST SUCKS! WHY SPEND ALL AFTERNOON FLUNKIN' IT, WHEN I CAN BE FINISHED RIGHT NOW?
YOU CALL THIS A TEST? IT'S NOTHING BUT CHICKEN FEET!
I'M OUTTA HERE!
FINE WITH ME. WHAT'S YOUR NAME?
YOU TELL ME, PROF!
MAPS

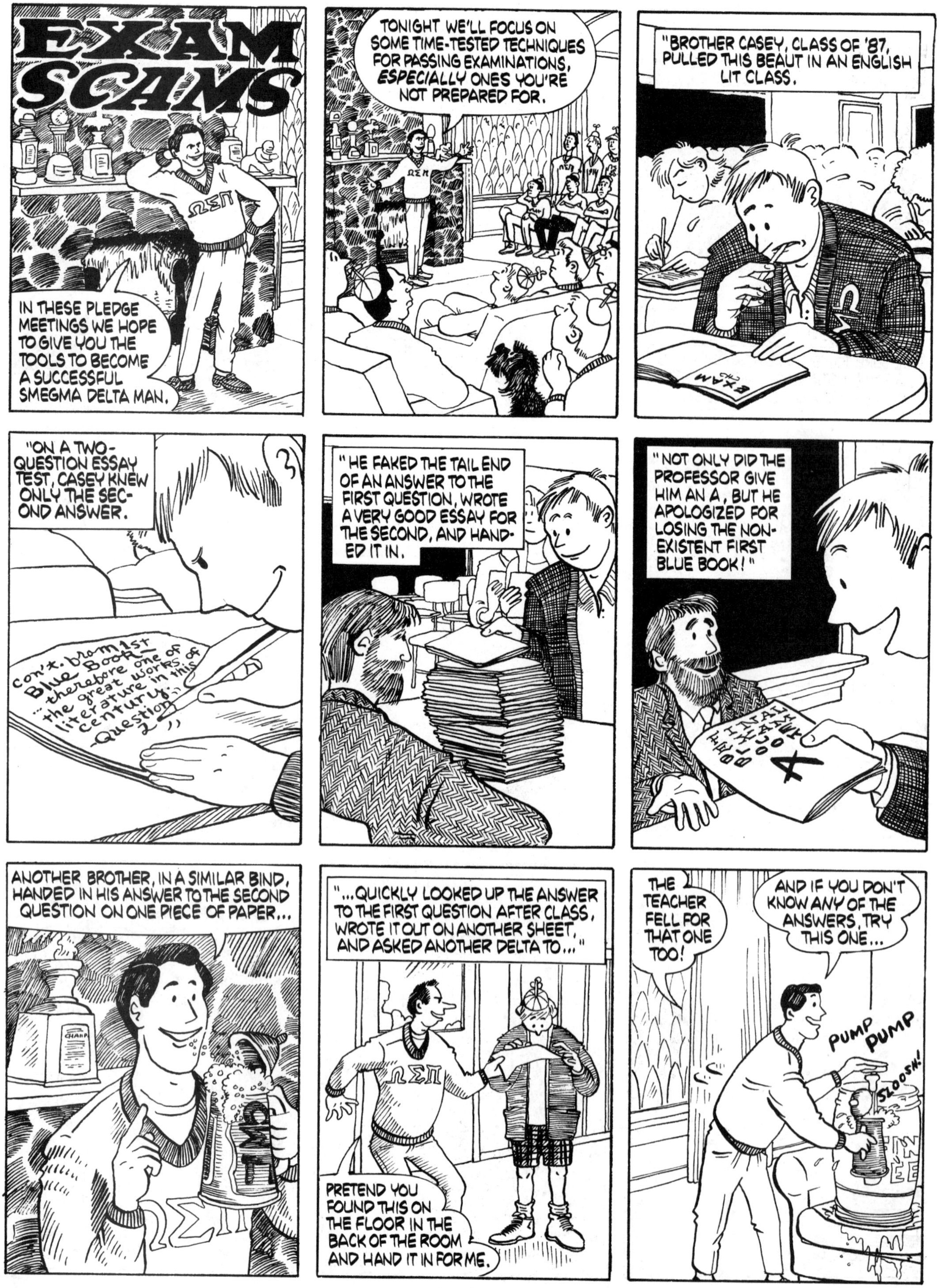
EXAM SCAMS
IN THESE PLEDGE MEETINGS WE HOPE TO GIVE YOU THE TOOLS TO BECOME A SUCCESSFUL SMEGMA DELTA MAN.
TONIGHT WE'LL FOCUS ON SOME TIME-TESTED TECHNIQUES FOR PASSING EXAMINATIONS, ESPECIALLY ONES YOU'RE NOT PREPARED FOR.
"BROTHER CASEY, CLASS OF '87, PULLED THIS BEAUT IN AN ENGLISH LIT CLASS.
"ON A TWO-QUESTION ESSAY TEST, CASEY KNEW ONLY THE SECOND ANSWER.
con't. from 1st Blue Book — ... therefore one of the great works of literature in this century." -Question 2
"HE FAKED THE TAIL END OF AN ANSWER TO THE FIRST QUESTION, WROTE A VERY GOOD ESSAY FOR THE SECOND, AND HANDED IT IN.
"NOT ONLY DID THE PROFESSOR GIVE HIM AN A, BUT HE APOLOGIZED FOR LOSING THE NON-EXISTENT FIRST BLUE BOOK!"
ANOTHER BROTHER, IN A SIMILAR BIND, HANDED IN HIS ANSWER TO THE SECOND QUESTION ON ONE PIECE OF PAPER...
"...QUICKLY LOOKED UP THE ANSWER TO THE FIRST QUESTION AFTER CLASS, WROTE IT OUT ON ANOTHER SHEET, AND ASKED ANOTHER DELTA TO..."
PRETEND YOU FOUND THIS ON THE FLOOR IN THE BACK OF THE ROOM AND HAND IT IN FOR ME.
THE TEACHER FELL FOR THAT ONE TOO!
AND IF YOU DON'T KNOW ANY OF THE ANSWERS, TRY THIS ONE...
PUMP PUMP
SLOOSH!

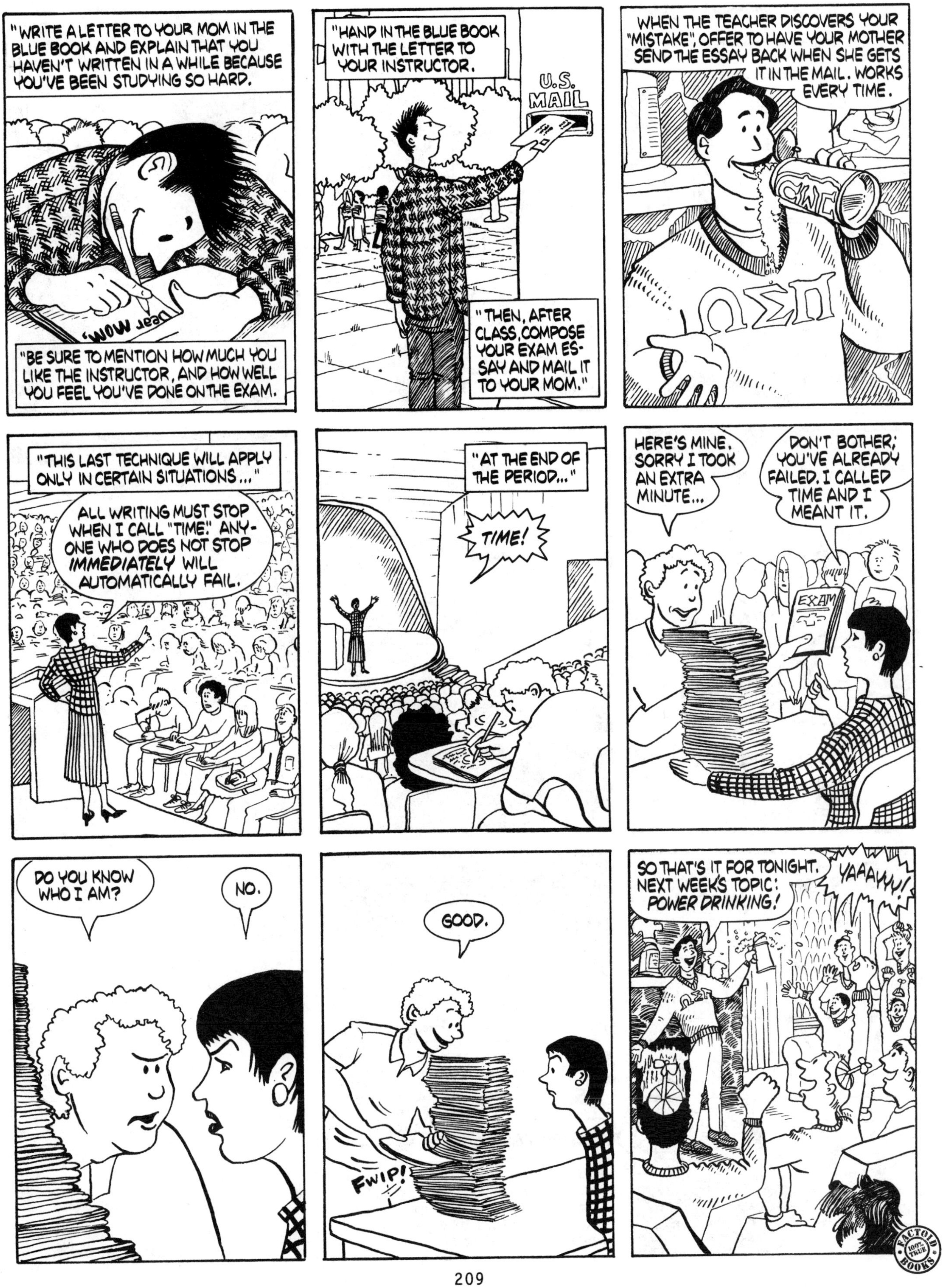

"WRITE A LETTER TO YOUR MOM IN THE BLUE BOOK AND EXPLAIN THAT YOU HAVEN'T WRITTEN IN A WHILE BECAUSE YOU'VE BEEN STUDYING SO HARD.
"BE SURE TO MENTION HOW MUCH YOU LIKE THE INSTRUCTOR, AND HOW WELL YOU FEEL YOU'VE DONE ON THE EXAM.
"HAND IN THE BLUE BOOK WITH THE LETTER TO YOUR INSTRUCTOR.
U.S. MAIL
"THEN, AFTER CLASS, COMPOSE YOUR EXAM ESSAY AND MAIL IT TO YOUR MOM."
WHEN THE TEACHER DISCOVERS YOUR "MISTAKE", OFFER TO HAVE YOUR MOTHER SEND THE ESSAY BACK WHEN SHE GETS IT IN THE MAIL. WORKS EVERY TIME.
"THIS LAST TECHNIQUE WILL APPLY ONLY IN CERTAIN SITUATIONS..."
ALL WRITING MUST STOP WHEN I CALL "TIME." ANYONE WHO DOES NOT STOP *IMMEDIATELY* WILL AUTOMATICALLY FAIL.
"AT THE END OF THE PERIOD..."
TIME!
HERE'S MINE. SORRY I TOOK AN EXTRA MINUTE...
DON'T BOTHER; YOU'VE ALREADY FAILED. I CALLED TIME AND I MEANT IT.
EXAM
DO YOU KNOW WHO I AM?
NO.
GOOD.
FWIP!
SO THAT'S IT FOR TONIGHT. NEXT WEEK'S TOPIC: *POWER DRINKING!*
YAAAAYY!

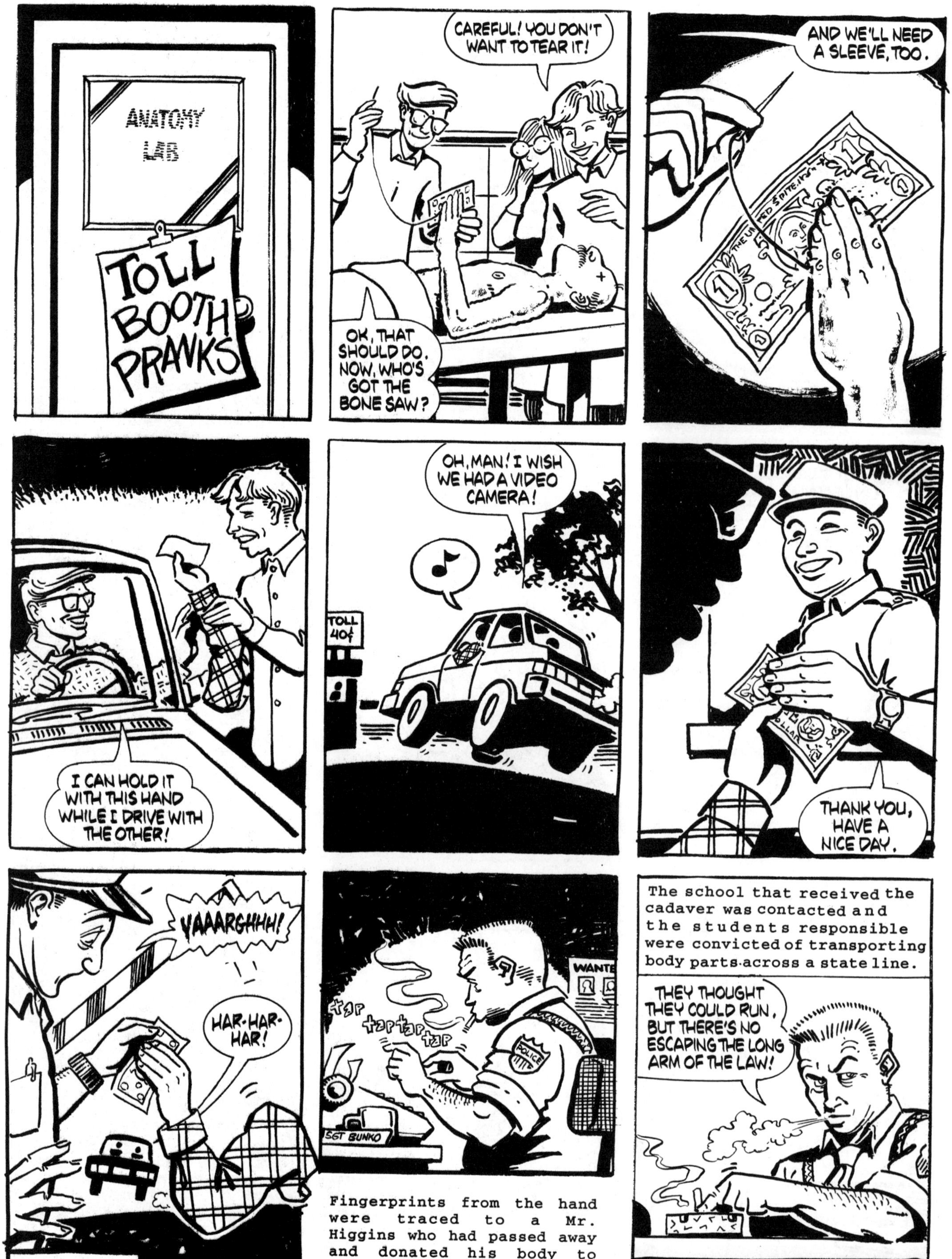
ANATOMY LAB
TOLL BOOTH PRANKS
CAREFUL! YOU DON'T WANT TO TEAR IT!
OK, THAT SHOULD DO. NOW, WHO'S GOT THE BONE SAW?
AND WE'LL NEED A SLEEVE, TOO.
I CAN HOLD IT WITH THIS HAND WHILE I DRIVE WITH THE OTHER!
OH, MAN! I WISH WE HAD A VIDEO CAMERA!
TOLL 40¢
THANK YOU, HAVE A NICE DAY.
YAAARGHHH!
HAR-HAR-HAR!
tap tap tap tap tap
SGT BUNKO
POLICE
Fingerprints from the hand were traced to a Mr. Higgins who had passed away and donated his body to medical science.
The school that received the cadaver was contacted and the students responsible were convicted of transporting body parts across a state line.
THEY THOUGHT THEY COULD RUN, BUT THERE'S NO ESCAPING THE LONG ARM OF THE LAW!

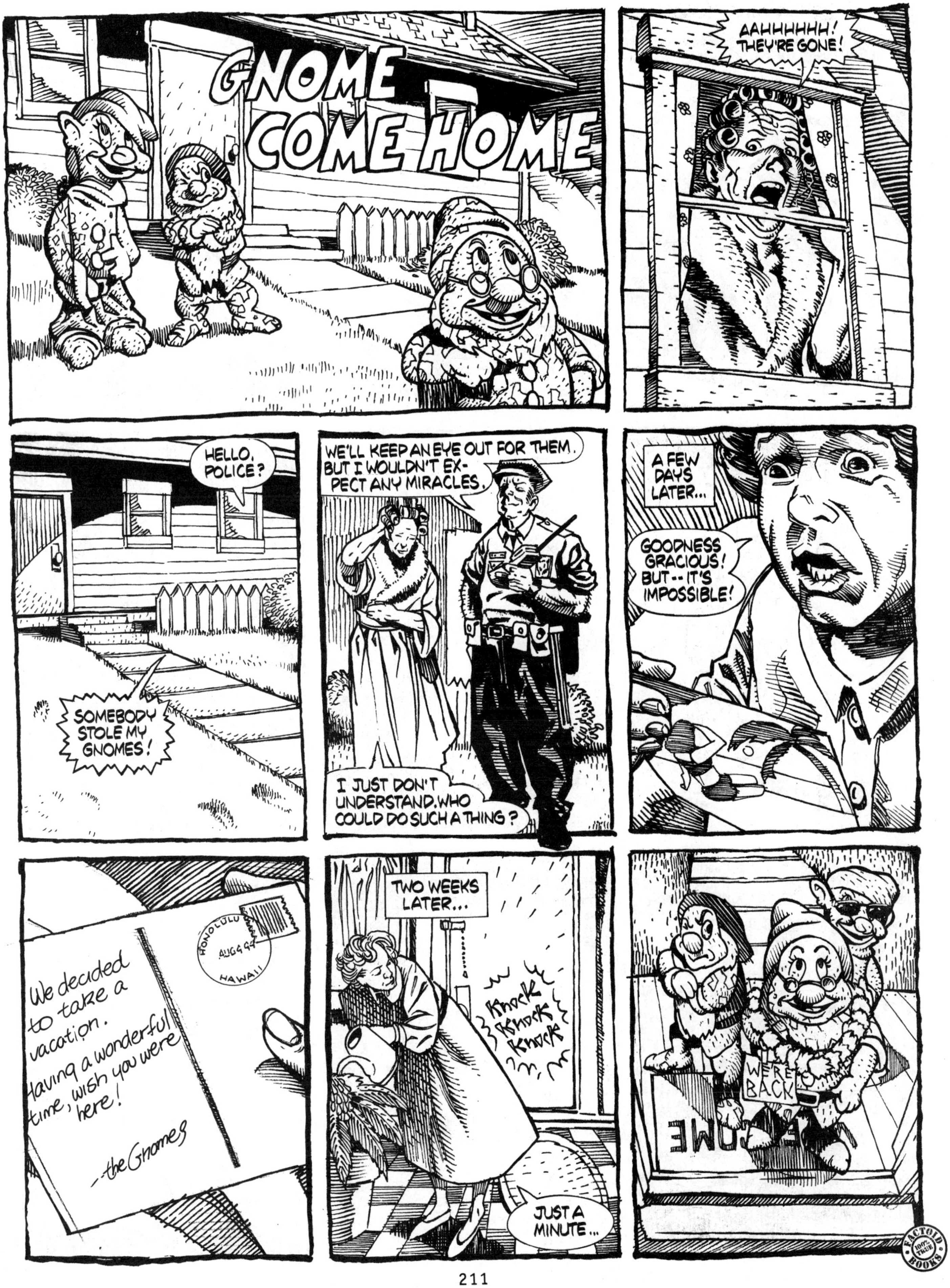
GNOME COME HOME
AAHHHHHH! THEY'RE GONE!
HELLO, POLICE?
SOMEBODY STOLE MY GNOMES!
WE'LL KEEP AN EYE OUT FOR THEM, BUT I WOULDN'T EXPECT ANY MIRACLES.
I JUST DON'T UNDERSTAND. WHO COULD DO SUCH A THING?
A FEW DAYS LATER...
GOODNESS GRACIOUS! BUT -- IT'S IMPOSSIBLE!
HONOLULU HAWAII AUG 4 94
We decided to take a vacation. Having a wonderful time, wish you were here!
-the Gnomes
TWO WEEKS LATER...
Knock Knock Knock
JUST A MINUTE...
WE'RE BACK

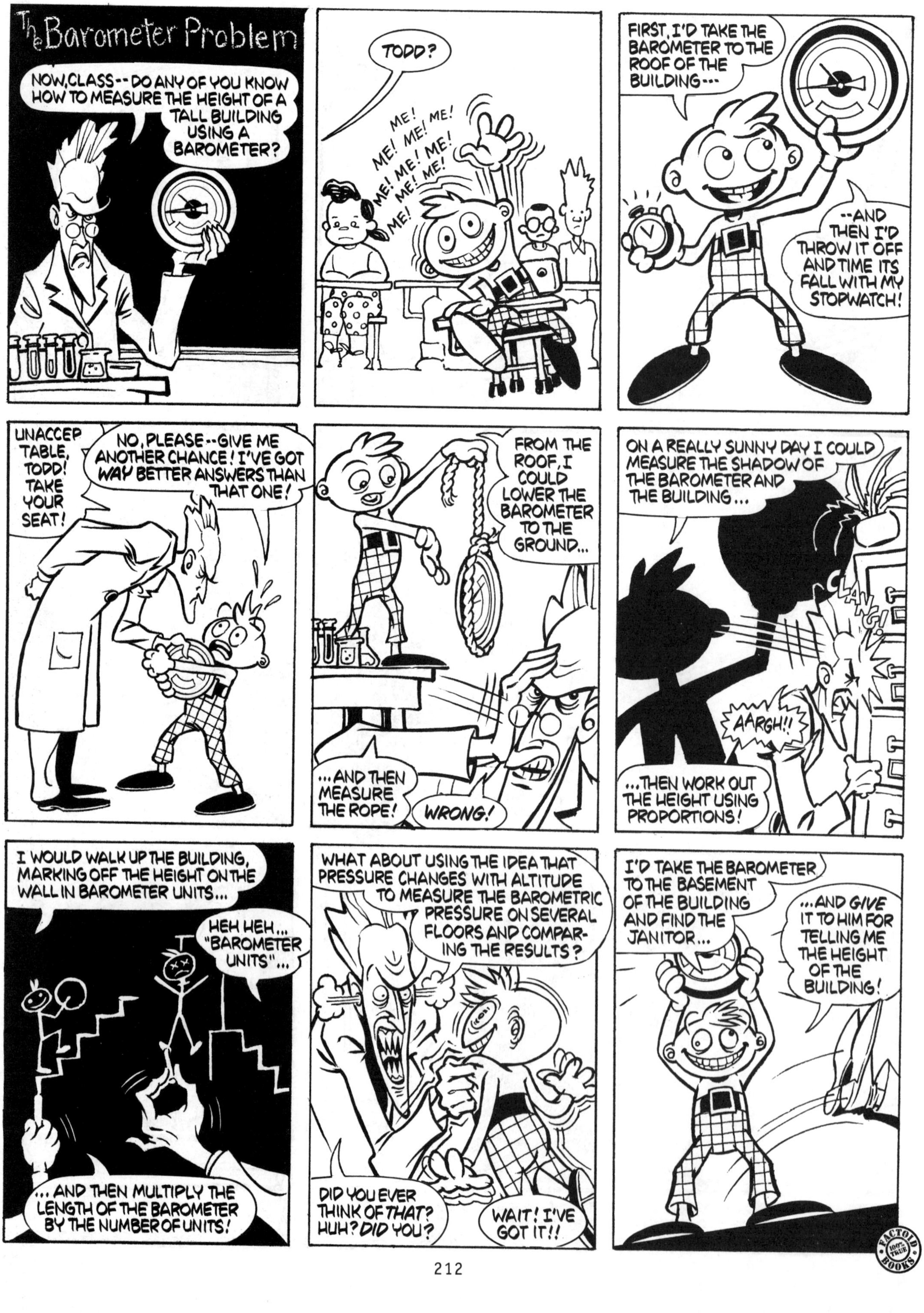
The Barometer Problem
NOW, CLASS -- DO ANY OF YOU KNOW HOW TO MEASURE THE HEIGHT OF A TALL BUILDING USING A BAROMETER?
TODD?
ME! ME! ME! ME! ME! ME! ME! ME! ME! ME!
FIRST, I'D TAKE THE BAROMETER TO THE ROOF OF THE BUILDING---
--AND THEN I'D THROW IT OFF AND TIME ITS FALL WITH MY STOPWATCH!
UNACCEPTABLE, TODD! TAKE YOUR SEAT!
NO, PLEASE -- GIVE ME ANOTHER CHANCE! I'VE GOT WAY BETTER ANSWERS THAN THAT ONE!
FROM THE ROOF, I COULD LOWER THE BAROMETER TO THE GROUND...
...AND THEN MEASURE THE ROPE!
WRONG!
ON A REALLY SUNNY DAY I COULD MEASURE THE SHADOW OF THE BAROMETER AND THE BUILDING...
CLANG!
AARGH!!
...THEN WORK OUT THE HEIGHT USING PROPORTIONS!
I WOULD WALK UP THE BUILDING, MARKING OFF THE HEIGHT ON THE WALL IN BAROMETER UNITS...
HEH HEH... "BAROMETER UNITS"...
...AND THEN MULTIPLY THE LENGTH OF THE BAROMETER BY THE NUMBER OF UNITS!
WHAT ABOUT USING THE IDEA THAT PRESSURE CHANGES WITH ALTITUDE TO MEASURE THE BAROMETRIC PRESSURE ON SEVERAL FLOORS AND COMPARING THE RESULTS?
DID YOU EVER THINK OF THAT? HUH? DID YOU?
WAIT! I'VE GOT IT!!
I'D TAKE THE BAROMETER TO THE BASEMENT OF THE BUILDING AND FIND THE JANITOR...
...AND GIVE IT TO HIM FOR TELLING ME THE HEIGHT OF THE BUILDING!
FACTOID BOOKS 100% TRUE

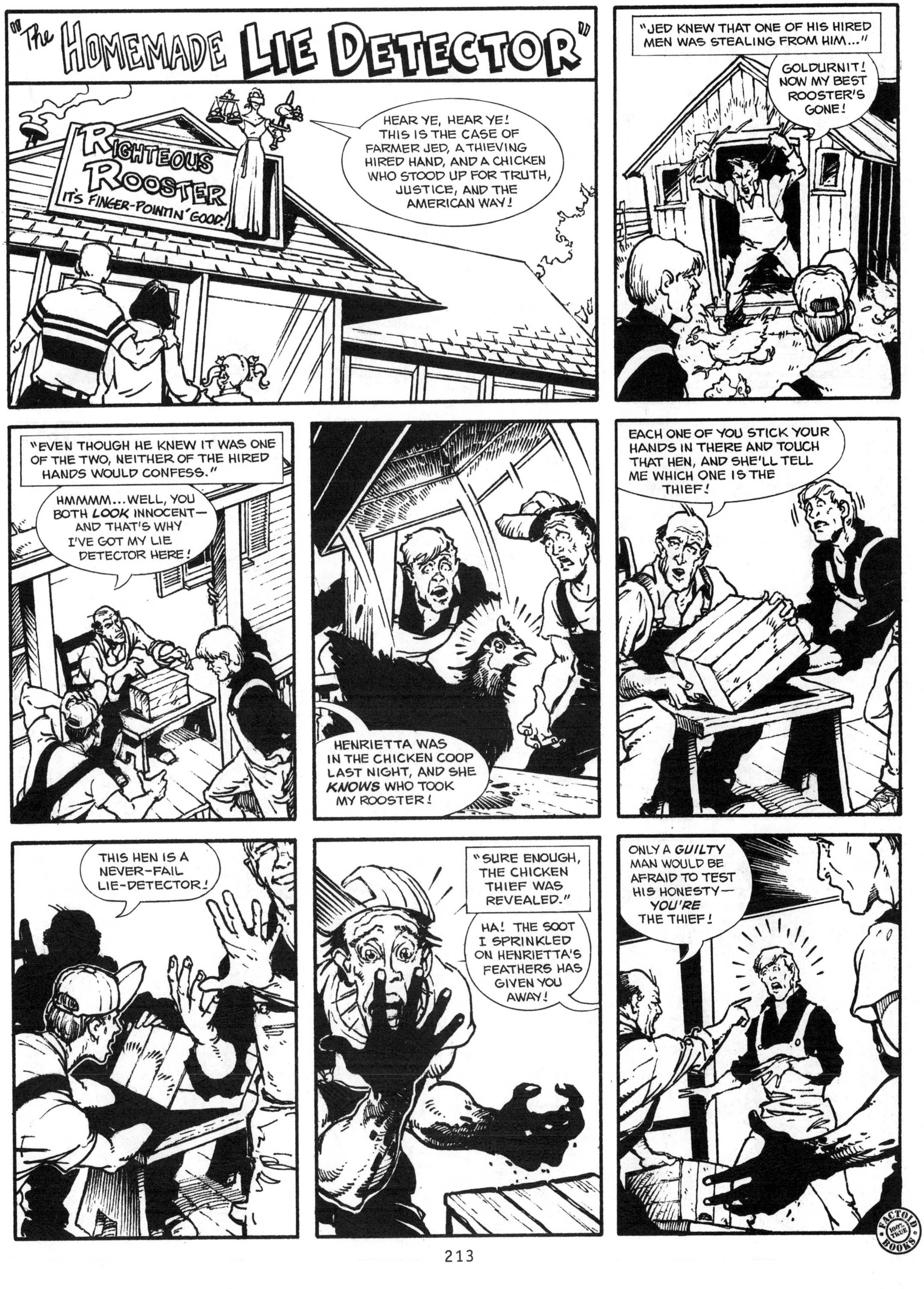
"The Homemade Lie Detector"
Righteous Rooster
It's finger-pointin' good!
HEAR YE, HEAR YE! THIS IS THE CASE OF FARMER JED, A THIEVING HIRED HAND, AND A CHICKEN WHO STOOD UP FOR TRUTH, JUSTICE, AND THE AMERICAN WAY!
"JED KNEW THAT ONE OF HIS HIRED MEN WAS STEALING FROM HIM..."
GOLDURNIT! NOW MY BEST ROOSTER'S GONE!
"EVEN THOUGH HE KNEW IT WAS ONE OF THE TWO, NEITHER OF THE HIRED HANDS WOULD CONFESS."
HMMMM...WELL, YOU BOTH LOOK INNOCENT— AND THAT'S WHY I'VE GOT MY LIE DETECTOR HERE!
HENRIETTA WAS IN THE CHICKEN COOP LAST NIGHT, AND SHE KNOWS WHO TOOK MY ROOSTER!
EACH ONE OF YOU STICK YOUR HANDS IN THERE AND TOUCH THAT HEN, AND SHE'LL TELL ME WHICH ONE IS THE THIEF!
THIS HEN IS A NEVER-FAIL LIE-DETECTOR!
"SURE ENOUGH, THE CHICKEN THIEF WAS REVEALED."
HA! THE SOOT I SPRINKLED ON HENRIETTA'S FEATHERS HAS GIVEN YOU AWAY!
ONLY A GUILTY MAN WOULD BE AFRAID TO TEST HIS HONESTY— YOU'RE THE THIEF!
FACTOID BOOKS 100% TRUE

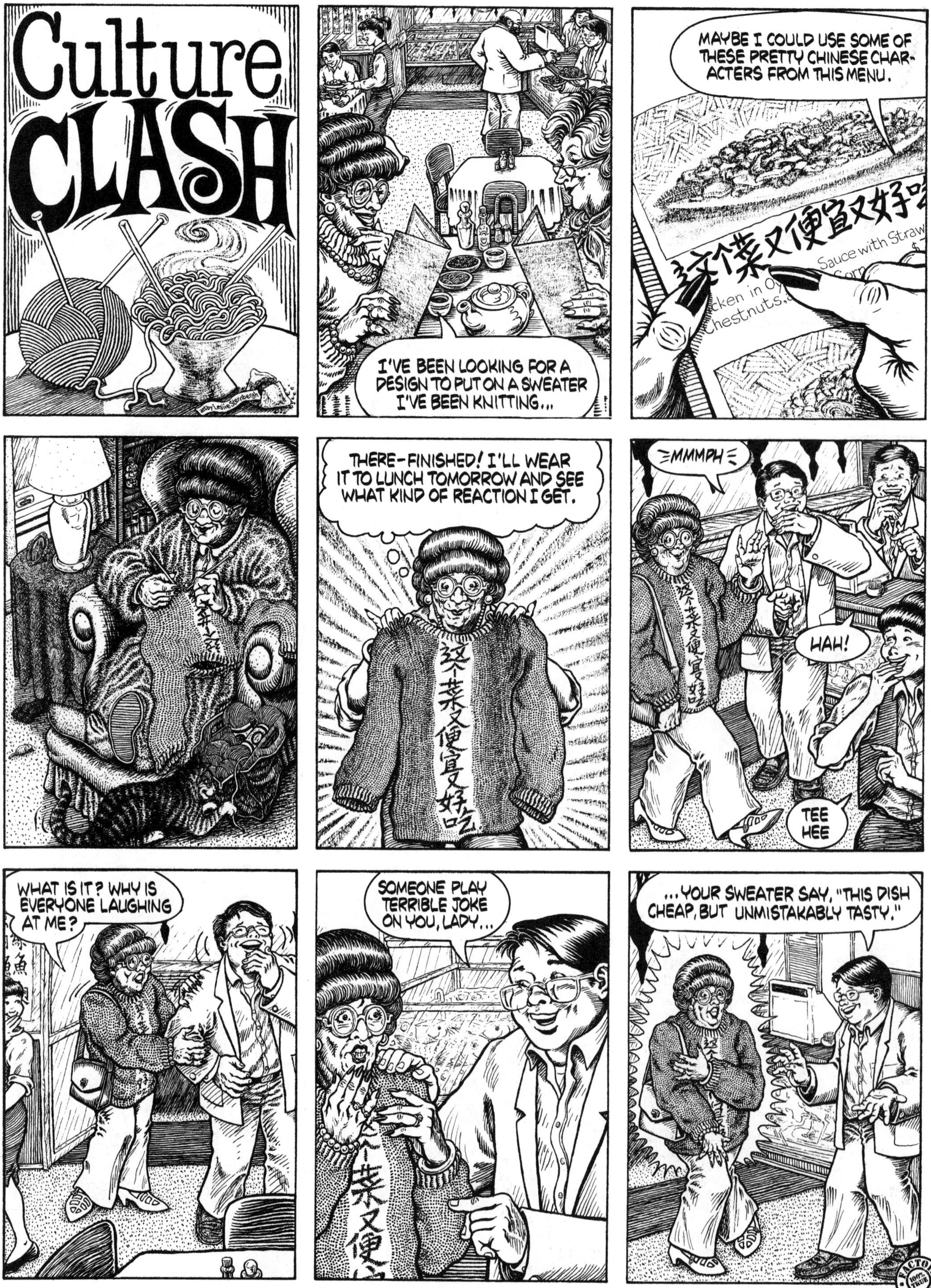
Culture CLASH
I'VE BEEN LOOKING FOR A DESIGN TO PUT ON A SWEATER I'VE BEEN KNITTING...
MAYBE I COULD USE SOME OF THESE PRETTY CHINESE CHARACTERS FROM THIS MENU.
THERE–FINISHED! I'LL WEAR IT TO LUNCH TOMORROW AND SEE WHAT KIND OF REACTION I GET.
MMMPH
HAH!
TEE HEE
WHAT IS IT? WHY IS EVERYONE LAUGHING AT ME?
SOMEONE PLAY TERRIBLE JOKE ON YOU, LADY...
...YOUR SWEATER SAY, "THIS DISH CHEAP, BUT UNMISTAKABLY TASTY."

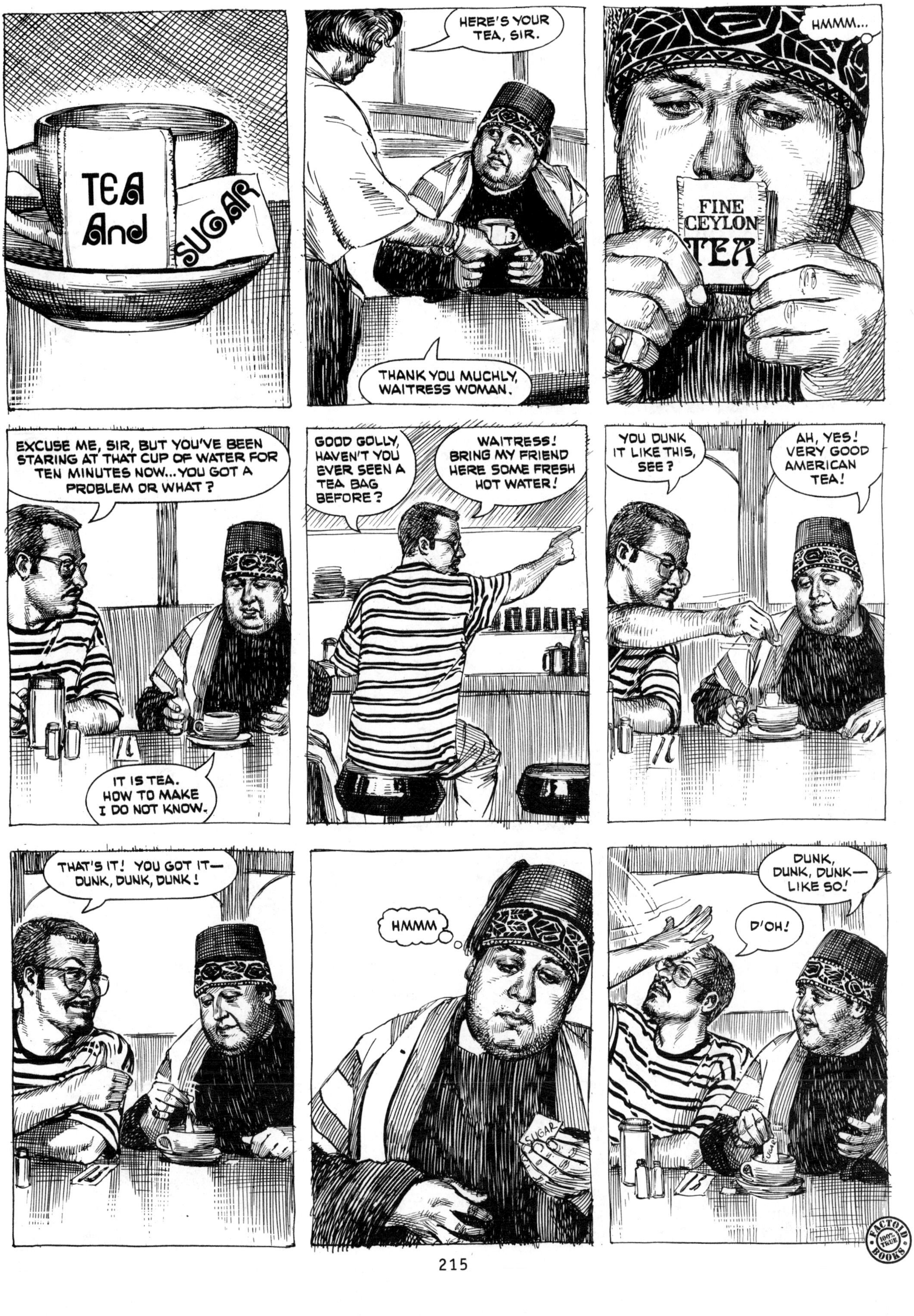
TEA And
SUGAR
HERE'S YOUR TEA, SIR.
THANK YOU MUCHLY, WAITRESS WOMAN.
HMMM...
FINE CEYLON TEA
EXCUSE ME, SIR, BUT YOU'VE BEEN STARING AT THAT CUP OF WATER FOR TEN MINUTES NOW... YOU GOT A PROBLEM OR WHAT?
IT IS TEA. HOW TO MAKE I DO NOT KNOW.
GOOD GOLLY, HAVEN'T YOU EVER SEEN A TEA BAG BEFORE?
WAITRESS! BRING MY FRIEND HERE SOME FRESH HOT WATER!
YOU DUNK IT LIKE THIS, SEE?
AH, YES! VERY GOOD AMERICAN TEA!
THAT'S IT! YOU GOT IT— DUNK, DUNK, DUNK!
HMMM
SUGAR
DUNK, DUNK, DUNK— LIKE SO!
D'OH!

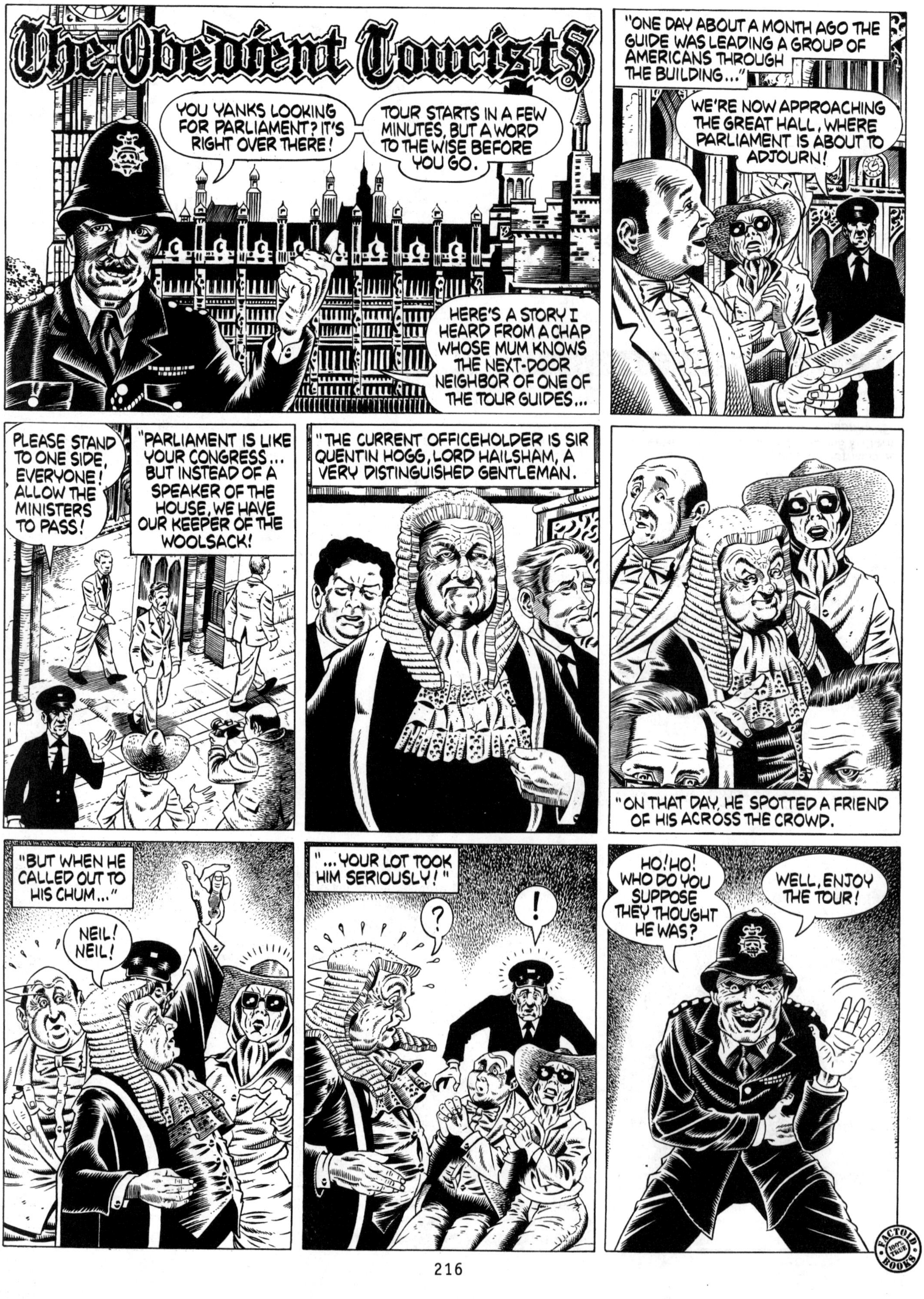
The Obedient Tourists
YOU YANKS LOOKING FOR PARLIAMENT? IT'S RIGHT OVER THERE!
TOUR STARTS IN A FEW MINUTES, BUT A WORD TO THE WISE BEFORE YOU GO.
HERE'S A STORY I HEARD FROM A CHAP WHOSE MUM KNOWS THE NEXT-DOOR NEIGHBOR OF ONE OF THE TOUR GUIDES...
"ONE DAY ABOUT A MONTH AGO THE GUIDE WAS LEADING A GROUP OF AMERICANS THROUGH THE BUILDING..."
WE'RE NOW APPROACHING THE GREAT HALL, WHERE PARLIAMENT IS ABOUT TO ADJOURN!
PLEASE STAND TO ONE SIDE, EVERYONE! ALLOW THE MINISTERS TO PASS!
"PARLIAMENT IS LIKE YOUR CONGRESS... BUT INSTEAD OF A SPEAKER OF THE HOUSE, WE HAVE OUR KEEPER OF THE WOOLSACK!
"THE CURRENT OFFICEHOLDER IS SIR QUENTIN HOGG, LORD HAILSHAM, A VERY DISTINGUISHED GENTLEMAN.
"ON THAT DAY, HE SPOTTED A FRIEND OF HIS ACROSS THE CROWD.
"BUT WHEN HE CALLED OUT TO HIS CHUM..."
NEIL! NEIL!
"...YOUR LOT TOOK HIM SERIOUSLY!"
?
!
HO! HO! WHO DO YOU SUPPOSE THEY THOUGHT HE WAS?
WELL, ENJOY THE TOUR!
FACTOID 100% TRUE BOOKS

BIO-GRAPHIES

WRITERS

ROBERT LOREN FLEMING
Robert Loren Fleming wrote *Thriller, Underworld, Ambush Bug, Aquaman, Ragman, Eclipso,* and *Valor* for DC. He's currently scripting *Legend of Supreme* for Image Comics and *The Cowl* for Marvel.

ROBERT F. BOYD, Jr.
Robert lives in Brooklyn, hosts an occasional radio program on WFMU-FM, contributes travel stories to *The New York Times* and photographs endangered commercial architecture. This is his first endeavor in comics.

LETTERERS

STEVE SMITH
Steve has been using the alphabet for many years. Other examples of his penmanship and pictures may be found in *Negative Burn, Aesop's Desecrated Fables,* and along the 101 freeway. He is also the artist of "The Toothbrush Story" in this volume. *(Page 169)*

GAIL BECKETT
Now a resident of northeast Georgia, Gail has worked as a letterer and colorist on the *Flash Gordon* and *Spider-Man* newspaper strips, and on comics by Dark Horse, Marvel, DC, Malibu, etc.

ARTISTS

ART ADAMS
Art Adams is currently working on *Monkey Man and O'Brien,* published by Dark Horse Comics, under the Legend imprint. *(Page 47)*

CHARLES ADLARD
A British comic artist who works in a small studio in the countryside with no social life except for his imaginary comic friends. It's all very sad, really... *(Page 17)*

CHRISTIAN ALAMY
"The French Guy" managed to draw *Lobo's Back* #4, *Lobo Annual* #1, and *Showcase '94* #1 and #2 in only two years! He lives in Brooklyn with his girl, Katerina, and his dog, Kuma. *(Page 141)*

GARY AMARO
Gary Amaro, tweed-clad and filled with *bonhomie,* is our generation's most ebullient Al Jolson impersonator and sous chef. *(Page 75)*

BRENT ANDERSON
June 15, 1955. Born. Grew. Read. Drew. Wrote. Drew more. Read comics. Wrote and drew comics. Published fanzines. 1976. Professional. Deadlines. 1994. Married. Tired. 'Bye. *(Page 86)*

TERRY AUSTIN
Award-winning inker of *X-Men, Star Wars, Batman vs. Predator II,* and more; writer of *Cloak and Dagger, Power Pack,* and *Excalibur,* penciller of comic book covers, *National Lampoon,* etc. "Will cartoon for cash." *(Page 160)*

MARK BADGER
Mark Badger has drawn lots of comics. Along with the coolest cartoonists in the world, his work appears in *Toy Piano: The Comic Just For The Fun Of It. (Page 24)*

GLENN BARR
Glenn's recent projects have included the graphic novels and comics *Cliff's Wild Life, Technocracy Blues, Mars on Earth,* and the upcoming *Brooklyn Dreams* for Paradox Press. His animation work includes *Ren and Stimpy* and *Baby Huey. (Page 46)*

DAN BARRY
A Golden Age artist who wrote and drew the *Flash Gordon* strip for 30 years, Dan recently did the comic book adaptation of *Young Indiana Jones.* He has also had about 150 showings as a fine artist. *(Page 104)*

HILARY BARTA
Hilary Barta is the culprit responsible for *Plastic Man* and *Stupid.* He spends most of his time walking his dog and thinking of reasons to avoid work. *(Pages 108-109)*

TERRY BEATTY
Terry Beatty's credits include *Ms. Tree, Wild Dog, Johnny Dynamite* (art), *Scary Monsters* (cover paintings), *Elfquest: New Blood* (script), and numerous short stories co-written with his mystery novelist wife, Wendi Lee. *(Page 83)*

ALLAN BEDNAR
I would love to say that philosophy, comparative religion, and literature were my other loves as well as comics, but it would sound too pretentious. *(Page 204)*

GREGORY BENTON
Gregory's illustrations have been seen in the *The New York Times* and *The Village Voice.* He self-publishes his own comix in a magazine called *Self Induced Narcosis.* He is 5' 4". *(Page 176)*

RON BOYD
Ron has been working on the *Legion of Super-Heroes* and other comics for the last four years. He and Kimberly are expecting their first baby in September. *(Page 72)*

RUSSELL BRAUN
Raised by wolves. *(Page 154)*

DANIEL BRERETON
Dan's first project, *The Black Terror,* started as a school assignment and ended as a new career painting comic books. Since then, he has illustrated comics, trading cards, and covers, and the upcoming *Nocturnals* for Malibu. *(Page 191)*

DAVID BREWER
David Brewer is a 23-year-old from Maine. He recently finished a story for Image called *Extremely Young Blood* (the characters portrayed as kids). *(Page 50)*

M.D. BRIGHT
M.D. Bright has pencilled *Green Lantern, G.I. Joe, Iron Man, Valor,* and *Power Man & Iron Fist.* Currently he pencils *Icon* for Milestone Media. *(Page 189)*

PAT BRODERICK
You know, I hate bios. I've always hated them. But Paradox Press insisted I supply one! And thirty words or *less!* Now I ask you, how can a person write — *(Page 162)*

TIM BURGARD
Currently Tim Burgard is storyboarding for big-budget movies, but has drawn, inked and/or written comics for DC, Marvel, Malibu and many others, with still more to come. *(Page 200)*

GUY BURWELL
Sagittarius, 12-13-65. This painter, penciller, and more has worked with Dark Horse Comics, A&M Records, Caliber, Boneyard, and others. Peace to the world. *(Page 150)*

ROBBIE BUSCH
Robbie Busch is a cartoonin' fool who has been known to delve into other artistic ventures. He's very happy that *Instant Piano* will see the light of day. *(Page 133)*

DON CAMERON
Since my break-up with Madonna, I have kept a low profile working as assistant to Howard "Pops" Chaykin. I am currently developing a Saturday morning cartoon based on the Suzanne Somers product, called *Thighmasters of the Universe.* *(Page 182)*

STEVE CARR
From *Conan* to *X-Factor,* from *Gameboy* to *Prince,* from *Silver Surfer* to *Green Lantern,* I've just about done it all. Also, special thanks to David Dace, whose pencils contributed enormously. *(Page 119)*

JOHN C. CEBOLLERO
Previous work: coloring on *X-O MANOWAR #0, Ninjak,* Topps trading cards, and several DC titles. This is John's first published sequential art. Future career goals: more pencilling opportunities — Please! *(Page 118)*

HOWARD CHAYKIN
Howard Chaykin pioneered the graphic novel form in the U.S. with *Empire, The Stars My Destination,* and *The Swords of Heaven, The Flowers of Hell,* and created the award-winning and influential *American Flagg!* and *Time².* He served on staff as executive script consultant on *The Flash* and *Viper* TV series. His most recent work includes *The Devil's Workshop* for DC, *Midnight Men* for Marvel, and *Power and Glory* for Bravura. *(Page 130)*

DAVID CHELSEA
Read David Chelsea's ultra-revealing graphic novel *David Chelsea In Love,* published by Eclipse. David's next book is *Welcome to the Zone,* from Kitchen Sink. *(Page 64)*

DAVID J. CHLYSTEK
I would like to dedicate this story (the artwork part) to my grandmother. Without her, I would never have had the desire to be an artist. *(Page 20)*

SCOTT COHN
I'm twenty, I'm from Philly, and when I'm not off saving the world I spend my time going to The School for Visual Arts in New York. *(Page 186)*

TOMM COKER
I live in California and have worked for Marvel, DC, and Dark Horse. Upcoming projects: *Midnight Sons* for Marvel, and a Harlan Ellison anthology for Dark Horse. Special thanks to Larry Ross. *(Page 174)*

MICHAEL COLLINS
Raised by Wolves (name of the local soccer team), Mike Collins now lives in a land that features a dragon on its flag. He draws and writes comic books. *(Page 21)*

JOHN COULTHART
John's previous work includes *Hawkwind* album cover designs and comics adaptations of H. P. Lovecraft stories. He is currently drawing the controversial Lord Horror epic *Reverbstorm* for Savoy Books. *(Page 58)*

DENYS COWAN
Denys worked on *The Question, Batman, Prince,* and *Deathlok,* among many other titles for Marvel and DC. He co-created the Milestone line of comics, draws *Hardware,* and is creative director at Milestone. *(Page 166)*

THOMAS CRIELLY
Previous comics work: trading cards and covers for Marvel U.K., and *Psychomancers* and *Relentless,* published by London Cartoon Centre. Hobbies include 5-a-side football and working out. *(Page 194)*

SCOTT CUNNINGHAM
Scott Cunningham is a regular contributor to *Heavy Metal* and *The Village Voice,* and to the now-defunct *Hyena.* He co-edits the political underground *World War 3 Illustrated.* *(Page 76)*

DONALD DAVID
Donald was imprisoned in the bowels of a Canadian art school for attempting to prove that comics were a valid medium for self-expression. To this day, he is haunted by the experience. *(Page 27)*

AL DAVISON
A black belt in karate who performs his own plays, Al Davison lives in London with his lover Maggie. Born paralyzed (spina-bifida), he wasn't expected to live/walk. Life's funny sometimes. *(Page 15)*

STEPHEN DeSTEFANO
Stephen DeStefano was born in 1966 in Queens, New York. He became a professional cartoonist at the age of fifteen, and by sixteen began regretting that decision like any old pro. *(Page 53)*

GUSTAVO DESIMONE
I live in Buenos Aires, Argentina, and got involved in comics when I was nine. I like stories with hard-hitting characters such as Lobo and Batman, and Erika Eleniak. *(Page 190)*

DAVE DeVRIES
Dave DeVries has illustrated for thirty years, producing countless award-winning comics and the successful children's book *Get Your Dog Out of My Crotch.* Unfortunately, this happened in another dimension. *(Page 167)*

D'ISRAELI D'EMON DRAUGHTSMAN
D'Israeli lives in Sheffield, England, with his Mummy and a nice Kitty. He was once nearly killed when a lesbian dressed as Tina Turner fell on his head. *(Page 114)*

FELIKS DOBRIN
I was born in Kiev and like to draw from my childhood. There was published couple of books by me: *Welcome Danger!, Dog's Kingdom,* and *The Dutch Schultz Story,* etc. Two years ago I came to the United States. I illustrated for DC Comics, and also won national Tektronix Print Illustration Contest in 1994. *(Page 94)*

EVAN DORKIN
Evan's cartoons have disgraced such magazines as *Esquire, Reflex,* and *Deadline.* His ongoing comic titles from Slave Labor Graphics include *Milk and Cheese, Hectic Planet,* and *Dork!* *(Page 41)*

RANDY DuBURKE
Randy is a cover artist for DC Comics, having worked on *Animal Man, Darkstars, Ms. Tree,* and *The Shadow.* He is also the artist on *Hunter's Heart,* a graphic novel to be published in the Paradox Mystery line. *(Page 198)*

LEO DURAÑONA
Leo Durañona was born in Buenos Aires, Argentina. His past work includes DC's *House of Horrors* and Warren's *Creepy* and *Eerie,* and *Race of Scorpions, Indiana Jones,* and *Predator* for Dark Horse. *(Page 183)*

KIERON DWYER
A professional for seven years, Kieron has pencilled, inked, colored and/or painted *Captain America, Batman, Robin, Hellraiser,* and *Lobo.* He is very proud of his work on *The Torch of Liberty.* *(Page 40)*

DUNCAN EAGLESON
The series of space-time events collectively labeled "Duncan Eagleson" have demonstrated a variety of reproducible results: his work has appeared in *Sandman* and *Shade* (Vertigo), *Storytellers* (Piranha), and *The Witching Hour* (Millennium). *(Page 124)*

TOMMY LEE EDWARDS
Tommy Lee Edwards resides in Los Angeles with his fiancee Melissa and their two cats. His previous work includes *System Shock;* he's currently pencilling a miniseries for DC/Milestone. *(Page 155)*

HUNT EMERSON
Hunt Emerson has drawn "underground" comics for twenty years, including Knockabout Comics' *Lady Chatterly's Lover, The Rime of The Ancient Mariner,* and the highly acclaimed *Casanova's Last Stand.* *(Page 10)*

JOHN ESTES
John Christian Estes is a graduate of the Academy of Art College, San Francisco. Primarily a painter, he's done two graphic novels, *Streets* (DC), and *Tales to Astonish* (Marvel), trading cards, and book covers. *(Pages 164-165)*

JIM FERN
Jim started as an inker on various Marvel titles in 1983. He began pencilling in 1987, and has drawn *L.E.G.I.O.N '90, Detective, Adventures of Superman,* and most recently the *Scarlett* series for DC. *(Page 81)*

BOB FINGERMAN
Bob Fingerman keeps his private life private, but would like to use this space to plug his series *White Like She,* published by Dark Horse Comics. *(Page 168)*

STUART FIRTH
Stuart Firth lives on the Scottish border.
Likes: motorcycles, old movies, peanut butter.
Dislikes: corruption, marzipan, filling in forms.
Ambition: To eat regular and pay the rent. *(Page 148)*

SHARY FLENNIKEN
Shary Flenniken is a cartoonist, screenwriter, and former editor of *National Lampoon.* Her latest project is *Seattle Laughs,* an anthology of original comic stories about her hometown. *(Pages 208-209)*

PHIL FOGLIO
Phil Foglio produces *Buck Godot — Zap Gun for Hire* and the Eisner Award-nominated *xxxenophile* for his own company, Palliard Press, as well as art for the game *Magic.* *(Page 107)*

DAVY FRANCIS
Davy Francis's work has appeared in *Oink, Knockabout Comics, The 3-D Zone,* and *Holy Cross* (written by Malachy Coney, from Fantagraphics Books). He's currently working on a Scottish cowboy comic, *Hoof Hearted.* *(Page 16)*

SIMON FRASER
Simon Fraser is from the Highlands of Scotland, living in Edinburgh, drawing comics set in London, New York, and Bavaria. He'd like to draw comics set in the Highlands of Scotland. *(Page 152)*

SAMUEL GANA
I was born in 1940 with a comic book under my arm, in Chile. Ever since then I've been filling my notebooks with cartoon characters and stories. Because of this, I was always punished. *(Page 79)*

JOHN GARCIA
I've drawn for *Open Space* (Marvel), *Medal of Honor* (Dark Horse) and Jim Vance's *Owlhoots* (Kitchen Sink). My finest work was for *Harvey Kurtzman's New Two-Fisted Tales* (Byron Preiss). *(Page 31)*

JOSÉ LUIS GARCÍA-LÓPEZ
García-López was born in Spain, reared in Argentina, and lives, works, hikes, fishes, and beachcombs in New York. His humble contribution: *Atari Force, Deadman, Twilight, Cinder & Ashe,* and others. *(Page 71)*

DAVID GARLAND
David produces and hosts wide-ranging music shows on WNYC-FM, the NPR affiliate in New York City. He's active as a composer and performer. This is his first work for a comics publisher. *(Page 192)*

RICK GEARY
Rick's comics and illustrations have appeared in various magazines, and his work has been collected in four volumes, including *Housebound with Rick Geary* and *Prairie Moon and Other Stories.* *(Page 99)*

EARL GEIER
Earl Geier has worked professionally since 1989, illustrating role-playing games such as *Battletech, Shadowrun,* and *Call of Cthulhu,* with comics work for Dark Horse Comics, Innovation, and Now. *(Page 97)*

KEITH GIFFEN
Born.
Draws comics.
Wishes he was dead. *(Page 132)*

SCOTT GILLIS
Scott Gillis moved to New York City in 1977, where he began freelance illustrating and dishwashing. He is a certified hypnotherapist and student of the martial arts, but a peaceful man. *(Page 85)*

CRAIG GILMORE
Craig Gilmore's specialty is horror and all things strange. He is an illustrator for *White Wolf* and Fasa Games and is also a penciller/inker for DC and Marvel Comics. *(Page 188)*

DICK GIORDANO
I was born July 20, 1932. The rest, as they say, is ancient history. *(Page 95)*

TREVOR GORING
Worked on early issues of *2000 AD, House of Hammer,* and *Dan Dare.* Went into advertising, moved from England to LA and did film storyboards, and returned to comics with *Pantera* (Malibu). *(Page 89)*

MARCUS GRAY
Marcus Gray is a Glaswegian who is working on a number of his own comics projects. He drinks large quantities of Guinness and loves the films of Hal Hartley. *(Page 44)*

JUSTIN GREEN
Justin Green began as an "underground cartoonist" in 1968. Since then, his work has appeared under the disclaimer: "Minors are forbidden to read any further. Put down this publication at once!" *(Page 201)*

D. ALEXANDER GREGORY
Alexander has worked on *Kilroy Is Here, The Twist, The Odyssey of Vladimir Illyich, Vampire: The Masquerade, Predator* for Dark Horse Comics, *Negative Burn,* and too much more. *(Page 203)*

DAERICK GRÖSS
Best known for his painted comics, Gröss received the Russ Manning Award for *The Vampire Lestat.* He has also done *Forbidden Planet, Necroscope,* and *Batman: Two-Face Strikes Twice* (for DC). *(Page 18)*

REBECCA GUAY
Rebecca's work has appeared in *Cricket Magazine for Children,* Topps's *Star Wars Series II,* and various Marvel and DC Comics. She is currently the regular penciller for DC/Vertigo's *Black Orchid.* *(Page 65)*

PIA GUERRA
Pia likes to think she can come up with witty comments about herself on demand, but really is much better suited to drawing the pictures. She doesn't wear earrings. *(Page 62)*

JACKSON GUICE
Jackson Guice and family live on twelve acres in the Smoky Mountains of North Carolina. He claims he has been a comics illustrator since dinosaurs walked the earth. *(Page 153)*

MIKE HADLEY
Credits include: *Deadline Magazine, Toxic, Sonic the Hedgehog, 2000 AD, Judge Dredd, Rogue Trooper* (as colorist), *Fervent & Lobe,* and *The Future King.* His ambition is to live off royalties. *(Page 23)*

KIM HAGEN
Kim is from Denmark, where he shares an art studio called "Pinligt Selskab" with eight other artists. His most recent work is for *Negative Burn,* "The Lad Who Wished to Meet Fear." *(Page 145)*

HAK
HAK has worked for various men's publications (*Screw,* etc.). Living in New Jersey, HAK lives a relatively monastic existence, going out only to obtain food, toilet paper, and more crayons. *(Page 91)*

BOB HALL
Bob Hall lives in New York City where he has been a theater director, playwright, actor, and cartoonist. He currently writes and draws *Shadowman* for Valiant Comics. *(Page 193)*

CRAIG HAMILTON
Craig Hamilton hates writing bios; he lives in the Deep South with three cats named Elrod, Paganini, and Ariel, and another human named Jody. Special thanks to Ray Snyder. *(Page 184)*

ED HANNIGAN
Over the years I've worked at almost every job in comics and done lots of stories for Marvel and DC. I'm really only in it for the free comics. *(Page 22)*

TONY HARRIS
Penciller, inker, cover painter Tony lives in Georgia with his wife Stacie, and his two dobermens, Natasha and Cleopatra. He's currently pencilling and painting covers on *Starman* (DC). *(Page 90)*

DANNY HELLMAN
Hail the new dawn! Early next year, Untermensch Hellman will be rocketed to the lunar surface to do battle with Wippy the Two-Headed Death Slarg. Never forget, he gives his life to save us all. *(Page 70)*

FRED HEMBECK
Fred Hembeck was reborn in the late seventies when he began using himself as a cartoon character to interview and kibbitz with the comic-book superstars he'd followed since childhood. *(Page 123)*

LEA HERNANDEZ
Has held scuzzy jobs in every work sector, including comics. Non-scuzzy work includes *Predator* and *Dirty Pair,* as well as prose fiction and articles on manga. Favorite saying: "Go limp or this will hurt." *(Page 206)*

GRAHAM HIGGINS
Graham Higgins regularly receives ten-dollar checks sent on the 10th of the month by perfect strangers who believe it will give him good luck. *(Page 117)*

JOHN HIGGINS
John Higgins is a pseudonym for John Higgins, a bit-part actor who played Charles Laughton's hump in *The Hunchback of Notre Dame.* *(Page 55)*

JAMES A. HODGKINS
Stylistically, "The Blind Man" marks a departure from my mainstream work: *Black Canary* and *Team Titans* for DC, and *Immortalis* for Marvel. I've enjoyed drawing it; I hope you enjoy reading it! *(Page 138)*

ALAN HOPKINS
I moved to Boston in '76 and embarked on an illustration career, but comic-book fever hit me in 1986. My claim to fame to date is drawing *Man-Eating Cow.* *(Page 213)*

FLOYD HUGHES
Floyd Hughes lives in Red Hook, Brooklyn with his wife Mayleen and daughter Sojourner. He believes all bigots should repent or die painfully. *(Page 74)*

MICHAEL JANTZE
When Michael draws, he thinks animals can talk and people can reason, that men are flexible and women are reasonable. He obviously doesn't make a lot of money at it. *(Page 126)*

PHIL JIMENEZ
Phil Jimenez hopes his family and friends know just how much their love, support, and guidance mean to him. *(Page 63)*

DAVE JOHNSON
Dave Johnson started Kudzu Tech Studio, named after his self-described style as used in *SuperPatriot.* Also did the sales-record-breaking *Chain Gang War* for DC. *(Page 137)*

LEIF JONES
Leif was raised by moths inside a windmill that was only visible during lightning storms. He lives and works in California, but plans to move closer to the North Pole. *(Page 207)*

RAFAEL KAYANAN
Rafael is currently drawing *Conan the Adventurer,* adapting Coppola's *Frankenstein* movie for Topps, and inking *Chiaroscuro* for Vertigo. He likes to read, paint, and get into knife fights. *(Page 173)*

NIGEL KITCHING
I have worked on a wide variety of British comics. Sometimes I write, sometimes I draw, and sometimes, if I'm lucky, I even get to do both. *(Page 196)*

DAVID G. KLEIN
David is an illustrator of magazines, books, and comics, including: *Frankenstein, The Scarlet Letter, Darker Than You Think, Humanoids, Eclipso, Batman: Legends of the Dark Knight* #51, and Marvel's 2099 Universe. *(Page 121)*

BILL KOEB
My work has appeared in *Hellraiser, Interface, The Hacker Files,* and various magazines including *Blur, Processed World* and *Ray Gun.* I'm currently working on *Faultlines* for Vertigo with writer Lee Marrs. *(Page 84)*

TEDDY KRISTIANSEN
Teddy lives in Copenhagen with his wife, daughter, two cats, and a huge phone bill from working abroad. He hopes to have more time for painting next year. *(Page 178)*

ALAN KUPPERBERG
Since 1971, New Yorker Alan Kupperberg has drawn *Justice League, Firestorm, Warlord,* et cetera (for DC Comics), and *Spider-Man, Thor, The Avengers, Captain America,* and others (for Marvel). *(Page 129)*

NGHIA LAM
Nghia was born in a country that no longer exists. He now lives in the deserts of San Diego, where he enjoys the company of blowfish and blonde women. *(Page 12)*

ROGER LANGRIDGE
Roger is the cartoonist of Fantagraphics' *Zoot.* His future goals include raising the number of people who have heard of him into three figures. *(Page 39)*

GREGORY B. LaROCQUE
Lots of super-heroes. *(Page 122)*

BATTON LASH
Batton Lash is the creator of *Wolf & Byrd, Counselors of the Macabre* and the writer of the *Archie/Punisher* crossovers. His cartooning appears in the other Factoid Big Books. *(Page 147)*

STEVE LEIALOHA
Other legends Steve's worked on include *The Hitchhiker's Guide to the Galaxy* and *The Illustrated Ray Bradbury,* as well as holding down the bass end of *The Seduction of the Innocent.* *(Page 19)*

MARK LEWIS
Mark Lewis is a longtime comics enthusiast and illustrator, and has contributed to Fantagraphics, Express Publications, and Big Bang Comics. Mark currently makes a living on the *X-Men* cartoon. *(Page 202)*

VINCENT LOCKE
Vincent Locke has done a few album covers and many comics, including *American Freak, Sandman, Sandman Mystery Theatre,* and *Deadworld.* When he's not working, he's wishing he was. *(Page 103)*

LENNIE MACE
Lennie Mace's ballpoint pen masterpieces continue crossing boundaries in his ongoing quest to build an artistic empire. His cartoon debut for DC marks another brick in the wall. *(Page 69)*

MADELEY
Madeley's first work appeared in Britain's *Weird City.* He illustrated *Flywheel, Shyster, Flywheel* for BBC, and his strip *Ashes,* co-written by Gavin Inglis, is soon to move onto television. *(Page 100)*

KEVIN MAGUIRE
Kevin began his career under the watchful eye of Andy Helfer during a two-year stint on *Justice League.* He is currently working on his creator-owned Bravura comic *Strikeback.* *(Page 136)*

GRAHAM MANLEY
Graham Manley lives and works in Scotland. His work has appeared in *Near Myths, Knockabout Comix, The Diceman, 'Max Overload,* many other unexpected places, and Paradox's Big Book series. *(Page 216)*

KIRK MANLEY
Kirk Manley has wanted to illustrate comics since age eight. He studied under Carmine Infantino at SVA and admires Frank Miller, Steve Rude, Adam Hughes, John Buscema, and John Byrne. *(Page 181)*

LEE MARRS
Lee is an Emmy award-winning TV art director, a humorist, artist, and a pioneer in the blending of traditional animation and computer graphics. She recently wrote *Zatanna* for DC. *(Page 93)*

NATHAN MASSENGILL
Nathan is known primarily for his pencilling work at DC (*Wonder Woman*) and Malibu, his watercolor painted work (Raven Publications), and his written work for Caliber Press (*Poets Prosper*). *(Page 177)*

ROBERT McCALLUM
Robert was born in 1971. He drew for *Electric Soup Humour Mag* while at the Glasgow School of Art. He is currently drawing *Lobo* for DC. *(Page 37)*

MAC McGILL
Mac is an editorial cartoonist/illustrator whose work has appeared in many progressive publications. He is a regular contributor to *High Times Magazine* and *World War 3 Illustrated.* *(Page 111)*

CHRIS McLOUGHLIN
Chris McLoughlin was born 1 November 1971. He was exposed to comics at an early age, but no one pressed charges. *(Page 134)*

ROBERT McNEILL
Robert McNeill is not what you'd expect. *(Page 67)*

LINDA MEDLEY
Little Linda would like to be a housewife when she grows up. *(Page 212)*

JASON MINOR
Name: Jason Temujin Minor
    Jason: Hebrew for Joshua, meaning "Jehovah is salvation."
    Temujin: Genghis Khan's birth name.
    Minor: Originally Bullman, changed in 1369 A.D.
    Occupation: Writer/artist *(Page 102)*

MARK MIRAGLIA
My major influences are EC Comics, Alex Raymond, and Mark Schultz — artists who draw in the heroic adventure genre. My other projects are *Solitare, Green Hornet* and *Green Arrow.* *(Page 26)*

GABRIEL MORRISSETTE
Gabriel worked on *Doc Savage, New Titans, Ragman,* and *Melody* for the American market, and the Quebec humor magazines *Anormal, Croc,* and *Safarir.* Of course he lives in Montreal. *(Page 51)*

SCOTT MUSGROVE
Scott's latest work is titled *Thirteen Fat, Russian Sailors With Butcher Knives Strapped to the Bottom of Their Boots Skated the Answers to Delicate Questions Across the Surface of a Frozen Rink of Porpoise Blood.* *(Page 175)*

TED NAIFEH
Ted is most noted for *The Machine* from Dark Horse's super-hero line. He is currently working on a creator-owned book with Epic called *The Exile of Abra Khan.* *(Page 211)*

MAT NASTOS
Artist and adventurer supreme, now spends much of his quiet time working on *ElfQuest: Blood of Ten Chiefs* for Warp Graphics. *(Page 78)*

BILL NAYLOR
Bill was reared in captivity on pints of "Wobbly Bob." Current work: this year's *Judge Dredd Annual,* and now DC. "I gotta be dreamin', or is it the 'Wobbly Bob?' Hic!" *(Page 113)*

MARK A. NELSON
Mark has worked on *Aliens, Feud, Nightbreed, Blood and Shadows,* and *From Pencils to Inks* in *Hero Illustrated.* He lives with his wife, two cats, a dog, and teaches at N.I.U. *(Page 49)*

JOSH NEUFELD
"Josh" is twenty-six and currently lives in Chicago. He draws comics and editorial illustrations, and he hates writing about himself in the third person. *(Page 149)*

MARK NEWGARDEN
Mark Newgarden is the real person to whom everything depicted in this book actually happened. He has been blessed with many, many friends. *(Page 32)*

ART NICHOLS
With a kick in the ass by Neal Adams and great advice from Bob Layton, Art doesn't just ink comics, he also pencils them. Sometimes both at the same time. *(Page 30)*

KEVIN NOWLAN
Previous work includes *New Mutants, Outsiders Annual,* the Man-Bat *Secret Origins, Grimwood's Daughter,* and *Batman: Sword of Azrael.* Currently working in obscurity on obscene material for a neo-fascist lunatic. *(Page 88)*

SHANE OAKLEY
Shane is a rich and successful cartoonist living in Bermuda. He spends his time wrestling sharks and writing his memoirs for a major TV adaptation. *(Page 195)*

MITCH O'CONNELL
Mitch is an award-winning fine artist whose work has appeared in *National Lampoon, Spy,* and *Playboy.* He has also published *Good Taste Gone Bad: The "Art" of Mitch O'Connell.* *(Page 163)*

MICHAEL AVON OEMING
As a small inking cog in the Marvel machine, I've worked on such titles as *Daredevil* and *The Avengers.* I'm currently drawing *Judge Dredd* for DC. *(Page 98)*

ROD OLLERENSHAW
After leaving art school, Rod managed to write and draw for Archie Comics and *Felix the Cat.* He enjoys old records and ancient cars. *(Page 116)*

KEVIN O'NEILL
Kevin co-created *Ro-Busters, The A.B.C. Warriors,* and *Nemesis the Warlock* for *2000 AD,* and *Metalzoic* for DC. Stints on *Green Lantern Corps, Lobo,* and *Bat-Mite.* Best known for co-creation *Marshall Law.* *(Page 35)*

JOE ORLANDO
A leading writer-editor-designer-cartoonist-illustrator in comics since 1950, Joe is also the Vice-President/Creative Director for DC Comics, and the Associate Publisher of *MAD Magazine*. (Page 139)

TAYYAR OZKAN
Tayyar is a Turkish-born Kurd, living in New York. His artwork has appeared in *World War 3 Illustrated* and *Heavy Metal,* and he is drawing *La Pacifica,* written by Joel Rose and Amos Poe, the first graphic novel in the Paradox Mystery line. (Page 52)

RICHARD PACE
Richard Pace used to draw big people hitting each other, to make money. He still does this, but he's better paid. (Page 92)

ANDREW PAQUETTE
Andrew Paquette, born 1965, married 1987, daughter 1992. Vegan diet since 1984 (and sick of getting advice about it). Work has appeared in *Hellraiser/Night Breed*. Co-creator/penciller of *Harsh Realm*. (Page 180)

RICK PARKER
Rick is the artist for *MTV's Beavis and Butt-Head* comic book from Marvel. Parker's comic strip *The Bossmen* and weekly cartoon *The Bullpen Bullseye* were also published by Marvel. (Page 11)

MIKE PAROBECK
Mike has worked on *El Diablo, The Fly, Justice Society of America,* and is presently working on *The Batman Adventures* and *Superman and Batman Magazine*. (Page 159)

PAUL PEART
Paul has worked like a dog on several titles, including *Slaughterbowl, Judge Dredd,* and *Kid.Eternity,* as well as several personal projects, while being big, brown and beautiful! (Page 110)

ANDREW PEPOY
Andrew has inked *Green Lantern* and *Iron Man,* is currently inking Roger Zelazny's *The Guns of Avalon* for Byron Preiss/DC Comics, and pencilling *G-8 and His Battle Aces* for Millennium. (Page 140)

OMAHA PÉREZ
Omaha Pérez (yes, that's his real name) is twenty-three. Any mention to him of a certain "Cat Dancer" and he will be forced to ignore you. (Page 66)

ERIC PETERSON
Eric's illustration credits include painting over 150 paperback covers. His most recent work in comics was nine painted cards for the *Superman: Forged in Steel* set. (Page 28)

JOE PHILLIPS
In nine years I've done over fifty issues and close to 120 covers and cards. Titles include: *Ex-Mutants, Speed Racer, Justice League, Fantastic Four,* and *Spider-Man*. Upcoming project: *The Heretic* from Dark Horse. (Page 60)

TOBY PHILP
These are a few of my favorite things: the human form, slick imagery, real artists, natural beauty, reliable friends, fax machines, sex, drugs, and blasphemy. (Page 80)

HOWARD PORTER
I work on *The Ray*. I like to snack on croutons. Oh yeah, I'm married to Heather. (Page 125)

GEORGE PRATT
George's graphic novel *Enemy Ace: War Idyll* is on the required reading list at West Point. He is currently working on *See You in Hell, Blind Boy! A Tale of the Blues*. (Page 68)

GORDON PURCELL
Credits include *Star Trek: The Next Generation/Deep Space Nine* crossover for DC/Malibu and the *Silver Sable* series for Marvel. Gordon lives with his wife Debra and a baby on the way. (Page 205)

BRIAN QUINN
This begins Brian's wonderful career in comics. After receiving his BA in fine art at Rutgers he decided to seek out a career that would actually pay the bills, but ended up here. (Page 112)

FRANK QUITELY
Born in Glasgow, Scotland 1968. Unsuccessful spell in Glasgow School of Art. Dabbled in small press while freelancing for several years. Became full-time comic artist in early 1993. (Page 36)

RICHARD PIERS RAYNER
Russ Manning Award-winner for Most Promising Newcomer in 1989, Richard has illustrated *Dr. Fate, L.E.G.I.O.N. '90, Swamp Thing* and *Hellblazer*. He is also drawing *Road to Perdition,* a graphic novel in the Paradox Mystery line, written by Max Allan Collins. (Page 13)

TRINA ROBBINS
Trina produced the first all-woman comic, *It Ain't Me Babe,* in 1970. Her latest projects are the book *A Century of Women Cartoonists* and the first CD-ROM for girls, *Hawaii High*. (Page 34)

DARICK ROBERTSON
Darick has pencilled many projects for DC, Marvel, and Malibu, including *Ripfire, Justice League, New Warriors, Wolverine, Cable* and *Spider-Man*. He is also embarking on a writing career. (Page 82)

DENIS RODIER
Denis's work was seen on the covers of *The Demon* and *Newstime Magazine*. He is currently inking a *Star Wars* mini-series for Dark Horse Comics and doing the finishes on *Action Comics*. (Page 161)

JAMES ROMBERGER
James's graphic novels include *Seven Miles a Second* with David Wojnarowicz, and *Ground Zero* with Marguerite Van Cook. His drawings are in many private and museum collections. (Page 96)

JOE RUBINSTEIN
I was born with a brush in one hand and a pen in the other. I hope to die having just finished inking a comic book faster than the Inky-poo — proving that no machine can beat a human. (Page 215)

GREG RUTH
After exiting the witness relocation program, Greg roamed across the southwest portion of Texas for 47 years before residing in the men's bathroom at the Dairy Queen outside of Houston. (Page 56)

TIM SALE
Tim is the artist on *Deathblow: Big Guns Guy,* and the *Legends of the Dark Knight* Halloween Specials. He lives in Seattle with his lovely dogs Hotspur and Shelby. (Page 142)

ADRIAN SALMON
Adrian's first professional commission was *Judge Karyn* in *Judge Dredd: The Megazine*. At present he is drawing her second series. Future projects include *The Cybermen* for *Doctor Who Magazine*. (Page 105)

ZINA SAUNDERS
Zina Saunders's illustrations have been used in advertising, theater posters, books, software, videocassette covers, and in the *Star Wars* trading card series. (Page 135)

TRISTAN SCHANE
Tristan Schane was born in Brooklyn, New York, October 1968. (Page 29)

CHRISTOPHER SCHENK
Thirty-one-year-old stud muffin. First job was assisting Mark Bodé drawing *Miami Mice*. (Ouch!) Recently did *Enemy* for Dark Horse. Enjoys espresso, landscape painting, espresso, R&B, and espresso. (Page 187)

VAL SEMEIKS
Val Semeiks is the current penciller of the *Lobo* monthly. Started in 1986 on *King Kull* and *Conan* for Marvel. Moved on to DC to draw *The Demon* and other projects. (Page 45)

ERIC SHANOWER
Eric's work has appeared in U.S. and European comics, in books, and on TV. He is best known for his *Oz* graphic novels. He lives in Bloomfield, NJ. *(Page 179)*

SCOTT SHAW!
An award-winning cartoonist whose work has spanned comic books (*Captain Carrot and his Amazing Zoo Crew!*), animation (*The Completely Mental Misadventures of Ed Grimley*), and advertising (Post Pebbles Cereal). *(Page 48)*

WILL SIMPSON
Will worked for *2000 AD* on *Chopper, Judge Dredd,* and *Rogue Trooper.* He worked on DC's *Hellblazer,* and then on *Aliens: Rogue* for Dark Horse. His most recent work is *Vamps* for DC/Vertigo. *(Page 131)*

PATRICK SINCLAIR
Patrick Melvin Sinclair has been in the business for 30 years and never had a heart attack. His past work has mostly appeared in British juvenile publications. *(Page 43)*

CIARAN SLAVIN
Ciaran is editor and commander of his own non-commercial comics company, Decay Comics. He is self-taught in art, a one-man maelstrom of comics ideas and stories. *(Page 14)*

BOB SMITH
Born: Aberdeen, Washington, 1951. Art education: BFA, Western Washington State University, 1974. I've been inking comics for DC since 1975. About every ten years, Andy Helfer lets me pencil something. *(Page 54)*

ROBIN SMITH
Robin was the art director for *2000 AD* and an artist on *Judge Dredd.* He also illustrated *Bogie Man.* Robin is drawing *Green Candles,* a graphic novel in the Paradox Mystery line. *(Page 146)*

NED SONNTAG
Since 1985 Ned has been the Betty Boop licensing artist for King Features and chief illustrator for *Outlaw Biker* and *Dimensions,* a fantasy/personals 'zine for fat women and admirers. *(Page 199)*

JOE STATON
Joe has worked for Marvel on *The Incredible Hulk,* and for DC illustrating *Superman, Batman, Plastic Man, Green Lantern,* and many others. Joe is the artist on *Family Man,* a graphic novel written by Jerome Charyn for the Paradox Mystery line. *(Page 144)*

ALEC STEVENS
Alec Stevens *almost* enjoys music more than art. He cites Bela Bartok, Stravinsky, Miles Davis, Coltrane, early Zappa/*Mothers,* Nick Drake, *Focus, Glassharp,* and Jukka Tolonen as favorites. *(Page 158)*

LESLIE STERNBERGH
It was a dark and stormy night when Leslie was born. Now she draws comix. See the *Twisted Sisters* collections for more of her work. She lives in New York. *(Page 214)*

JIM SULLIVAN
Jim has been published in Pacific Comics' *Alien Worlds,* Eclipse's *Alien Encounters,* and Topps' *Cadillacs and Dinosaurs.* Early inspirations include DC Silver Age greats Dick Sprang, Curt Swan, and Ramona Boone. *(Page 170)*

SÉAN TAGGART
Known for his "Ichabod's Magic Fairyland" theme parks dotted all about South America, Sean takes a crack at the North American marketplace with this piece. *(Page 73)*

BRAD TEARE
In addition to creating and publishing the comic *Cypher,* Teare has created art for *The New York Times,* as well as covers for books by James Michener and Ann Tyler. *(Page 57)*

TY TEMPLETON
Ty "The Guy" Templeton has worked on *Superman, Batman, Spider-Man, X-Men, Ren and Stimpy,* and his personal favorite, *Mad Dog.* He lives with Keiren, their son Kellam, and three cats. *(Page 185)*

GREG THEAKSTON
Greg has been working in comics since 1970. He's also known for his work bleaching classic comics, his work at *Mad Magazine,* and as editor/publisher of *The Betty Pages.* *(Page 61)*

JAMIE TOLAGSON
Mr. Tolagson (a lean, strapping 7' 2", 215 lbs.) believes that his large form distracts people from his true artistic nature. Jamie now lives in Phuket, Thailand with his four lovable dobermen. *(Page 42)*

CHAS TRUOG
Chas is known for his work on DC's *Animal Man* and is currently at work on *Chiaroscuro,* a ten-issue series for Vertigo due out in the summer of '95. *(Page 210)*

COLIN UPTON
After producing over sixty minicomics, Colin self-published his first *Big Thing* comic book in 1990. Four more *Big Things* have been published by Fantagraphics Books and another by Aeon Press. *(Page 156)*

JOHN VAN FLEET
Look for *Shadows Fall* for Halloween '94, a six-part Vertigo book written by John Ney Rieber. *(Page 151)*

ALEX WALD
A former teenage blues legend and later First Comics art director, Alex has been published in *American Splendor, The Comics Journal, Highball, Monster International,* and *Secret Agent Man.* *(Page 120)*

ALAN WEISS
Alan has worked for DC, Marvel, and Defiant, and has split his time between comics and advertising. He is the creator of *War Dancer* for Defiant, which he co-writes and draws. *(Page 128)*

ANDREW WENDEL
Former portraitist for *The New Yorker,* fueled by passions for music, cycling, and the bizarre, Andrew here makes his DC/Paradox debut. He is currently employed by a rival company. *(Page 77)*

ART WETHERELL
Can't think of anything to write. Check out his *Indiana Jones* book from Dark Horse Comics. *(Page 38)*

SHANE WHITE
I like vegetables. I like bald phat guys in jock straps with suspenders. I like smoking midgets and tough women named bitch. White trash, too. All these things inspire me! *(Page 106)*

KEITH S. WILSON
Keith does not believe in bios. *(Page 25)*

KENT WILLIAMS
Born 1962. Other books: *Tell Me, Dark; Wolverine: Killing; Meltdown; Blood: A Tale; Kent Williams: Drawings* and *Monotypes.* *(Page 172)*

GLENN WONG
I work as both a comic book artist (*The Young Cynics Club*) and a toy sculptor (action figures). My goals are world domination and understanding the Tao. *(Page 127)*

JEFF WONG
Jeff Wong is a long, lanky gad-about, looking to meet chicks. *(Page 157)*

BILL WRAY
Bill has worked as a penciller, inker, and colorist. He is currently directing cartoons for *The Ren and Stimpy Show* and still wondering why *Mad Magazine* won't hire him. *(Page 101)*